P9-DYY-811

# SANITY & TALLULAH

# Sanity &

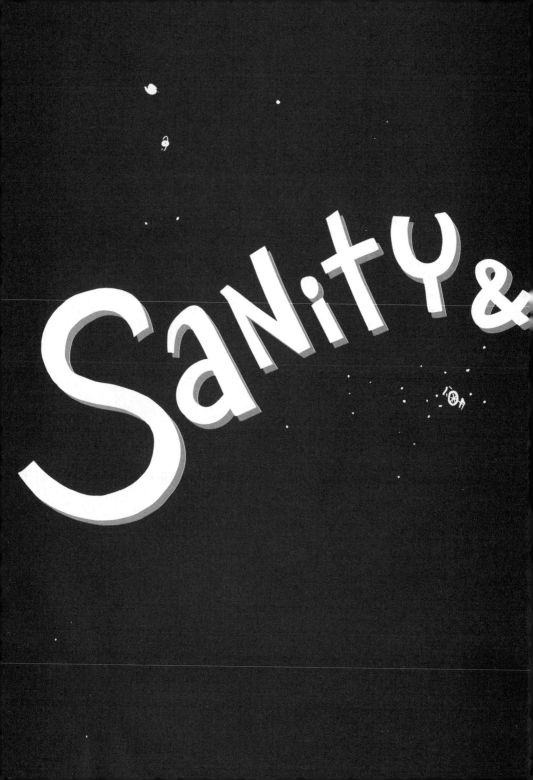

# TALLULAH

MOLLY BROOKS

𝒟ɪꜱɴᴇʏ • **Hyperion**

LOS ANGELES    NEW YORK

Copyright © 2018 by Molly Brooks
All rights reserved. Published by Disney • Hyperion, an imprint of Disney Book Group.
No part of this book may be reproduced or transmitted in any form or by any means,
electronic or mechanical, including photocopying, recording, or by any information
storage and retrieval system, without written permission from the publisher.
For information address Disney • Hyperion, 125 West End Avenue, New York, New York 10023.

First Edition, October 2018
10 9 8 7 6 5 4 3 2 1
FAC-008598-18250
Printed in the United States of America

This book is set in 9-pt Gargle/Fontspring
Designed by Maria Elias

Library of Congress Cataloging-in-Publication Data
Names: Brooks, Molly (Molly Grayson), author, illustrator.
Title: Sanity & Tallulah / Molly Brooks.
Other titles: Sanity and Tallulah
Description: First edition. • Los Angeles ; New York : Disney-Hyperion, 2018.
Summary: "Sanity and Tallulah live in a space station at the end of the galaxy.
When Sanity's illegally created three-headed kitten escapes, the girls have to turn
their home upside down to find her in this graphic novel"—Provided by publisher.
Identifiers: LCCN 2017056156• ISBN 9781368008440 (hardcover) • ISBN 1368008445 (hardcover)
Subjects: LCSH: Graphic novels. • CYAC: Graphic novels. • Space stations—Fiction. •
Cats—Fiction. • Animals—Infancy—Fiction. • Lost and found possessions—Fiction. • Science fiction.
Classification: LCC PZ7.7.B765 San 2018 • DDC 741.5/973—dc23
LC record available at https://lccn.loc.gov/2017056156

Reinforced binding
Visit www.DisneyBooks.com

SUSTAINABLE FORESTRY INITIATIVE    Certified Sourcing
www.sfiprogram.org
SFI-00993

THIS LABEL APPLIES TO TEXT STOCK

**for my parents, Kix and Barbara Brooks.**
they are the kind, creative, and practical people upon whom
every kind, creative, and practical character in this book is based.


**super huge thanks to:**

Andrea Tsurumi for giving me the excuse to invent Sanity and Tallulah
in 2014 by agreeing to do a minicomic zine with me and then
suggesting our theme should be "science fiction teen girl detectives."

Rotem Moscovich and Maria Elias for hand-holding me through
the editorial process and making this a much better book than
I would have made on my own.

The small army of color flatters whose quick and stellar work helped me
to get this project done *very nearly* on time, most especially:
Kory Bing, Ashanti Fortson, Paloma Hernando, Alexandra Beguez,
Olivia Stephens, Molly Murakami, and Alberto Hernandez.

# SANITY & TALLULAH

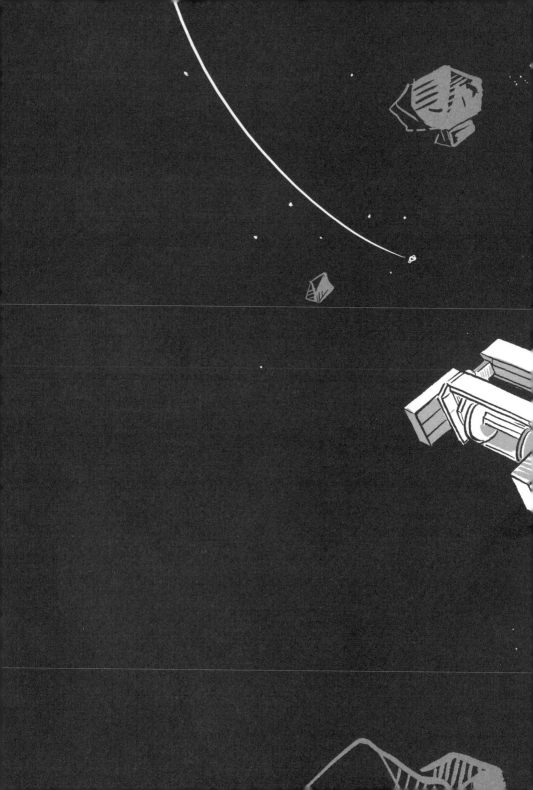

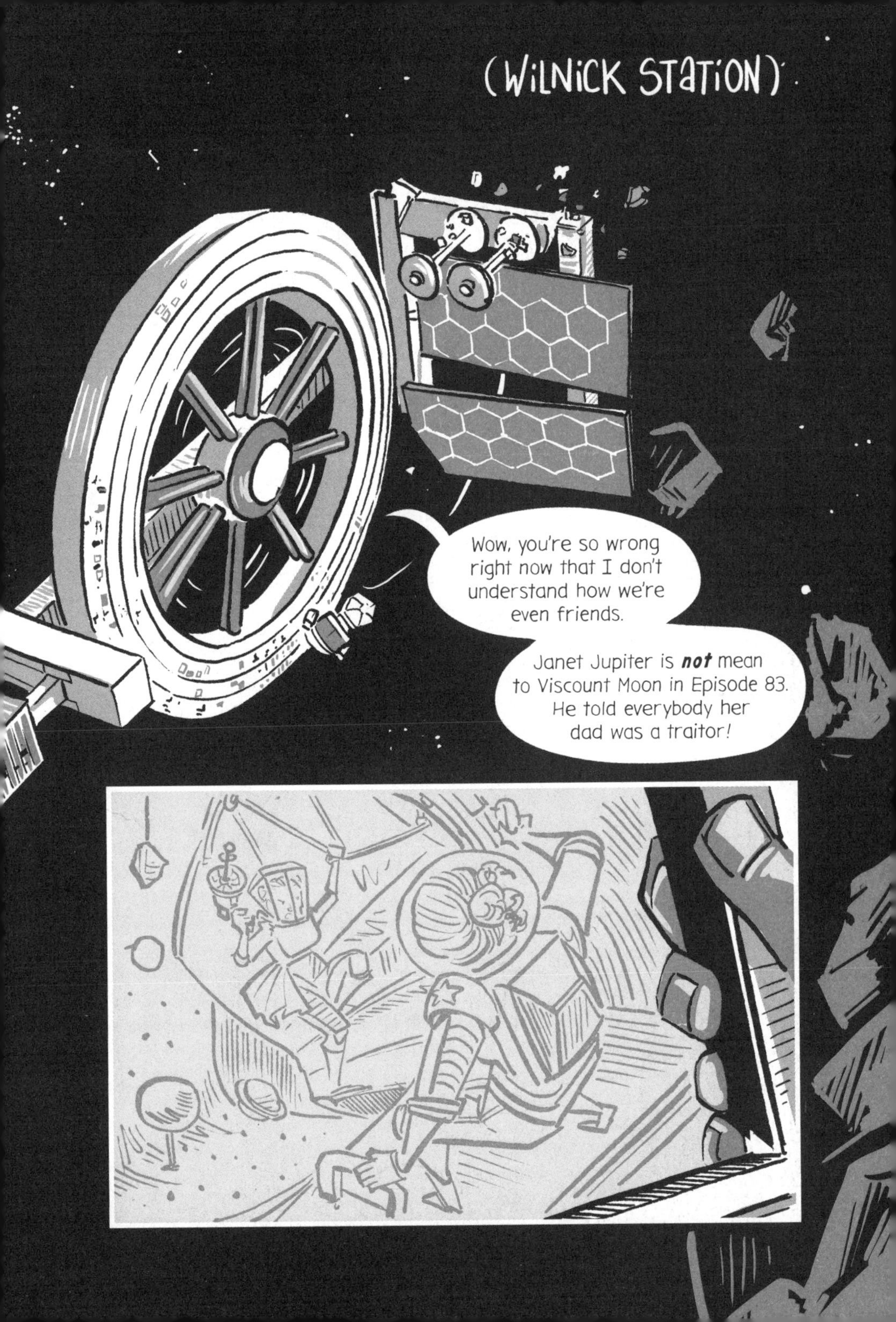
(WILNICK STATION)
Wow, you're so wrong right now that I don't understand how we're even friends.
Janet Jupiter is ***not*** mean to Viscount Moon in Episode 83. He told everybody her dad was a traitor!

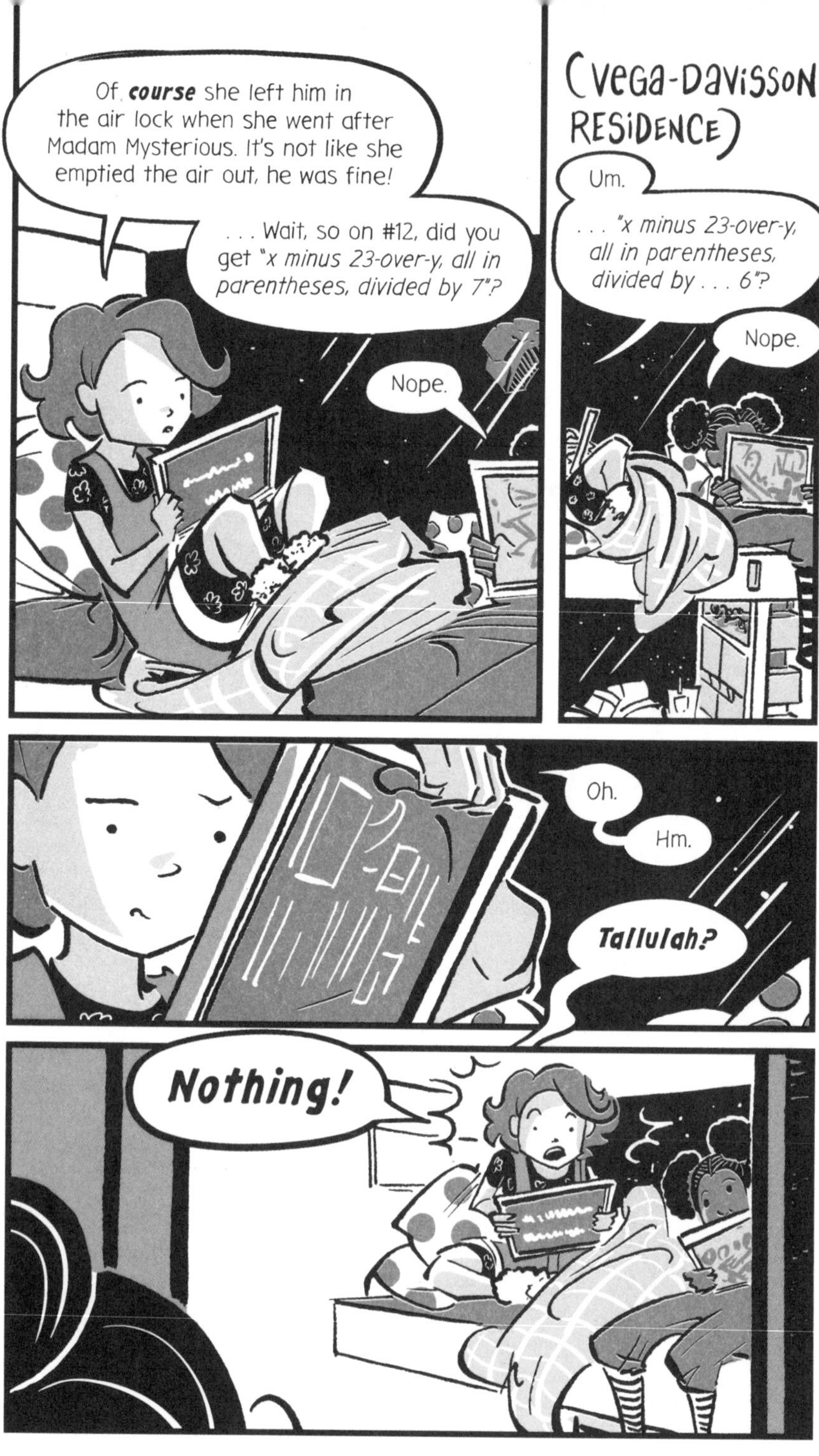
Of **course** she left him in the air lock when she went after Madam Mysterious. It's not like she emptied the air out, he was fine!
. . . Wait, so on #12, did you get *"x minus 23-over-y, all in parentheses, divided by 7"*?
Nope.
(VEGA-DAVISSON RESIDENCE)
Um.
. . . *"x minus 23-over-y, all in parentheses, divided by . . . 6"*?
Nope.
Oh.
Hm.
***Tallulah?***
***Nothing!***

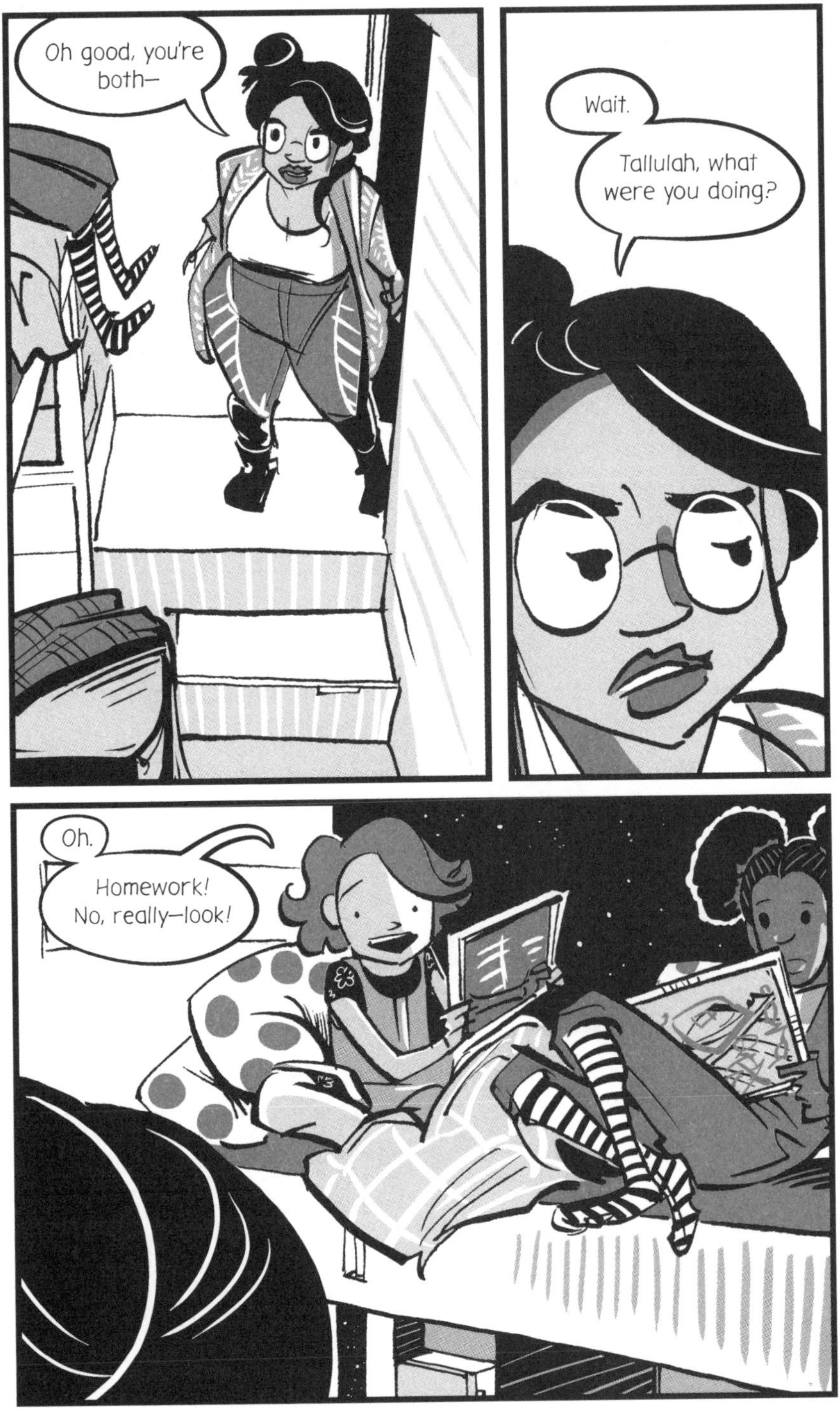
Oh good, you're both—
Wait.
Tallulah, what were you doing?
Oh.
Homework! No, really—look!

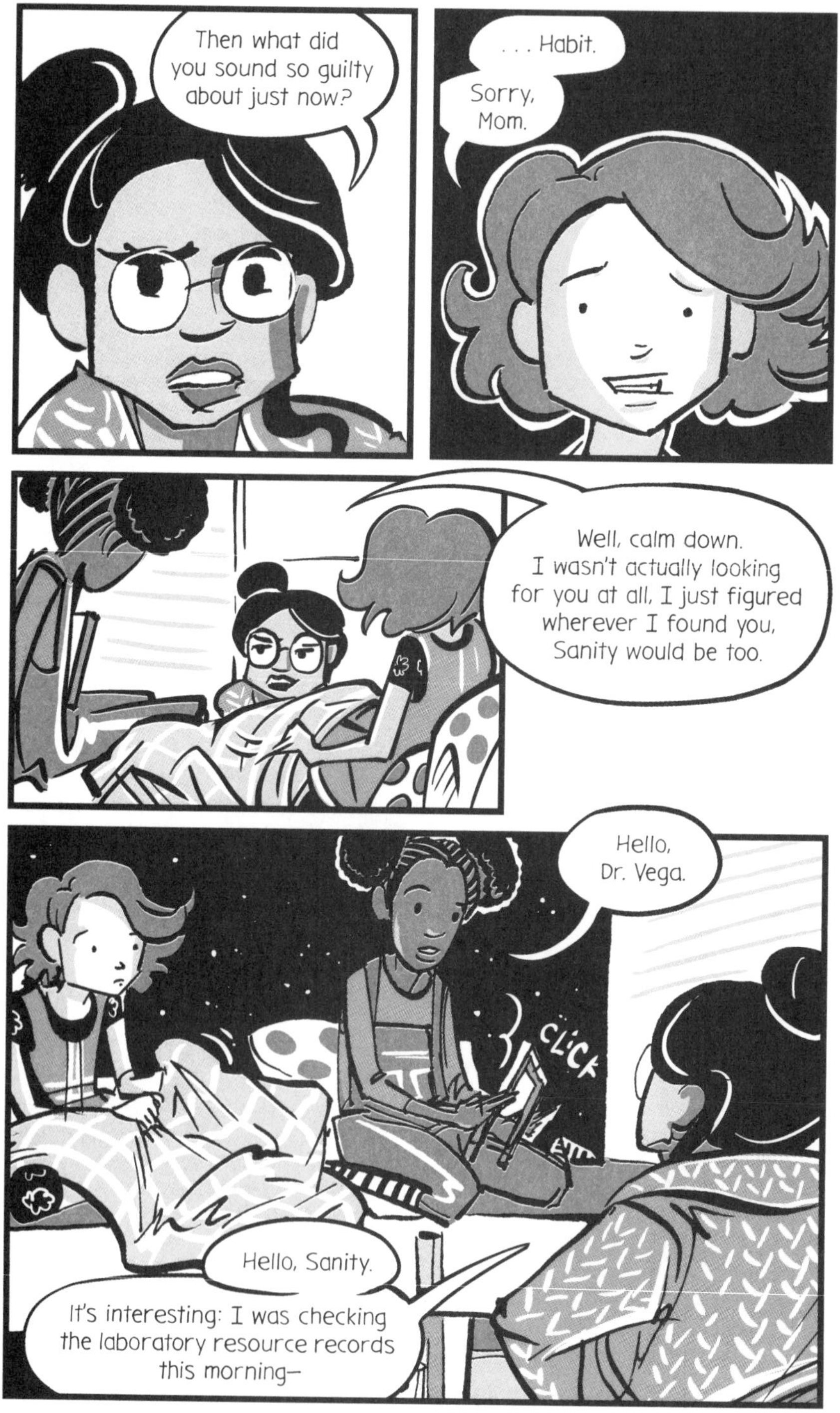
Then what did you sound so guilty about just now?
. . . Habit.
Sorry, Mom.
Well, calm down. I wasn't actually looking for you at all, I just figured wherever I found you, Sanity would be too.
Hello, Dr. Vega.
CLICK
Hello, Sanity.
It's interesting: I was checking the laboratory resource records this morning—

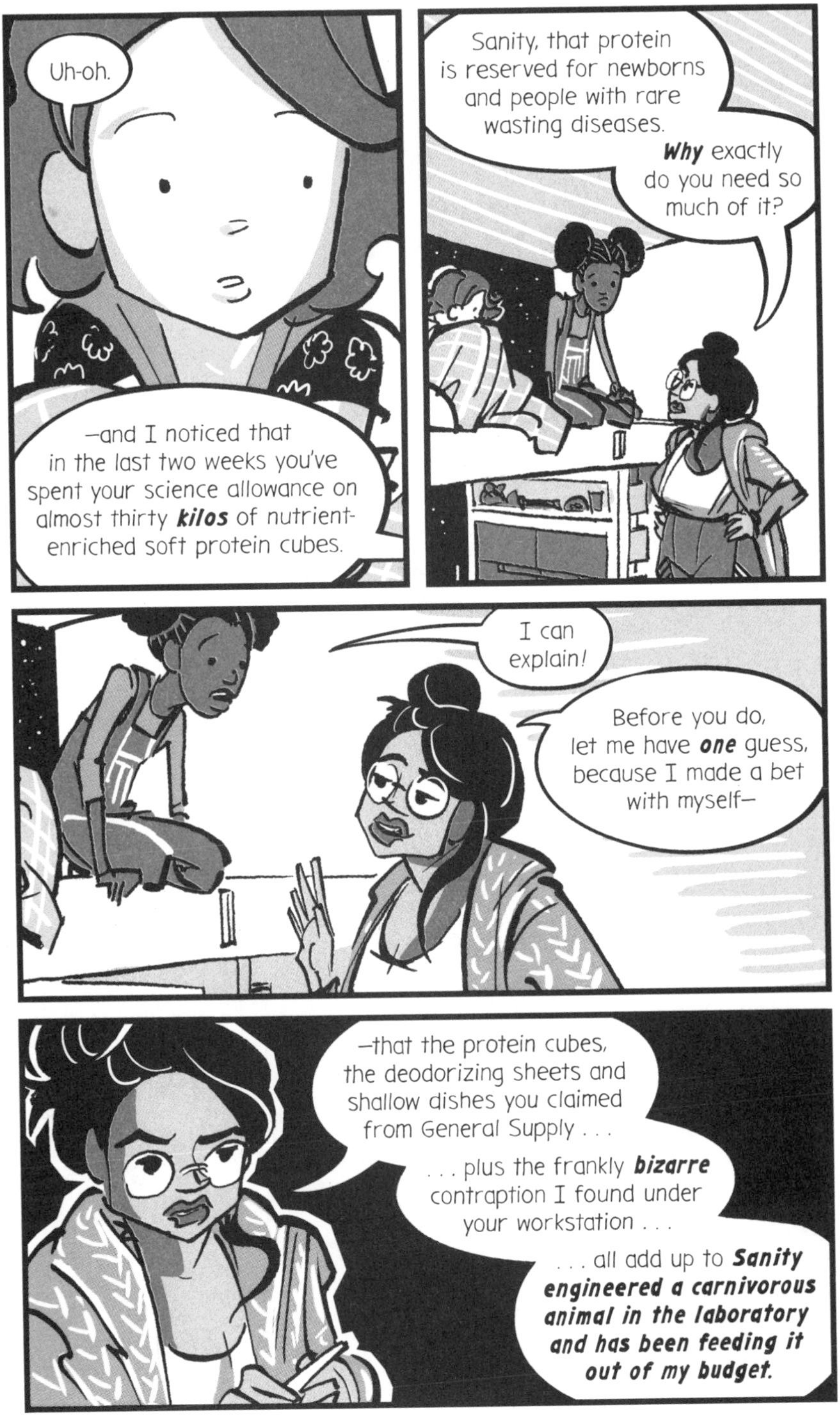
Uh-oh.
—and I noticed that in the last two weeks you've spent your science allowance on almost thirty **kilos** of nutrient-enriched soft protein cubes.
Sanity, that protein is reserved for newborns and people with rare wasting diseases.
**Why** exactly do you need so much of it?
I can explain!
Before you do, let me have **one** guess, because I made a bet with myself—
—that the protein cubes, the deodorizing sheets and shallow dishes you claimed from General Supply . . .
. . . plus the frankly **bizarre** contraption I found under your workstation . . .
. . . all add up to **Sanity engineered a carnivorous animal in the laboratory and has been feeding it out of my budget.**

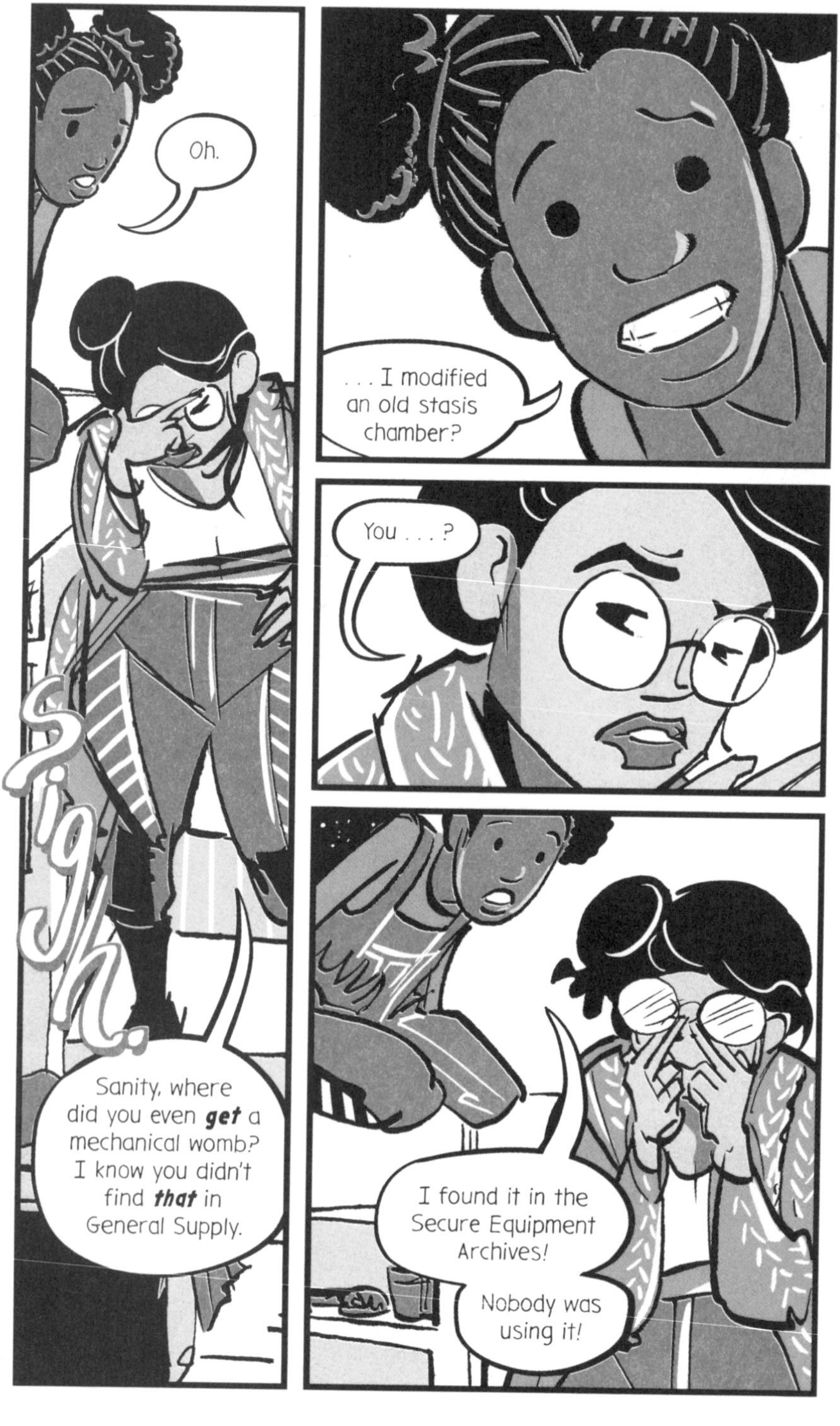
Oh.
. . . I modified an old stasis chamber?
You . . . ?
Sigh.
Sanity, where did you even **get** a mechanical womb? I know you didn't find **that** in General Supply.
I found it in the Secure Equipment Archives!
Nobody was using it!

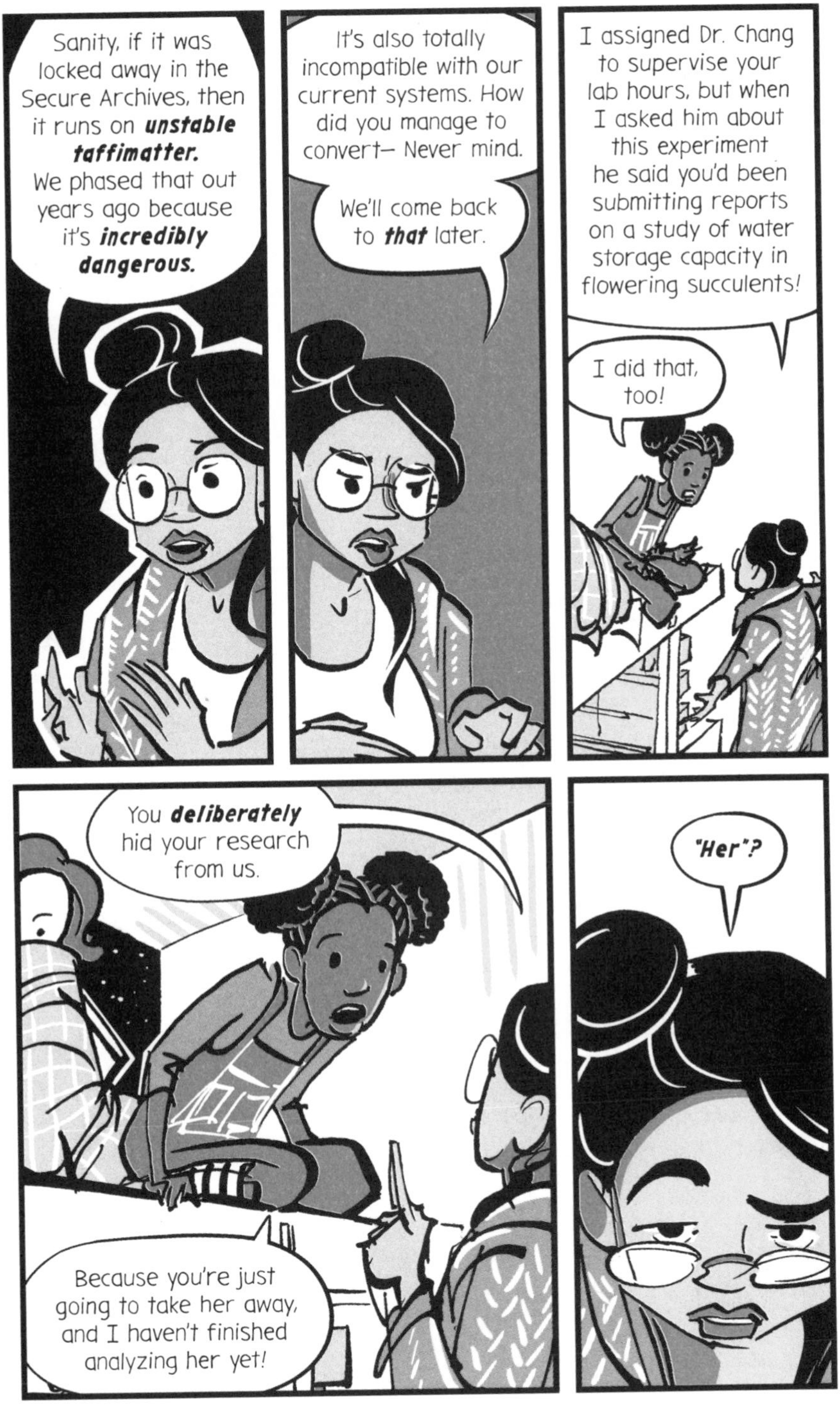
Sanity, if it was locked away in the Secure Archives, then it runs on **unstable taffimatter.** We phased that out years ago because it's **incredibly dangerous.**
It's also totally incompatible with our current systems. How did you manage to convert— Never mind.
We'll come back to **that** later.
I assigned Dr. Chang to supervise your lab hours, but when I asked him about this experiment he said you'd been submitting reports on a study of water storage capacity in flowering succulents!
I did that, too!
You **deliberately** hid your research from us.
Because you're just going to take her away, and I haven't finished analyzing her yet!
**"Her"?**

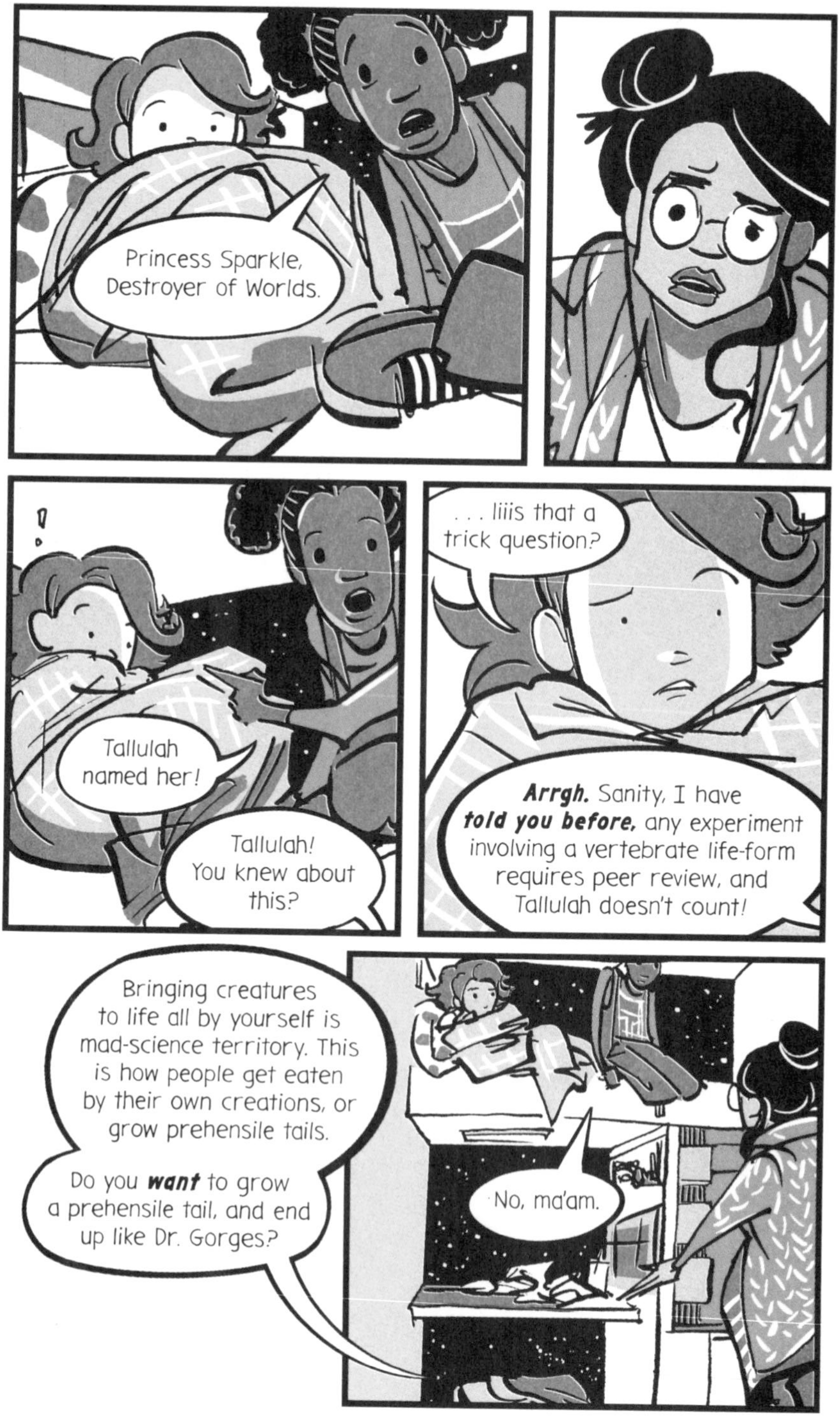
Princess Sparkle, Destroyer of Worlds.
!
Tallulah named her!
Tallulah! You knew about this?
. . . liiis that a trick question?
**Arrgh.** Sanity, I have ***told you before,*** any experiment involving a vertebrate life-form requires peer review, and Tallulah doesn't count!
Bringing creatures to life all by yourself is mad-science territory. This is how people get eaten by their own creations, or grow prehensile tails.
Do you ***want*** to grow a prehensile tail, and end up like Dr. Gorges?
No, ma'am.

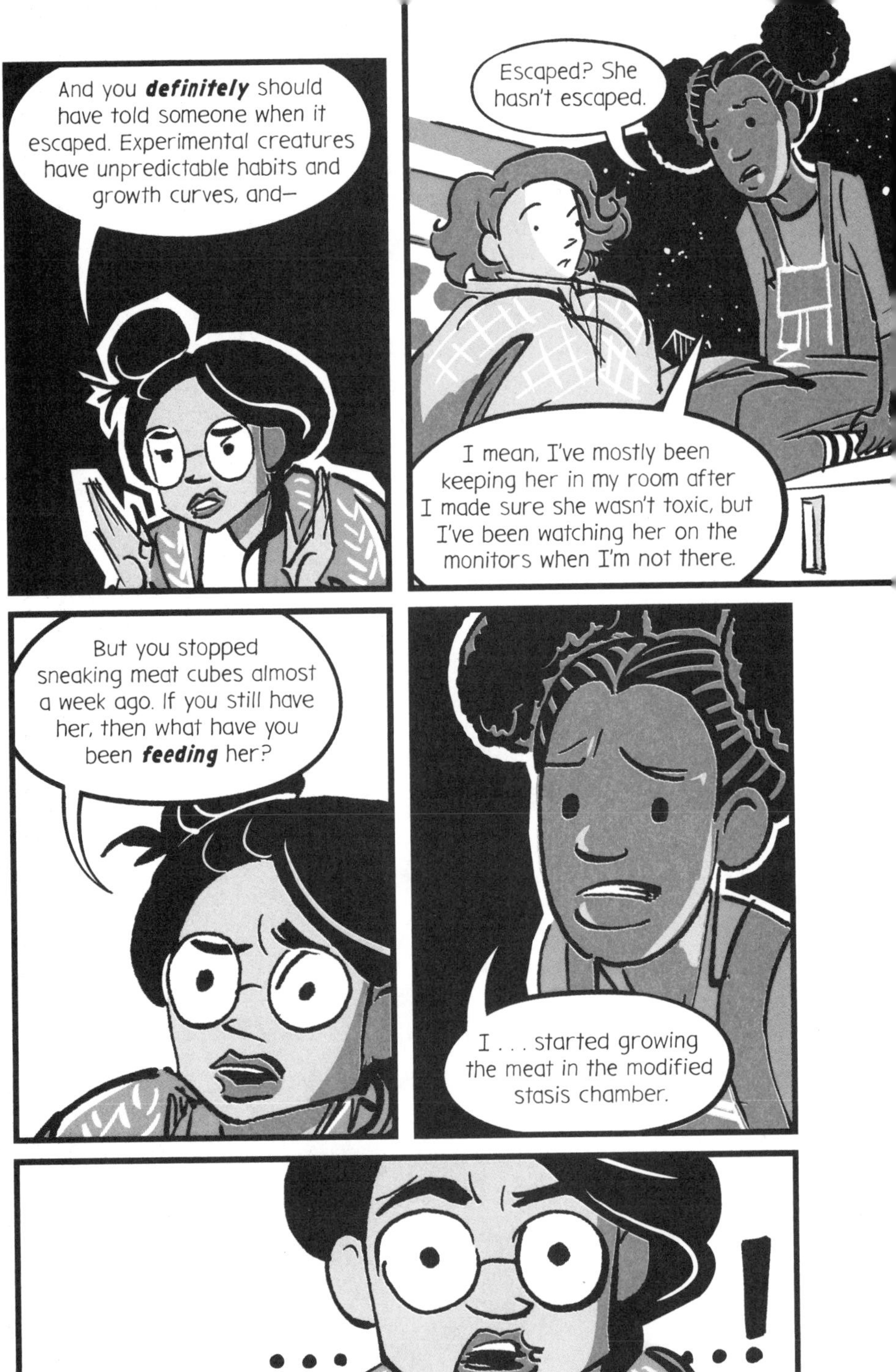
And you **definitely** should have told someone when it escaped. Experimental creatures have unpredictable habits and growth curves, and—
Escaped? She hasn't escaped.
I mean, I've mostly been keeping her in my room after I made sure she wasn't toxic, but I've been watching her on the monitors when I'm not there.
But you stopped sneaking meat cubes almost a week ago. If you still have her, then what have you been **feeding** her?
I . . . started growing the meat in the modified stasis chamber.
. . .
. . !

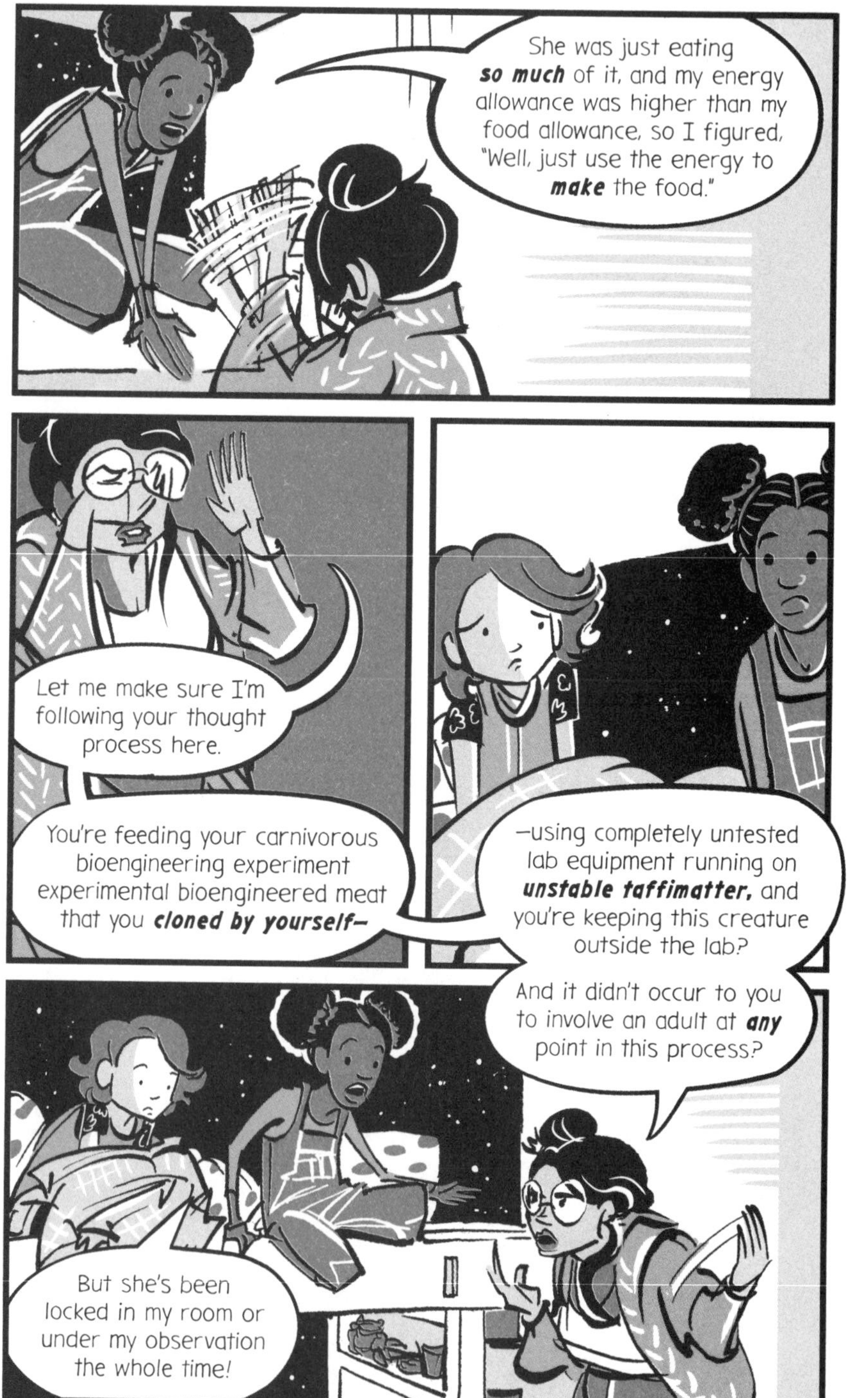
She was just eating **so much** of it, and my energy allowance was higher than my food allowance, so I figured, "Well, just use the energy to **make** the food."
Let me make sure I'm following your thought process here.
You're feeding your carnivorous bioengineering experiment experimental bioengineered meat that you **cloned by yourself**—
—using completely untested lab equipment running on **unstable taffimatter,** and you're keeping this creature outside the lab?
And it didn't occur to you to involve an adult at **any** point in this process?
But she's been locked in my room or under my observation the whole time!

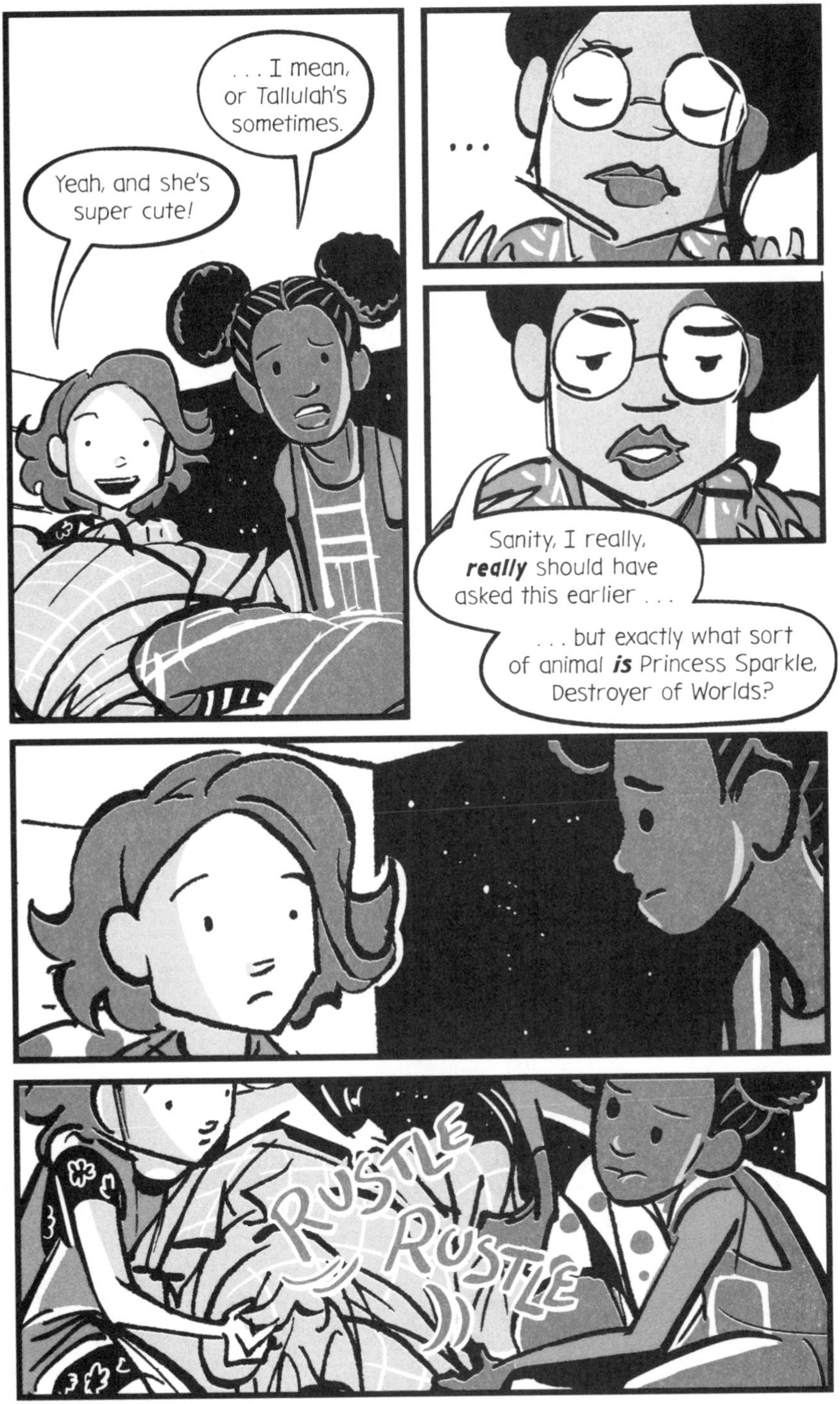
Yeah, and she's super cute!
. . . I mean, or Tallulah's sometimes.
. . .
Sanity, I really, **really** should have asked this earlier . . .
. . . but exactly what sort of animal ***is*** Princess Sparkle, Destroyer of Worlds?
RUSTLE
RUSTLE

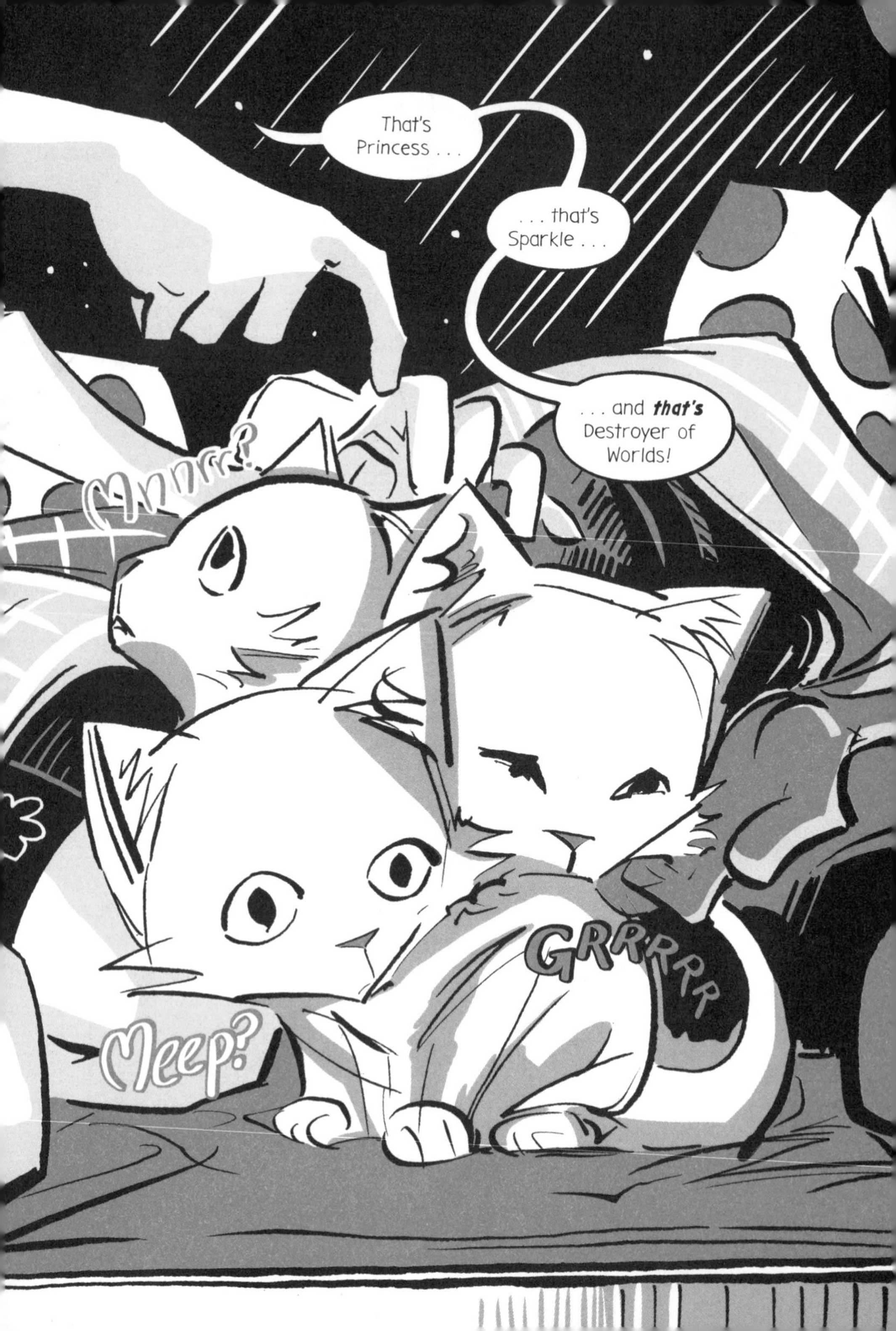

That's Princess . . .
. . . that's Sparkle . . .
. . . and **that's** Destroyer of Worlds!
Mnnrr?
GRRRRR
Meep?

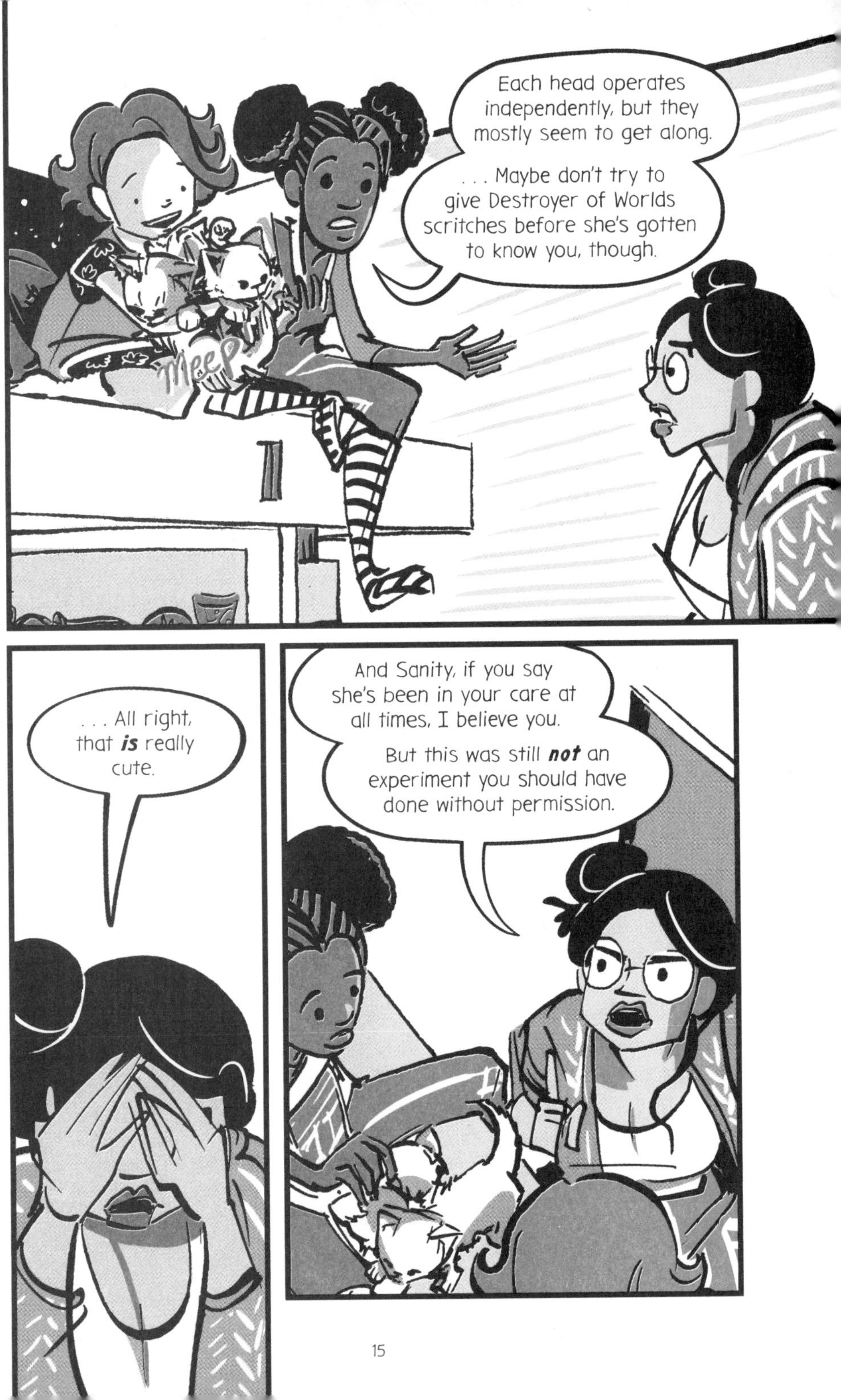
Each head operates independently, but they mostly seem to get along.
. . . Maybe don't try to give Destroyer of Worlds scritches before she's gotten to know you, though.
Meep
. . . All right, that *is* really cute.
And Sanity, if you say she's been in your care at all times, I believe you.
But this was still ***not*** an experiment you should have done without permission.

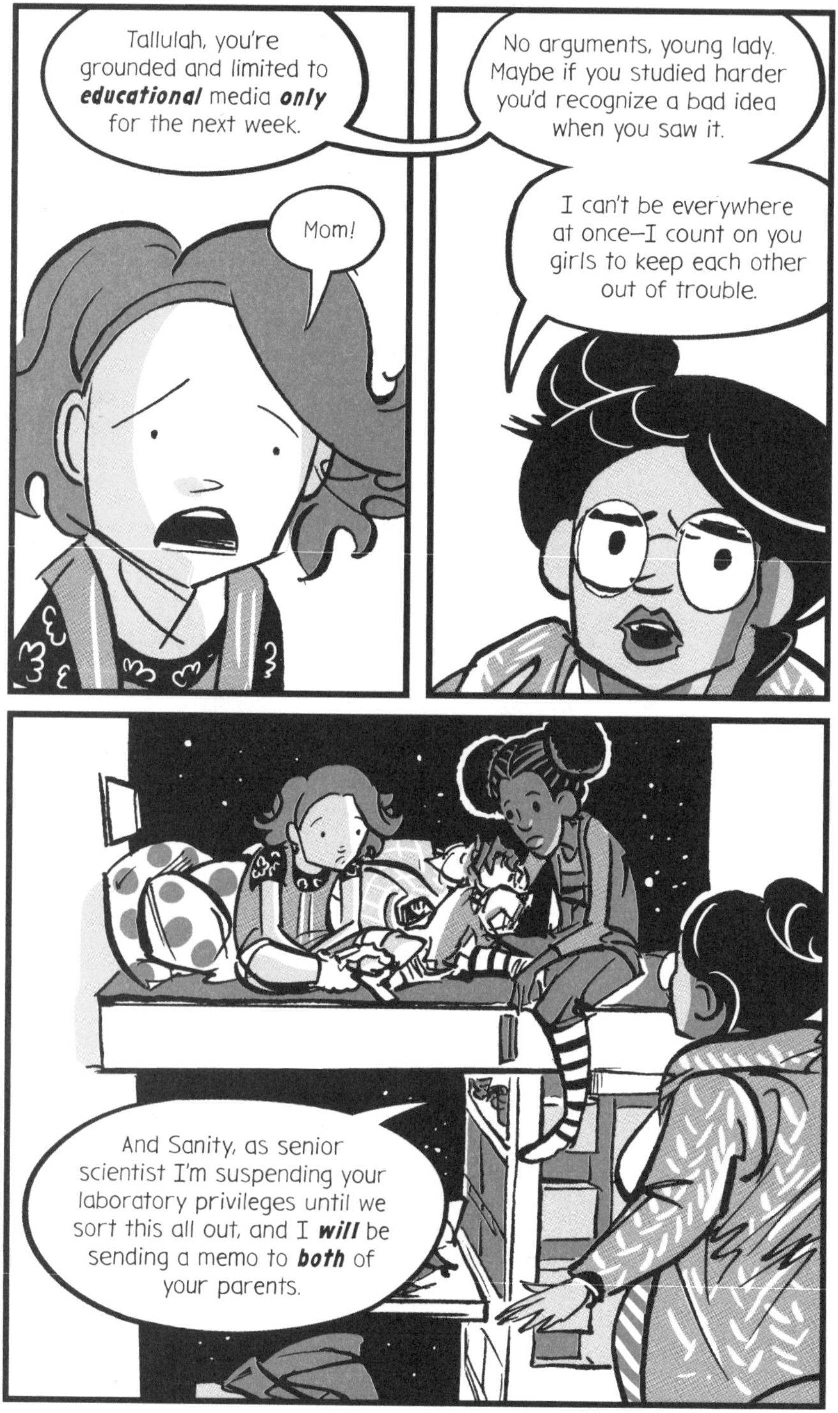
Tallulah, you're grounded and limited to **educational** media **only** for the next week.
Mom!
No arguments, young lady. Maybe if you studied harder you'd recognize a bad idea when you saw it.
I can't be everywhere at once—I count on you girls to keep each other out of trouble.
And Sanity, as senior scientist I'm suspending your laboratory privileges until we sort this all out, and I **will** be sending a memo to **both** of your parents.

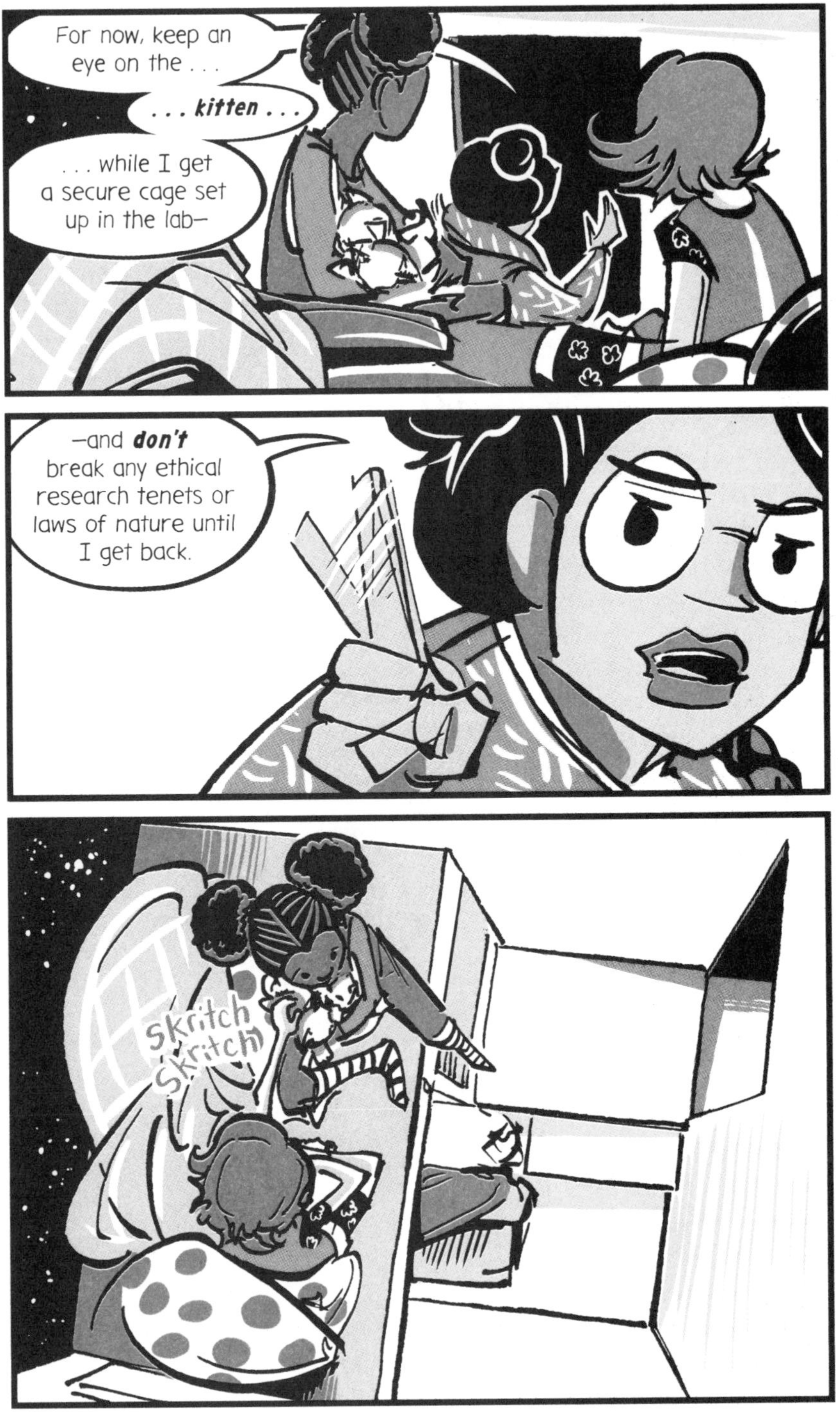
For now, keep an eye on the . . .
. . . kitten . . .
. . . while I get a secure cage set up in the lab—
—and **don't** break any ethical research tenets or laws of nature until I get back.
SKRITCH SKRITCH

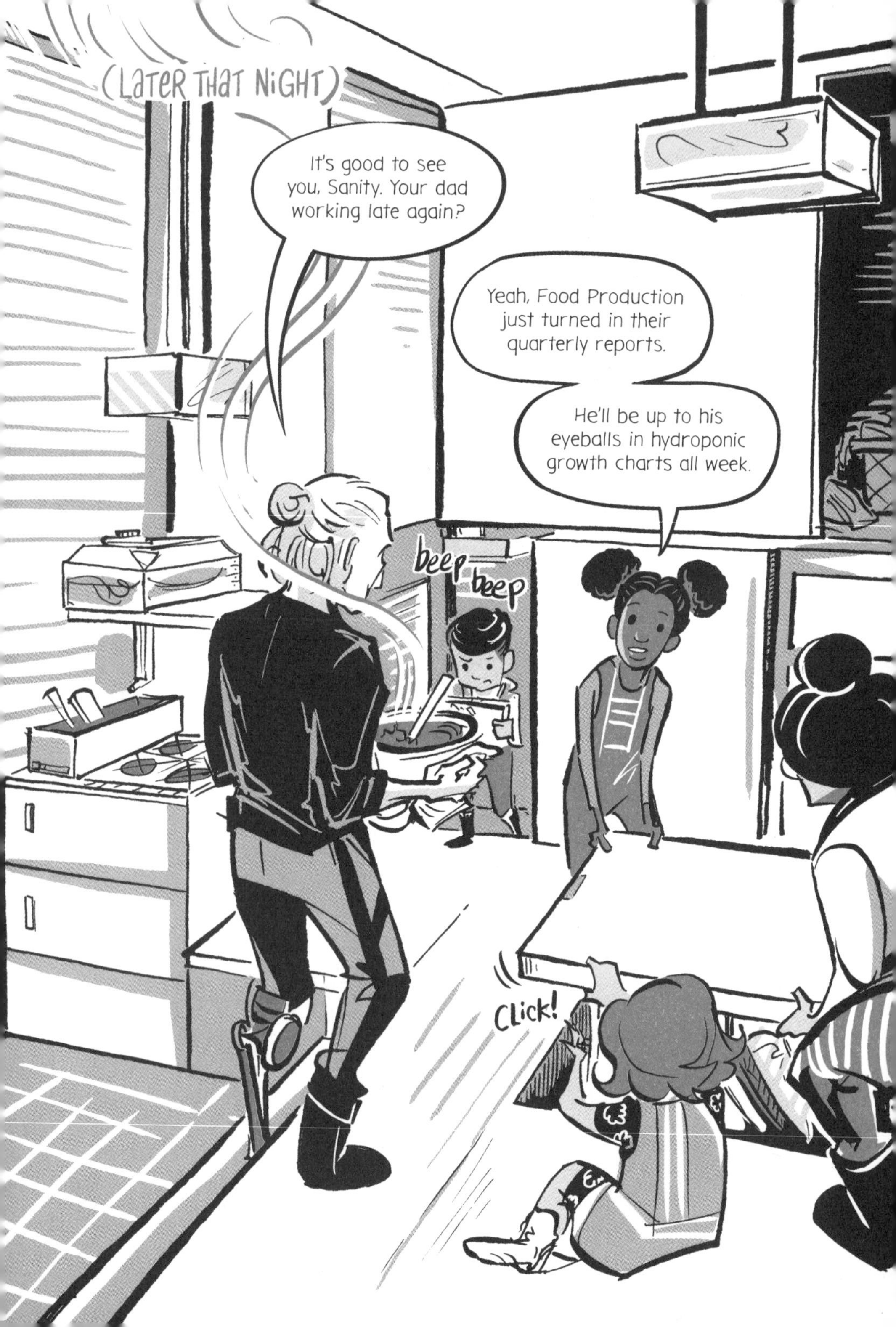
(LATER THAT NIGHT)
It's good to see you, Sanity. Your dad working late again?
Yeah, Food Production just turned in their quarterly reports.
He'll be up to his eyeballs in hydroponic growth charts all week.
beep beep
CLICK!

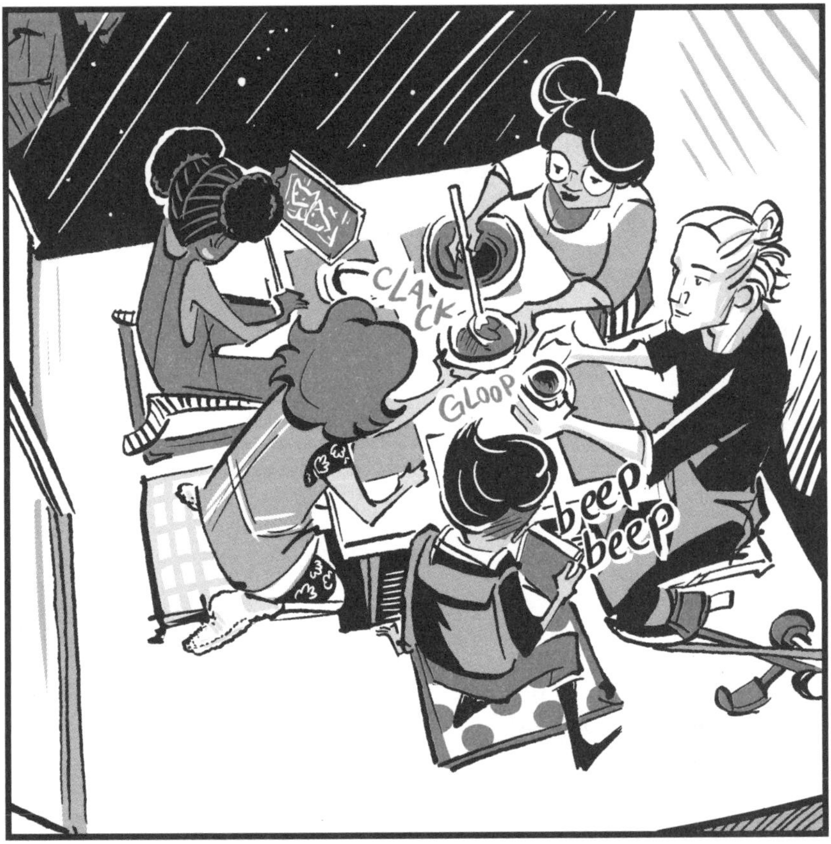
CLACK
GLOOP
beep
beep

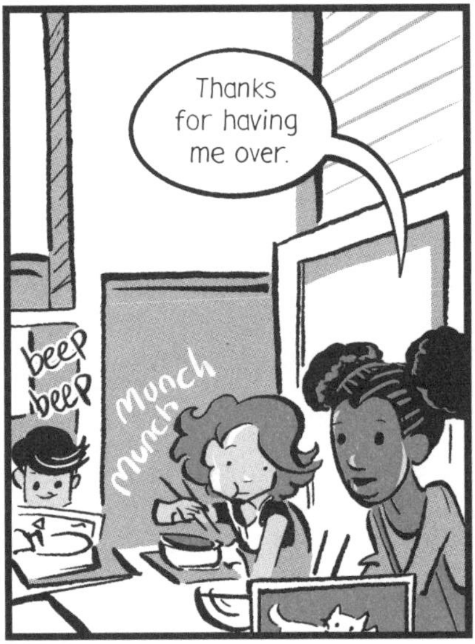
Thanks for having me over.
beep
beep
munch
munch

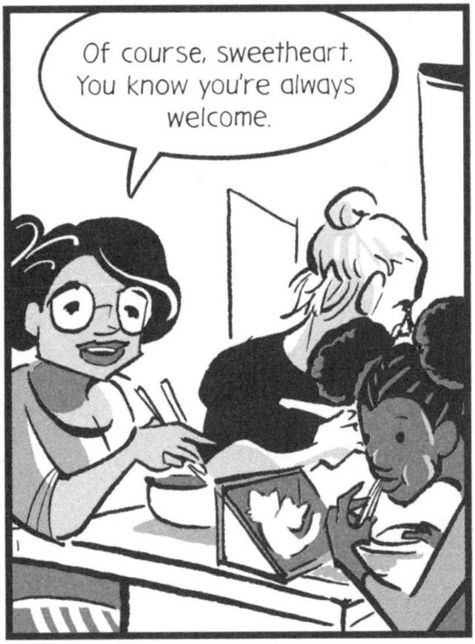
Of course, sweetheart. You know you're always welcome.

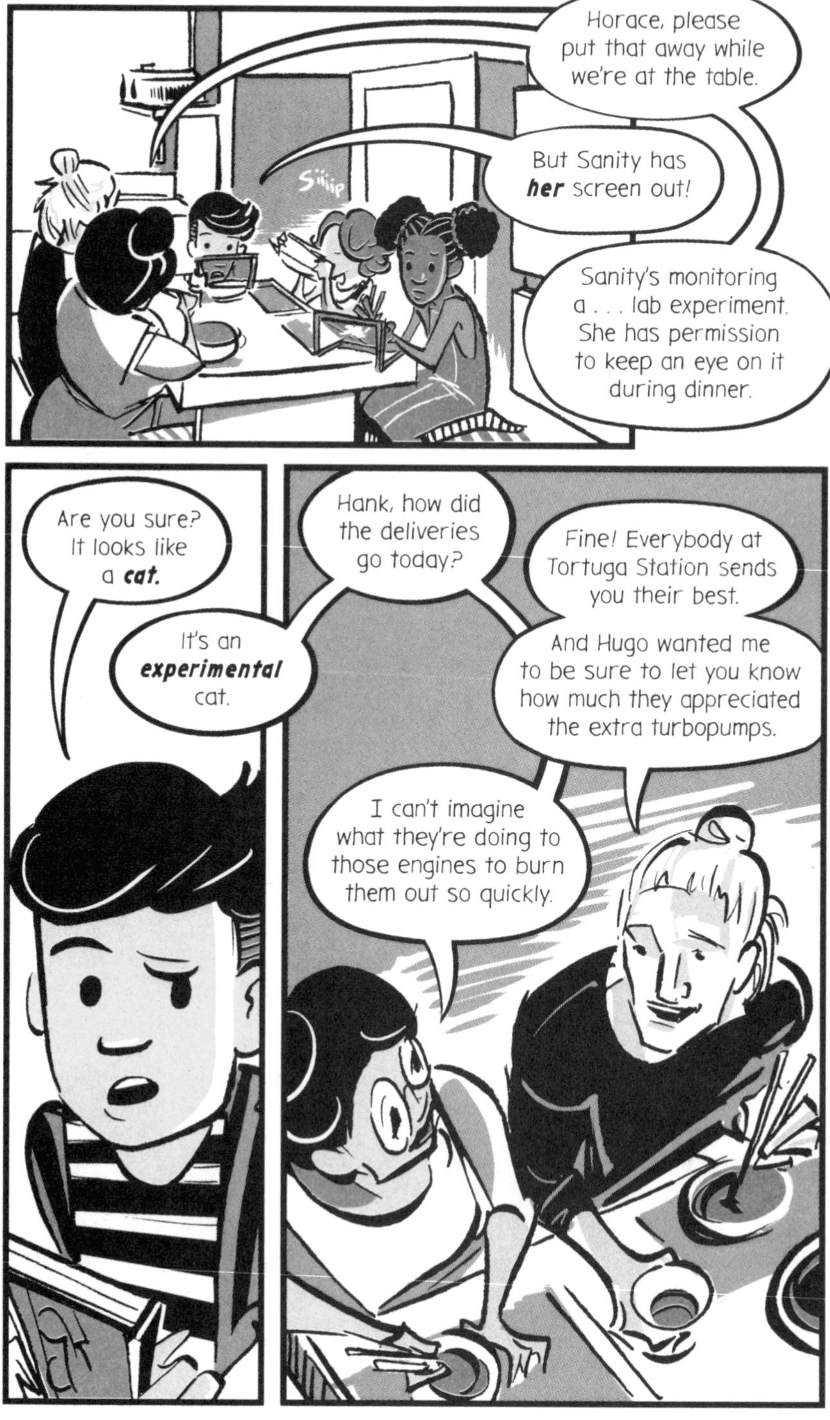
Horace, please put that away while we're at the table.
Siiiip
But Sanity has **her** screen out!
Sanity's monitoring a . . . lab experiment. She has permission to keep an eye on it during dinner.
Are you sure? It looks like a **cat.**
It's an **experimental** cat.
Hank, how did the deliveries go today?
Fine! Everybody at Tortuga Station sends you their best.
And Hugo wanted me to be sure to let you know how much they appreciated the extra turbopumps.
I can't imagine what they're doing to those engines to burn them out so quickly.

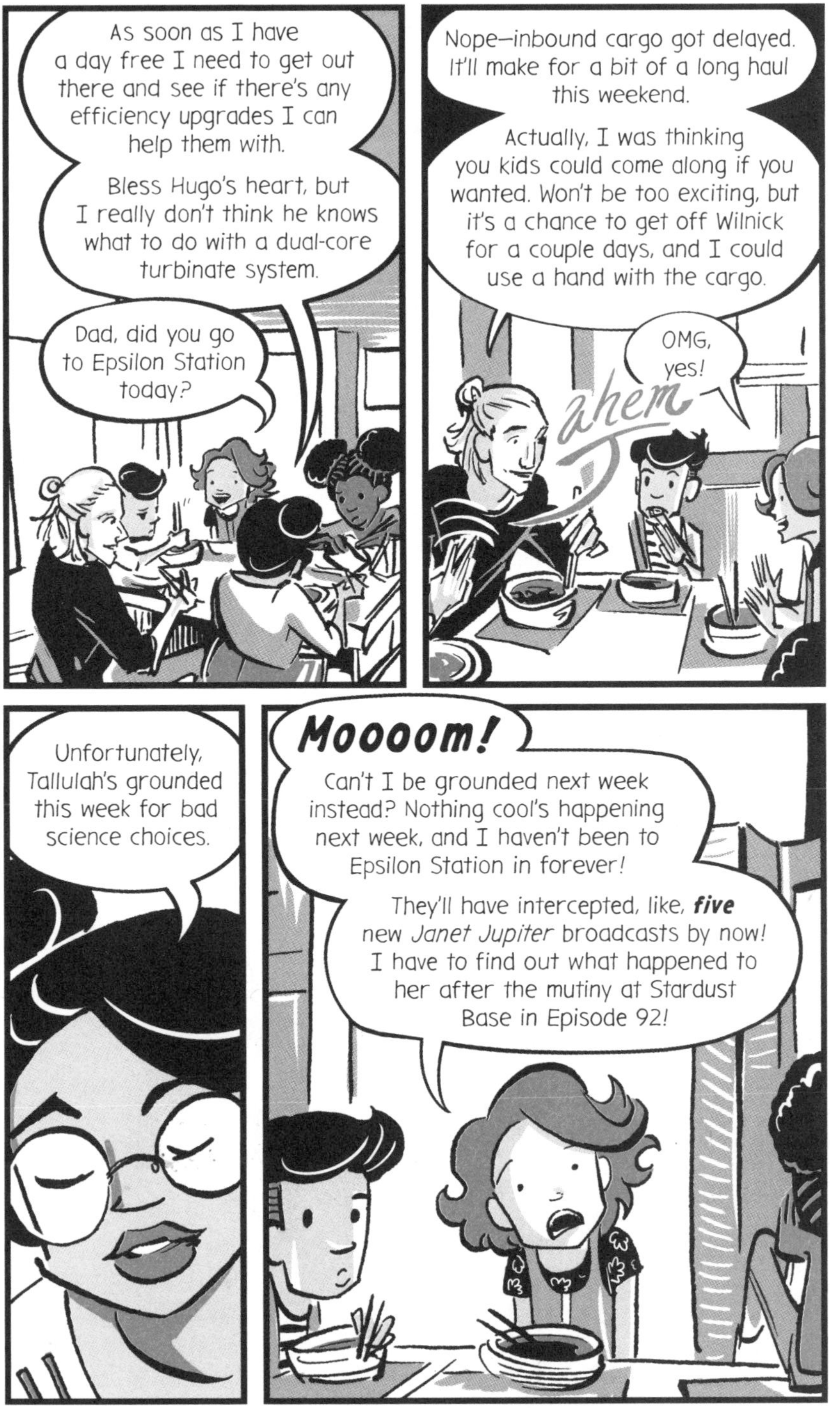
As soon as I have a day free I need to get out there and see if there's any efficiency upgrades I can help them with.
Bless Hugo's heart, but I really don't think he knows what to do with a dual-core turbinate system.
Dad, did you go to Epsilon Station today?
Nope—inbound cargo got delayed. It'll make for a bit of a long haul this weekend.
Actually, I was thinking you kids could come along if you wanted. Won't be too exciting, but it's a chance to get off Wilnick for a couple days, and I could use a hand with the cargo.
OMG, yes!
ahem
Unfortunately, Tallulah's grounded this week for bad science choices.
Moooom!
Can't I be grounded next week instead? Nothing cool's happening next week, and I haven't been to Epsilon Station in forever!
They'll have intercepted, like, **five** new *Janet Jupiter* broadcasts by now! I have to find out what happened to her after the mutiny at Stardust Base in Episode 92!

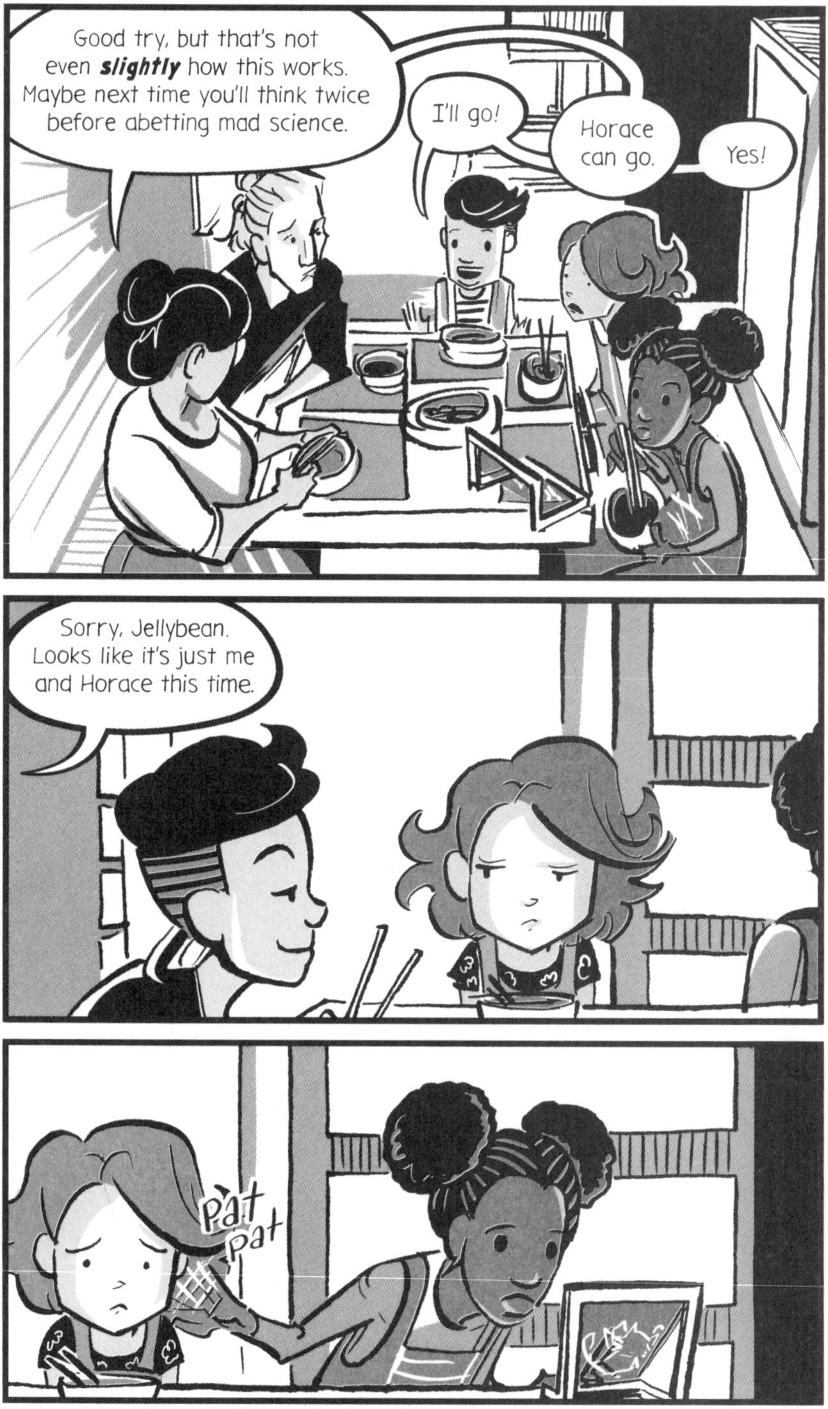
Good try, but that's not even **slightly** how this works. Maybe next time you'll think twice before abetting mad science.
I'll go!
Horace can go.
Yes!
Sorry, Jellybean. Looks like it's just me and Horace this time.
Pat pat

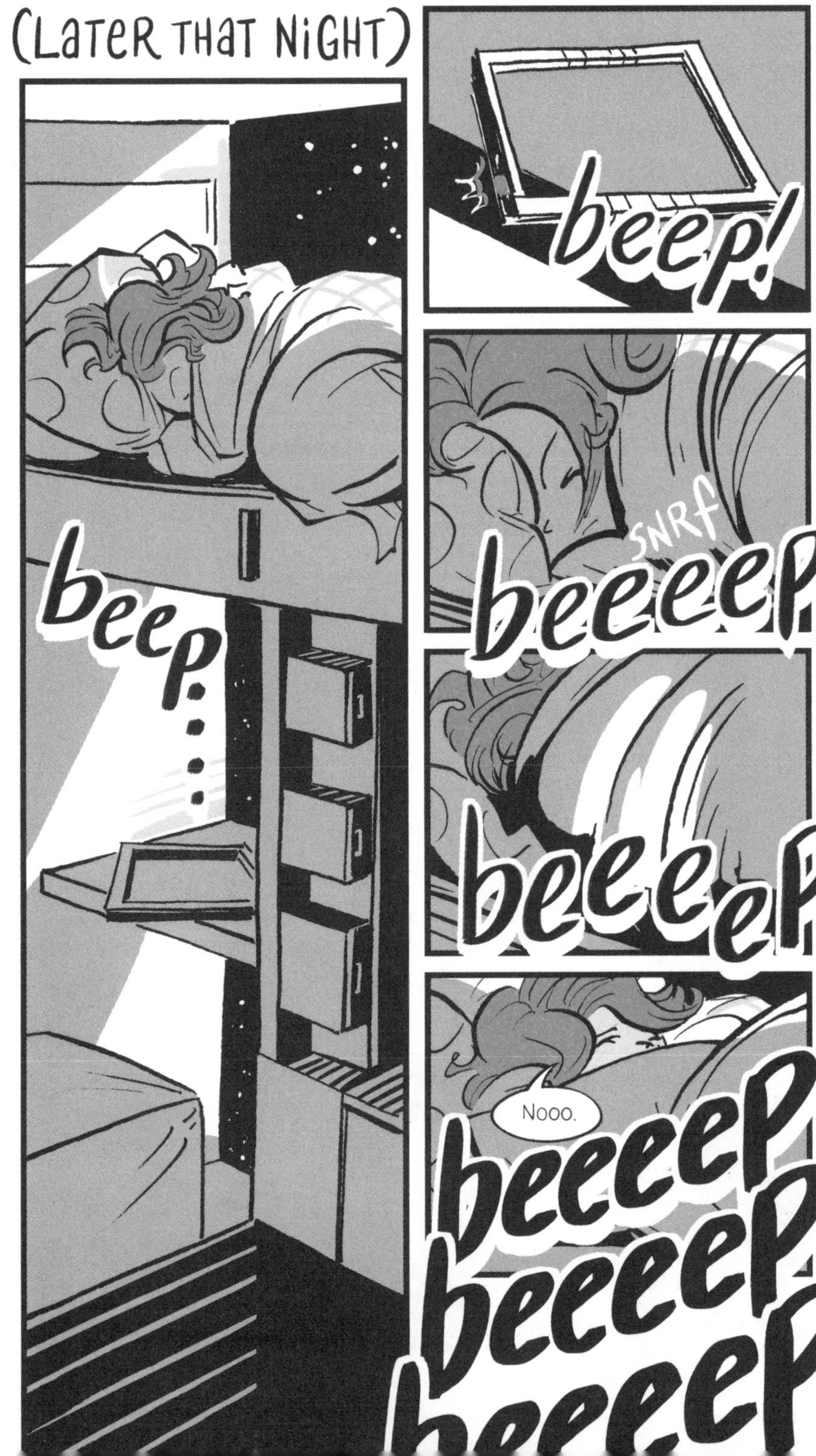

(LATER THAT NIGHT)
beep!
beep.....
SNRf
beeeeep
beeeeep
Nooo.
beeeeep
beeeeep
beeeeep

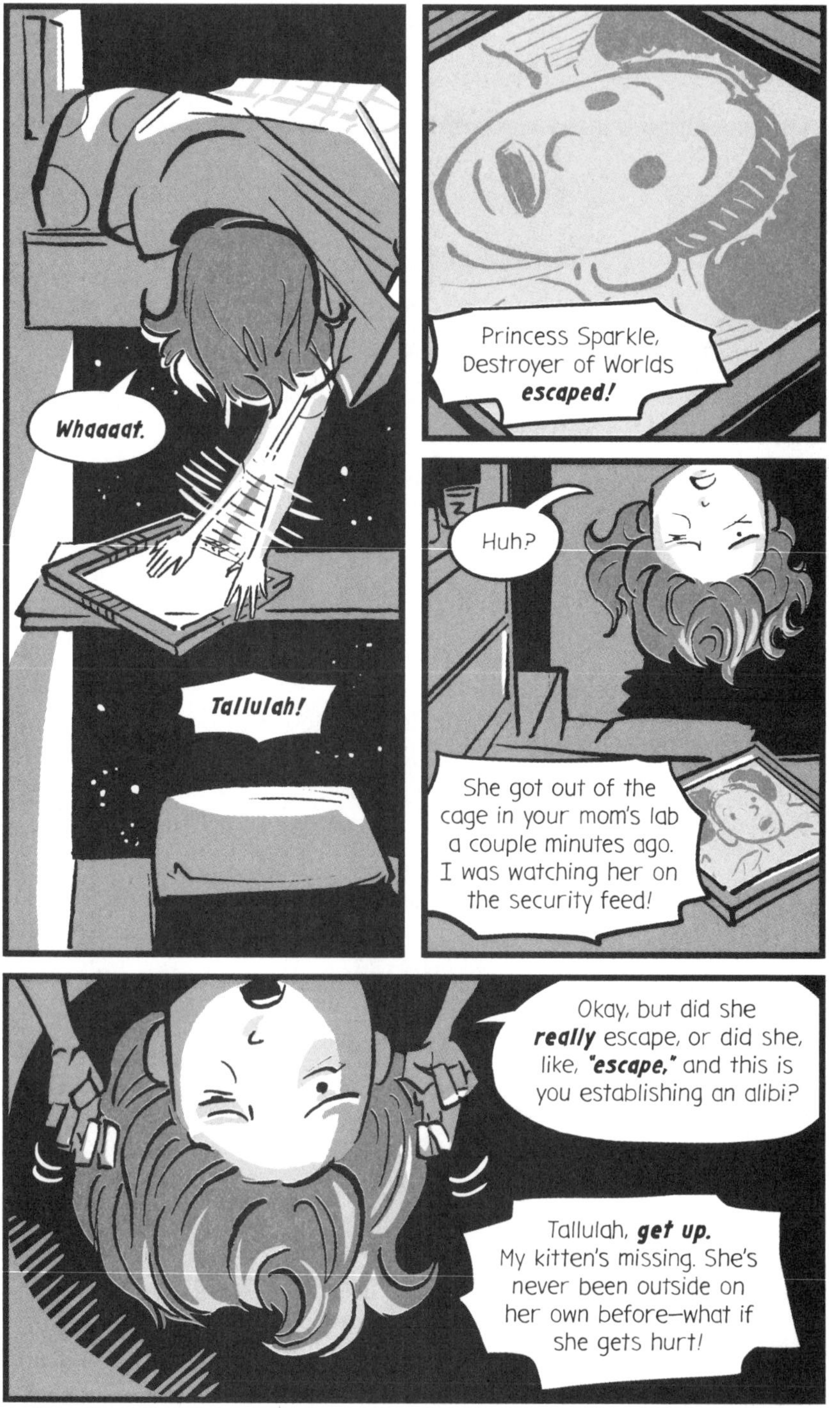
Whaaaat.
Princess Sparkle, Destroyer of Worlds **escaped!**
Tallulah!
Huh?
She got out of the cage in your mom's lab a couple minutes ago. I was watching her on the security feed!
Okay, but did she **really** escape, or did she, like, **"escape,"** and this is you establishing an alibi?
Tallulah, **get up.** My kitten's missing. She's never been outside on her own before—what if she gets hurt!

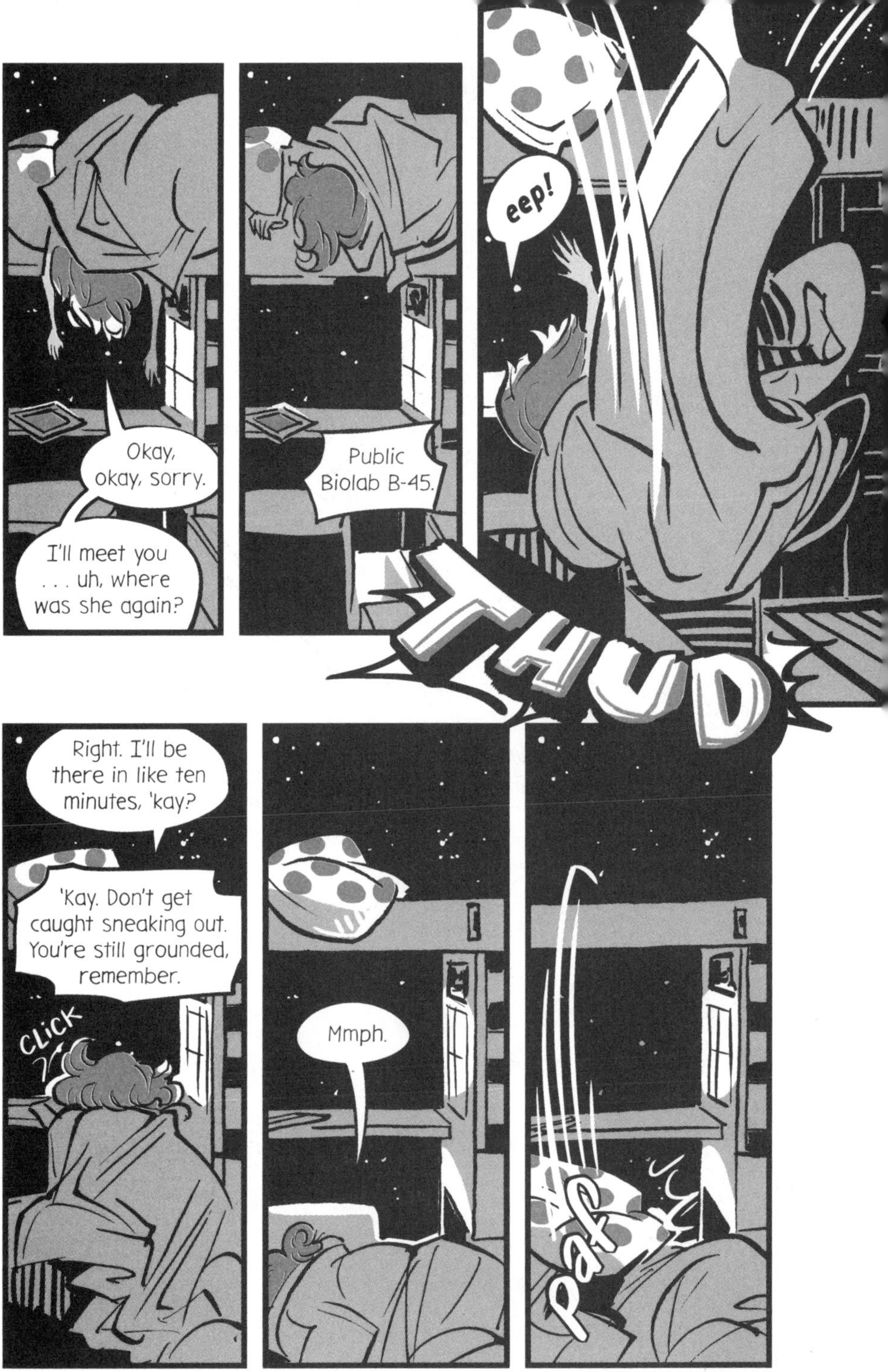
Okay, okay, sorry.
I'll meet you . . . uh, where was she again?
Public Biolab B-45.
eep!
THUD
Right. I'll be there in like ten minutes, 'kay?
'Kay. Don't get caught sneaking out. You're still grounded, remember.
CLICK
Mmph.
paf

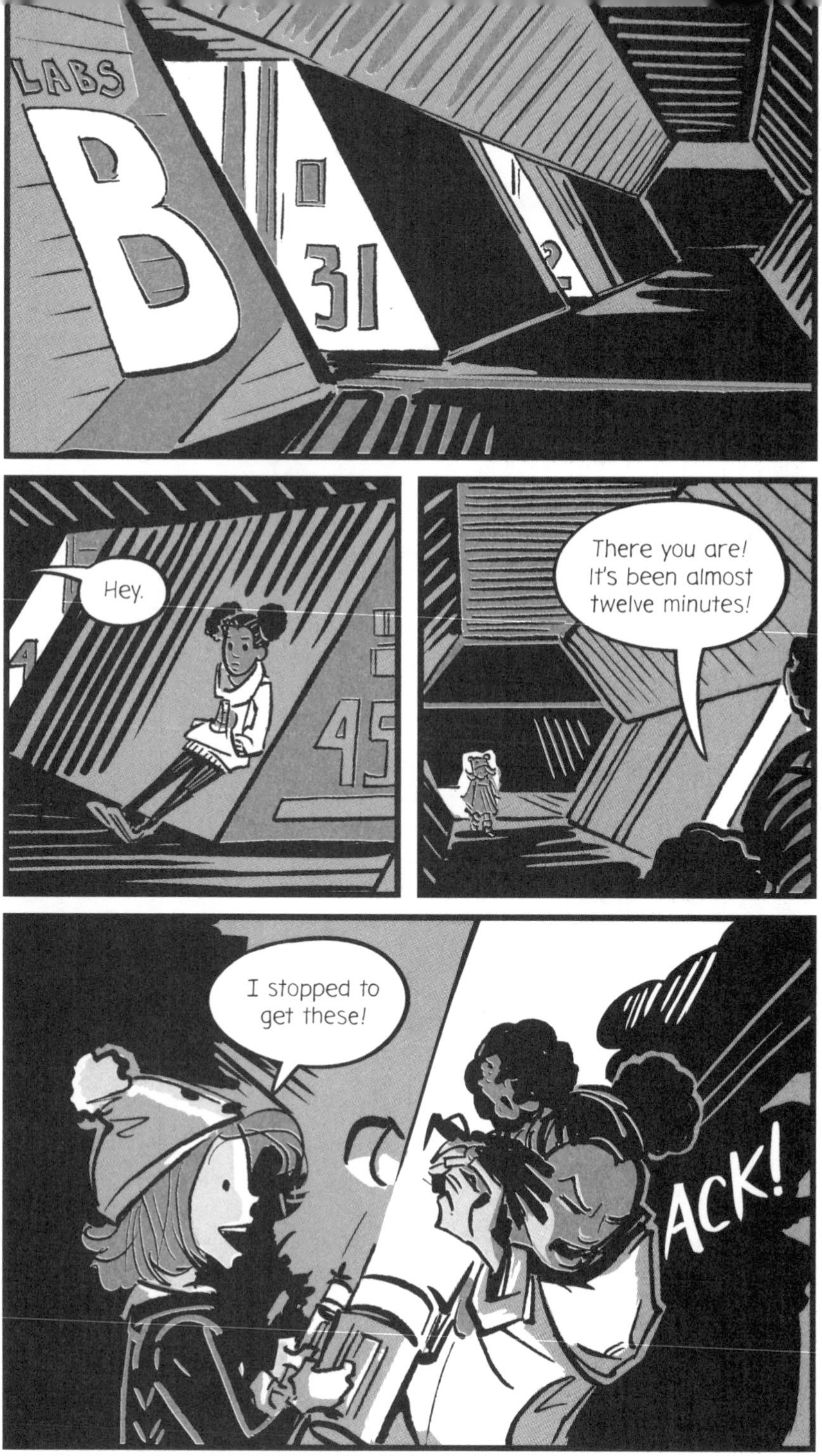
LABS
B
31
Hey.
45
There you are! It's been almost twelve minutes!
I stopped to get these!
ACK!

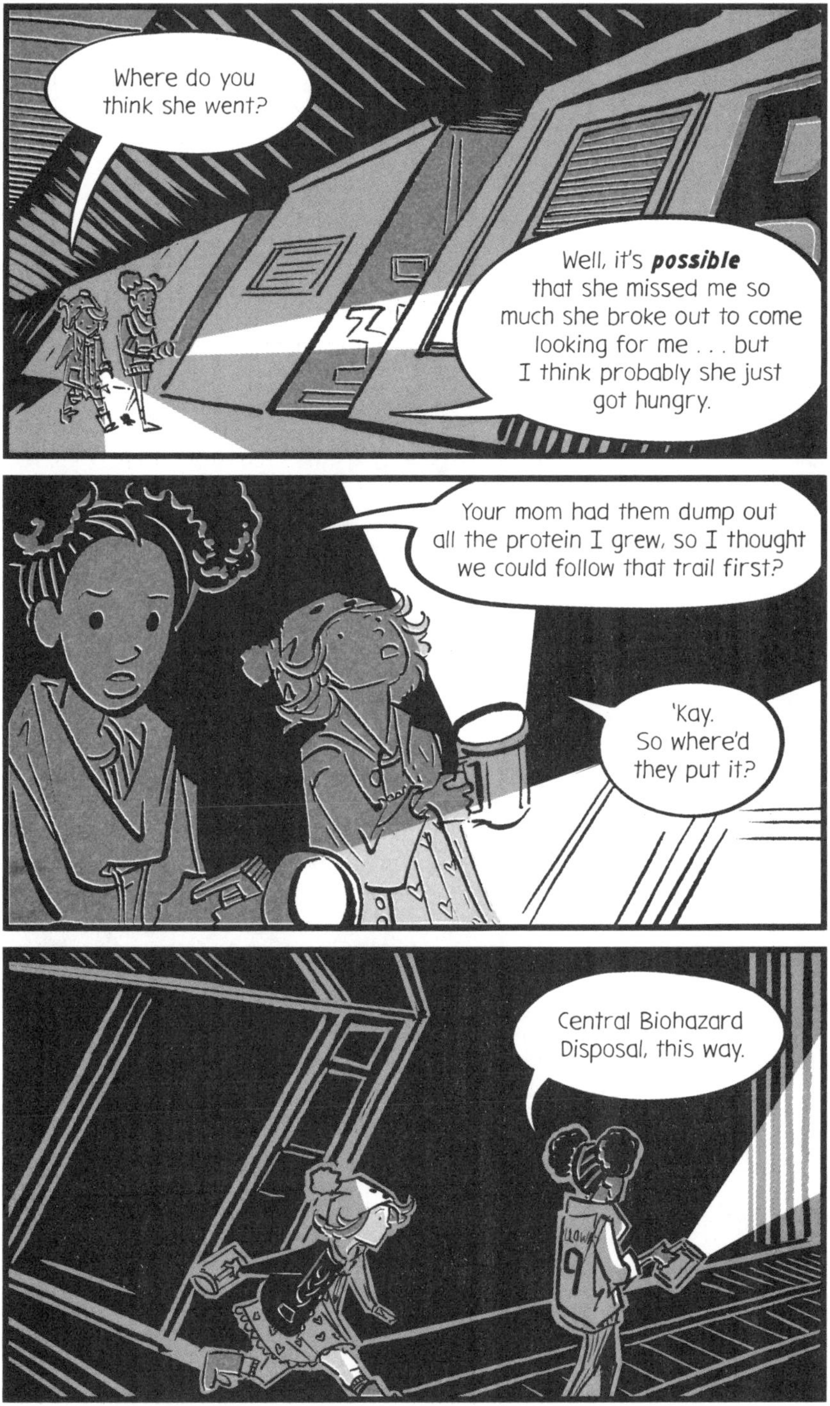
Where do you think she went?
Well, it's **possible** that she missed me so much she broke out to come looking for me . . . but I think probably she just got hungry.
Your mom had them dump out all the protein I grew, so I thought we could follow that trail first?
'Kay. So where'd they put it?
Central Biohazard Disposal, this way.

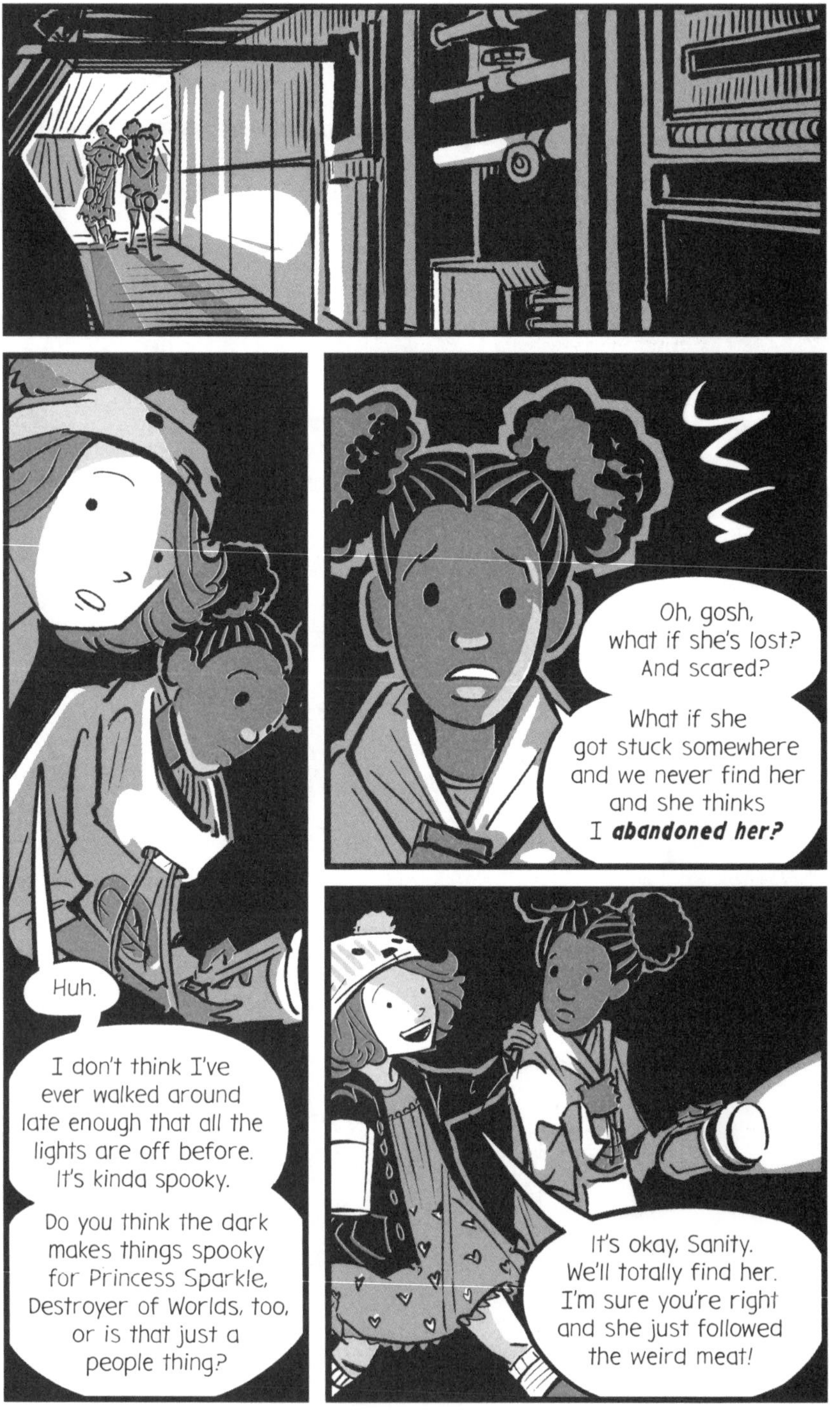
Huh.
I don't think I've ever walked around late enough that all the lights are off before. It's kinda spooky.
Do you think the dark makes things spooky for Princess Sparkle, Destroyer of Worlds, too, or is that just a people thing?
Oh, gosh, what if she's lost? And scared?
What if she got stuck somewhere and we never find her and she thinks I ***abandoned her?***
It's okay, Sanity. We'll totally find her. I'm sure you're right and she just followed the weird meat!

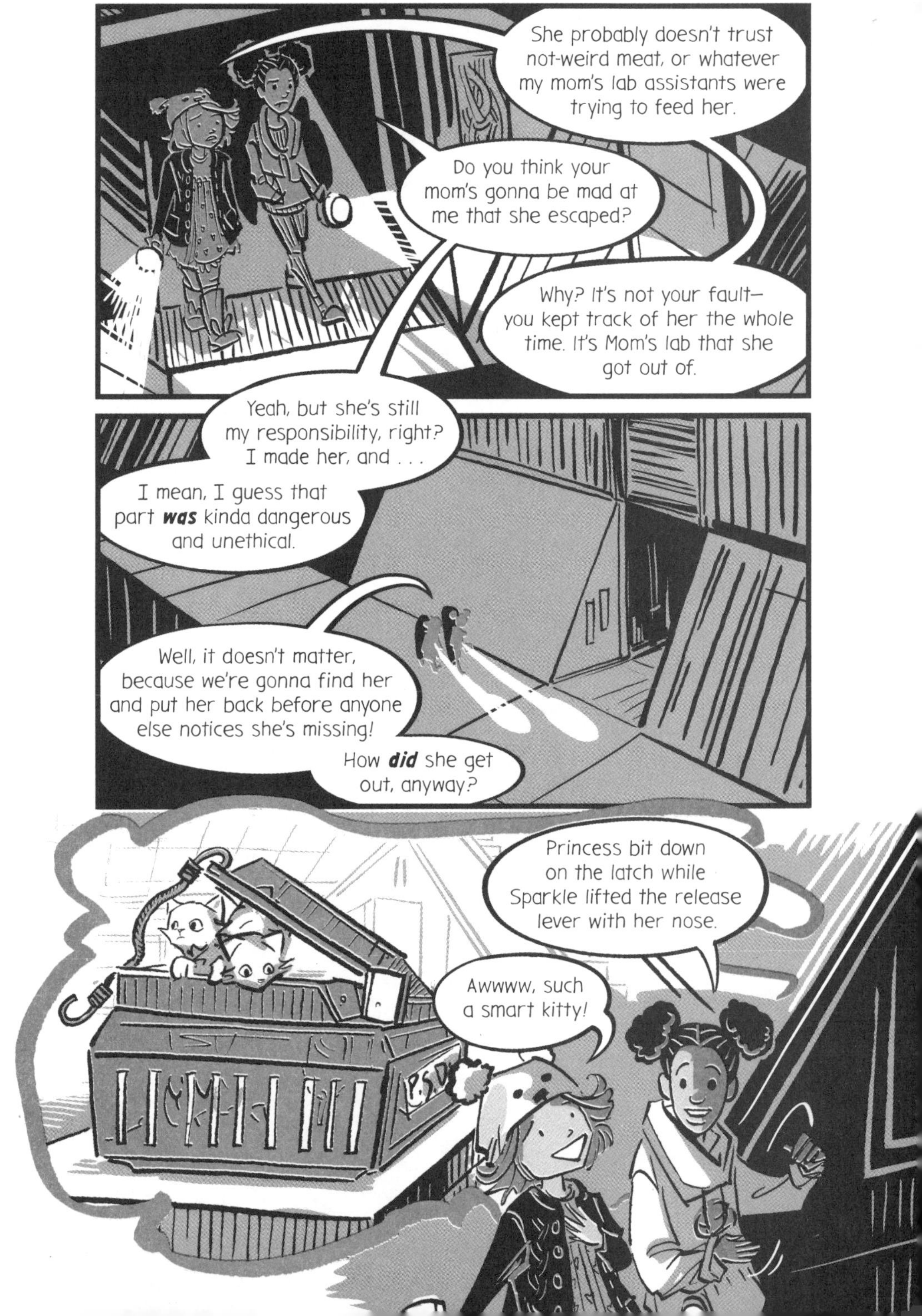
She probably doesn't trust not-weird meat, or whatever my mom's lab assistants were trying to feed her.
Do you think your mom's gonna be mad at me that she escaped?
Why? It's not your fault— you kept track of her the whole time. It's Mom's lab that she got out of.
Yeah, but she's still my responsibility, right? I made her, and . . .
I mean, I guess that part **was** kinda dangerous and unethical.
Well, it doesn't matter, because we're gonna find her and put her back before anyone else notices she's missing!
How **did** she get out, anyway?
Princess bit down on the latch while Sparkle lifted the release lever with her nose.
Awwww, such a smart kitty!
P.S.D.

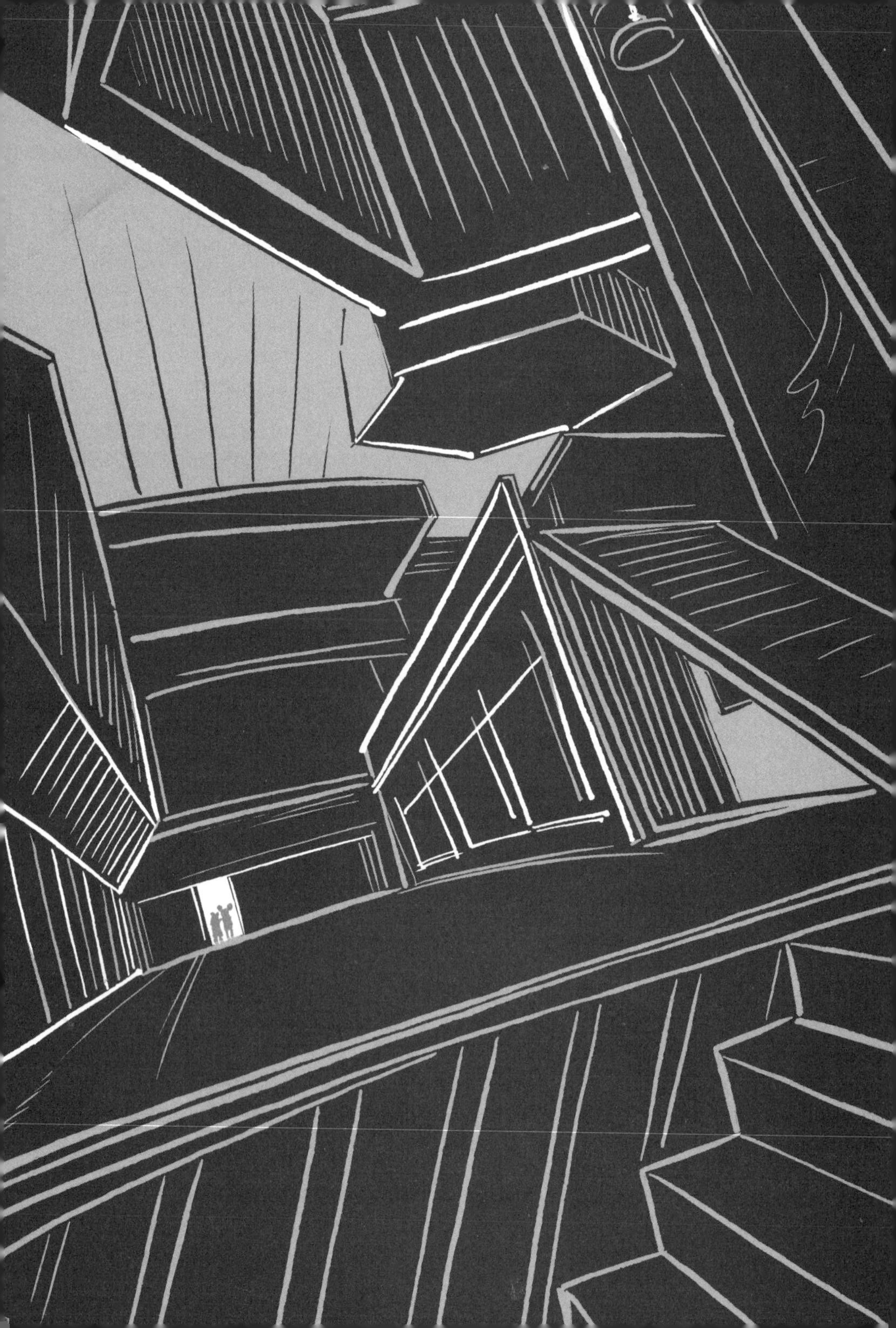

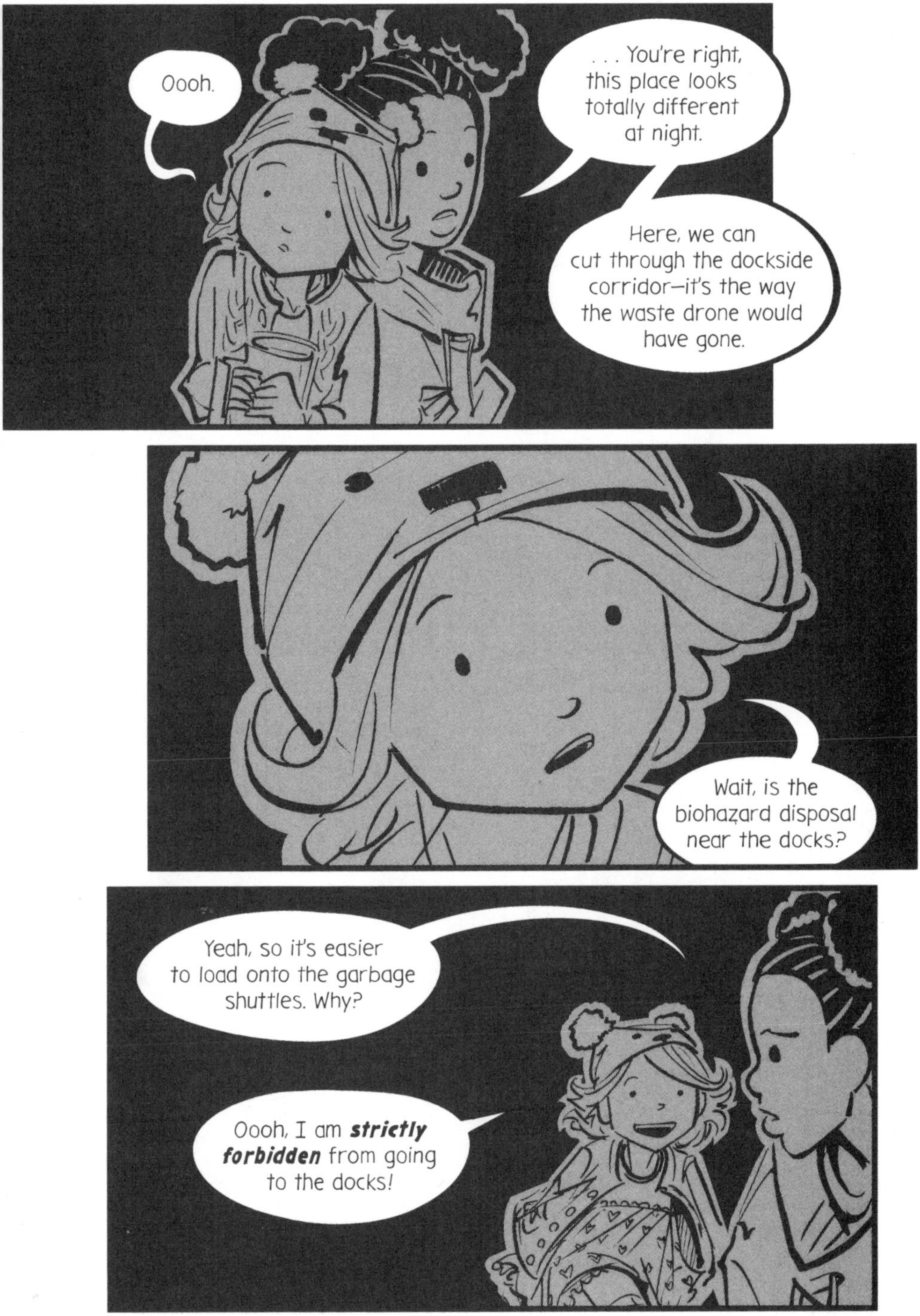
Oooh.
. . . You're right, this place looks totally different at night.
Here, we can cut through the dockside corridor—it's the way the waste drone would have gone.
Wait, is the biohazard disposal near the docks?
Yeah, so it's easier to load onto the garbage shuttles. Why?
Oooh, I am ***strictly forbidden*** from going to the docks!

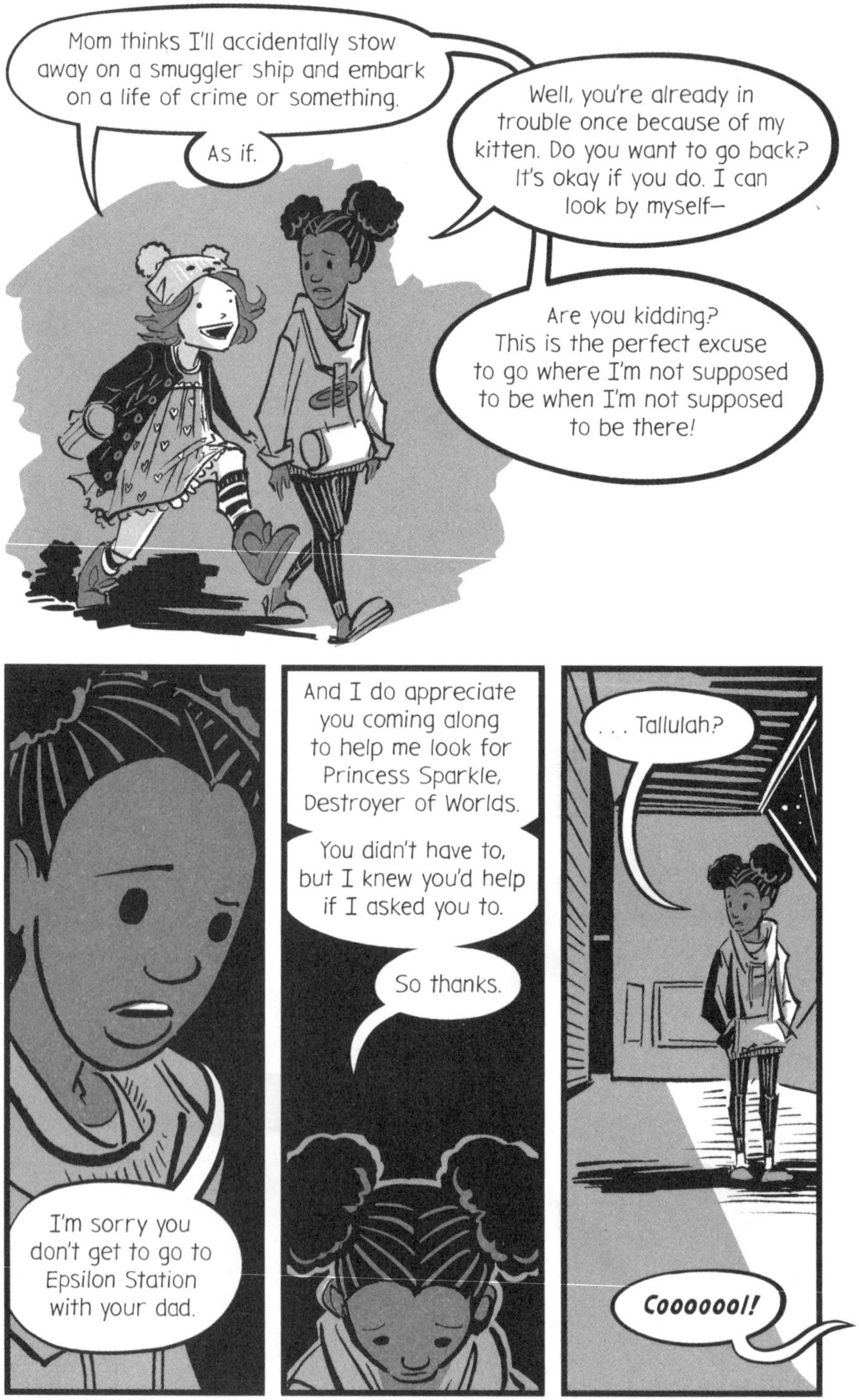
Mom thinks I'll accidentally stow away on a smuggler ship and embark on a life of crime or something.
As if.
Well, you're already in trouble once because of my kitten. Do you want to go back? It's okay if you do. I can look by myself—
Are you kidding? This is the perfect excuse to go where I'm not supposed to be when I'm not supposed to be there!
I'm sorry you don't get to go to Epsilon Station with your dad.
And I do appreciate you coming along to help me look for Princess Sparkle, Destroyer of Worlds.
You didn't have to, but I knew you'd help if I asked you to.
So thanks.
. . . Tallulah?
Cooooool!

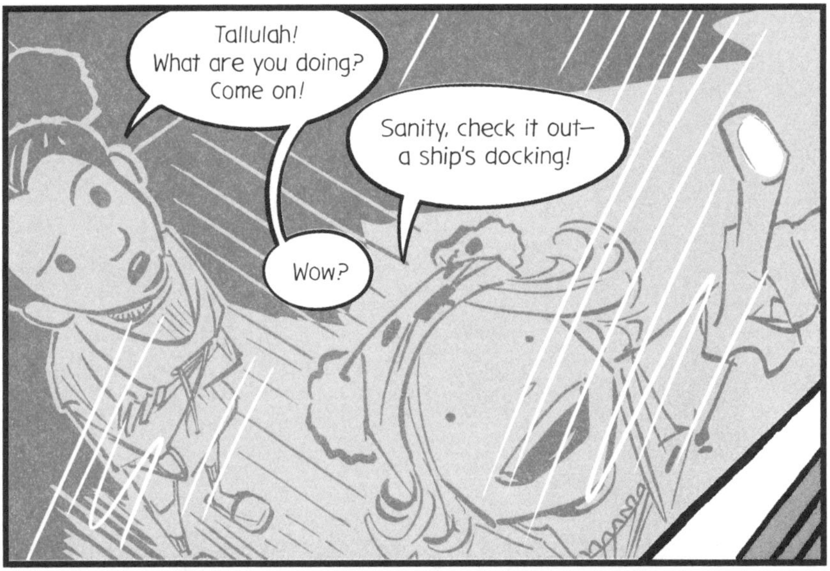
Tallulah! What are you doing? Come on!
Sanity, check it out—a ship's docking!
Wow?

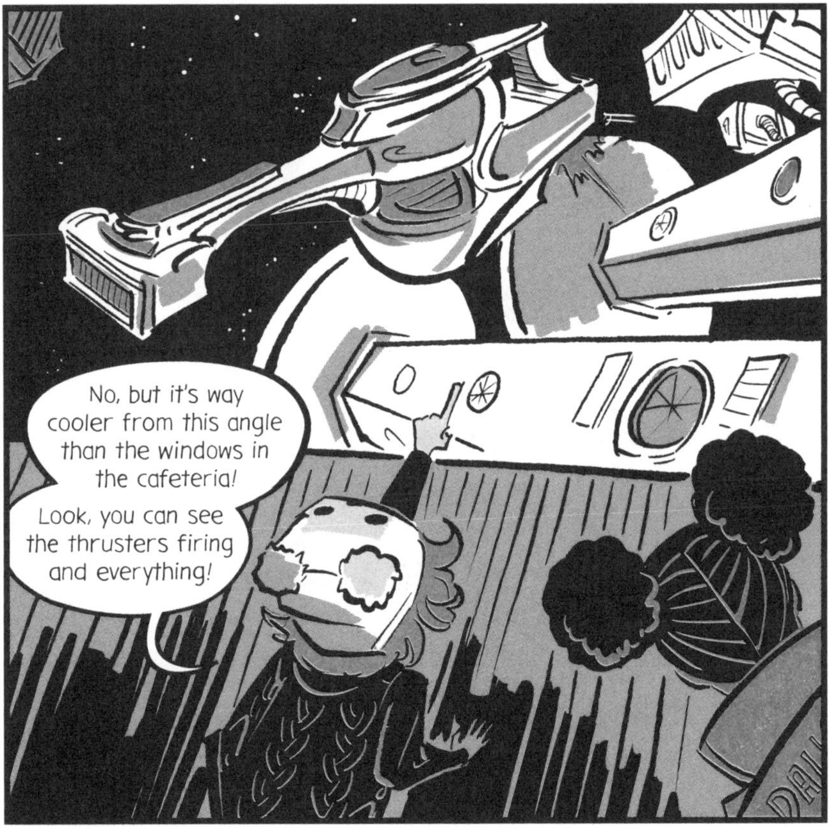
No, but it's way cooler from this angle than the windows in the cafeteria!
Look, you can see the thrusters firing and everything!

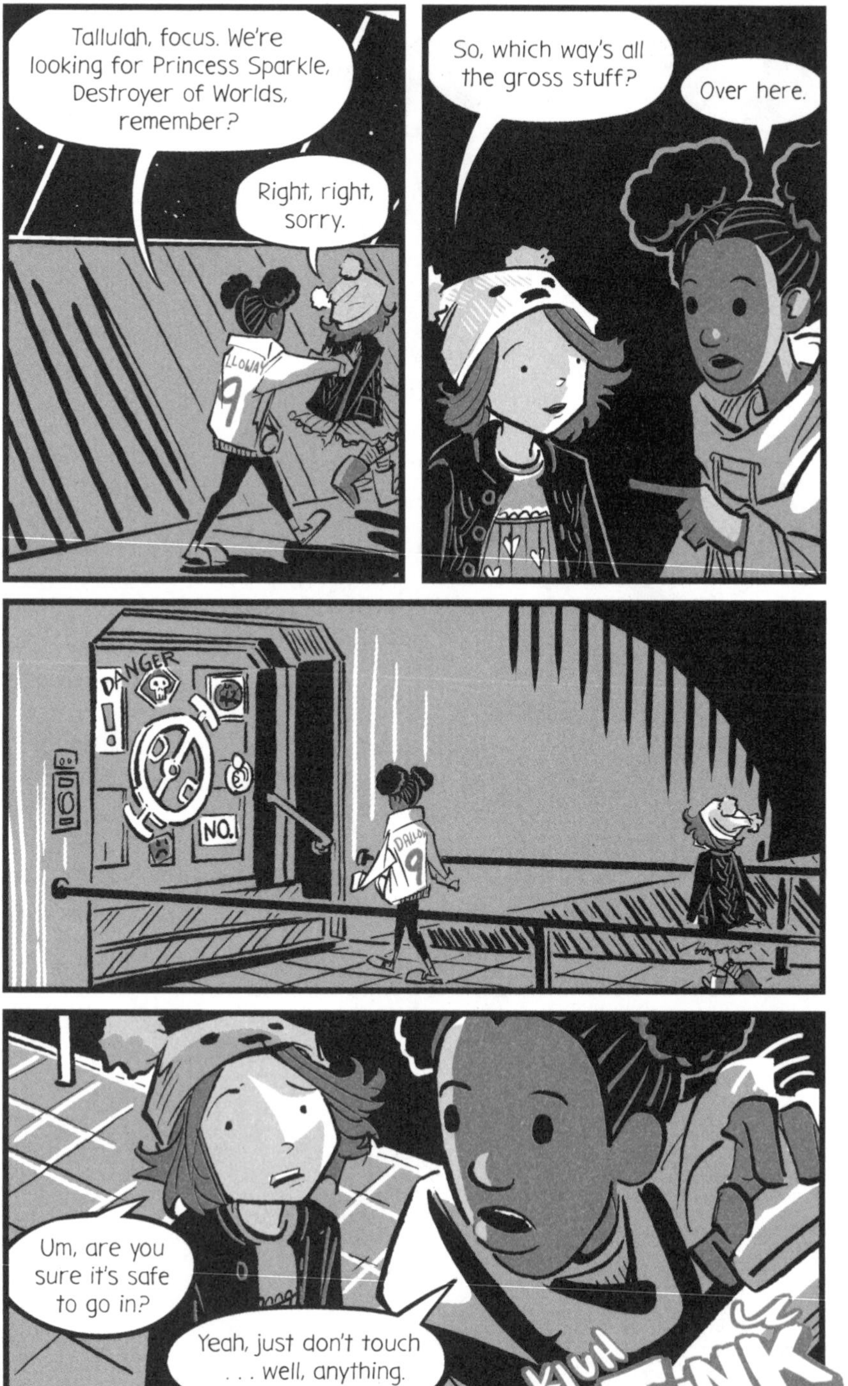
Tallulah, focus. We're looking for Princess Sparkle, Destroyer of Worlds, remember?
Right, right, sorry.
So, which way's all the gross stuff?
Over here.
DANGER
!
NO.
Um, are you sure it's safe to go in?
Yeah, just don't touch . . . well, anything.
KLUH
TUNK

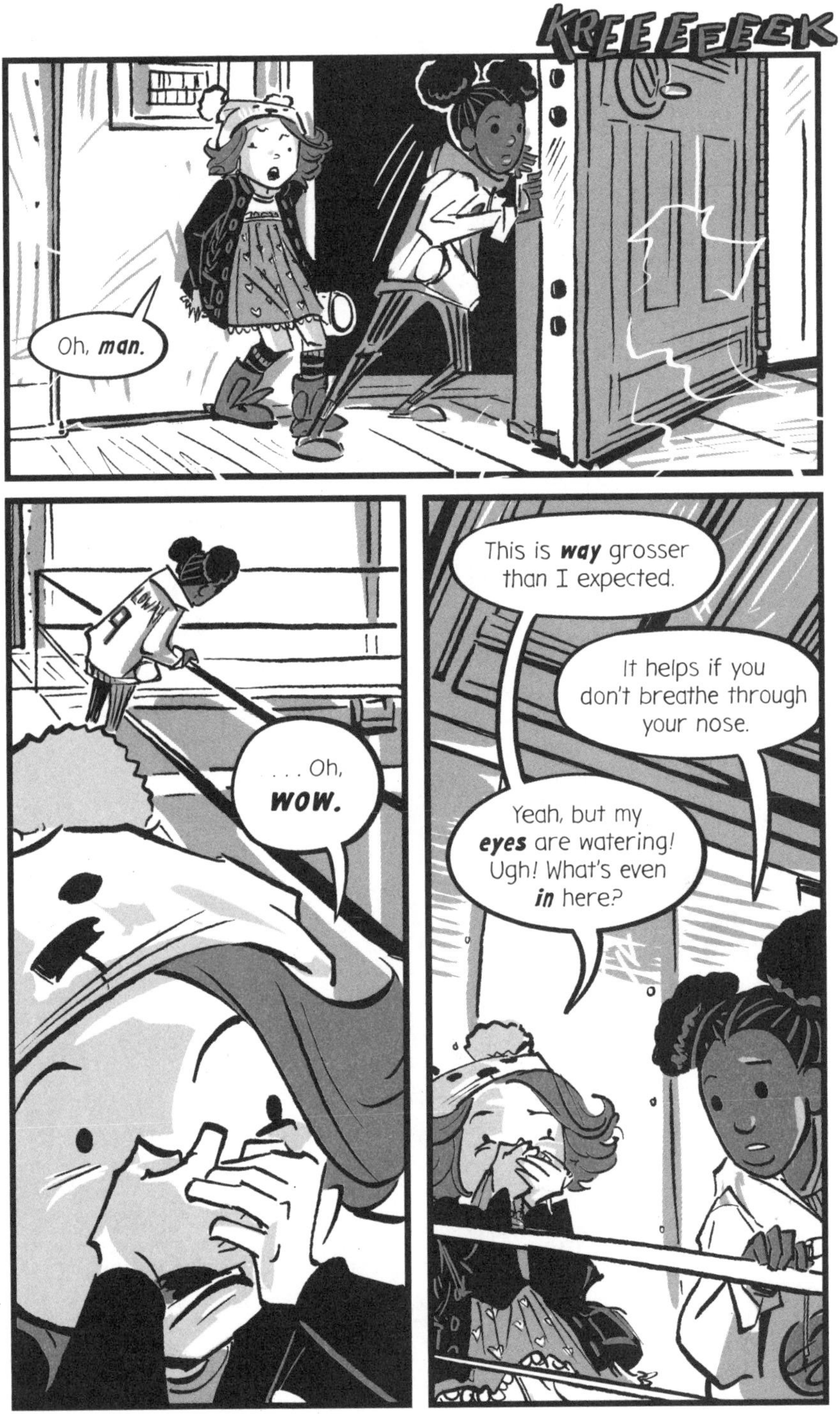
KREEEEEEK
Oh, man.
. . . Oh, WOW.
This is way grosser than I expected.
It helps if you don't breathe through your nose.
Yeah, but my eyes are watering! Ugh! What's even in here?

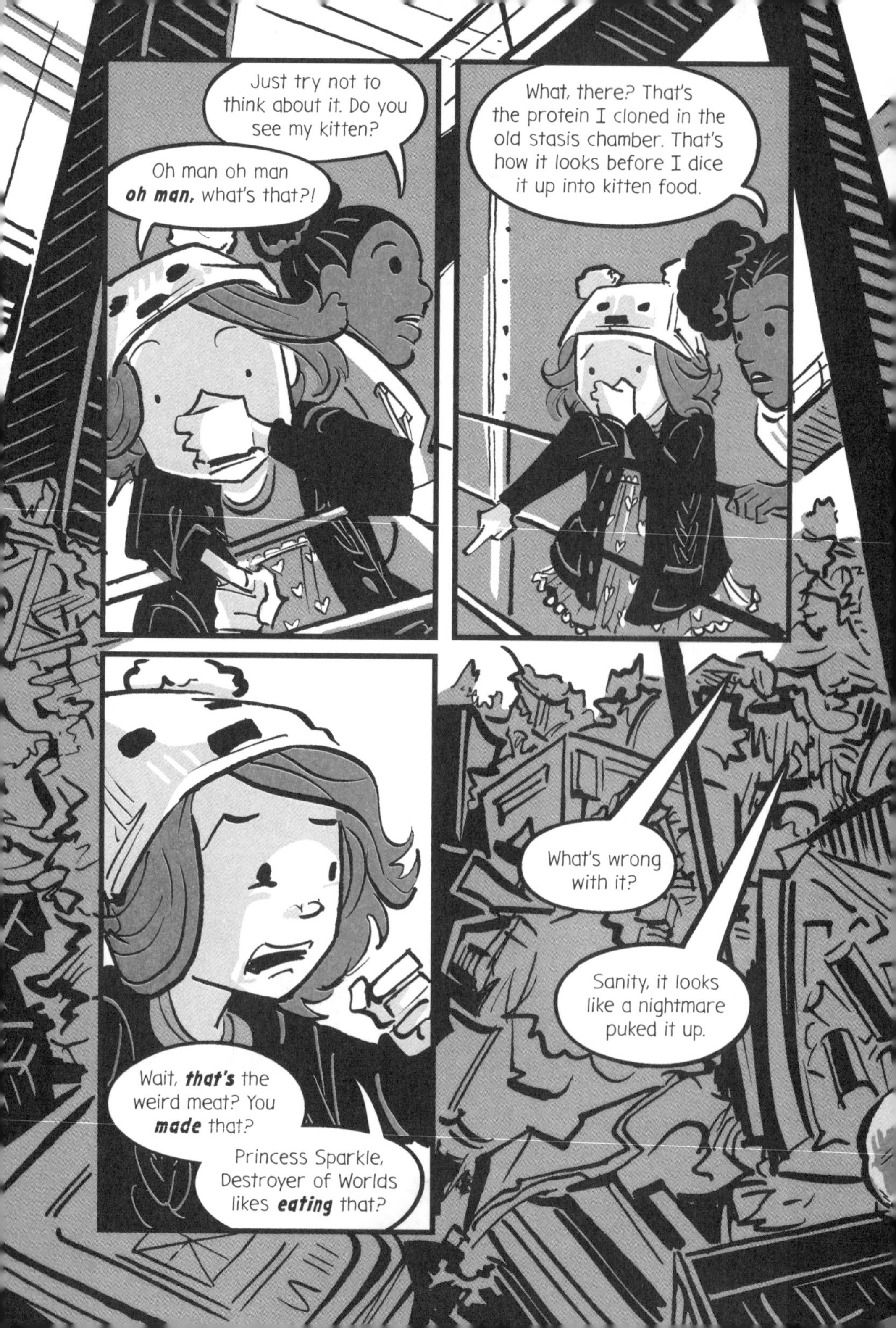
Just try not to think about it. Do you see my kitten?
Oh man oh man **oh man,** what's that?!
What, there? That's the protein I cloned in the old stasis chamber. That's how it looks before I dice it up into kitten food.
What's wrong with it?
Sanity, it looks like a nightmare puked it up.
Wait, ***that's*** the weird meat? You ***made*** that?
Princess Sparkle, Destroyer of Worlds likes ***eating*** that?

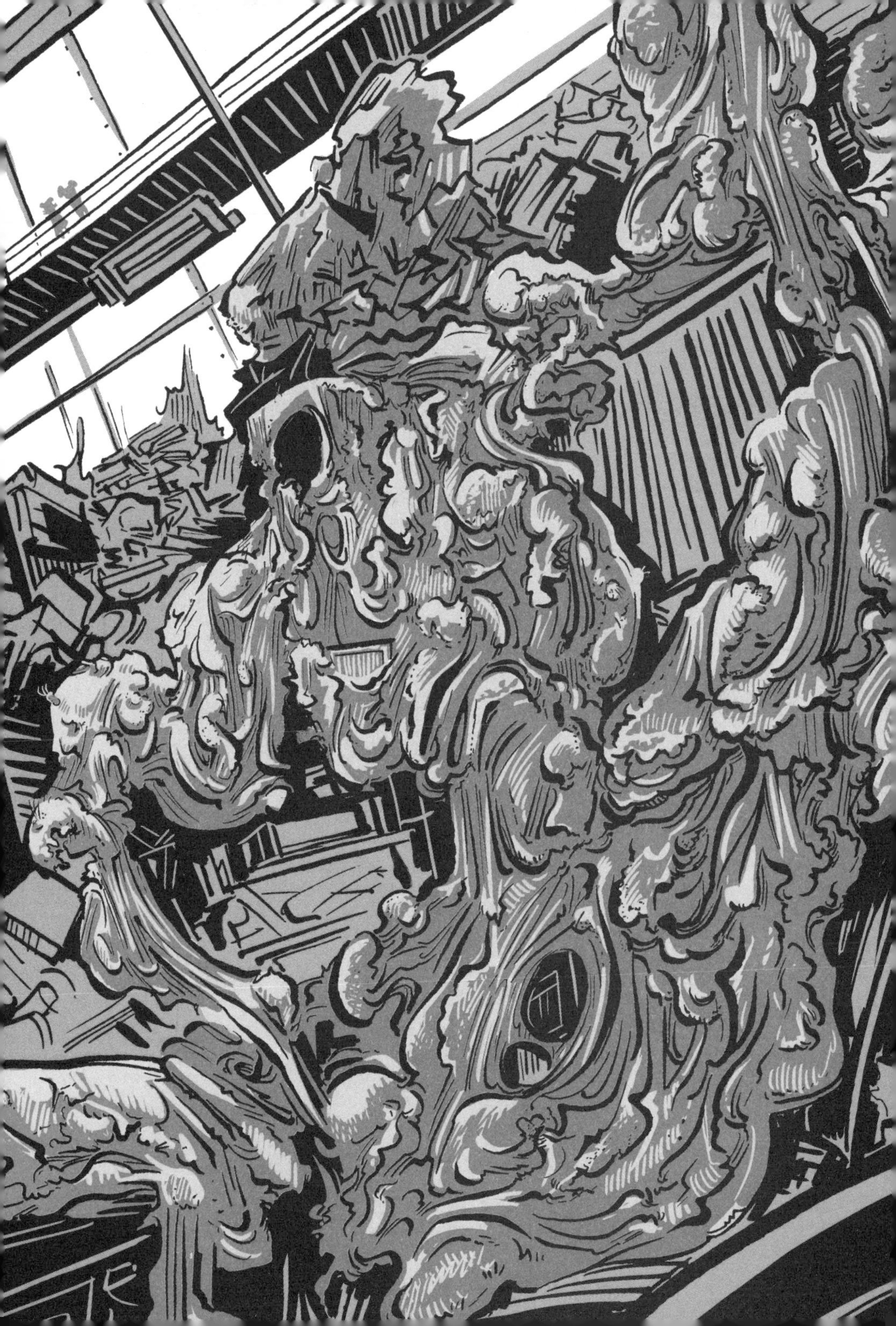

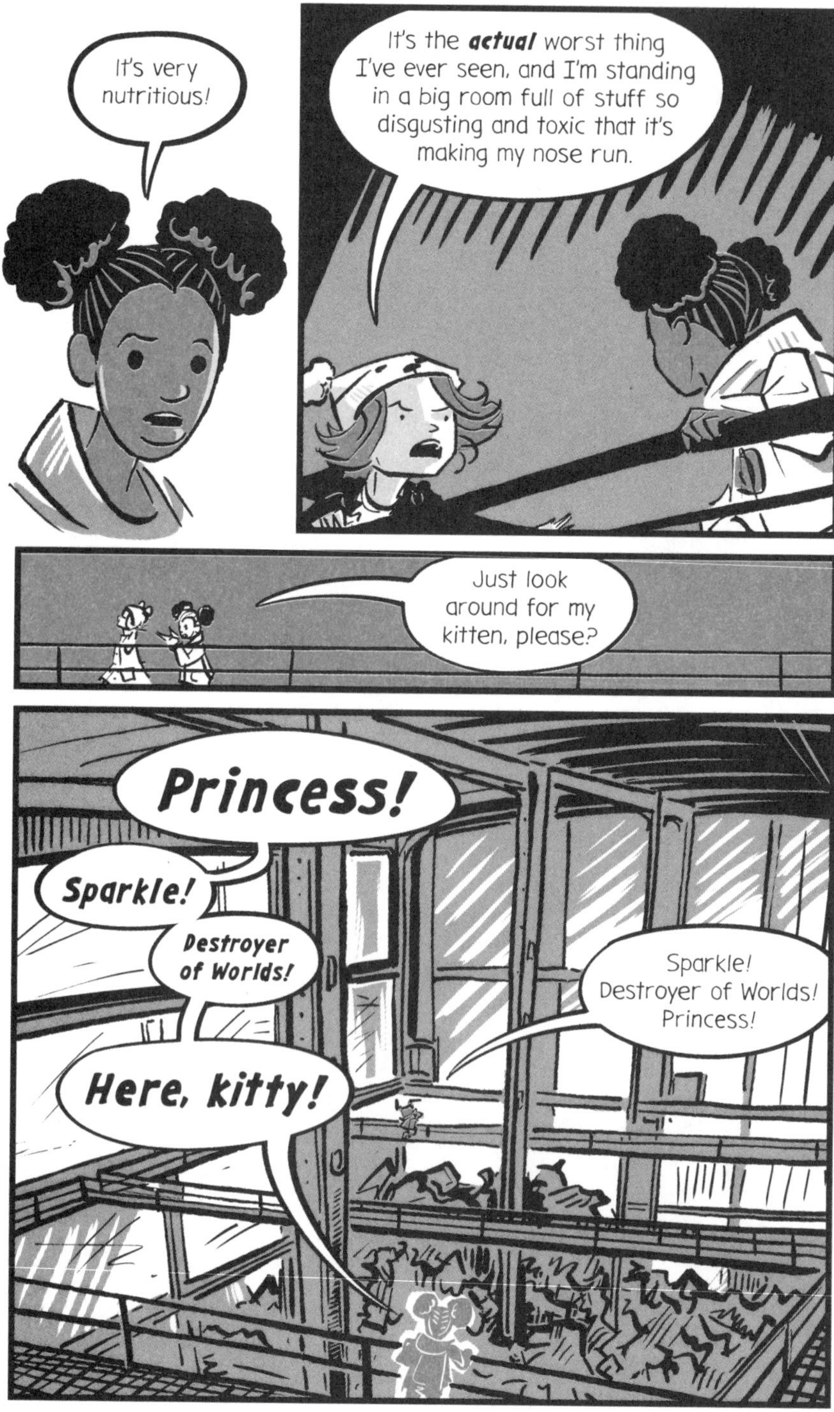
It's very nutritious!
It's the ***actual*** worst thing I've ever seen, and I'm standing in a big room full of stuff so disgusting and toxic that it's making my nose run.
Just look around for my kitten, please?
Princess!
Sparkle!
Destroyer of Worlds!
Here, kitty!
Sparkle! Destroyer of Worlds! Princess!

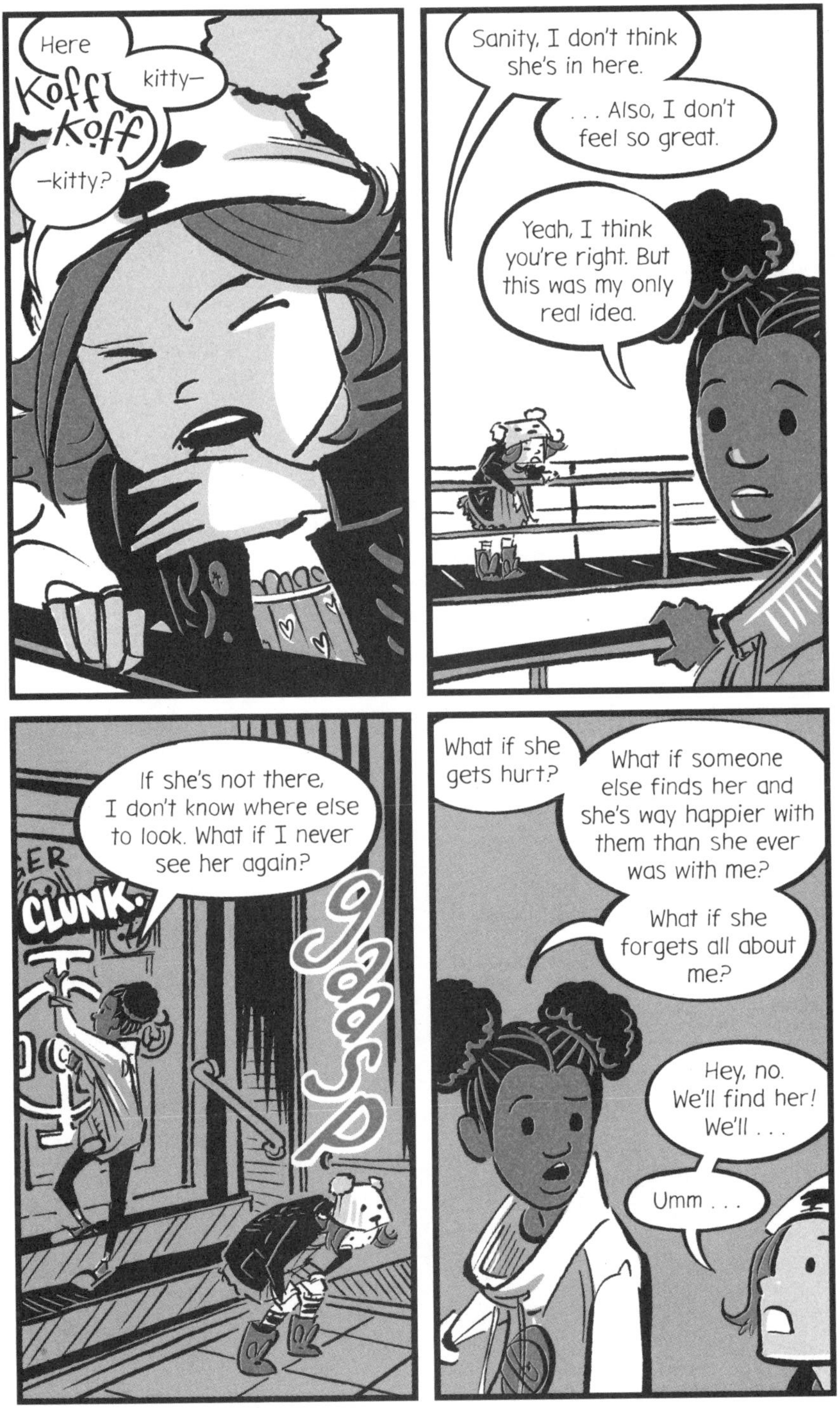

Here
Koff koff
kitty—
—kitty?
Sanity, I don't think she's in here.
. . . Also, I don't feel so great.
Yeah, I think you're right. But this was my only real idea.
If she's not there, I don't know where else to look. What if I never see her again?
CLUNK.
gaasp
What if she gets hurt?
What if someone else finds her and she's way happier with them than she ever was with me?
What if she forgets all about me?
Hey, no. We'll find her! We'll . . .
Umm . . .

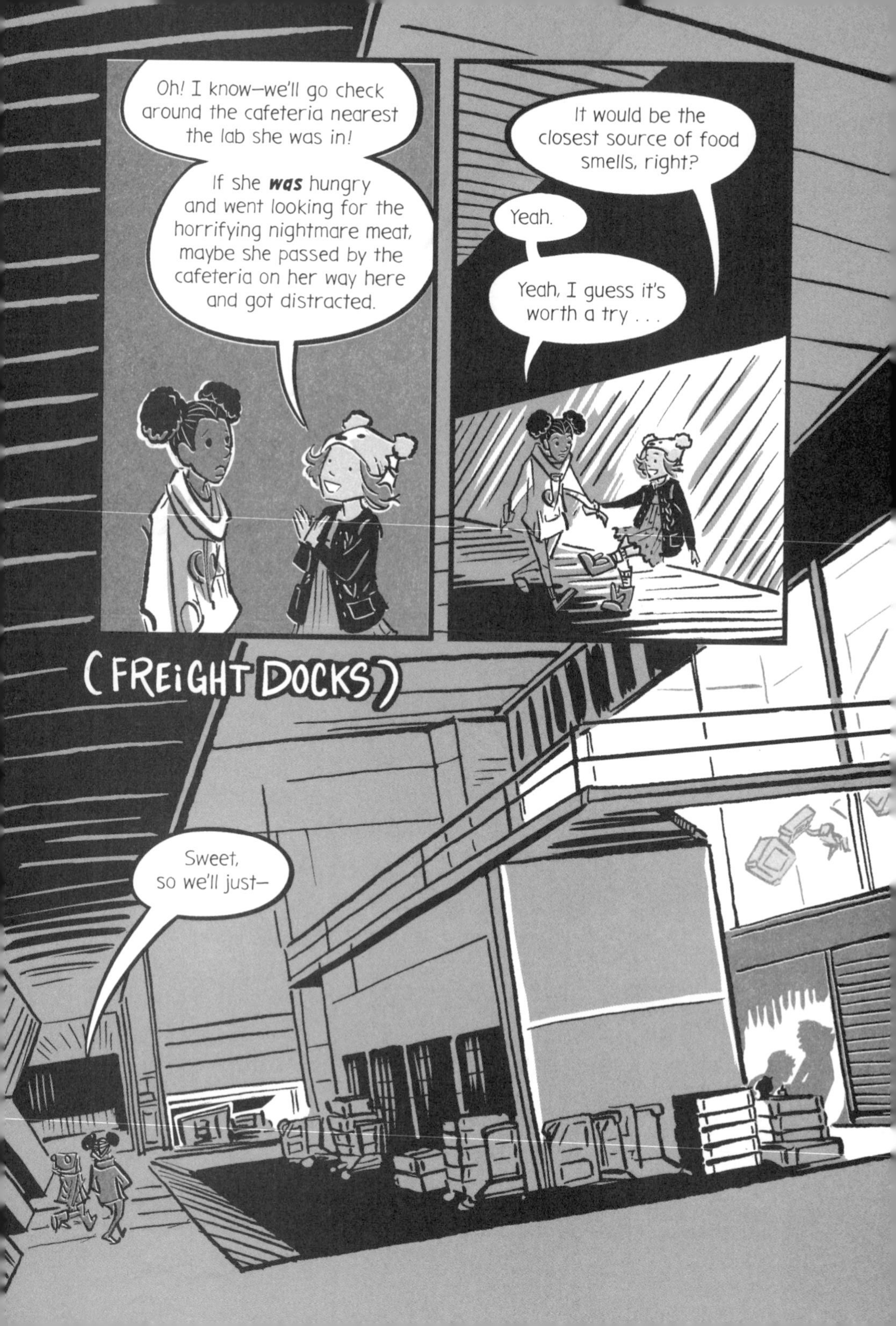

Oh! I know—we'll go check around the cafeteria nearest the lab she was in!
If she **was** hungry and went looking for the horrifying nightmare meat, maybe she passed by the cafeteria on her way here and got distracted.
It would be the closest source of food smells, right?
Yeah.
Yeah, I guess it's worth a try . . .
(FREIGHT DOCKS)
Sweet, so we'll just—

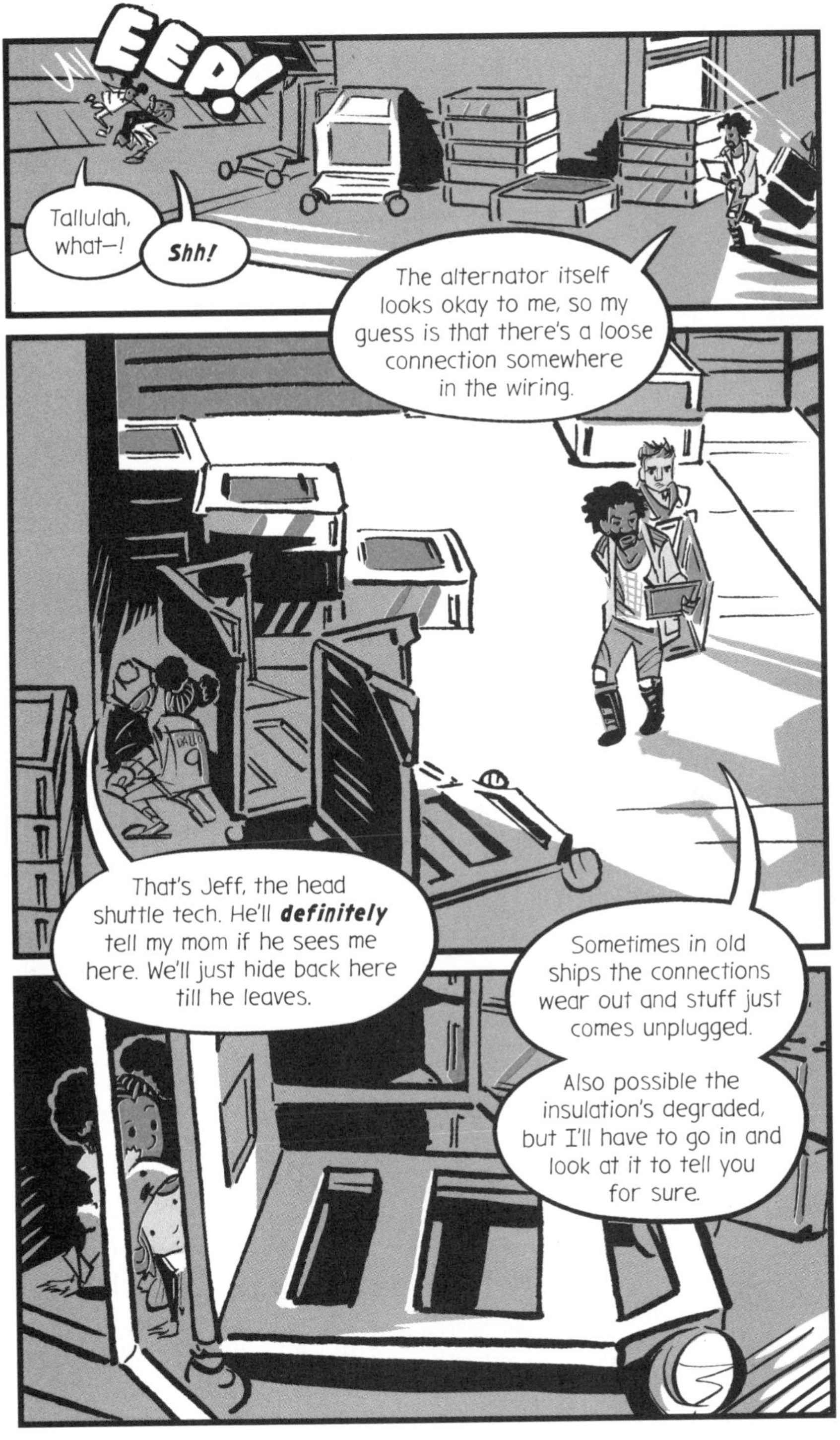
EEP!
Tallulah, what—!
Shh!
The alternator itself looks okay to me, so my guess is that there's a loose connection somewhere in the wiring.
That's Jeff, the head shuttle tech. He'll **definitely** tell my mom if he sees me here. We'll just hide back here till he leaves.
Sometimes in old ships the connections wear out and stuff just comes unplugged.
Also possible the insulation's degraded, but I'll have to go in and look at it to tell you for sure.

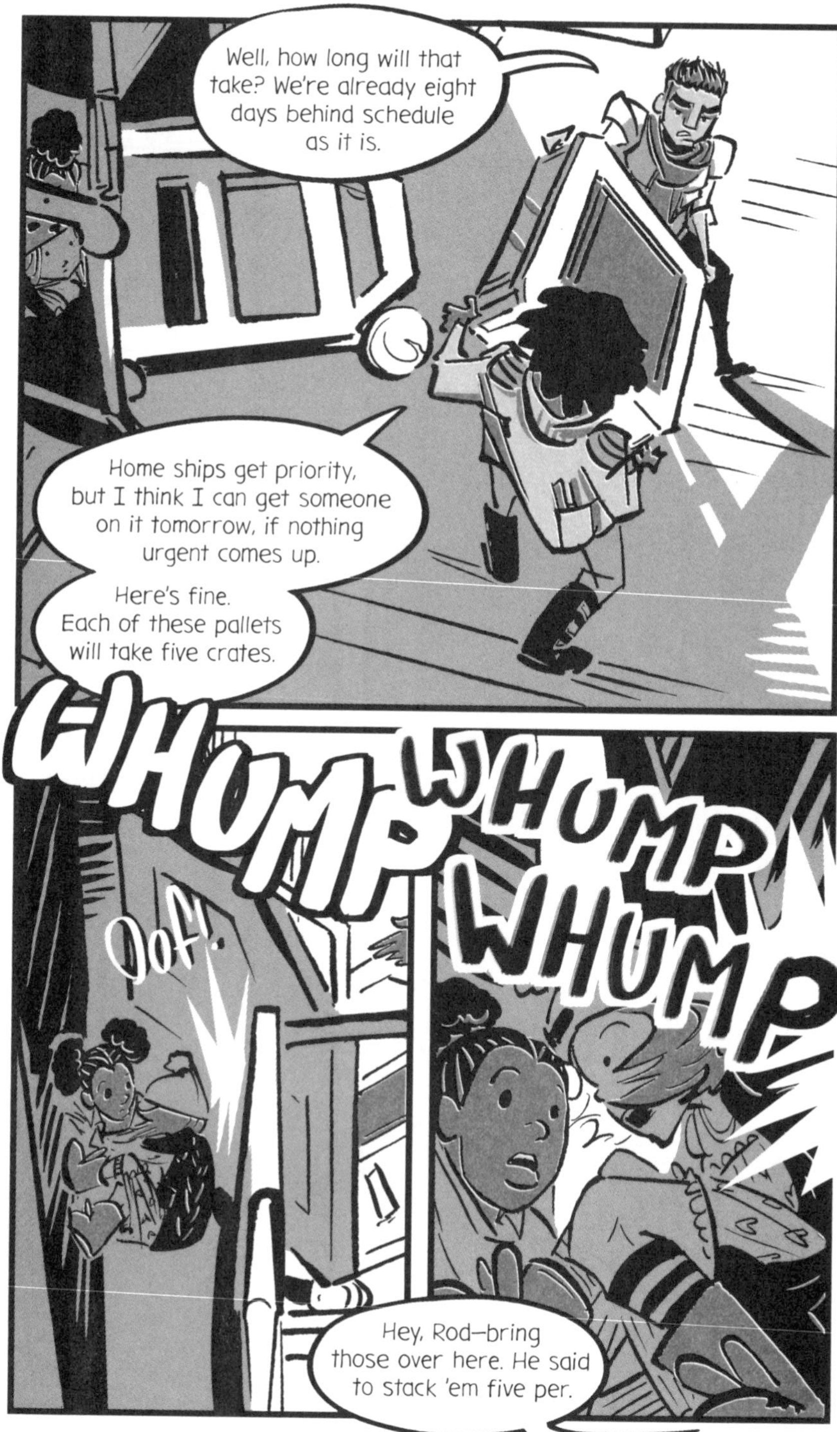
Well, how long will that take? We're already eight days behind schedule as it is.
Home ships get priority, but I think I can get someone on it tomorrow, if nothing urgent comes up.
Here's fine. Each of these pallets will take five crates.
WHUMP
WHUMP
WHUMP
WHUMP
Oof!
Hey, Rod—bring those over here. He said to stack 'em five per.

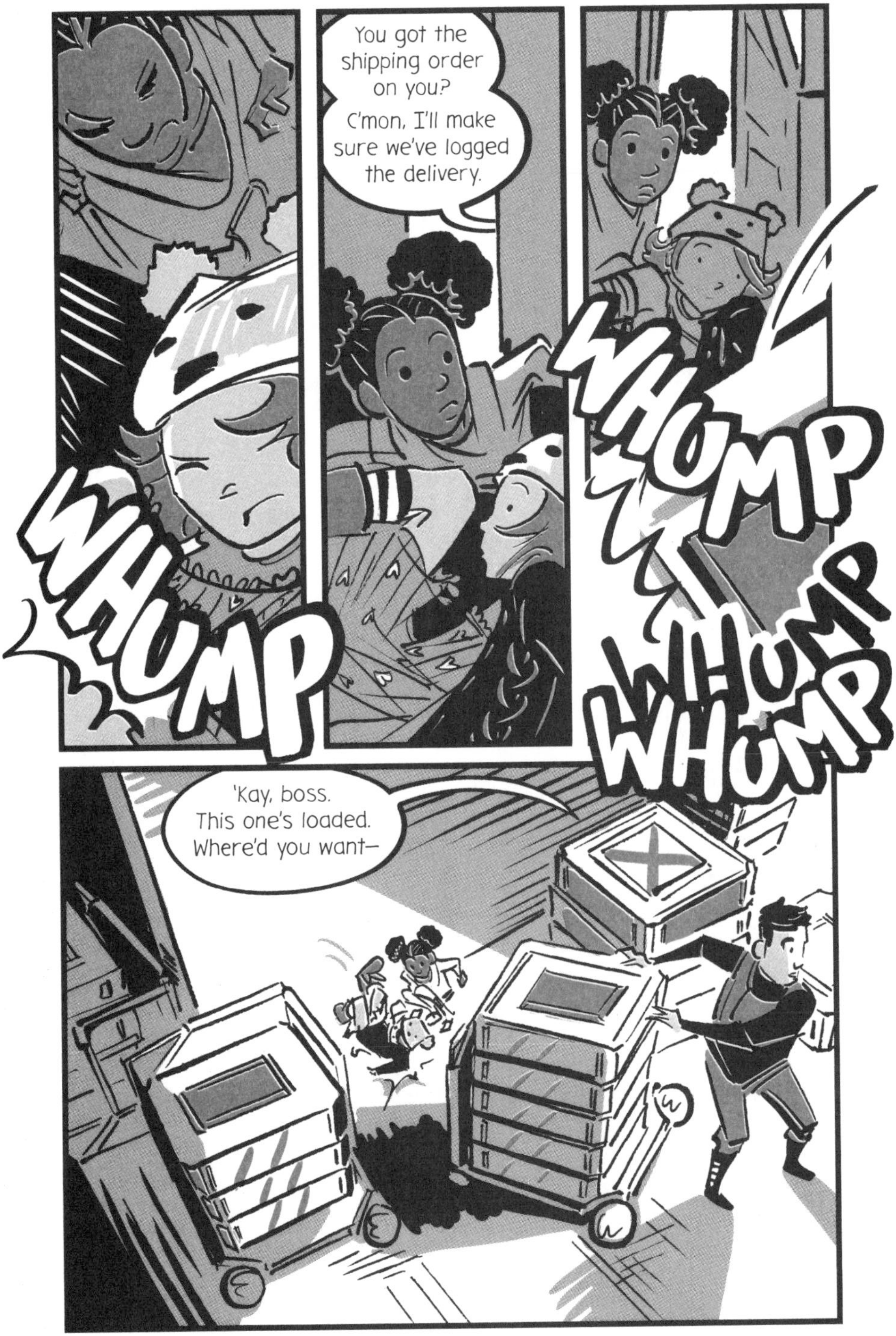
You got the shipping order on you?
C'mon, I'll make sure we've logged the delivery.
WHUMP
WHUMP
WHUMP
WHUMP
'Kay, boss. This one's loaded. Where'd you want–

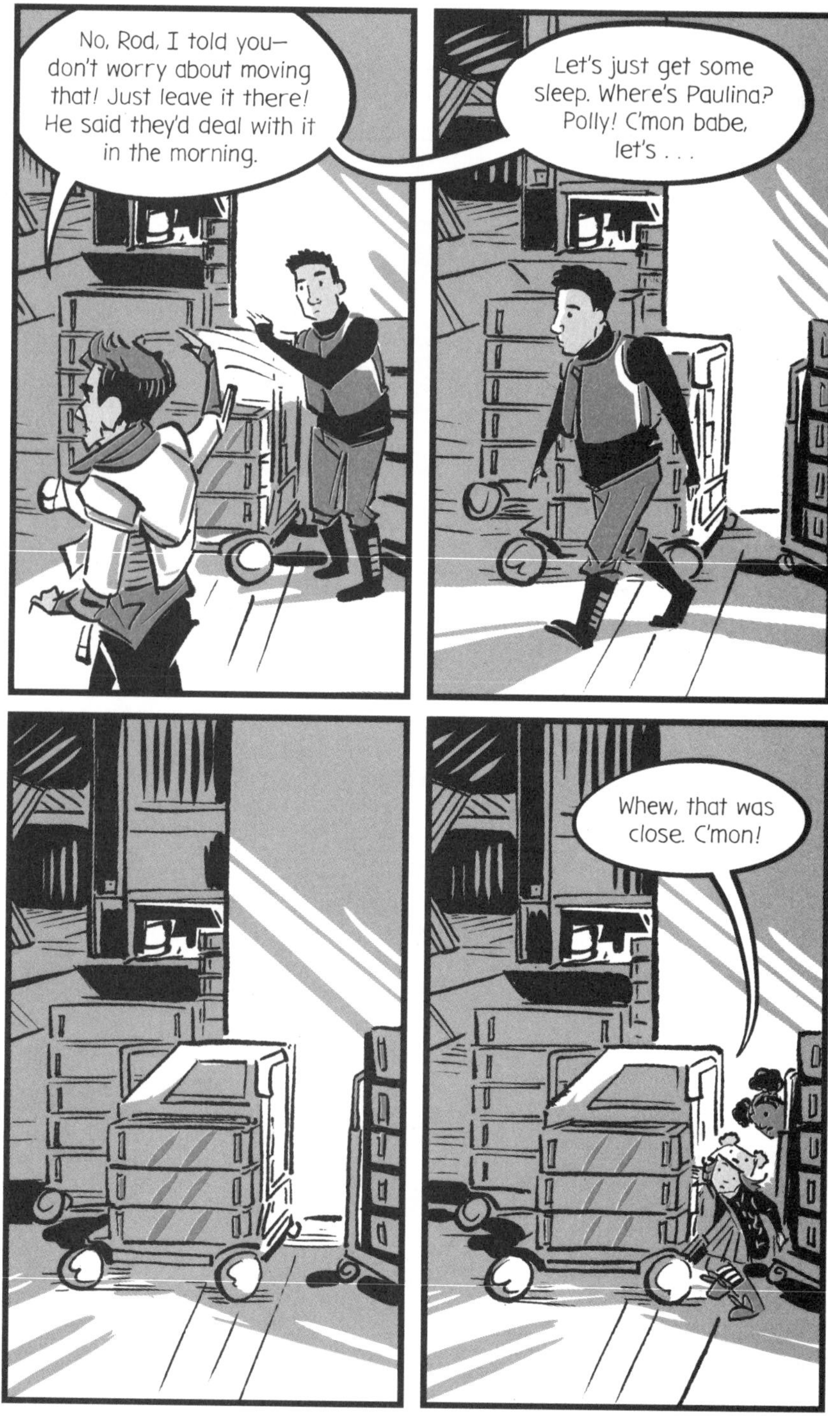
No, Rod, I told you—
don't worry about moving
that! Just leave it there!
He said they'd deal with it
in the morning.
Let's just get some
sleep. Where's Paulina?
Polly! C'mon babe,
let's . . .
Whew, that was
close. C'mon!

(RESEARCH CAFE)

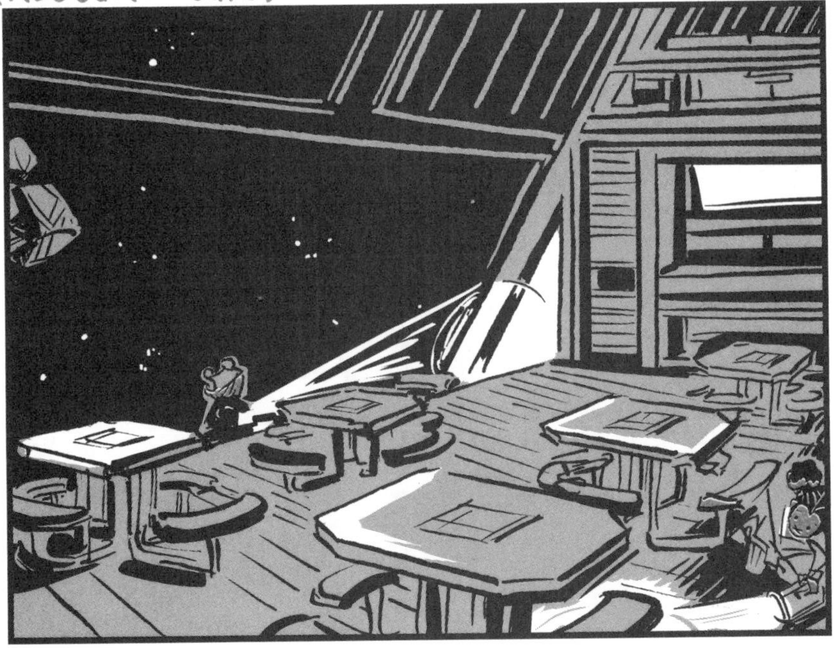

(ENGINEERING CAFE)

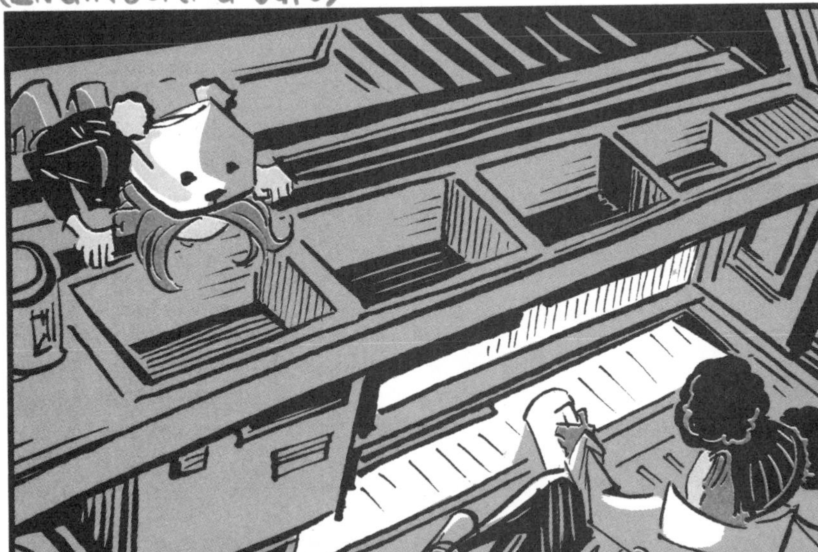
DALLOWAY

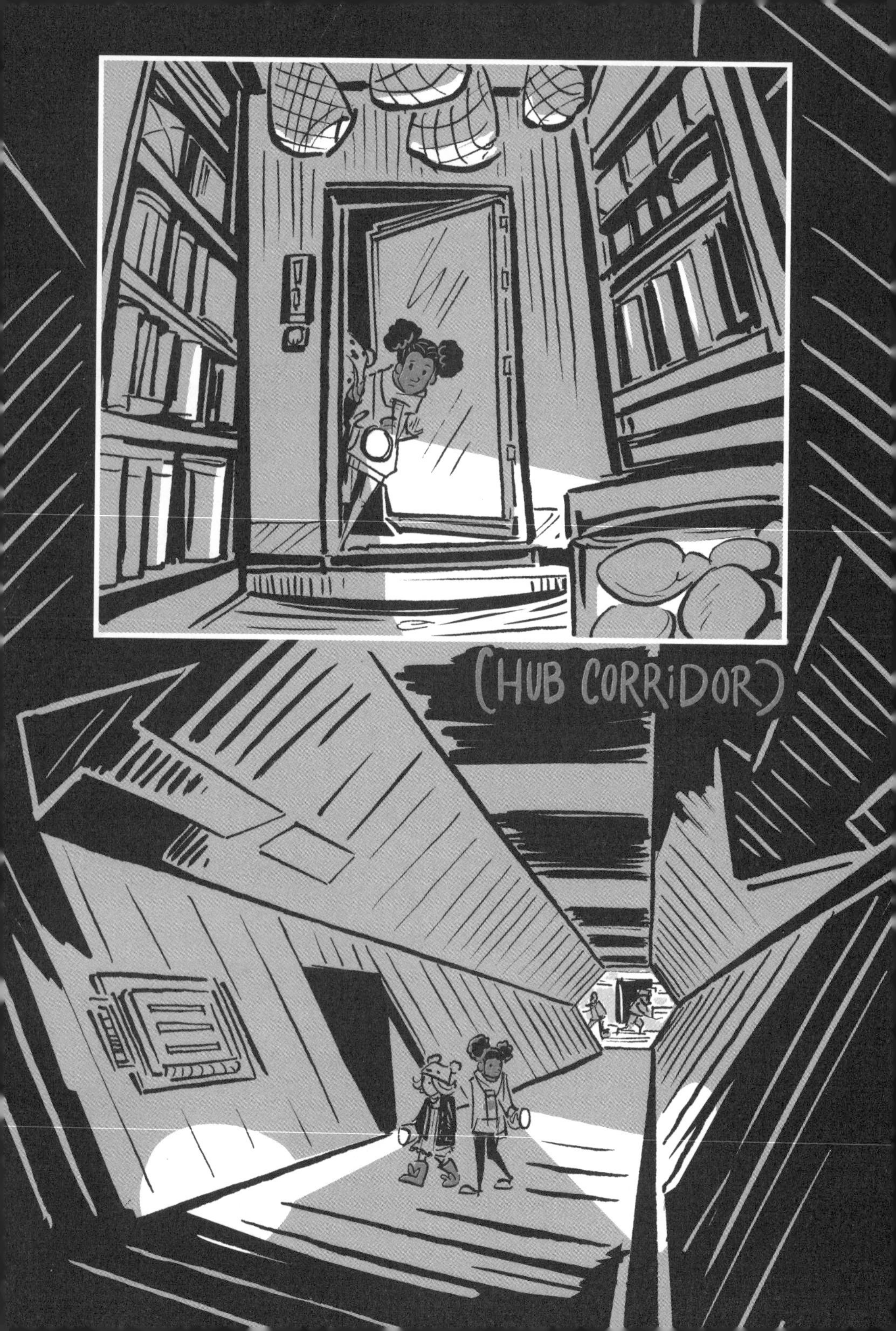
(HUB CORRIDOR)

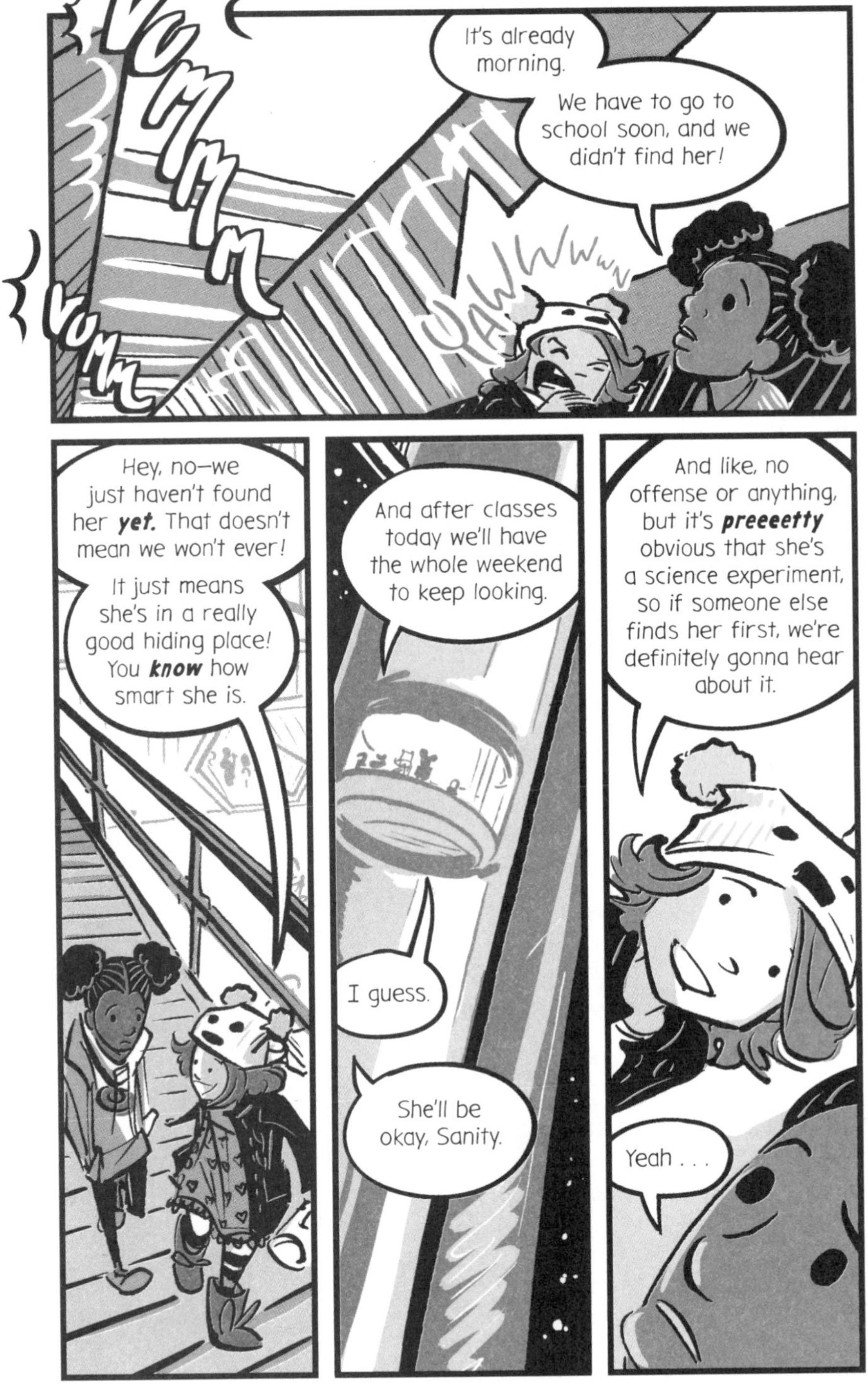
VOMMM
VOMM
It's already morning.
We have to go to school soon, and we didn't find her!
YAWWWWN
Hey, no—we just haven't found her **yet.** That doesn't mean we won't ever!
It just means she's in a really good hiding place! You **know** how smart she is.
And after classes today we'll have the whole weekend to keep looking.
I guess.
She'll be okay, Sanity.
And like, no offense or anything, but it's **preeeetty** obvious that she's a science experiment, so if someone else finds her first, we're definitely gonna hear about it.
Yeah . . .

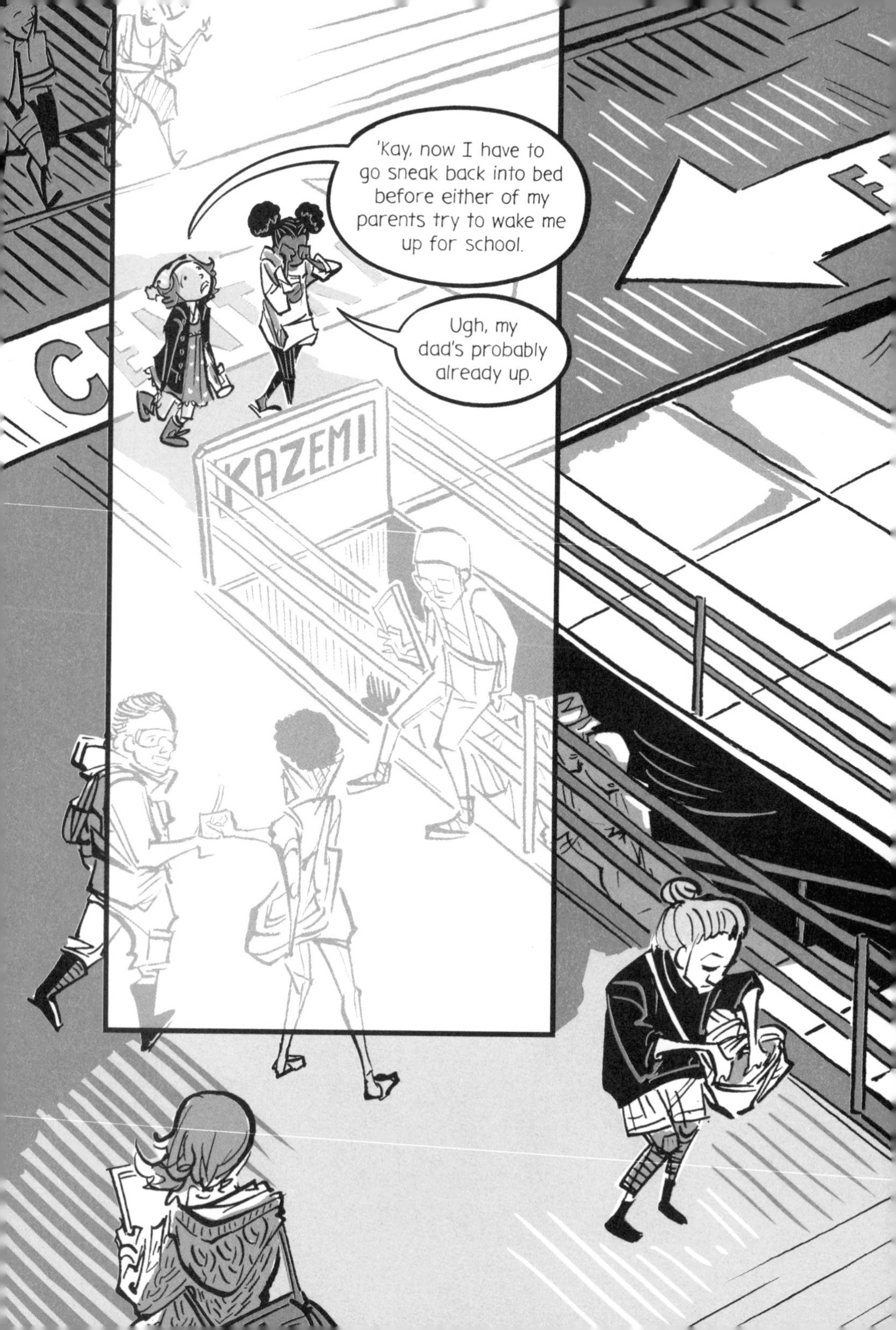
'Kay, now I have to go sneak back into bed before either of my parents try to wake me up for school.
Ugh, my dad's probably already up.
KAZEMI

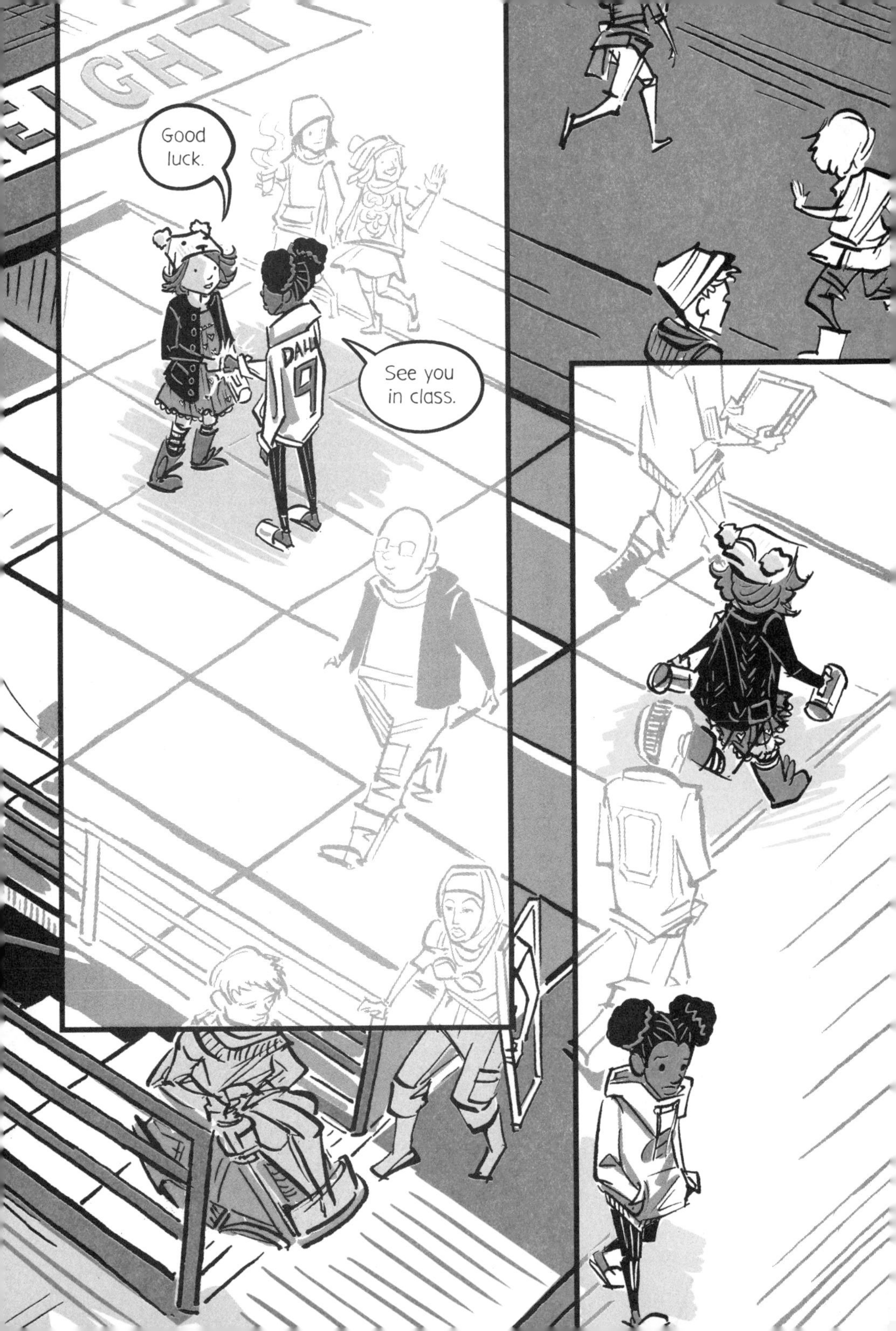
EIGHT
Good luck.
DALL
9
See you in class.

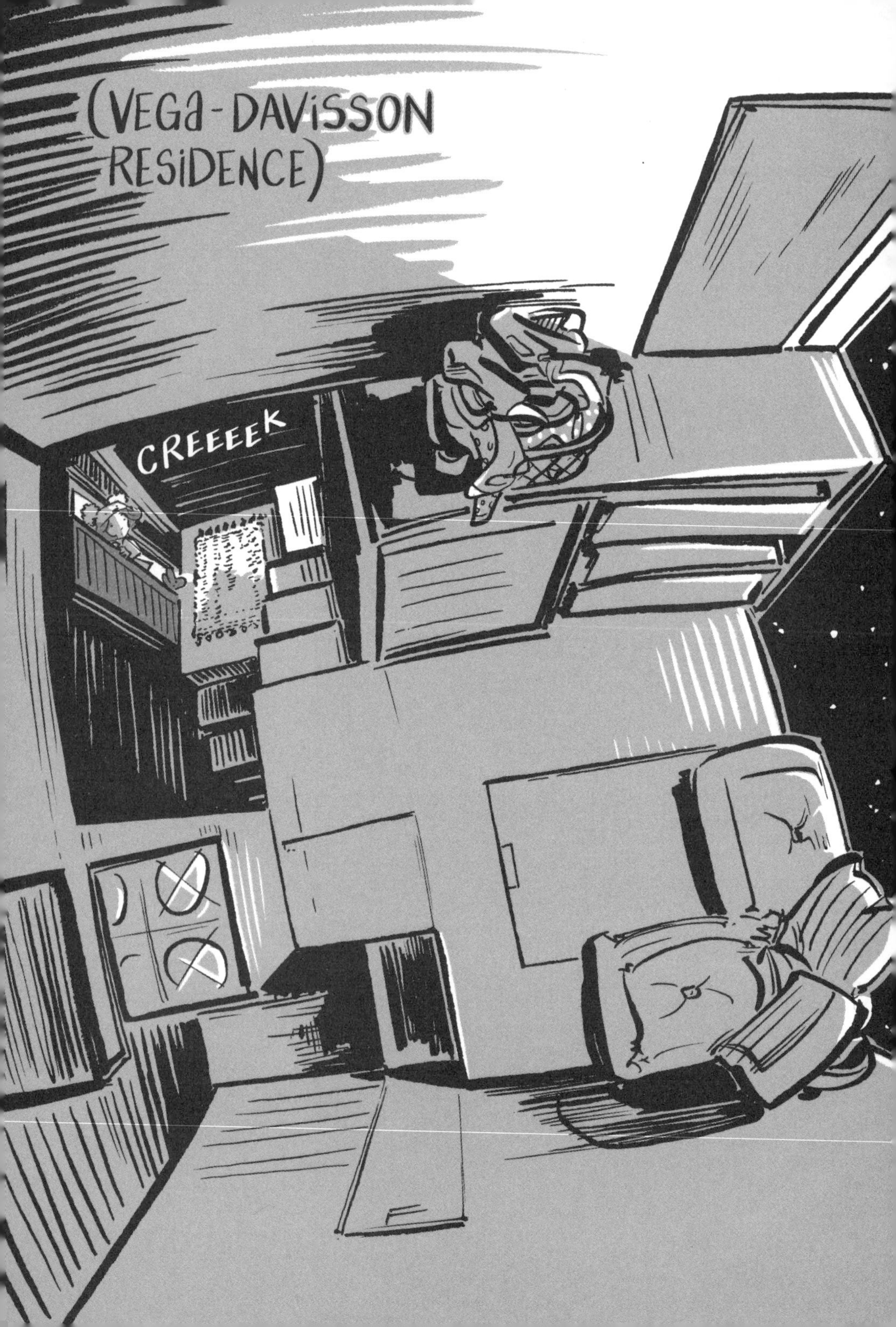
(VEGA-DAVISSON RESIDENCE)
CREEEEK

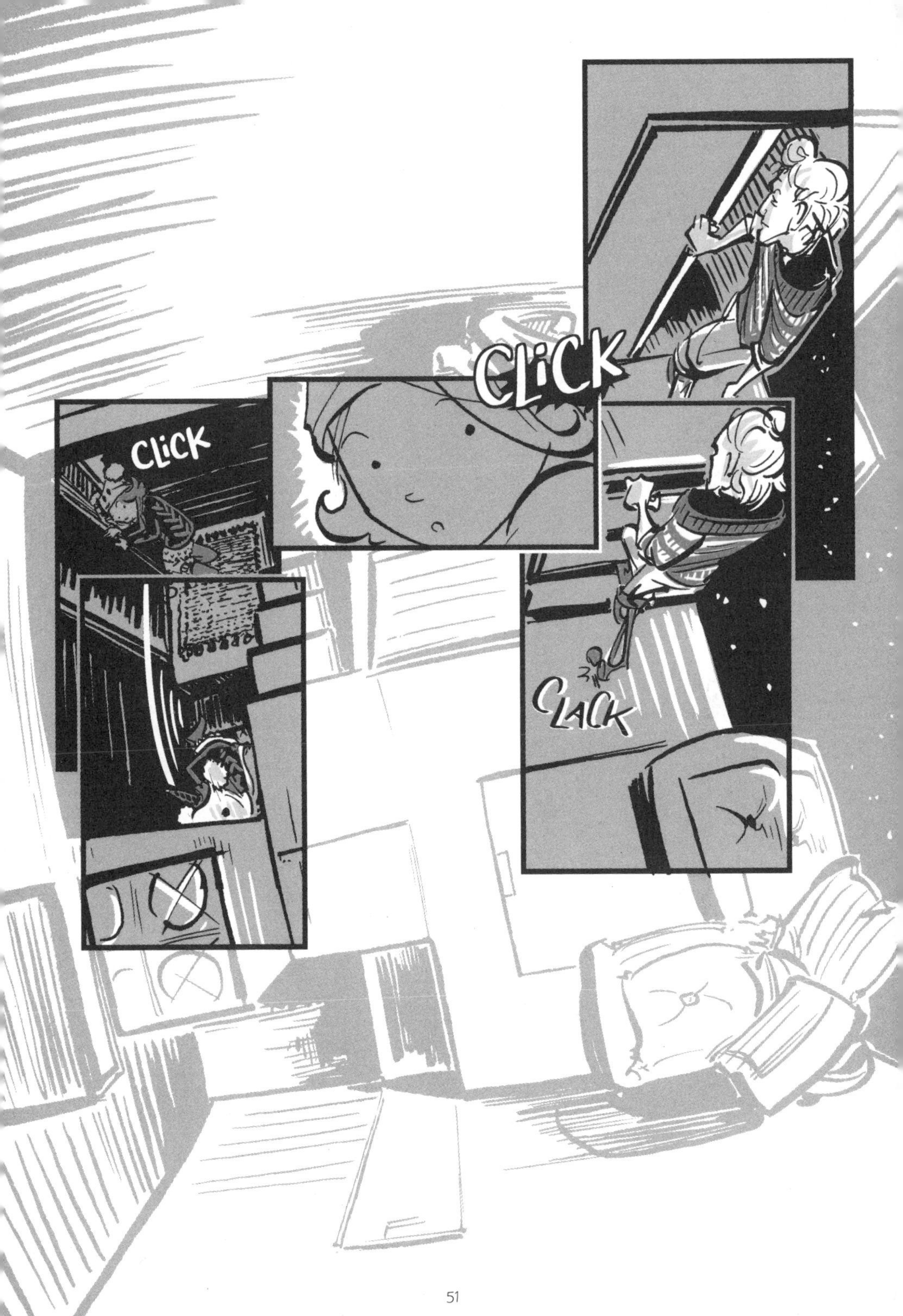
CLICK
CLICK
CLACK

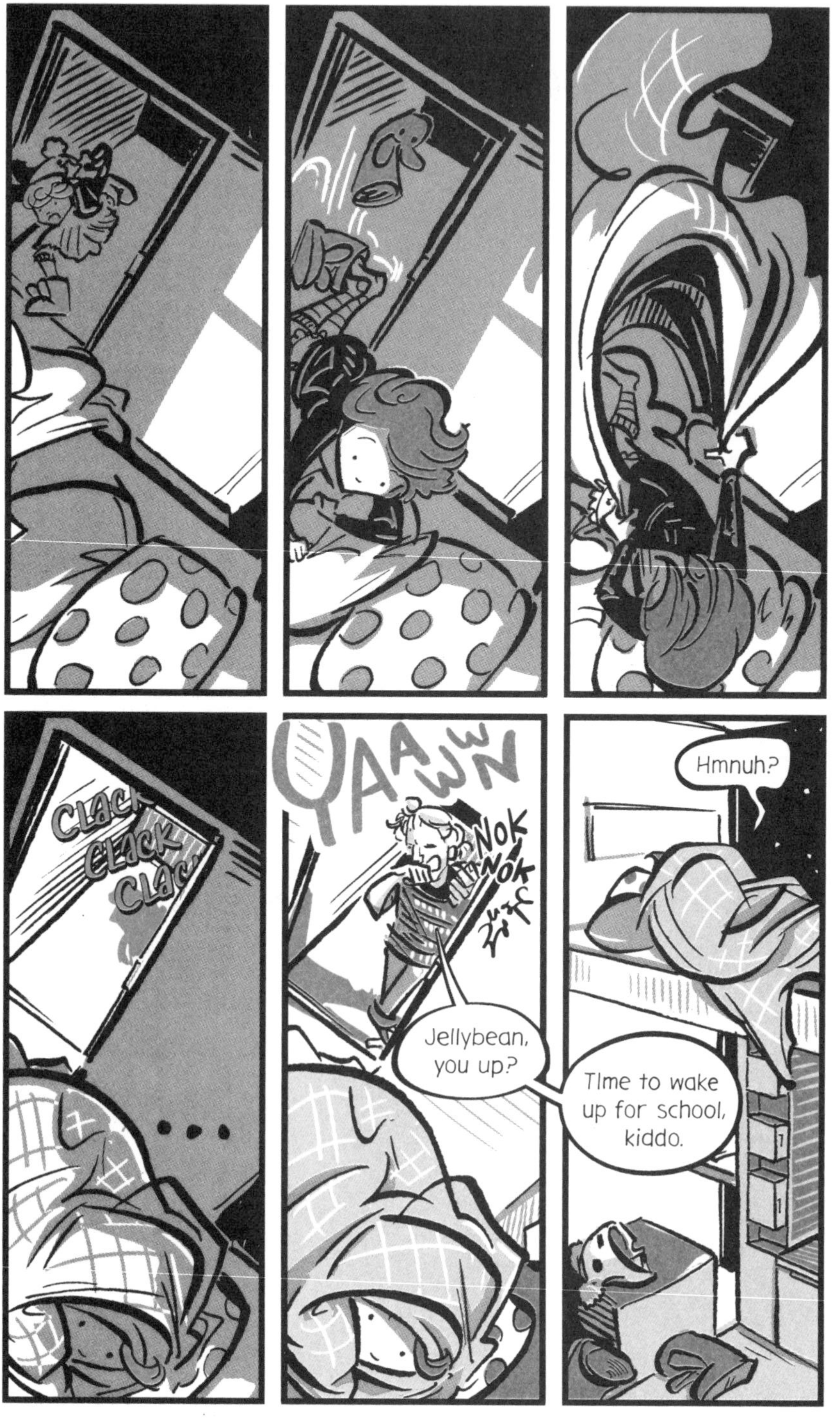
CLACK
CLACK
CLACK
YAAWWN
NOK NOK
Jellybean, you up?
Time to wake up for school, kiddo.
Hmnuh?

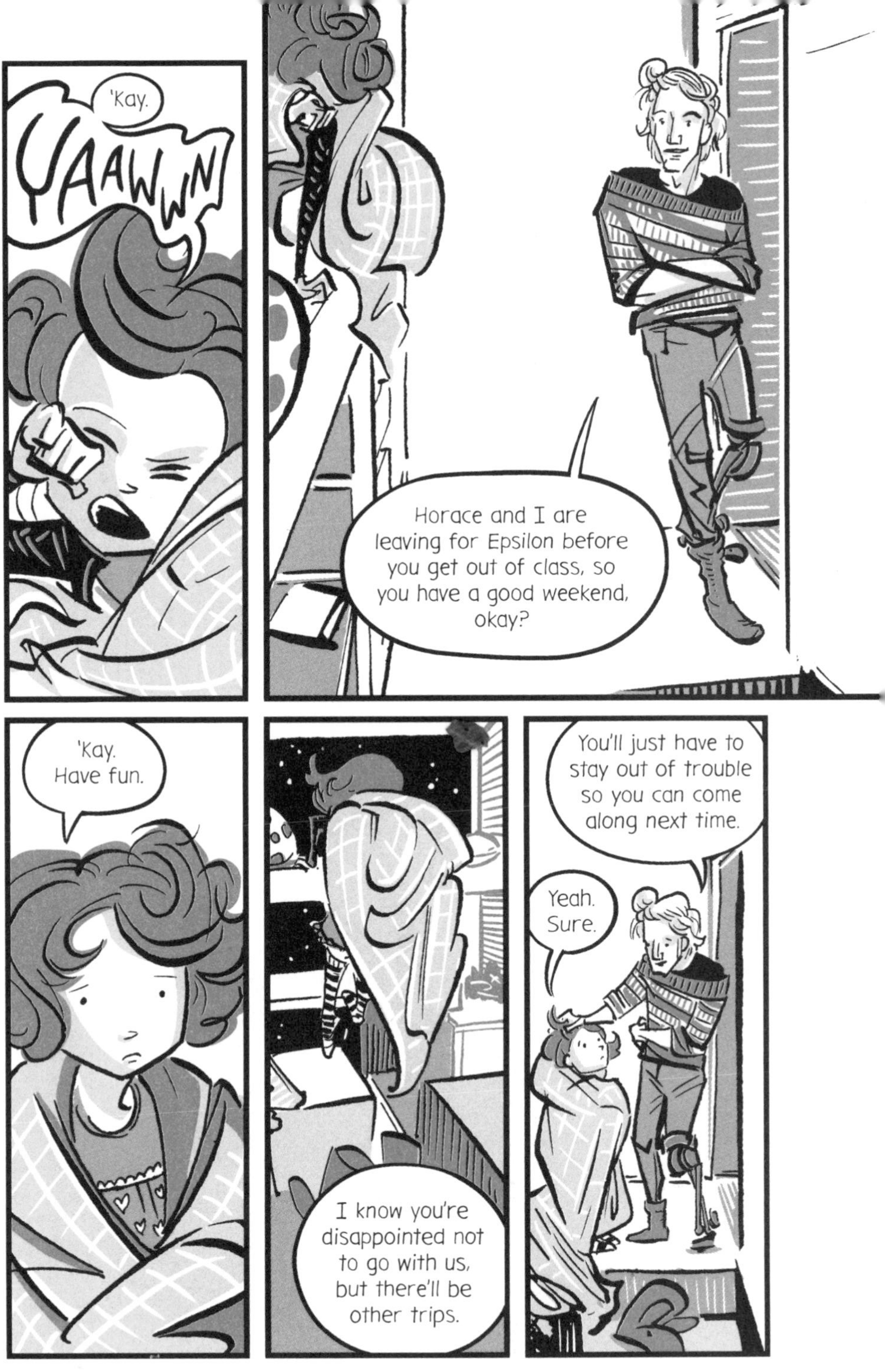
'Kay.
YAAWWN
Horace and I are leaving for Epsilon before you get out of class, so you have a good weekend, okay?
'Kay. Have fun.
I know you're disappointed not to go with us, but there'll be other trips.
You'll just have to stay out of trouble so you can come along next time.
Yeah. Sure.

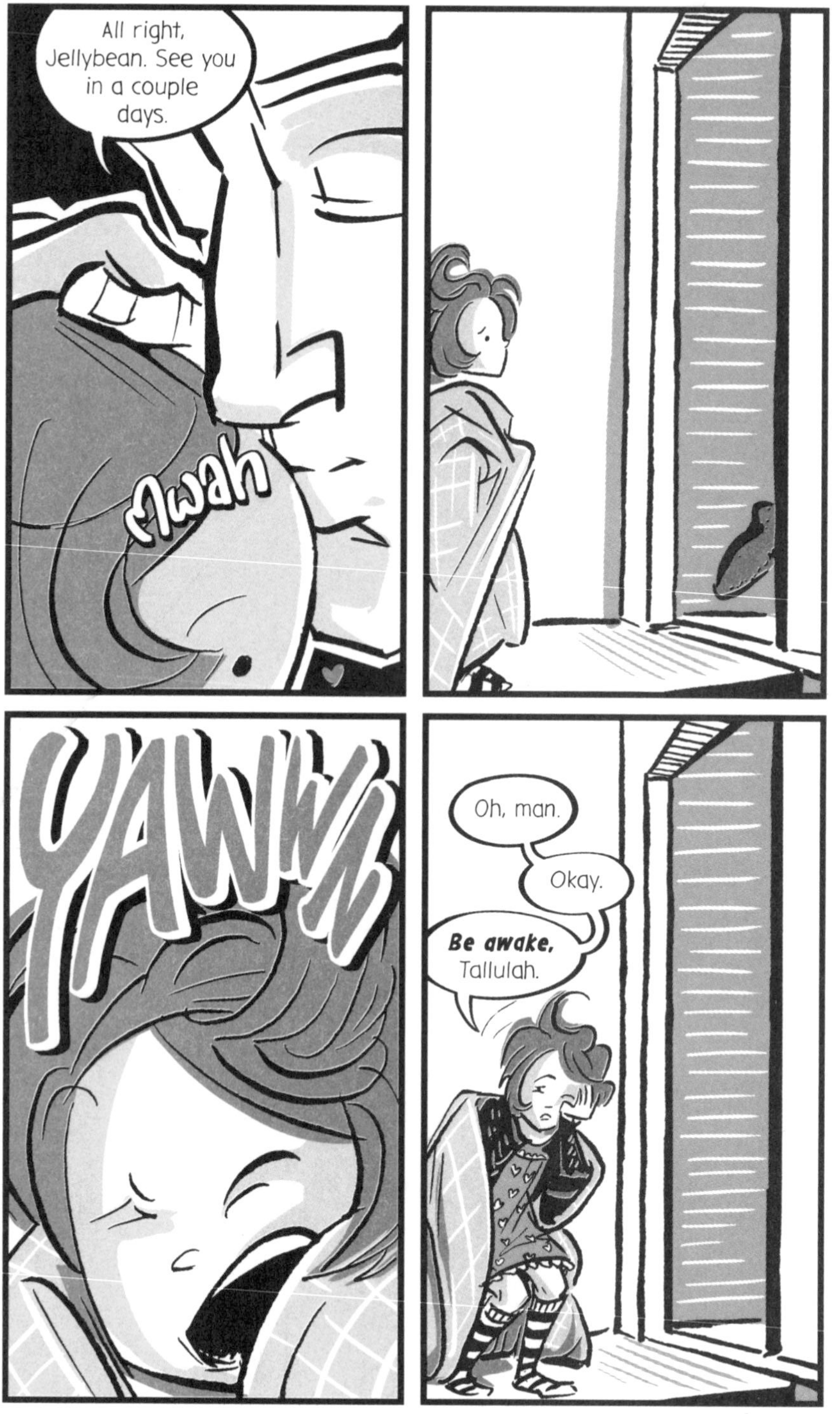
All right, Jellybean. See you in a couple days.
Mwah
YAWWN
Oh, man.
Okay.
**Be awake,** Tallulah.

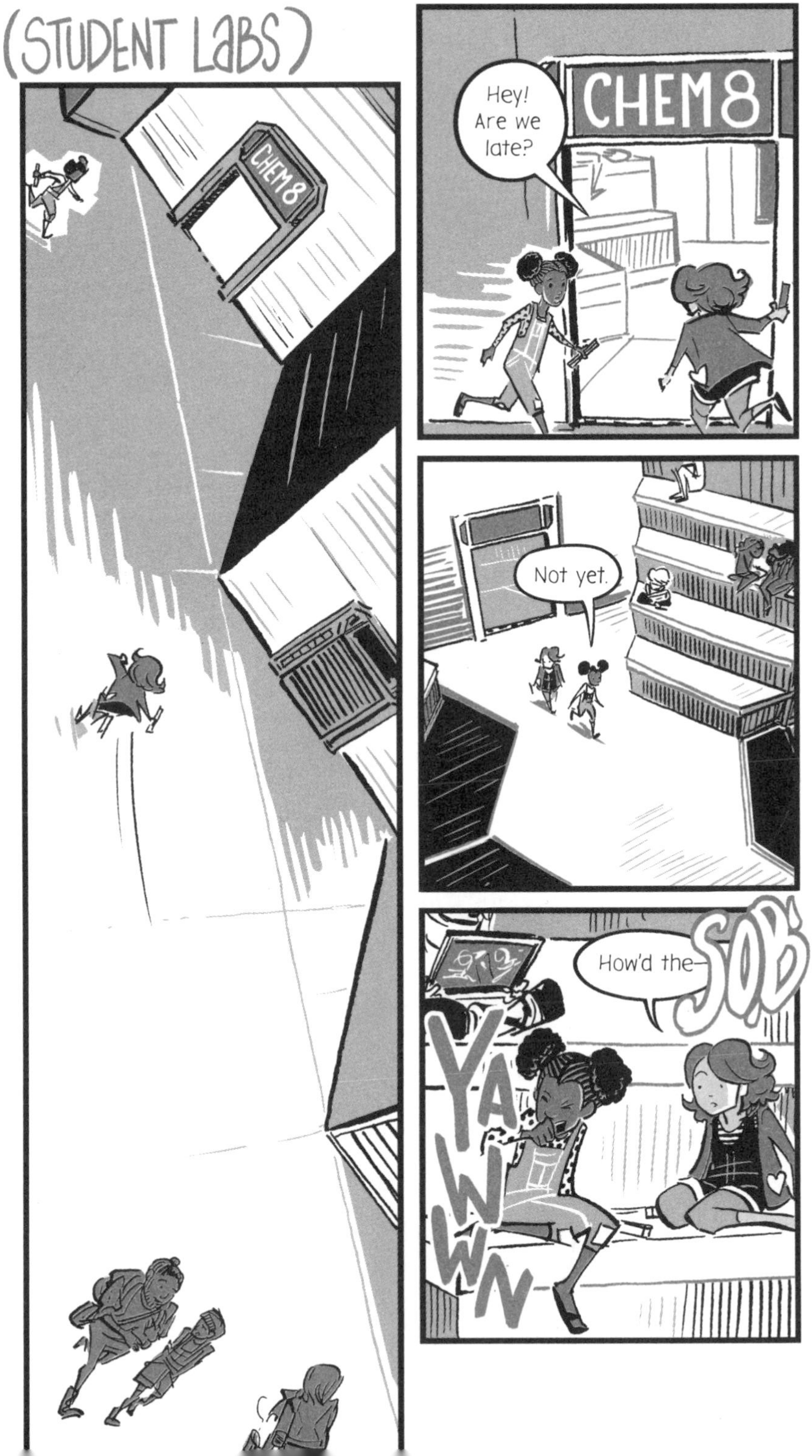
(STUDENT LABS)
CHEM 8
CHEM 8
Hey! Are we late?
Not yet.
How'd the—
SOB
YAWWN

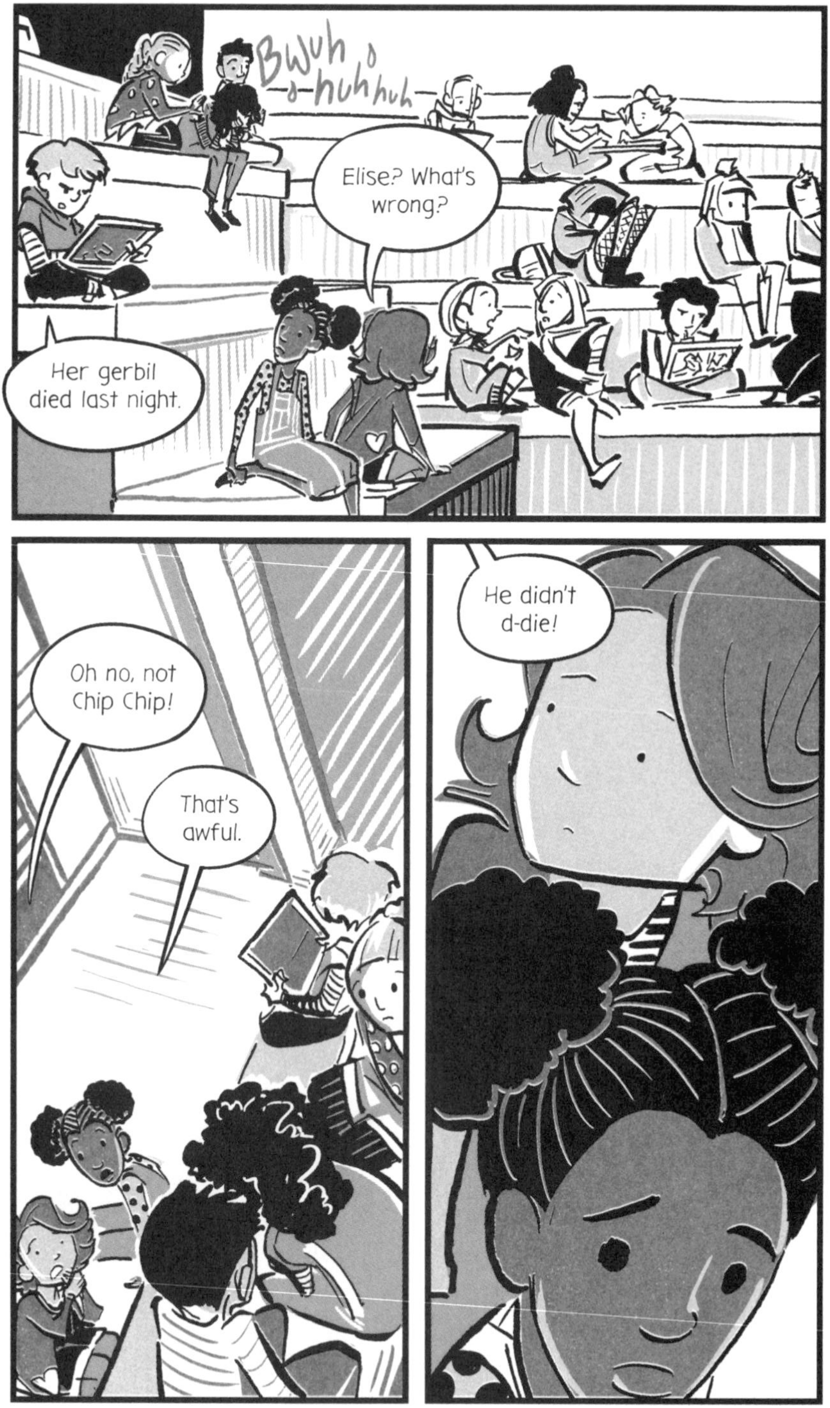
Bwuh o o-huhhuh
Elise? What's wrong?
Her gerbil died last night.
Oh no, not Chip Chip!
That's awful.
He didn't d-die!

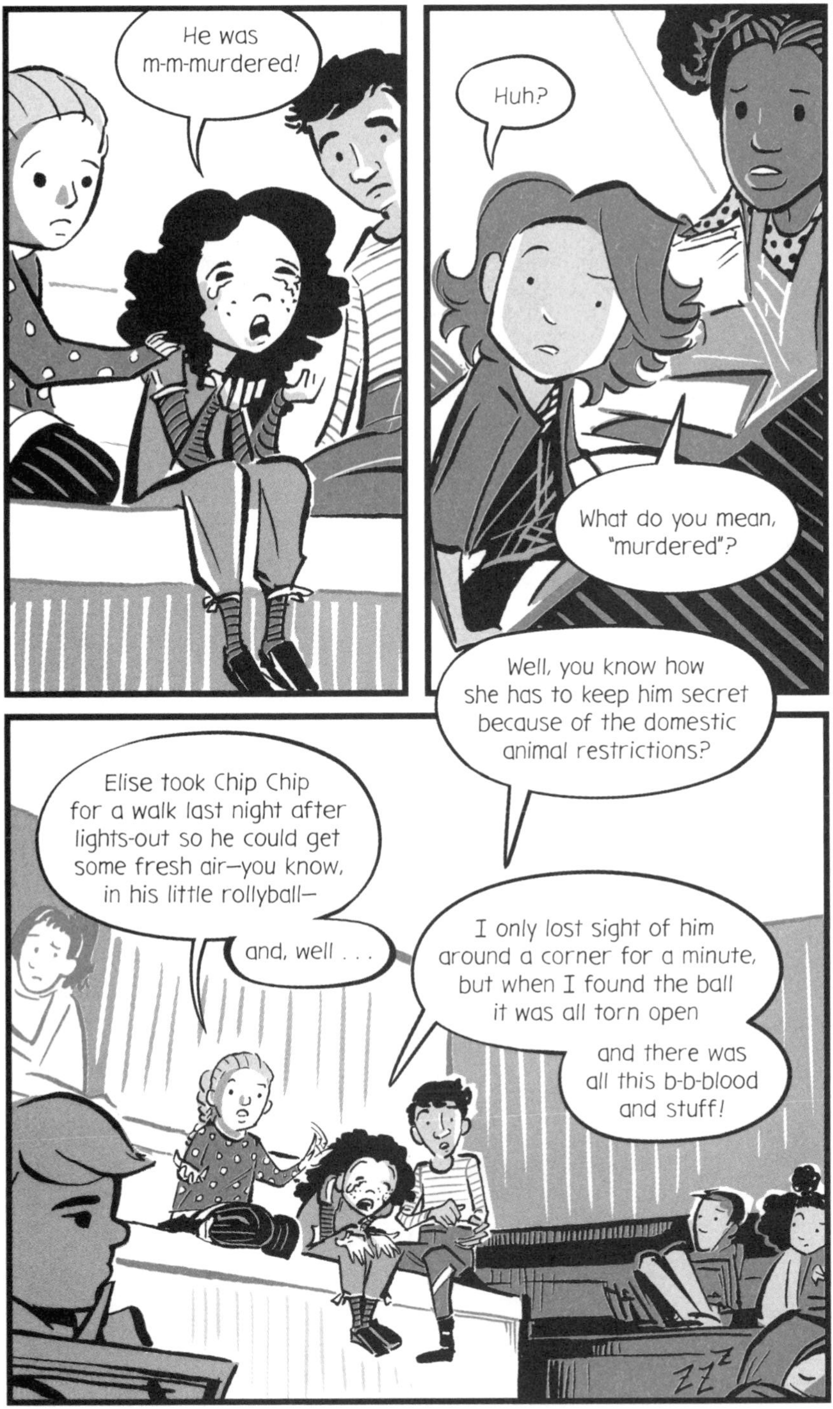
He was m-m-murdered!
Huh?
What do you mean, "murdered"?
Well, you know how she has to keep him secret because of the domestic animal restrictions?
Elise took Chip Chip for a walk last night after lights-out so he could get some fresh air—you know, in his little rollyball—
and, well . . .
I only lost sight of him around a corner for a minute, but when I found the ball it was all torn open
and there was all this b-b-blood and stuff!
ZZZ

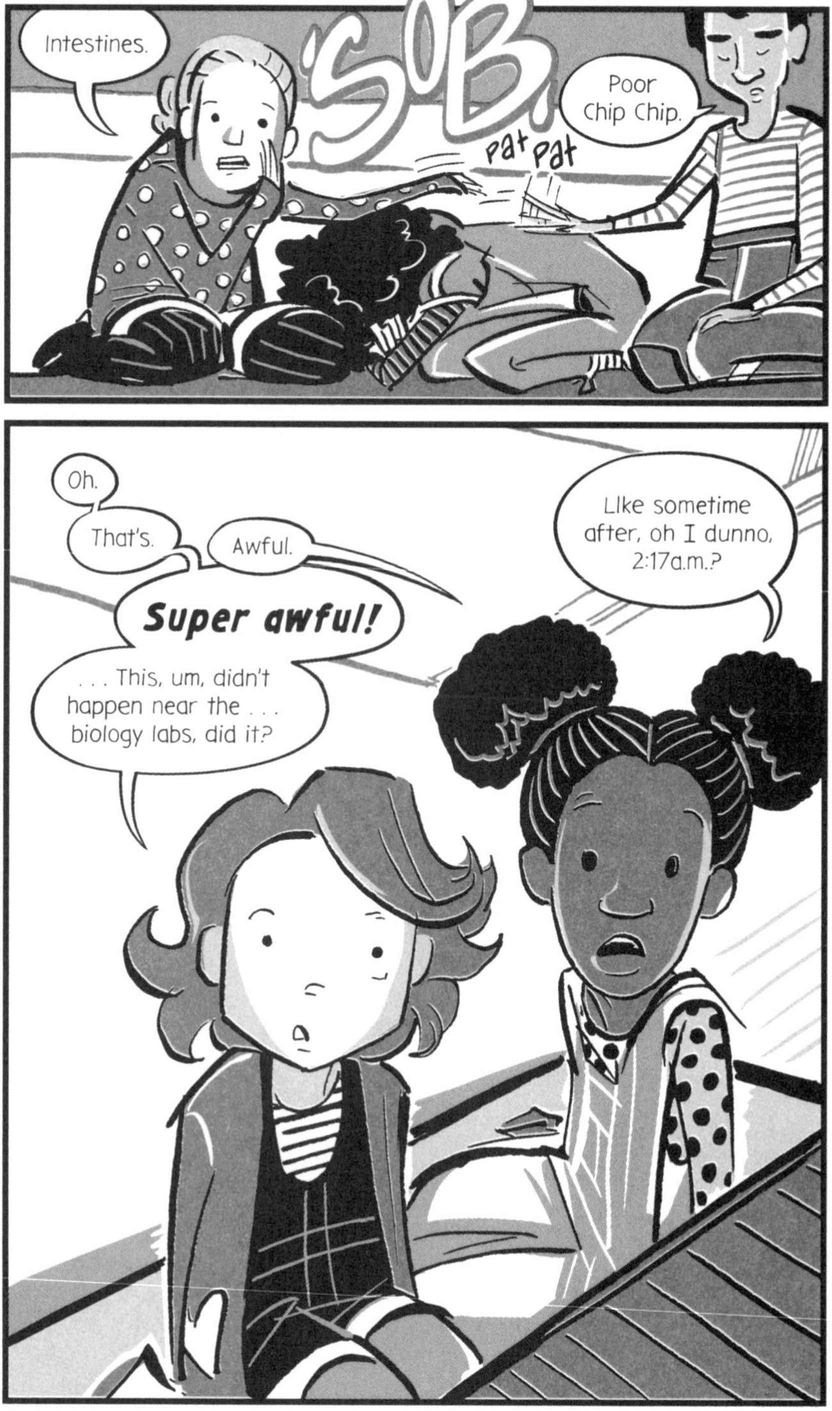
Intestines.
SOB
Poor Chip Chip.
Pat Pat
Oh.
That's.
Awful.
**Super awful!**
. . . This, um, didn't happen near the . . . biology labs, did it?
Like sometime after, oh I dunno, 2:17a.m.?

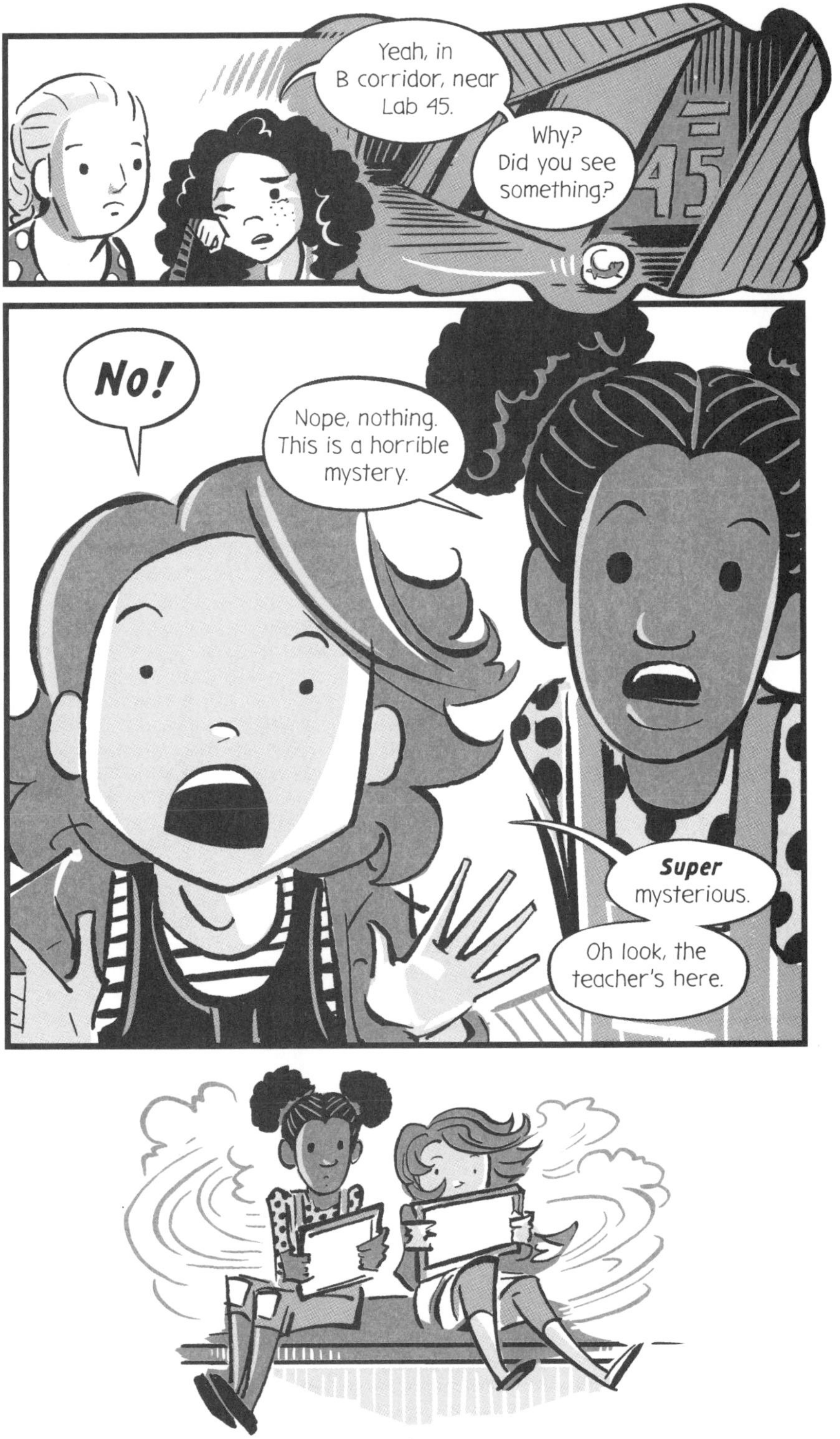
Yeah, in B corridor, near Lab 45.
Why? Did you see something?
45
No!
Nope, nothing. This is a horrible mystery.
Super mysterious.
Oh look, the teacher's here.

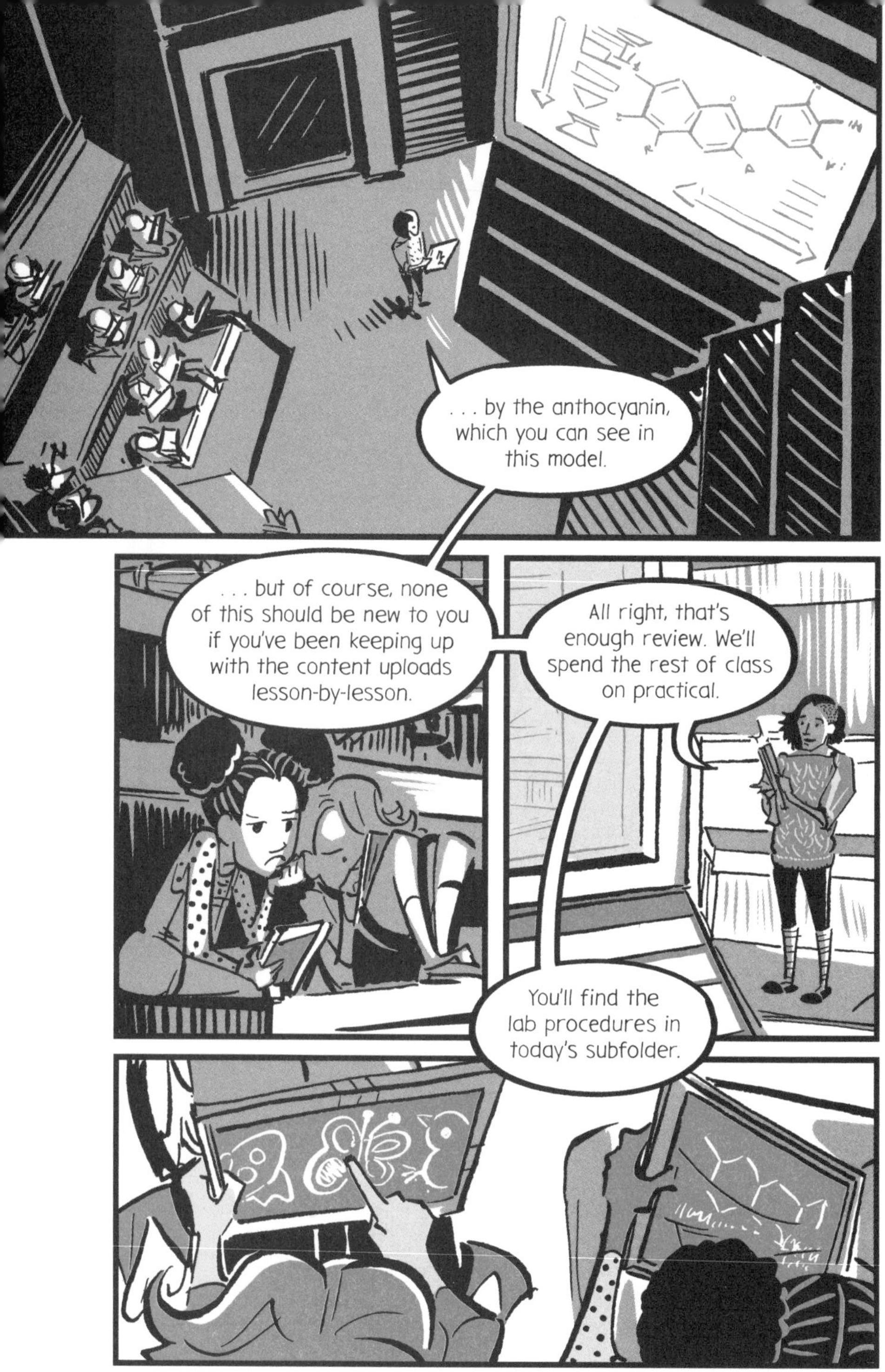
. . . by the anthocyanin, which you can see in this model.
. . . but of course, none of this should be new to you if you've been keeping up with the content uploads lesson-by-lesson.
All right, that's enough review. We'll spend the rest of class on practical.
You'll find the lab procedures in today's subfolder.

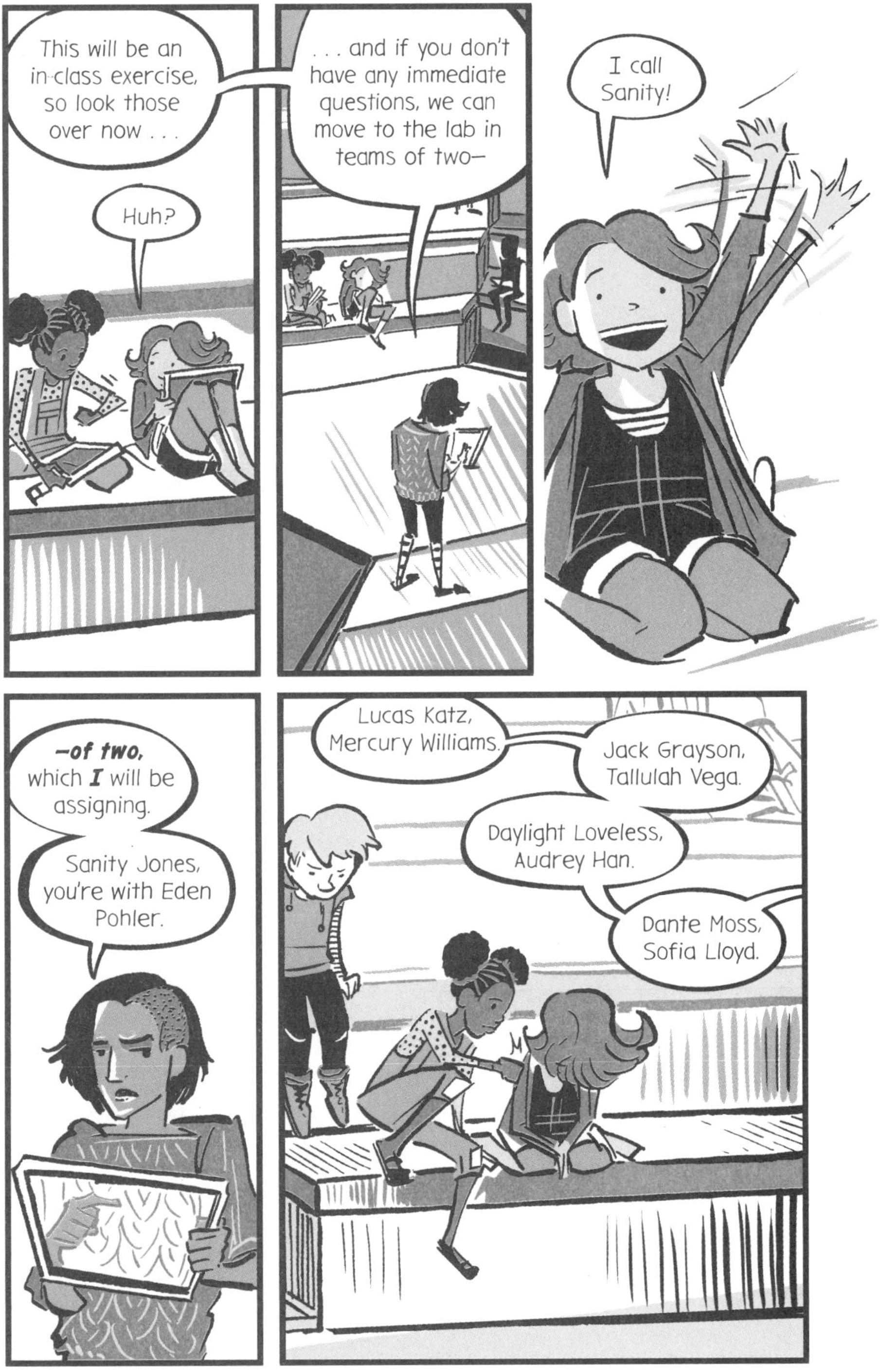
This will be an in-class exercise, so look those over now . . .
Huh?
. . . and if you don't have any immediate questions, we can move to the lab in teams of two—
I call Sanity!
—of two, which I will be assigning.
Sanity Jones, you're with Eden Pohler.
Lucas Katz, Mercury Williams.
Jack Grayson, Tallulah Vega.
Daylight Loveless, Audrey Han.
Dante Moss, Sofia Lloyd.

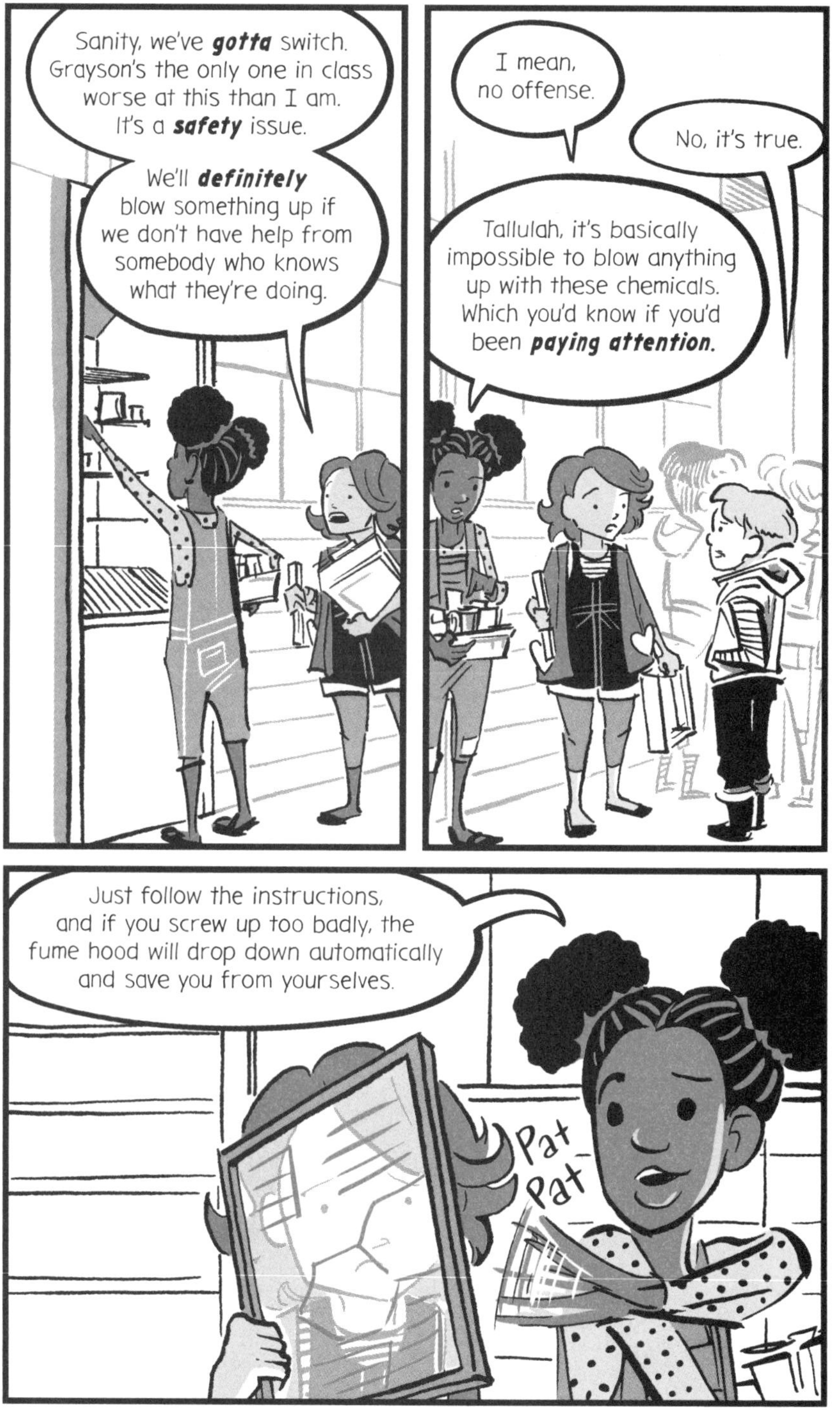

Sanity, we've **gotta** switch. Grayson's the only one in class worse at this than I am. It's a **safety** issue.
We'll **definitely** blow something up if we don't have help from somebody who knows what they're doing.
I mean, no offense.
No, it's true.
Tallulah, it's basically impossible to blow anything up with these chemicals. Which you'd know if you'd been **paying attention.**
Just follow the instructions, and if you screw up too badly, the fume hood will drop down automatically and save you from yourselves.
Pat Pat

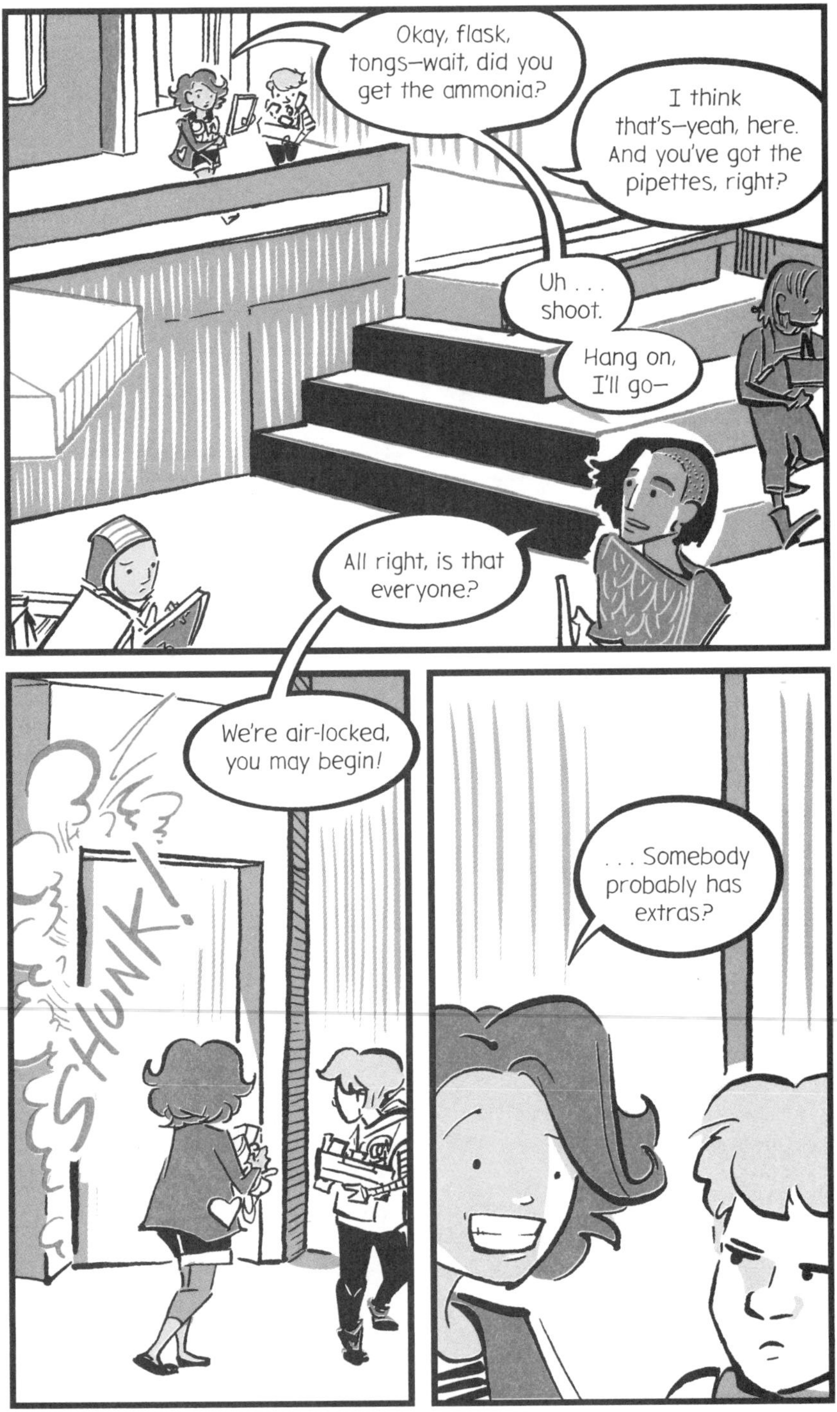
Okay, flask, tongs—wait, did you get the ammonia?
I think that's—yeah, here. And you've got the pipettes, right?
Uh . . . shoot.
Hang on, I'll go—
All right, is that everyone?
We're air-locked, you may begin!
SHUNK!
. . . Somebody probably has extras?

# (FREIGHT DOCKS)

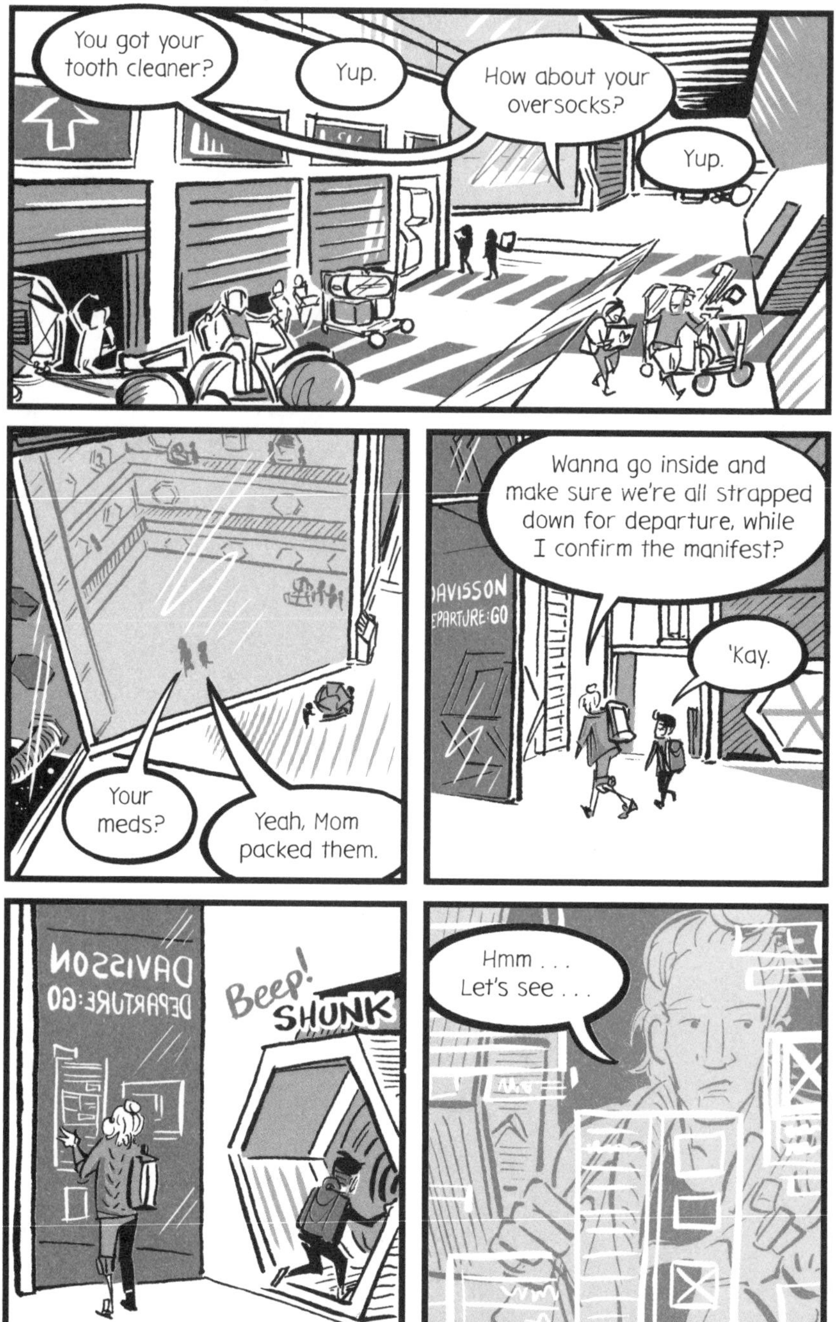
You got your tooth cleaner?
Yup.
How about your oversocks?
Yup.
Your meds?
Yeah, Mom packed them.
Wanna go inside and make sure we're all strapped down for departure, while I confirm the manifest?
'Kay.
Beep!
SHUNK
Hmm . . . Let's see . . .

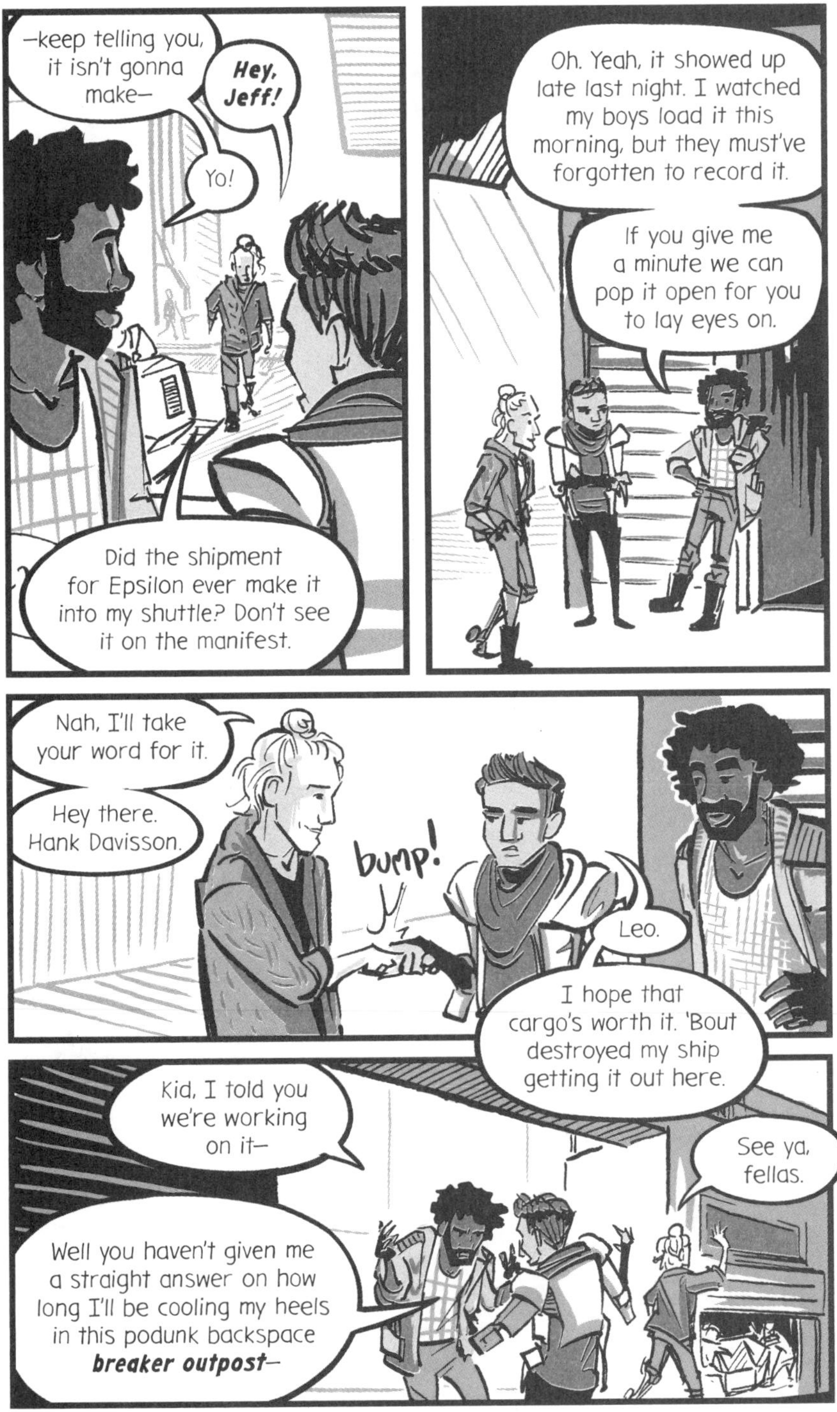

—keep telling you, it isn't gonna make—
***Hey, Jeff!***
Yo!
Did the shipment for Epsilon ever make it into my shuttle? Don't see it on the manifest.
Oh. Yeah, it showed up late last night. I watched my boys load it this morning, but they must've forgotten to record it.
If you give me a minute we can pop it open for you to lay eyes on.
Nah, I'll take your word for it.
Hey there. Hank Davisson.
bump!
Leo.
I hope that cargo's worth it. 'Bout destroyed my ship getting it out here.
Kid, I told you we're working on it—
Well you haven't given me a straight answer on how long I'll be cooling my heels in this podunk backspace ***breaker outpost***—
See ya, fellas.

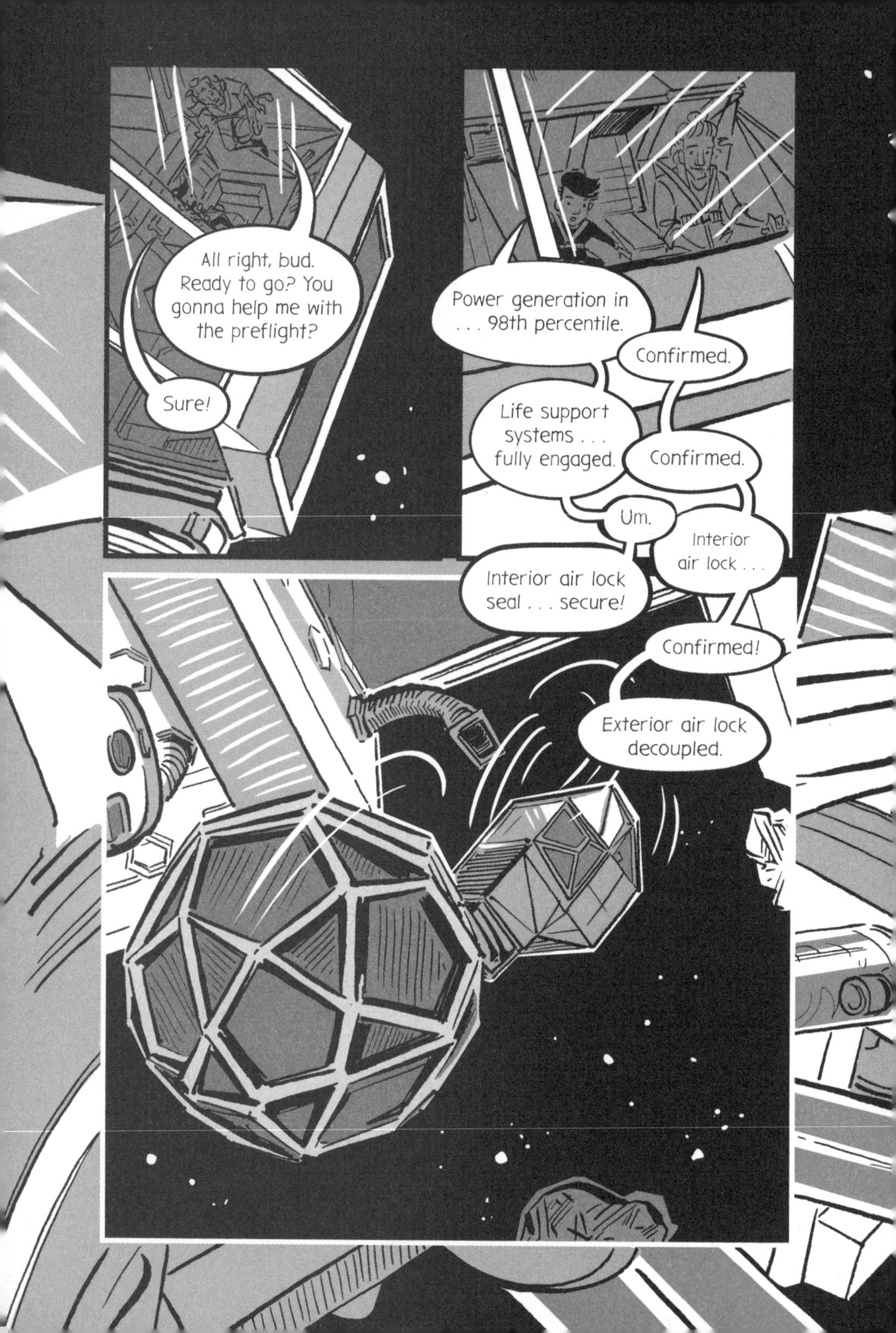
All right, bud. Ready to go? You gonna help me with the preflight?
Sure!
Power generation in . . . 98th percentile.
Confirmed.
Life support systems . . . fully engaged.
Confirmed.
Um.
Interior air lock . . .
Interior air lock seal . . . secure!
Confirmed!
Exterior air lock decoupled.

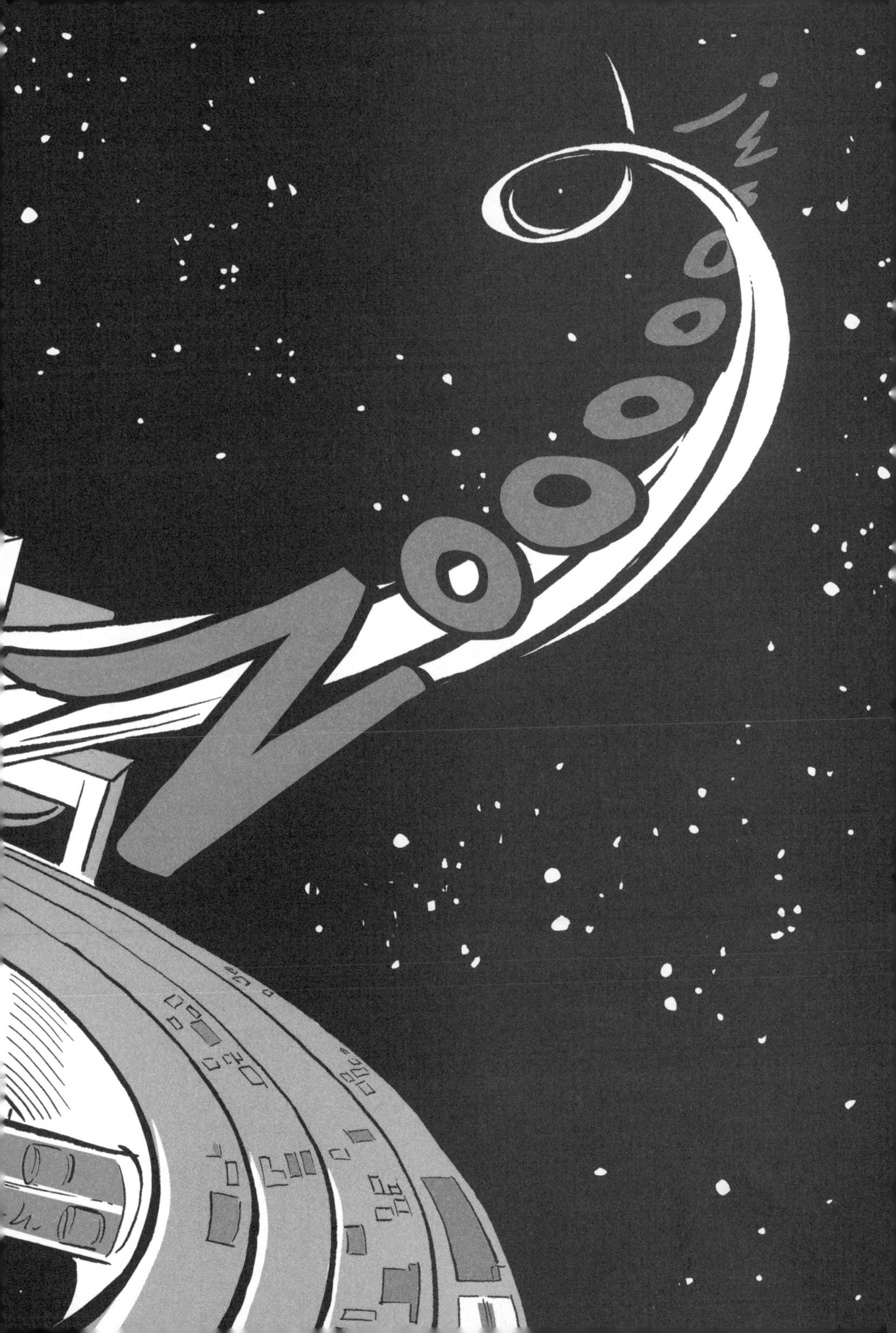
ZOOOOOM!

( ENGINEERING LAB C-12 )

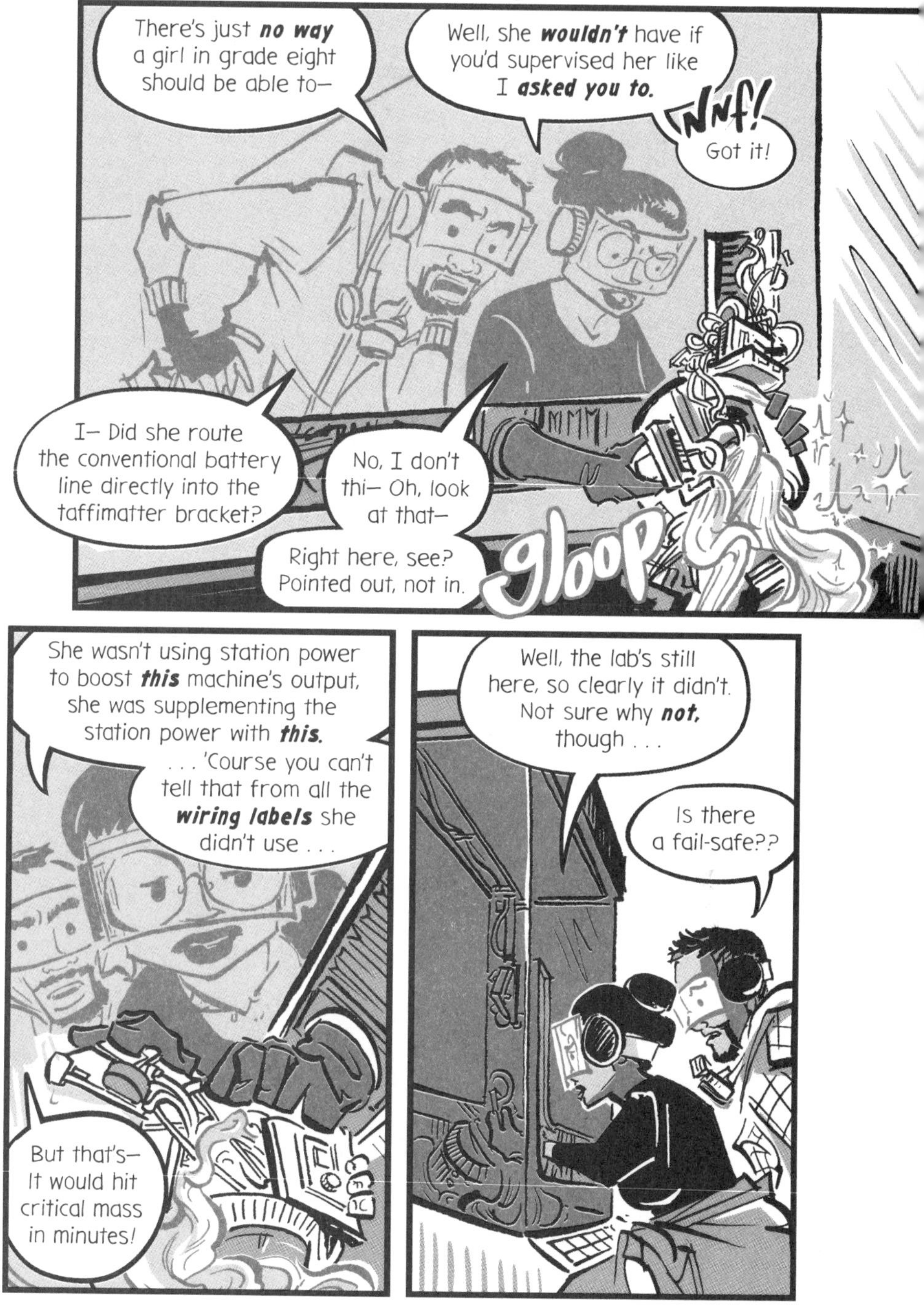
There's just **no way** a girl in grade eight should be able to—
Well, she **wouldn't** have if you'd supervised her like I **asked you to.**
Wnf!
Got it!
I— Did she route the conventional battery line directly into the taffimatter bracket?
No, I don't thi— Oh, look at that—
Right here, see? Pointed out, not in.
gloop
She wasn't using station power to boost **this** machine's output, she was supplementing the station power with **this.**
. . . 'Course you can't tell that from all the **wiring labels** she didn't use . . .
But that's— It would hit critical mass in minutes!
Well, the lab's still here, so clearly it didn't. Not sure why **not,** though . . .
Is there a fail-safe??

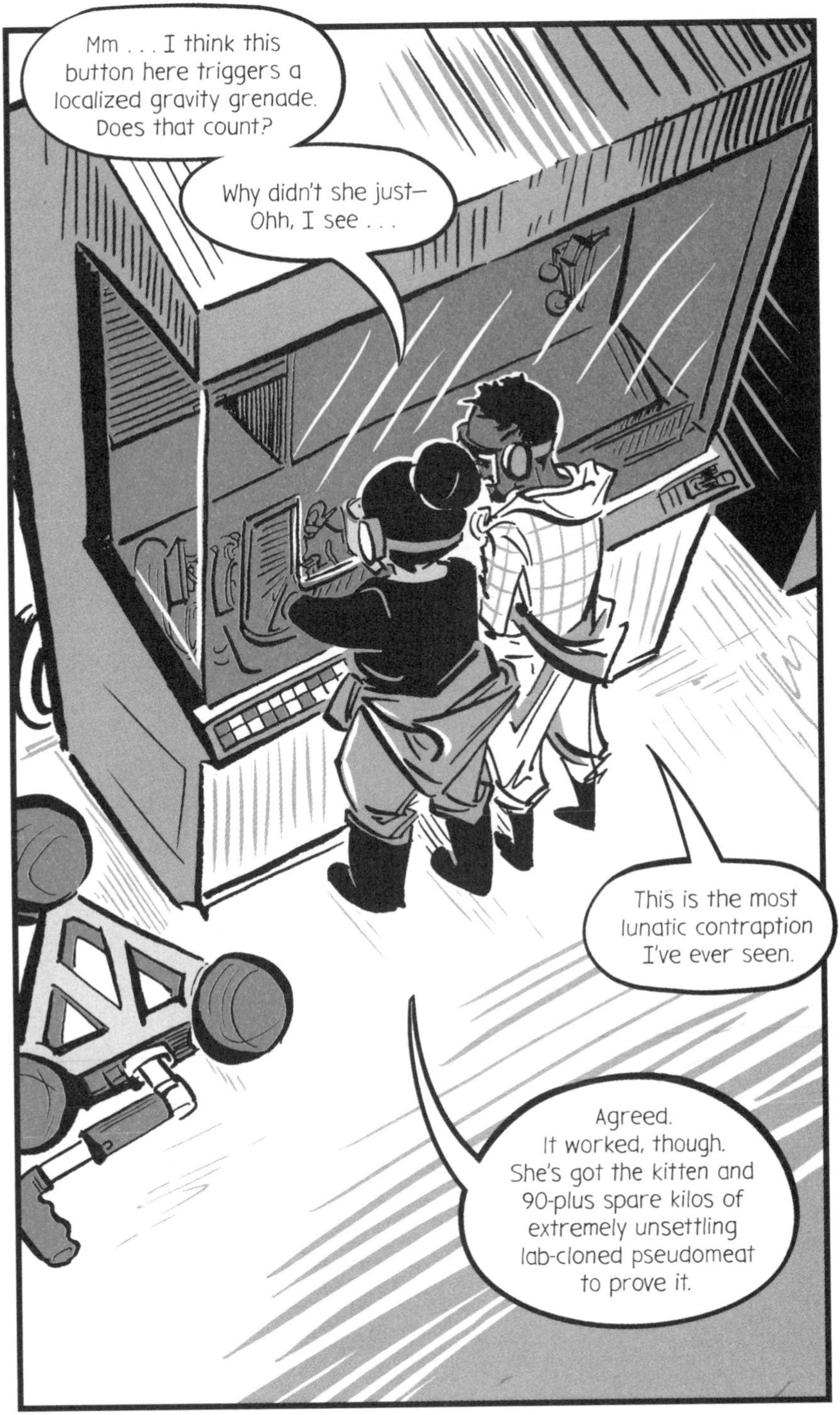
Mm . . . I think this button here triggers a localized gravity grenade. Does that count?
Why didn't she just— Ohh, I see . . .
This is the most lunatic contraption I've ever seen.
Agreed. It worked, though. She's got the kitten and 90-plus spare kilos of extremely unsettling lab-cloned pseudomeat to prove it.

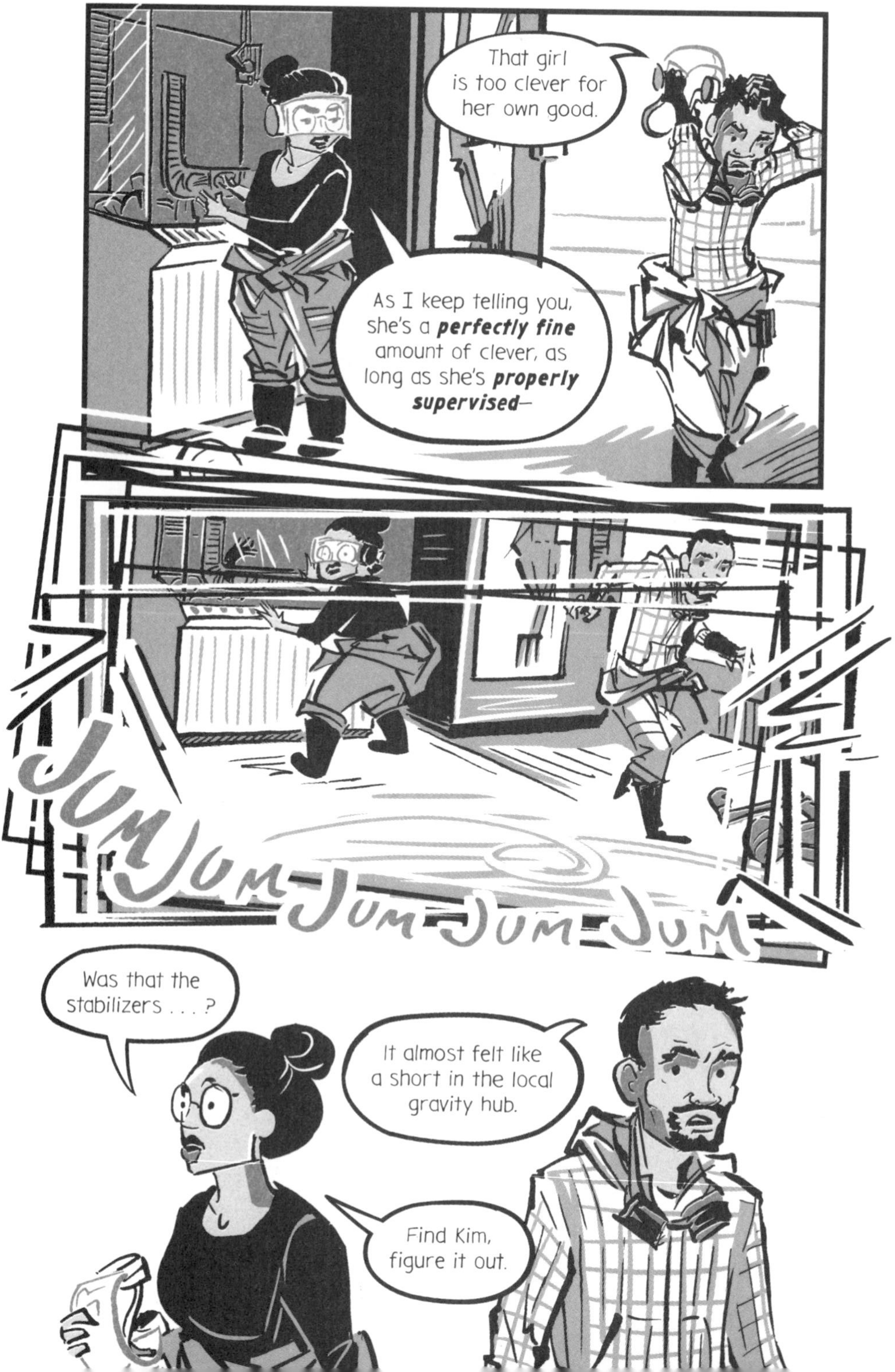

That girl is too clever for her own good.
As I keep telling you, she's a **perfectly fine** amount of clever, as long as she's **properly supervised**—
JUM JUM-JUM-JUM-JUM
Was that the stabilizers . . . ?
It almost felt like a short in the local gravity hub.
Find Kim, figure it out.

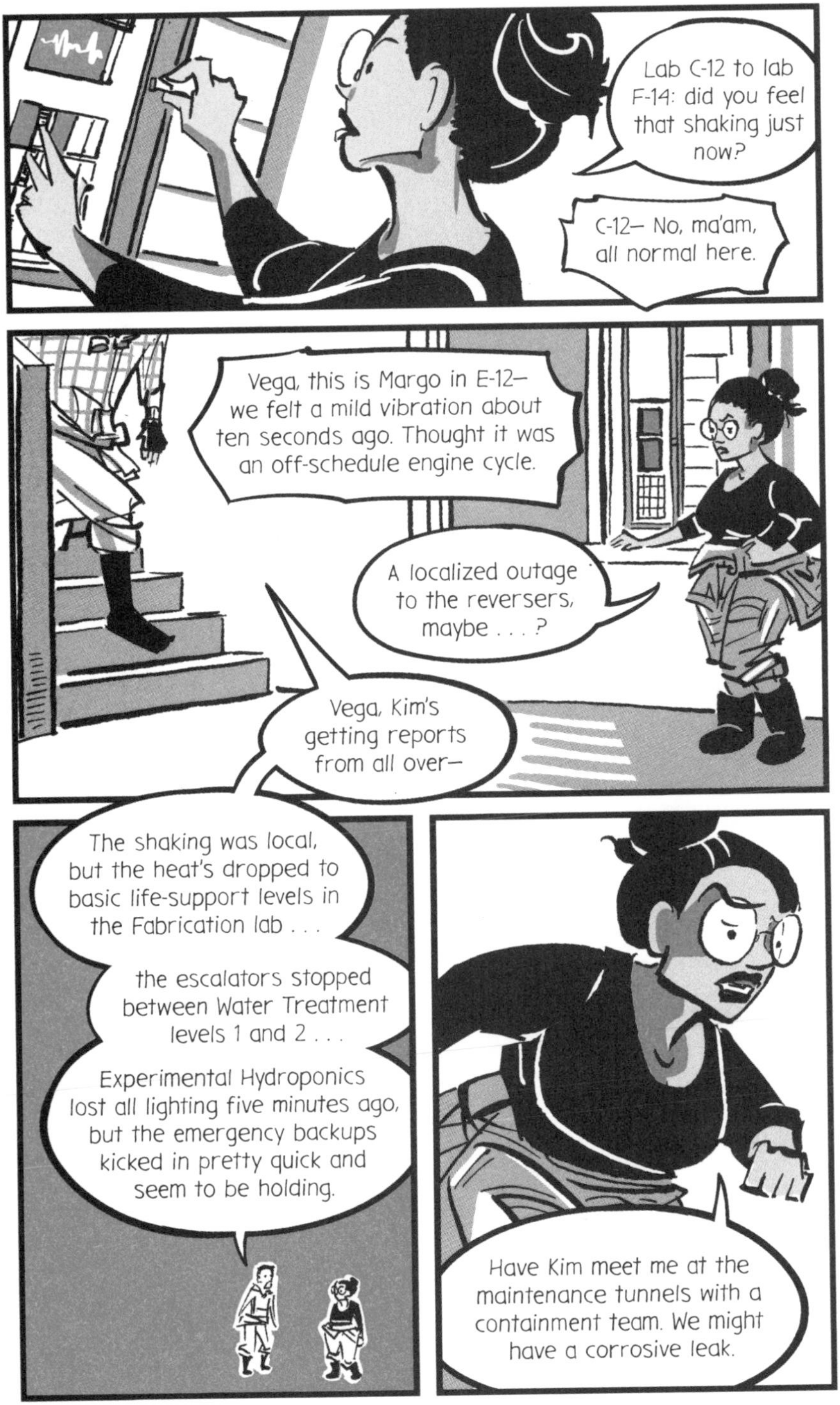
Lab C-12 to lab F-14: did you feel that shaking just now?
C-12— No, ma'am, all normal here.
Vega, this is Margo in E-12— we felt a mild vibration about ten seconds ago. Thought it was an off-schedule engine cycle.
A localized outage to the reversers, maybe . . . ?
Vega, Kim's getting reports from all over—
The shaking was local, but the heat's dropped to basic life-support levels in the Fabrication lab . . .
the escalators stopped between Water Treatment levels 1 and 2 . . .
Experimental Hydroponics lost all lighting five minutes ago, but the emergency backups kicked in pretty quick and seem to be holding.
Have Kim meet me at the maintenance tunnels with a containment team. We might have a corrosive leak.

## (STUDENT LABS, END OF CLASS)

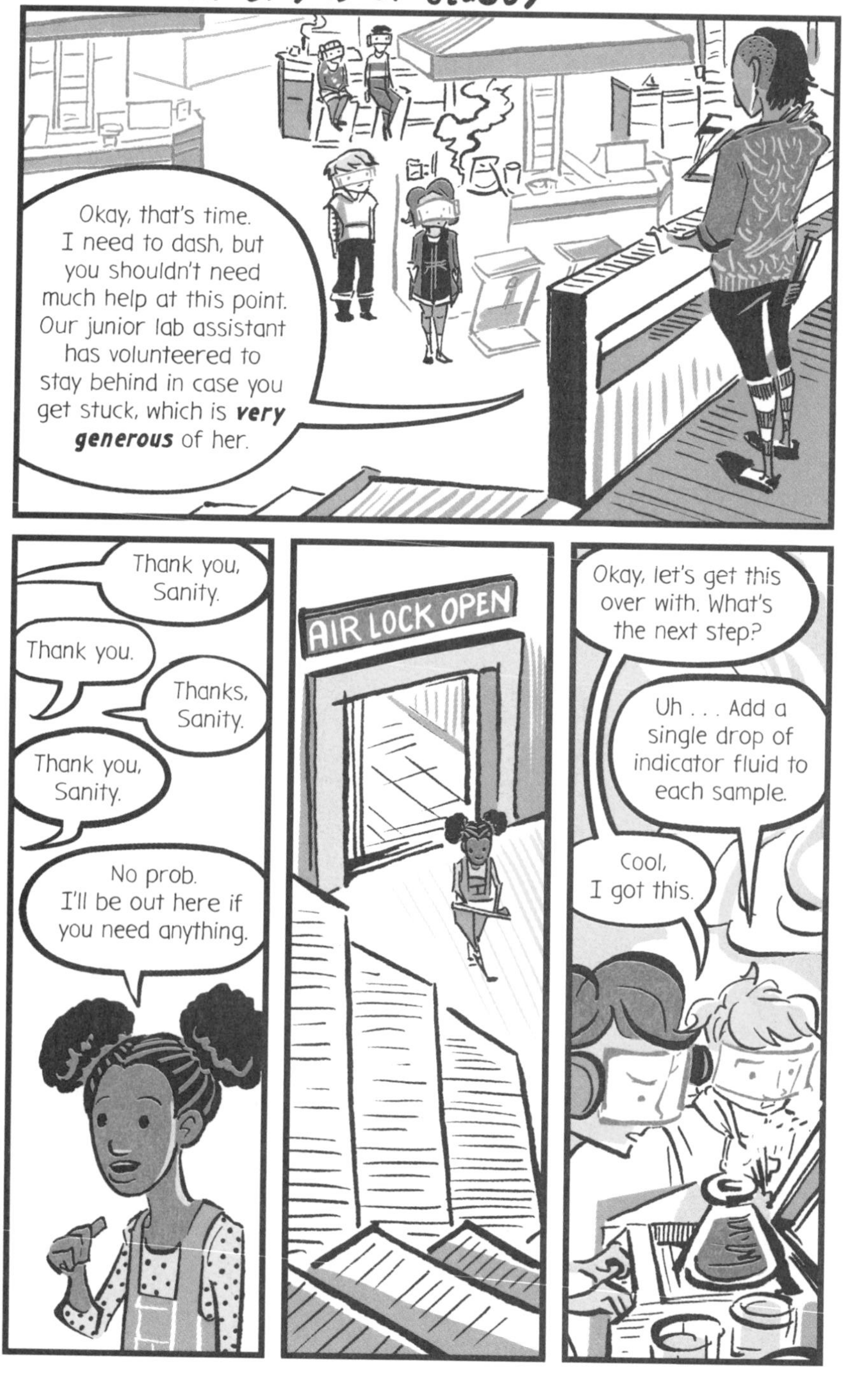

Okay, that's time. I need to dash, but you shouldn't need much help at this point. Our junior lab assistant has volunteered to stay behind in case you get stuck, which is ***very generous*** of her.
Thank you, Sanity.
Thank you.
Thanks, Sanity.
Thank you, Sanity.
No prob. I'll be out here if you need anything.
AIR LOCK OPEN
Okay, let's get this over with. What's the next step?
Uh . . . Add a single drop of indicator fluid to each sample.
Cool, I got this.

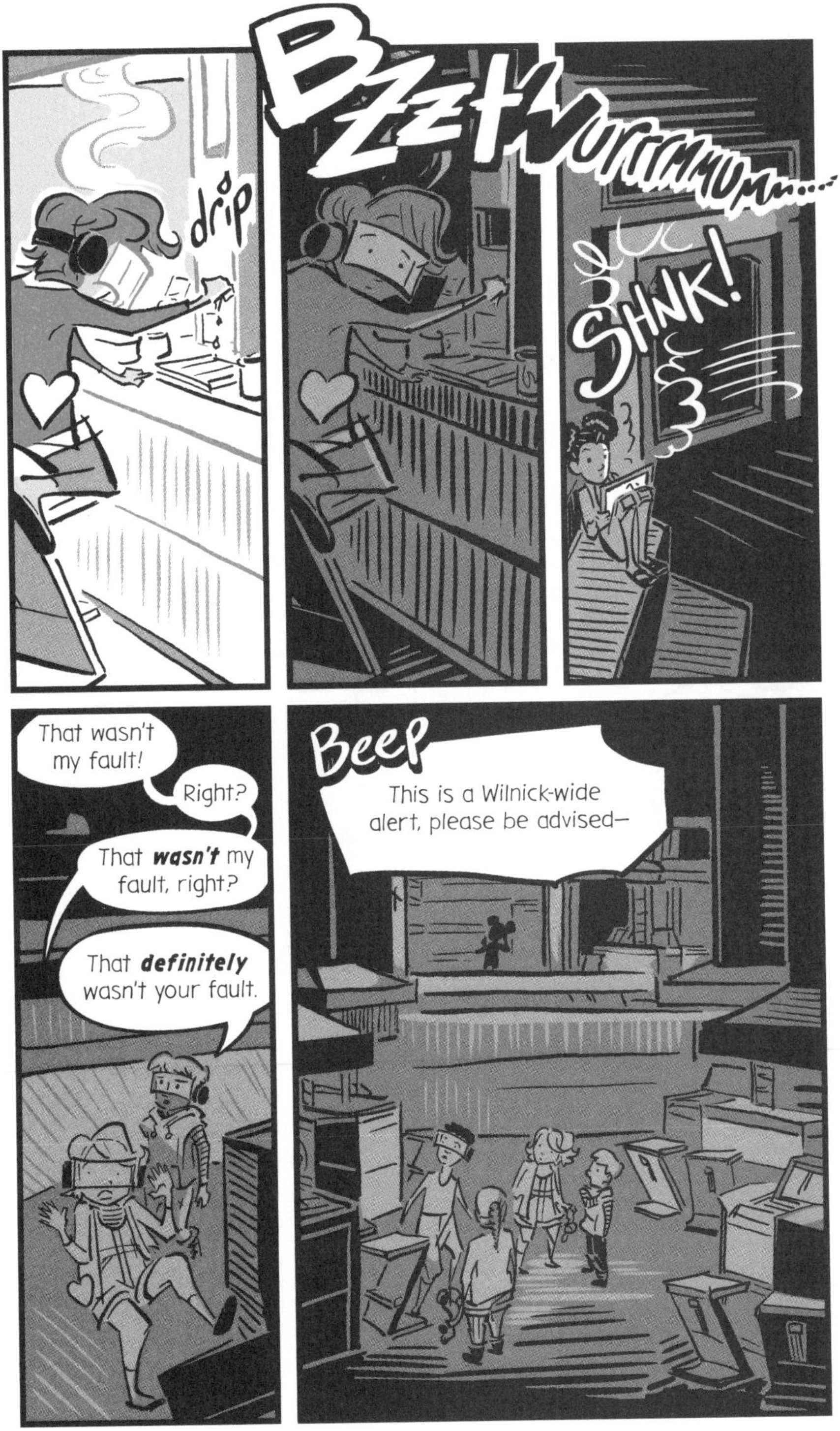
drip
BZZT'WUTTTMUM.....
SHNK!
That wasn't my fault!
Right?
That **wasn't** my fault, right?
That **definitely** wasn't your fault.
Beep
This is a Wilnick-wide alert, please be advised—

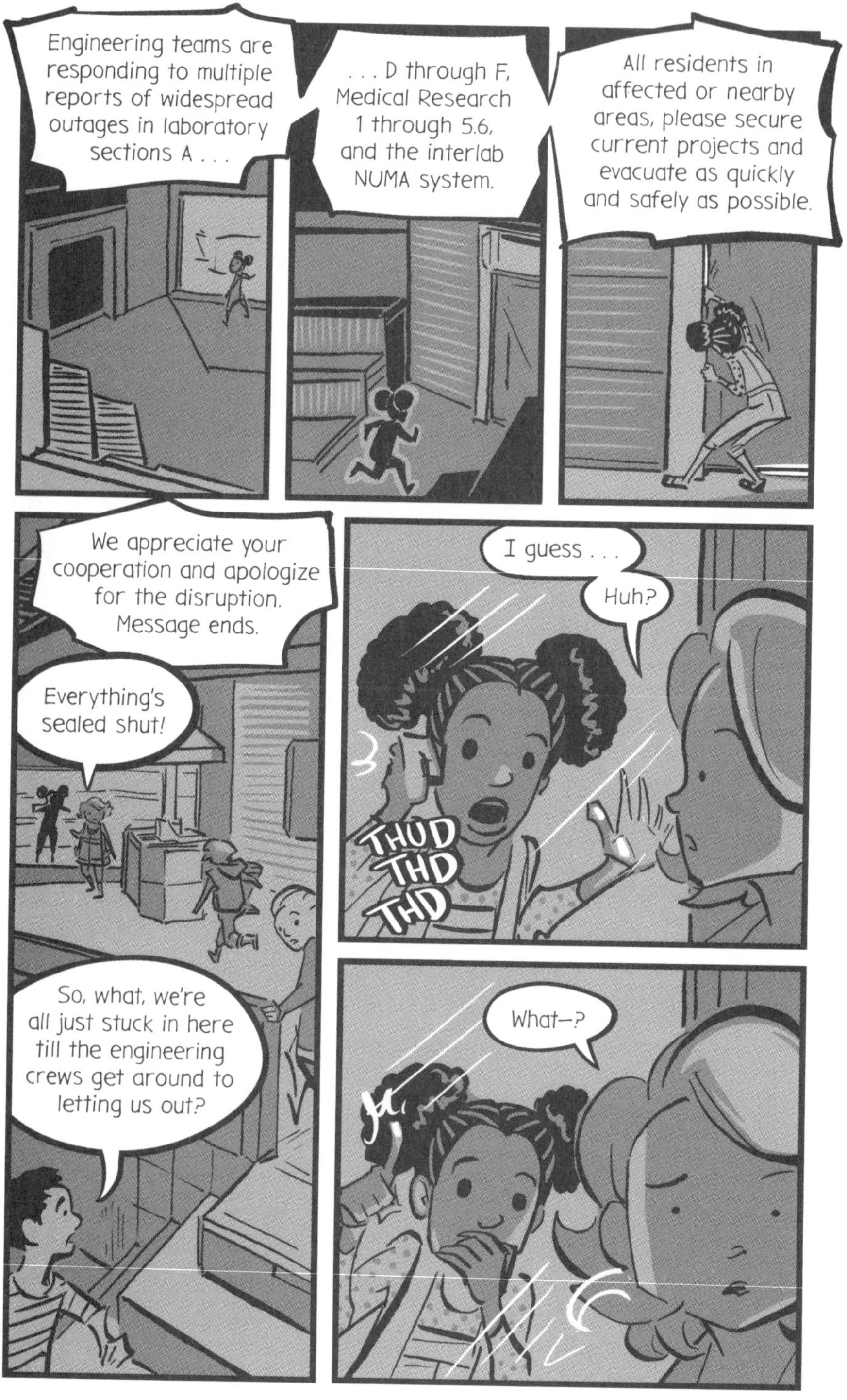
Engineering teams are responding to multiple reports of widespread outages in laboratory sections A . . .
. . . D through F, Medical Research 1 through 5.6, and the interlab NUMA system.
All residents in affected or nearby areas, please secure current projects and evacuate as quickly and safely as possible.
We appreciate your cooperation and apologize for the disruption. Message ends.
Everything's sealed shut!
So, what, we're all just stuck in here till the engineering crews get around to letting us out?
I guess . . .
Huh?
THUD
THD
THD
What–?

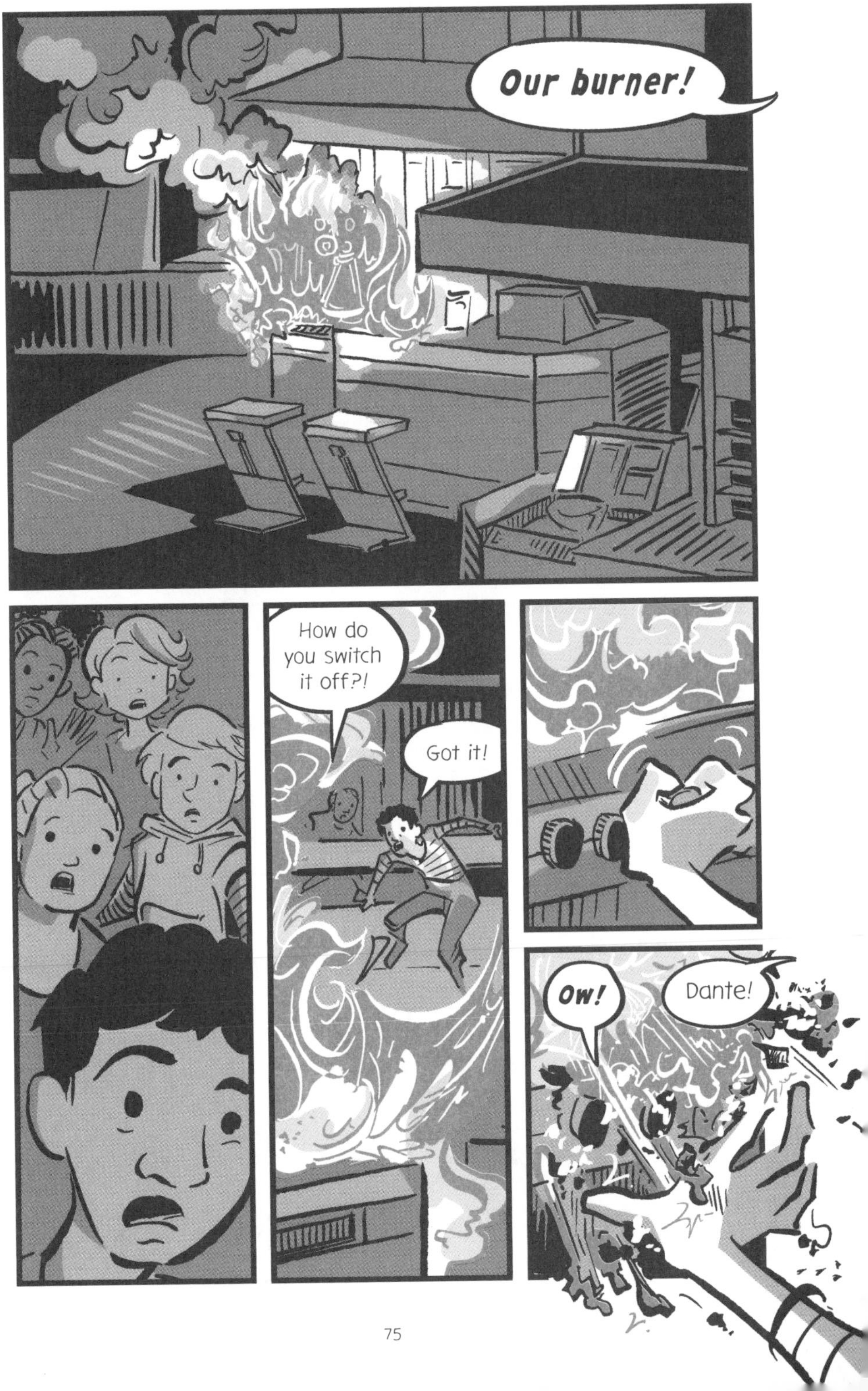
Our burner!
How do you switch it off?!
Got it!
Ow!
Dante!

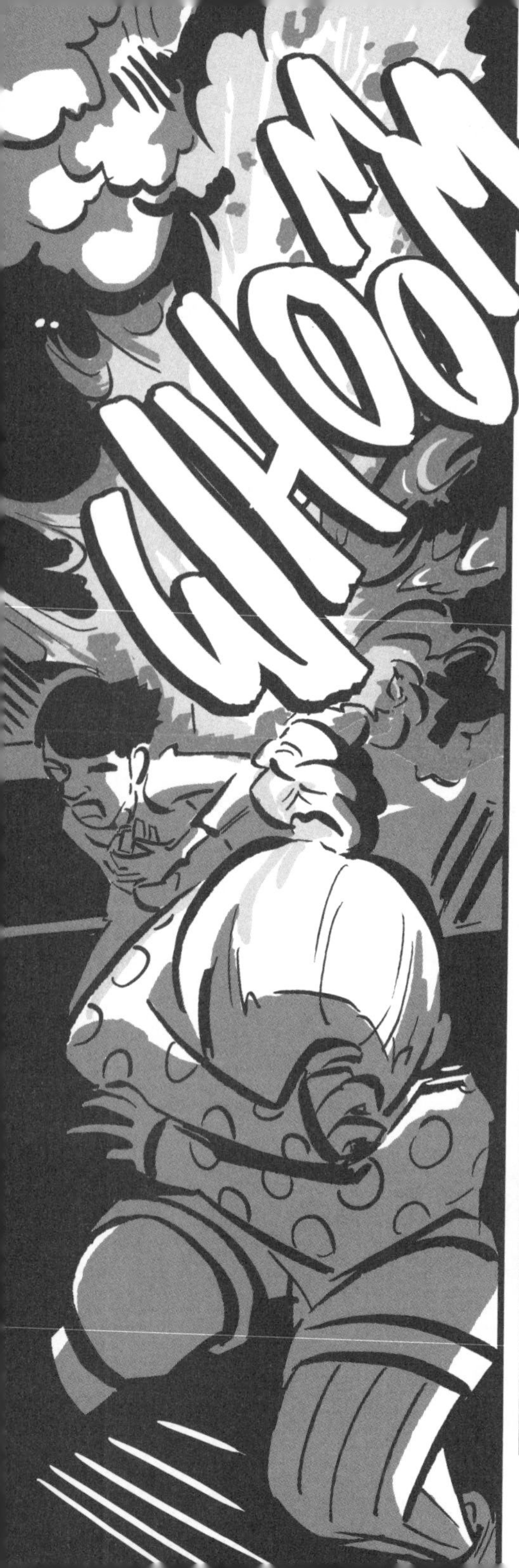
WHOOM

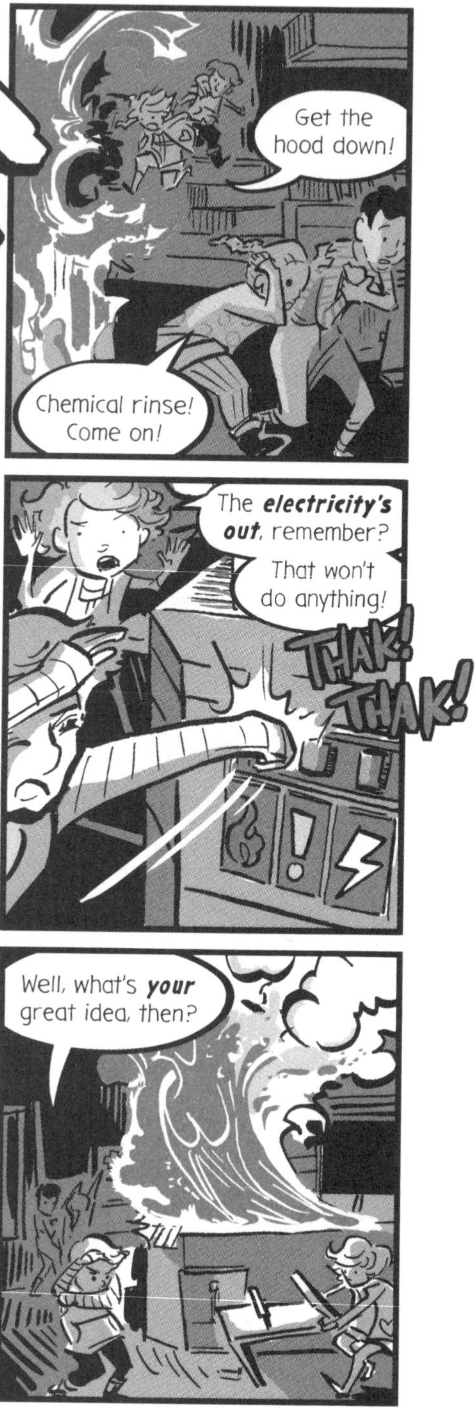
Get the hood down!
Chemical rinse! Come on!
The ***electricity's out***, remember?
That won't do anything!
THAK! THAK!
Well, what's ***your*** great idea, then?

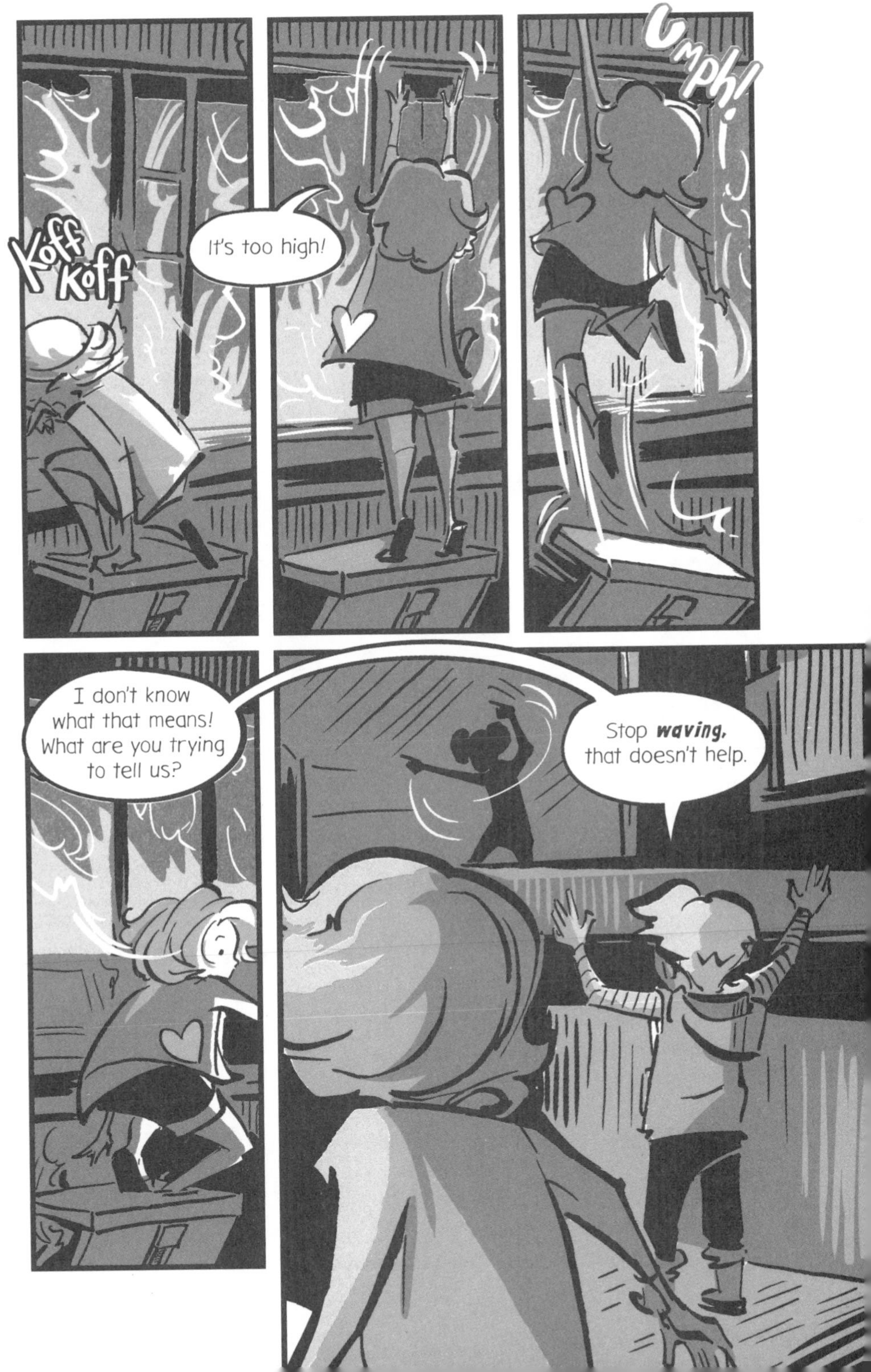
Koff Koff
It's too high!
Umph!
I don't know what that means! What are you trying to tell us?
Stop **waving,** that doesn't help.

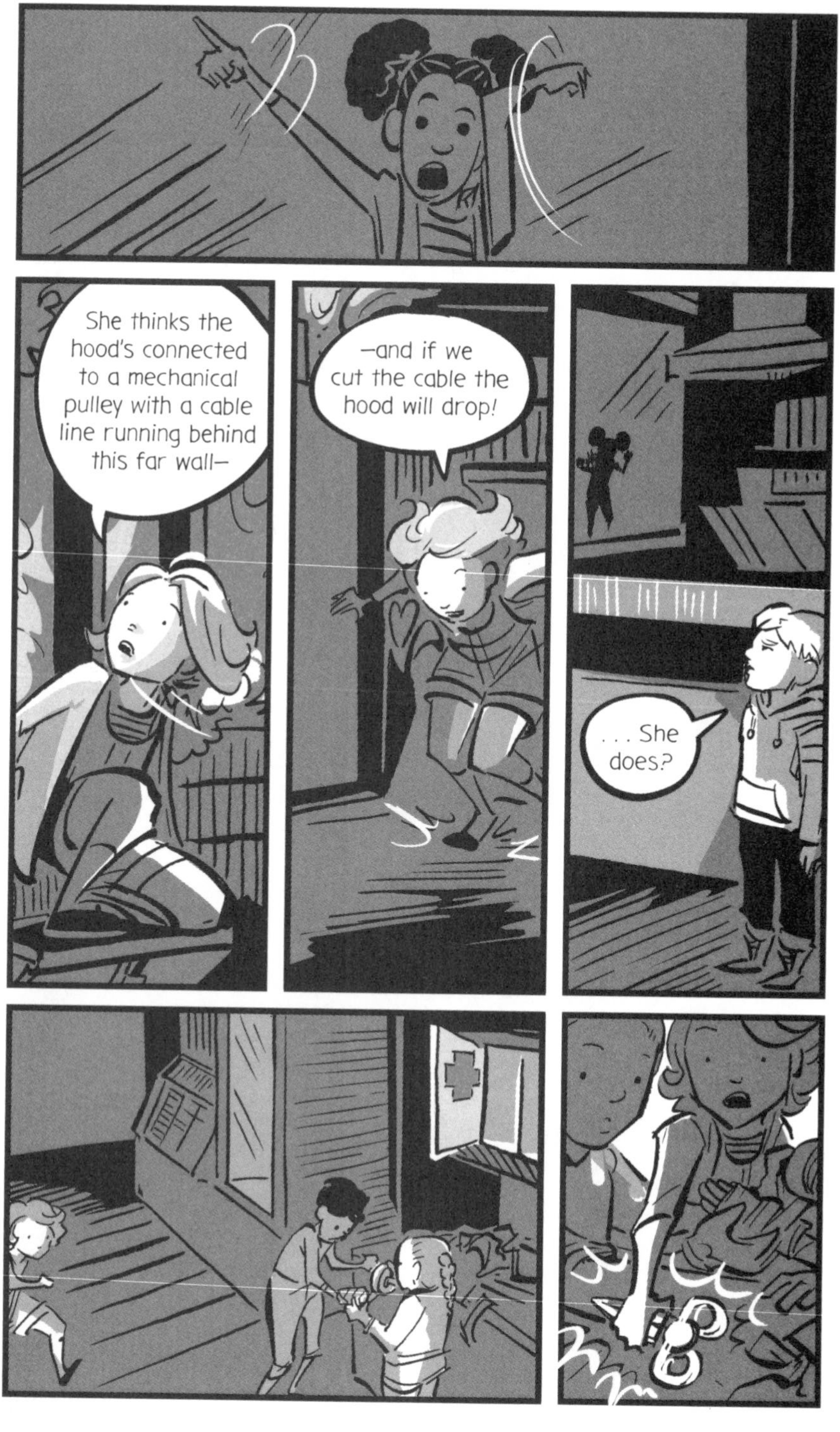
She thinks the hood's connected to a mechanical pulley with a cable line running behind this far wall—
—and if we cut the cable the hood will drop!
. . . She does?

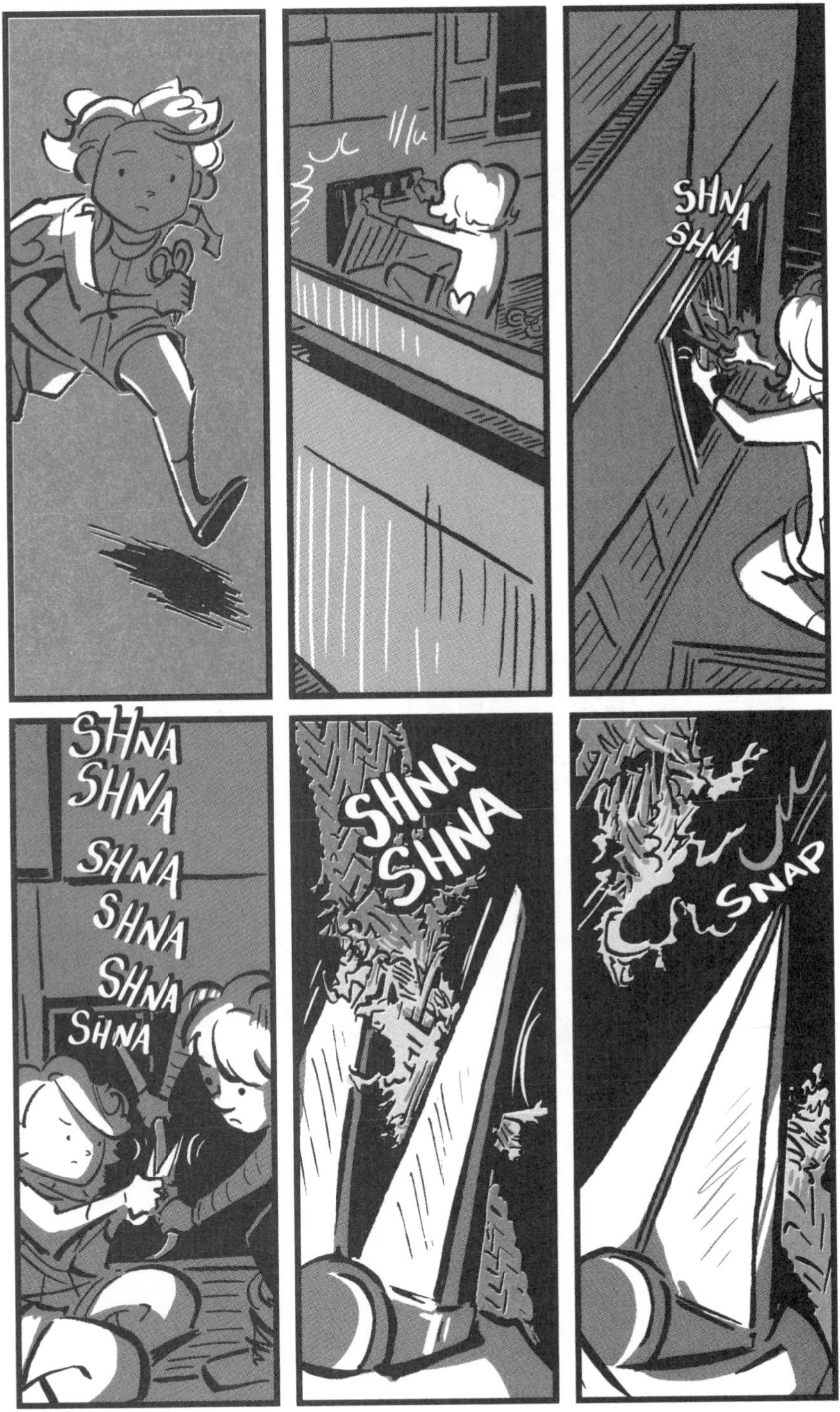
SHNA
SHNA
SHNA
SHNA
SHNA
SHNA
SHNA
SHNA
SHNA
SHNA
SNAP

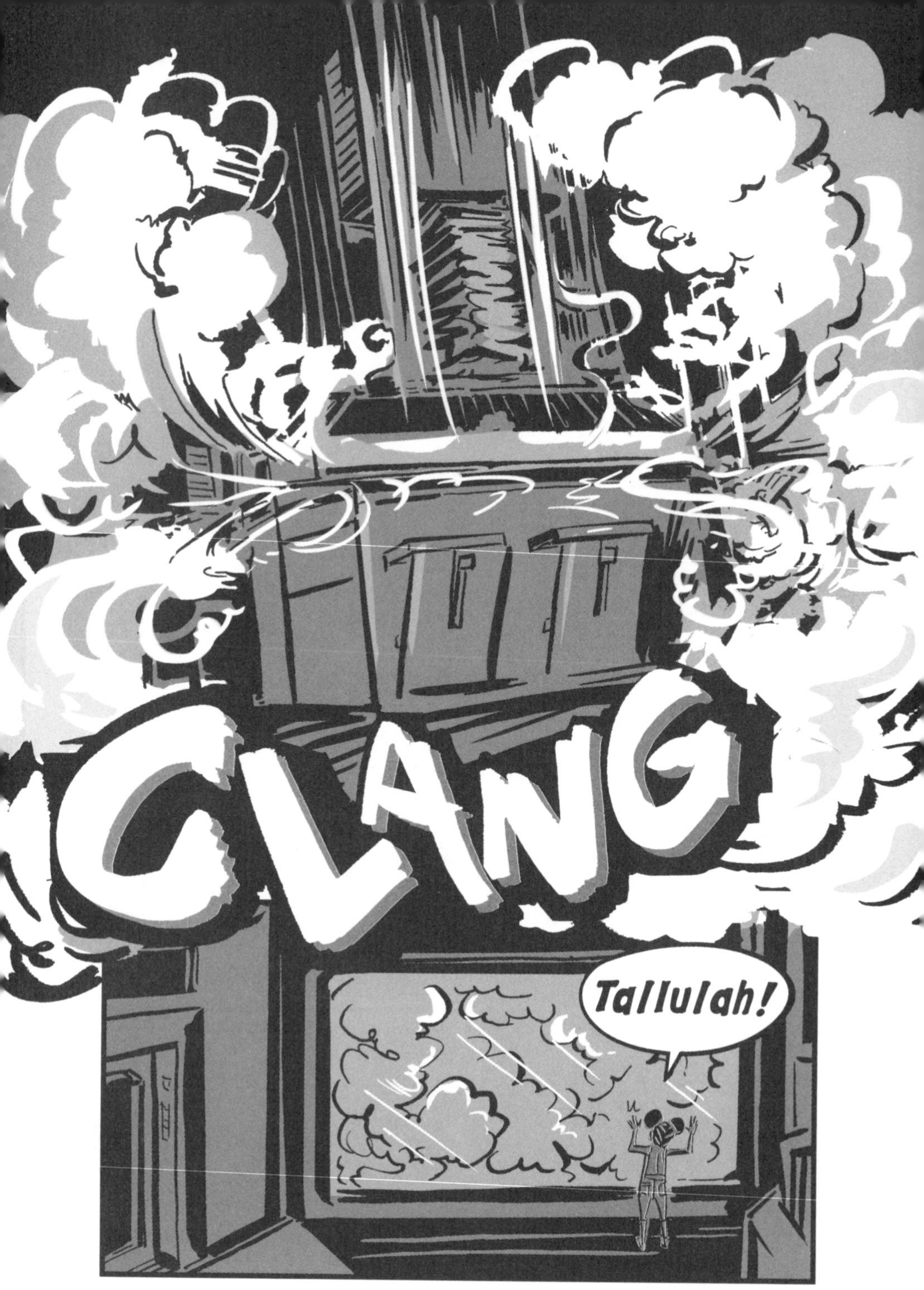
CLANG
Tallulah!

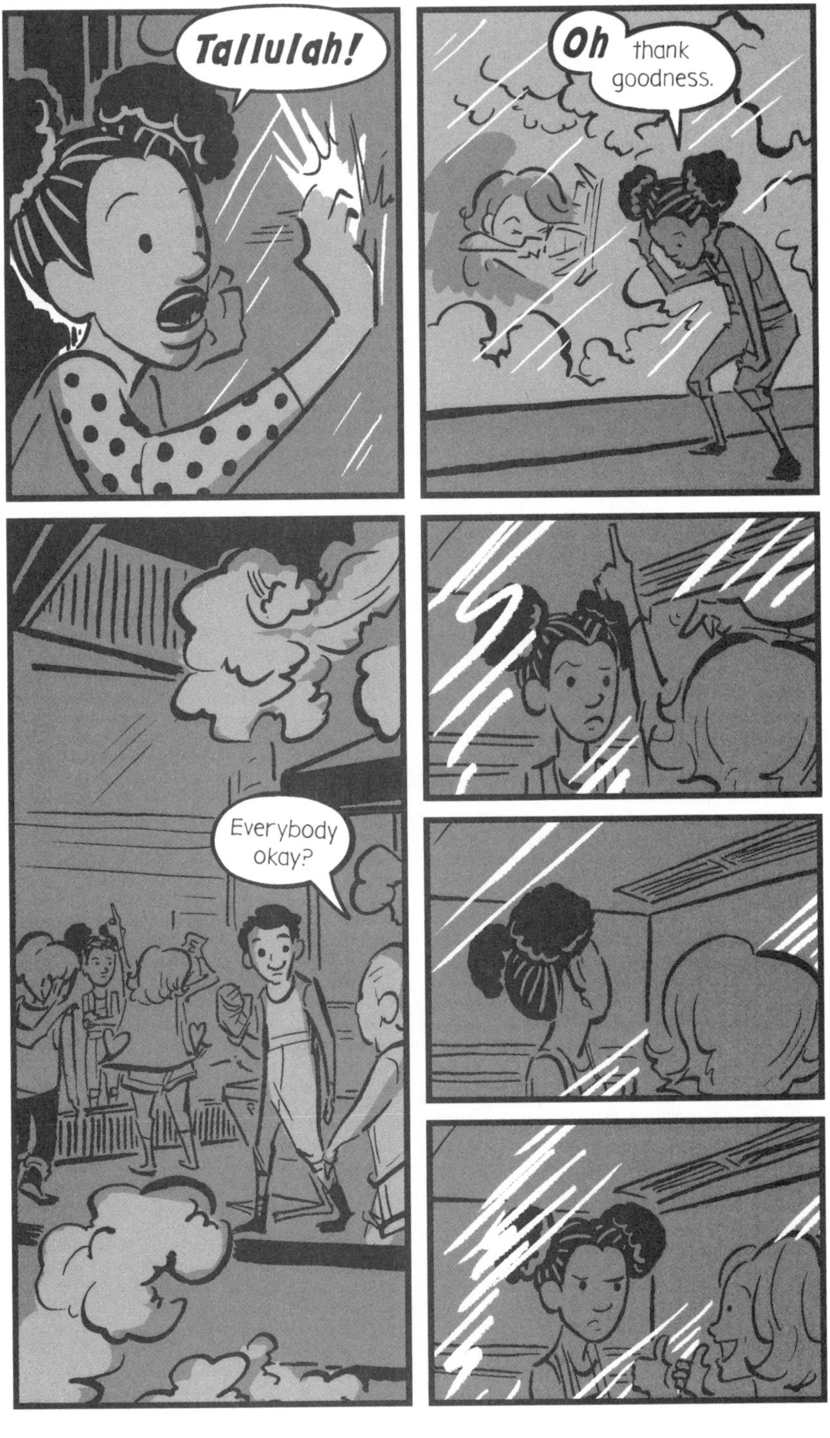
Tallulah!
Oh thank goodness.
Everybody okay?

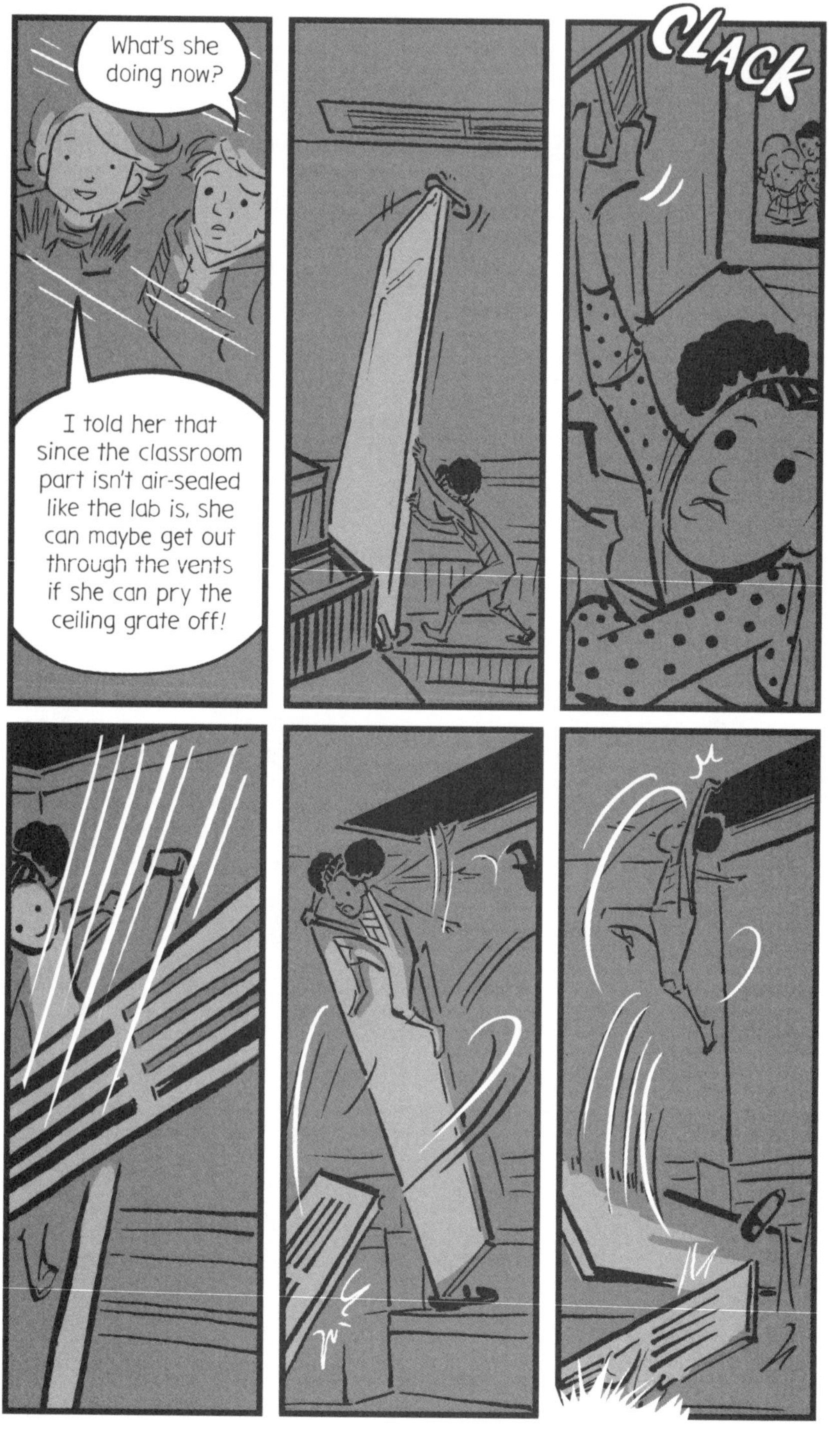
What's she doing now?
I told her that since the classroom part isn't air-sealed like the lab is, she can maybe get out through the vents if she can pry the ceiling grate off!
CLACK

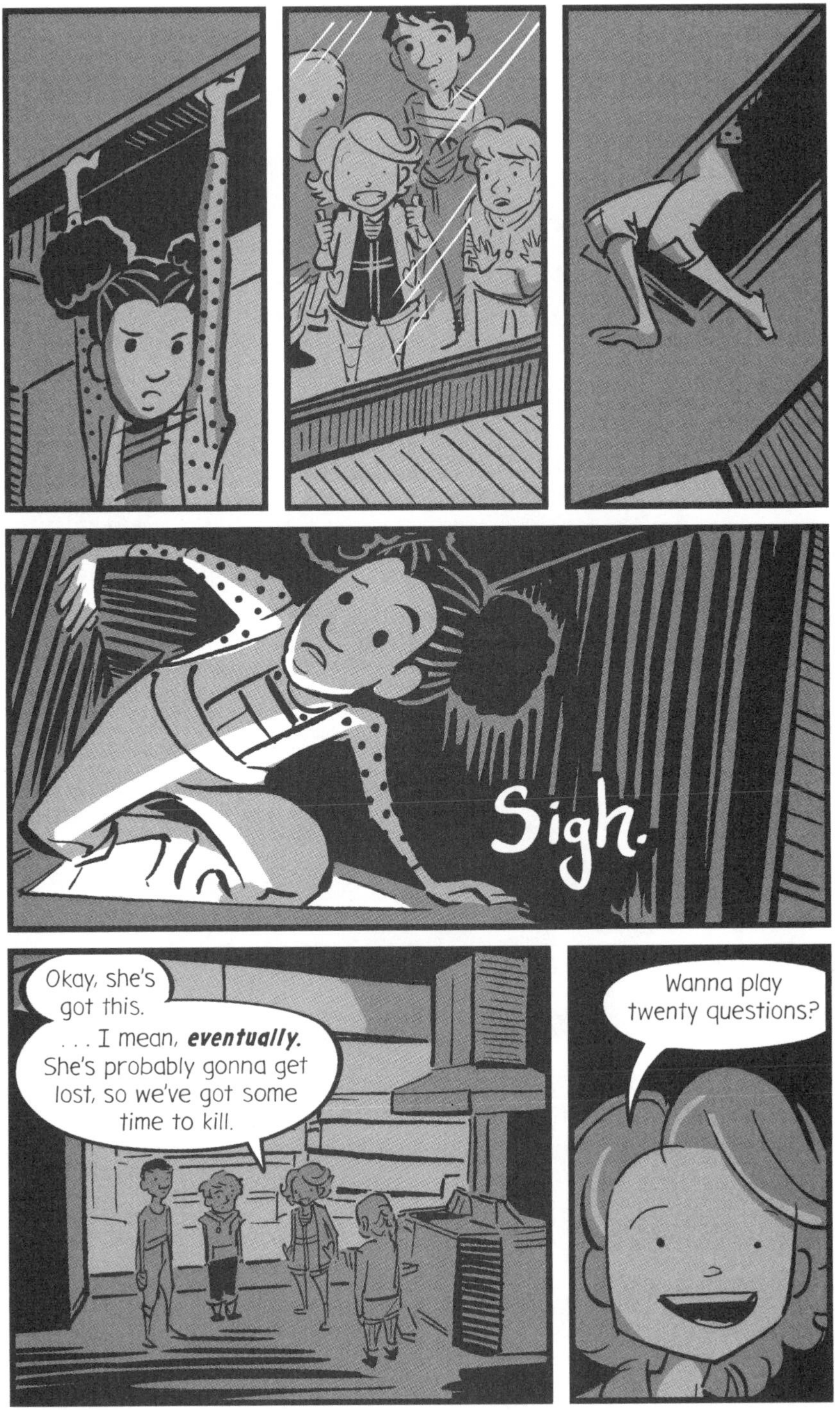
Sigh.
Okay, she's got this.
. . . I mean, **eventually.** She's probably gonna get lost, so we've got some time to kill.
Wanna play twenty questions?

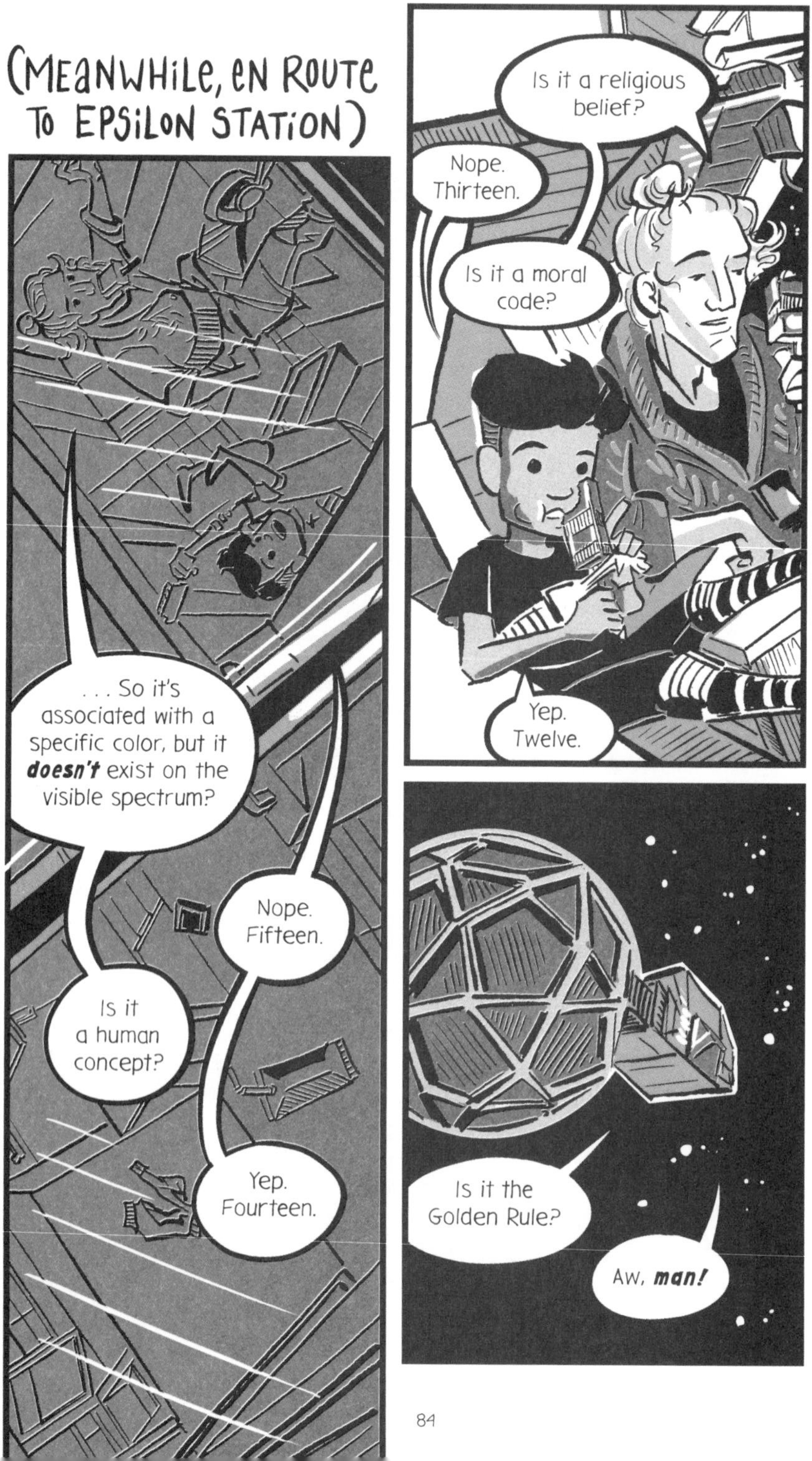
(MEANWHILE, EN ROUTE TO EPSILON STATION)
. . . So it's associated with a specific color, but it **doesn't** exist on the visible spectrum?
Nope. Fifteen.
Is it a human concept?
Yep. Fourteen.
Is it a religious belief?
Nope. Thirteen.
Is it a moral code?
Yep. Twelve.
Is it the Golden Rule?
Aw, **man!**

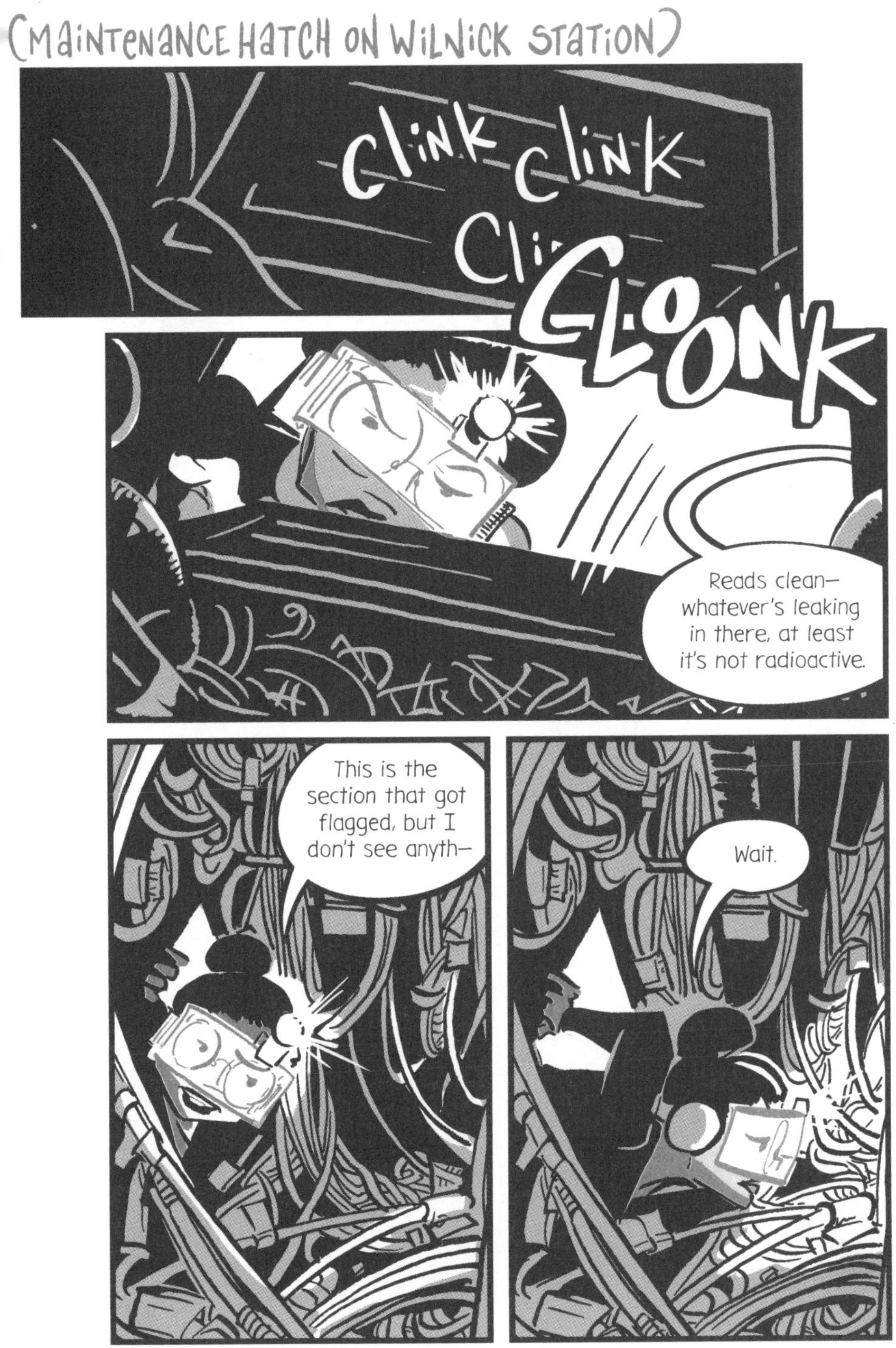
(MAINTENANCE HATCH ON WILNICK STATION)
CLINK CLINK
CLI
CLOONK
Reads clean— whatever's leaking in there, at least it's not radioactive.
This is the section that got flagged, but I don't see anyth—
Wait.

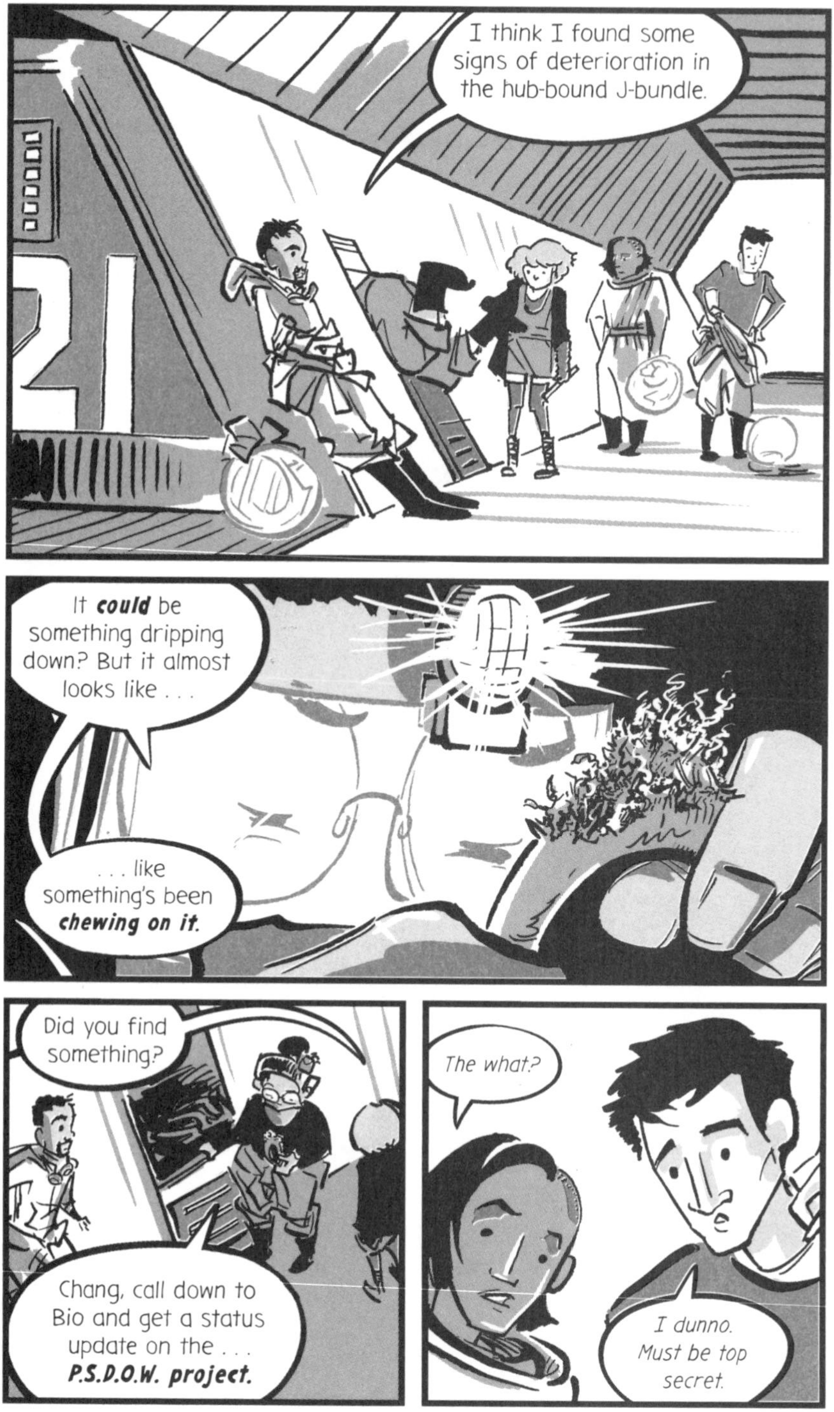
I think I found some signs of deterioration in the hub-bound J-bundle.
It **could** be something dripping down? But it almost looks like . . .
. . . like something's been **chewing on it.**
Did you find something?
Chang, call down to Bio and get a status update on the . . . **P.S.D.O.W. project.**
*The what?*
*I dunno. Must be top secret.*

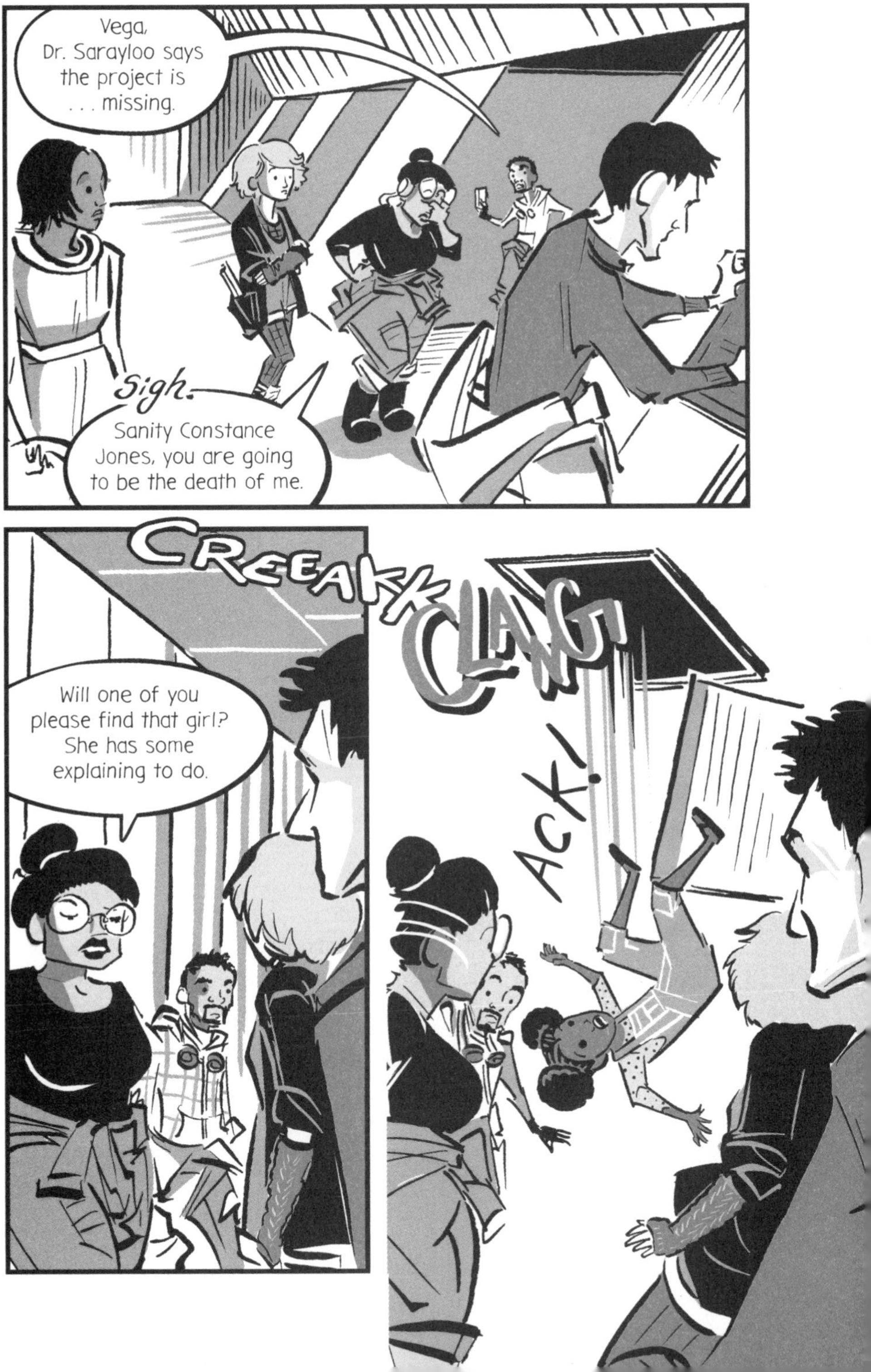
Vega, Dr. Sarayloo says the project is . . . missing.
Sigh.
Sanity Constance Jones, you are going to be the death of me.
CREEAKK
CLANG!
Will one of you please find that girl? She has some explaining to do.
ACK!

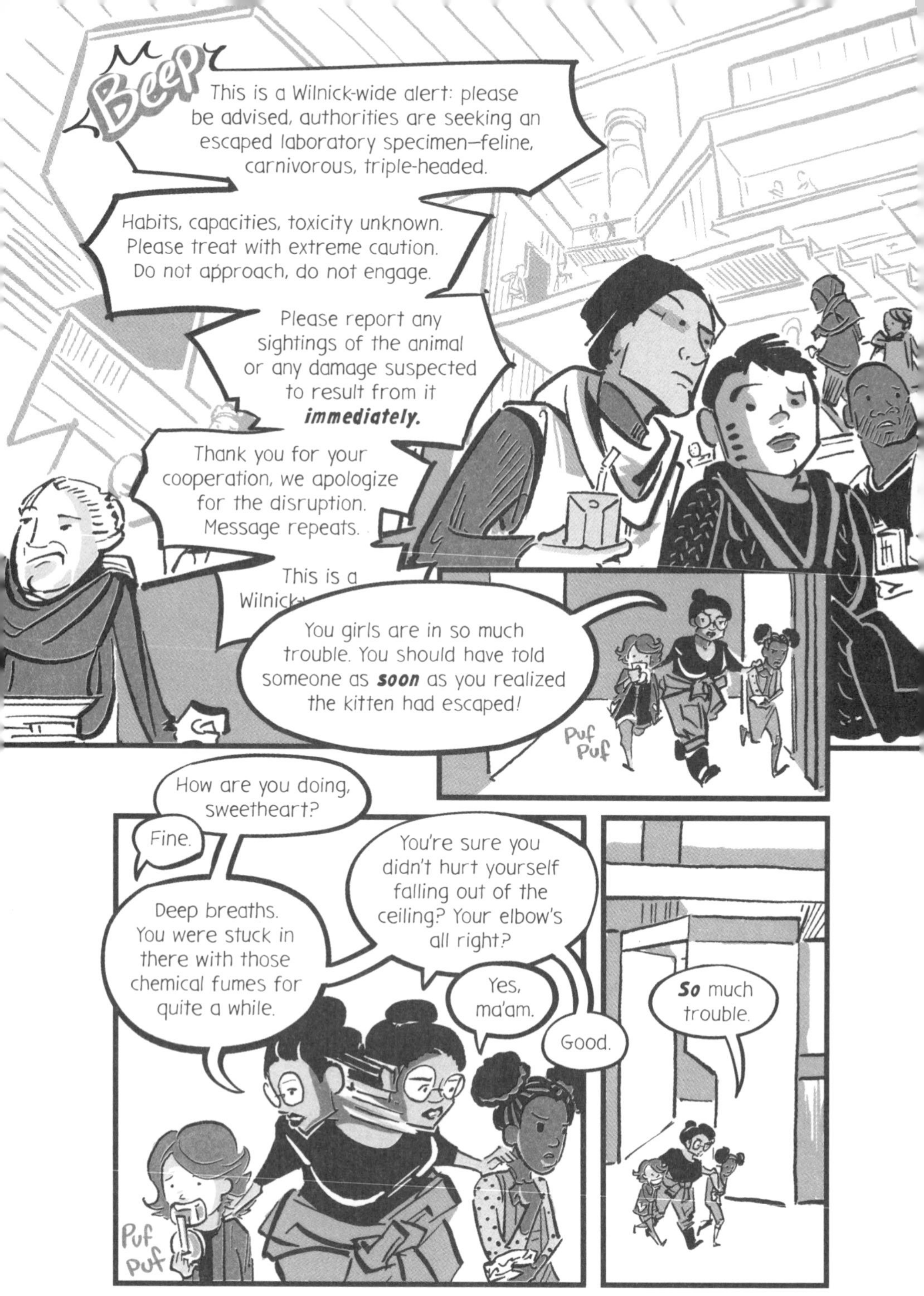
Beep
This is a Wilnick-wide alert: please be advised, authorities are seeking an escaped laboratory specimen—feline, carnivorous, triple-headed.
Habits, capacities, toxicity unknown. Please treat with extreme caution. Do not approach, do not engage.
Please report any sightings of the animal or any damage suspected to result from it **immediately.**
Thank you for your cooperation, we apologize for the disruption. Message repeats.
This is a Wilnick
You girls are in so much trouble. You should have told someone as **soon** as you realized the kitten had escaped!
Puf Puf
How are you doing, sweetheart?
Fine.
Deep breaths. You were stuck in there with those chemical fumes for quite a while.
You're sure you didn't hurt yourself falling out of the ceiling? Your elbow's all right?
Yes, ma'am.
Good.
Puf Puf
**So** much trouble.

(Station Administration)

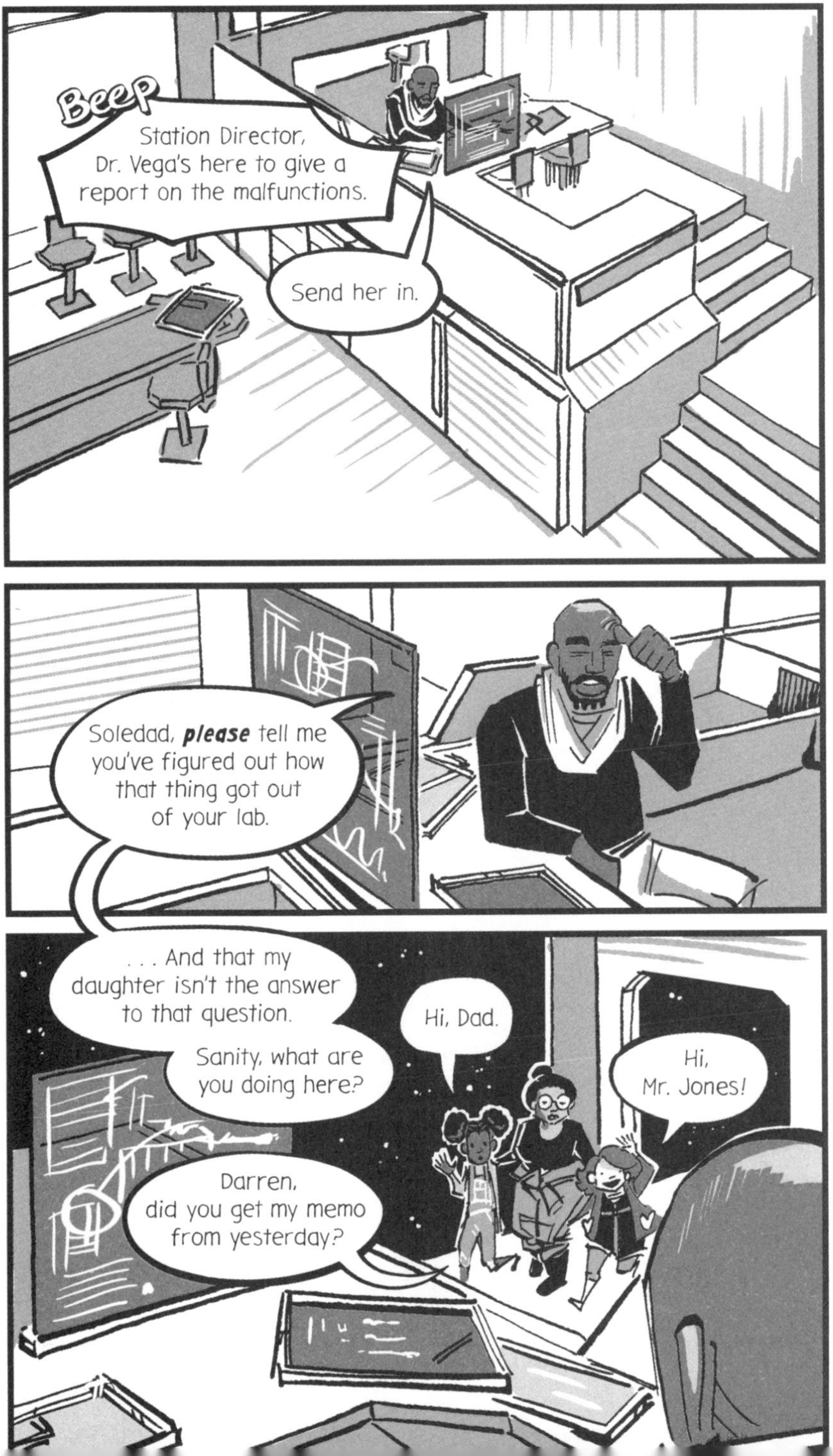
Beep
Station Director, Dr. Vega's here to give a report on the malfunctions.
Send her in.
Soledad, *please* tell me you've figured out how that thing got out of your lab.
. . . And that my daughter isn't the answer to that question.
Sanity, what are you doing here?
Hi, Dad.
Hi, Mr. Jones!
Darren, did you get my memo from yesterday?

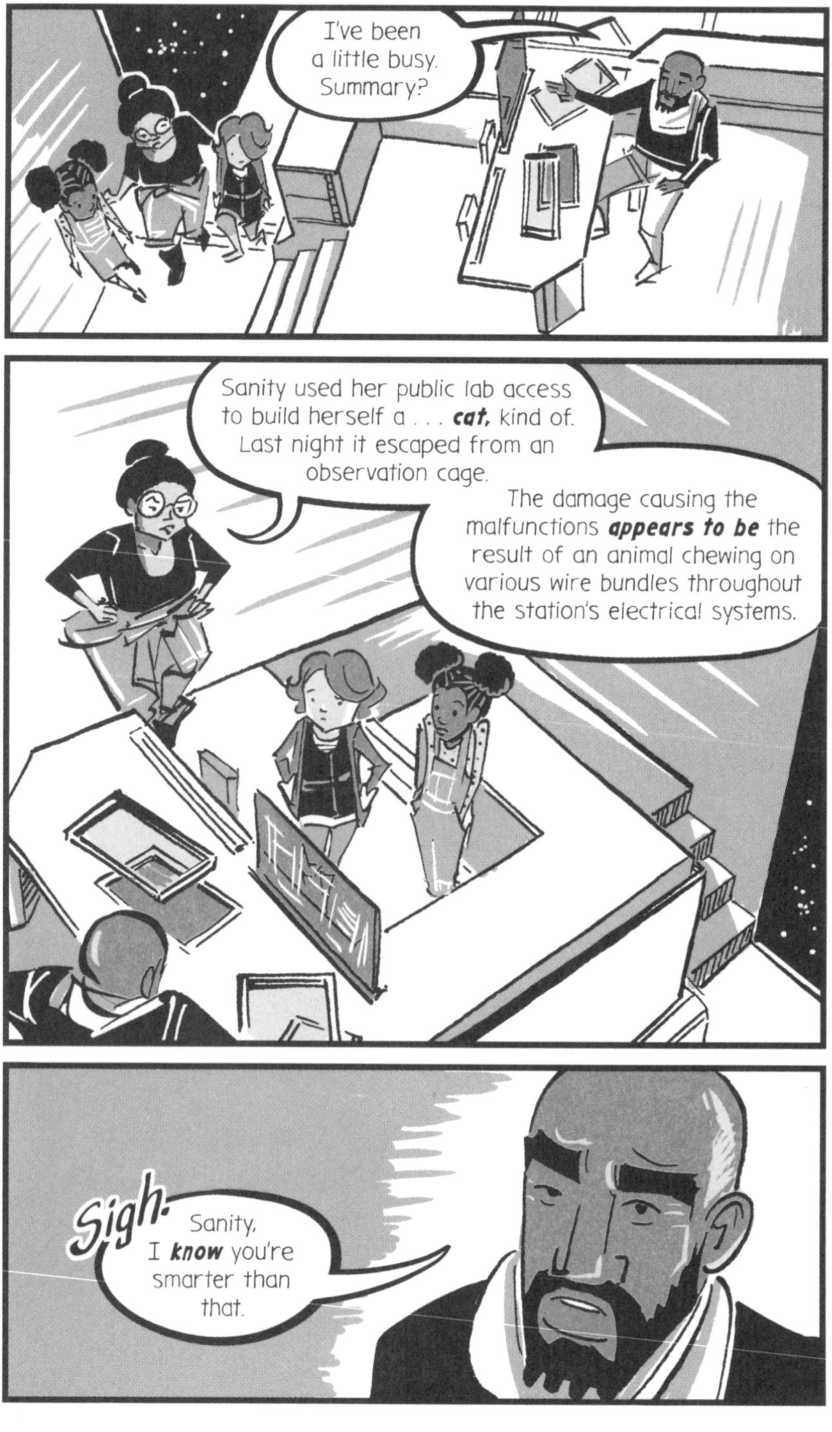

I've been a little busy. Summary?
Sanity used her public lab access to build herself a . . . **cat,** kind of. Last night it escaped from an observation cage.
The damage causing the malfunctions **appears to be** the result of an animal chewing on various wire bundles throughout the station's electrical systems.
Sigh.
Sanity, I **know** you're smarter than that.

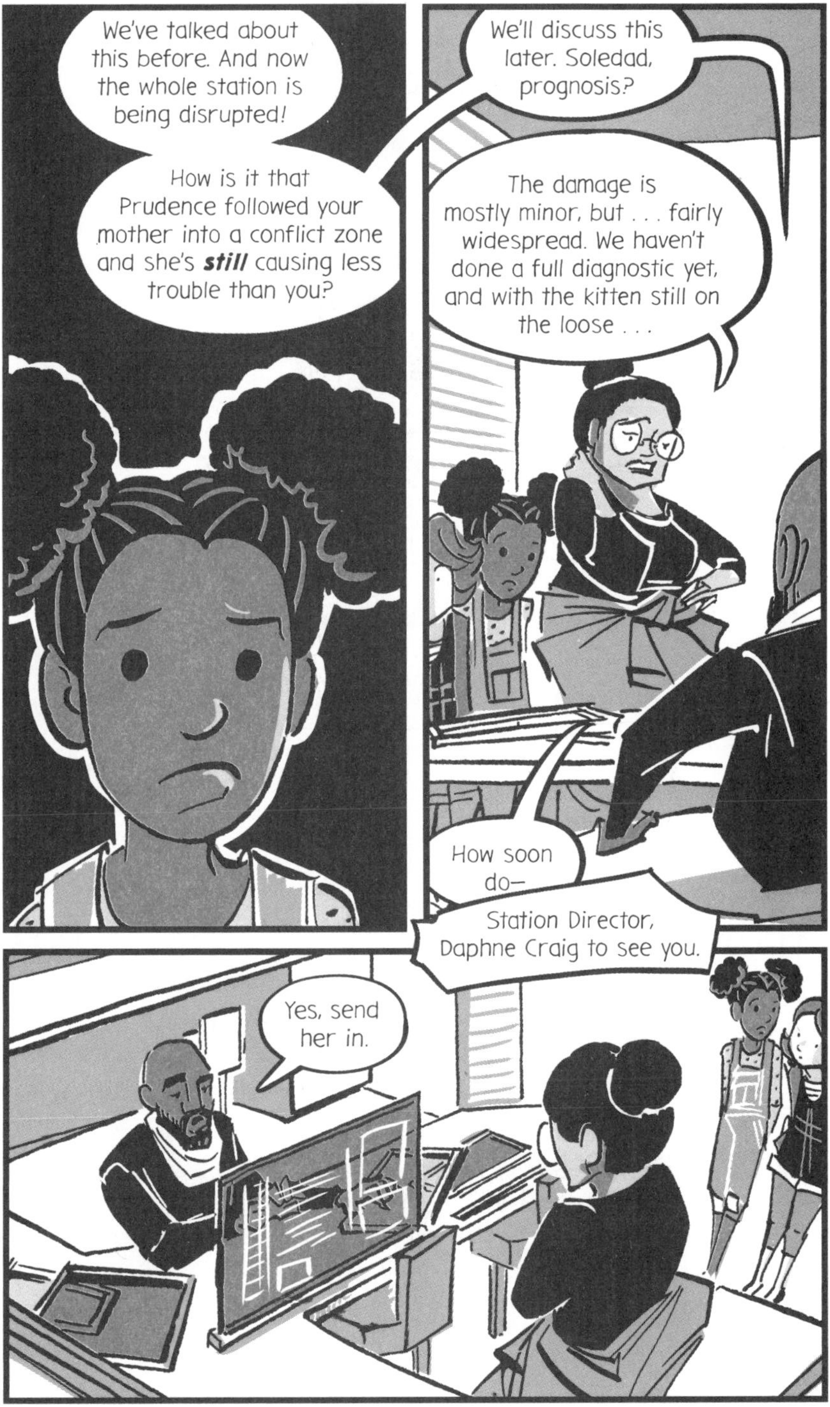
We've talked about this before. And now the whole station is being disrupted!
How is it that Prudence followed your mother into a conflict zone and she's ***still*** causing less trouble than you?
We'll discuss this later. Soledad, prognosis?
The damage is mostly minor, but . . . fairly widespread. We haven't done a full diagnostic yet, and with the kitten still on the loose . . .
How soon do—
Station Director, Daphne Craig to see you.
Yes, send her in.

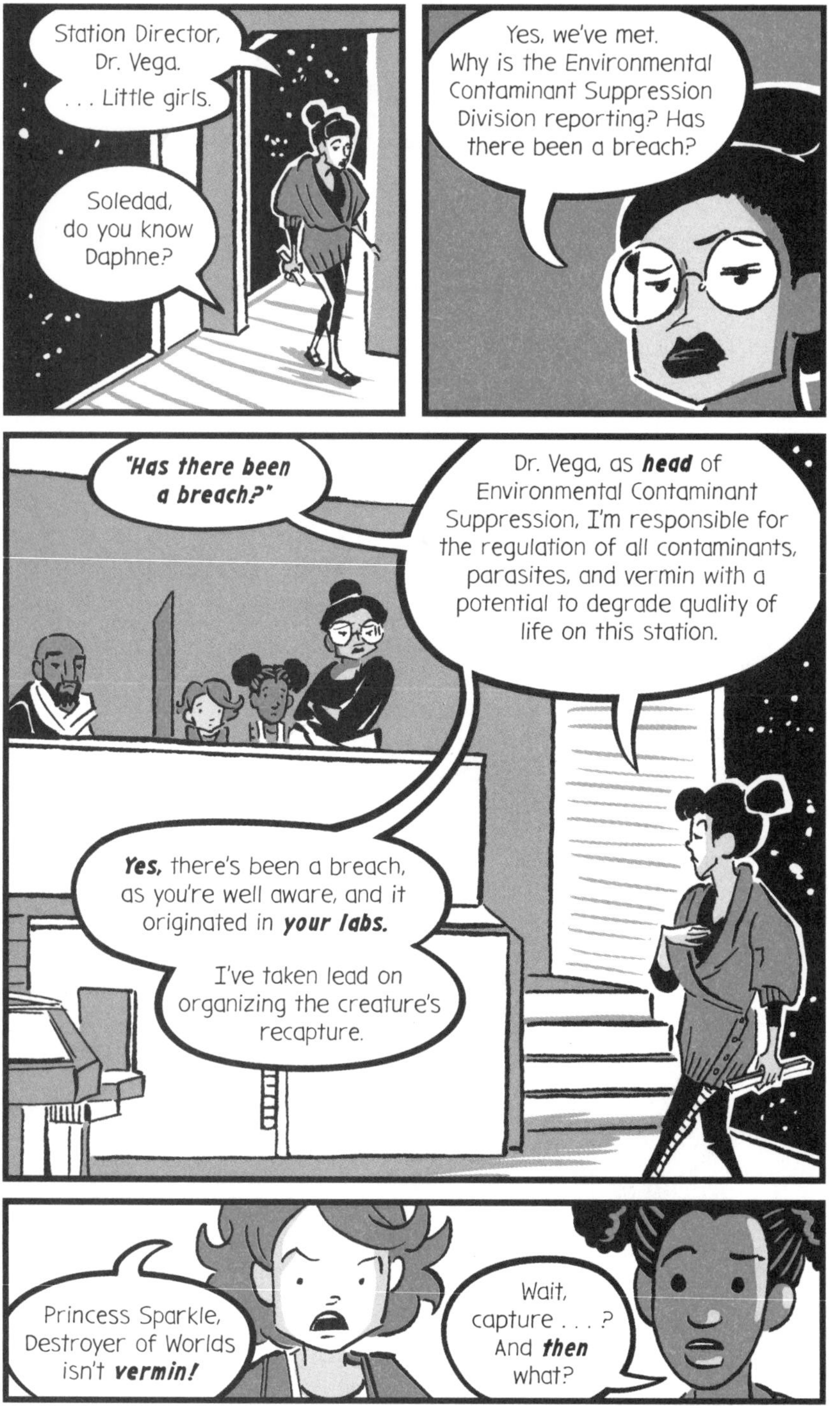

Station Director, Dr. Vega.
. . . Little girls.
Soledad, do you know Daphne?
Yes, we've met. Why is the Environmental Contaminant Suppression Division reporting? Has there been a breach?
*"Has there been a breach?"*
Dr. Vega, as ***head*** of Environmental Contaminant Suppression, I'm responsible for the regulation of all contaminants, parasites, and vermin with a potential to degrade quality of life on this station.
***Yes,*** there's been a breach, as you're well aware, and it originated in ***your labs.***
I've taken lead on organizing the creature's recapture.
Princess Sparkle, Destroyer of Worlds isn't ***vermin!***
Wait, capture . . . ? And ***then*** what?

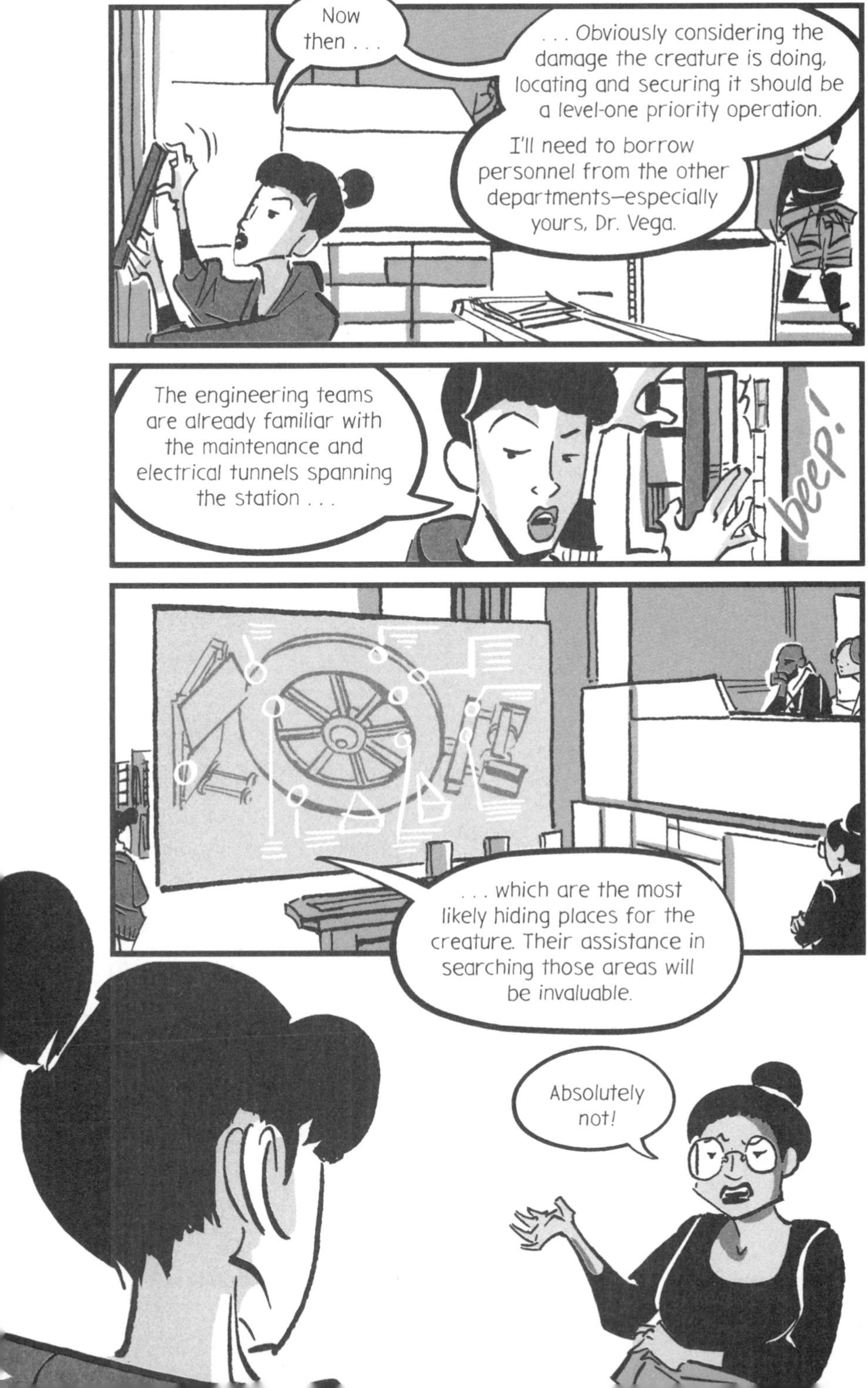
Now then . . .
. . . Obviously considering the damage the creature is doing, locating and securing it should be a level-one priority operation.
I'll need to borrow personnel from the other departments—especially yours, Dr. Vega.
The engineering teams are already familiar with the maintenance and electrical tunnels spanning the station . . .
beep!
. . . which are the most likely hiding places for the creature. Their assistance in searching those areas will be invaluable.
Absolutely not!

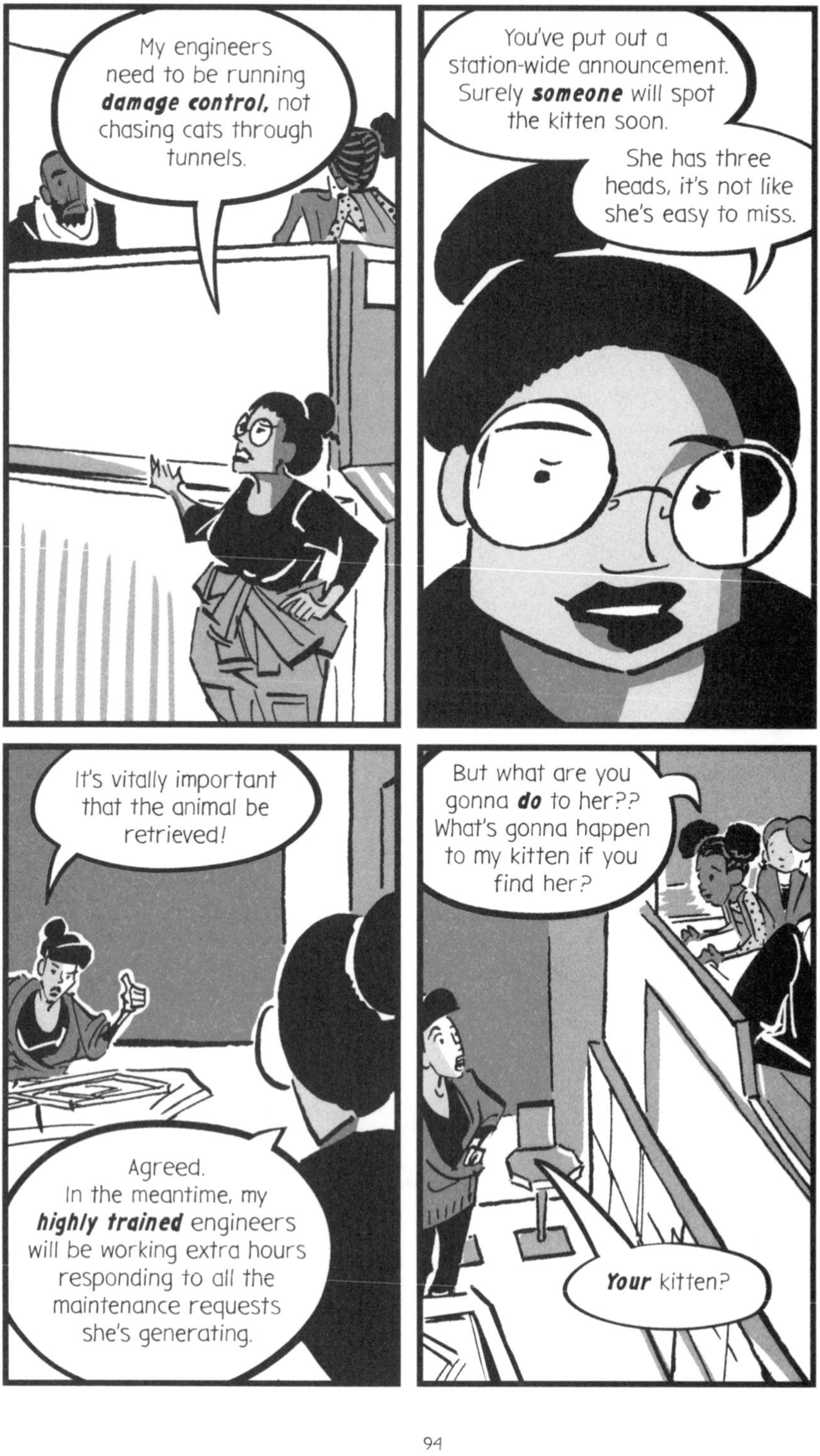
My engineers need to be running **damage control,** not chasing cats through tunnels.
You've put out a station-wide announcement. Surely **someone** will spot the kitten soon.
She has three heads, it's not like she's easy to miss.
It's vitally important that the animal be retrieved!
Agreed. In the meantime, my **highly trained** engineers will be working extra hours responding to all the maintenance requests she's generating.
But what are you gonna **do** to her?? What's gonna happen to my kitten if you find her?
**Your** kitten?

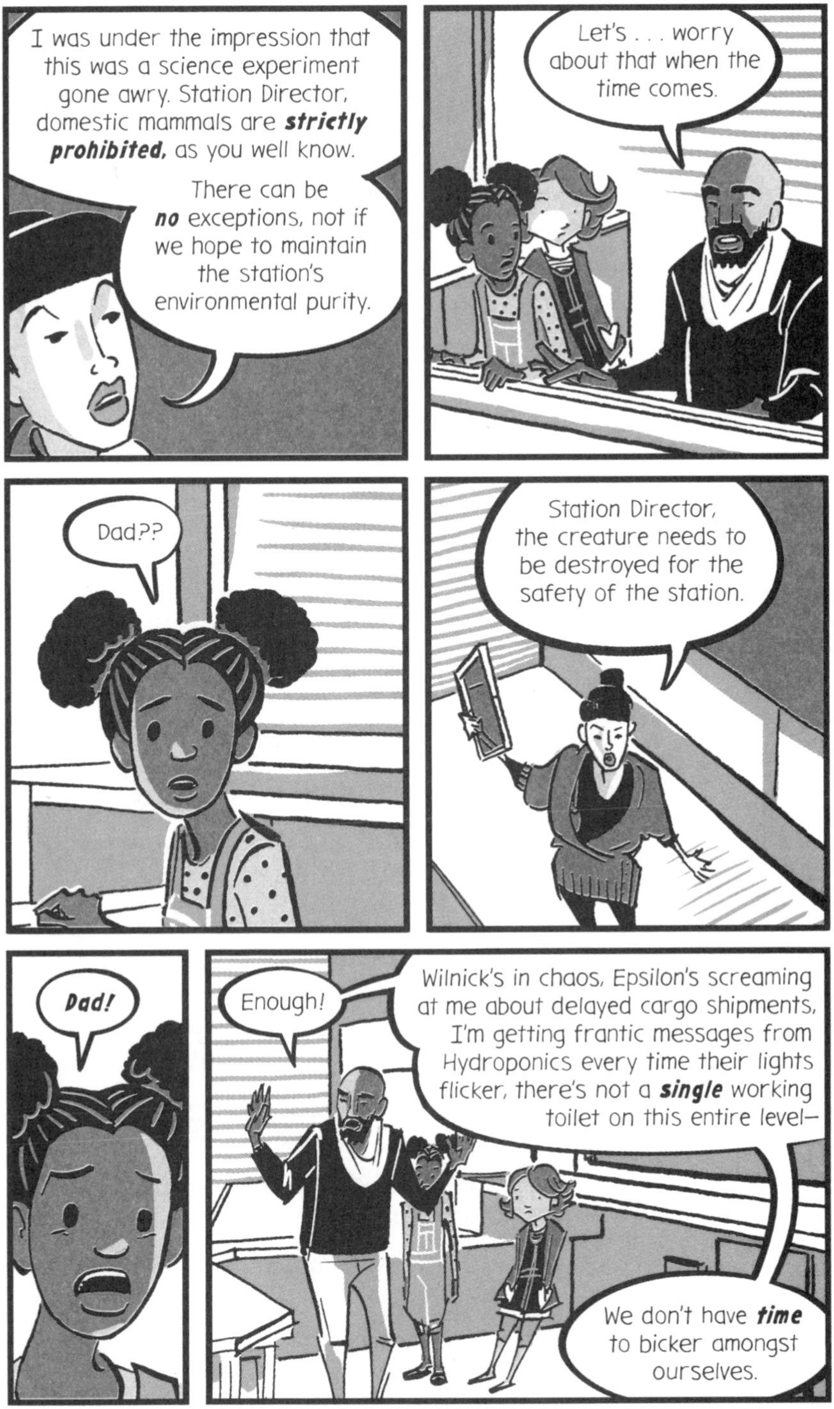
I was under the impression that this was a science experiment gone awry. Station Director, domestic mammals are **strictly prohibited,** as you well know.
There can be **no** exceptions, not if we hope to maintain the station's environmental purity.
Let's . . . worry about that when the time comes.
Dad??
Station Director, the creature needs to be destroyed for the safety of the station.
**Dad!**
Enough!
Wilnick's in chaos, Epsilon's screaming at me about delayed cargo shipments, I'm getting frantic messages from Hydroponics every time their lights flicker, there's not a **single** working toilet on this entire level—
We don't have **time** to bicker amongst ourselves.

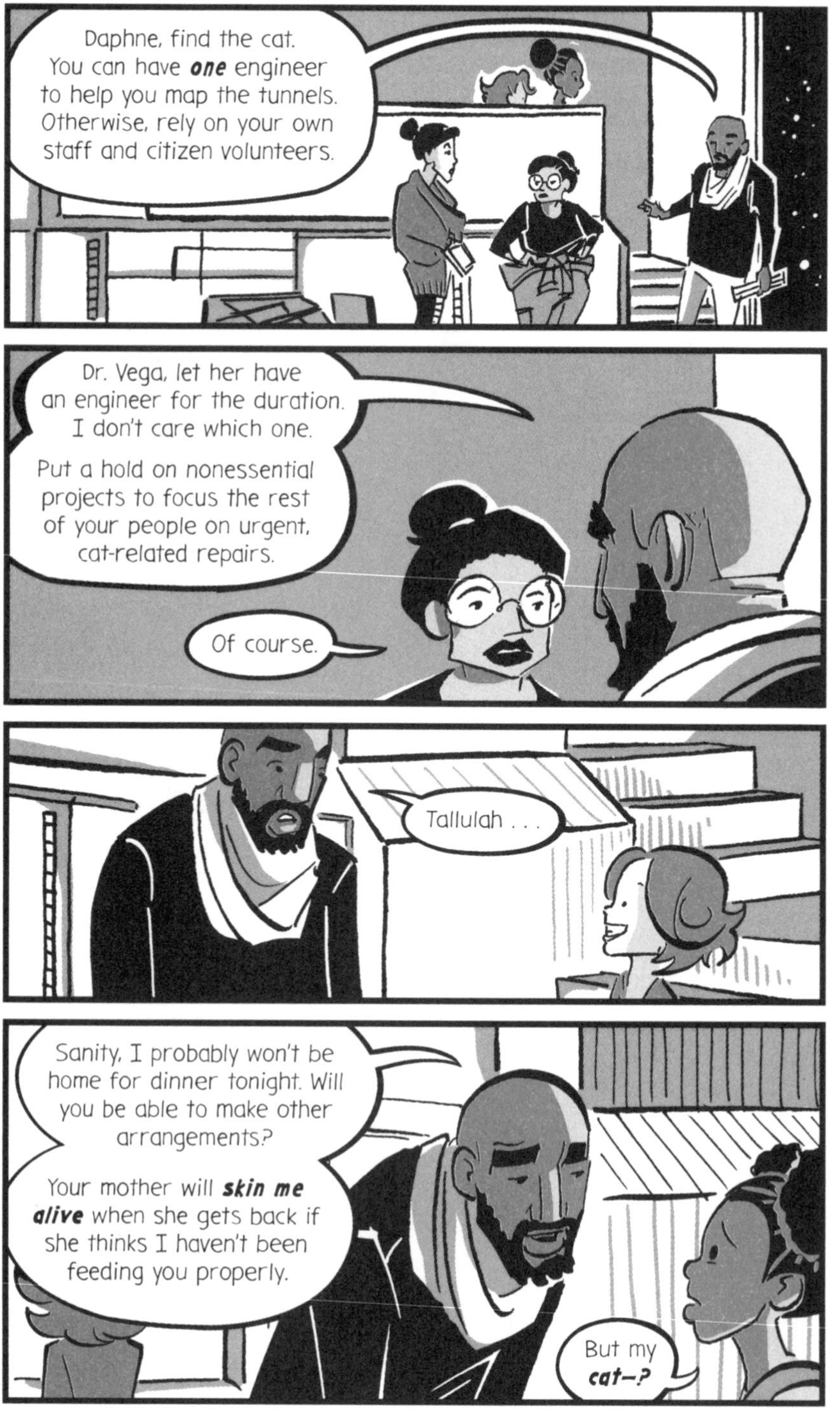

Daphne, find the cat. You can have **one** engineer to help you map the tunnels. Otherwise, rely on your own staff and citizen volunteers.
Dr. Vega, let her have an engineer for the duration. I don't care which one.
Put a hold on nonessential projects to focus the rest of your people on urgent, cat-related repairs.
Of course.
Tallulah . . .
Sanity, I probably won't be home for dinner tonight. Will you be able to make other arrangements?
Your mother will **skin me alive** when she gets back if she thinks I haven't been feeding you properly.
But my **cat—?**

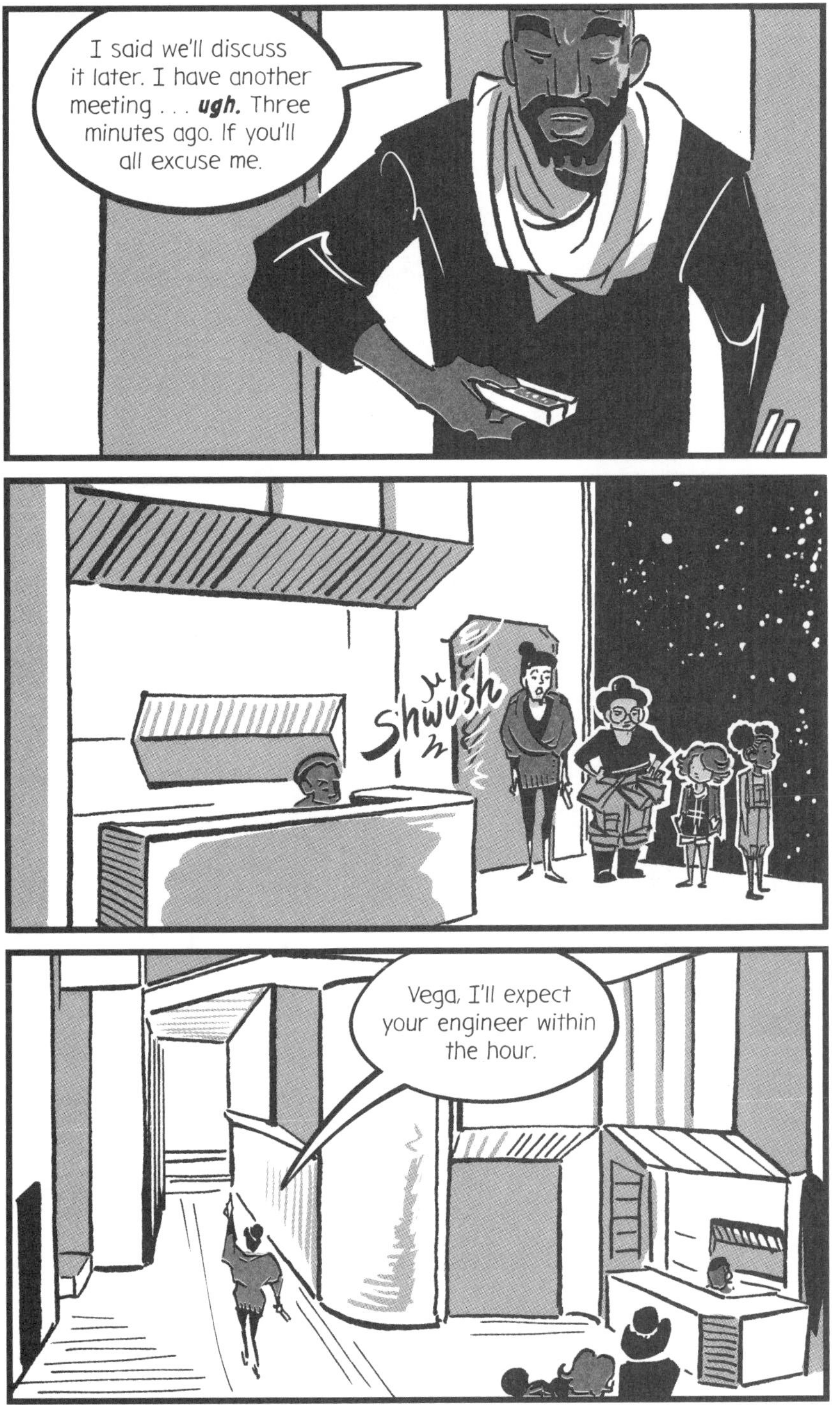

I said we'll discuss it later. I have another meeting . . . **ugh.** Three minutes ago. If you'll all excuse me.
Shwush
Vega, I'll expect your engineer within the hour.

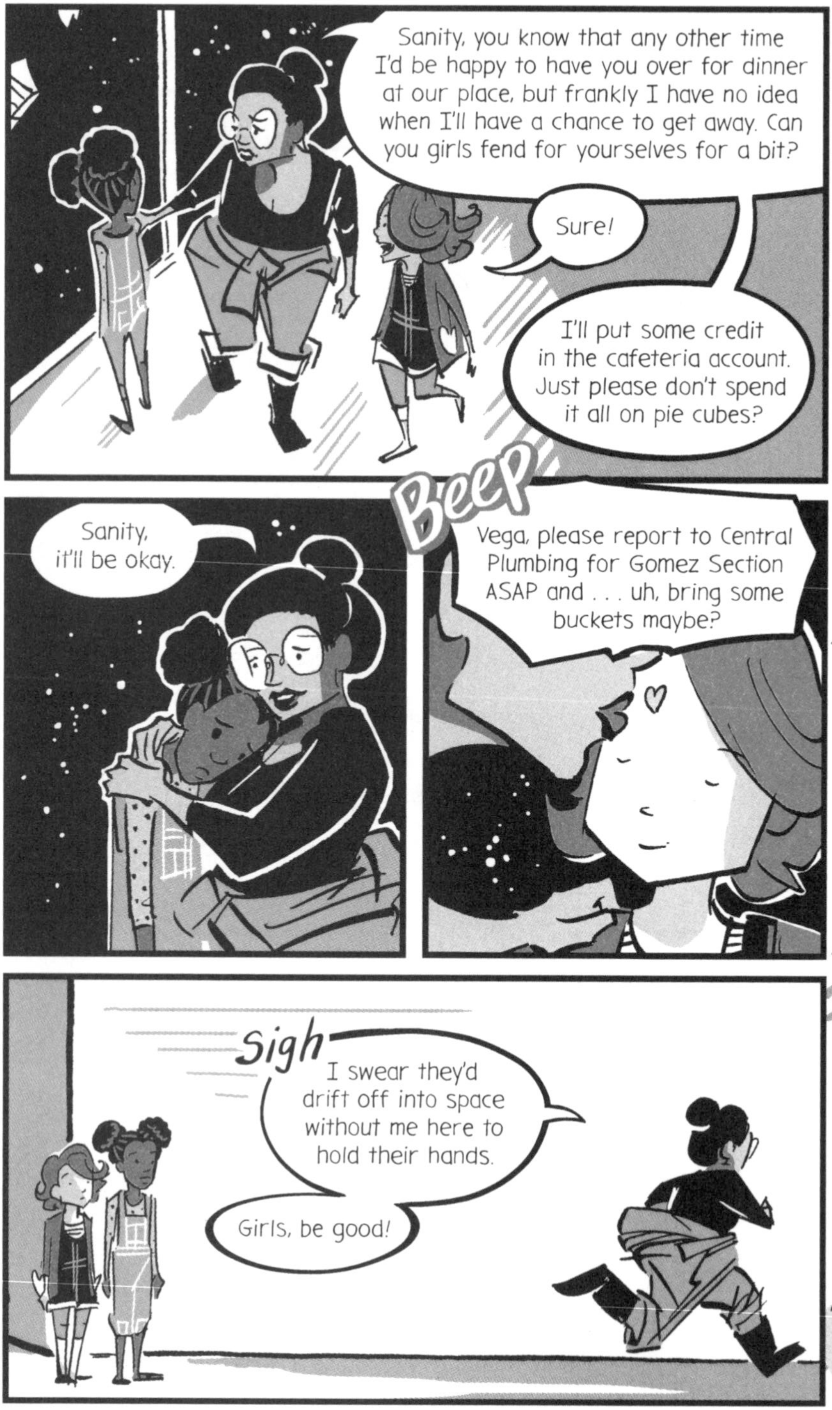
Sanity, you know that any other time I'd be happy to have you over for dinner at our place, but frankly I have no idea when I'll have a chance to get away. Can you girls fend for yourselves for a bit?
Sure!
I'll put some credit in the cafeteria account. Just please don't spend it all on pie cubes?
Beep
Sanity, it'll be okay.
Vega, please report to Central Plumbing for Gomez Section ASAP and . . . uh, bring some buckets maybe?
Sigh
I swear they'd drift off into space without me here to hold their hands.
Girls, be good!

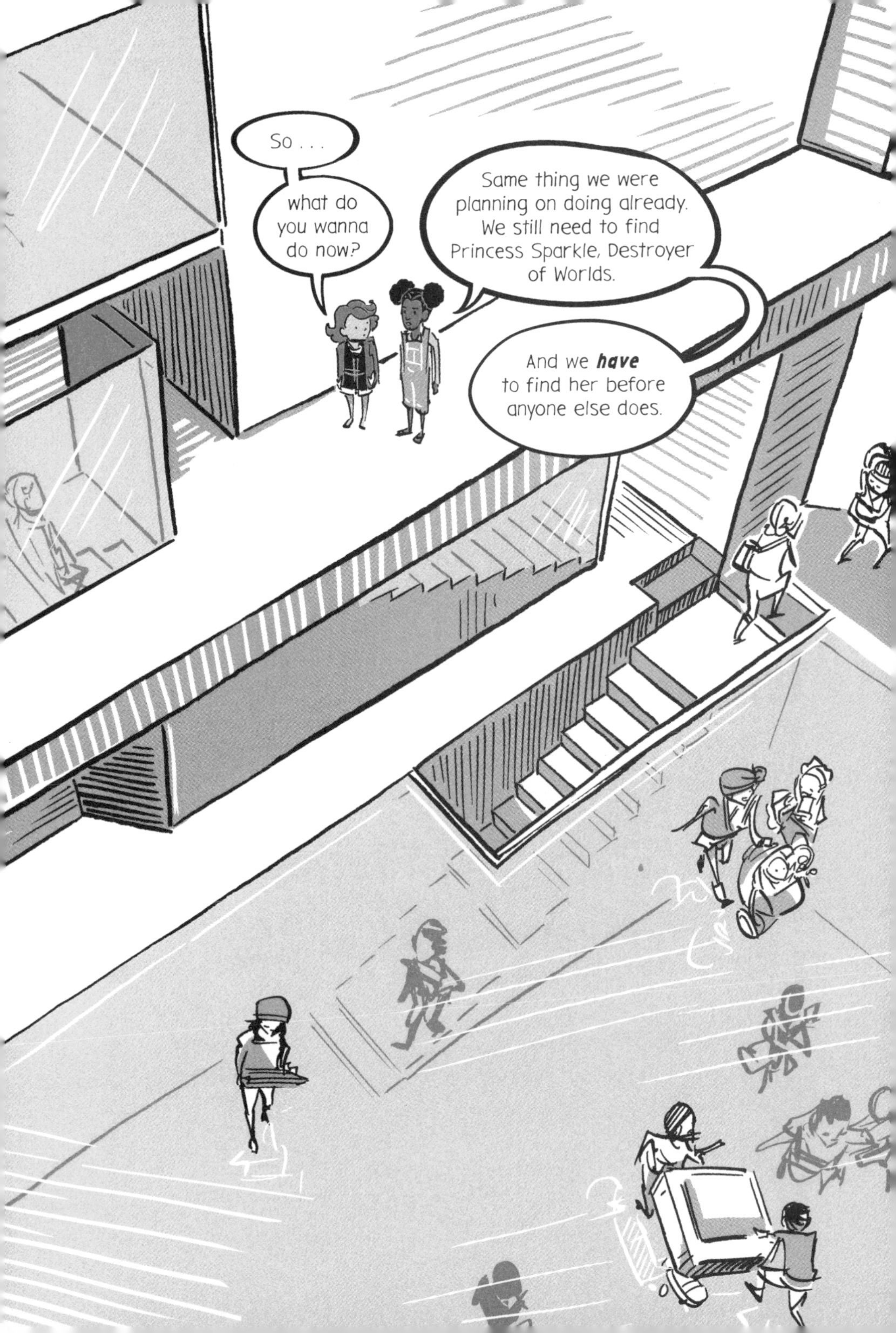
So . . .
what do you wanna do now?
Same thing we were planning on doing already. We still need to find Princess Sparkle, Destroyer of Worlds.
And we ***have*** to find her before anyone else does.

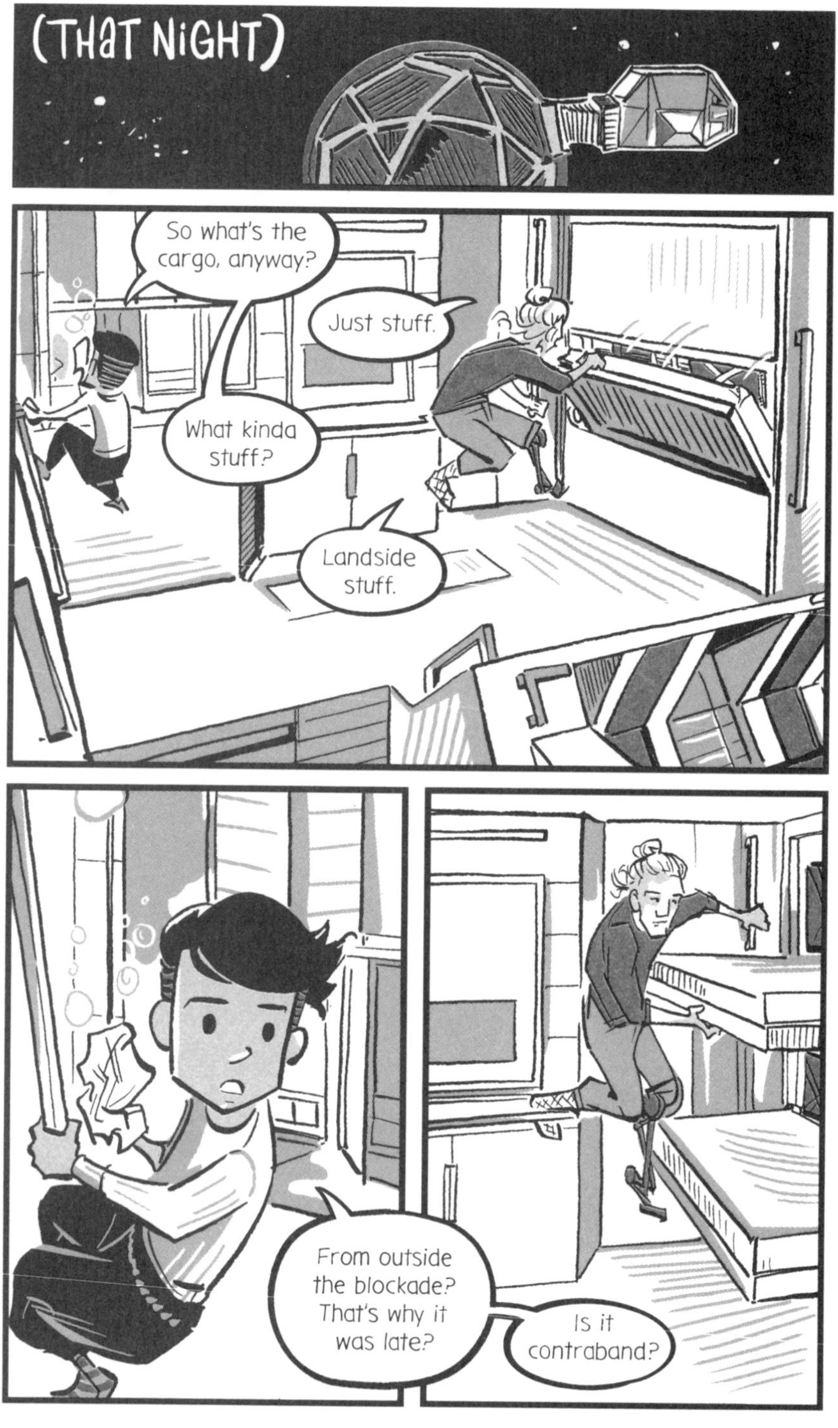
(THAT NIGHT)
So what's the cargo, anyway?
Just stuff.
What kinda stuff?
Landside stuff.
From outside the blockade? That's why it was late?
Is it contraband?

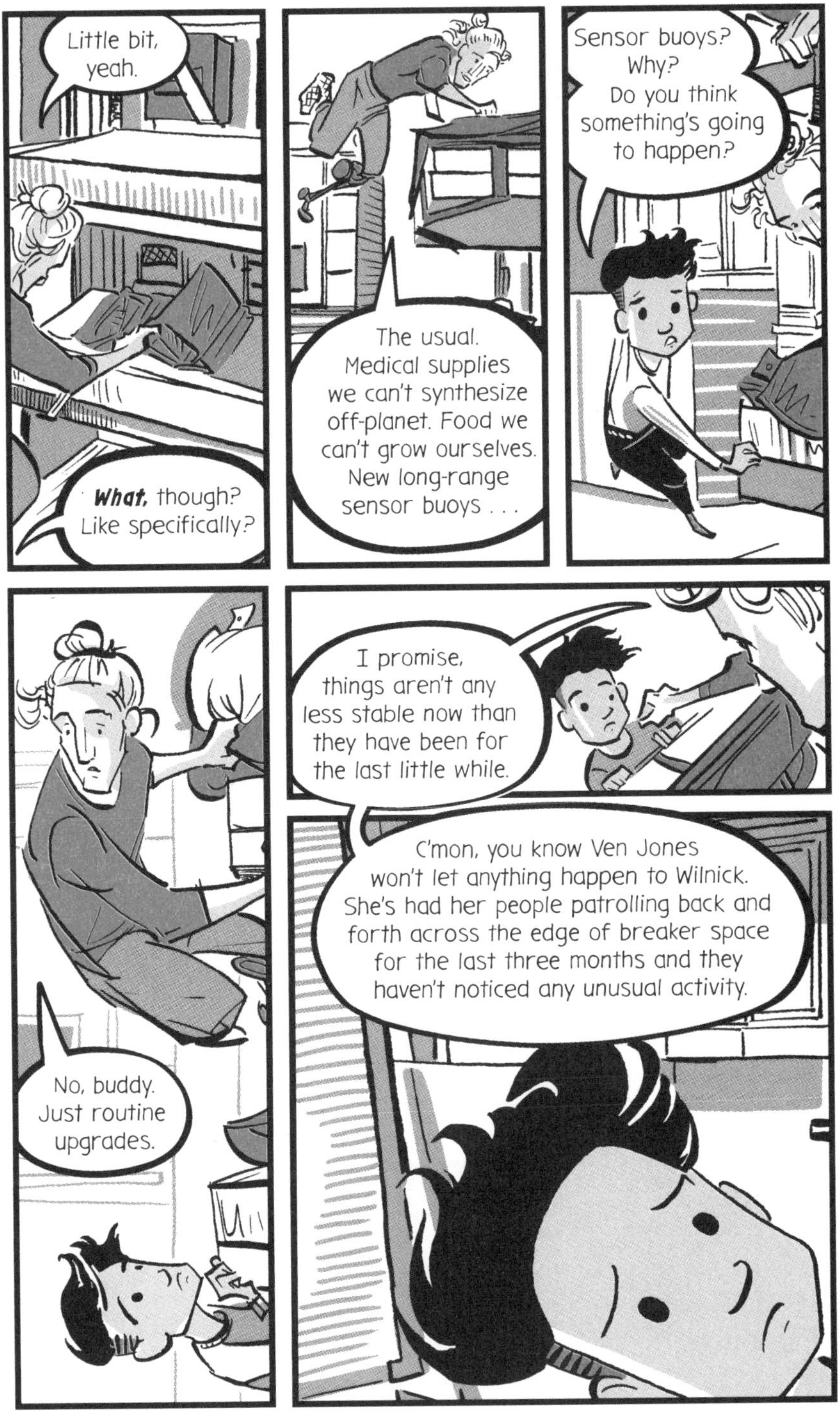
Little bit, yeah.
**What,** though? Like specifically?
The usual. Medical supplies we can't synthesize off-planet. Food we can't grow ourselves. New long-range sensor buoys . . .
Sensor buoys? Why? Do you think something's going to happen?
No, buddy. Just routine upgrades.
I promise, things aren't any less stable now than they have been for the last little while.
C'mon, you know Ven Jones won't let anything happen to Wilnick. She's had her people patrolling back and forth across the edge of breaker space for the last three months and they haven't noticed any unusual activity.

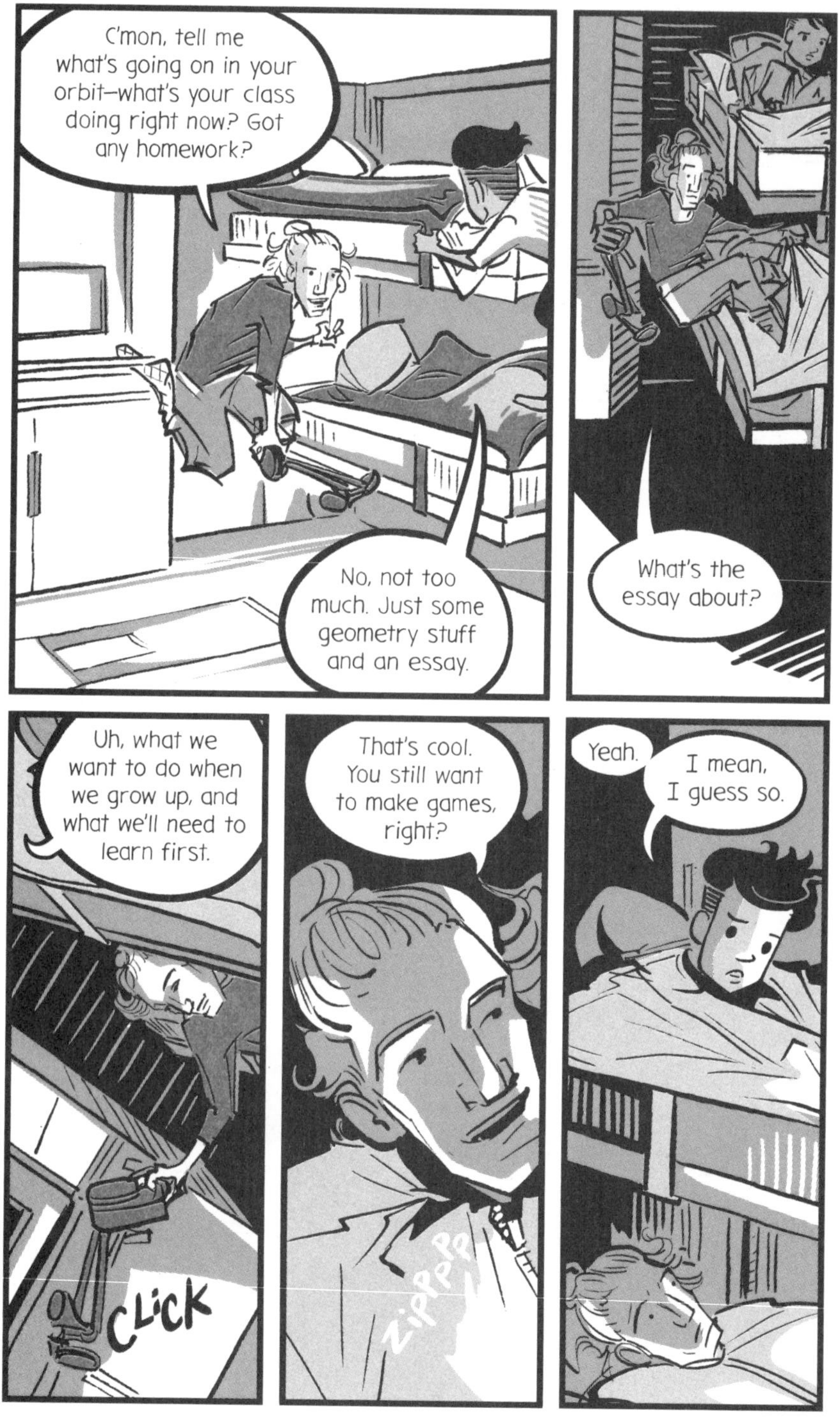
C'mon, tell me what's going on in your orbit—what's your class doing right now? Got any homework?
No, not too much. Just some geometry stuff and an essay.
What's the essay about?
Uh, what we want to do when we grow up, and what we'll need to learn first.
CLICK
That's cool. You still want to make games, right?
ZIPPPP
Yeah.
I mean, I guess so.

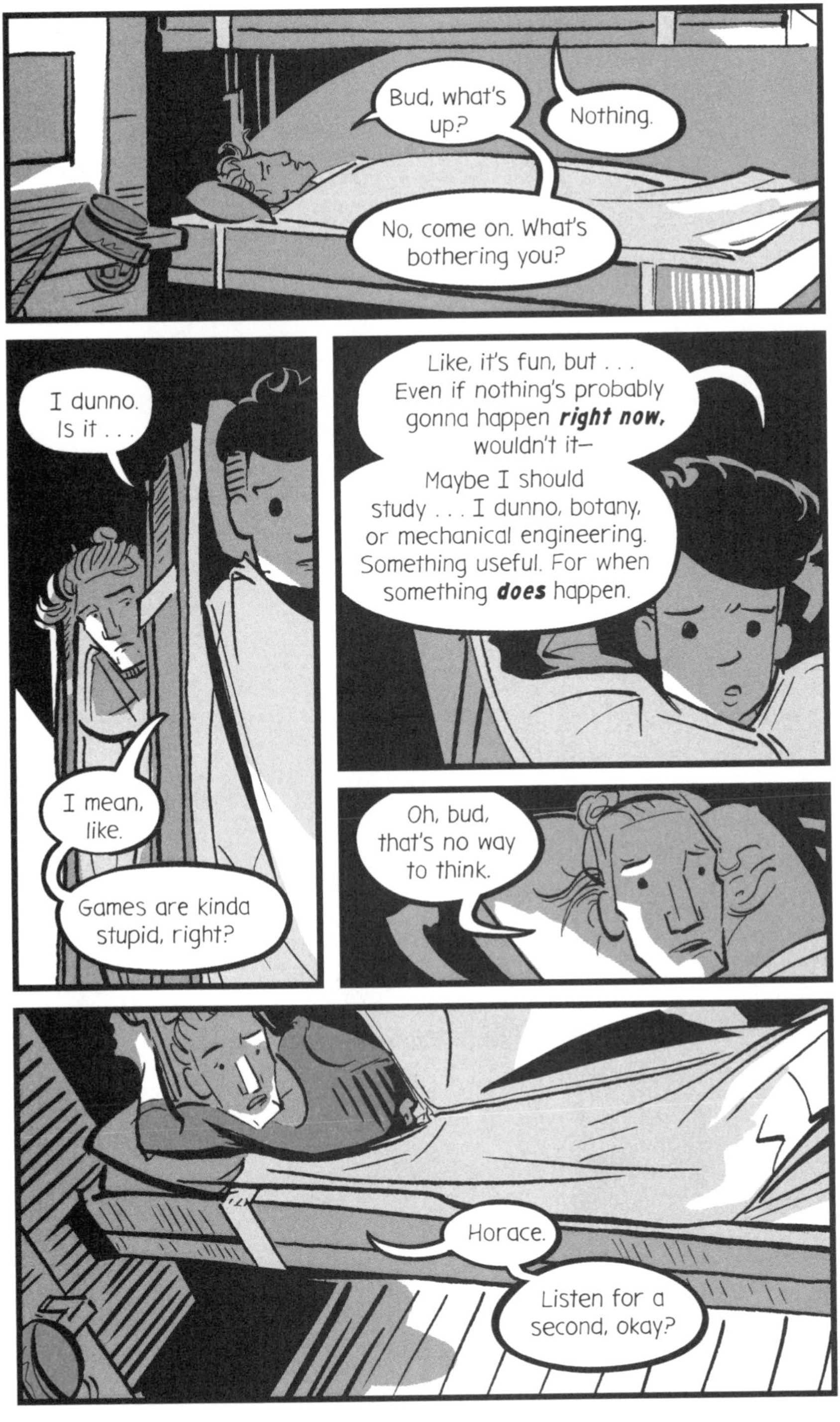

Bud, what's up?
Nothing.
No, come on. What's bothering you?
I dunno. Is it . . .
I mean, like.
Games are kinda stupid, right?
Like, it's fun, but . . . Even if nothing's probably gonna happen **right now,** wouldn't it—
Maybe I should study . . . I dunno, botany, or mechanical engineering. Something useful. For when something **does** happen.
Oh, bud, that's no way to think.
Horace.
Listen for a second, okay?

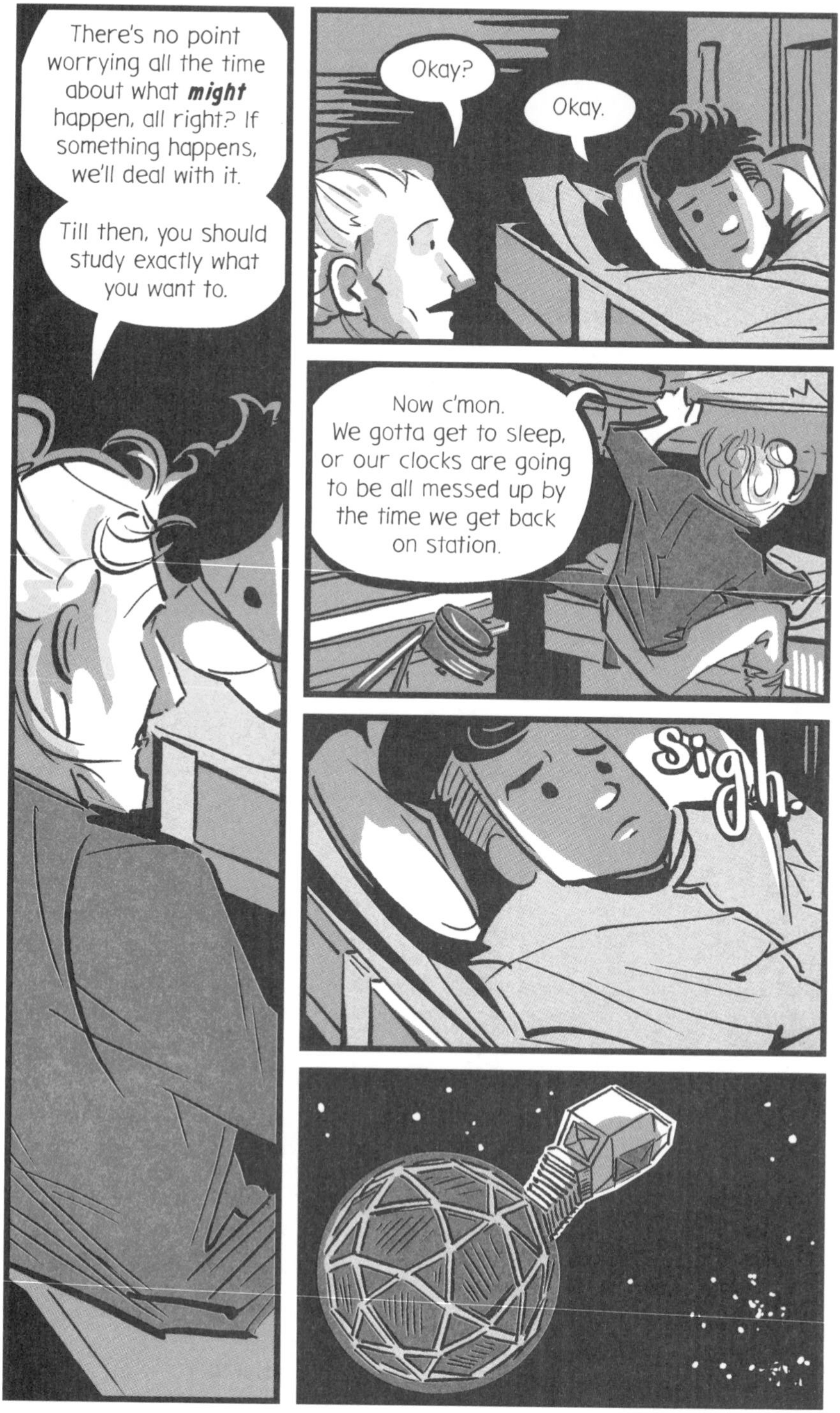
There's no point worrying all the time about what **might** happen, all right? If something happens, we'll deal with it.
Till then, you should study exactly what you want to.
Okay?
Okay.
Now c'mon. We gotta get to sleep, or our clocks are going to be all messed up by the time we get back on station.
Sigh.

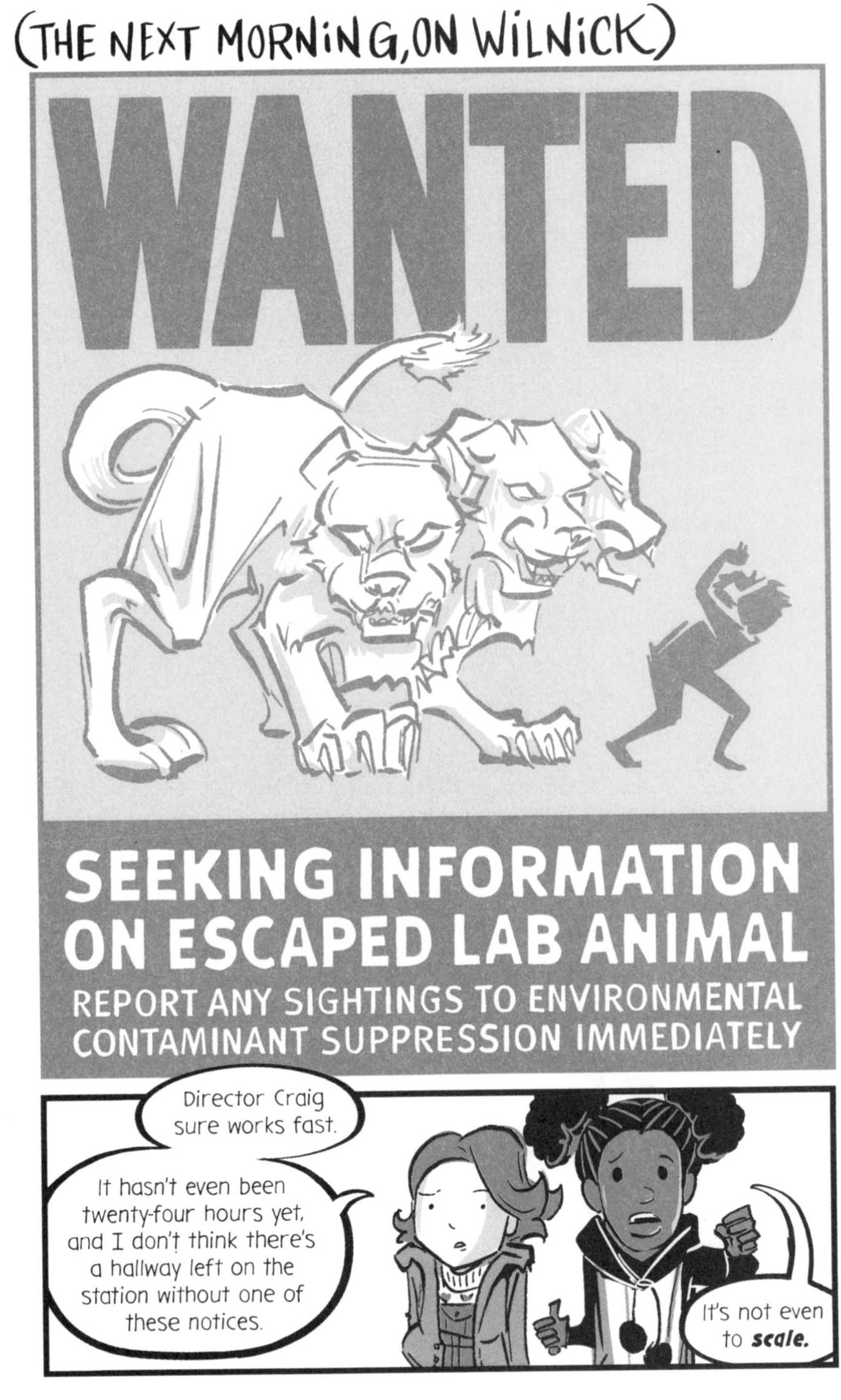
(THE NEXT MORNING, ON WILNICK)
WANTED
SEEKING INFORMATION ON ESCAPED LAB ANIMAL
REPORT ANY SIGHTINGS TO ENVIRONMENTAL CONTAMINANT SUPPRESSION IMMEDIATELY
Director Craig sure works fast.
It hasn't even been twenty-four hours yet, and I don't think there's a hallway left on the station without one of these notices.
It's not even to **scale.**

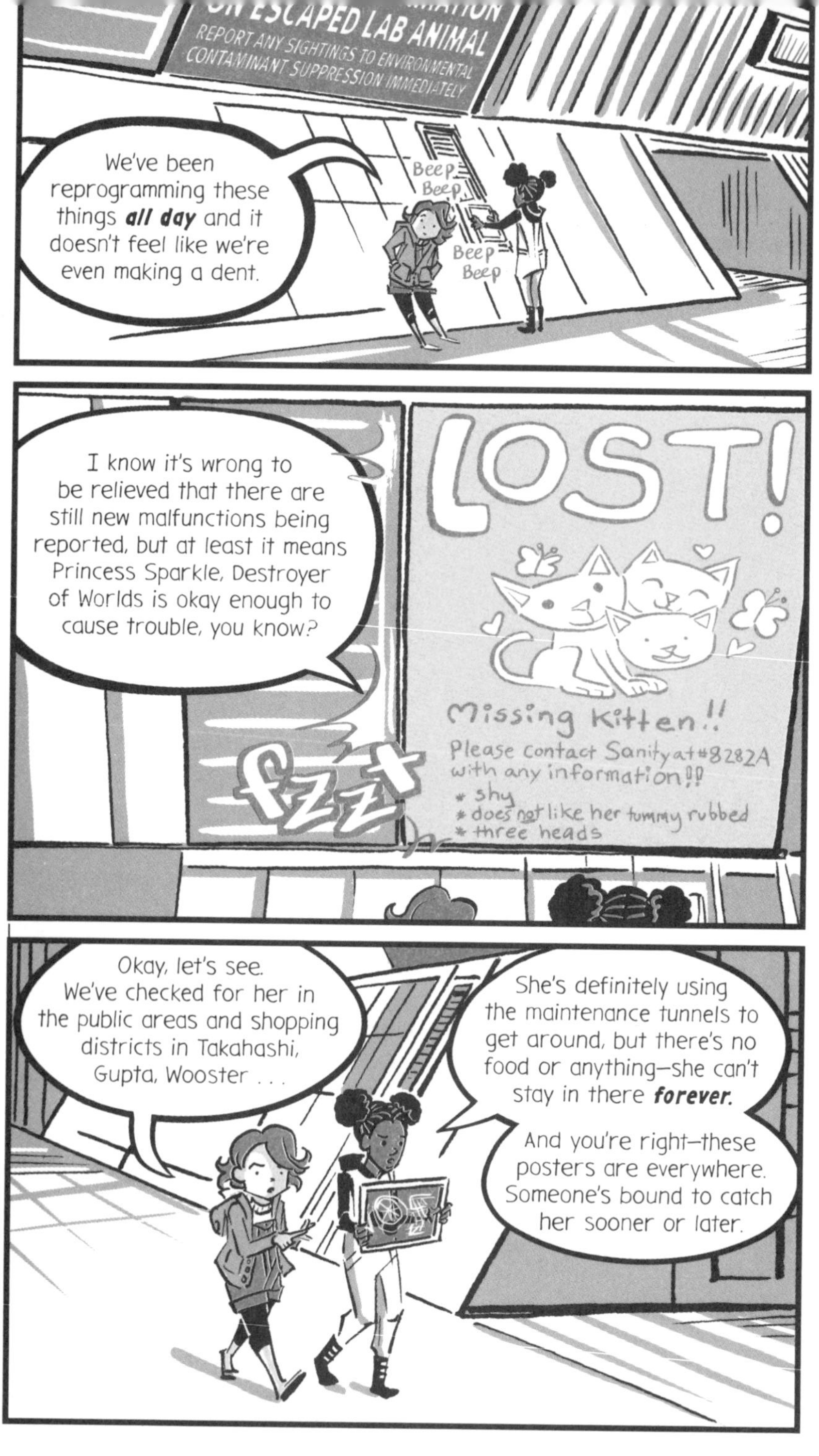
ESCAPED LAB ANIMAL
REPORT ANY SIGHTINGS TO ENVIRONMENTAL CONTAMINANT SUPPRESSION IMMEDIATELY
We've been reprogramming these things **all day** and it doesn't feel like we're even making a dent.
Beep Beep
Beep Beep
I know it's wrong to be relieved that there are still new malfunctions being reported, but at least it means Princess Sparkle, Destroyer of Worlds is okay enough to cause trouble, you know?
LOST!
Missing Kitten!!
Please contact Sanity at #8282A with any information!!
* shy
* does not like her tummy rubbed
* three heads
fzzt
Okay, let's see. We've checked for her in the public areas and shopping districts in Takahashi, Gupta, Wooster . . .
She's definitely using the maintenance tunnels to get around, but there's no food or anything—she can't stay in there **forever.**
And you're right—these posters are everywhere. Someone's bound to catch her sooner or later.

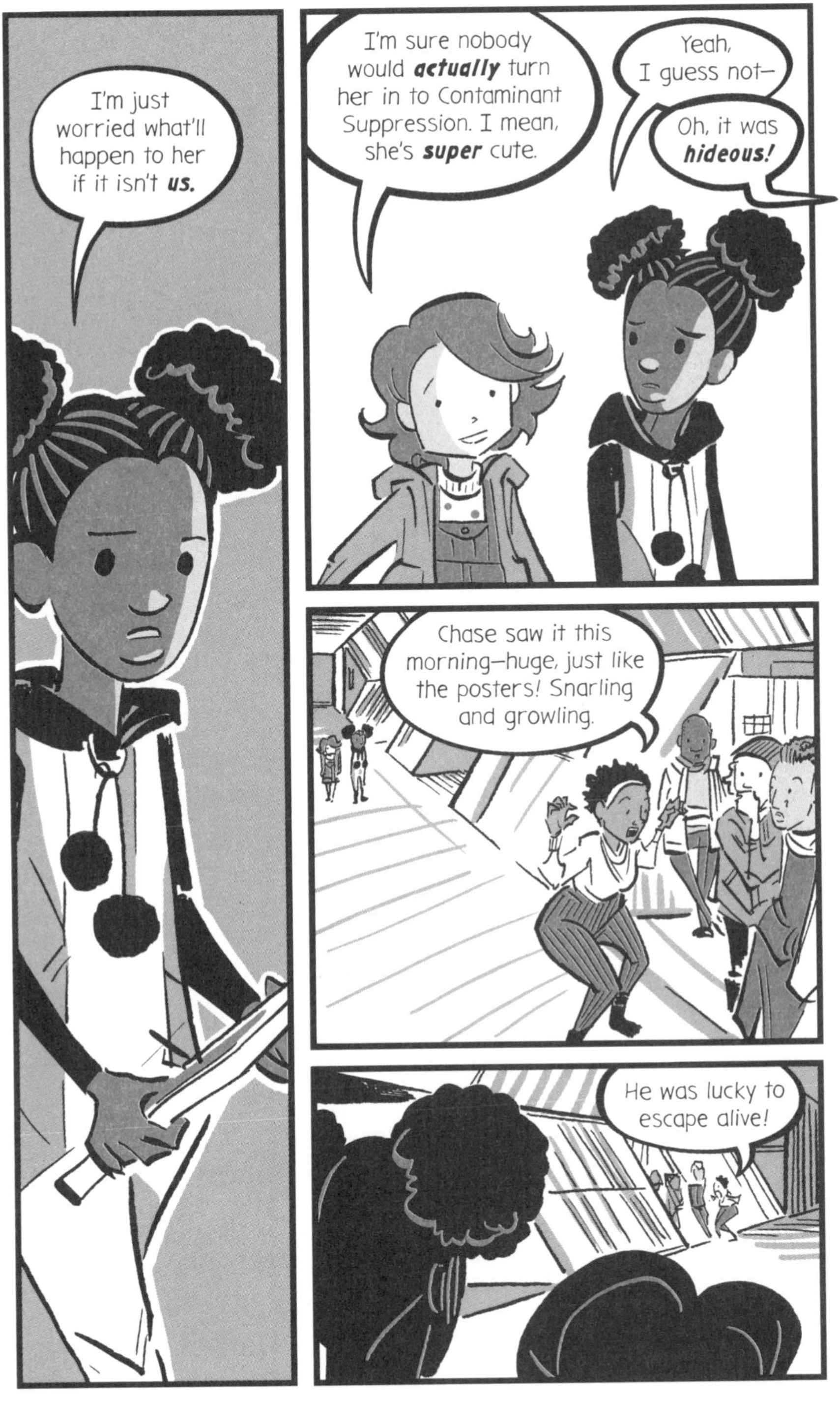
I'm just worried what'll happen to her if it isn't **us.**
I'm sure nobody would ***actually*** turn her in to Contaminant Suppression. I mean, she's ***super*** cute.
Yeah, I guess not—
Oh, it was ***hideous!***
Chase saw it this morning—huge, just like the posters! Snarling and growling.
He was lucky to escape alive!

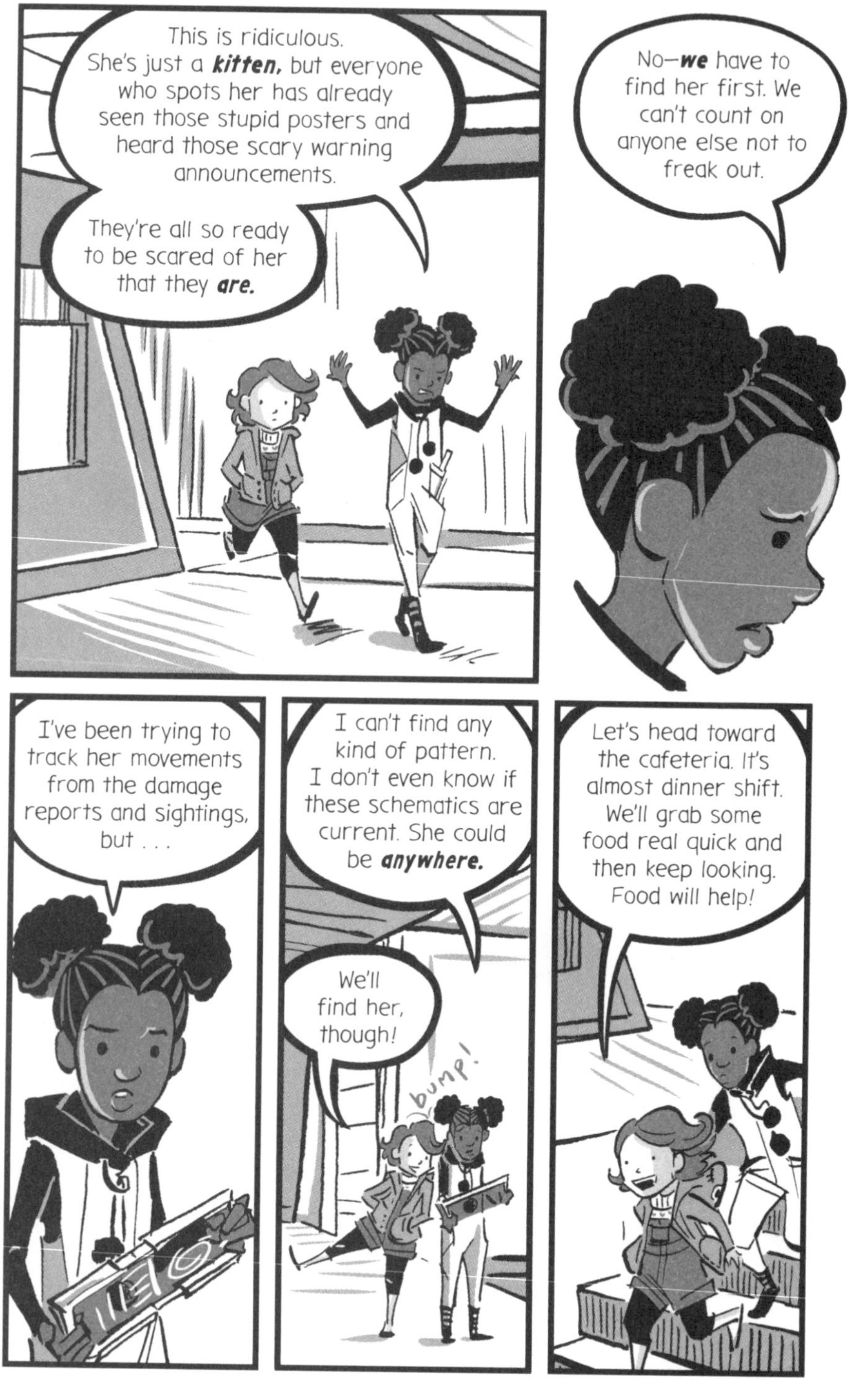
This is ridiculous. She's just a kitten, but everyone who spots her has already seen those stupid posters and heard those scary warning announcements.
They're all so ready to be scared of her that they are.
No—we have to find her first. We can't count on anyone else not to freak out.
I've been trying to track her movements from the damage reports and sightings, but . . .
I can't find any kind of pattern. I don't even know if these schematics are current. She could be anywhere.
We'll find her, though!
bump!
Let's head toward the cafeteria. It's almost dinner shift. We'll grab some food real quick and then keep looking. Food will help!

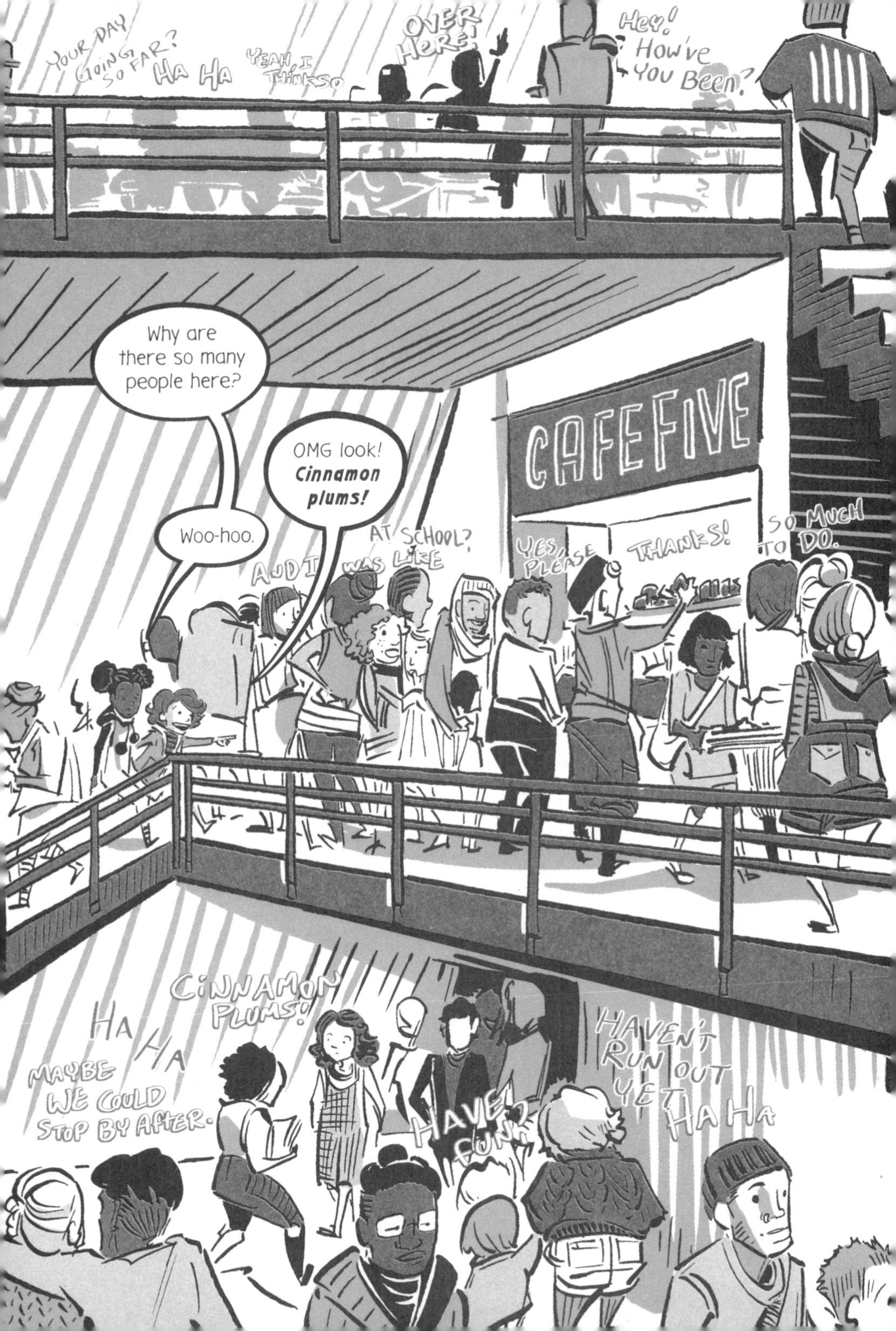
YOUR DAY GOING SO FAR?
HA HA
YEAH I THINK SO
OVER HERE!
Hey! How've You Been?
Why are there so many people here?
OMG look! Cinnamon plums!
Woo-hoo.
CAFE FIVE
AND I WAS LIKE
AT SCHOOL?
YES, PLEASE
THANKS!
SO MUCH TO DO.
CINNAMON PLUMS!
HA HA
MAYBE WE COULD STOP BY AFTER.
HAVE FUN
HAVEN'T RUN OUT YET
HA HA

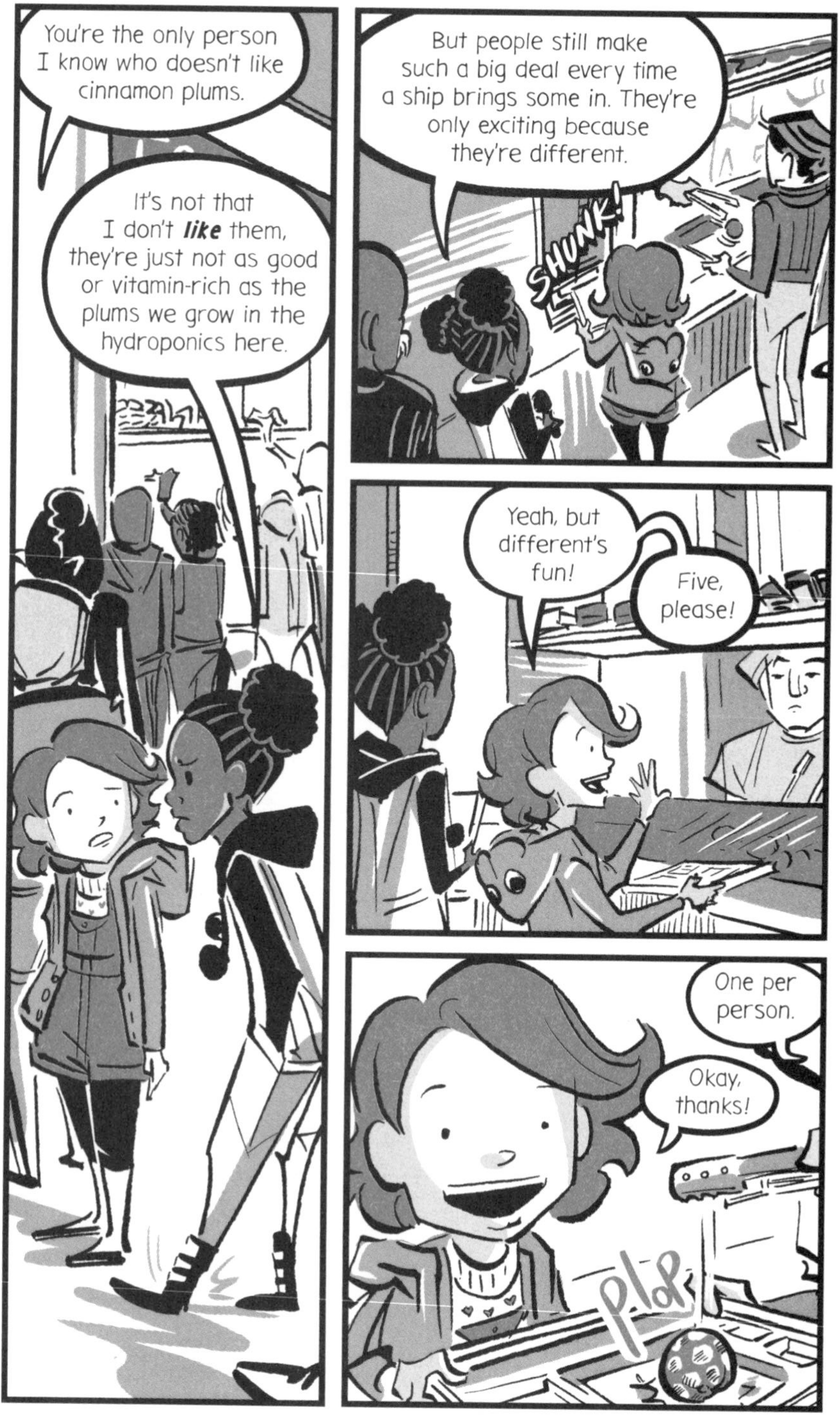
You're the only person I know who doesn't like cinnamon plums.
It's not that I don't **like** them, they're just not as good or vitamin-rich as the plums we grow in the hydroponics here.
But people still make such a big deal every time a ship brings some in. They're only exciting because they're different.
SHUNK!
Yeah, but different's fun!
Five, please!
One per person.
Okay, thanks!
PLOP

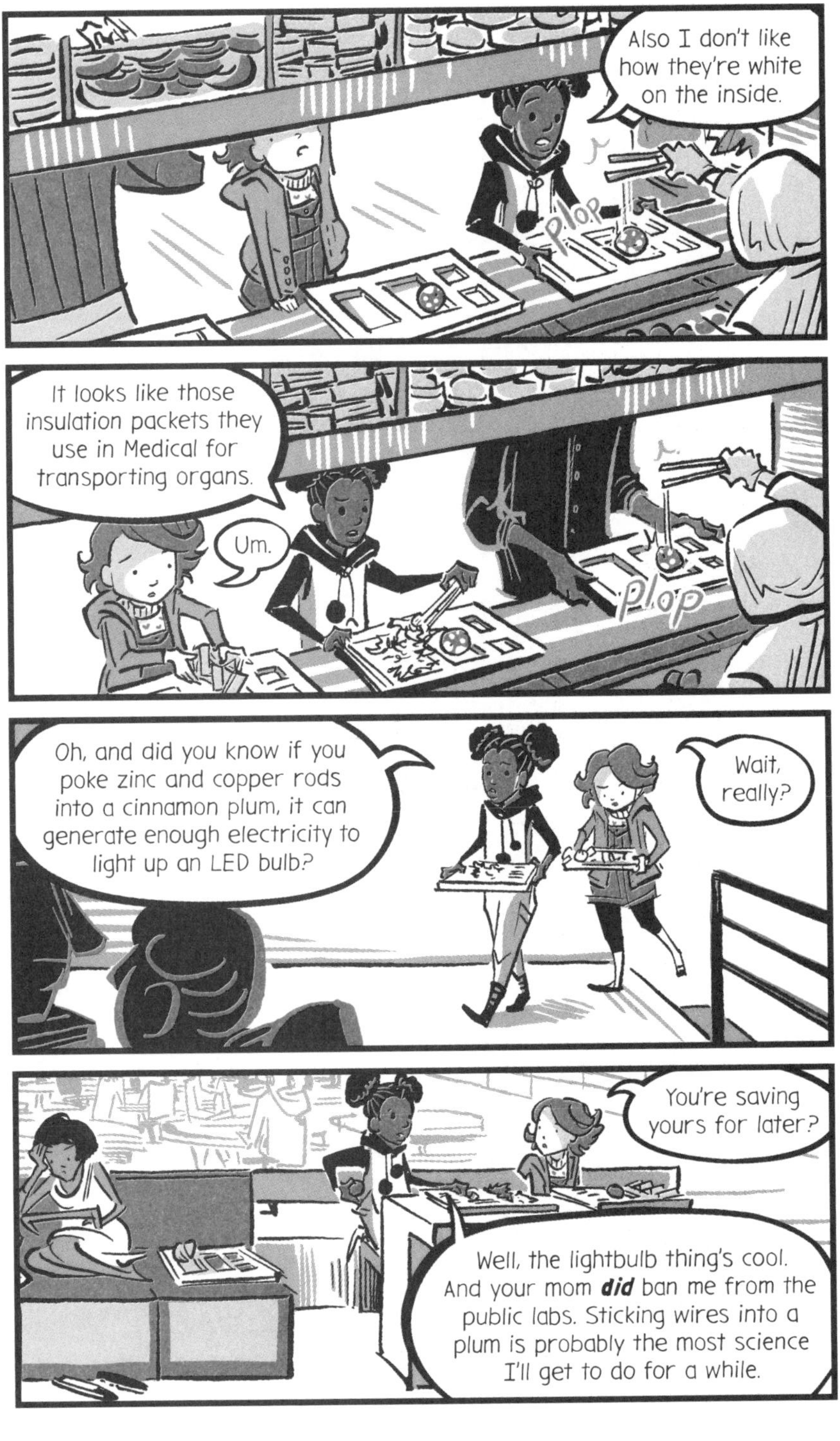
Also I don't like how they're white on the inside.
PLOP
It looks like those insulation packets they use in Medical for transporting organs.
Um.
PLOP
Oh, and did you know if you poke zinc and copper rods into a cinnamon plum, it can generate enough electricity to light up an LED bulb?
Wait, really?
You're saving yours for later?
Well, the lightbulb thing's cool. And your mom ***did*** ban me from the public labs. Sticking wires into a plum is probably the most science I'll get to do for a while.

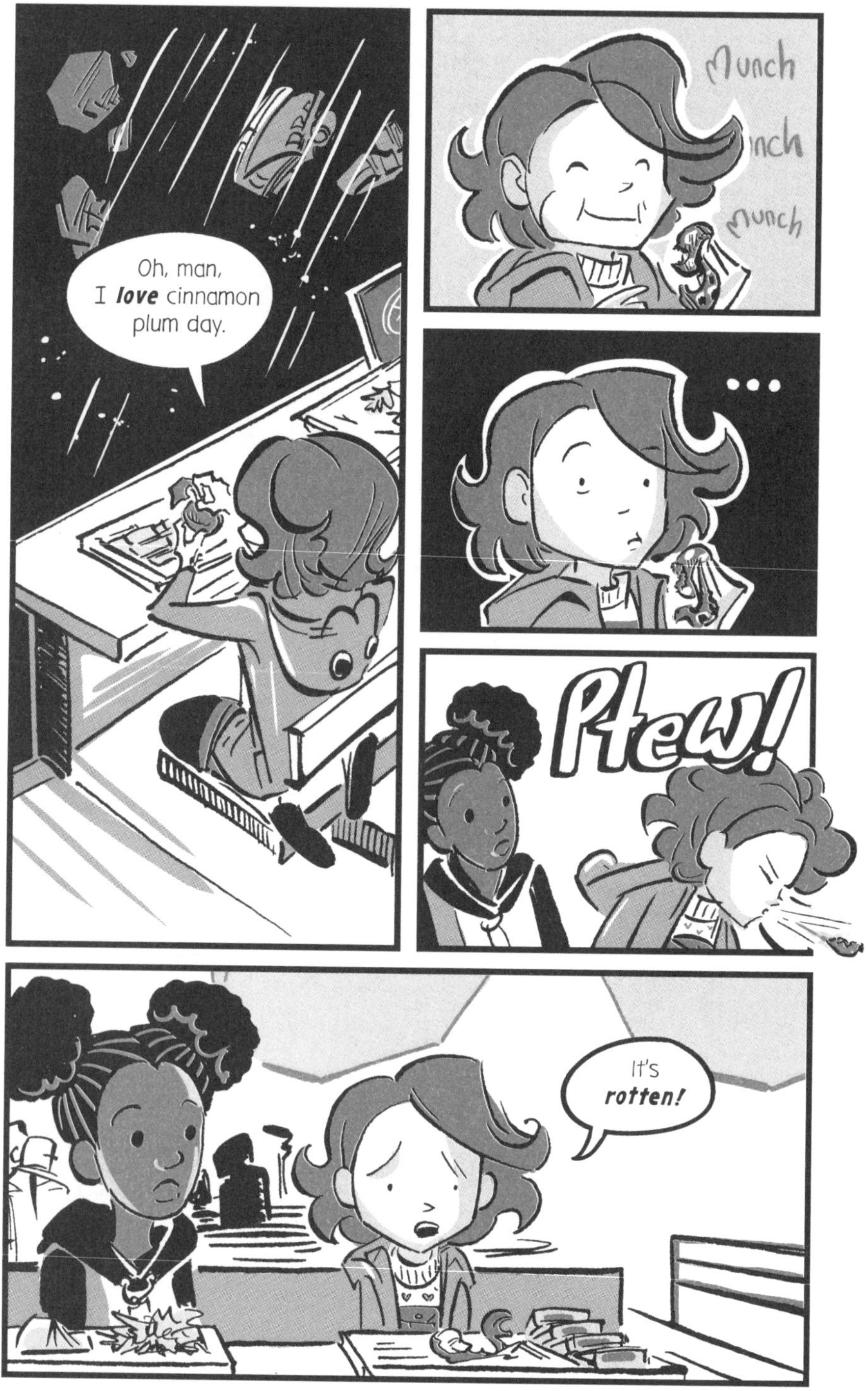
Oh, man, I *love* cinnamon plum day.
Munch
unch
Munch
...
Ptew!
It's *rotten!*

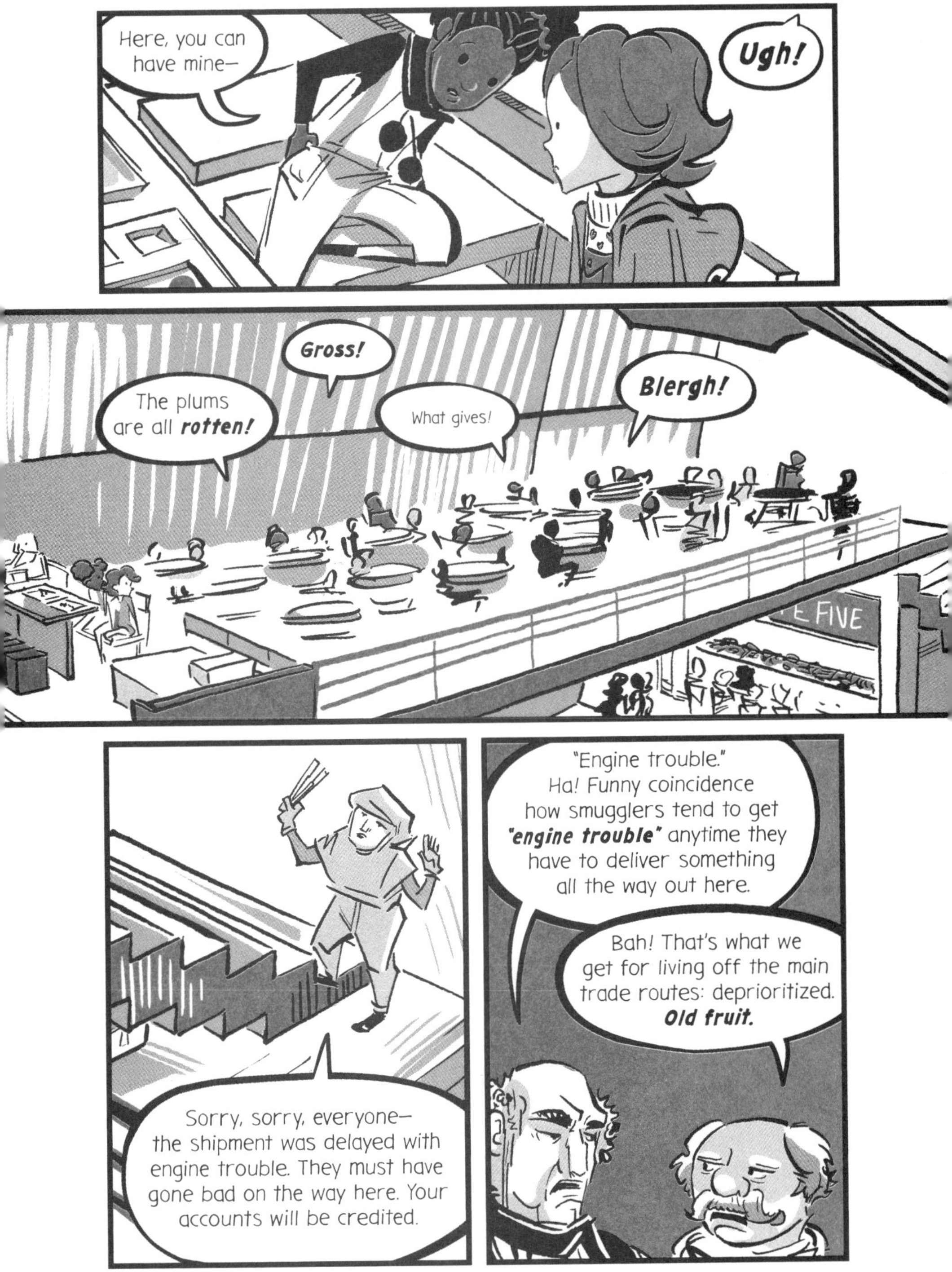
Here, you can have mine—
Ugh!
The plums are all **rotten!**
Gross!
What gives!
Blergh!
FIVE
Sorry, sorry, everyone— the shipment was delayed with engine trouble. They must have gone bad on the way here. Your accounts will be credited.
"Engine trouble." Ha! Funny coincidence how smugglers tend to get **"engine trouble"** anytime they have to deliver something all the way out here.
Bah! That's what we get for living off the main trade routes: deprioritized. **Old fruit.**

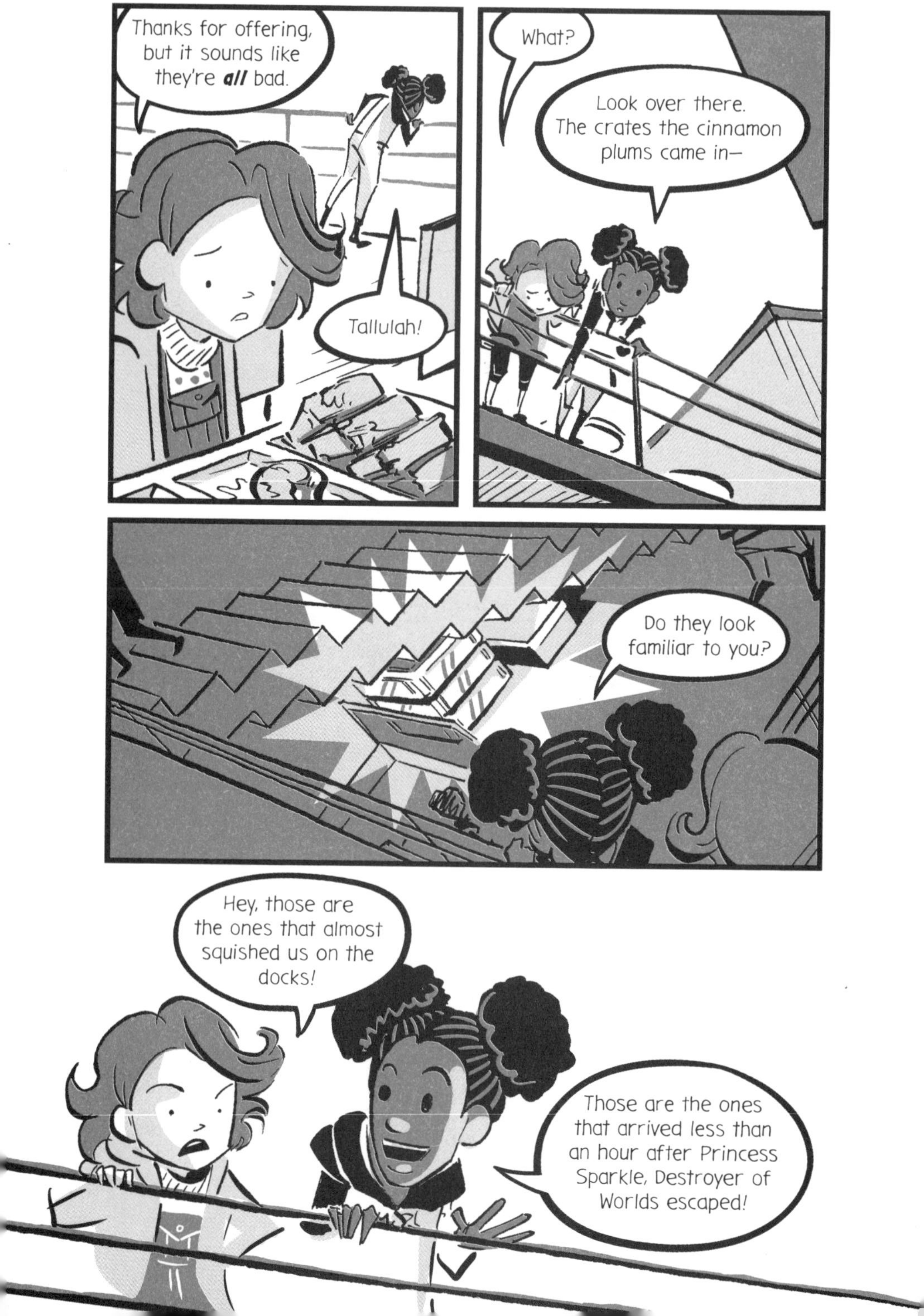

Thanks for offering, but it sounds like they're ***all*** bad.
Tallulah!
What?
Look over there. The crates the cinnamon plums came in—
Do they look familiar to you?
Hey, those are the ones that almost squished us on the docks!
Those are the ones that arrived less than an hour after Princess Sparkle, Destroyer of Worlds escaped!

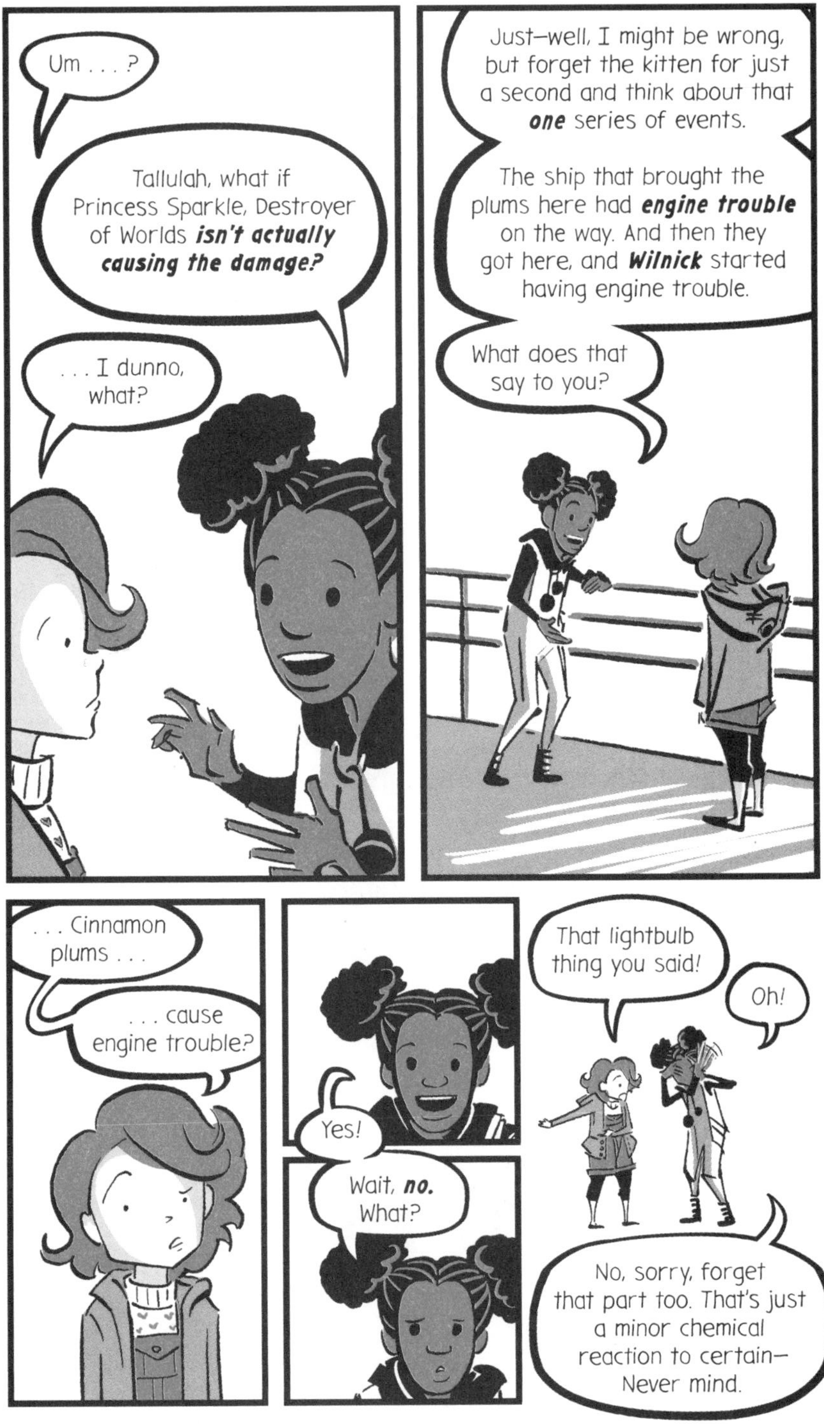
Um . . . ?
Tallulah, what if Princess Sparkle, Destroyer of Worlds **isn't actually causing the damage?**
. . . I dunno, what?
Just—well, I might be wrong, but forget the kitten for just a second and think about that **one** series of events.
The ship that brought the plums here had **engine trouble** on the way. And then they got here, and **Wilnick** started having engine trouble.
What does that say to you?
. . . Cinnamon plums . . .
. . . cause engine trouble?
Yes!
Wait, **no.** What?
That lightbulb thing you said!
Oh!
No, sorry, forget that part too. That's just a minor chemical reaction to certain— Never mind.

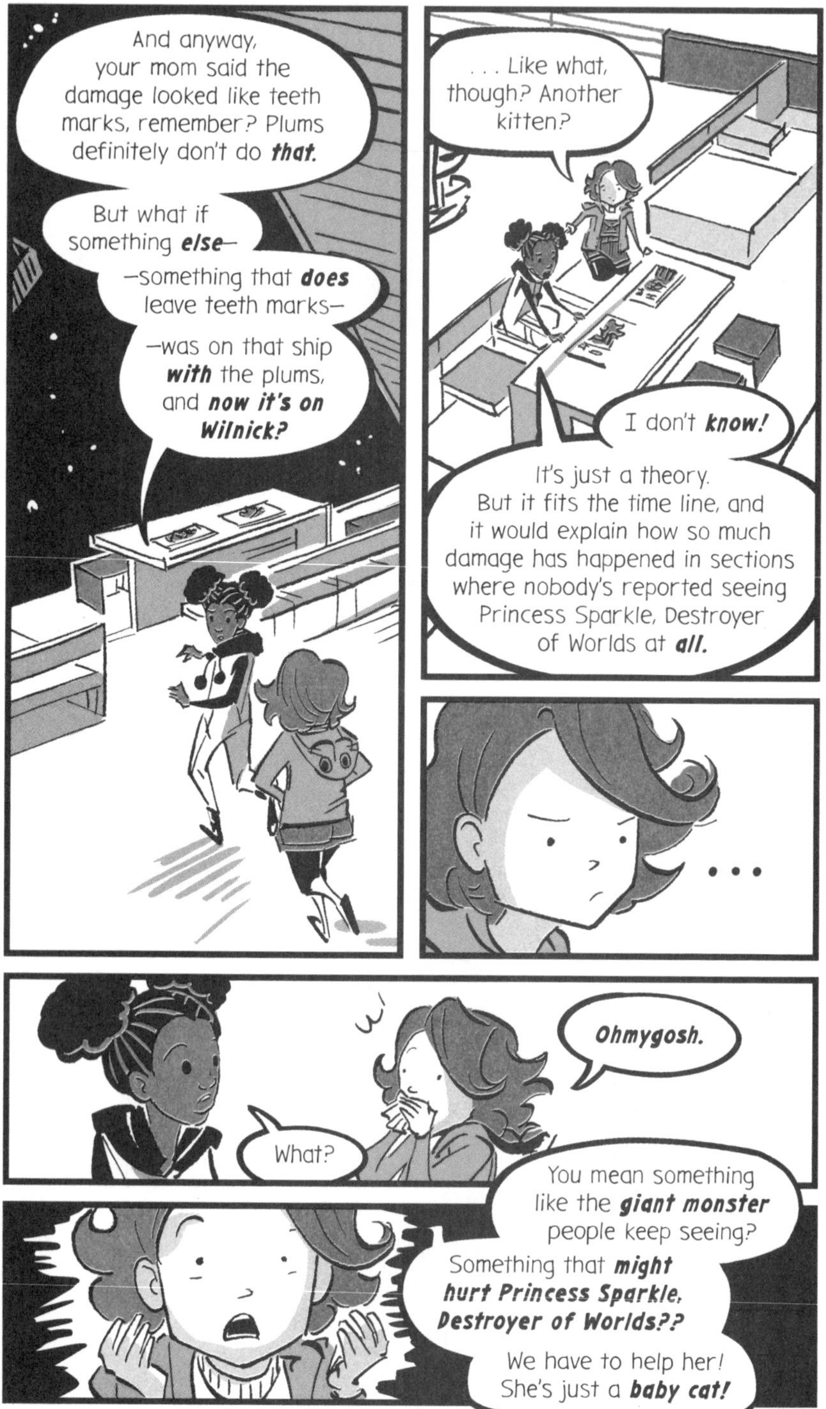
And anyway, your mom said the damage looked like teeth marks, remember? Plums definitely don't do **that.**
But what if something **else**—
—something that **does** leave teeth marks—
—was on that ship **with** the plums, and **now it's on Wilnick?**
. . . Like what, though? Another kitten?
I don't **know!**
It's just a theory. But it fits the time line, and it would explain how so much damage has happened in sections where nobody's reported seeing Princess Sparkle, Destroyer of Worlds at **all.**
. . .
**Ohmygosh.**
What?
You mean something like the **giant monster** people keep seeing?
Something that **might hurt Princess Sparkle, Destroyer of Worlds??**
We have to help her! She's just a **baby cat!**

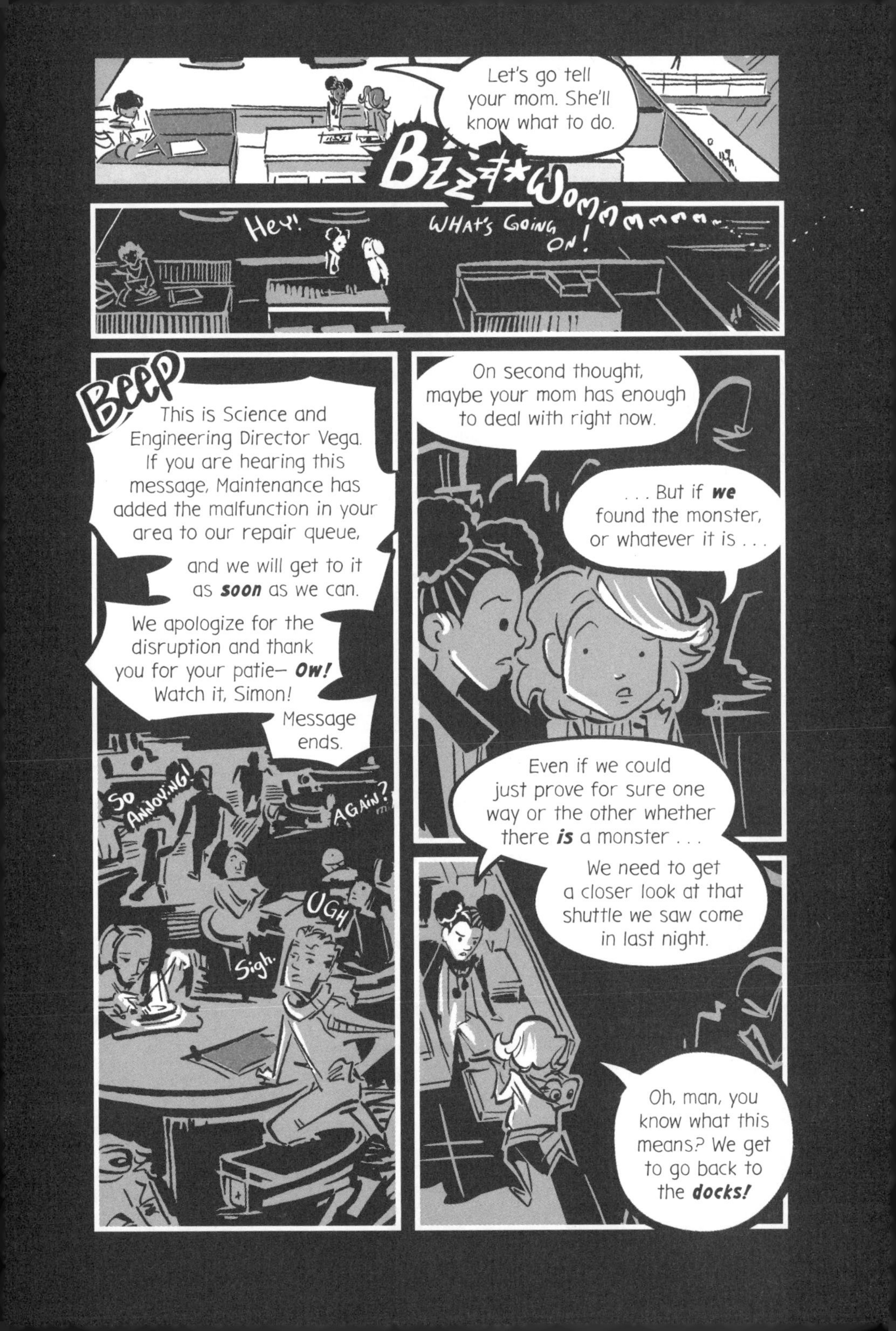
Let's go tell your mom. She'll know what to do.
Bzzt*Wommmmmm...
Hey!
WHAT's GOING ON!
Beep
This is Science and Engineering Director Vega. If you are hearing this message, Maintenance has added the malfunction in your area to our repair queue,
and we will get to it as **soon** as we can.
We apologize for the disruption and thank you for your patie– **Ow!** Watch it, Simon!
Message ends.
SO ANNOYING!
AGAIN?
UGH
Sigh.
On second thought, maybe your mom has enough to deal with right now.
. . . But if **we** found the monster, or whatever it is . . .
Even if we could just prove for sure one way or the other whether there ***is*** a monster . . .
We need to get a closer look at that shuttle we saw come in last night.
Oh, man, you know what this means? We get to go back to the ***docks!***

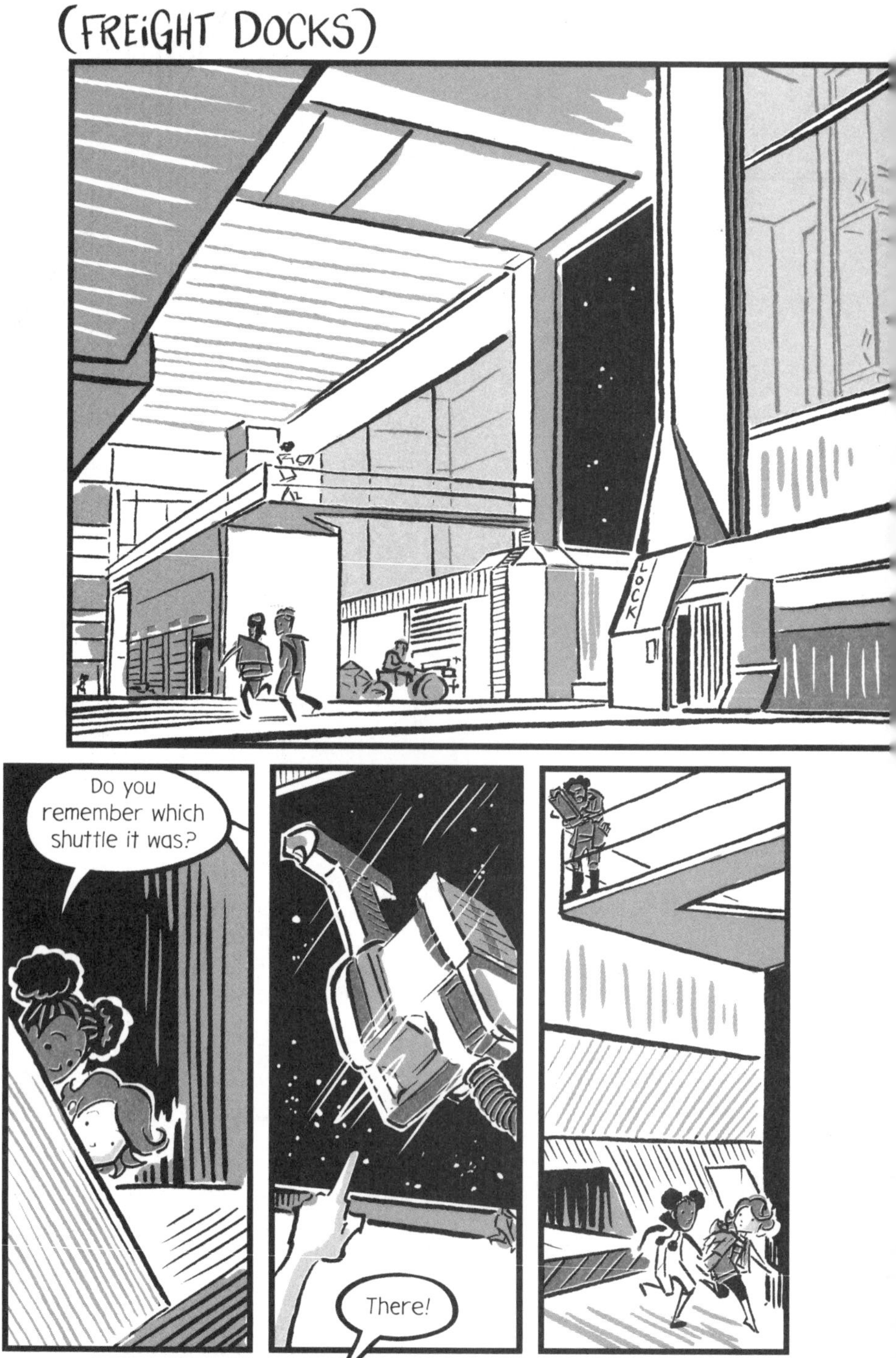
(FREIGHT DOCKS)
LOCK
Do you remember which shuttle it was?
There!

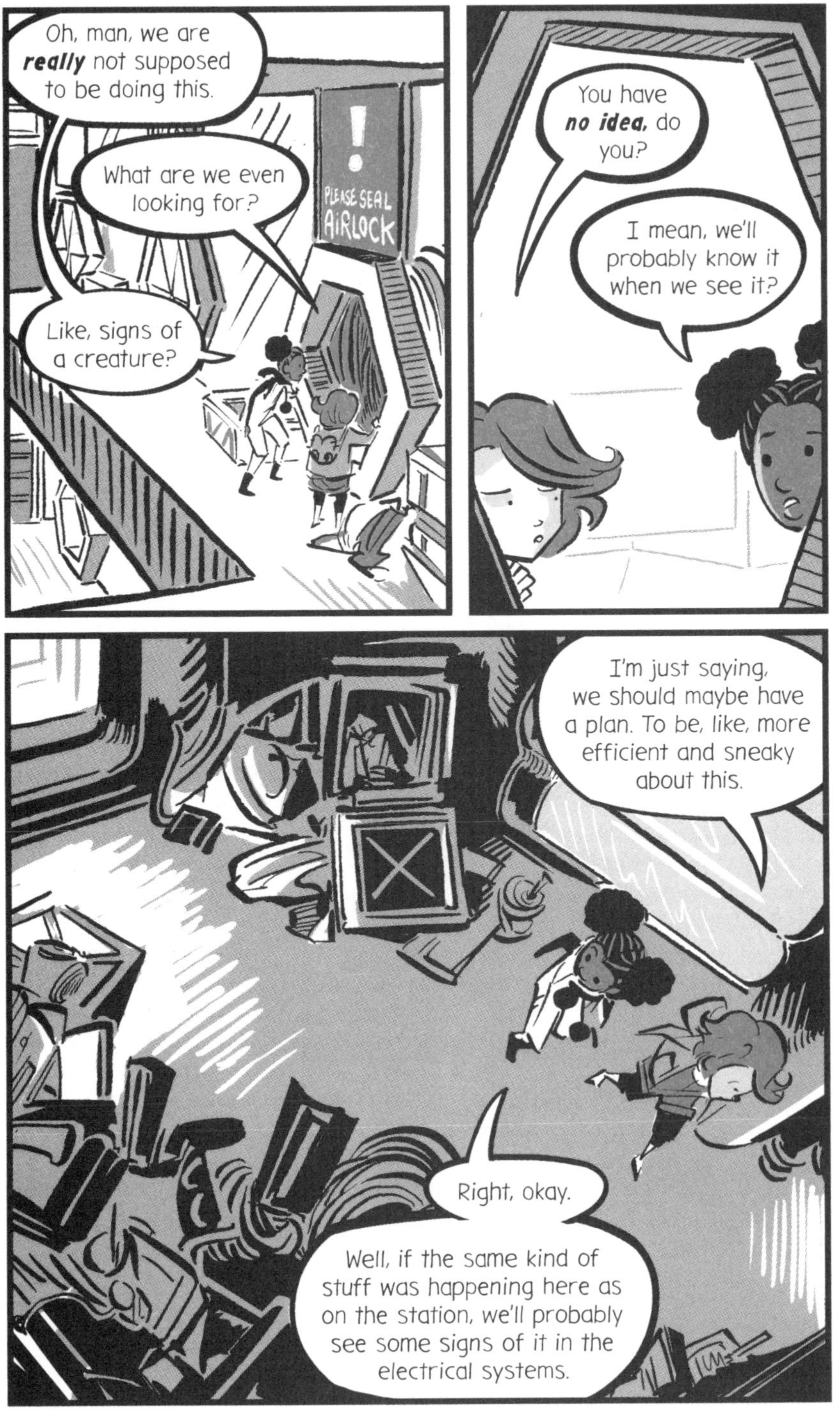
Oh, man, we are **really** not supposed to be doing this.
What are we even looking for?
Like, signs of a creature?
PLEASE SEAL AIRLOCK
You have **no idea,** do you?
I mean, we'll probably know it when we see it?
I'm just saying, we should maybe have a plan. To be, like, more efficient and sneaky about this.
Right, okay.
Well, if the same kind of stuff was happening here as on the station, we'll probably see some signs of it in the electrical systems.

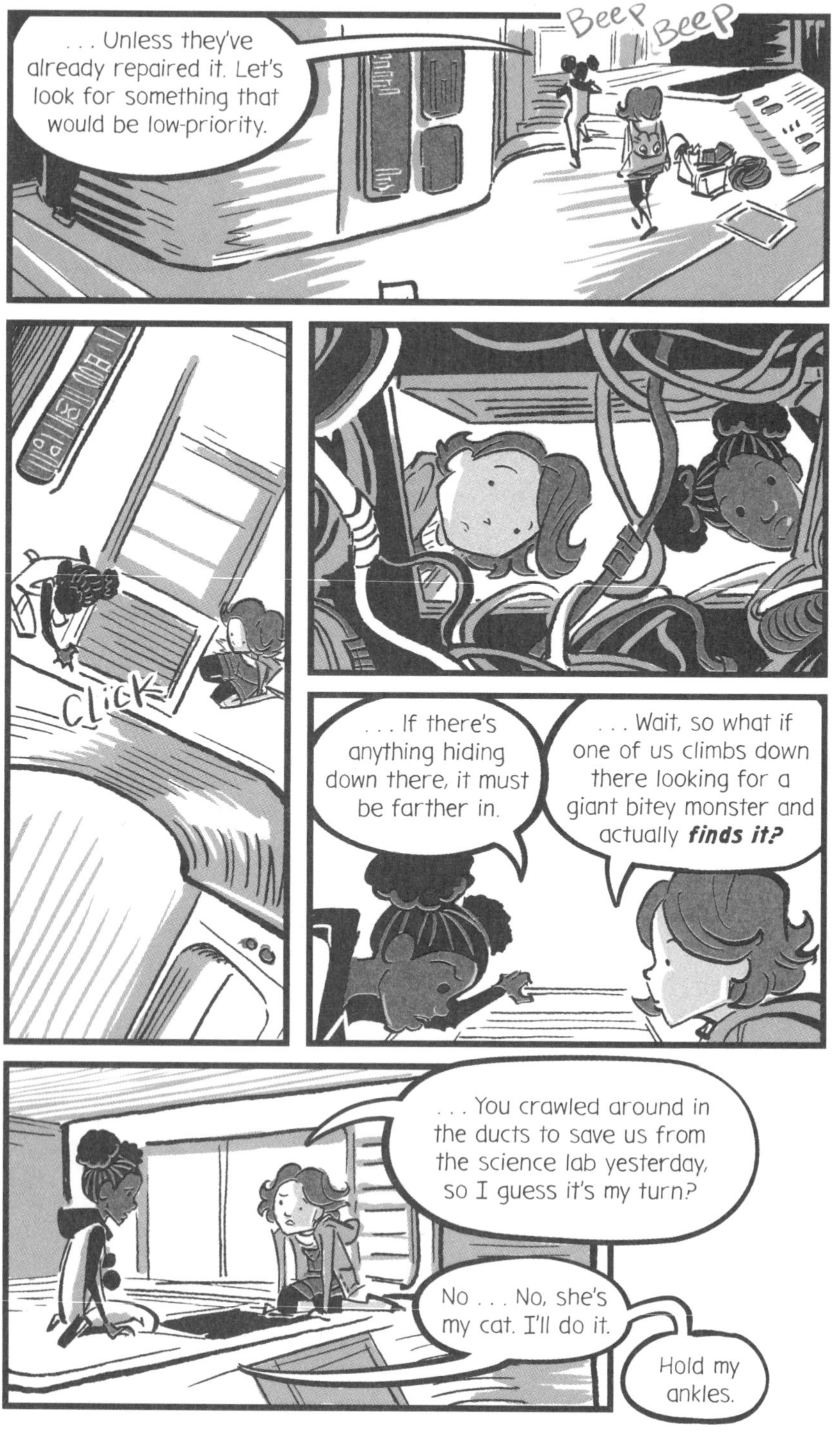
. . . Unless they've already repaired it. Let's look for something that would be low-priority.
Beep Beep
CLICK
. . . If there's anything hiding down there, it must be farther in.
. . . Wait, so what if one of us climbs down there looking for a giant bitey monster and actually ***finds it?***
. . . You crawled around in the ducts to save us from the science lab yesterday, so I guess it's my turn?
No . . . No, she's my cat. I'll do it.
Hold my ankles.

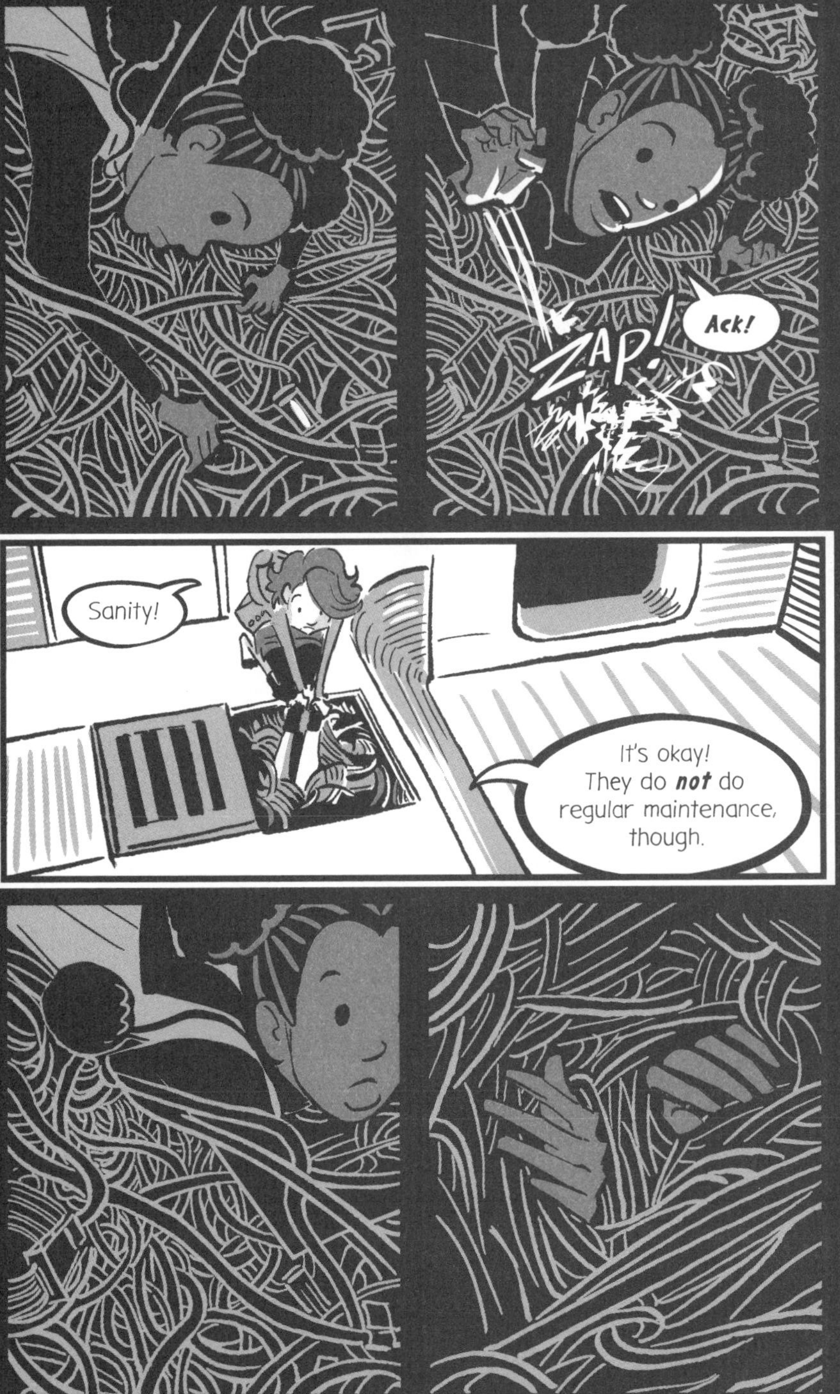

ZAP!
Ack!
Sanity!
It's okay!
They do **not** do
regular maintenance,
though.

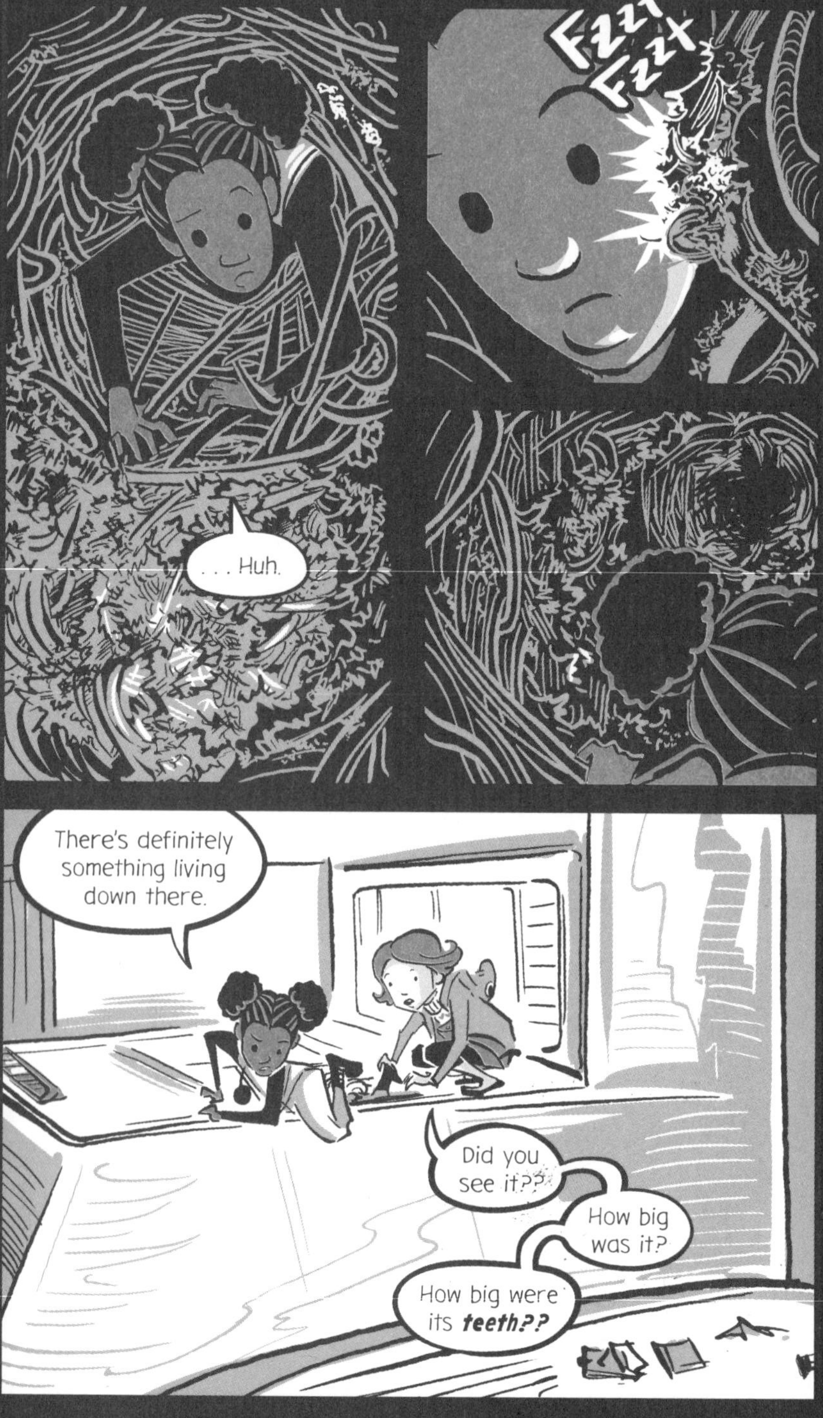
Fzzt
Fzzt
. . . Huh.
There's definitely something living down there.
Did you see it??
How big was it?
How big were its ***teeth??***

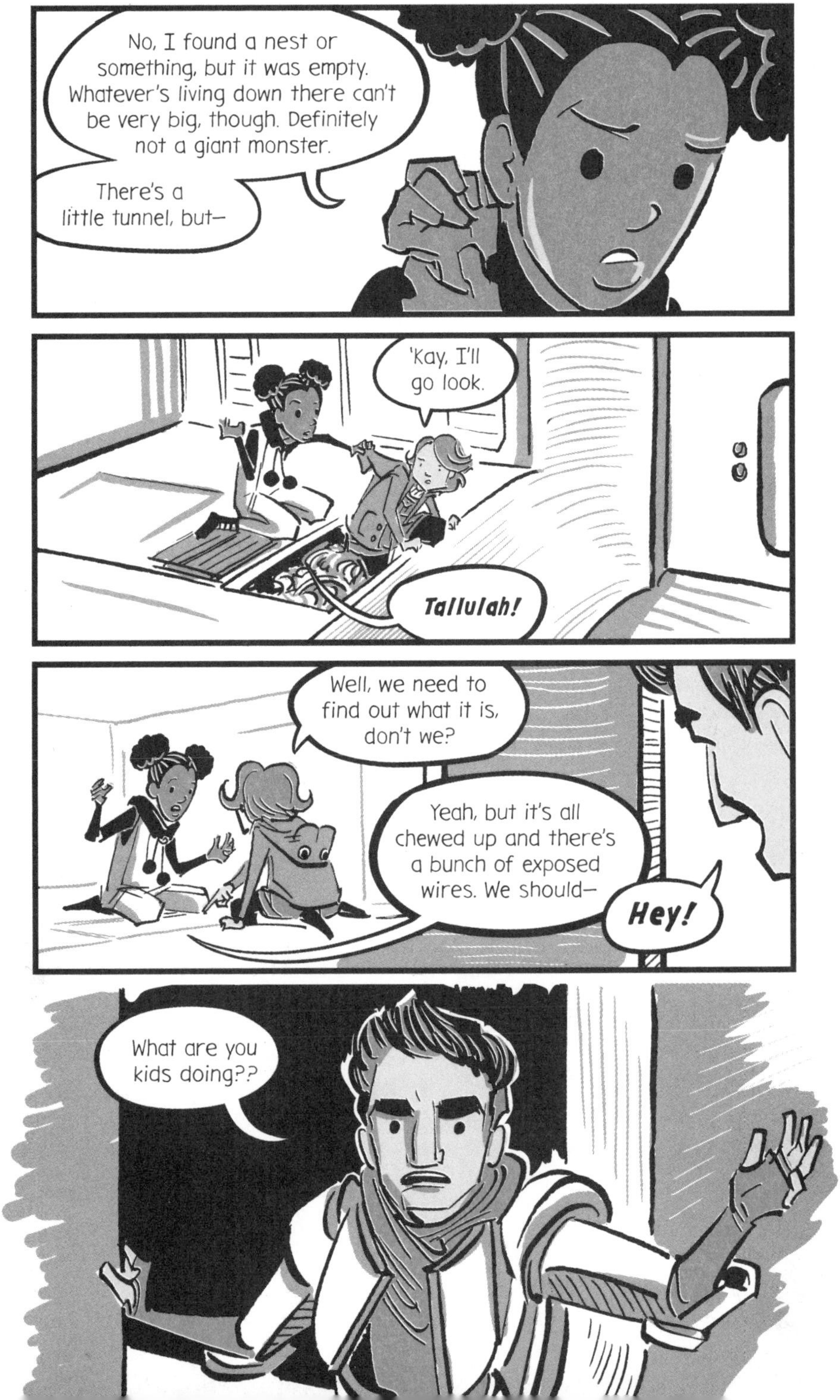
No, I found a nest or something, but it was empty. Whatever's living down there can't be very big, though. Definitely not a giant monster.
There's a little tunnel, but—
'Kay, I'll go look.
Tallulah!
Well, we need to find out what it is, don't we?
Yeah, but it's all chewed up and there's a bunch of exposed wires. We should—
Hey!
What are you kids doing??

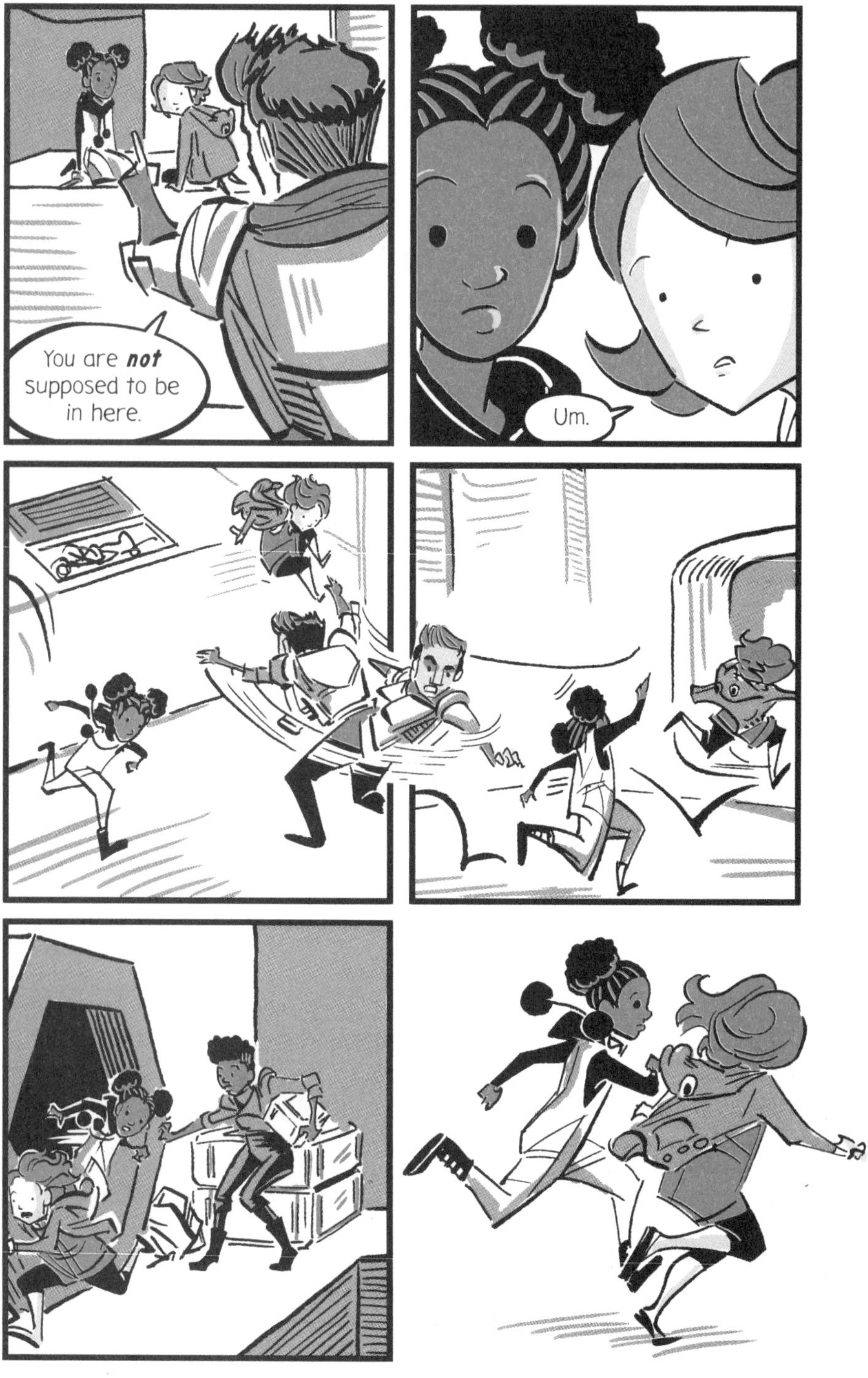
You are **not** supposed to be in here.
Um.

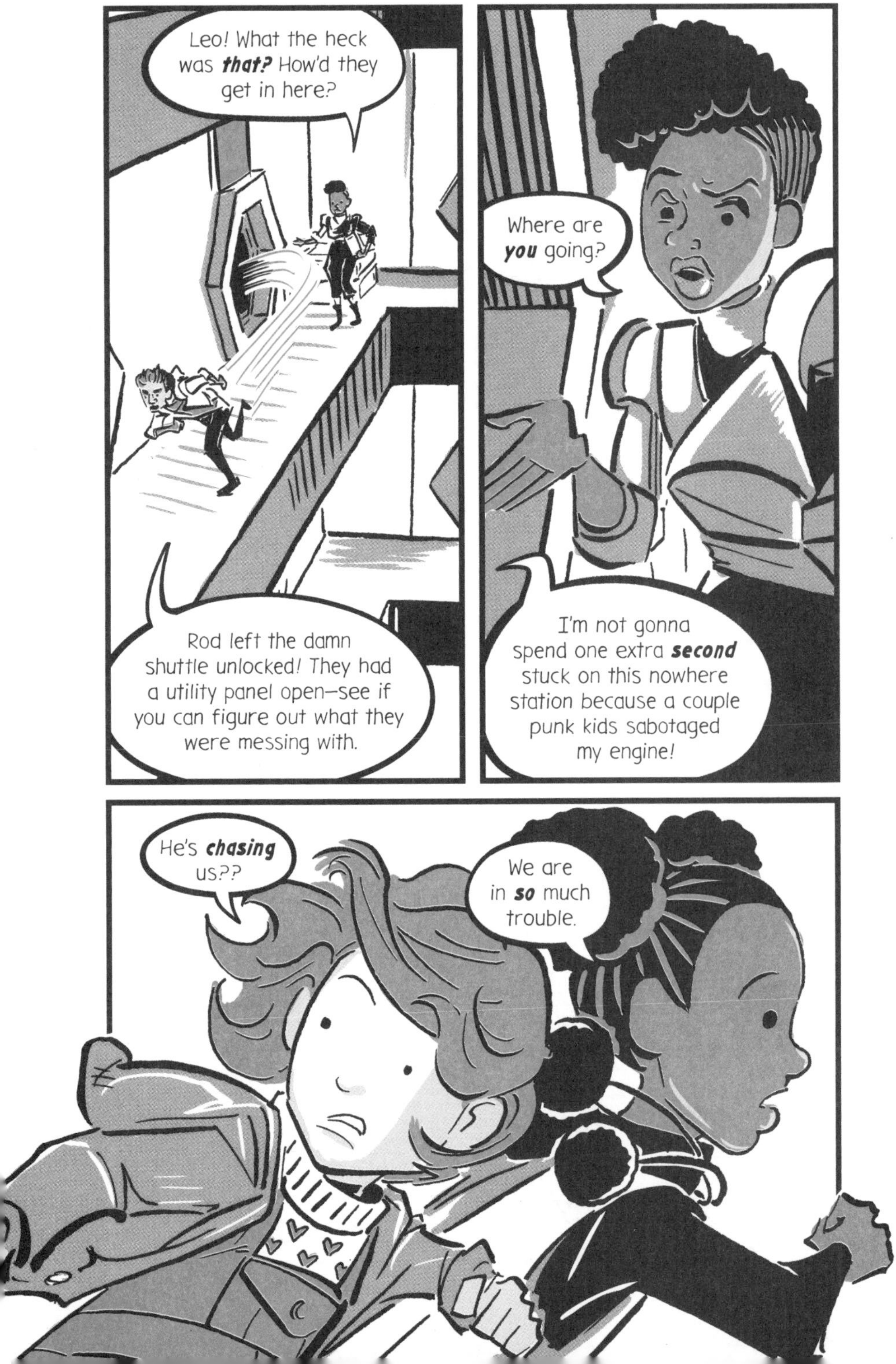
Leo! What the heck was *that?* How'd they get in here?
Rod left the damn shuttle unlocked! They had a utility panel open—see if you can figure out what they were messing with.
Where are *you* going?
I'm not gonna spend one extra *second* stuck on this nowhere station because a couple punk kids sabotaged my engine!
He's *chasing* us??
We are in *so* much trouble.

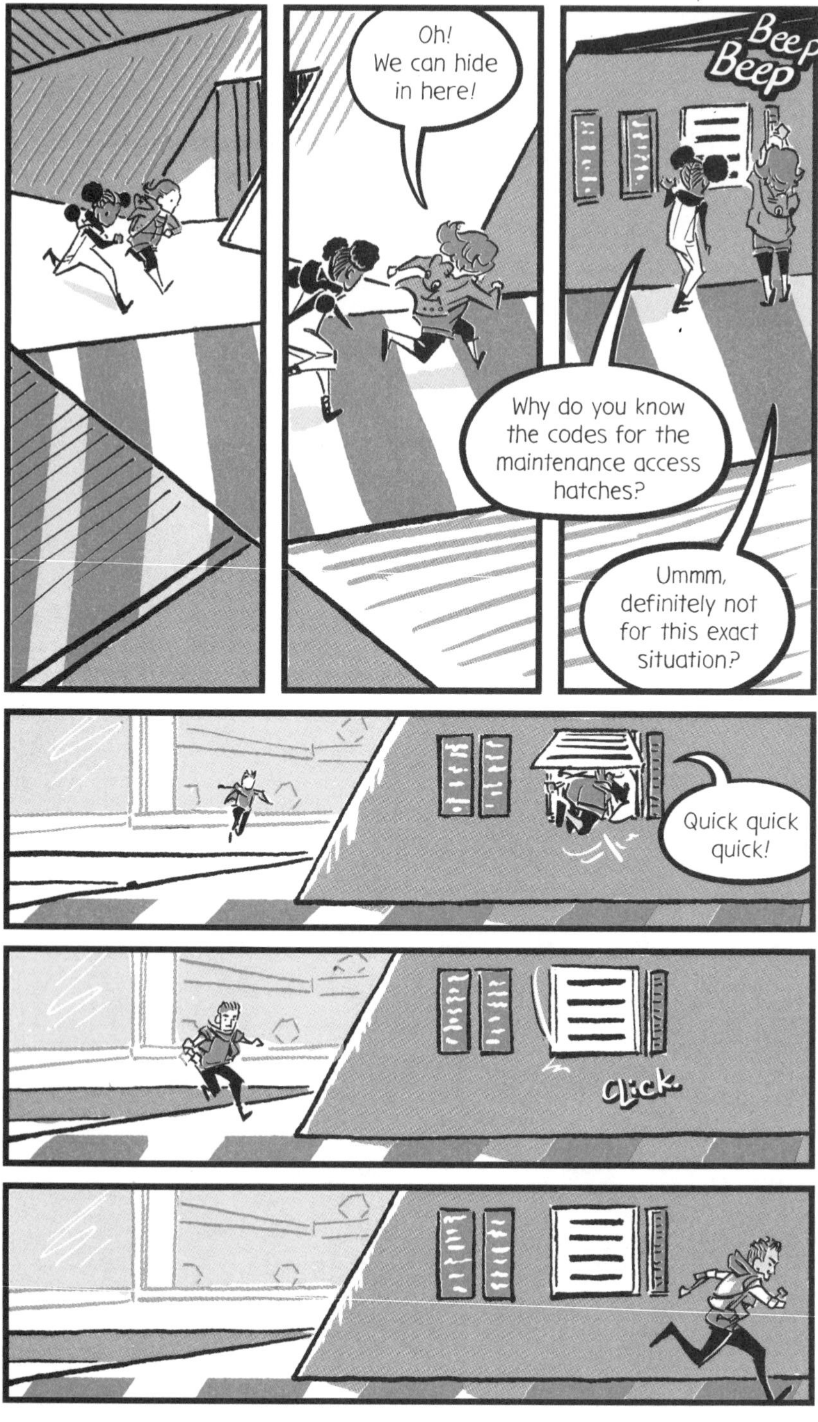
Oh! We can hide in here!
Beep Beep
Why do you know the codes for the maintenance access hatches?
Ummm, definitely not for this exact situation?
Quick quick quick!
Click.

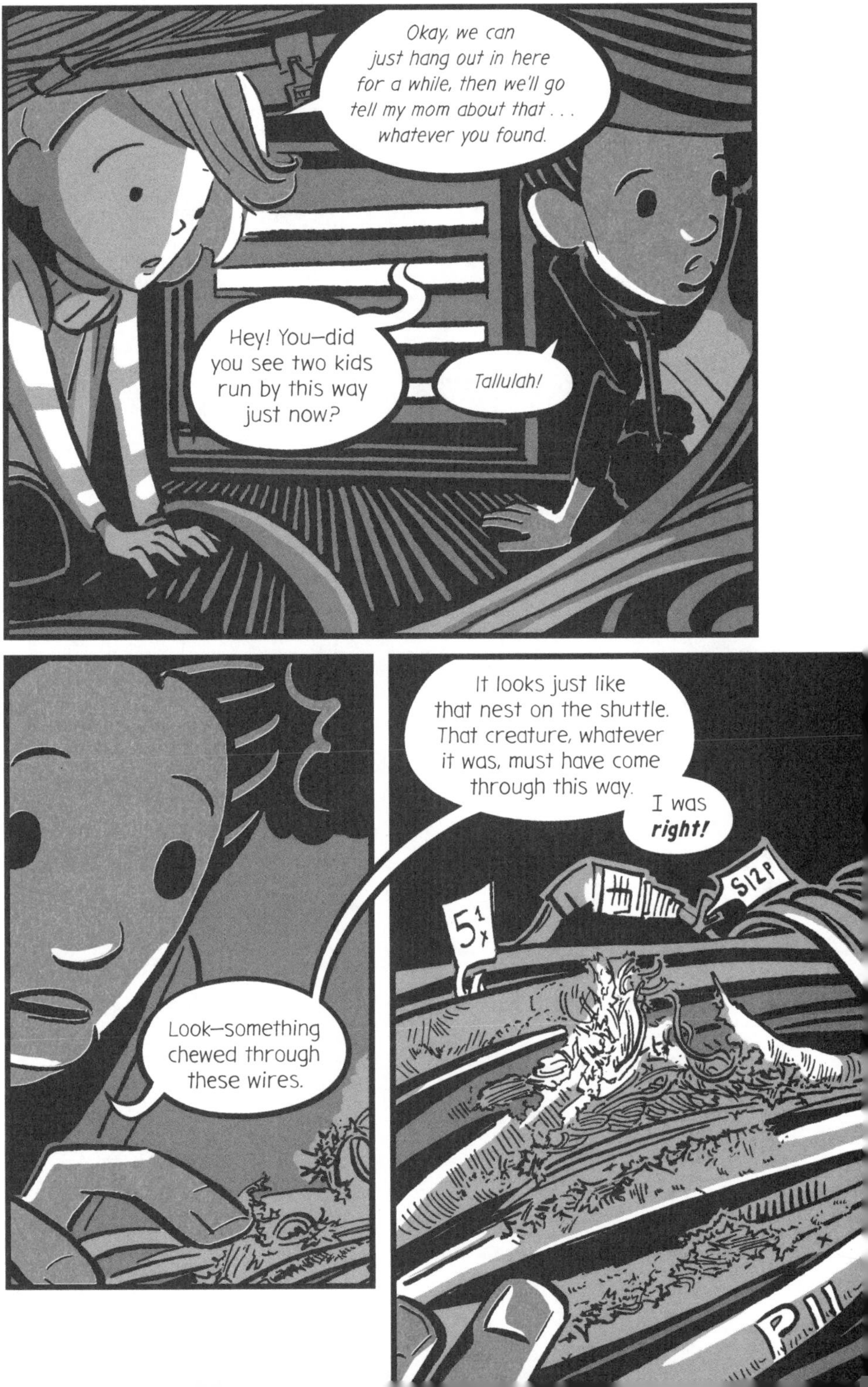
Okay, we can just hang out in here for a while, then we'll go tell my mom about that . . . whatever you found.
Hey! You—did you see two kids run by this way just now?
Tallulah!
Look—something chewed through these wires.
It looks just like that nest on the shuttle. That creature, whatever it was, must have come through this way.
I was **right!**
S12P
P11

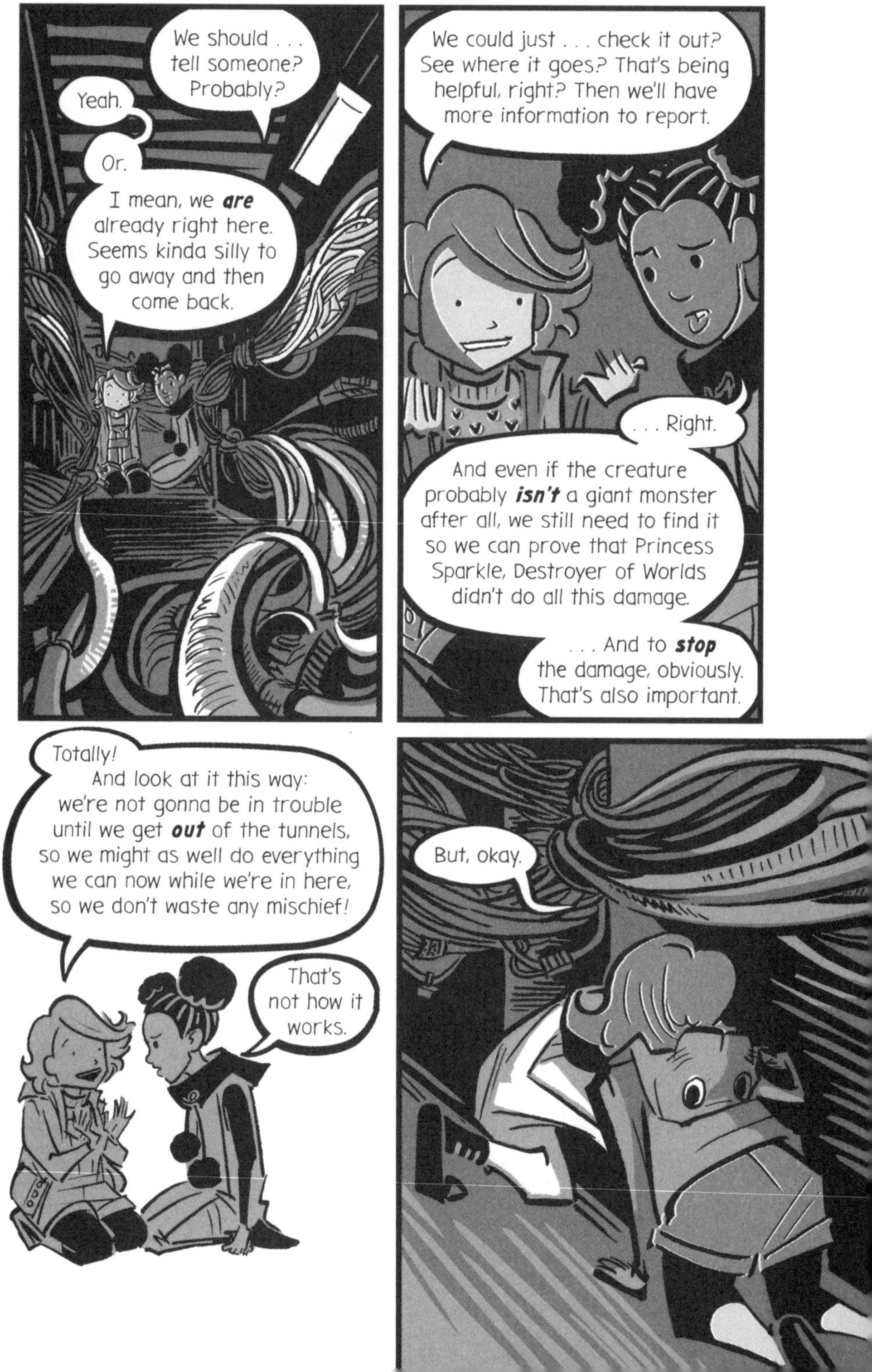
We should . . . tell someone? Probably?
Yeah.
Or.
I mean, we **are** already right here. Seems kinda silly to go away and then come back.
We could just . . . check it out? See where it goes? That's being helpful, right? Then we'll have more information to report.
. . . Right.
And even if the creature probably **isn't** a giant monster after all, we still need to find it so we can prove that Princess Sparkle, Destroyer of Worlds didn't do all this damage.
. . . And to **stop** the damage, obviously. That's also important.
Totally! And look at it this way: we're not gonna be in trouble until we get **out** of the tunnels, so we might as well do everything we can now while we're in here, so we don't waste any mischief!
That's not how it works.
But, okay.

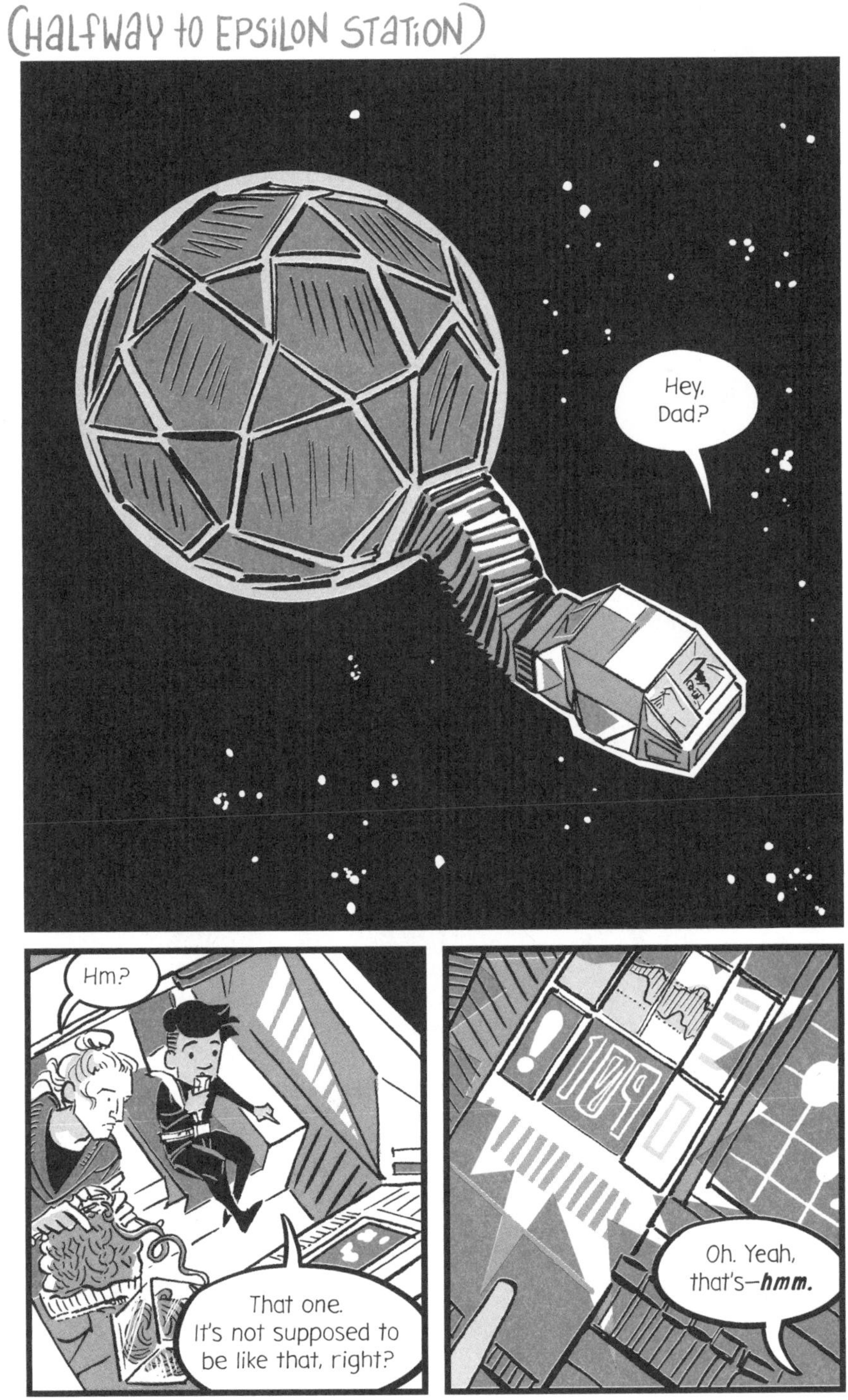
(Halfway to Epsilon Station)
Hey, Dad?
Hm?
That one. It's not supposed to be like that, right?
Oh. Yeah, that's—*hmm.*

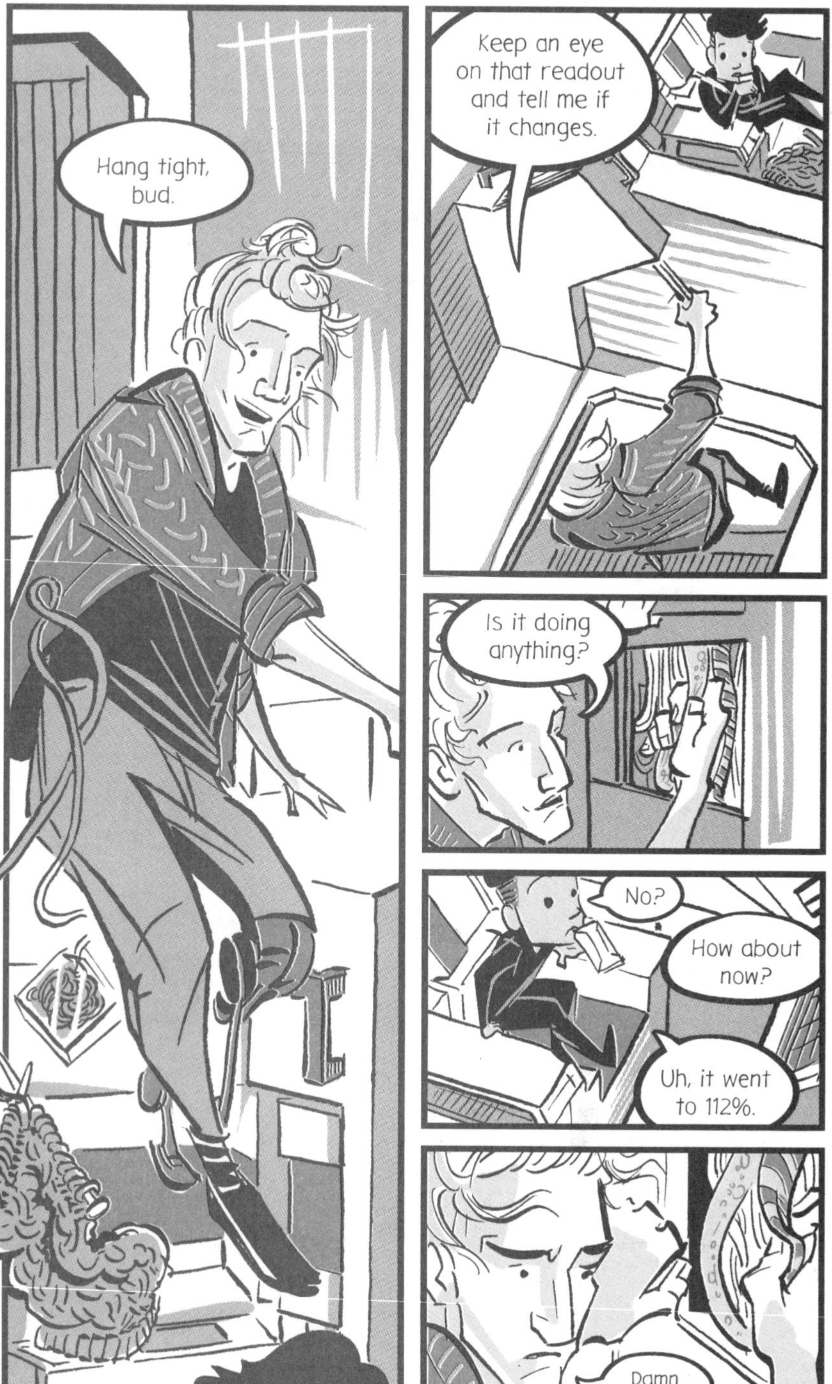
Hang tight, bud.
Keep an eye on that readout and tell me if it changes.
Is it doing anything?
No?
How about now?
Uh, it went to 112%.
Damn.

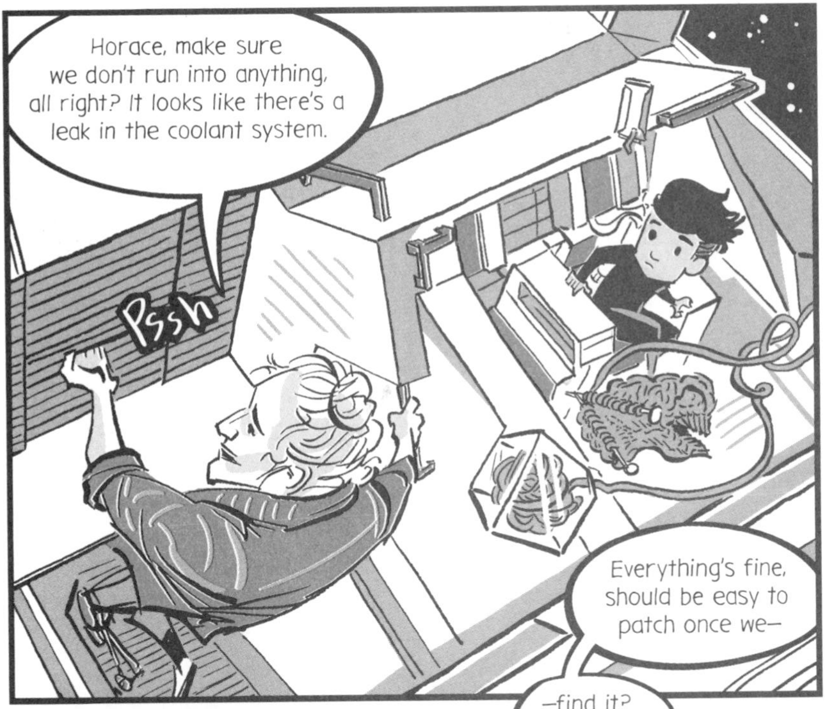
Horace, make sure we don't run into anything, all right? It looks like there's a leak in the coolant system.
Pssh
Everything's fine, should be easy to patch once we—

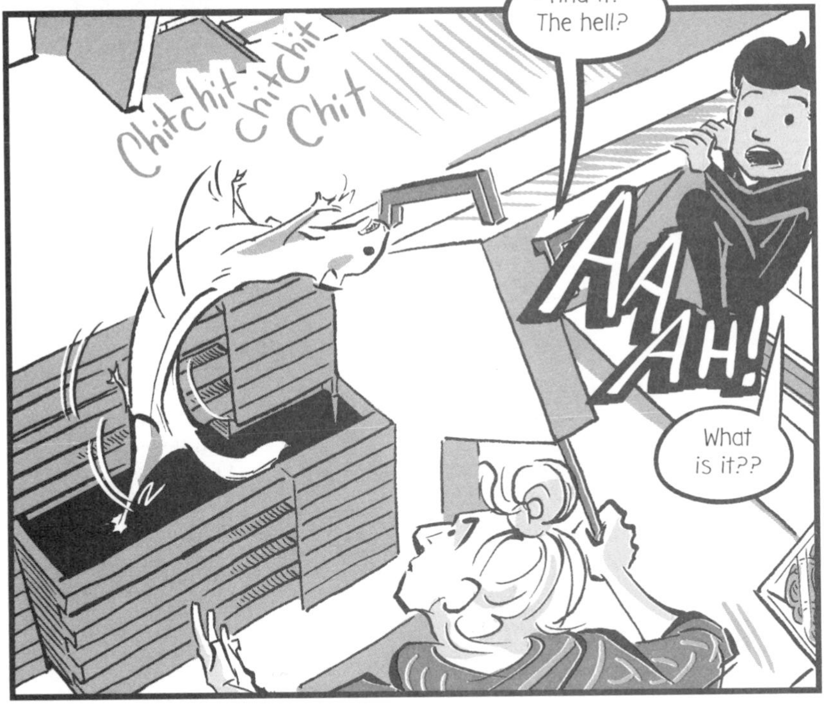
—find it? The hell?
Chitchit chitchit Chit
AAAH!
What is it??

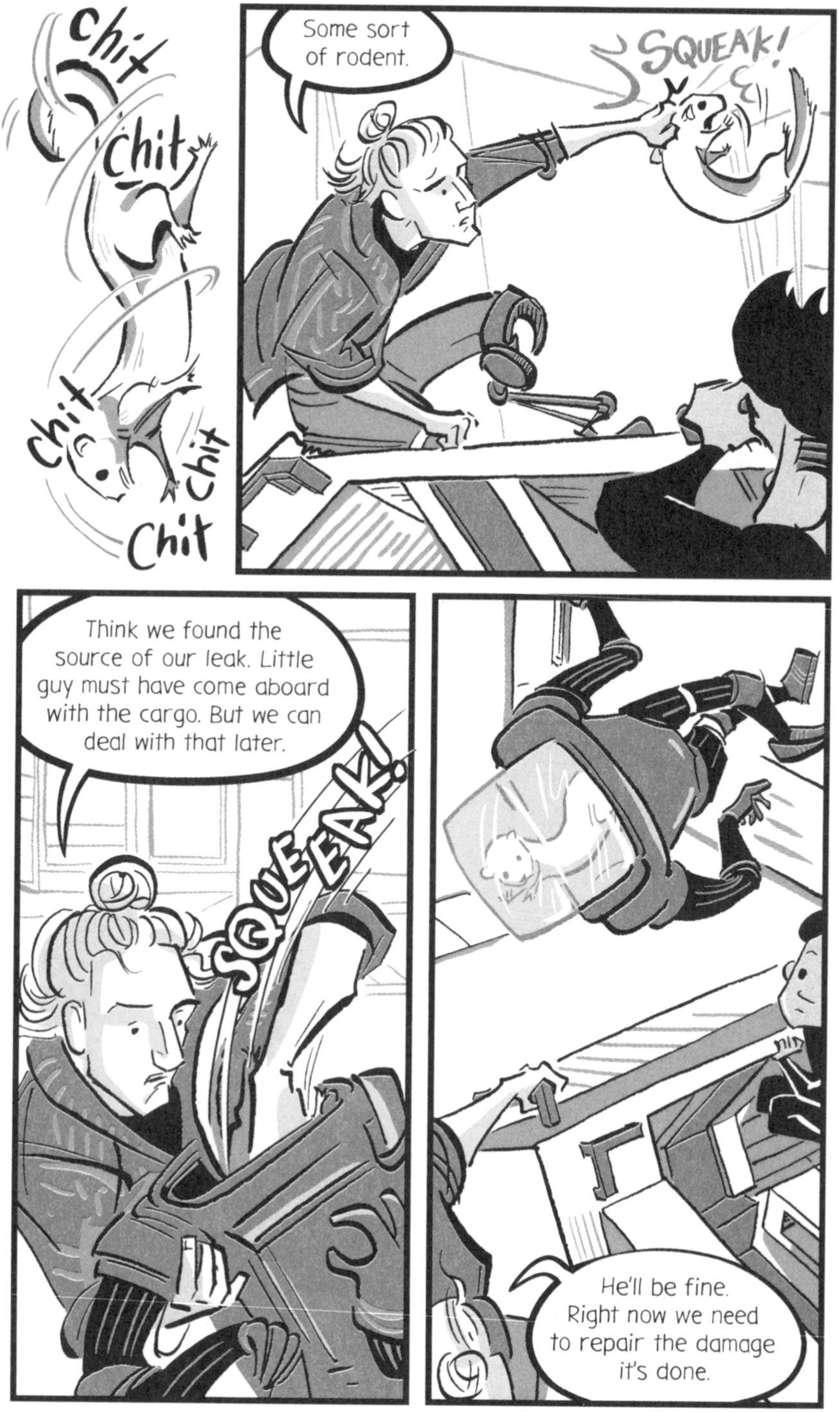
Chit
Chit
Chit
Chit
Chit
Some sort of rodent.
SQUEAK!
Think we found the source of our leak. Little guy must have come aboard with the cargo. But we can deal with that later.
SQUEEAK!
He'll be fine. Right now we need to repair the damage it's done.

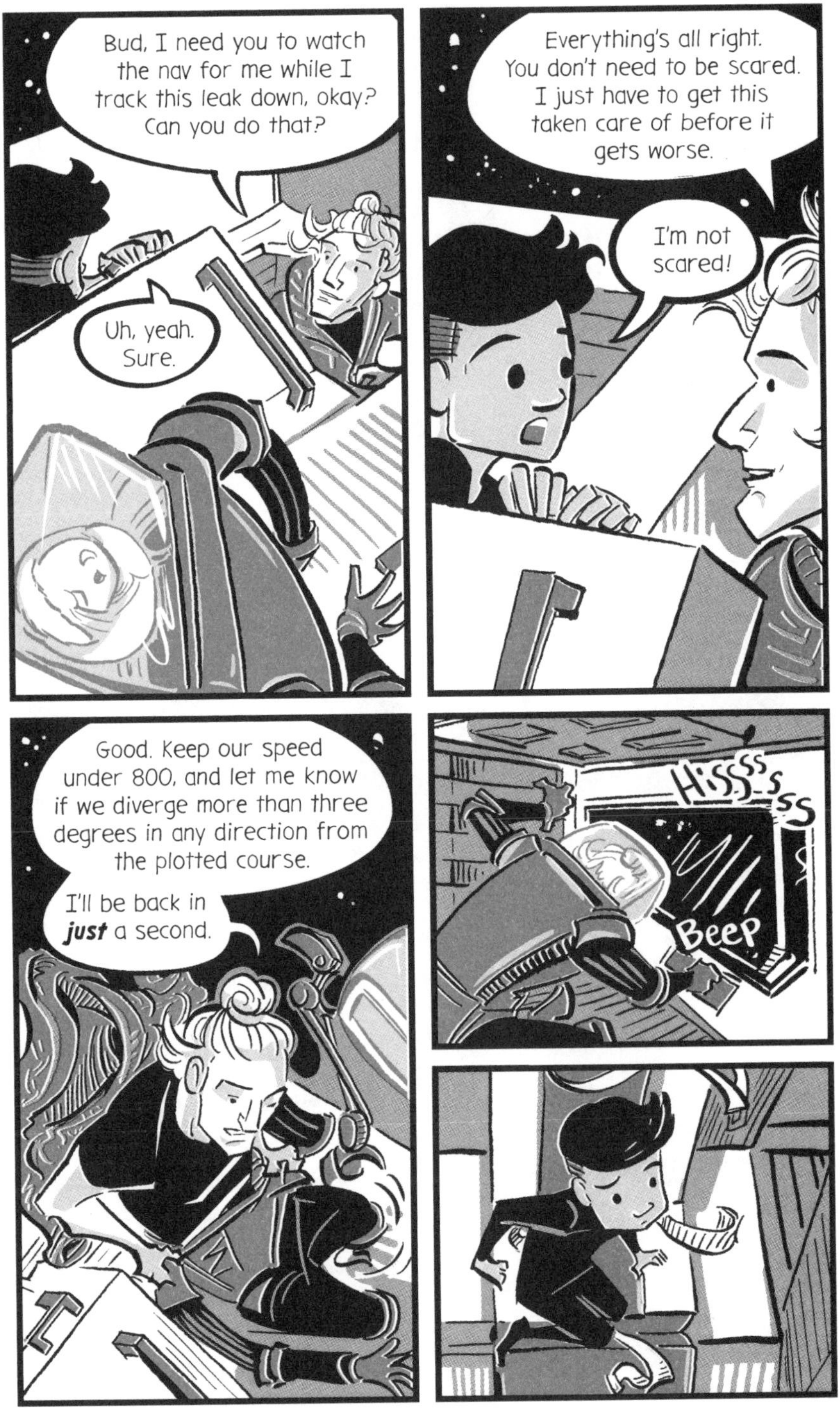
Bud, I need you to watch the nav for me while I track this leak down, okay? Can you do that?
Uh, yeah. Sure.
Everything's all right. You don't need to be scared. I just have to get this taken care of before it gets worse.
I'm not scared!
Good. Keep our speed under 800, and let me know if we diverge more than three degrees in any direction from the plotted course.
I'll be back in **just** a second.
HiSSSsSSS
Beep

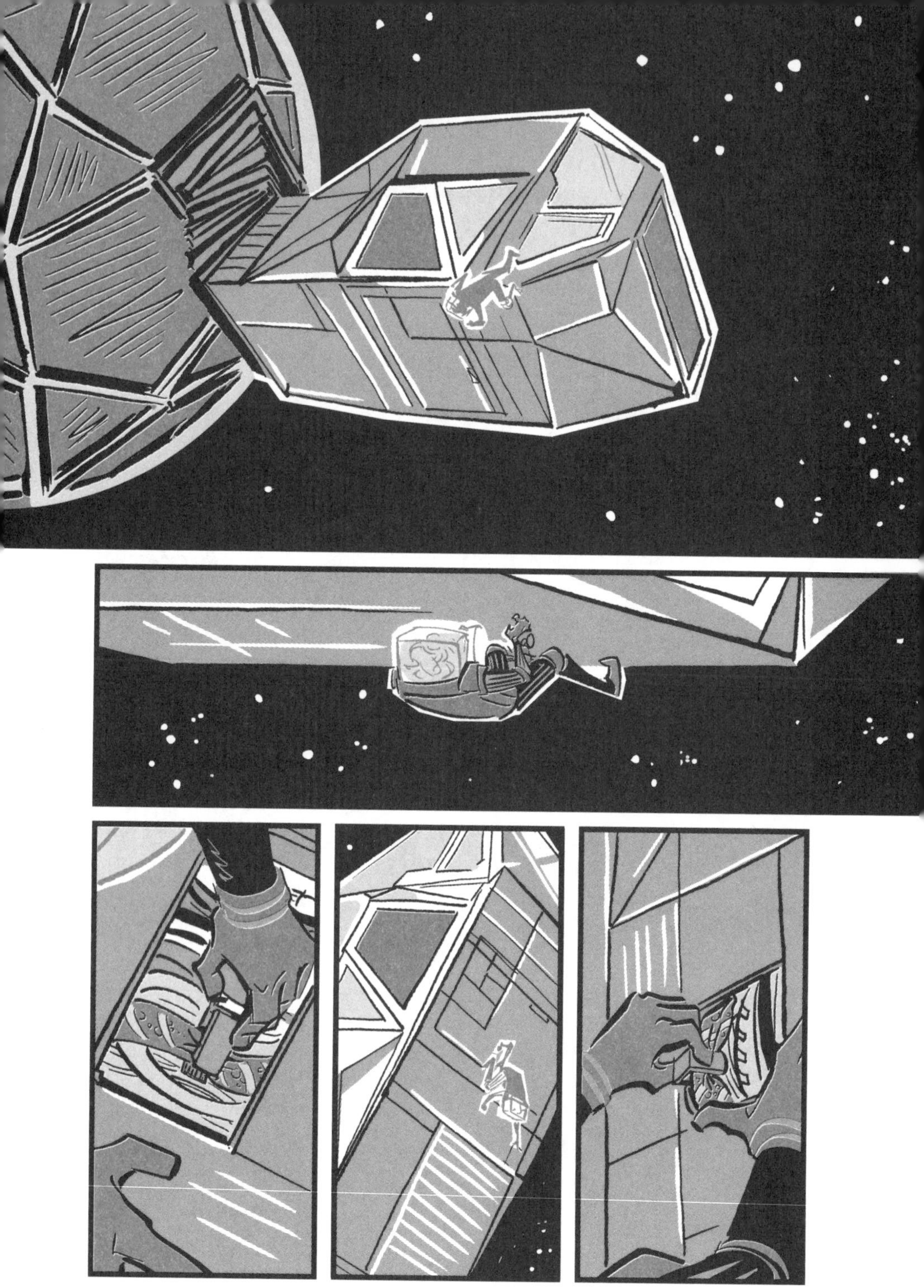

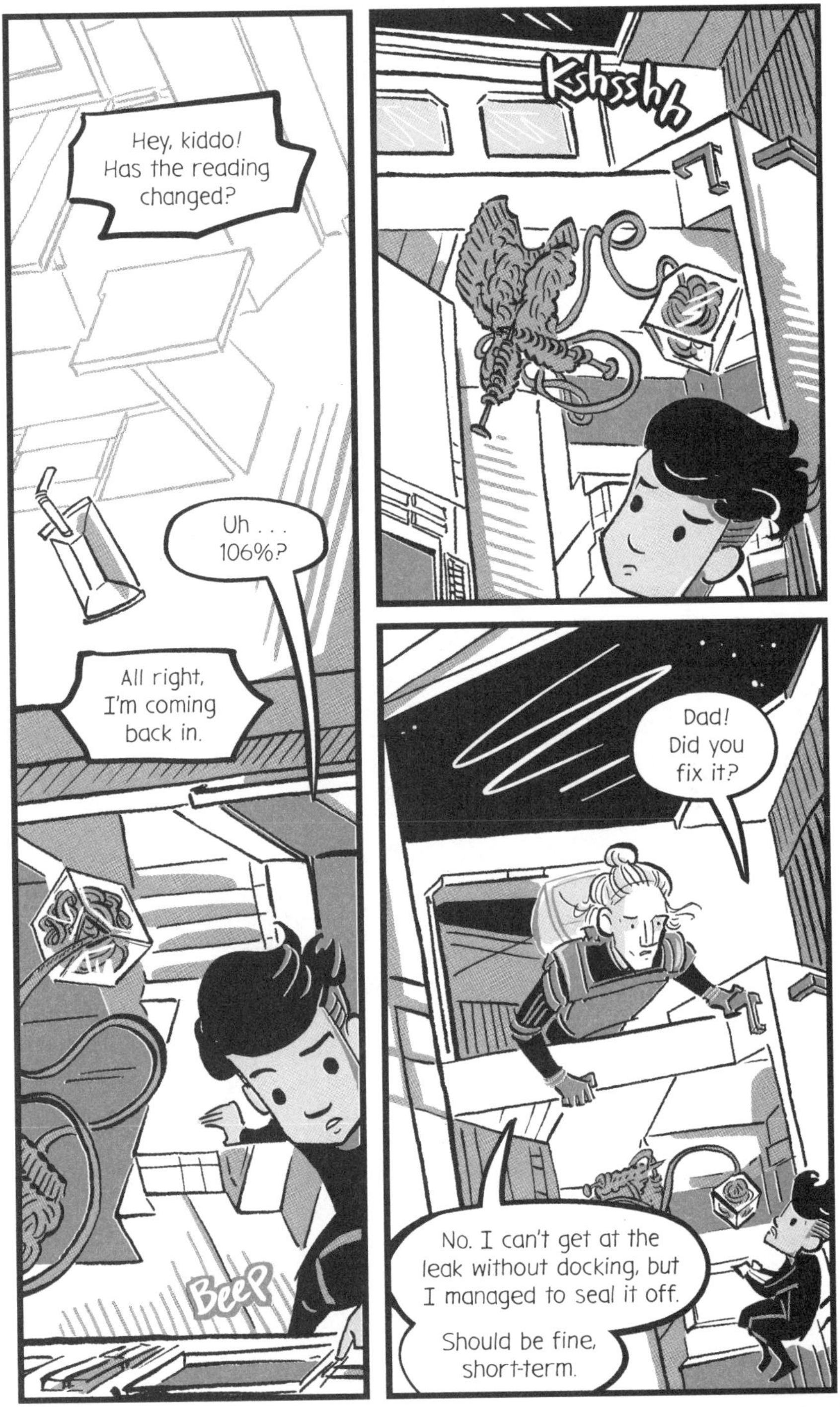

Hey, kiddo! Has the reading changed?
Uh . . . 106%?
All right, I'm coming back in.
Beep
Kshsshh
Dad! Did you fix it?
No. I can't get at the leak without docking, but I managed to seal it off.
Should be fine, short-term.

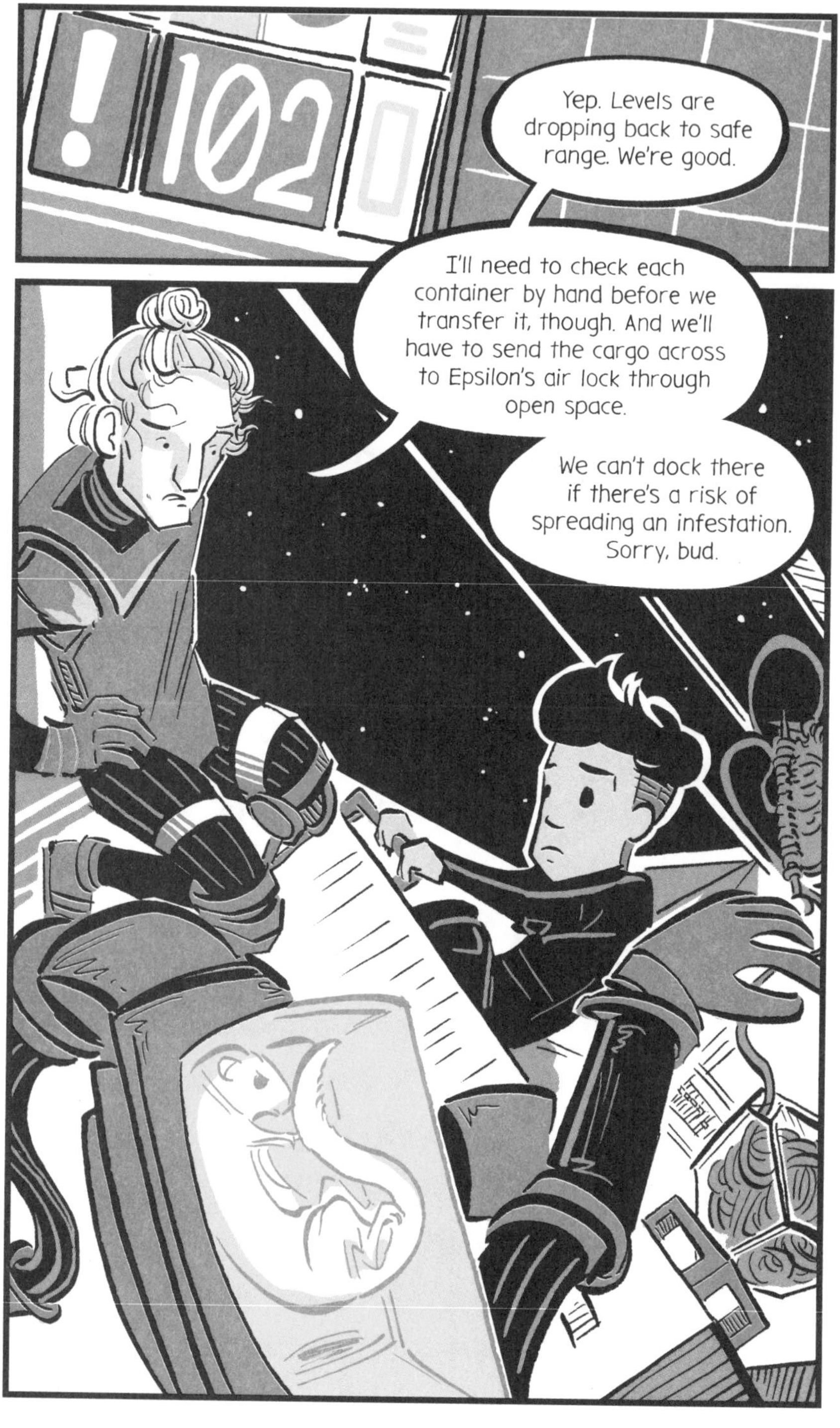
!102
Yep. Levels are dropping back to safe range. We're good.
I'll need to check each container by hand before we transfer it, though. And we'll have to send the cargo across to Epsilon's air lock through open space.
We can't dock there if there's a risk of spreading an infestation. Sorry, bud.

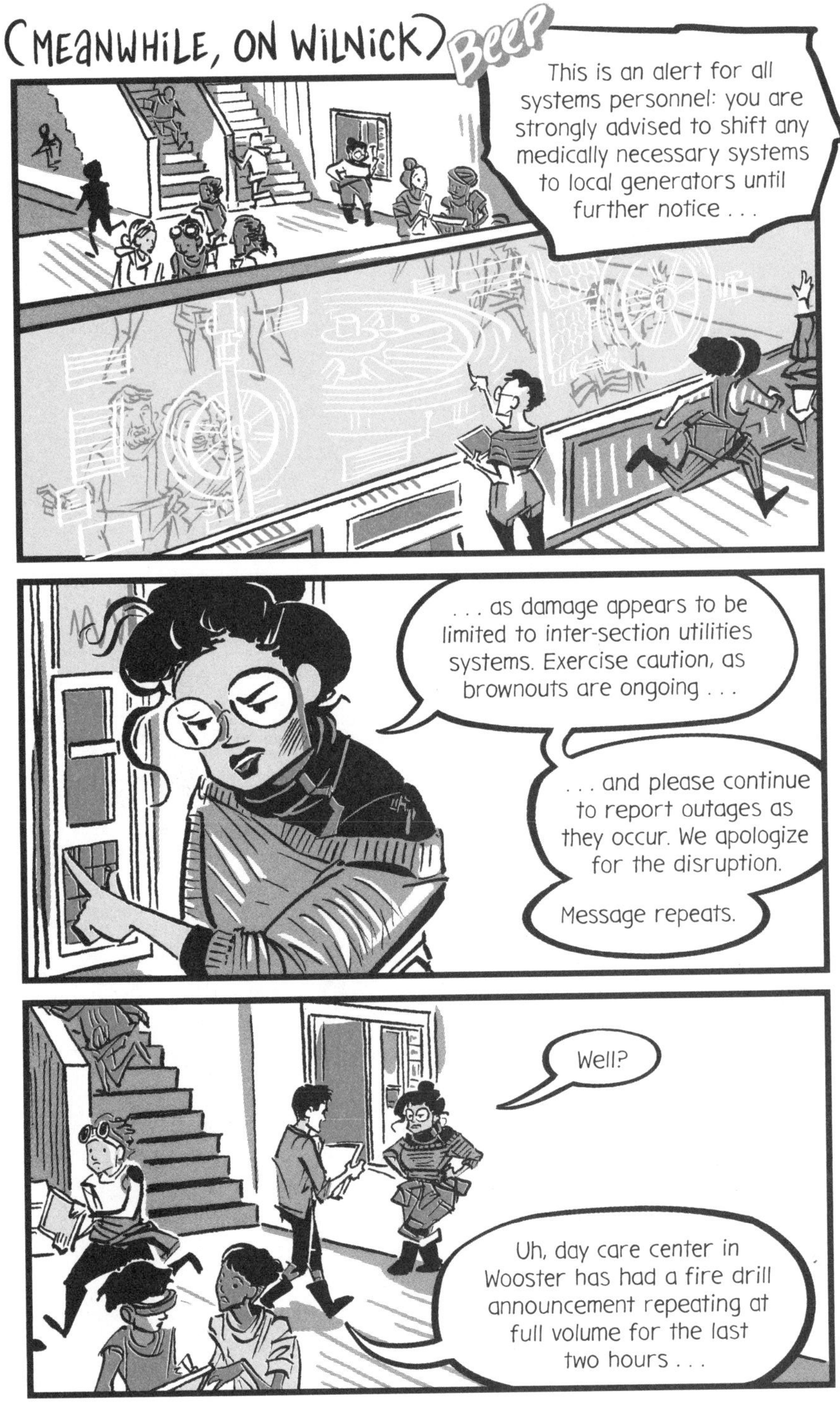
(MEANWHILE, ON WILNICK)
Beep
This is an alert for all systems personnel: you are strongly advised to shift any medically necessary systems to local generators until further notice . . .
. . . as damage appears to be limited to inter-section utilities systems. Exercise caution, as brownouts are ongoing . . .
. . . and please continue to report outages as they occur. We apologize for the disruption.
Message repeats.
Well?
Uh, day care center in Wooster has had a fire drill announcement repeating at full volume for the last two hours . . .

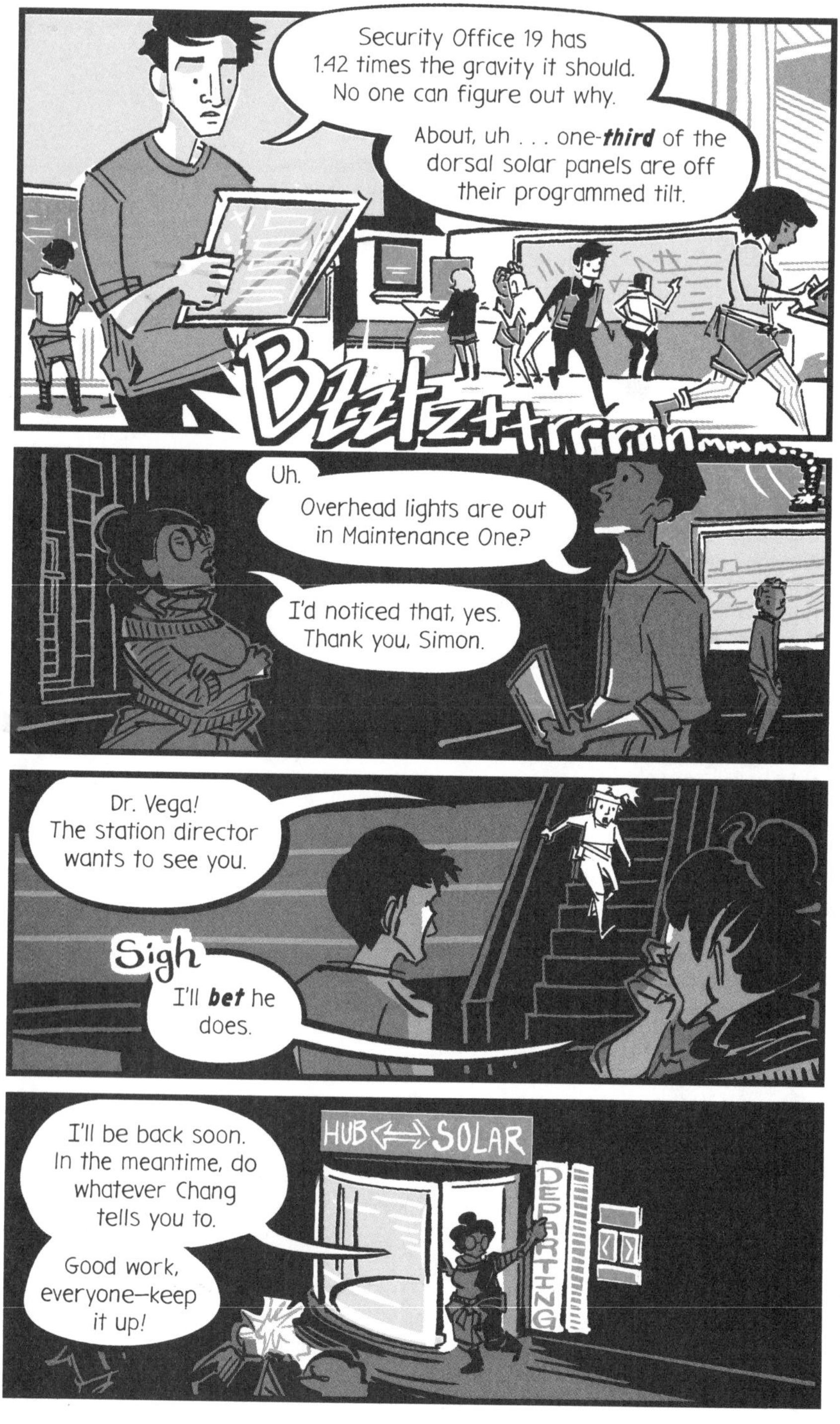
Security Office 19 has 1.42 times the gravity it should. No one can figure out why.
About, uh . . . one-***third*** of the dorsal solar panels are off their programmed tilt.
Bzztzttrrrrnnmmm...
Uh.
Overhead lights are out in Maintenance One?
I'd noticed that, yes. Thank you, Simon.
Dr. Vega! The station director wants to see you.
Sigh
I'll ***bet*** he does.
HUB ⟺ SOLAR
DEPARTING
I'll be back soon. In the meantime, do whatever Chang tells you to.
Good work, everyone—keep it up!

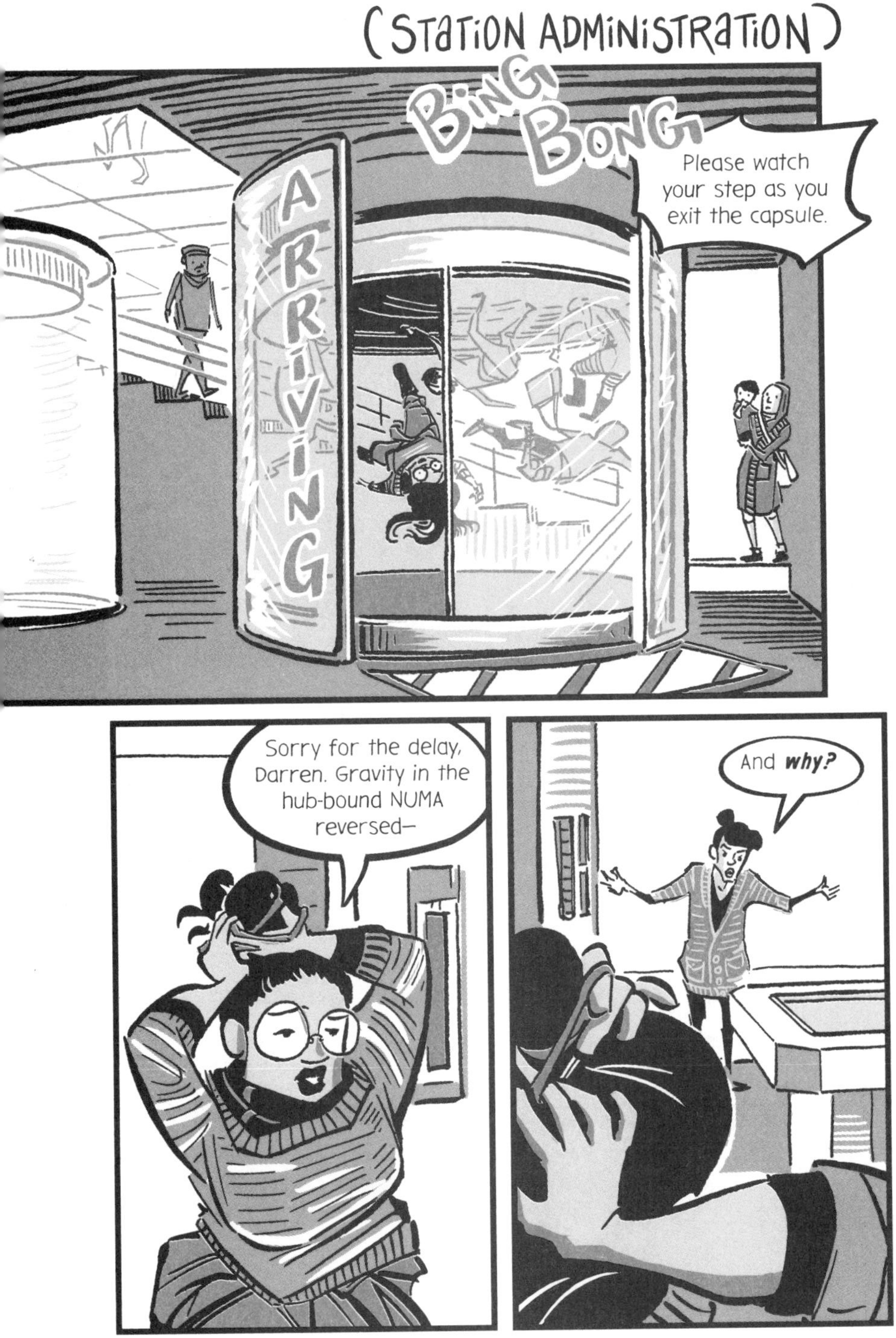
(STATION ADMINISTRATION)
BING BONG
Please watch your step as you exit the capsule.
ARRIVING
Sorry for the delay, Darren. Gravity in the hub-bound NUMA reversed–
And **why?**

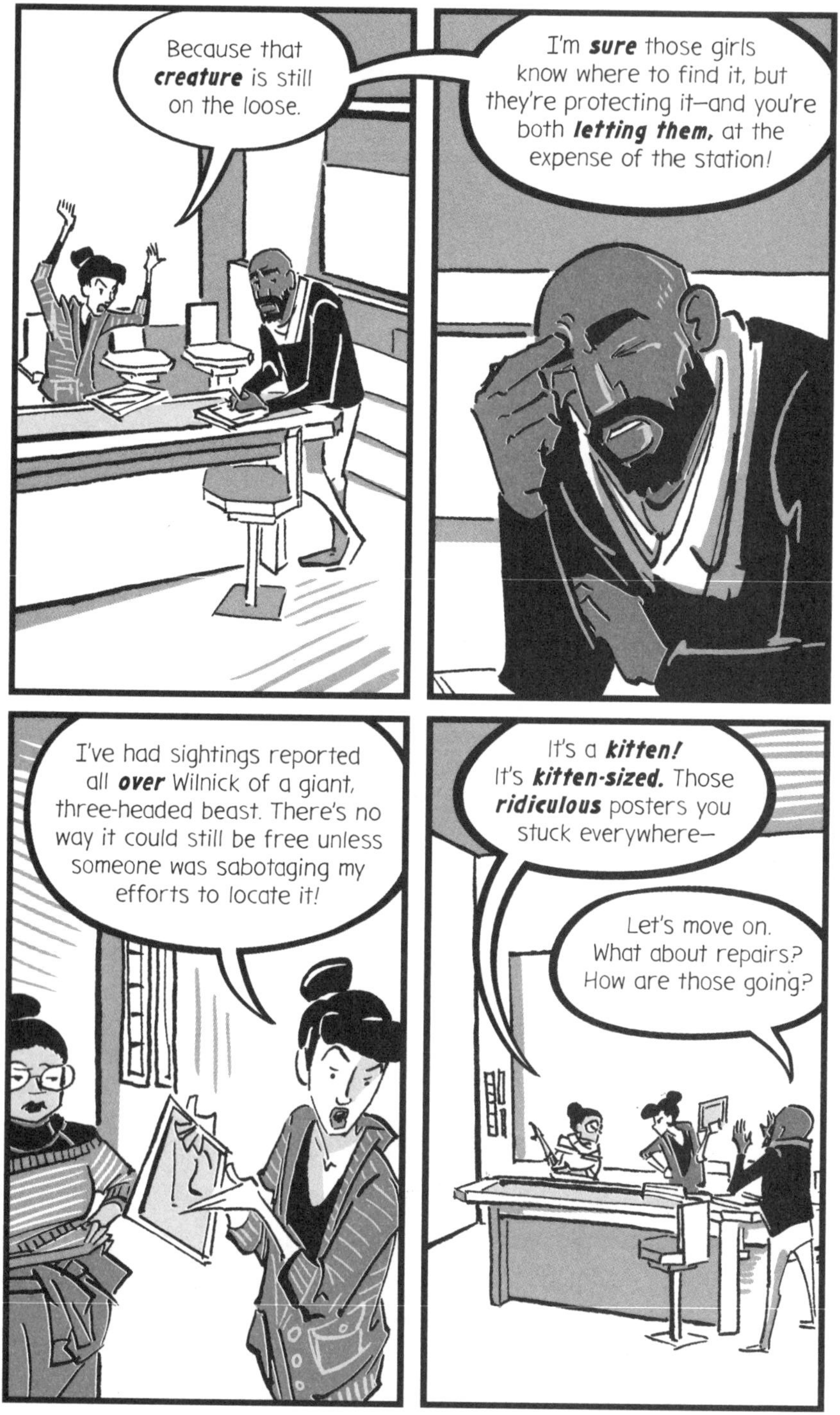
Because that **creature** is still on the loose.
I'm **sure** those girls know where to find it, but they're protecting it—and you're both **letting them,** at the expense of the station!
I've had sightings reported all **over** Wilnick of a giant, three-headed beast. There's no way it could still be free unless someone was sabotaging my efforts to locate it!
It's a **kitten!** It's **kitten-sized.** Those **ridiculous** posters you stuck everywhere—
Let's move on. What about repairs? How are those going?

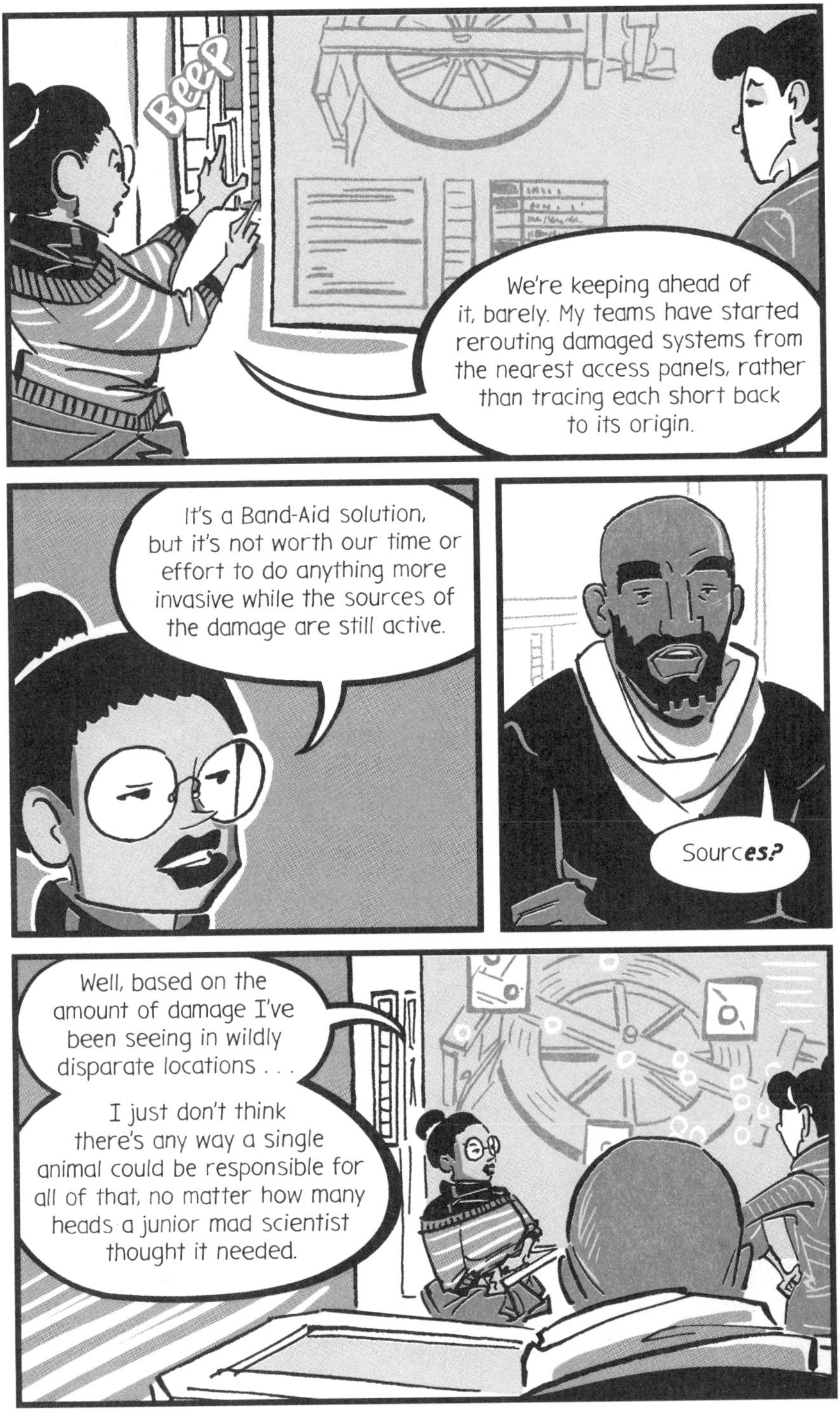

BEEP
We're keeping ahead of it, barely. My teams have started rerouting damaged systems from the nearest access panels, rather than tracing each short back to its origin.
It's a Band-Aid solution, but it's not worth our time or effort to do anything more invasive while the sources of the damage are still active.
Sourc**es?**
Well, based on the amount of damage I've been seeing in wildly disparate locations . . .
I just don't think there's any way a single animal could be responsible for all of that, no matter how many heads a junior mad scientist thought it needed.

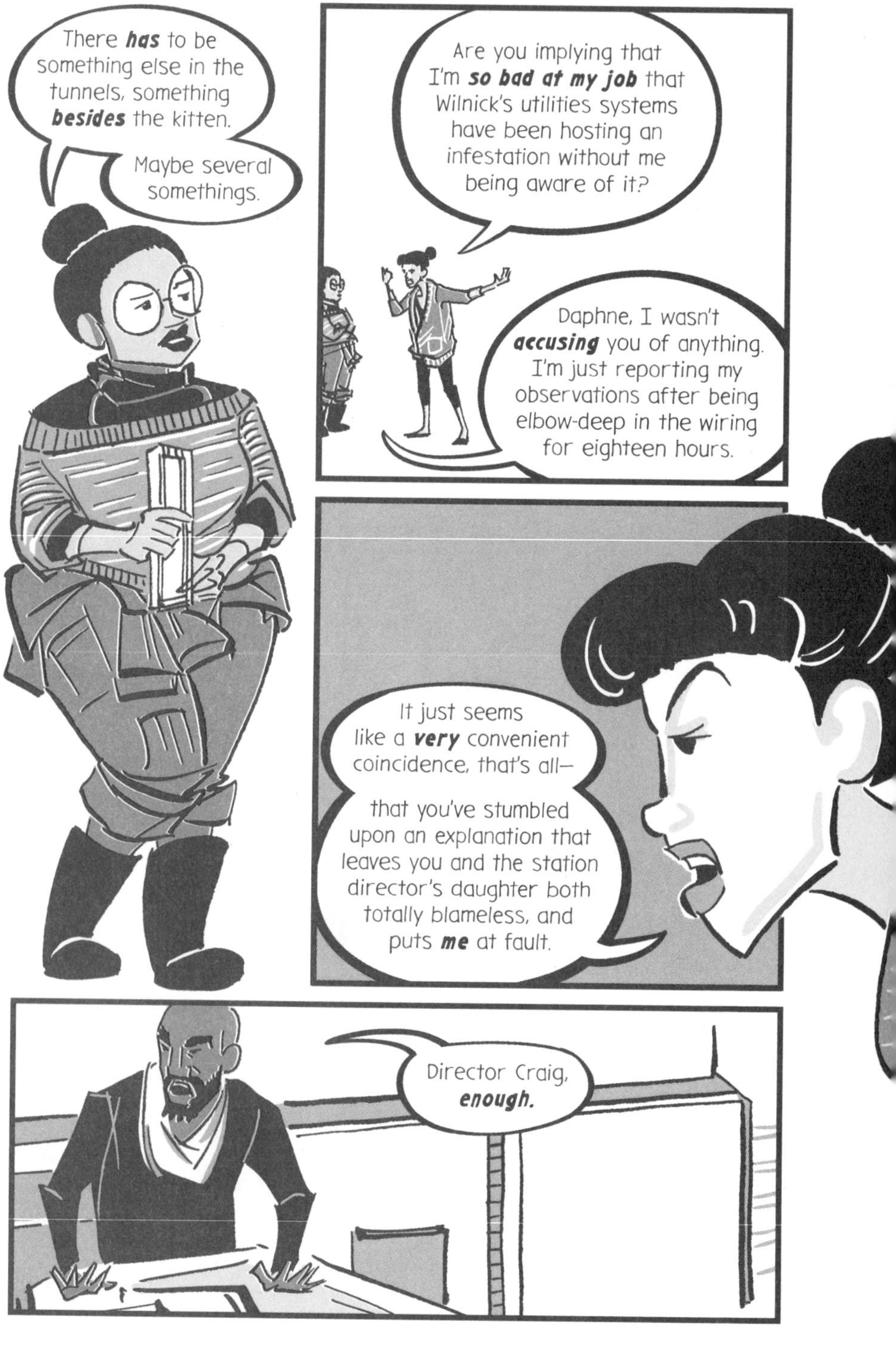
There **has** to be something else in the tunnels, something **besides** the kitten.
Maybe several somethings.
Are you implying that I'm **so bad at my job** that Wilnick's utilities systems have been hosting an infestation without me being aware of it?
Daphne, I wasn't **accusing** you of anything. I'm just reporting my observations after being elbow-deep in the wiring for eighteen hours.
It just seems like a **very** convenient coincidence, that's all—
that you've stumbled upon an explanation that leaves you and the station director's daughter both totally blameless, and puts **me** at fault.
Director Craig, **enough.**

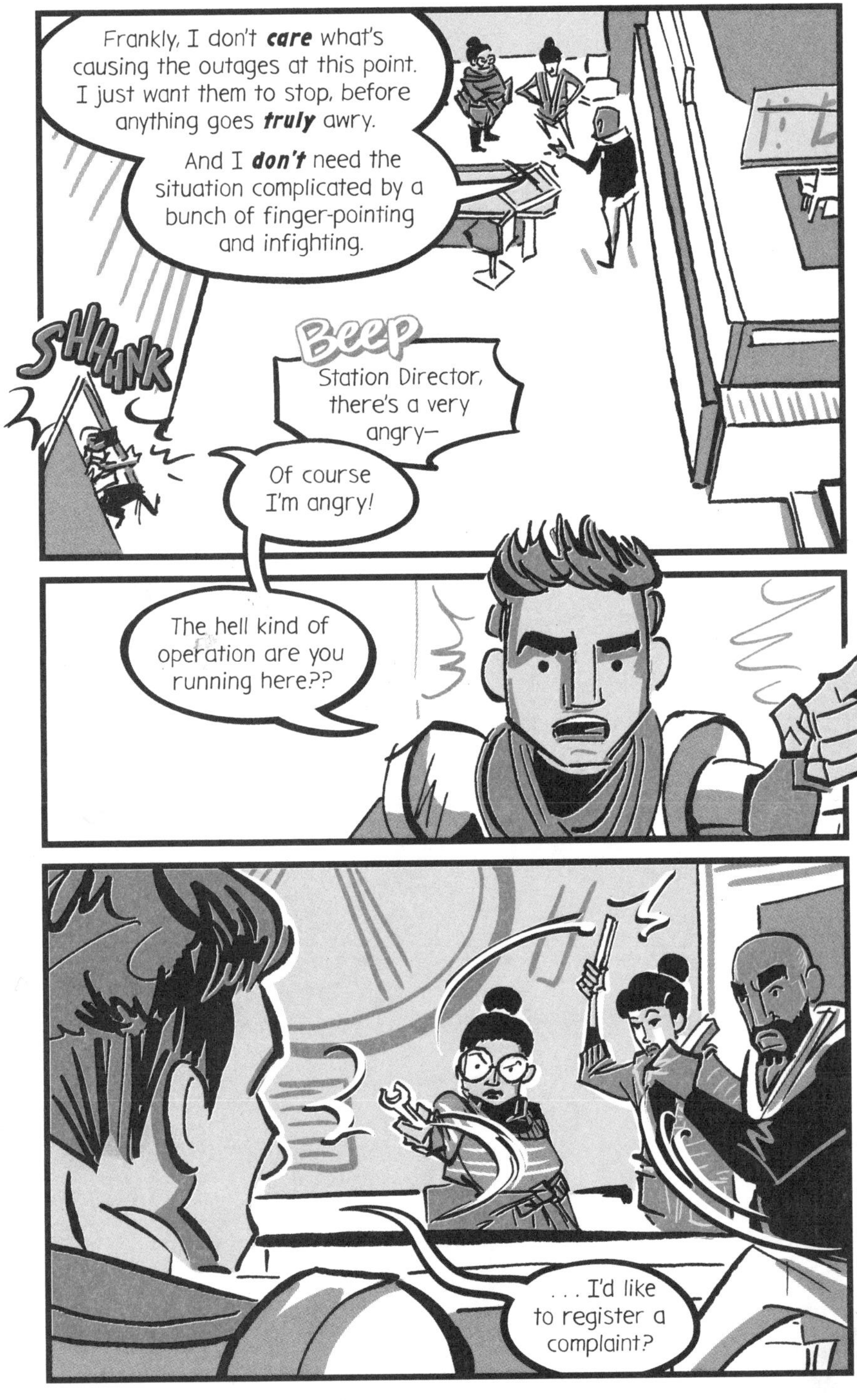
Frankly, I don't **care** what's causing the outages at this point. I just want them to stop, before anything goes **truly** awry.
And I **don't** need the situation complicated by a bunch of finger-pointing and infighting.
SHHHNK
Beep
Station Director, there's a very angry—
Of course I'm angry!
The hell kind of operation are you running here??
. . . I'd like to register a complaint?

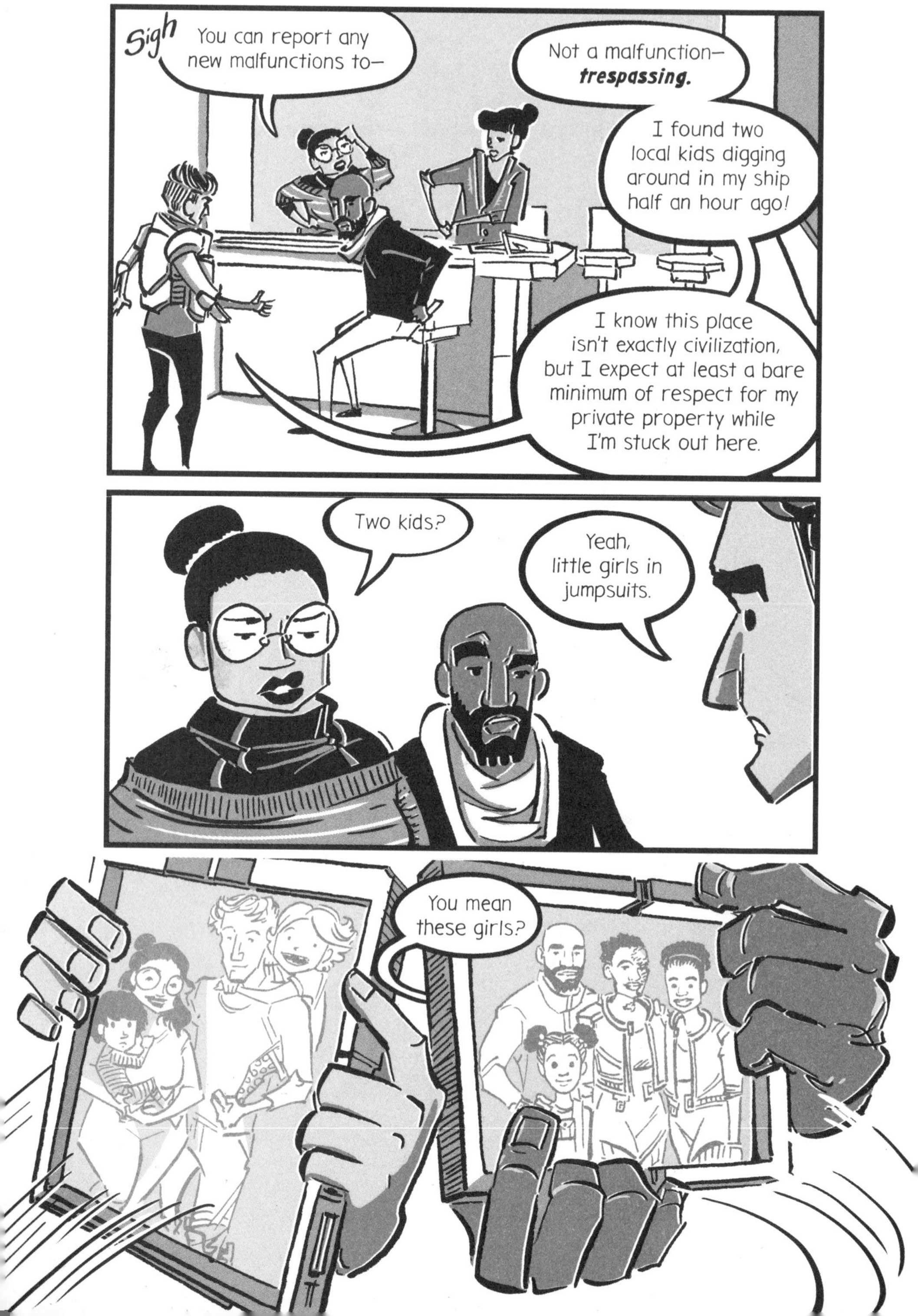
Sigh
You can report any new malfunctions to—
Not a malfunction— **trespassing.**
I found two local kids digging around in my ship half an hour ago!
I know this place isn't exactly civilization, but I expect at least a bare minimum of respect for my private property while I'm stuck out here.
Two kids?
Yeah, little girls in jumpsuits.
You mean these girls?

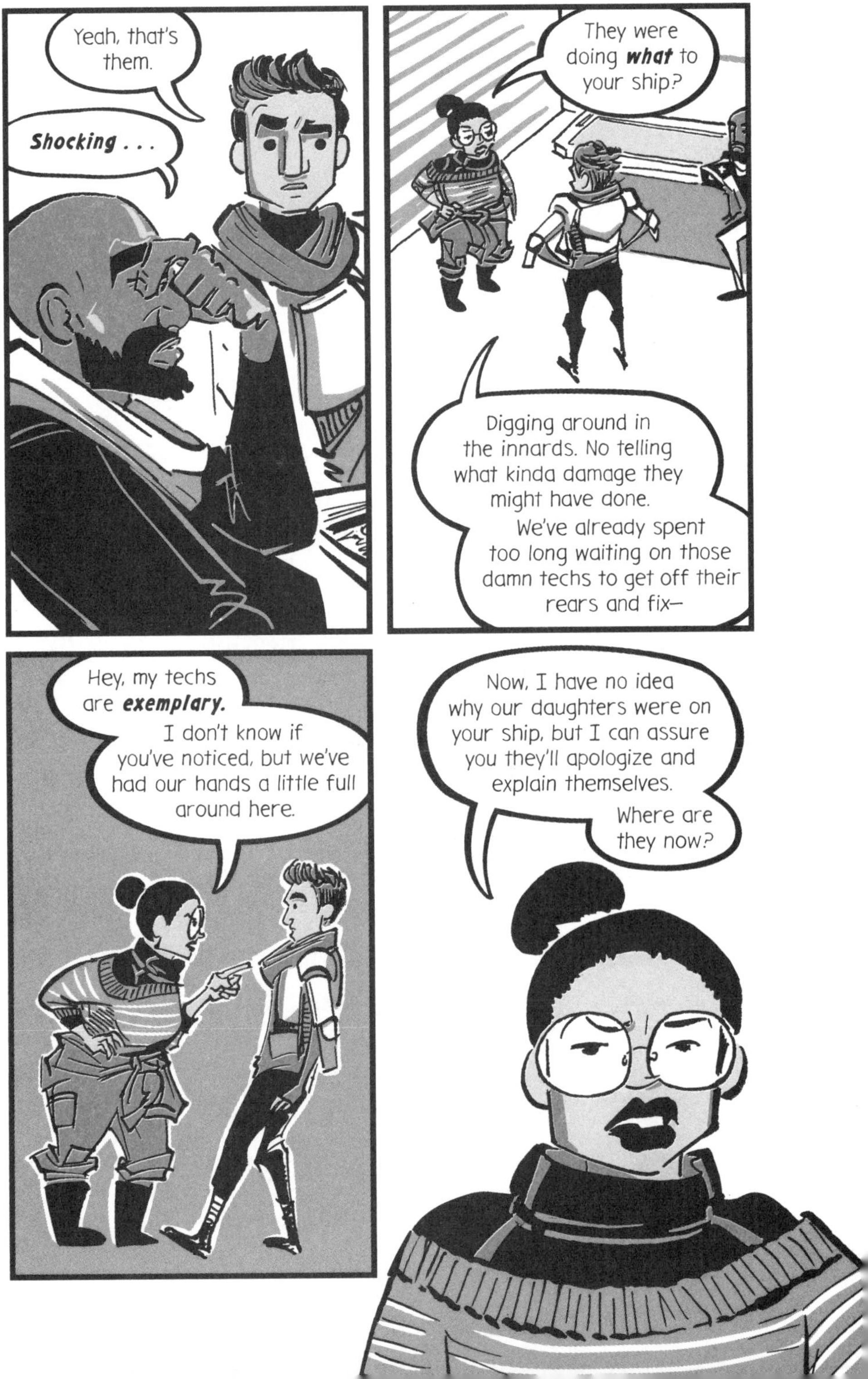
Yeah, that's them.
Shocking . . .
They were doing **what** to your ship?
Digging around in the innards. No telling what kinda damage they might have done.
We've already spent too long waiting on those damn techs to get off their rears and fix—
Hey, my techs are **exemplary.**
I don't know if you've noticed, but we've had our hands a little full around here.
Now, I have no idea why our daughters were on your ship, but I can assure you they'll apologize and explain themselves.
Where are they now?

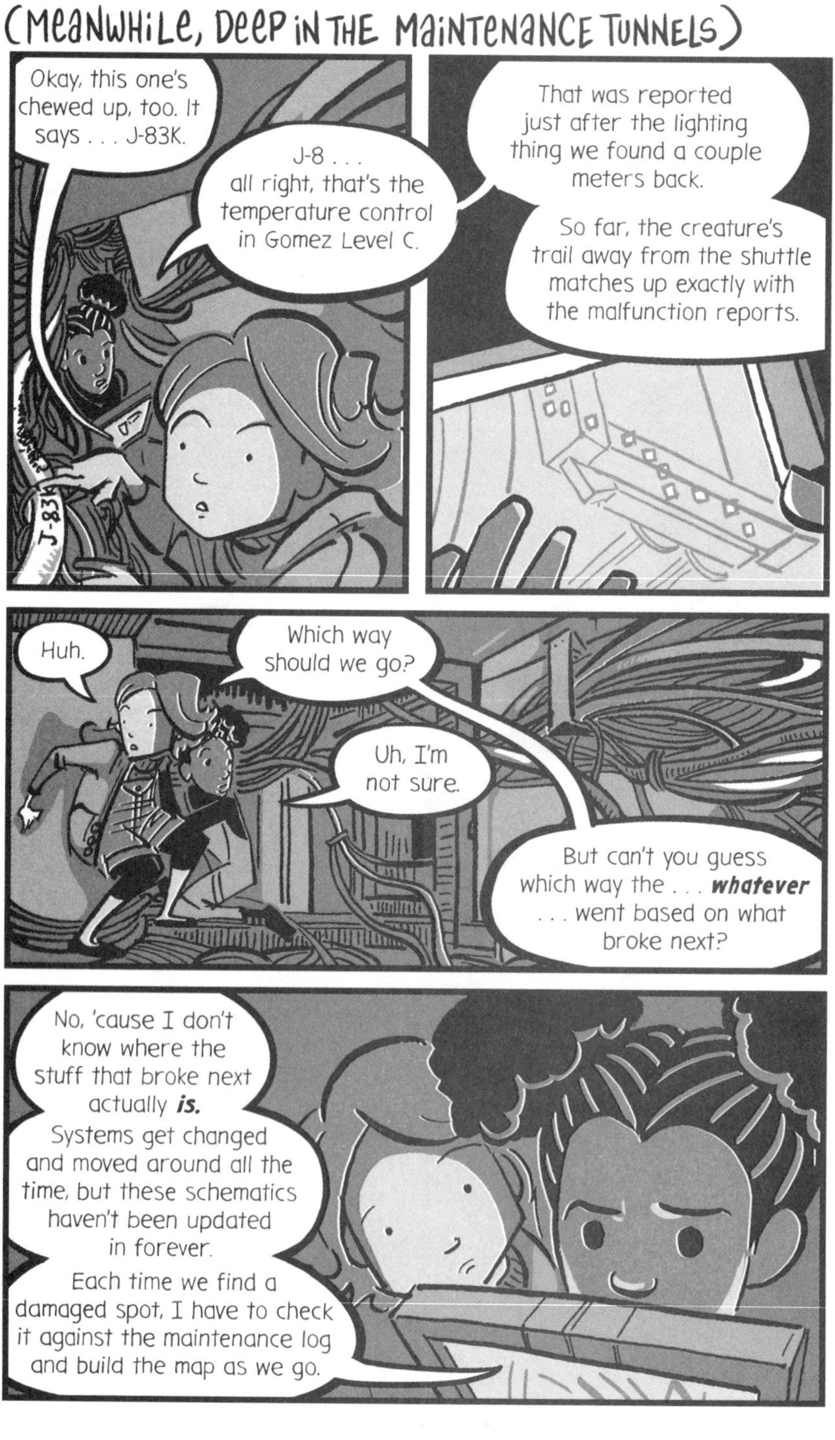
(MEANWHILE, DEEP IN THE MAINTENANCE TUNNELS)
Okay, this one's chewed up, too. It says . . . J-83K.
J-83K
J-8 . . . all right, that's the temperature control in Gomez Level C.
That was reported just after the lighting thing we found a couple meters back.
So far, the creature's trail away from the shuttle matches up exactly with the malfunction reports.
Huh.
Which way should we go?
Uh, I'm not sure.
But can't you guess which way the . . . ***whatever*** . . . went based on what broke next?
No, 'cause I don't know where the stuff that broke next actually ***is.***
Systems get changed and moved around all the time, but these schematics haven't been updated in forever.
Each time we find a damaged spot, I have to check it against the maintenance log and build the map as we go.

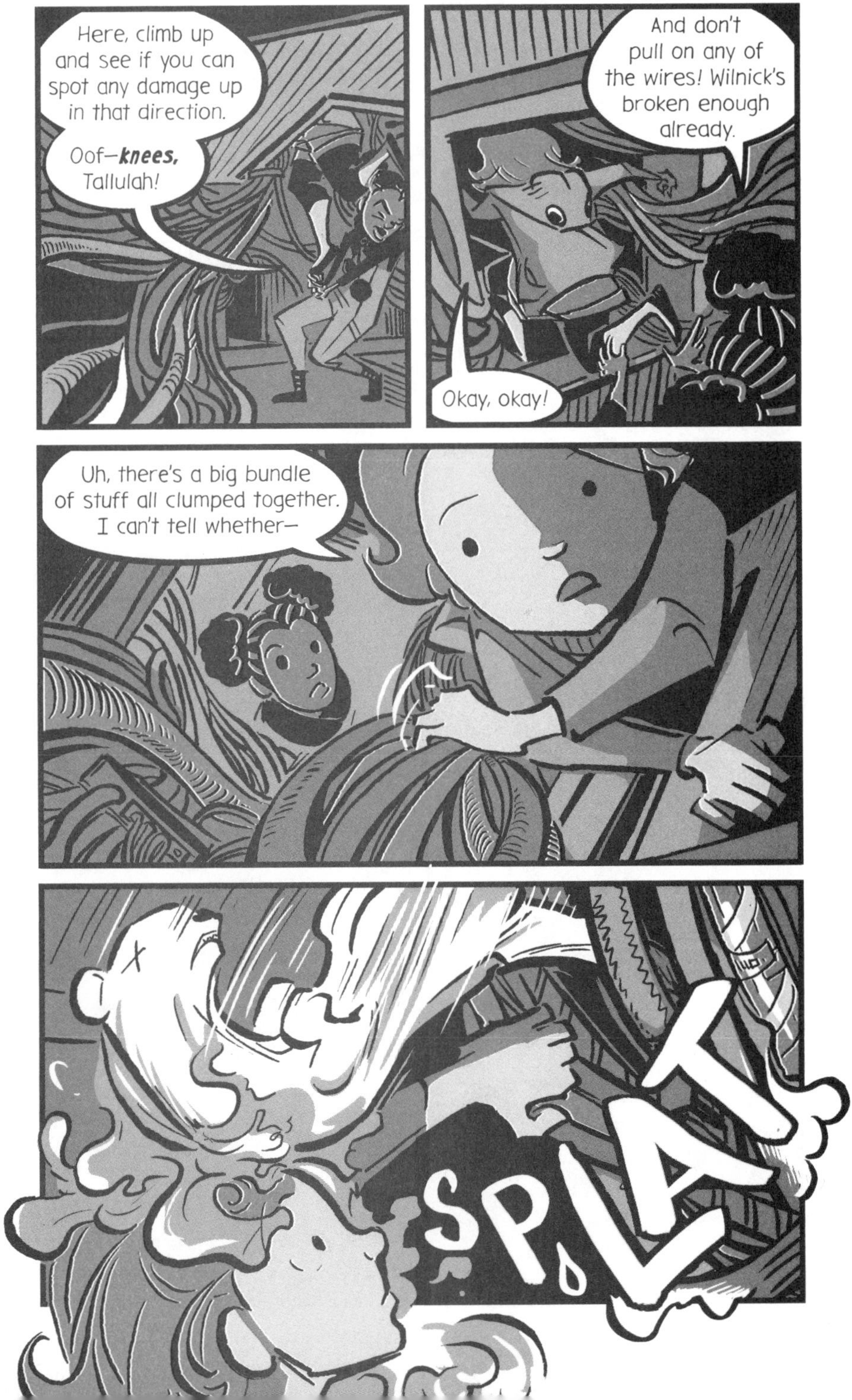
Here, climb up and see if you can spot any damage up in that direction.
Oof—**knees,** Tallulah!
And don't pull on any of the wires! Wilnick's broken enough already.
Okay, okay!
Uh, there's a big bundle of stuff all clumped together. I can't tell whether—
SPLAT

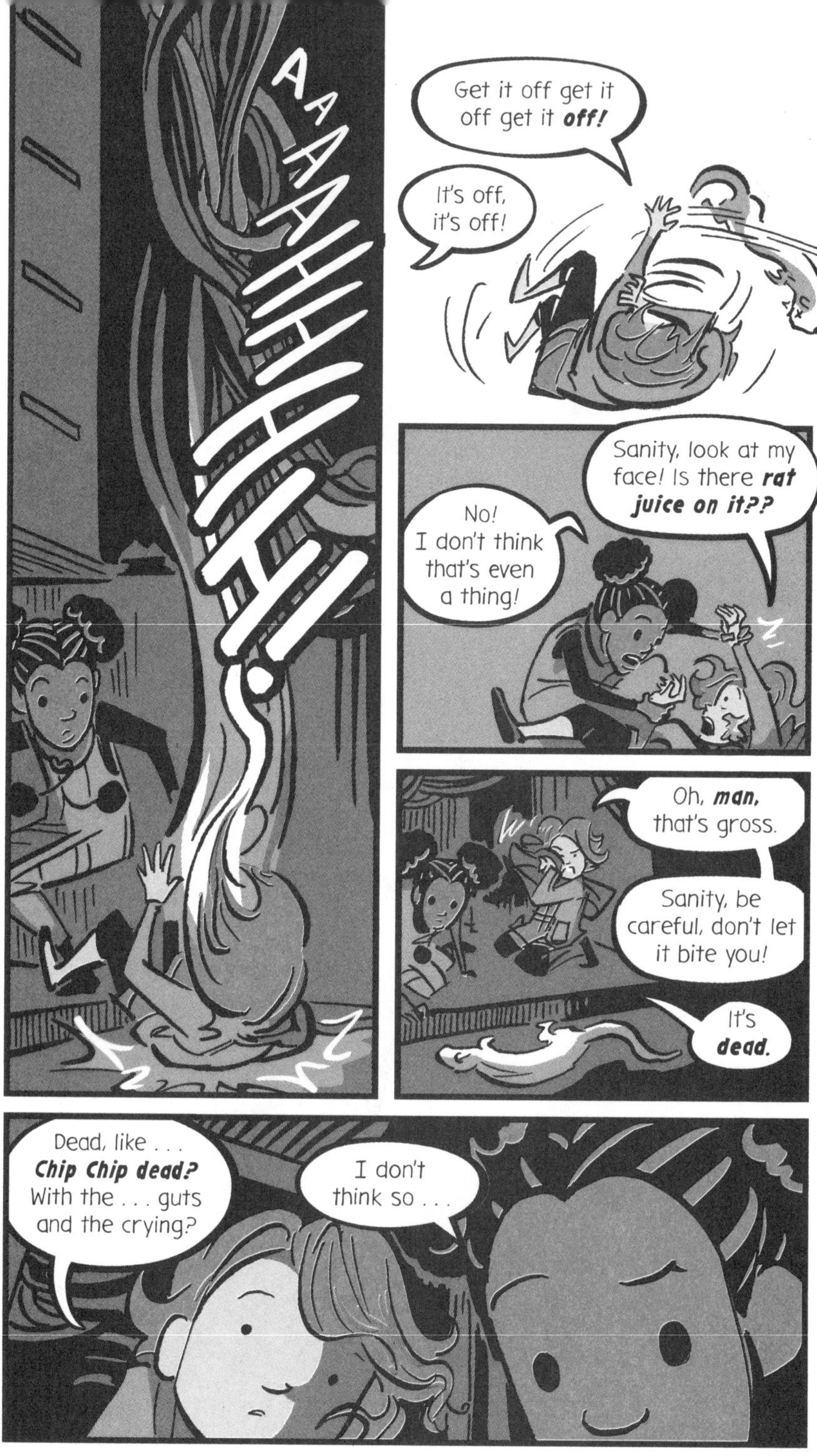

AAAAHHHHHHH!
Get it off get it off get it **off!**
It's off, it's off!
Sanity, look at my face! Is there **rat juice on it??**
No! I don't think that's even a thing!
Oh, **man,** that's gross.
Sanity, be careful, don't let it bite you!
It's **dead.**
Dead, like . . . **Chip Chip dead?** With the . . . guts and the crying?
I don't think so . . .

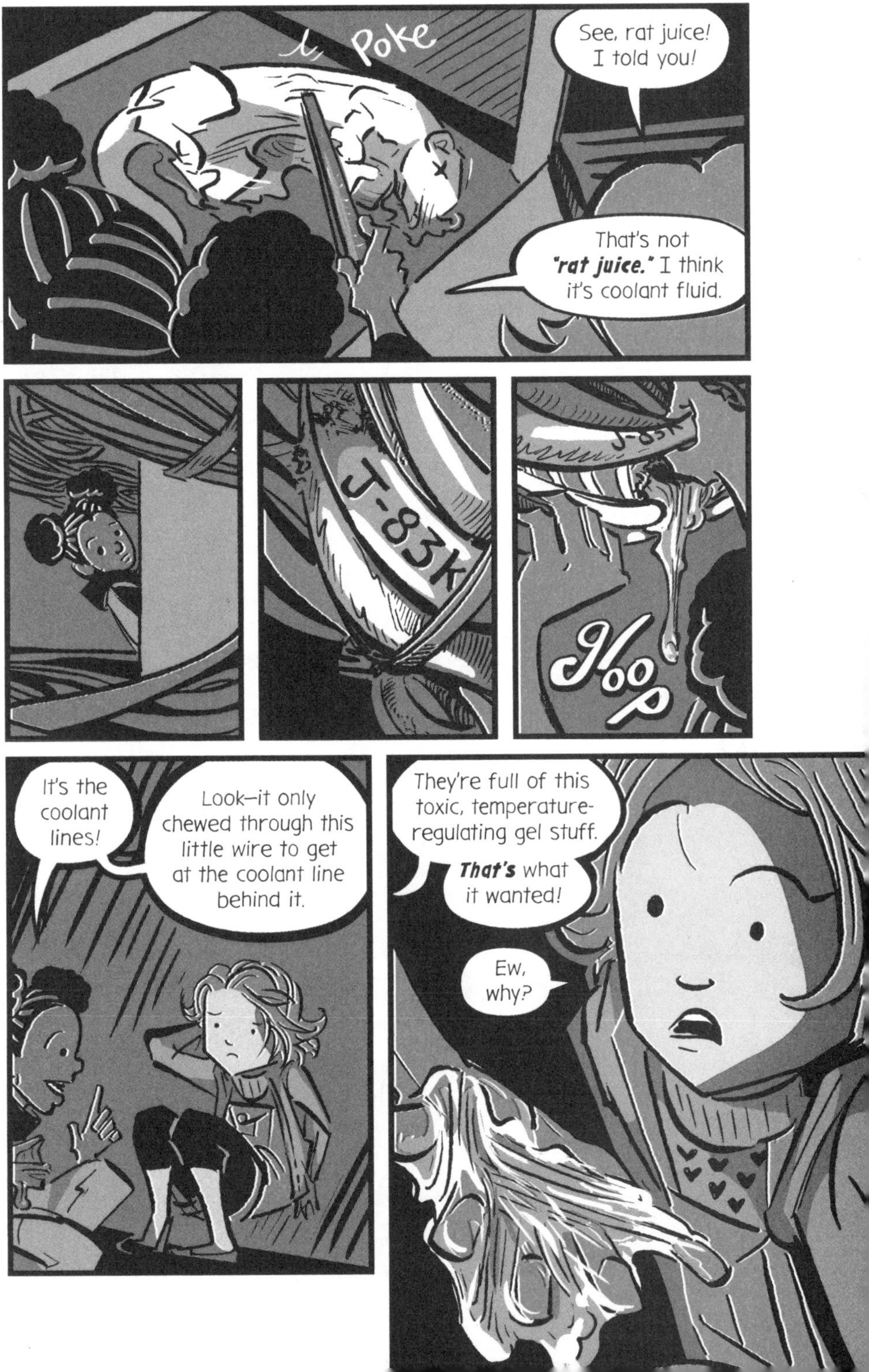
Poke
See, rat juice! I told you!
That's not **"rat juice."** I think it's coolant fluid.
J-83K
J-83K
Gloop
It's the coolant lines!
Look—it only chewed through this little wire to get at the coolant line behind it.
They're full of this toxic, temperature-regulating gel stuff.
***That's*** what it wanted!
Ew, why?

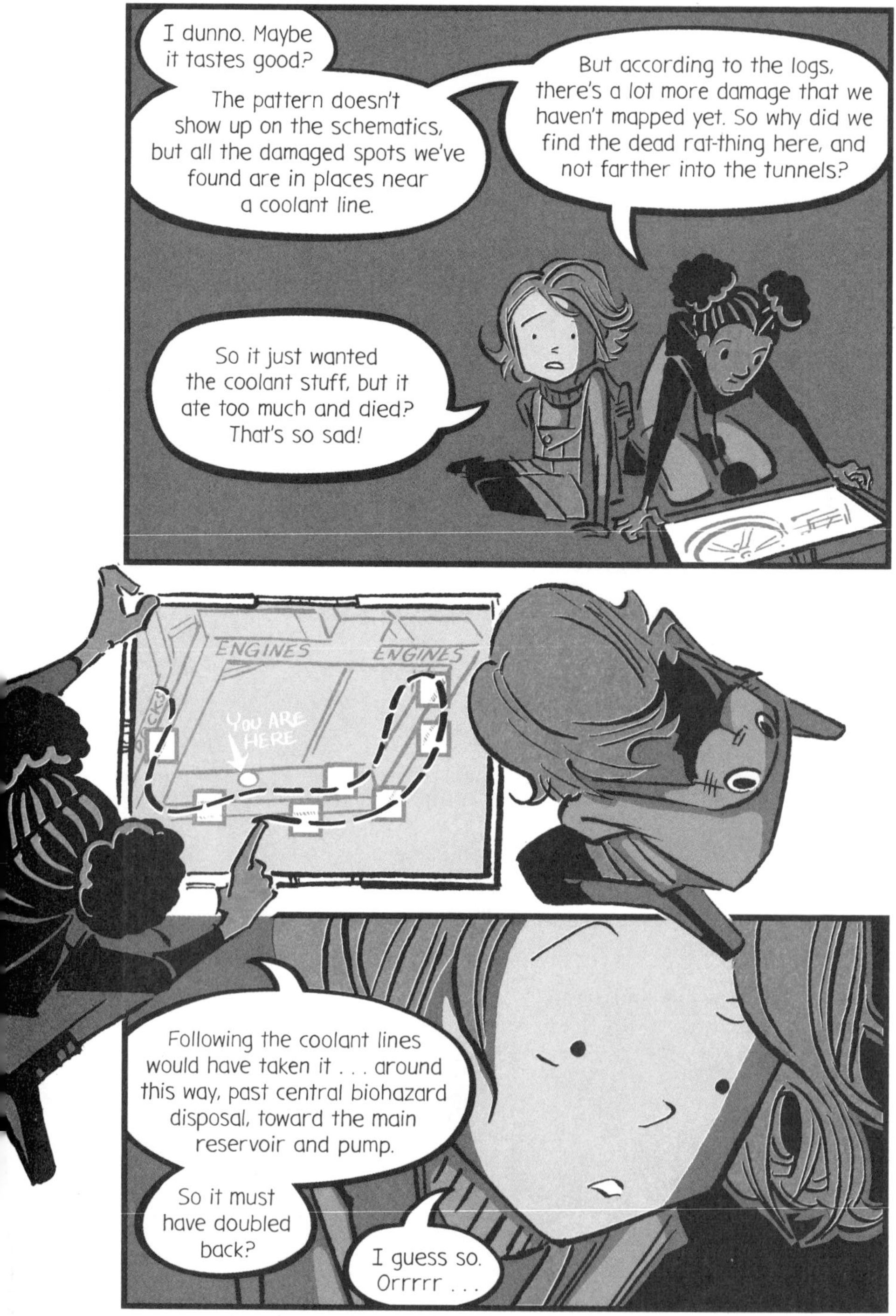
I dunno. Maybe it tastes good?
The pattern doesn't show up on the schematics, but all the damaged spots we've found are in places near a coolant line.
But according to the logs, there's a lot more damage that we haven't mapped yet. So why did we find the dead rat-thing here, and not farther into the tunnels?
So it just wanted the coolant stuff, but it ate too much and died? That's so sad!
ENGINES
ENGINES
YOU ARE HERE
Following the coolant lines would have taken it . . . around this way, past central biohazard disposal, toward the main reservoir and pump.
So it must have doubled back?
I guess so. Orrrrr . . .

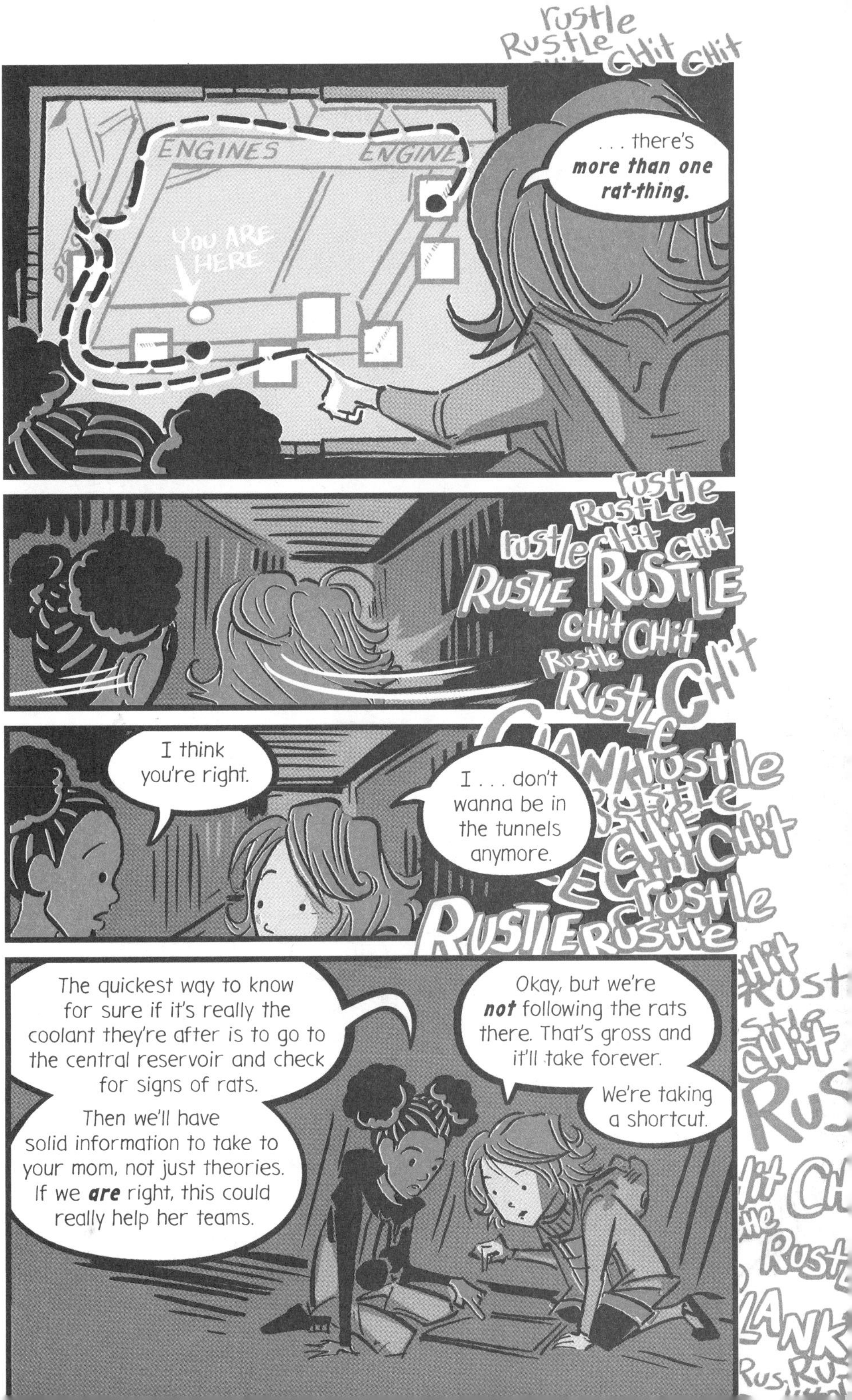
rustle
RUSTLE
CHIT CHIT
ENGINES
ENGINE
YOU ARE HERE
. . . there's **more than one rat-thing.**
rustle
RUSTLE
rustle CHIT CHIT
RUSTLE RUSTLE
CHIT CHIT
Rustle
RUSTLE CHIT
I think you're right.
I . . . don't wanna be in the tunnels anymore.
rustle
CHIT CHIT
rustle
RUSTLE RUSTLE
The quickest way to know for sure if it's really the coolant they're after is to go to the central reservoir and check for signs of rats.
Then we'll have solid information to take to your mom, not just theories. If we ***are*** right, this could really help her teams.
Okay, but we're ***not*** following the rats there. That's gross and it'll take forever.
We're taking a shortcut.
CHIT
RUST
CHIT
RUS
CH
Rust
LANK
RUS, RU

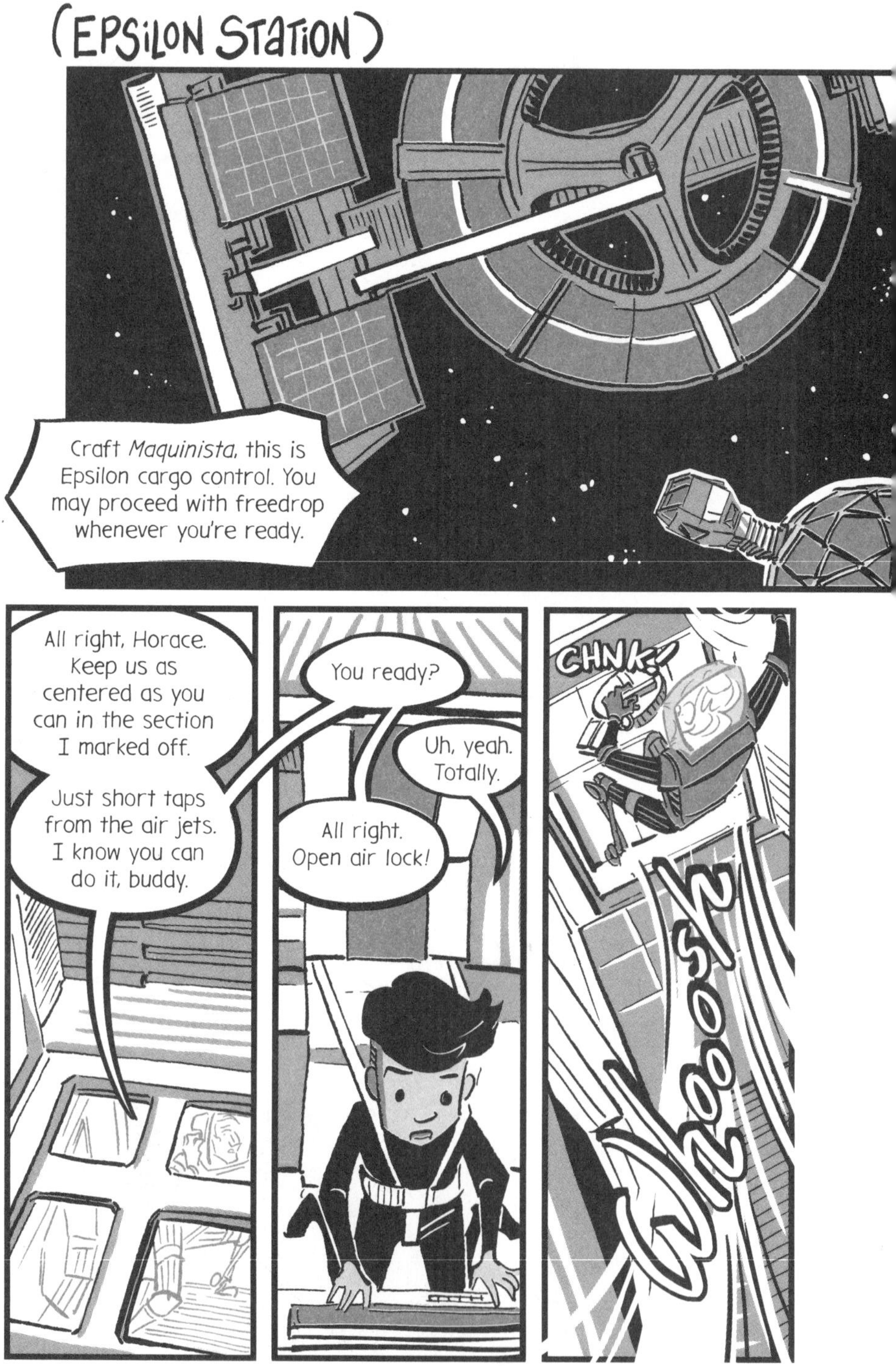
(EPSILON STATION)
Craft *Maquinista*, this is Epsilon cargo control. You may proceed with freedrop whenever you're ready.
All right, Horace. Keep us as centered as you can in the section I marked off.
Just short taps from the air jets. I know you can do it, buddy.
You ready?
Uh, yeah. Totally.
All right. Open air lock!
CHNK!
whoooosh

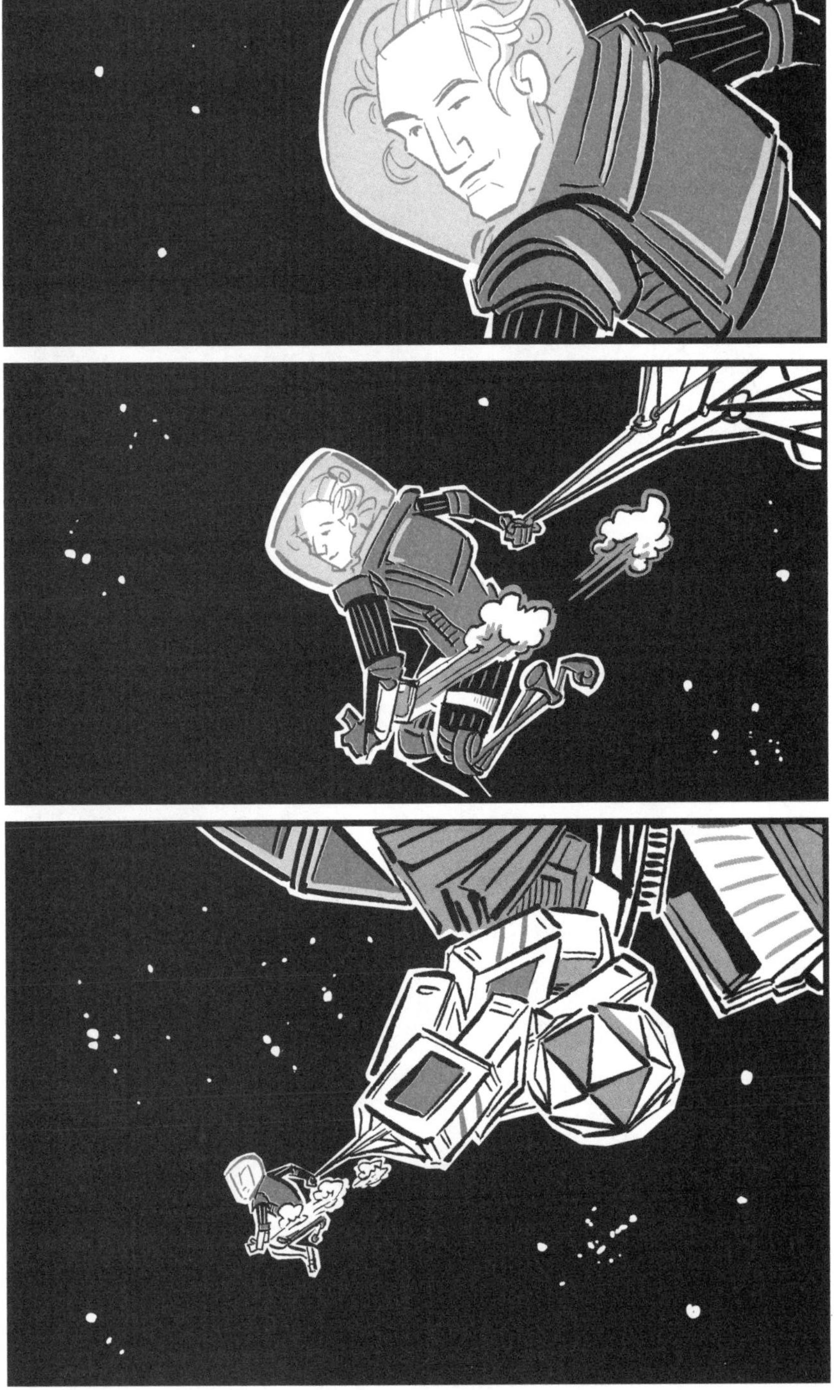

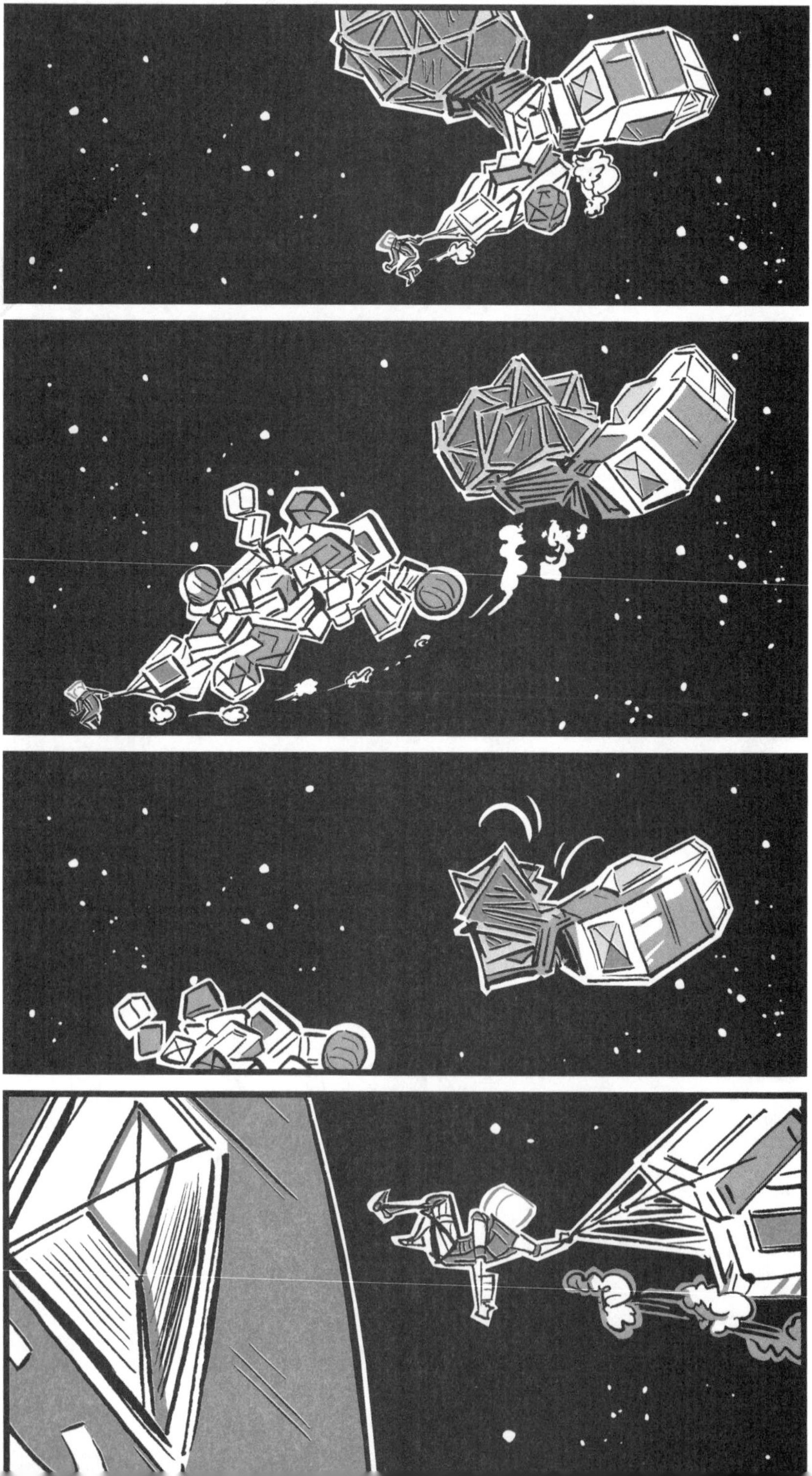

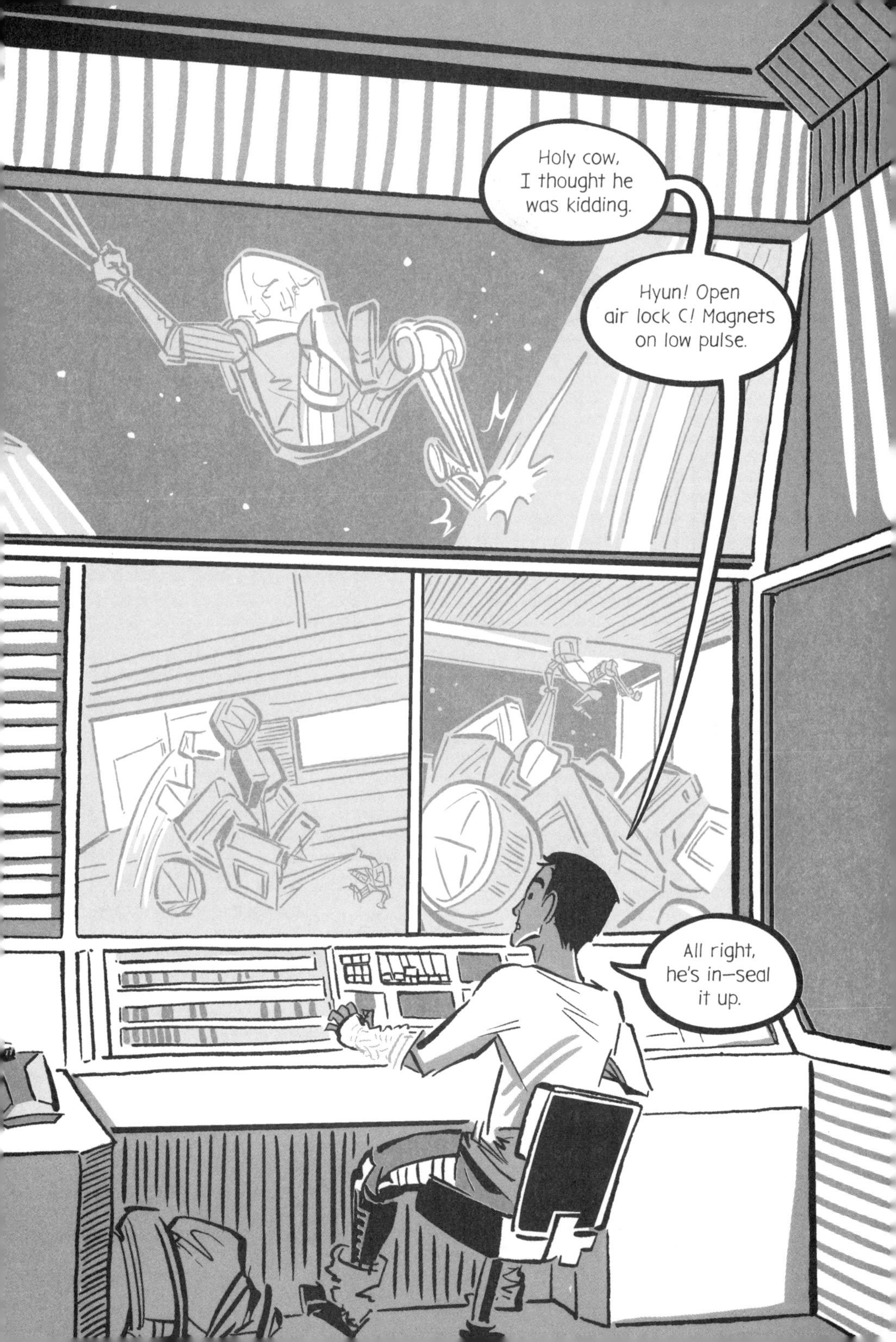
Holy cow, I thought he was kidding.
Hyun! Open air lock C! Magnets on low pulse.
All right, he's in—seal it up.

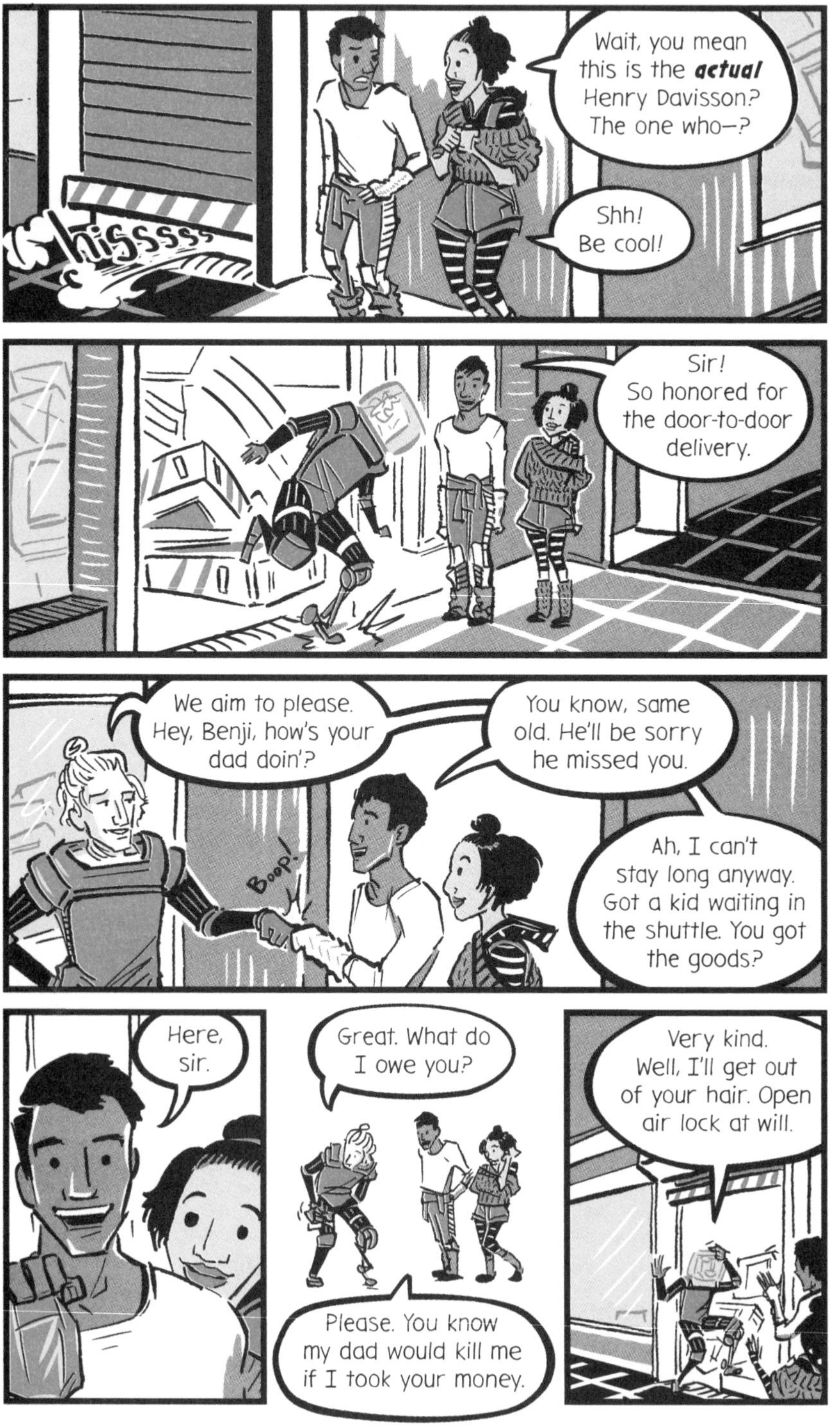
hissss
Wait, you mean this is the ***actual*** Henry Davisson? The one who—?
Shh! Be cool!
Sir! So honored for the door-to-door delivery.
We aim to please. Hey, Benji, how's your dad doin'?
You know, same old. He'll be sorry he missed you.
Boop!
Ah, I can't stay long anyway. Got a kid waiting in the shuttle. You got the goods?
Here, sir.
Great. What do I owe you?
Please. You know my dad would kill me if I took your money.
Very kind. Well, I'll get out of your hair. Open air lock at will.

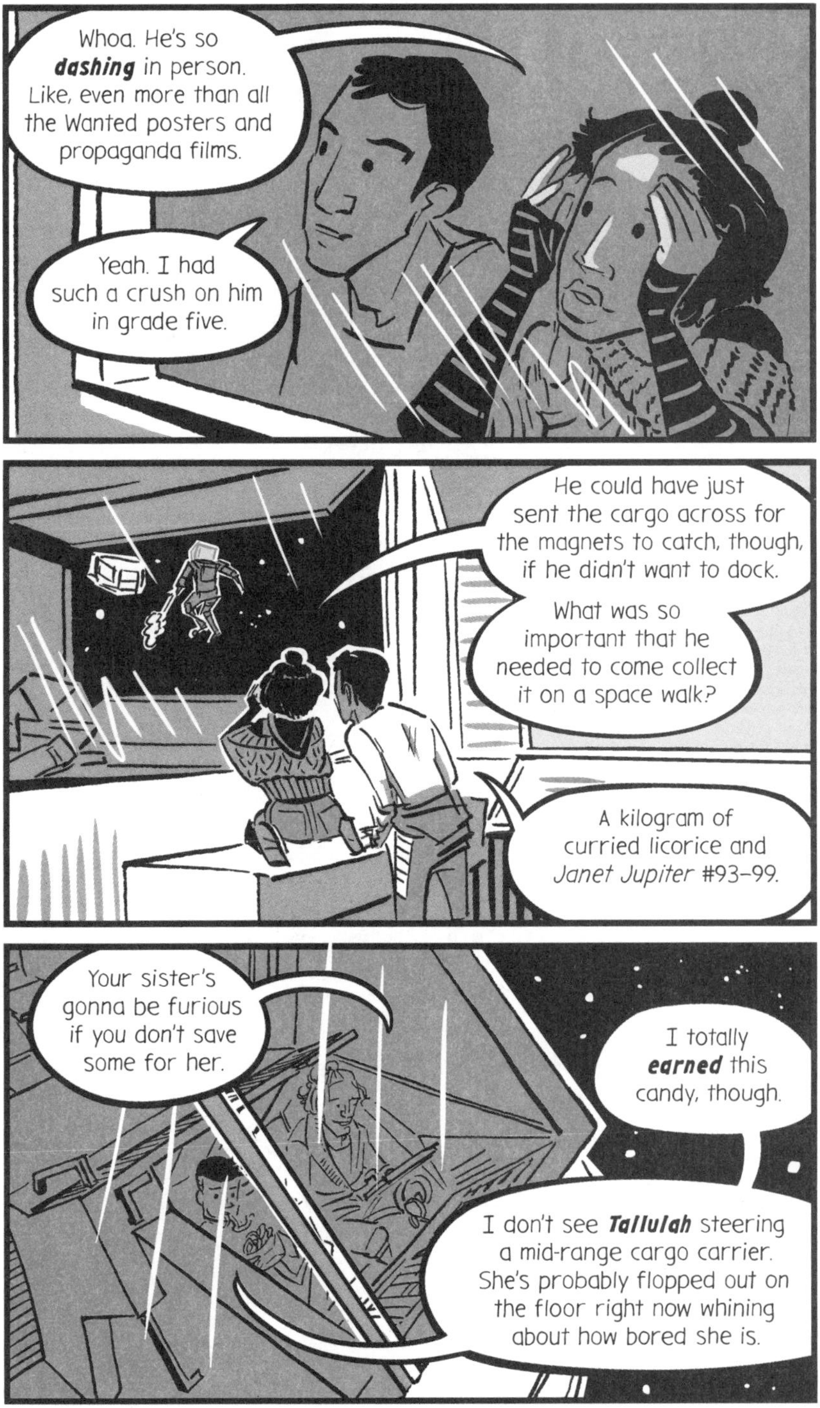
Whoa. He's so **dashing** in person. Like, even more than all the Wanted posters and propaganda films.
Yeah. I had such a crush on him in grade five.
He could have just sent the cargo across for the magnets to catch, though, if he didn't want to dock.
What was so important that he needed to come collect it on a space walk?
A kilogram of curried licorice and *Janet Jupiter* #93–99.
Your sister's gonna be furious if you don't save some for her.
I totally **earned** this candy, though.
I don't see **Tallulah** steering a mid-range cargo carrier. She's probably flopped out on the floor right now whining about how bored she is.

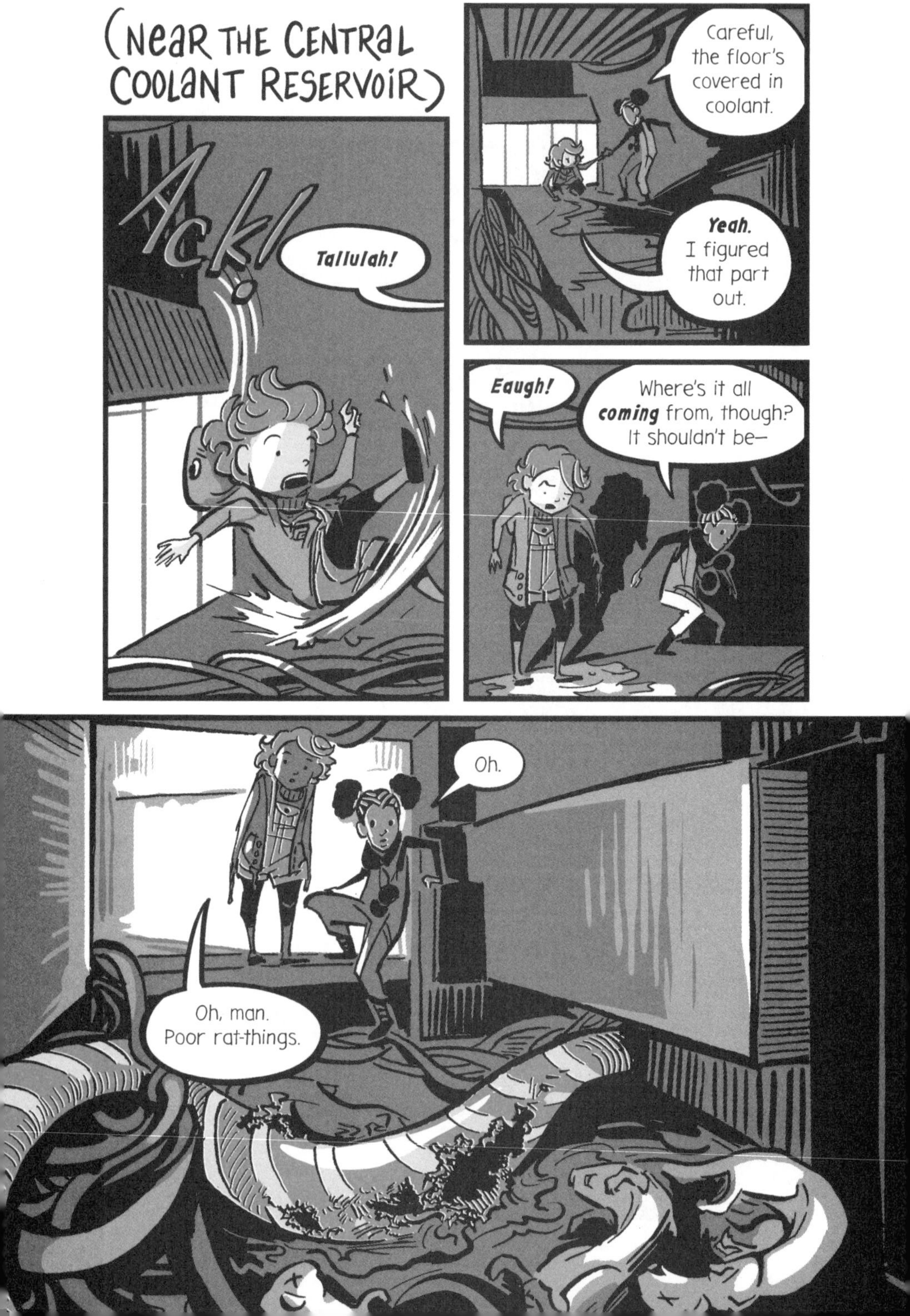
(Near the Central Coolant Reservoir)
Ack!
Tallulah!
Careful, the floor's covered in coolant.
Yeah. I figured that part out.
Eaugh!
Where's it all coming from, though? It shouldn't be—
Oh.
Oh, man. Poor rat-things.

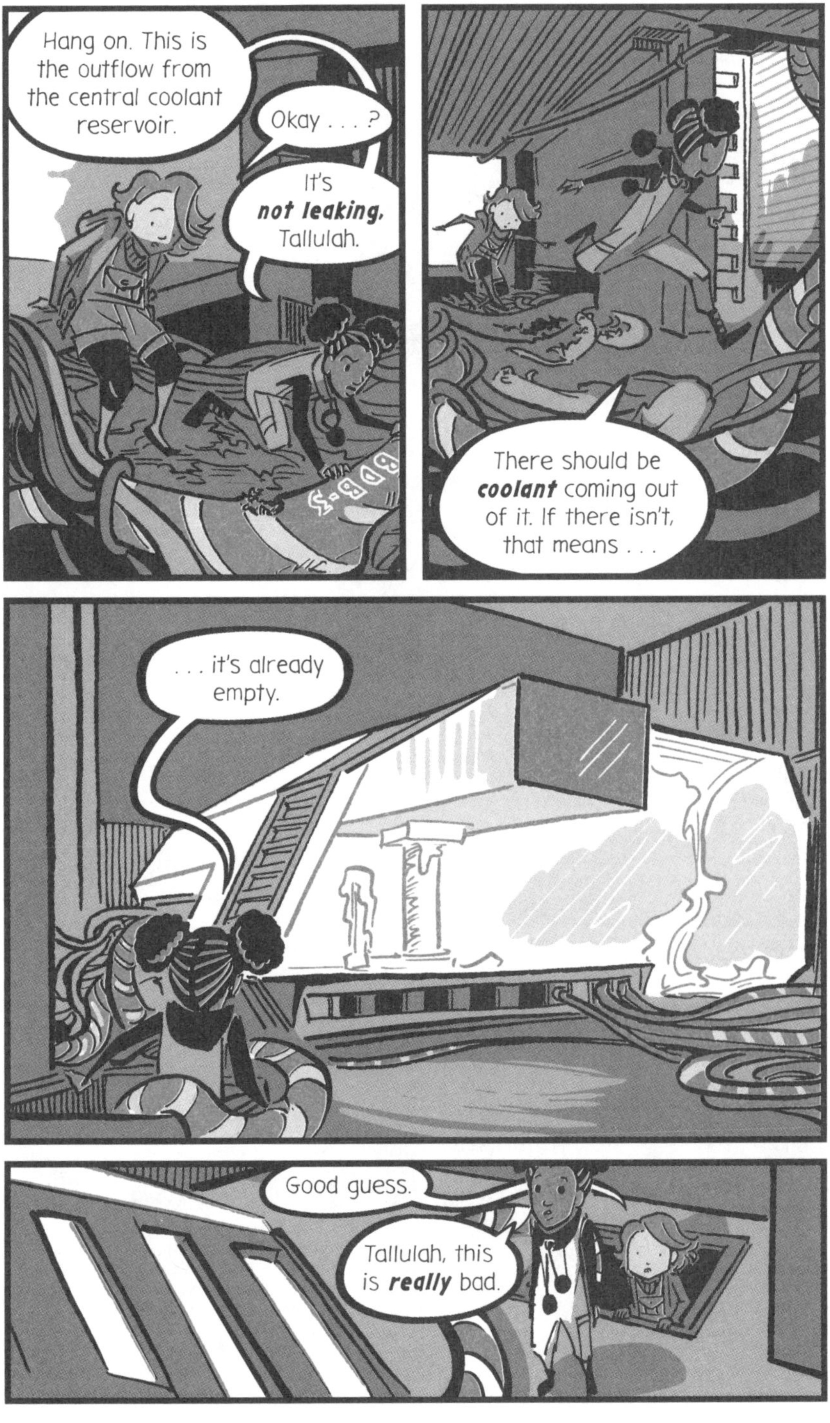
Hang on. This is the outflow from the central coolant reservoir.
Okay . . . ?
It's **not leaking,** Tallulah.
There should be **coolant** coming out of it. If there isn't, that means . . .
. . . it's already empty.
Good guess.
Tallulah, this is **really** bad.

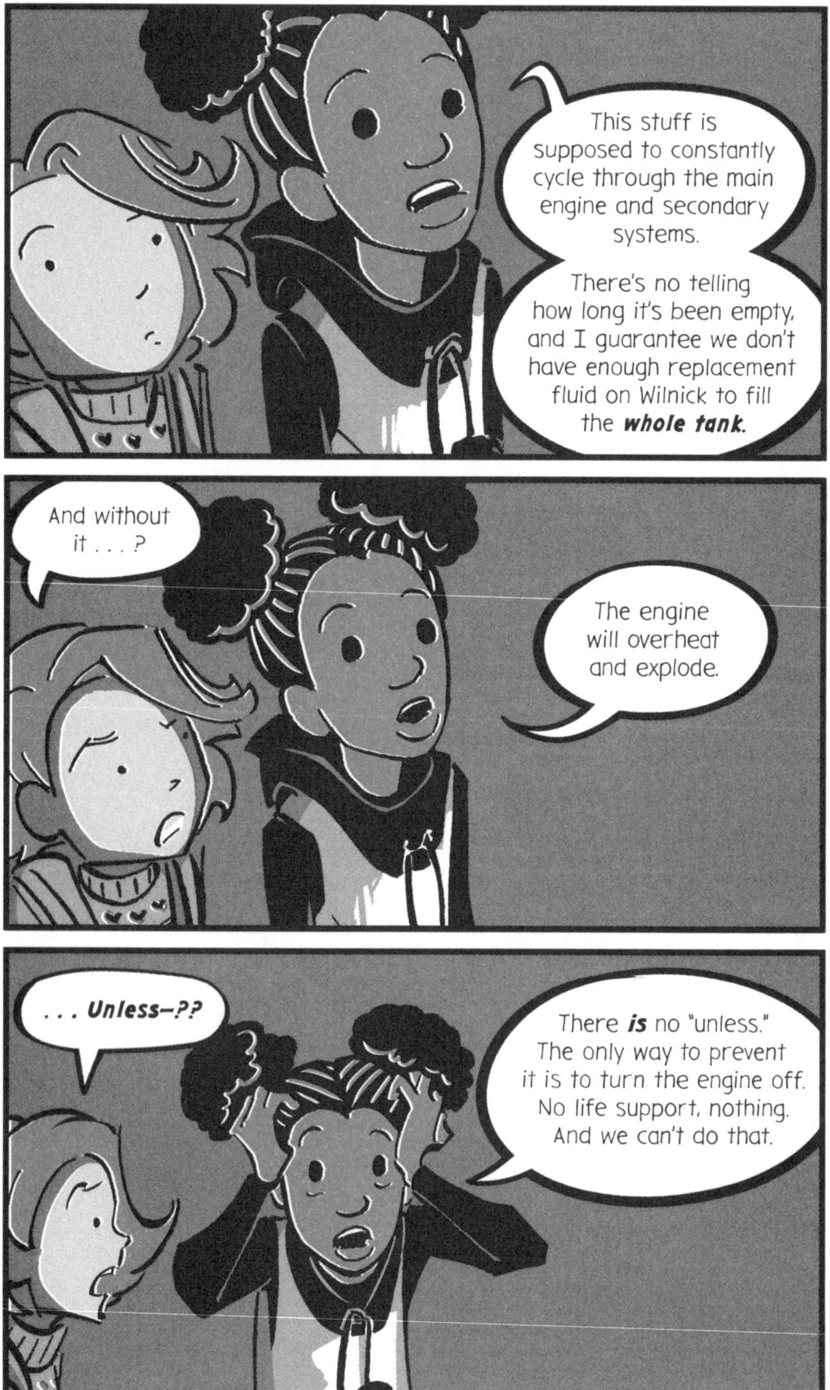
This stuff is supposed to constantly cycle through the main engine and secondary systems.
There's no telling how long it's been empty, and I guarantee we don't have enough replacement fluid on Wilnick to fill the ***whole tank.***
And without it . . . ?
The engine will overheat and explode.
***. . . Unless–??***
There ***is*** no "unless." The only way to prevent it is to turn the engine off. No life support, nothing. And we can't do that.

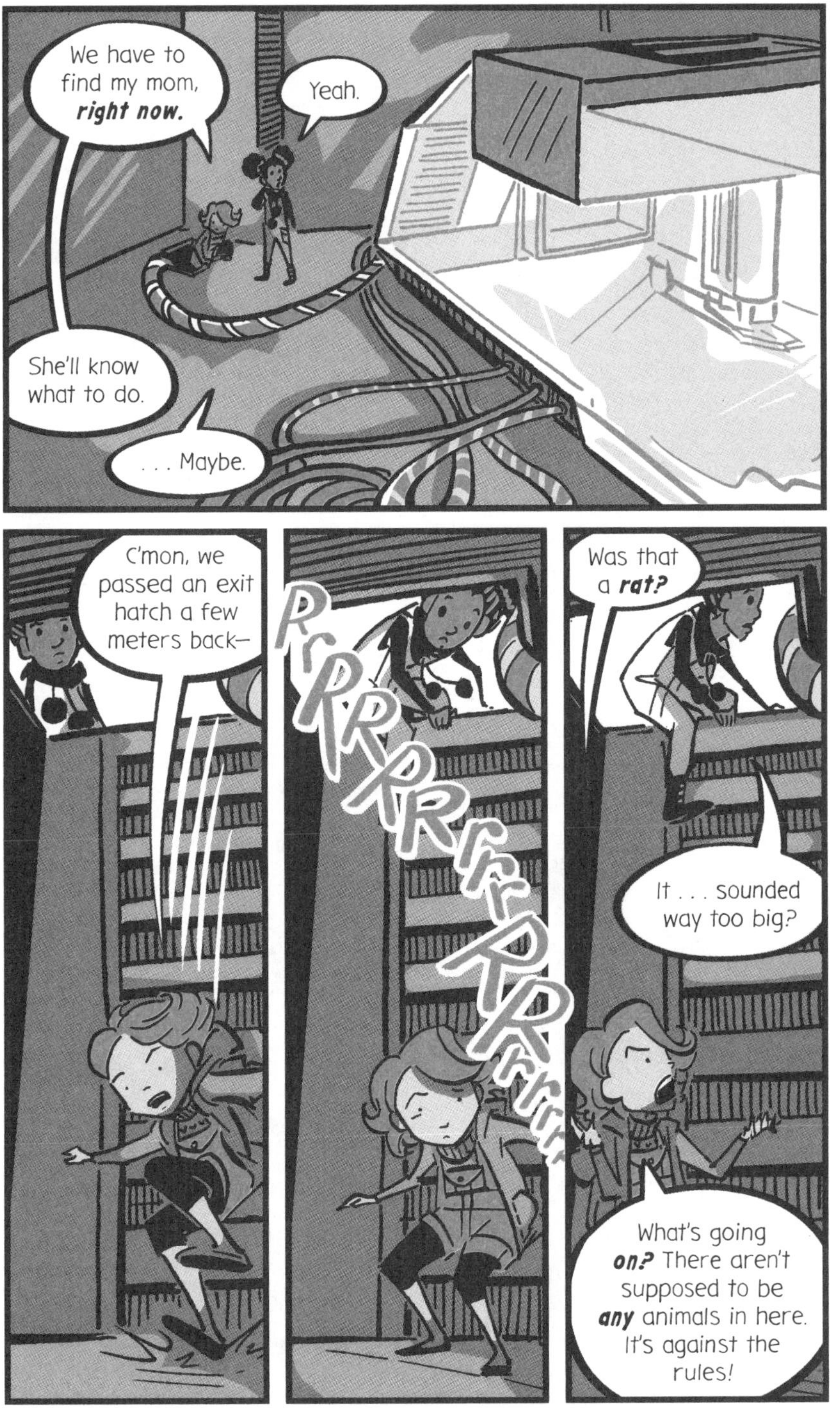
We have to find my mom, **right now.**
Yeah.
She'll know what to do.
. . . Maybe.
C'mon, we passed an exit hatch a few meters back—
RrRRRRrrrRRrrrr
Was that a **rat?**
It . . . sounded way too big?
What's going **on?** There aren't supposed to be **any** animals in here. It's against the rules!

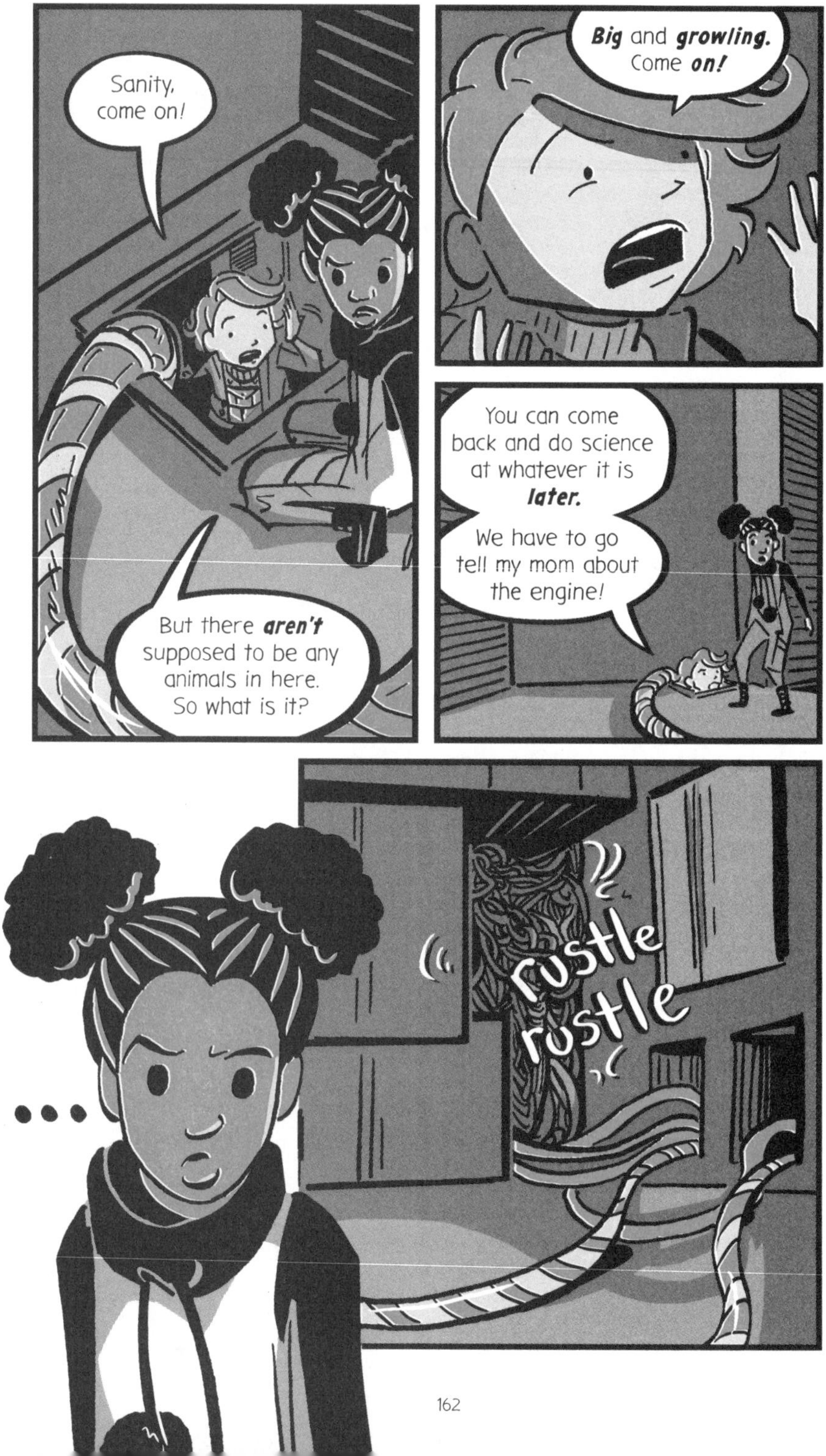
Sanity, come on!
But there **aren't** supposed to be any animals in here. So what is it?
**Big** and **growling.** Come **on!**
You can come back and do science at whatever it is **later.**
We have to go tell my mom about the engine!
rustle rustle
...

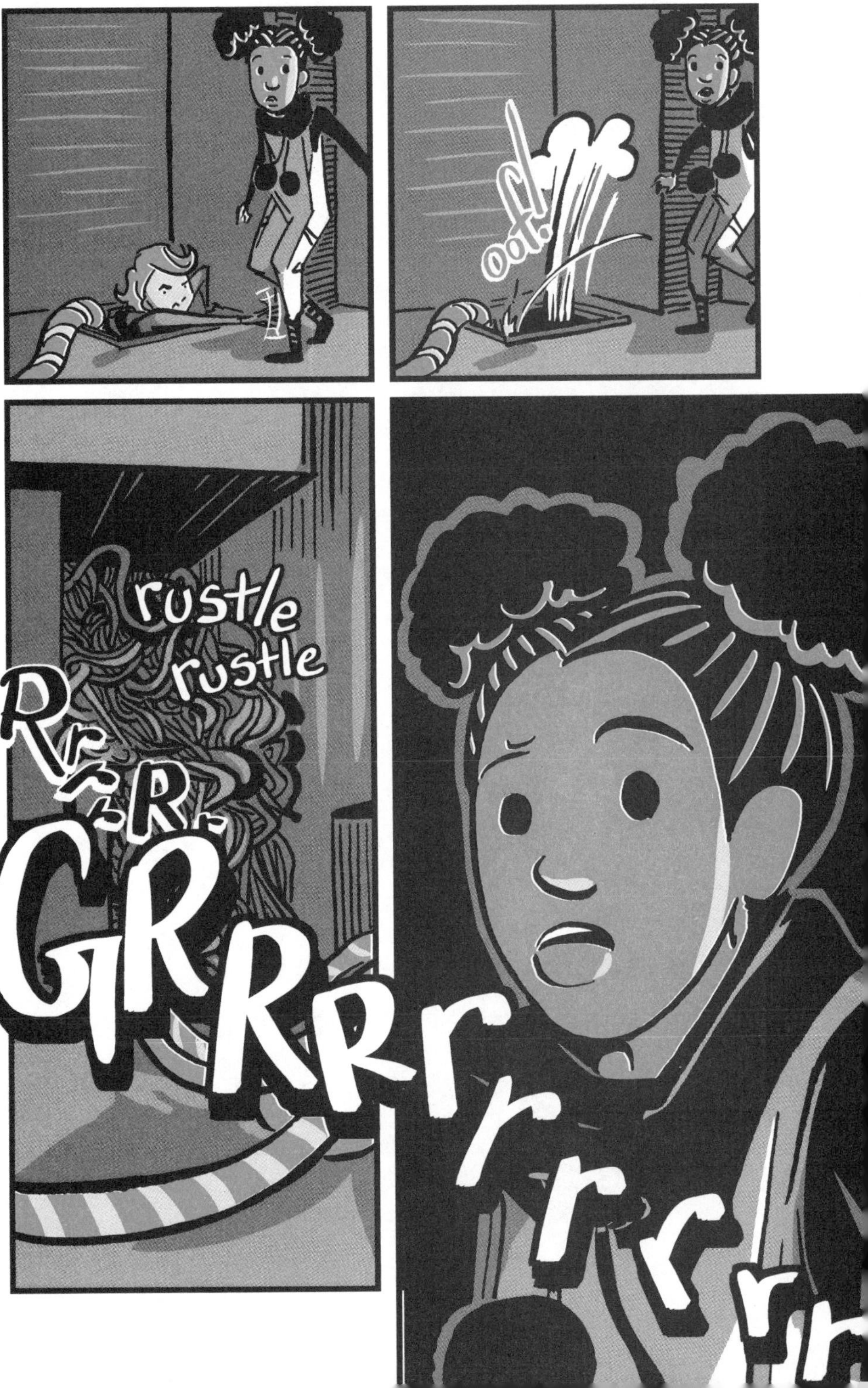
oof!
rustle
rustle
GRRRrrrr

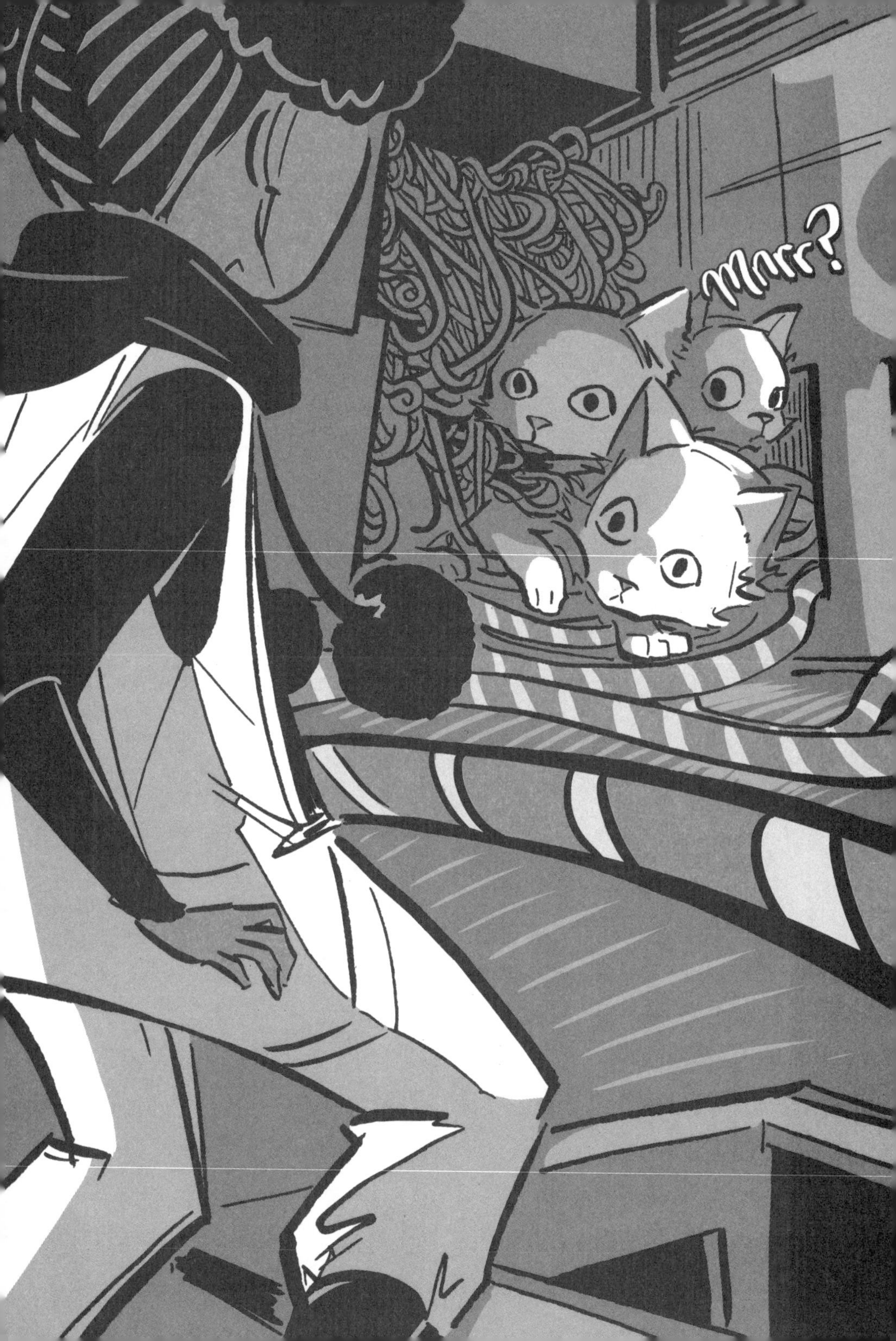
Mrrr?

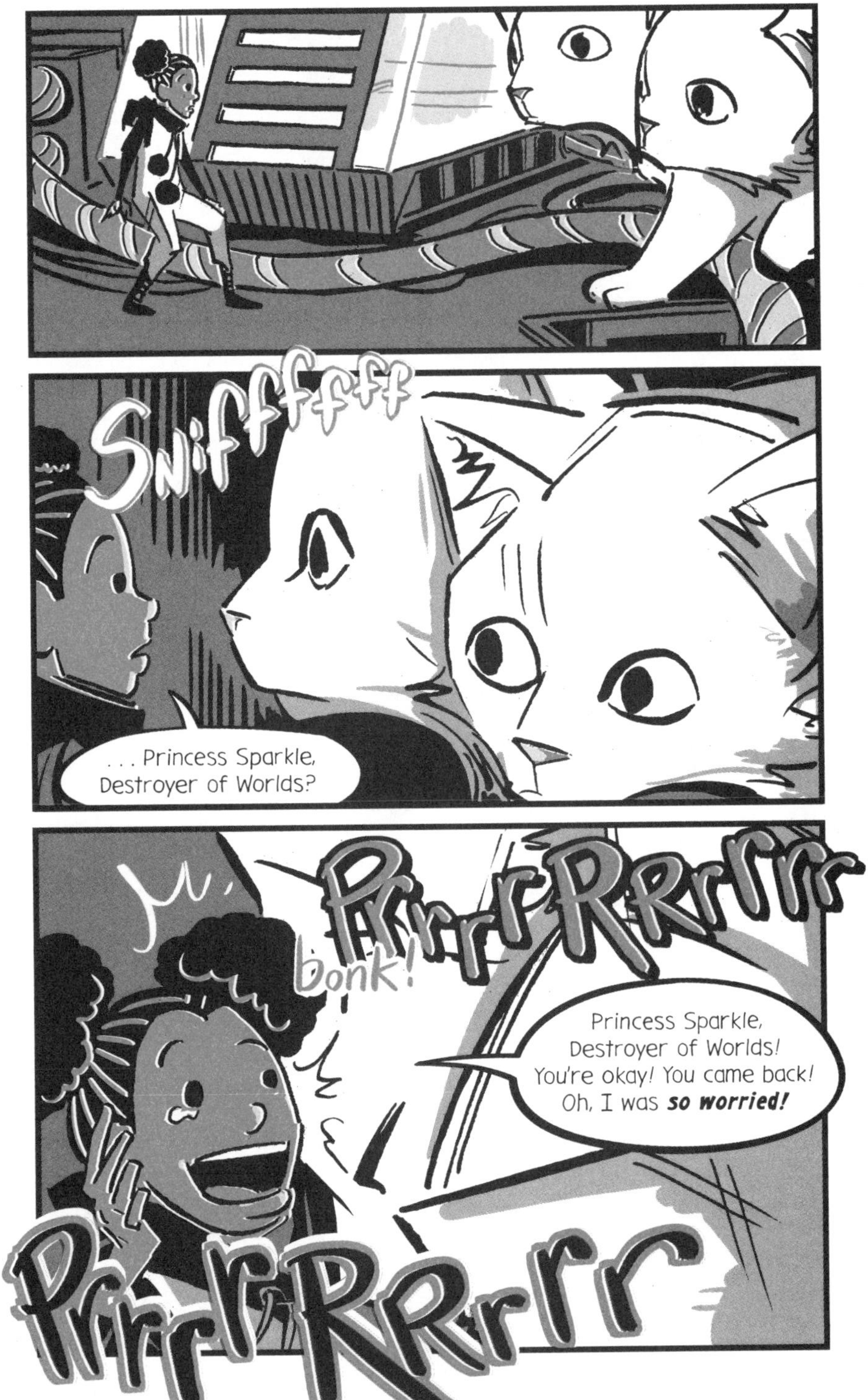
Sniffffff
. . . Princess Sparkle, Destroyer of Worlds?
PrrrrRRrrrr
bonk!
Princess Sparkle, Destroyer of Worlds! You're okay! You came back! Oh, I was ***so worried!***
PrrrrRRrrrr

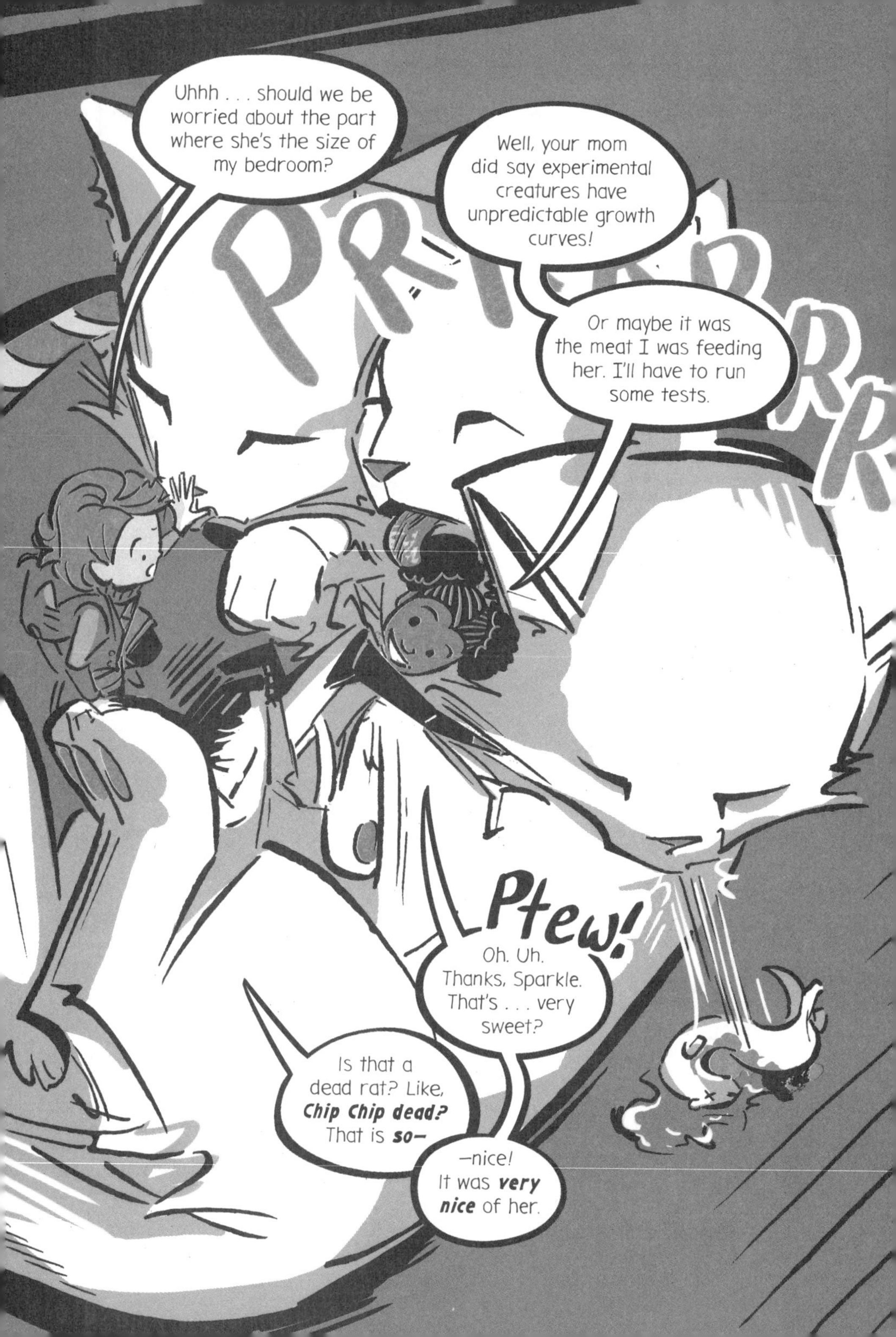
Uhhh . . . should we be worried about the part where she's the size of my bedroom?
Well, your mom did say experimental creatures have unpredictable growth curves!
PRRRRR
Or maybe it was the meat I was feeding her. I'll have to run some tests.
Ptew!
Oh. Uh. Thanks, Sparkle. That's . . . very sweet?
Is that a dead rat? Like, **Chip Chip dead?** That is **so—**
—nice! It was **very nice** of her.

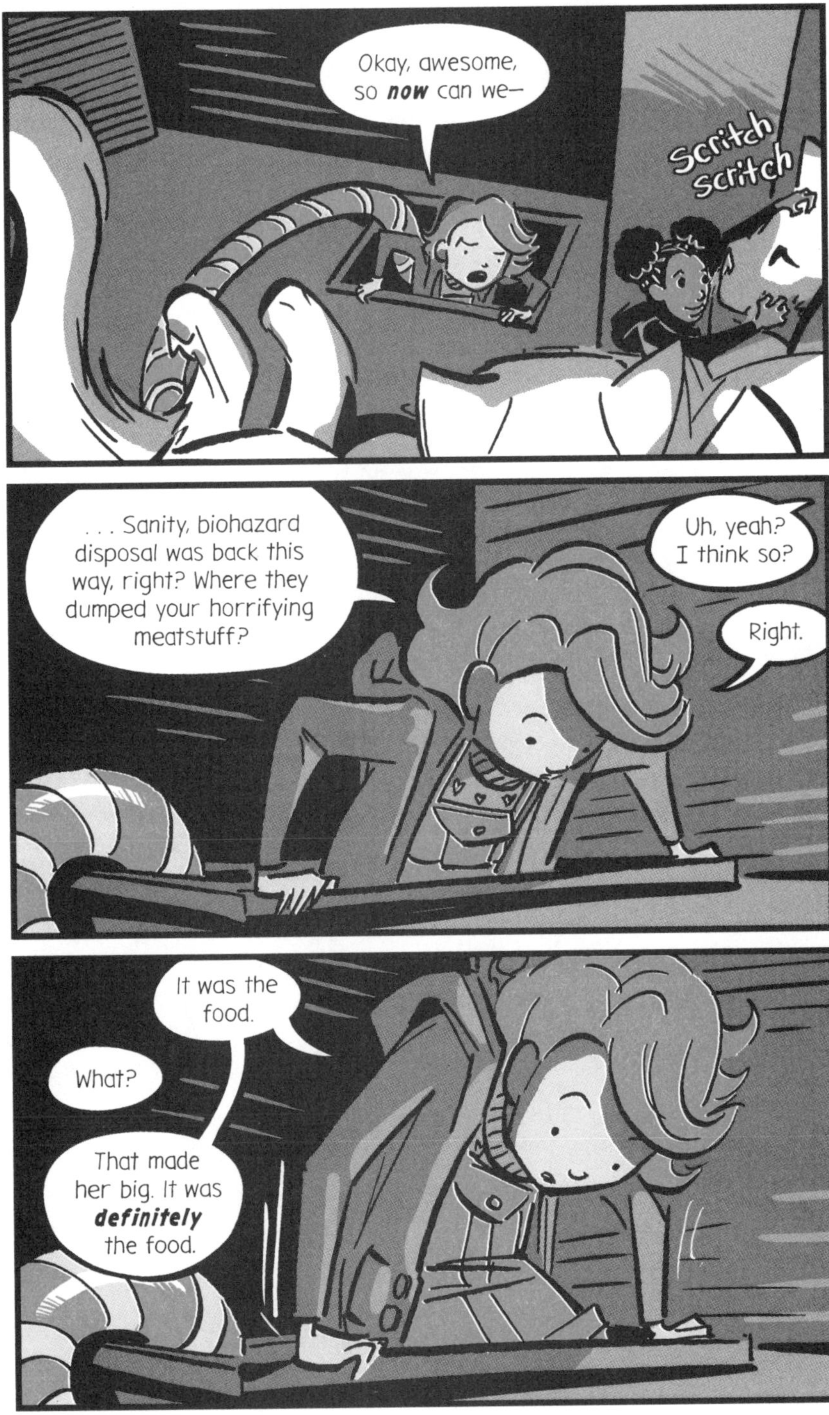
Okay, awesome, so **now** can we—
Scritch scritch
. . . Sanity, biohazard disposal was back this way, right? Where they dumped your horrifying meatstuff?
Uh, yeah? I think so?
Right.
It was the food.
What?
That made her big. It was ***definitely*** the food.

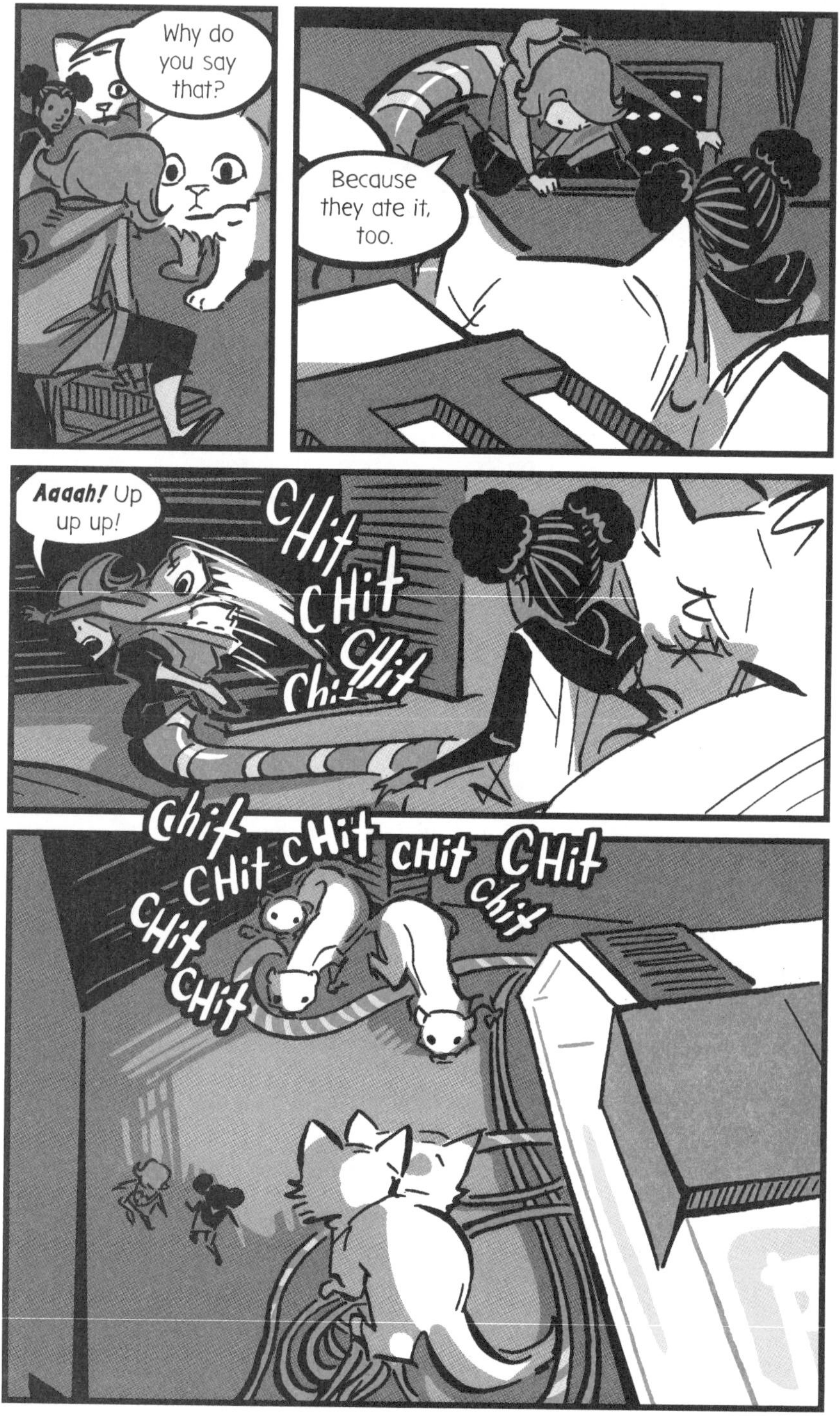
Why do you say that?
Because they ate it, too.
**Aaaah!** Up up up!
CHit CHit CHit Chit
Chit CHit CHit chit CHit CHit chit CHit CHit

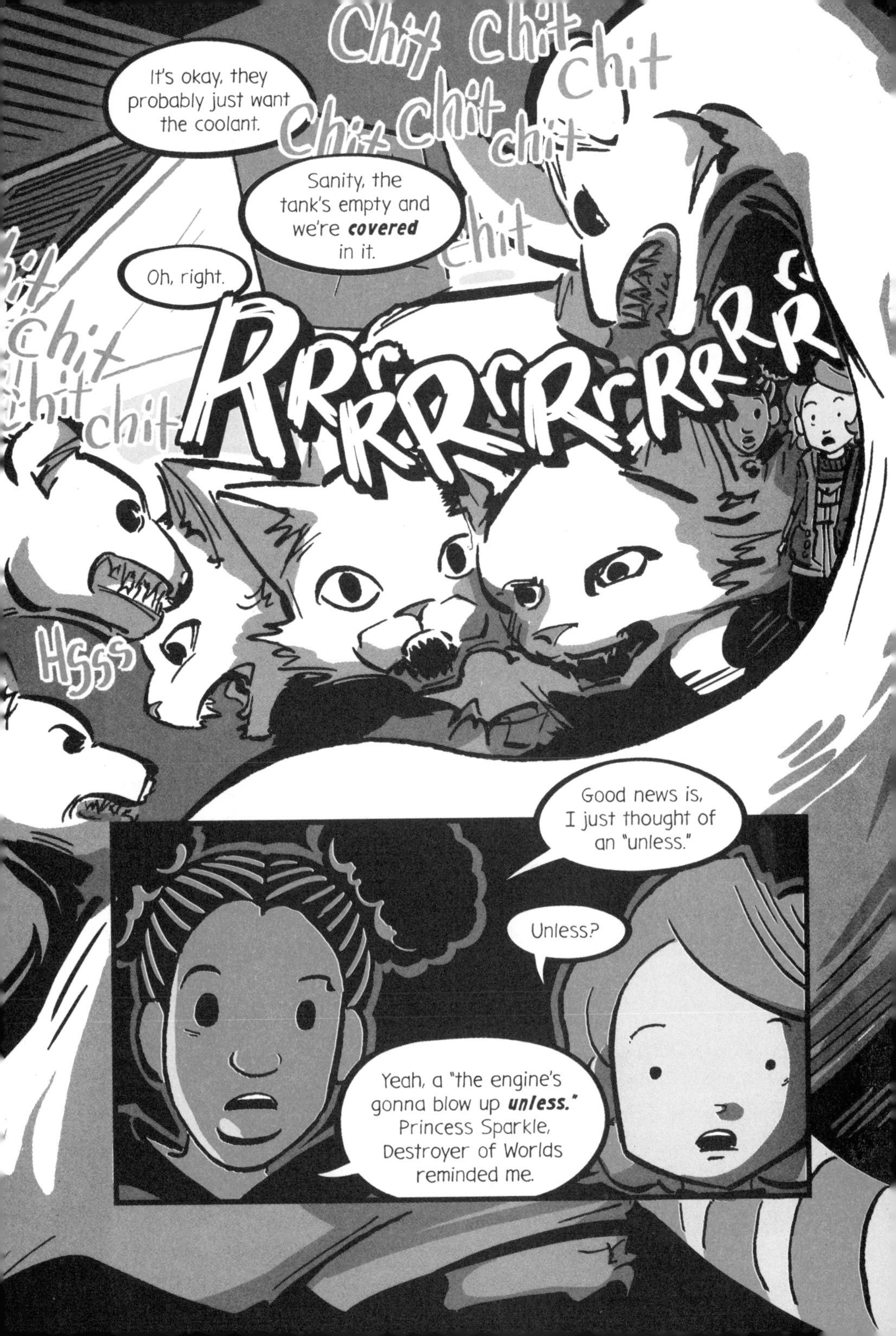
Chit chit
chit
It's okay, they probably just want the coolant.
Chit chit chit
Sanity, the tank's empty and we're **covered** in it.
chit
Oh, right.
chit
chit
chit
chit
RRrRRrRRrRRRR
Hsss
Good news is, I just thought of an "unless."
Unless?
Yeah, a "the engine's gonna blow up ***unless.***" Princess Sparkle, Destroyer of Worlds reminded me.

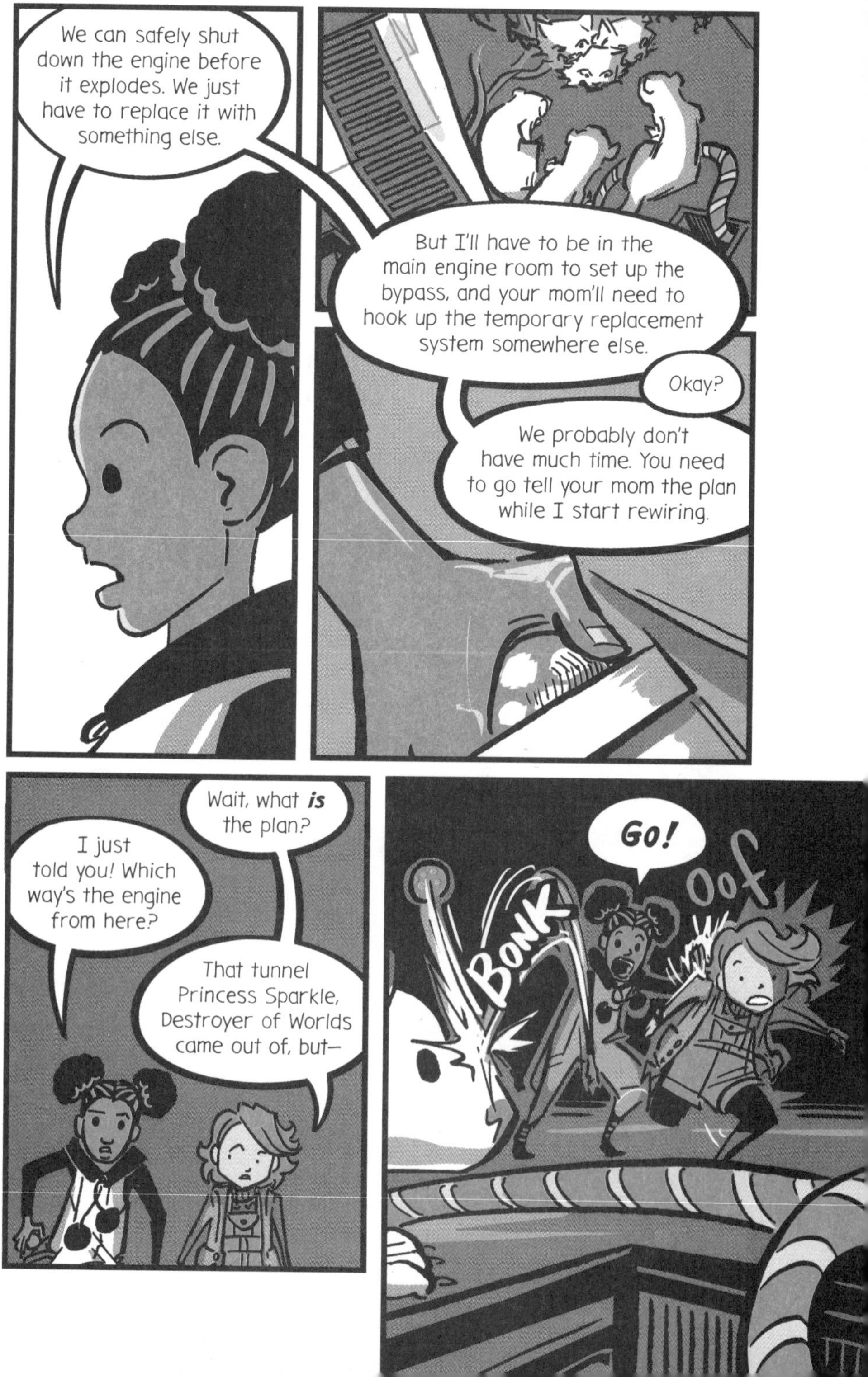
We can safely shut down the engine before it explodes. We just have to replace it with something else.
But I'll have to be in the main engine room to set up the bypass, and your mom'll need to hook up the temporary replacement system somewhere else.
Okay?
We probably don't have much time. You need to go tell your mom the plan while I start rewiring.
Wait, what *is* the plan?
I just told you! Which way's the engine from here?
That tunnel Princess Sparkle, Destroyer of Worlds came out of, but—
Go!
BONK
Oof

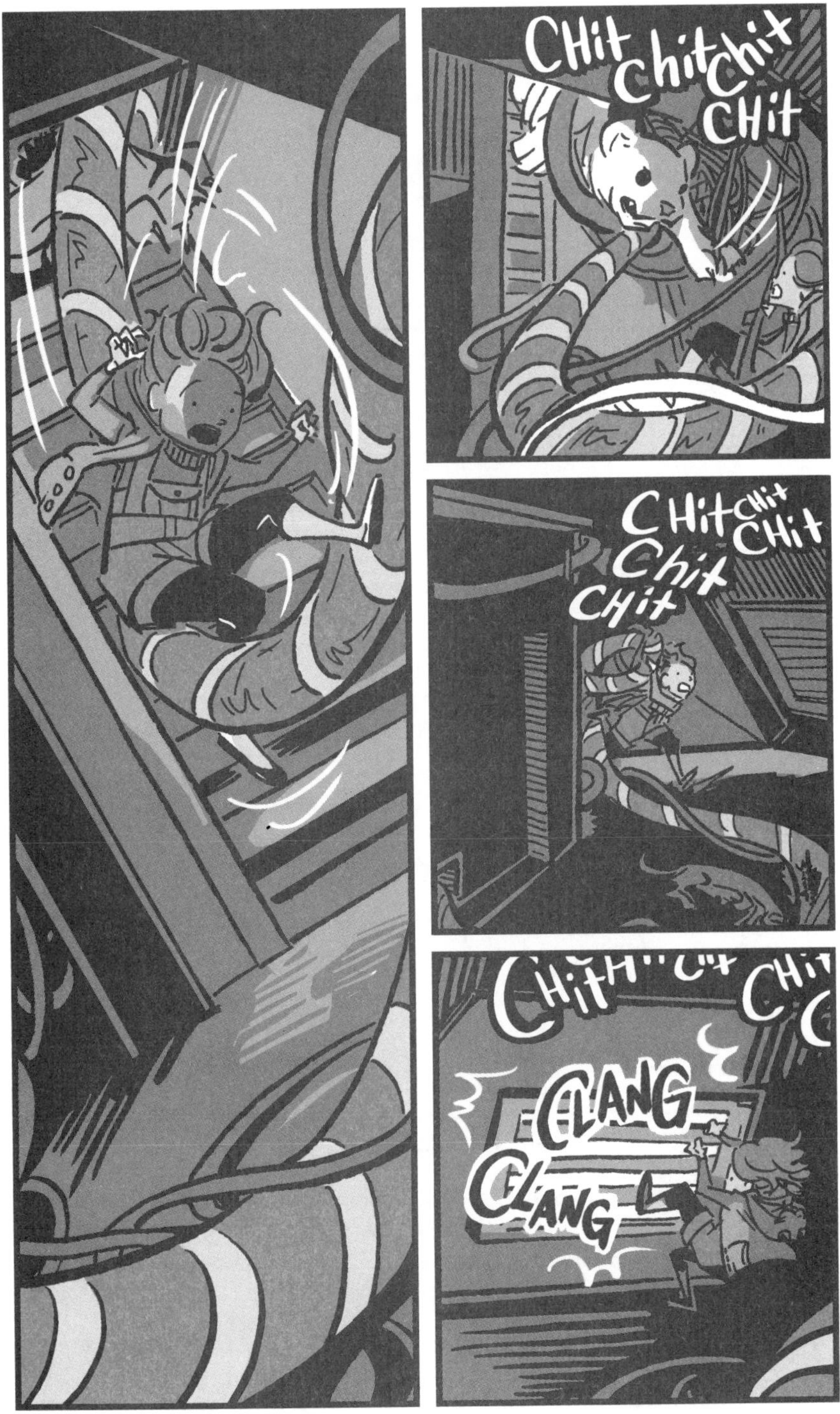
CHIT chit chit CHIT
CHIT chit CHIT Chit CHIT
CLANG CLANG

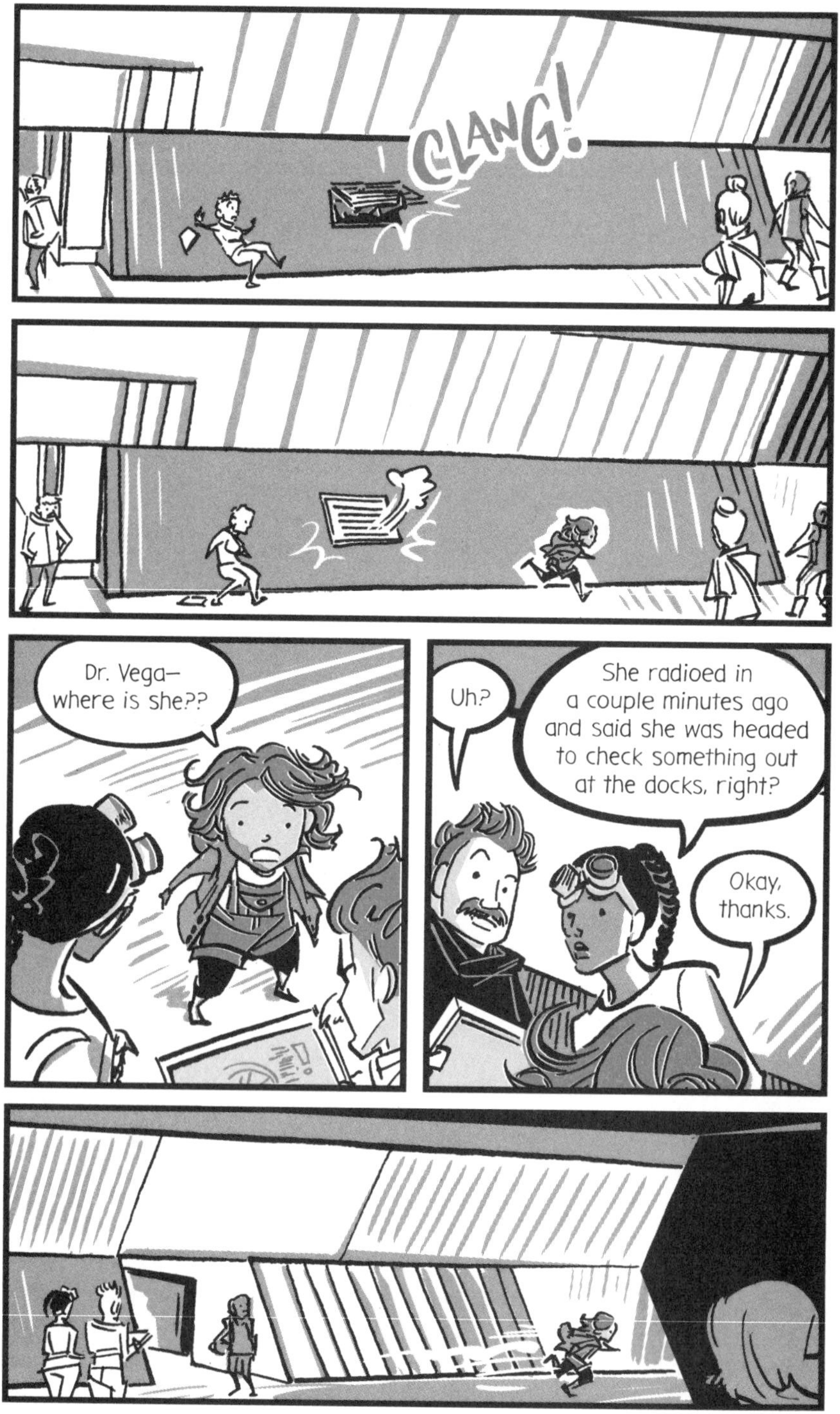
CLANG!
Dr. Vega—where is she??
Uh?
She radioed in a couple minutes ago and said she was headed to check something out at the docks, right?
Okay, thanks.

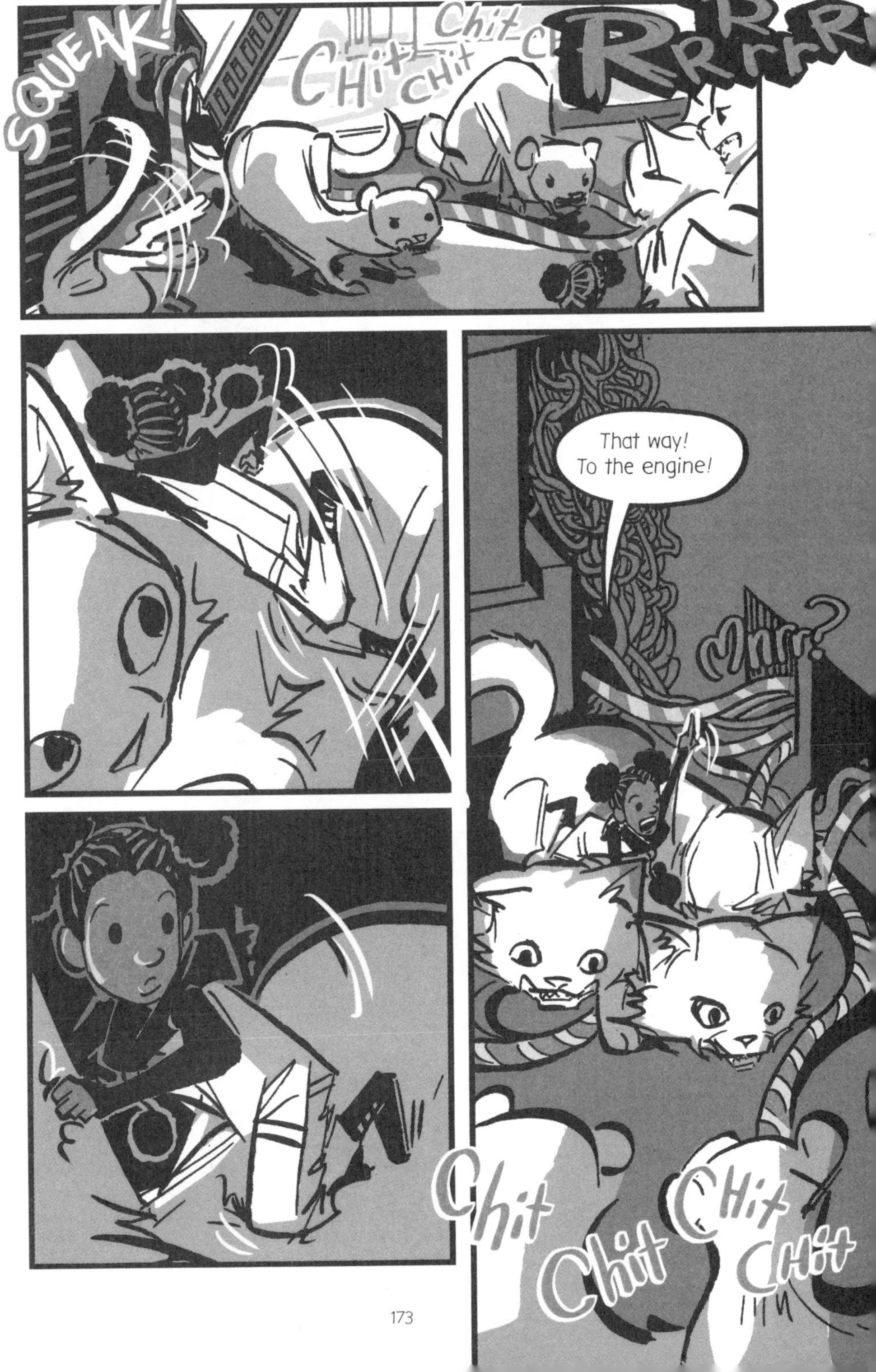
SQUEAK!
Chit Chit Chit Chit
RRRRRR
That way! To the engine!
Mrrr?
Chit Chit Chit Chit

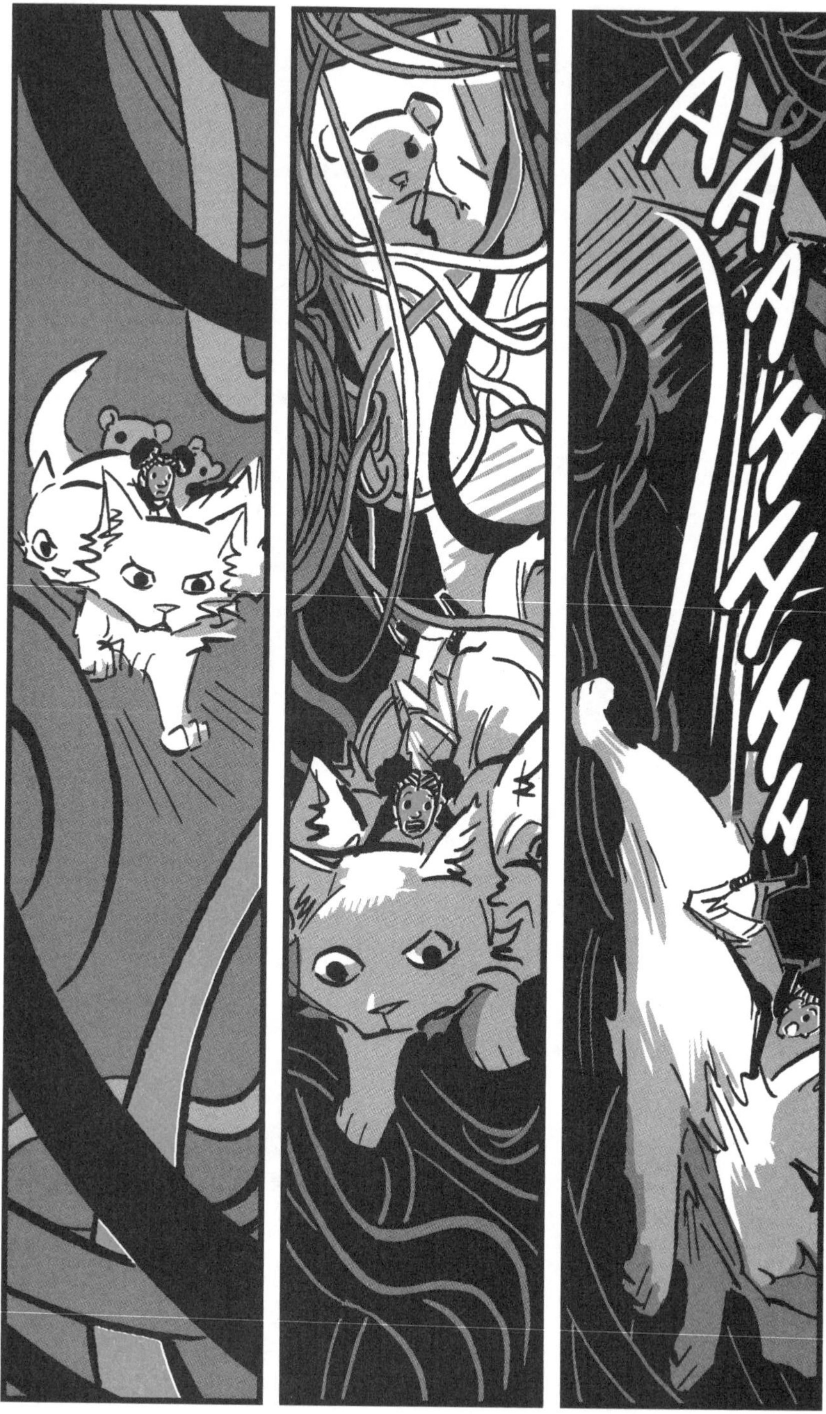
AAAAHHHHHH

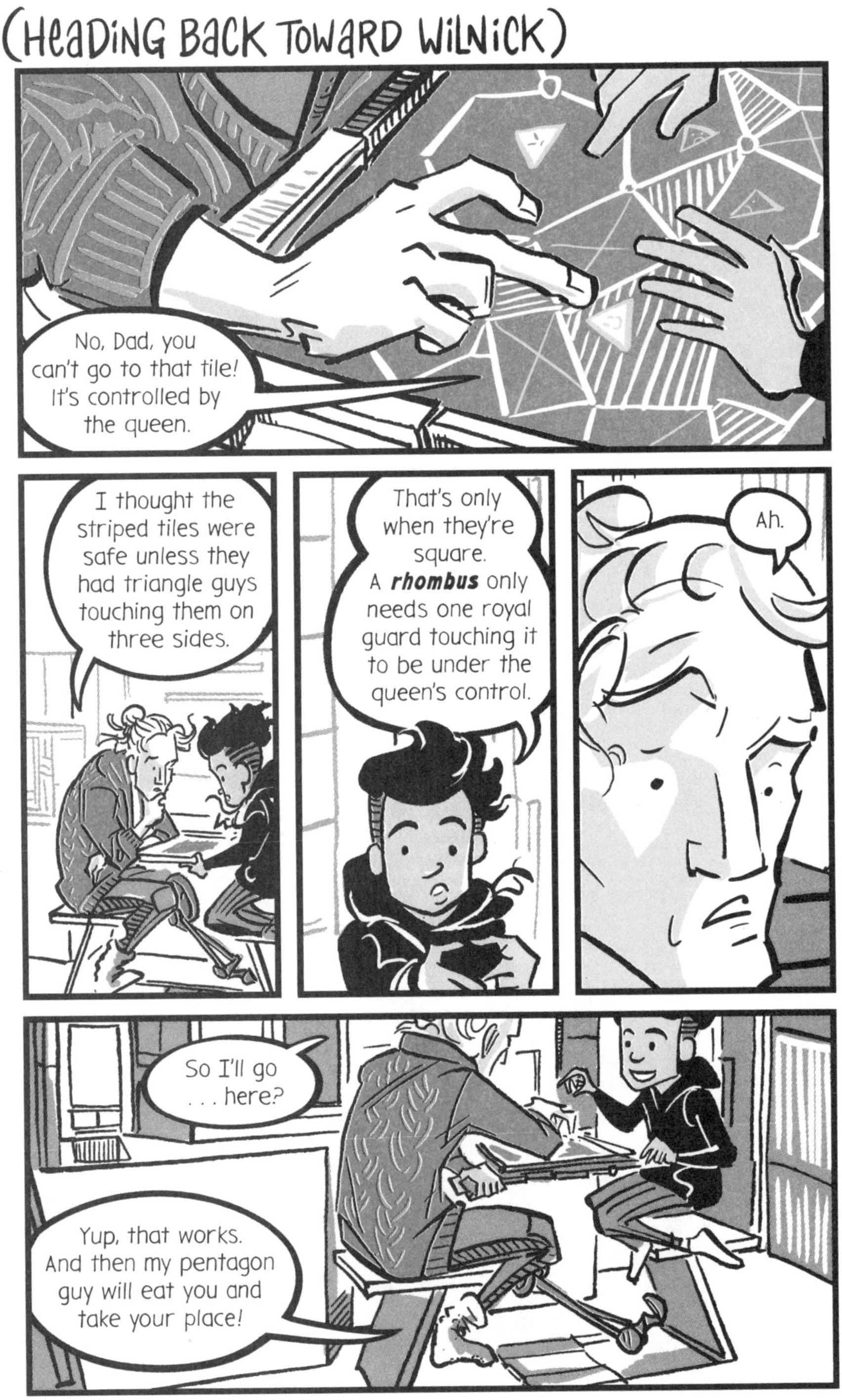
(HEADING BACK TOWARD WILNICK)
No, Dad, you can't go to that tile! It's controlled by the queen.
I thought the striped tiles were safe unless they had triangle guys touching them on three sides.
That's only when they're square. A **rhombus** only needs one royal guard touching it to be under the queen's control.
Ah.
So I'll go . . . here?
Yup, that works. And then my pentagon guy will eat you and take your place!

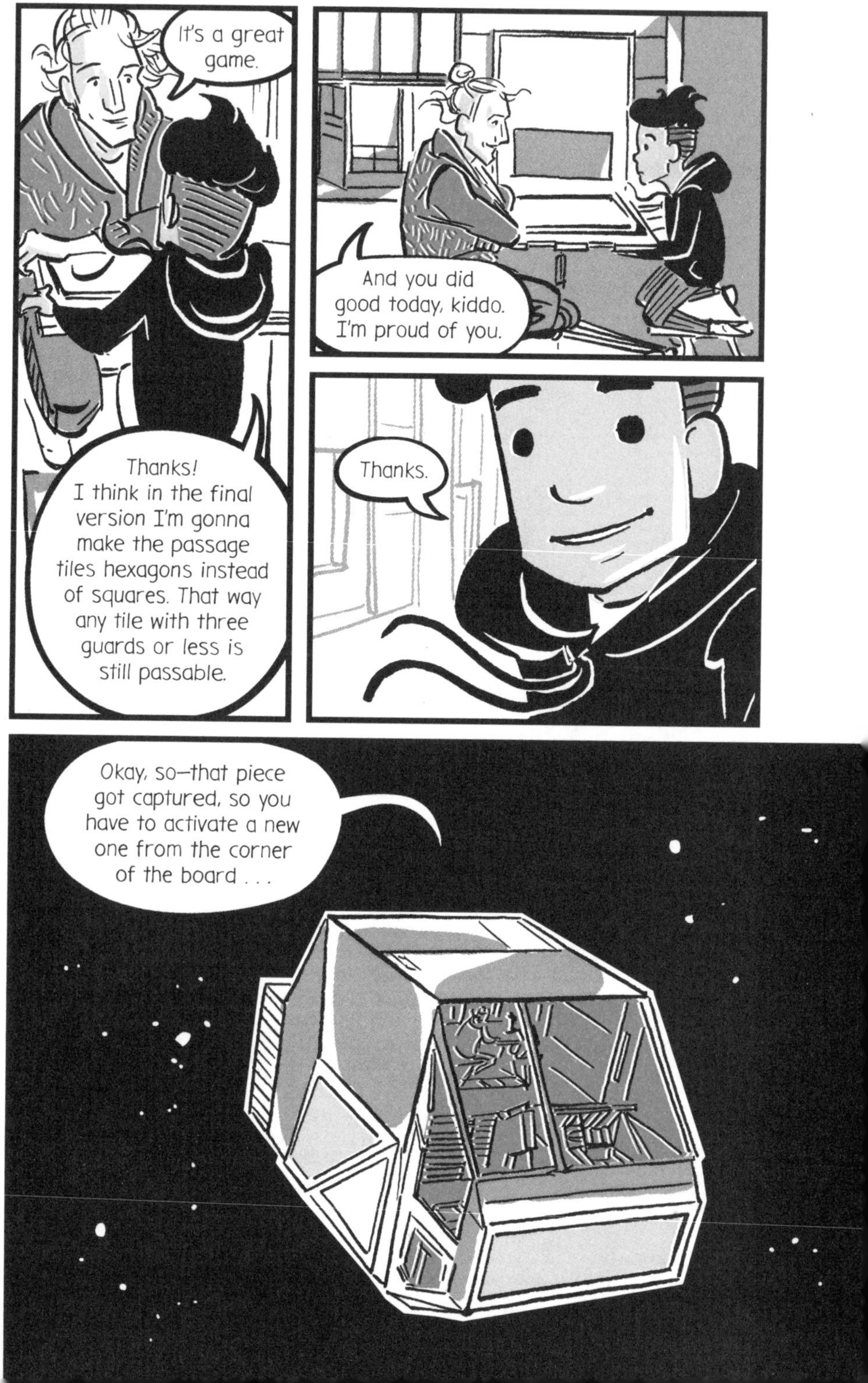
It's a great game.
And you did good today, kiddo. I'm proud of you.
Thanks! I think in the final version I'm gonna make the passage tiles hexagons instead of squares. That way any tile with three guards or less is still passable.
Thanks.
Okay, so—that piece got captured, so you have to activate a new one from the corner of the board . . .

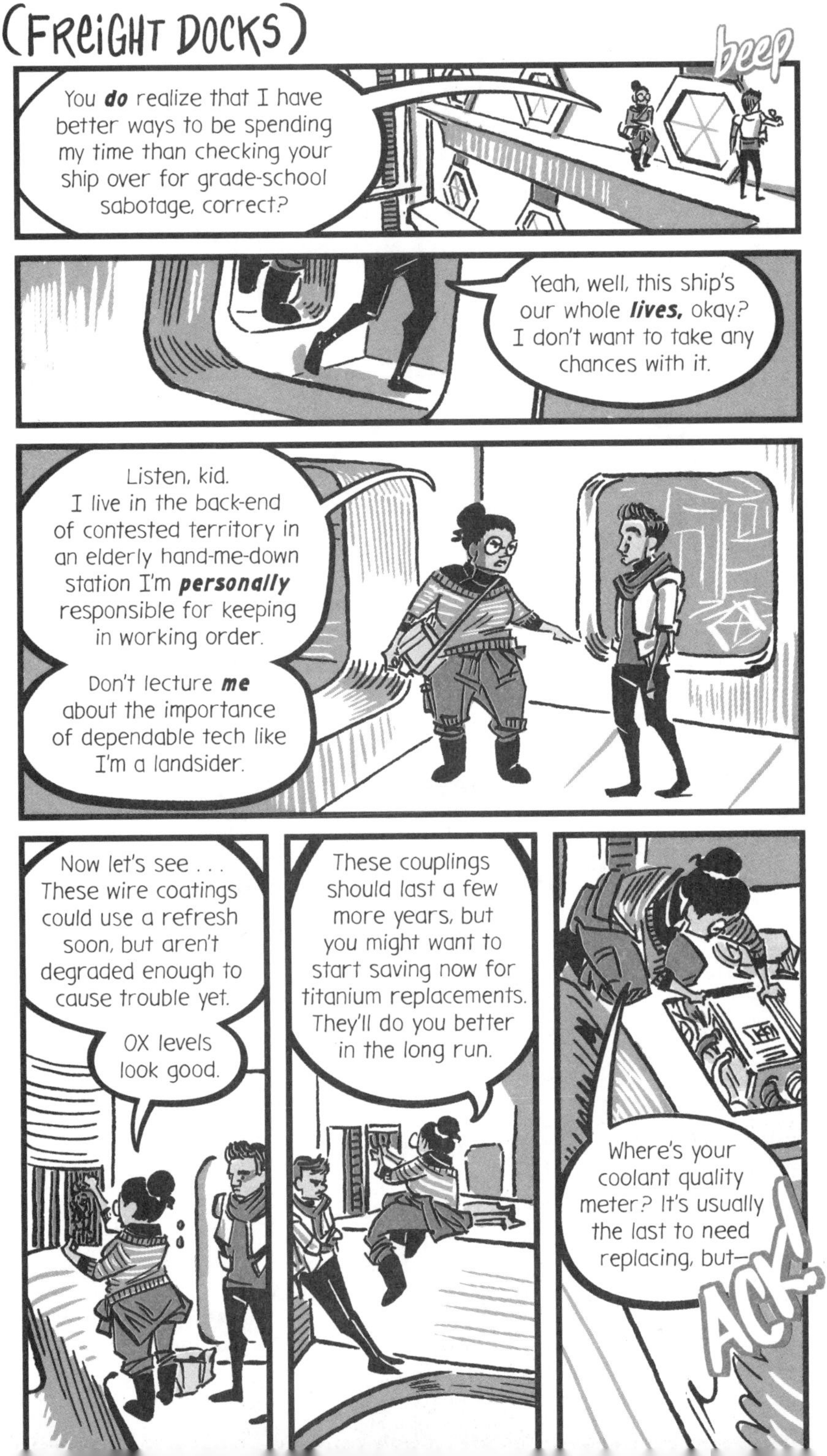
(FREIGHT DOCKS)
beep
You **do** realize that I have better ways to be spending my time than checking your ship over for grade-school sabotage, correct?
Yeah, well, this ship's our whole **lives,** okay? I don't want to take any chances with it.
Listen, kid. I live in the back-end of contested territory in an elderly hand-me-down station I'm **personally** responsible for keeping in working order.
Don't lecture **me** about the importance of dependable tech like I'm a landsider.
Now let's see . . . These wire coatings could use a refresh soon, but aren't degraded enough to cause trouble yet.
OX levels look good.
These couplings should last a few more years, but you might want to start saving now for titanium replacements. They'll do you better in the long run.
Where's your coolant quality meter? It's usually the last to need replacing, but—
ACK!

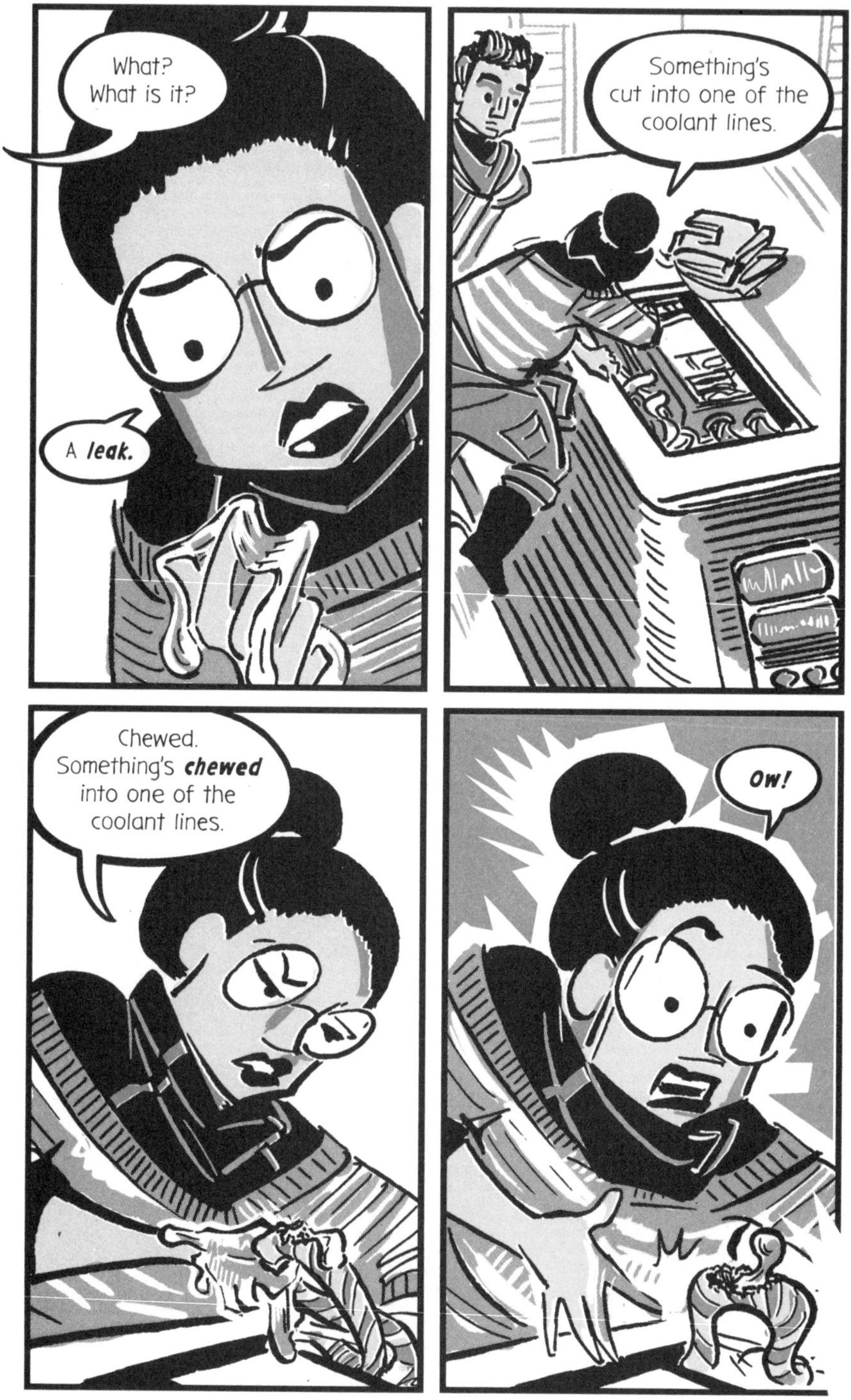
What? What is it?
A **leak.**
Something's cut into one of the coolant lines.
Chewed. Something's **chewed** into one of the coolant lines.
**Ow!**

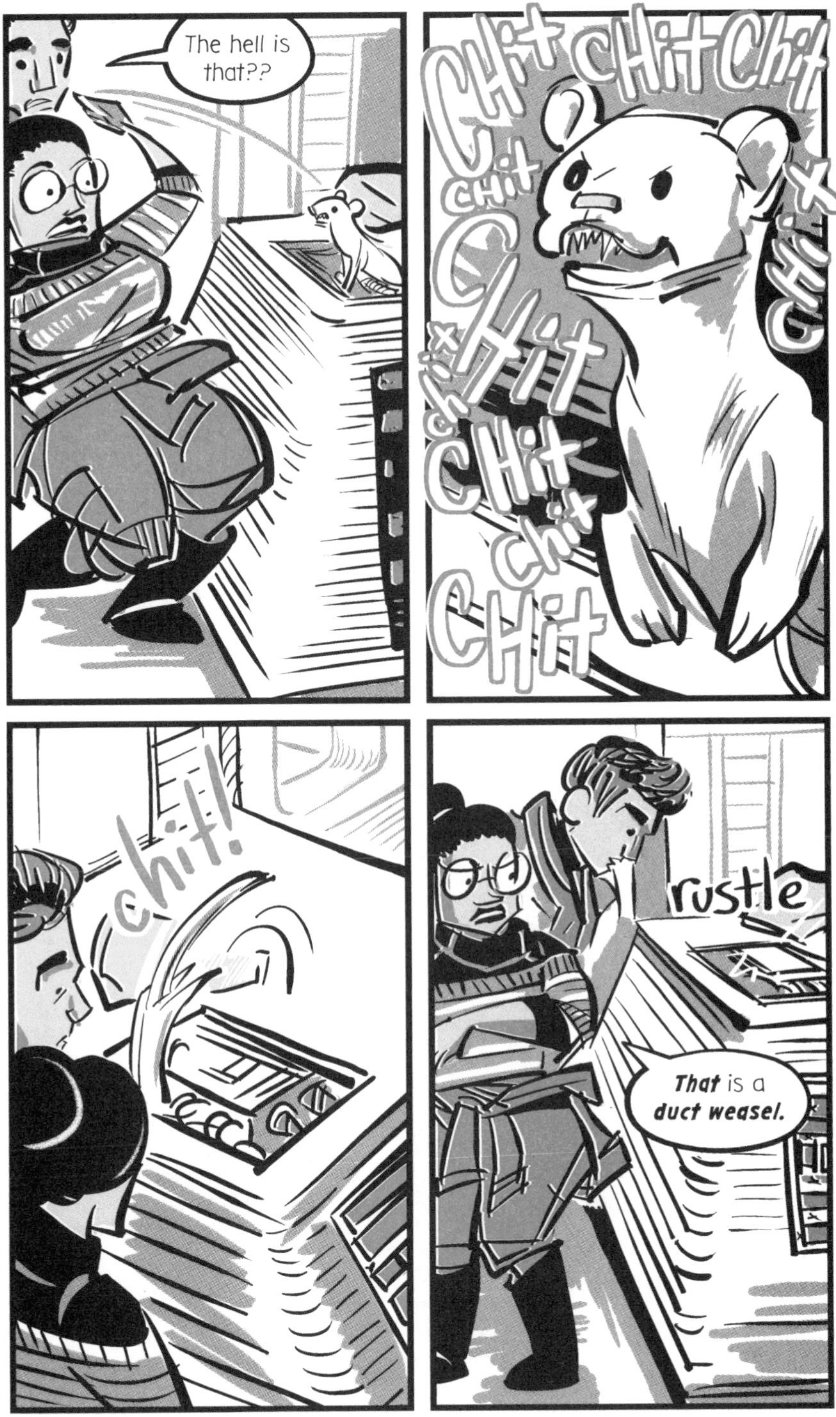
The hell is that??
CHit CHit CHit
CHit
CHit
CHit
CHit
chit
CHit
CHit
chit!
rustle
**That** is a **duct weasel.**

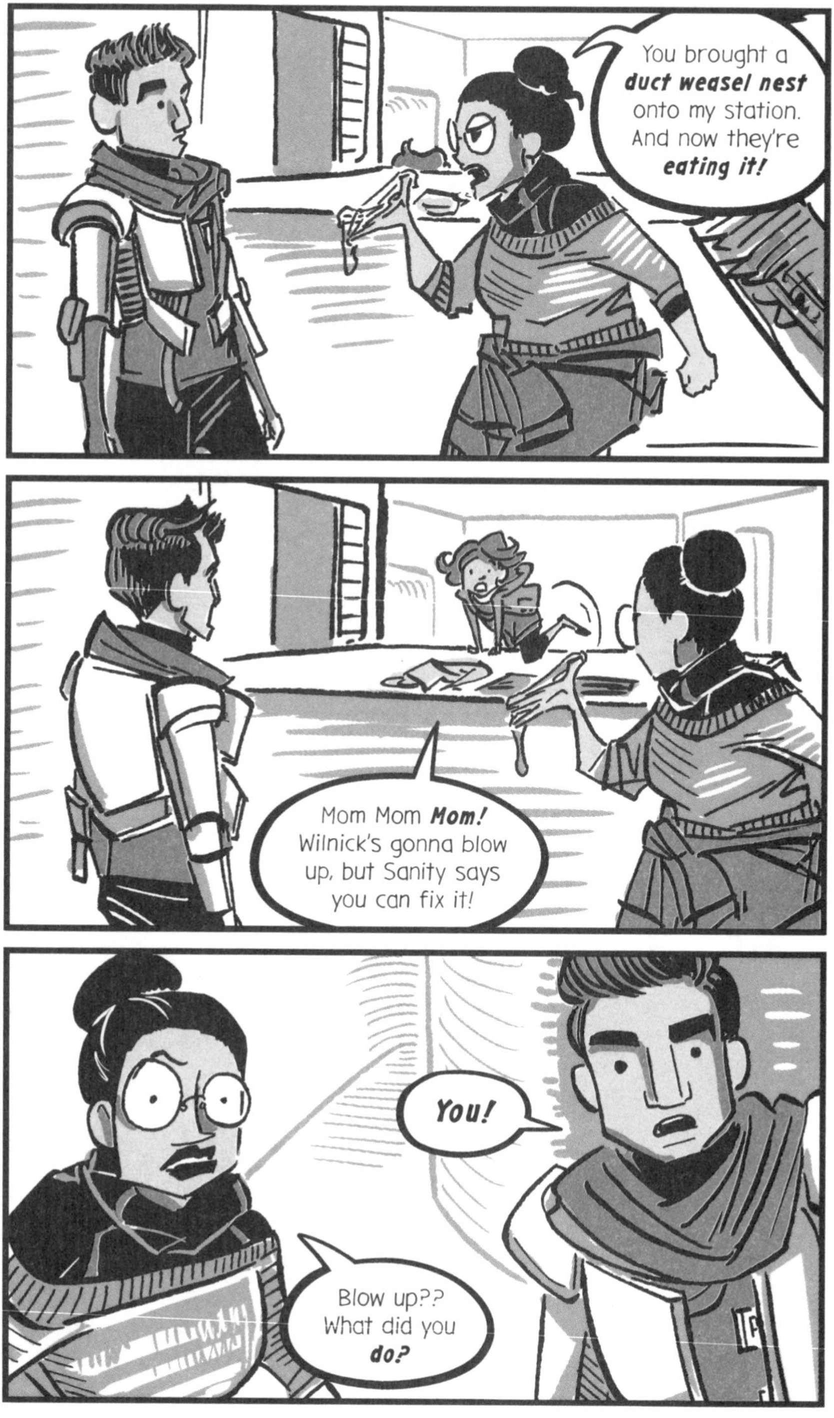
You brought a **duct weasel nest** onto my station. And now they're ***eating it!***
Mom Mom Mom ***Mom!*** Wilnick's gonna blow up, but Sanity says you can fix it!
***You!***
Blow up?? What did you ***do?***

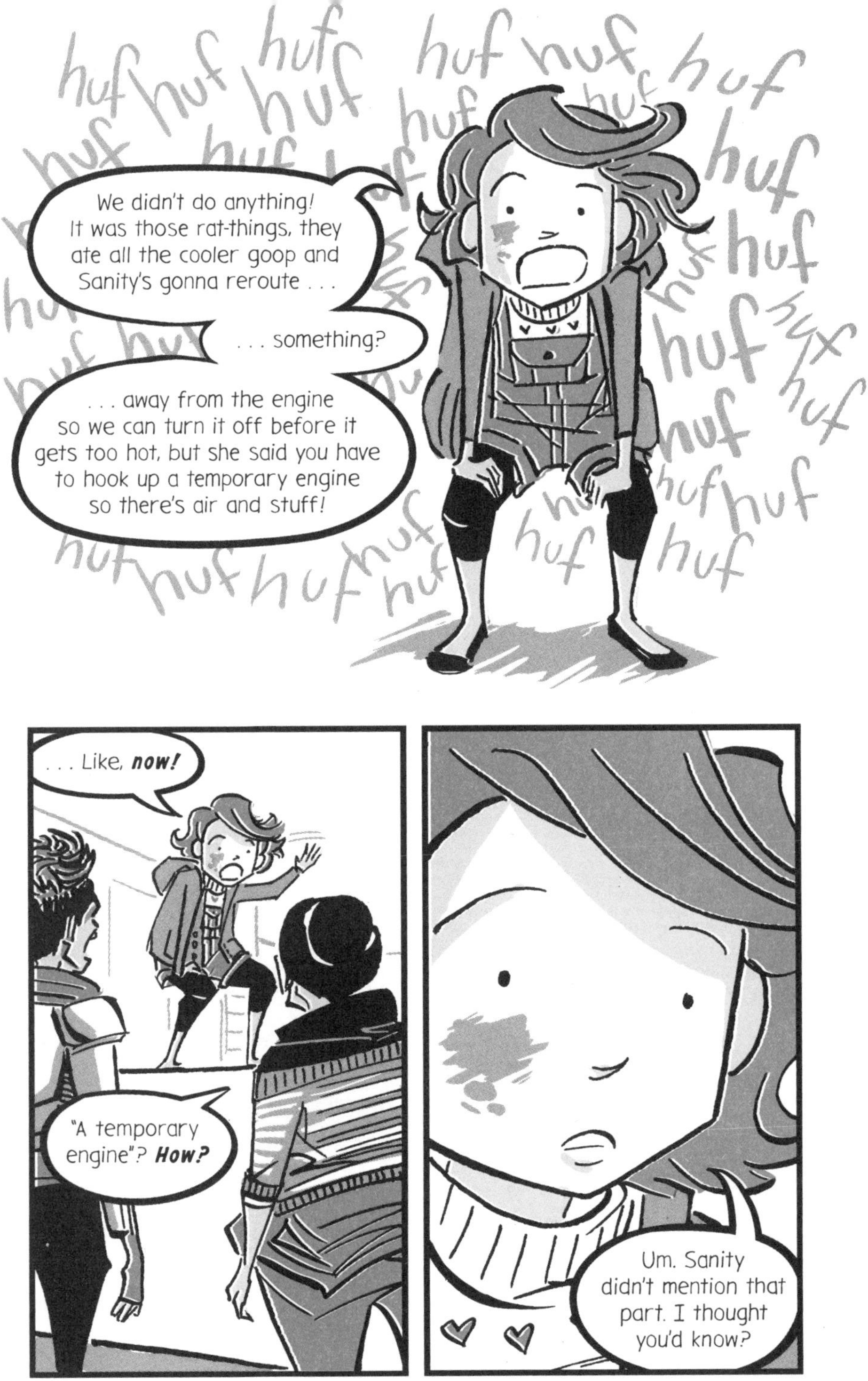
huf huf huf huf huf huf huf huf huf huf huf huf huf huf huf huf huf huf huf huf huf huf huf huf huf
We didn't do anything! It was those rat-things, they ate all the cooler goop and Sanity's gonna reroute . . .
. . . something?
. . . away from the engine so we can turn it off before it gets too hot, but she said you have to hook up a temporary engine so there's air and stuff!
. . . Like, ***now!***
"A temporary engine"? ***How?***
Um. Sanity didn't mention that part. I thought you'd know?

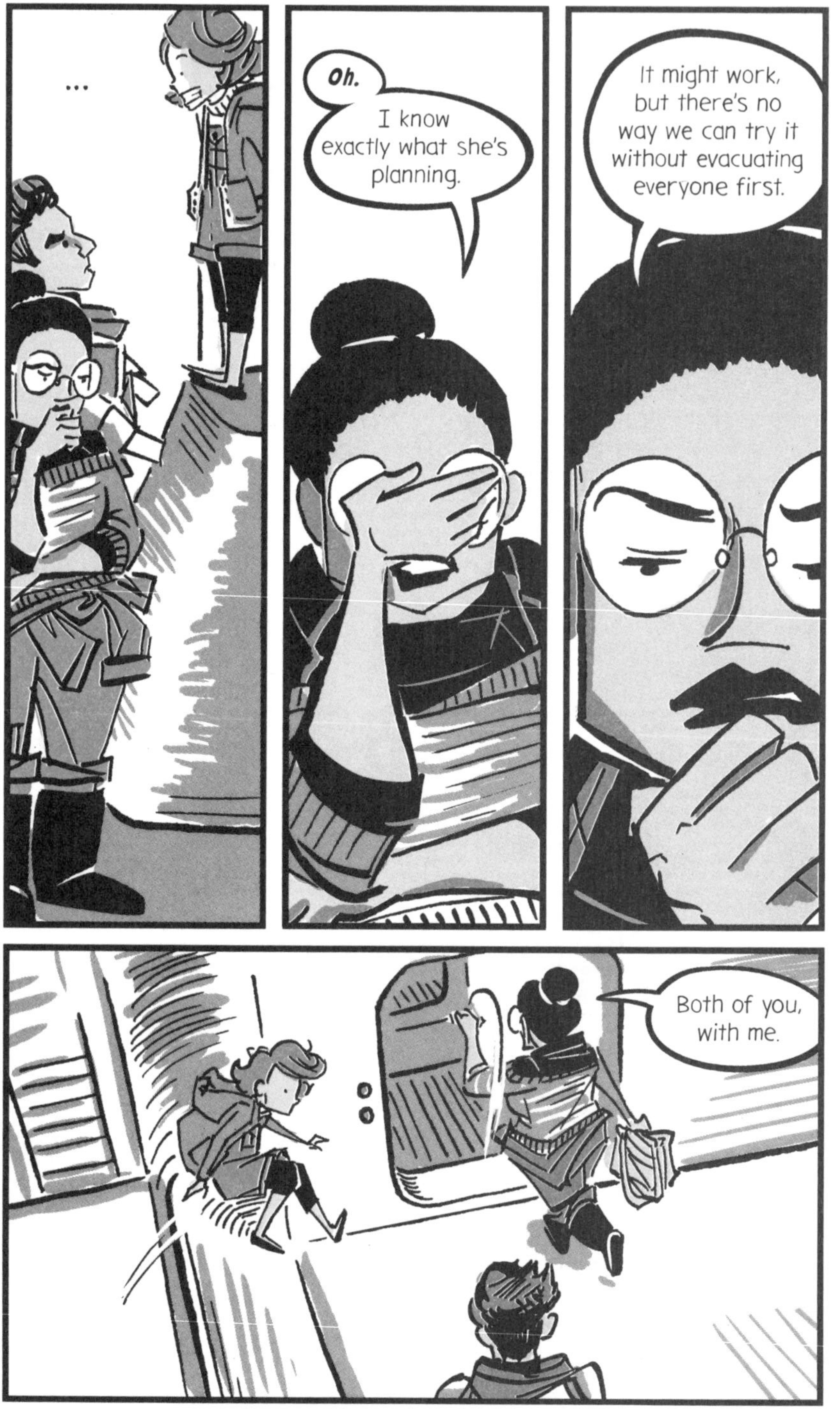
...
Oh.
I know exactly what she's planning.
It might work, but there's no way we can try it without evacuating everyone first.
Both of you, with me.

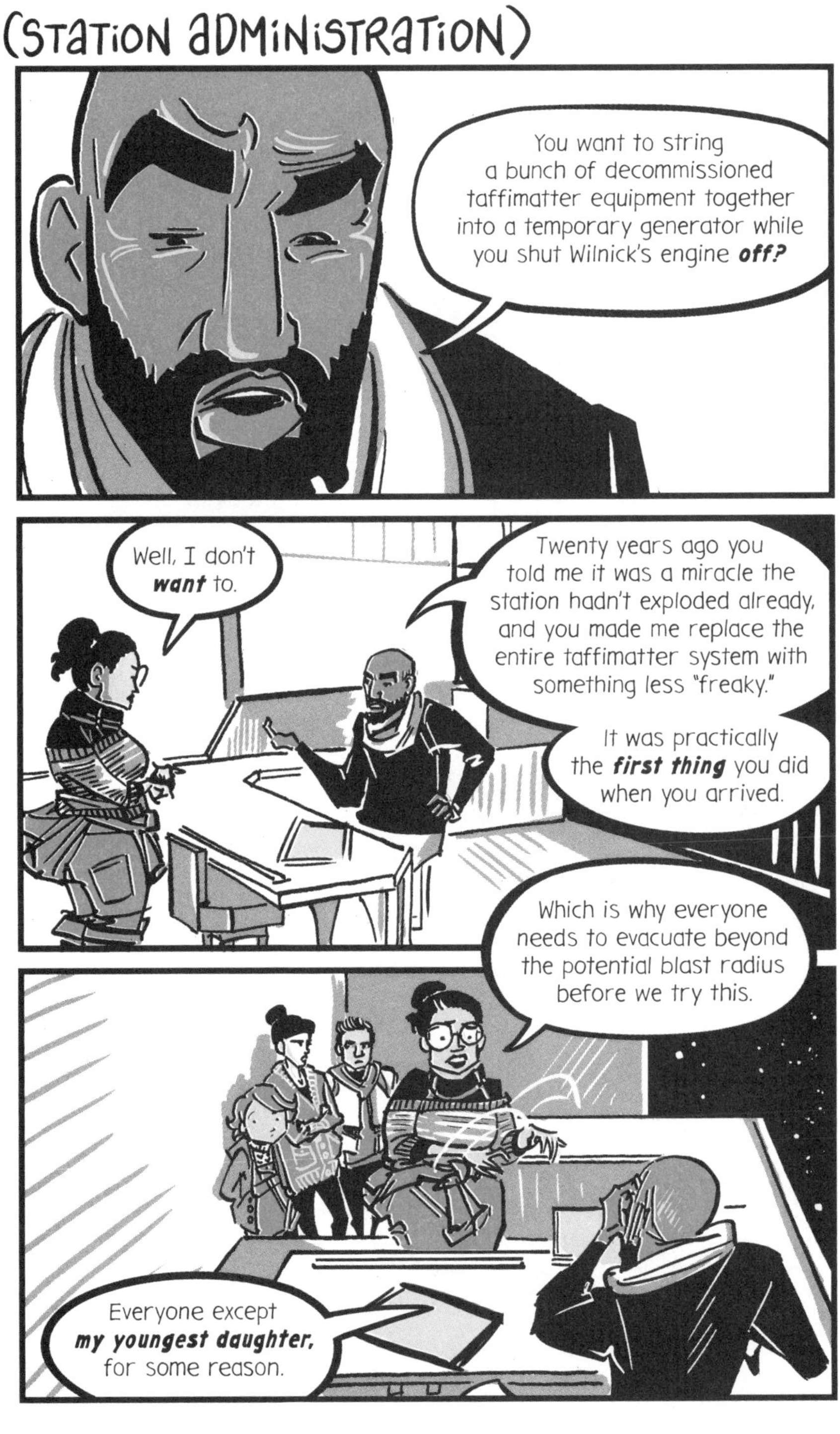
(STATION ADMINISTRATION)
You want to string a bunch of decommissioned taffimatter equipment together into a temporary generator while you shut Wilnick's engine ***off?***
Well, I don't ***want*** to.
Twenty years ago you told me it was a miracle the station hadn't exploded already, and you made me replace the entire taffimatter system with something less "freaky."
It was practically the ***first thing*** you did when you arrived.
Which is why everyone needs to evacuate beyond the potential blast radius before we try this.
Everyone except ***my youngest daughter,*** for some reason.

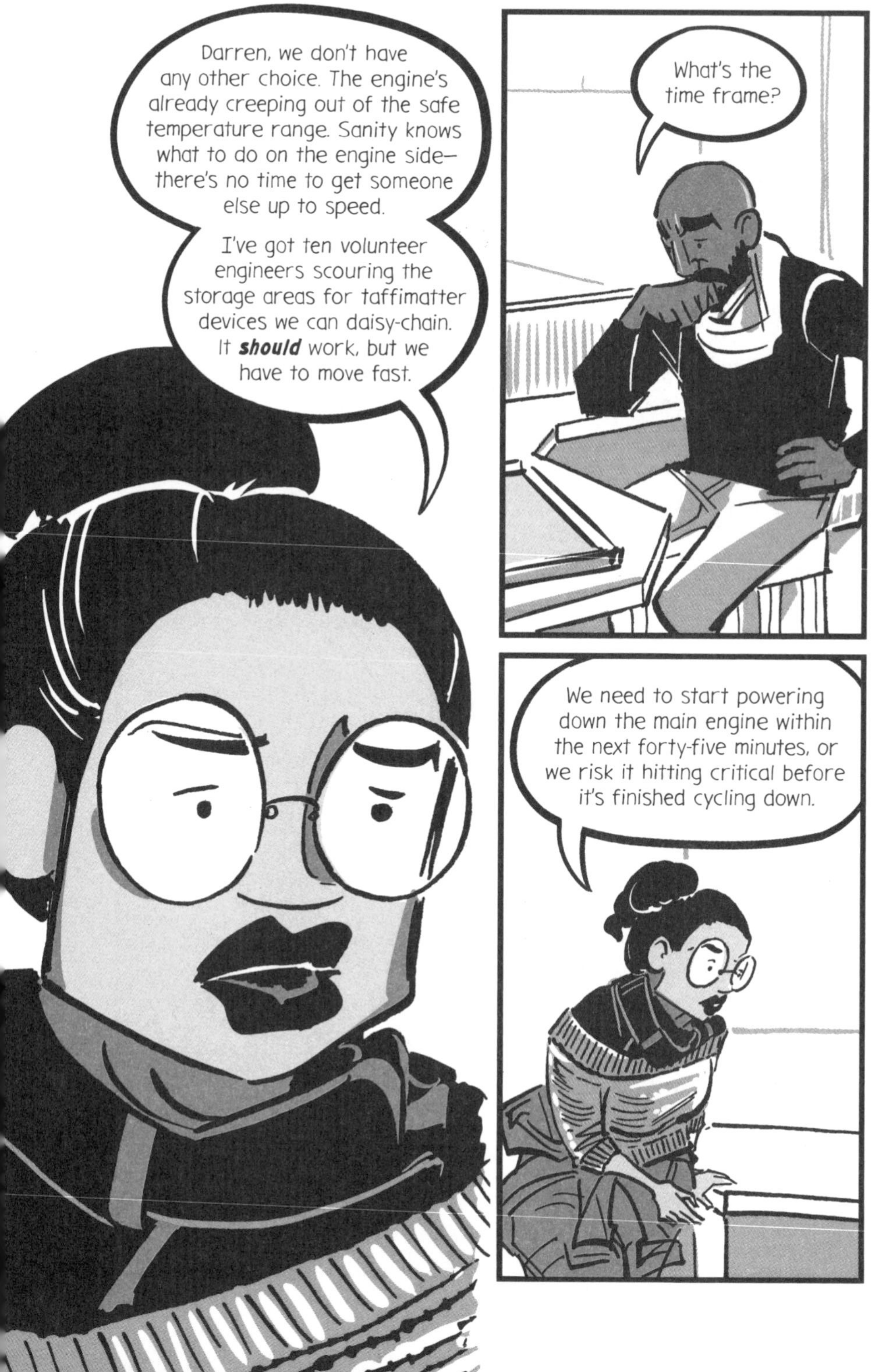
Darren, we don't have any other choice. The engine's already creeping out of the safe temperature range. Sanity knows what to do on the engine side—there's no time to get someone else up to speed.
I've got ten volunteer engineers scouring the storage areas for taffimatter devices we can daisy-chain. It ***should*** work, but we have to move fast.
What's the time frame?
We need to start powering down the main engine within the next forty-five minutes, or we risk it hitting critical before it's finished cycling down.

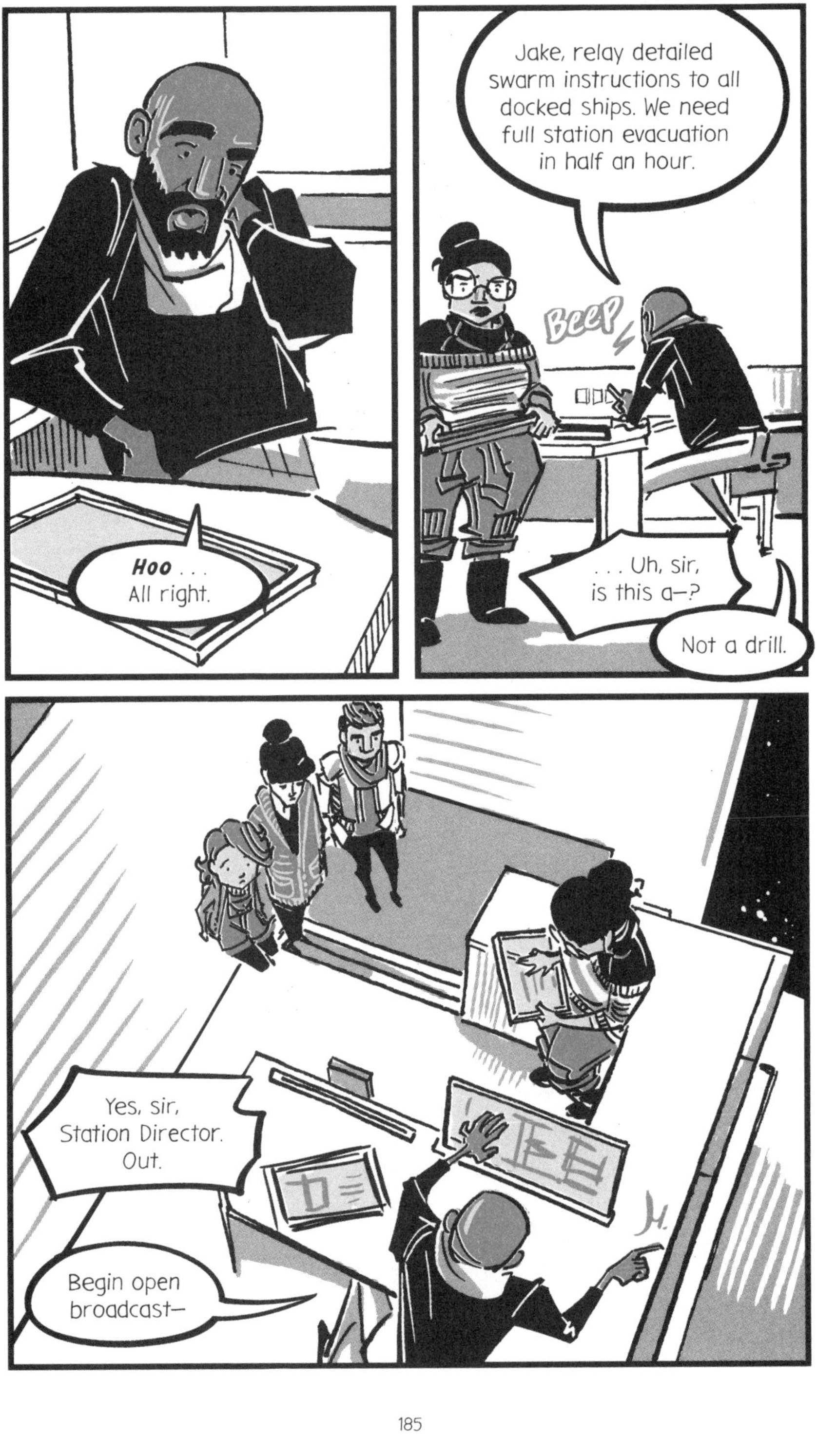
Hoo . . . All right.
Jake, relay detailed swarm instructions to all docked ships. We need full station evacuation in half an hour.
Beep
. . . Uh, sir, is this a—?
Not a drill.
Yes, sir, Station Director. Out.
Begin open broadcast—

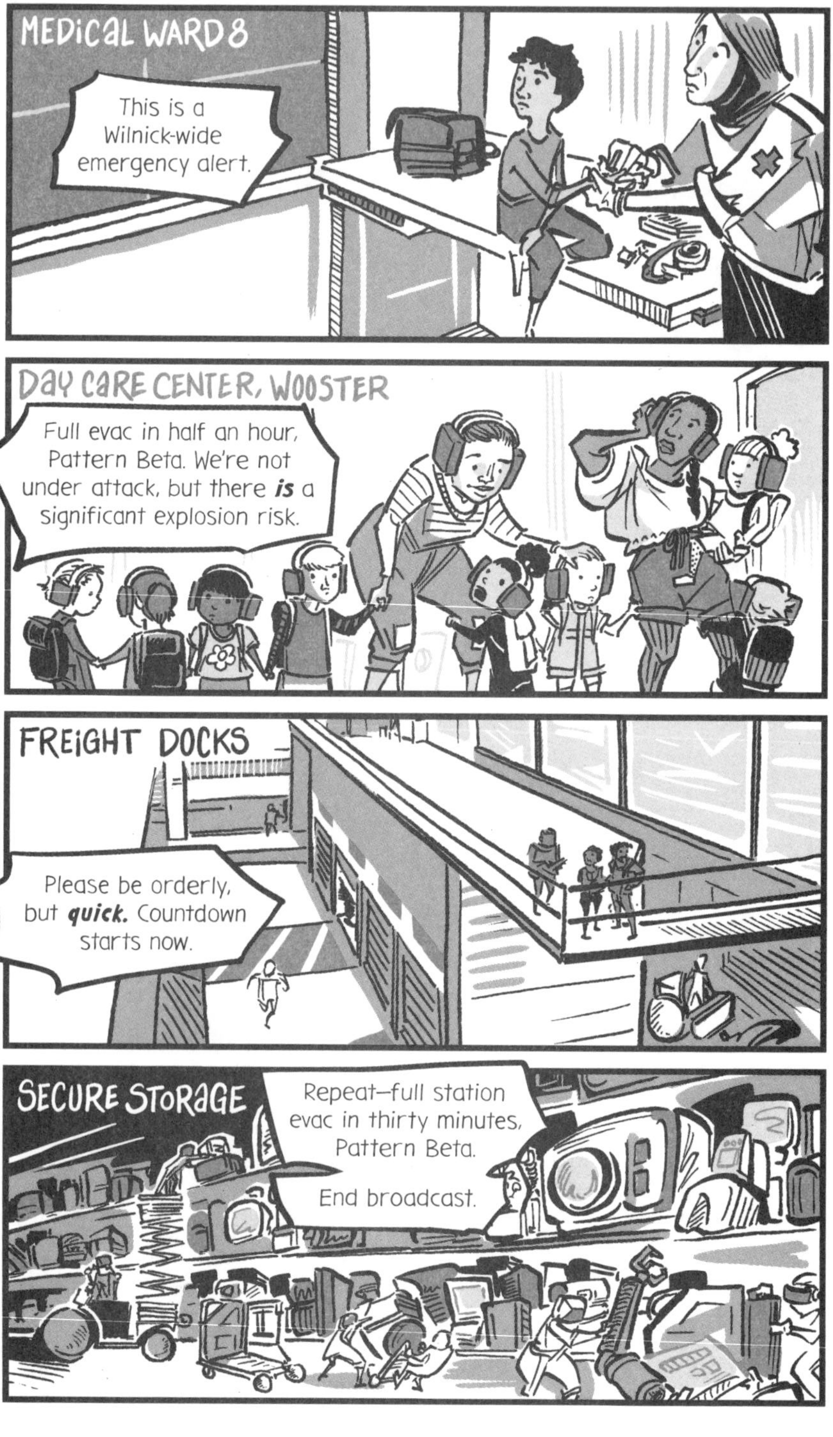
MEDICAL WARD 8
This is a Wilnick-wide emergency alert.
DAY CARE CENTER, WOOSTER
Full evac in half an hour, Pattern Beta. We're not under attack, but there *is* a significant explosion risk.
FREIGHT DOCKS
Please be orderly, but **quick.** Countdown starts now.
SECURE STORAGE
Repeat—full station evac in thirty minutes, Pattern Beta.
End broadcast.

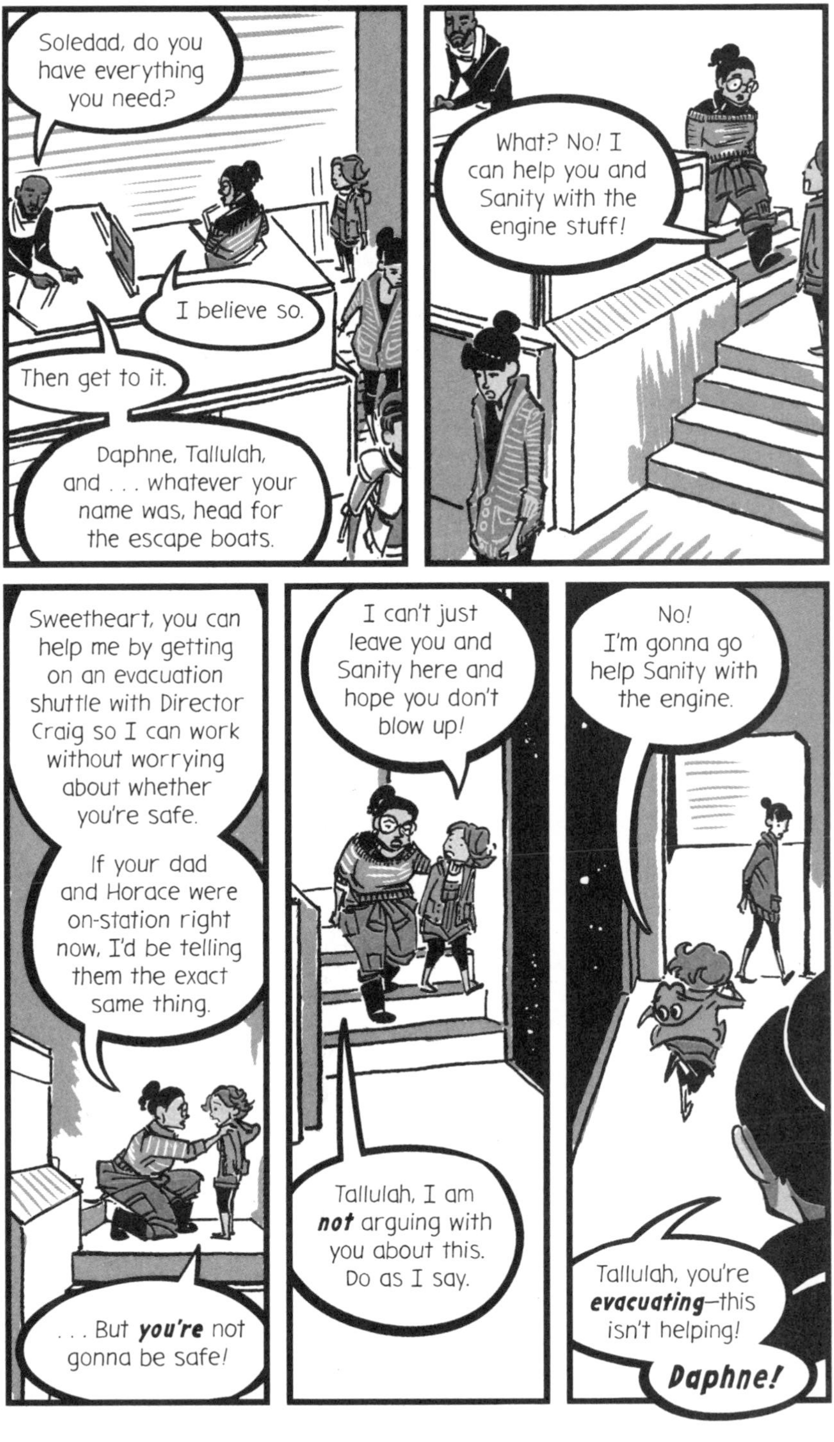
Soledad, do you have everything you need?
I believe so.
Then get to it.
Daphne, Tallulah, and . . . whatever your name was, head for the escape boats.
What? No! I can help you and Sanity with the engine stuff!
Sweetheart, you can help me by getting on an evacuation shuttle with Director Craig so I can work without worrying about whether you're safe.
If your dad and Horace were on-station right now, I'd be telling them the exact same thing.
. . . But ***you're*** not gonna be safe!
I can't just leave you and Sanity here and hope you don't blow up!
Tallulah, I am ***not*** arguing with you about this. Do as I say.
No! I'm gonna go help Sanity with the engine.
Tallulah, you're ***evacuating***—this isn't helping!
***Daphne!***

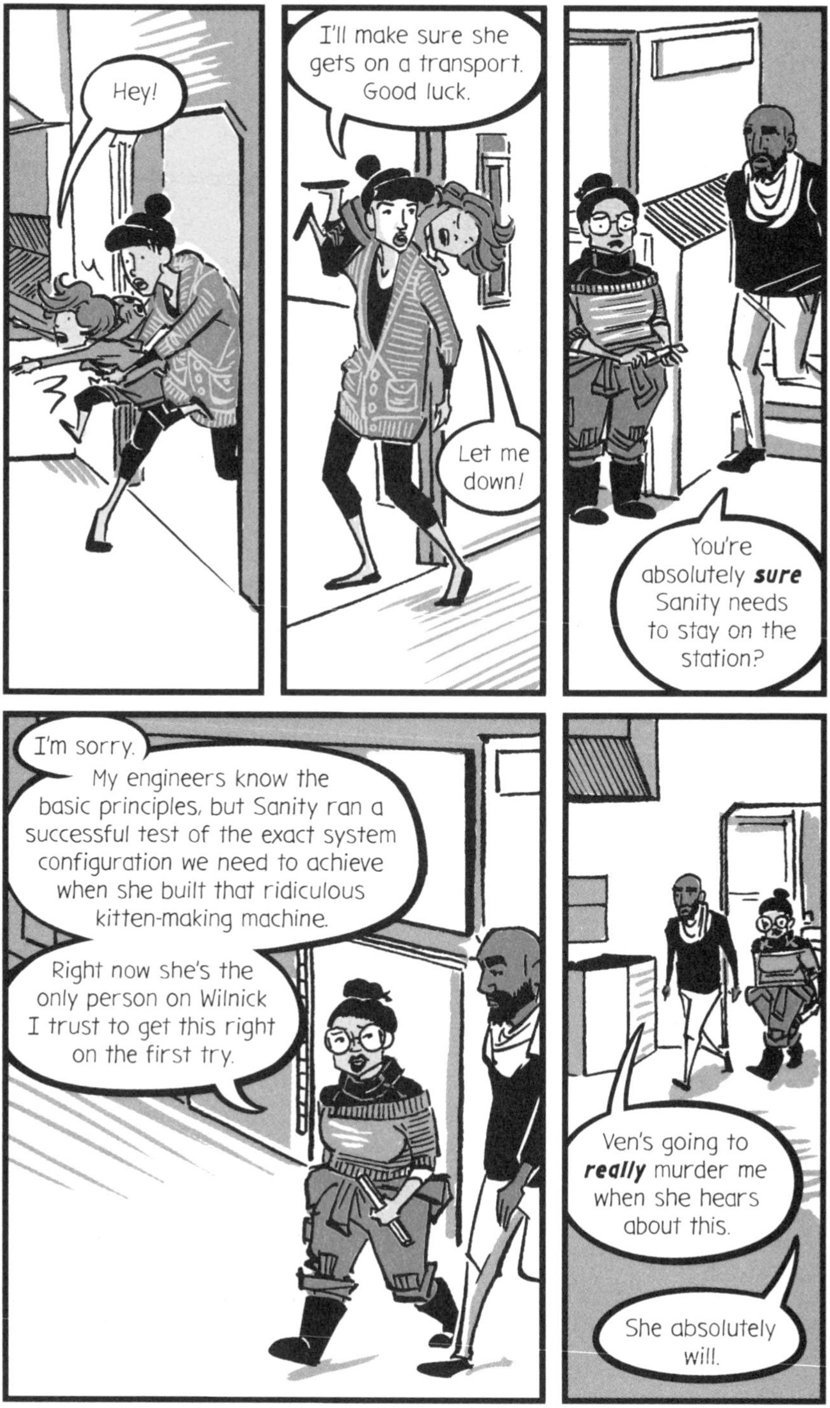
Hey!
I'll make sure she gets on a transport. Good luck.
Let me down!
You're absolutely **sure** Sanity needs to stay on the station?
I'm sorry.
My engineers know the basic principles, but Sanity ran a successful test of the exact system configuration we need to achieve when she built that ridiculous kitten-making machine.
Right now she's the only person on Wilnick I trust to get this right on the first try.
Ven's going to **really** murder me when she hears about this.
She absolutely will.

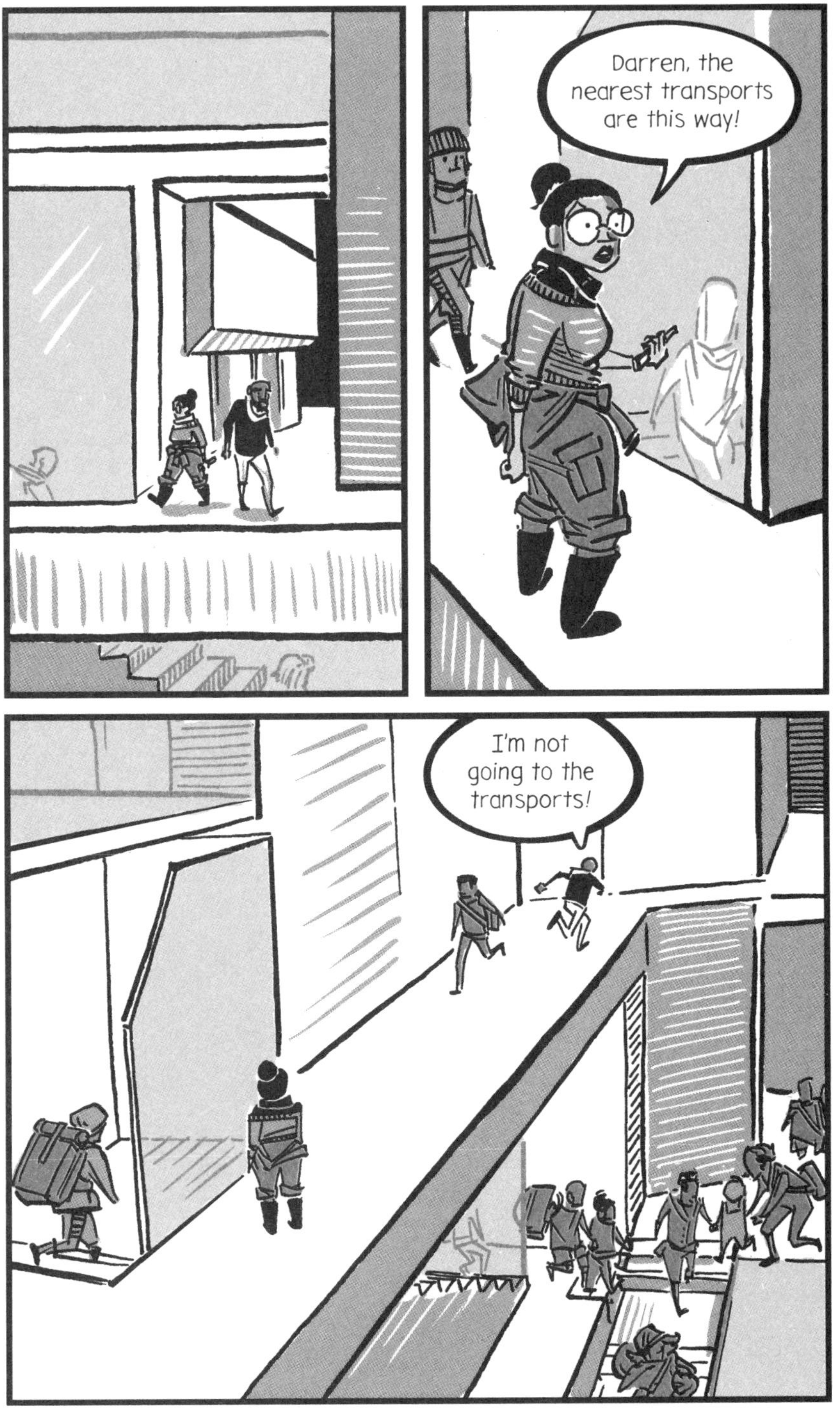
Darren, the nearest transports are this way!
I'm not going to the transports!

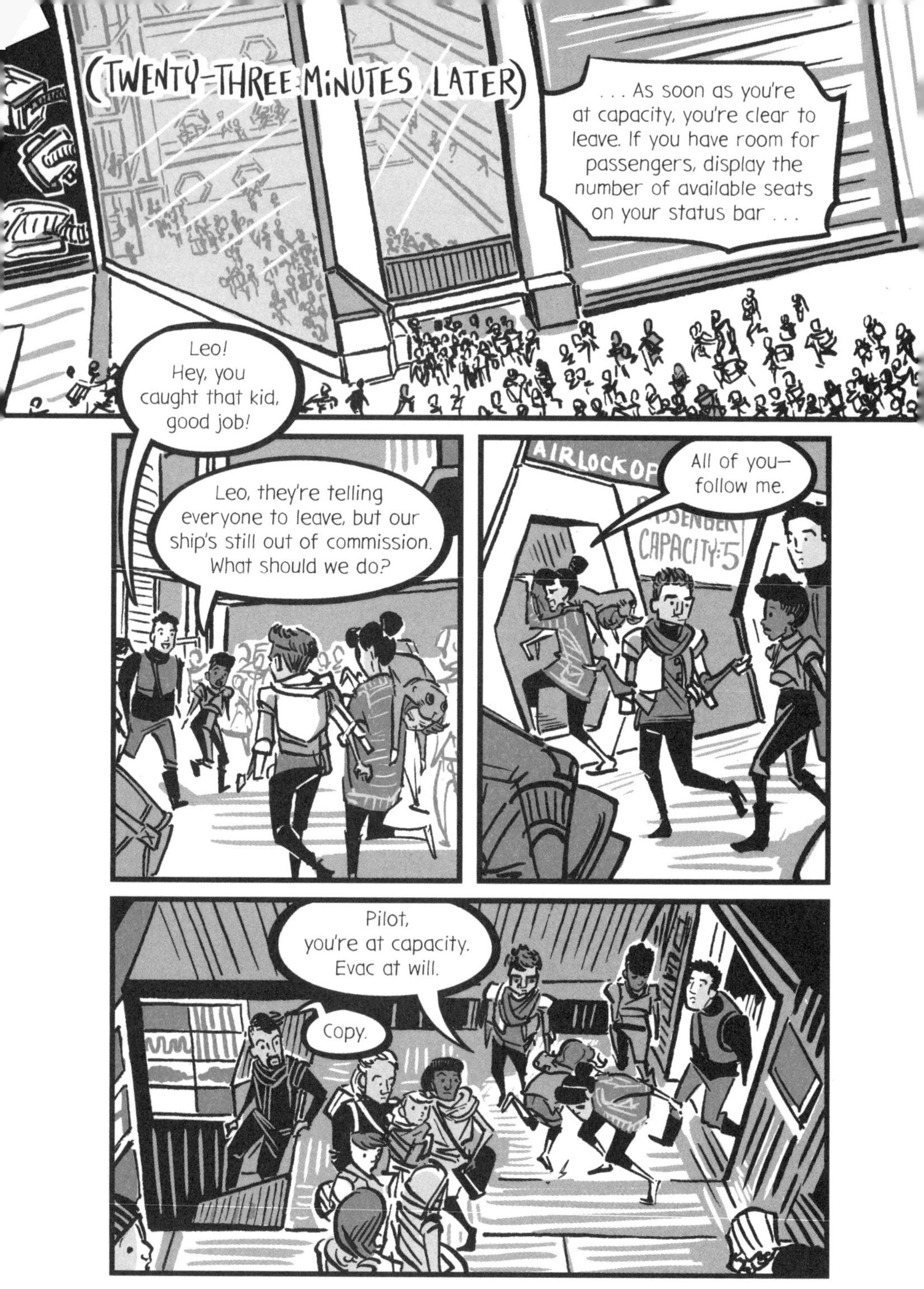
(TWENTY-THREE MINUTES LATER)
. . . As soon as you're at capacity, you're clear to leave. If you have room for passengers, display the number of available seats on your status bar . . .
Leo! Hey, you caught that kid, good job!
Leo, they're telling everyone to leave, but our ship's still out of commission. What should we do?
AIRLOCK OP
All of you—follow me.
PASSENGER CAPACITY: 5
Pilot, you're at capacity. Evac at will.
Copy.

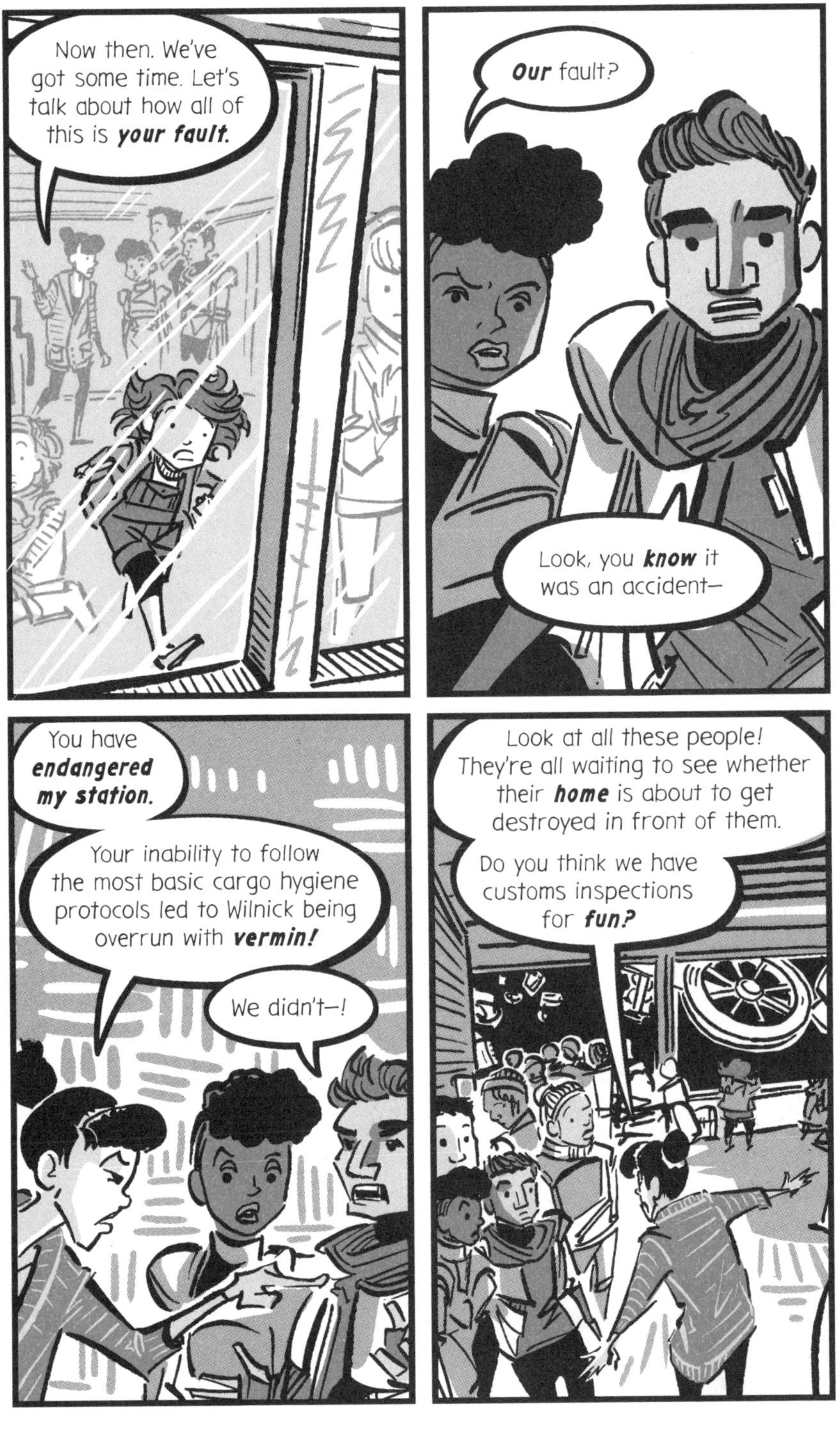
Now then. We've got some time. Let's talk about how all of this is **your fault.**
**Our** fault?
Look, you **know** it was an accident—
You have **endangered my station.**
Your inability to follow the most basic cargo hygiene protocols led to Wilnick being overrun with **vermin!**
We didn't—!
Look at all these people! They're all waiting to see whether their **home** is about to get destroyed in front of them.
Do you think we have customs inspections for **fun?**

(ENGINE ROOM)

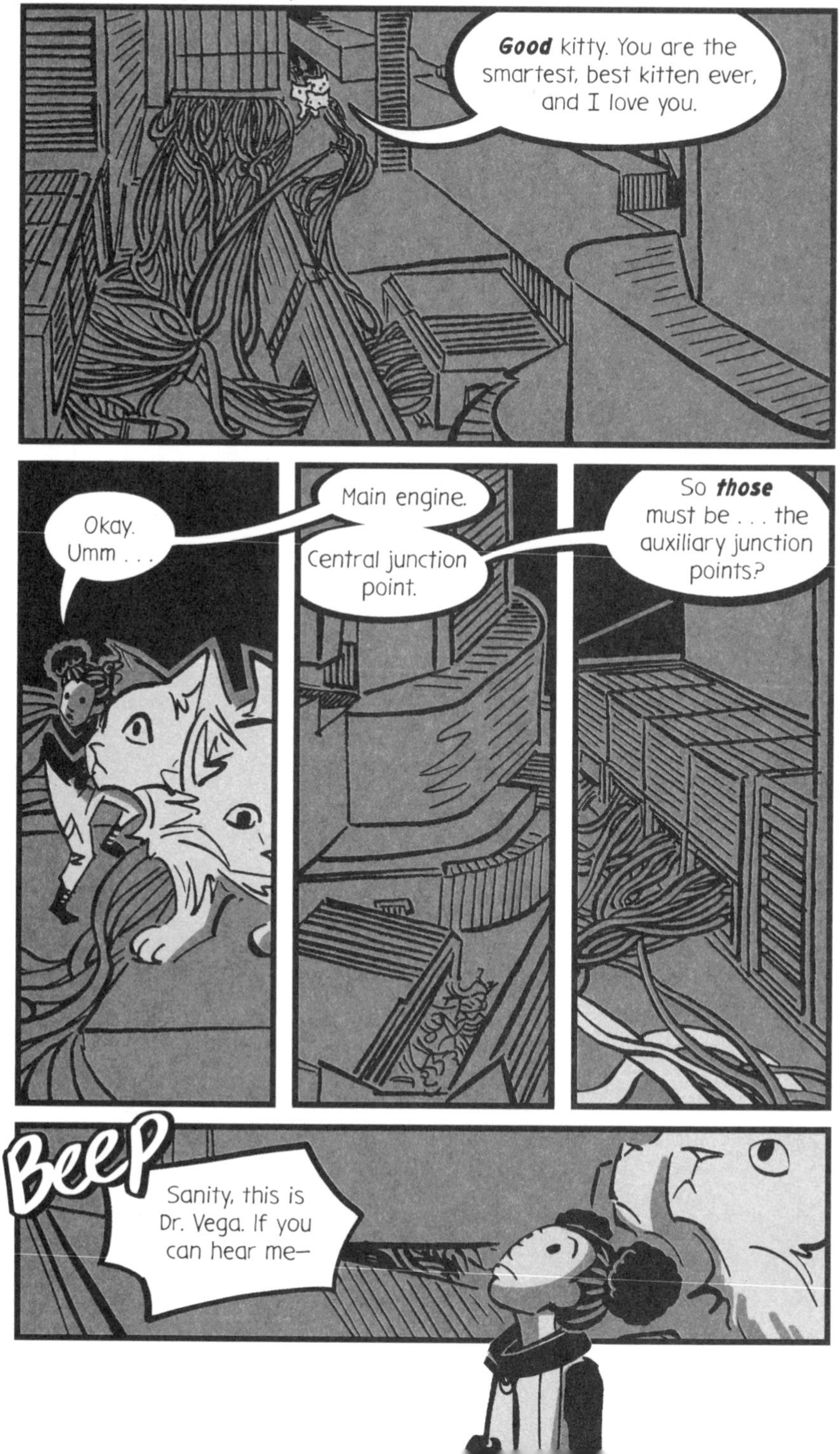

**Good** kitty. You are the smartest, best kitten ever, and I love you.
Okay. Umm . . .
Main engine.
Central junction point.
So **those** must be . . . the auxiliary junction points?
Beep
Sanity, this is Dr. Vega. If you can hear me—

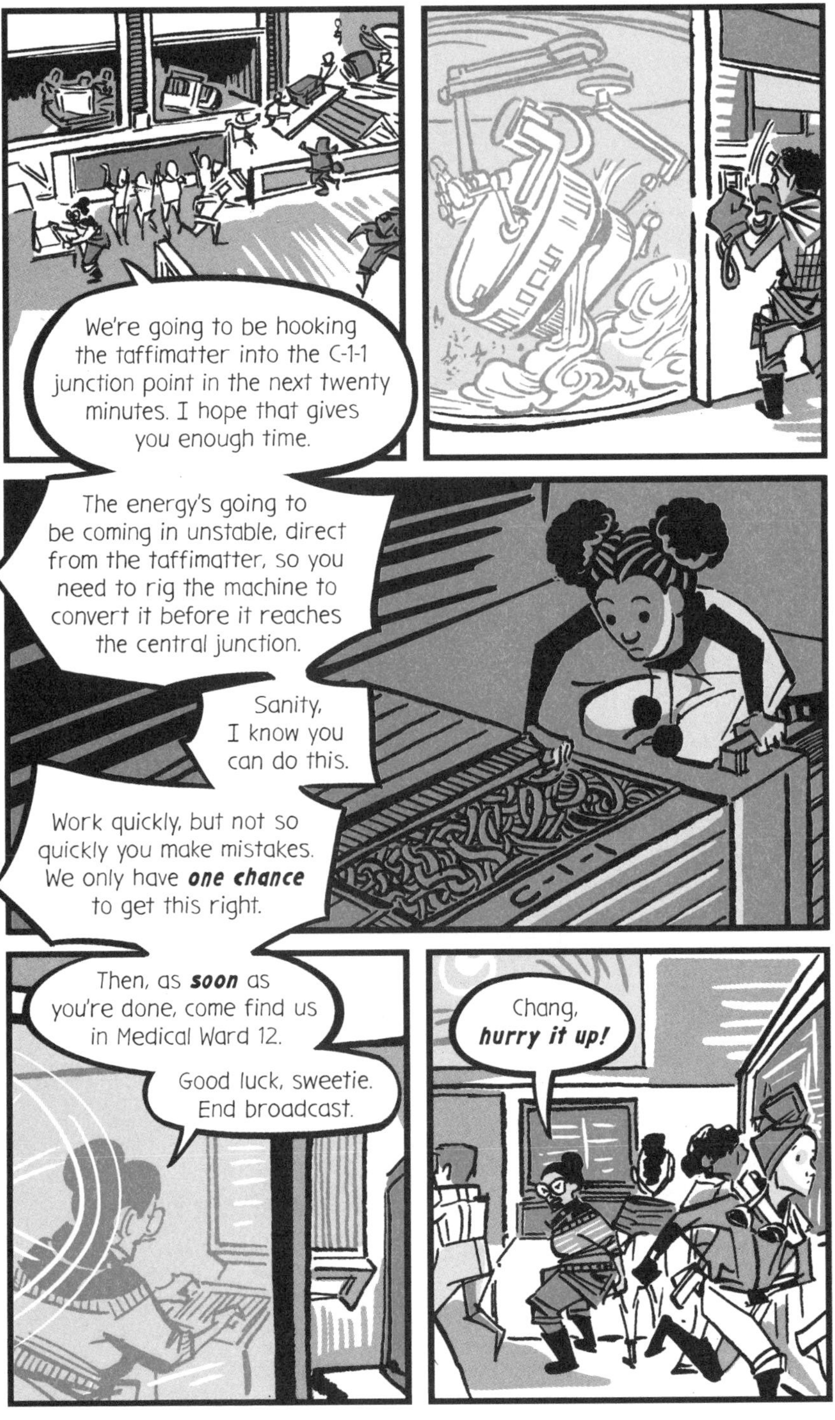
We're going to be hooking the taffimatter into the C-1-1 junction point in the next twenty minutes. I hope that gives you enough time.
The energy's going to be coming in unstable, direct from the taffimatter, so you need to rig the machine to convert it before it reaches the central junction.
Sanity, I know you can do this.
Work quickly, but not so quickly you make mistakes. We only have **one chance** to get this right.
C-1-1
Then, as **soon** as you're done, come find us in Medical Ward 12.
Good luck, sweetie. End broadcast.
Chang, **hurry it up!**

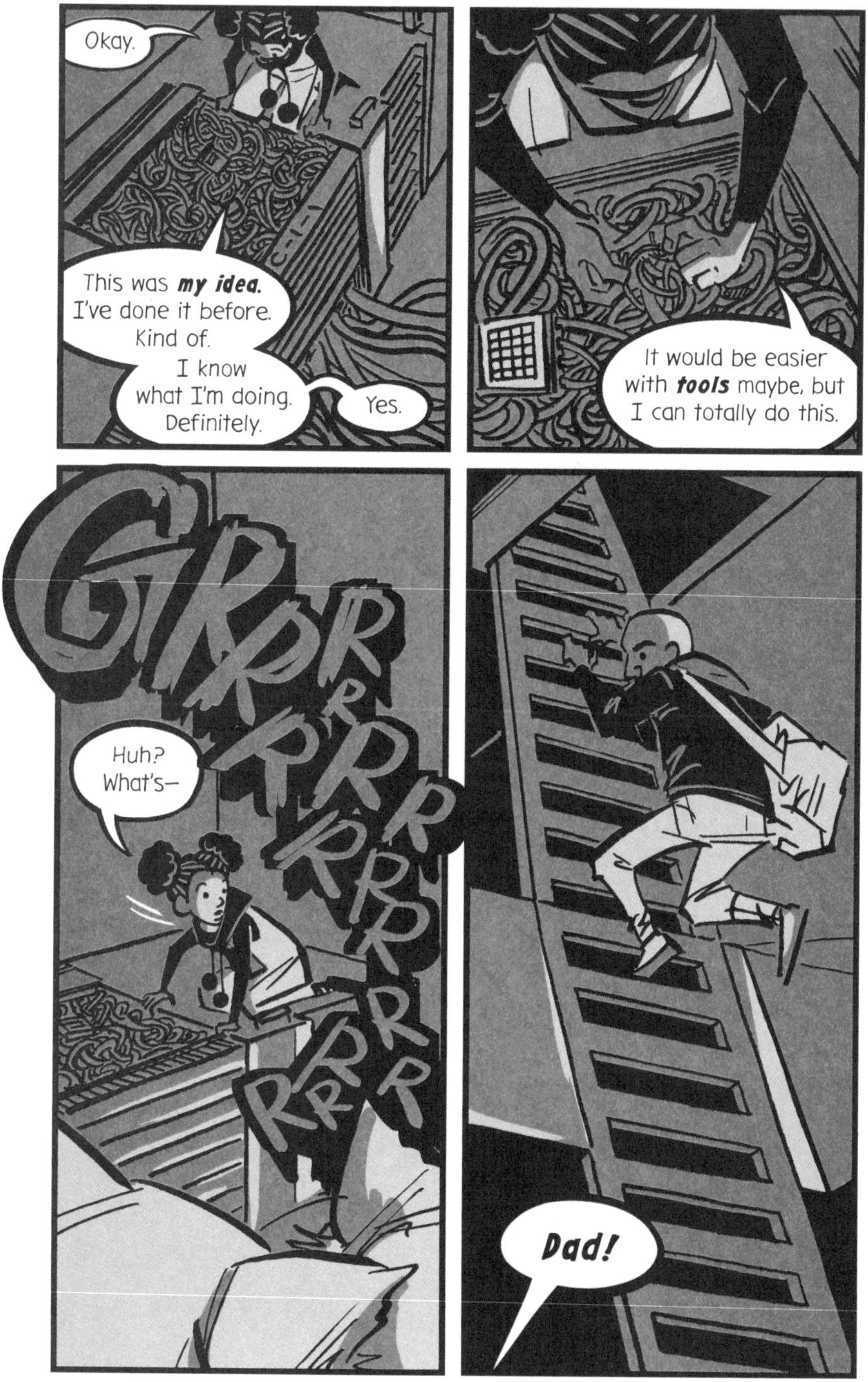
Okay.
This was **my idea.** I've done it before. Kind of.
I know what I'm doing. Definitely.
Yes.
It would be easier with **tools** maybe, but I can totally do this.
GRRRRRRRRRRRRRRRRR
Huh? What's—
**Dad!**

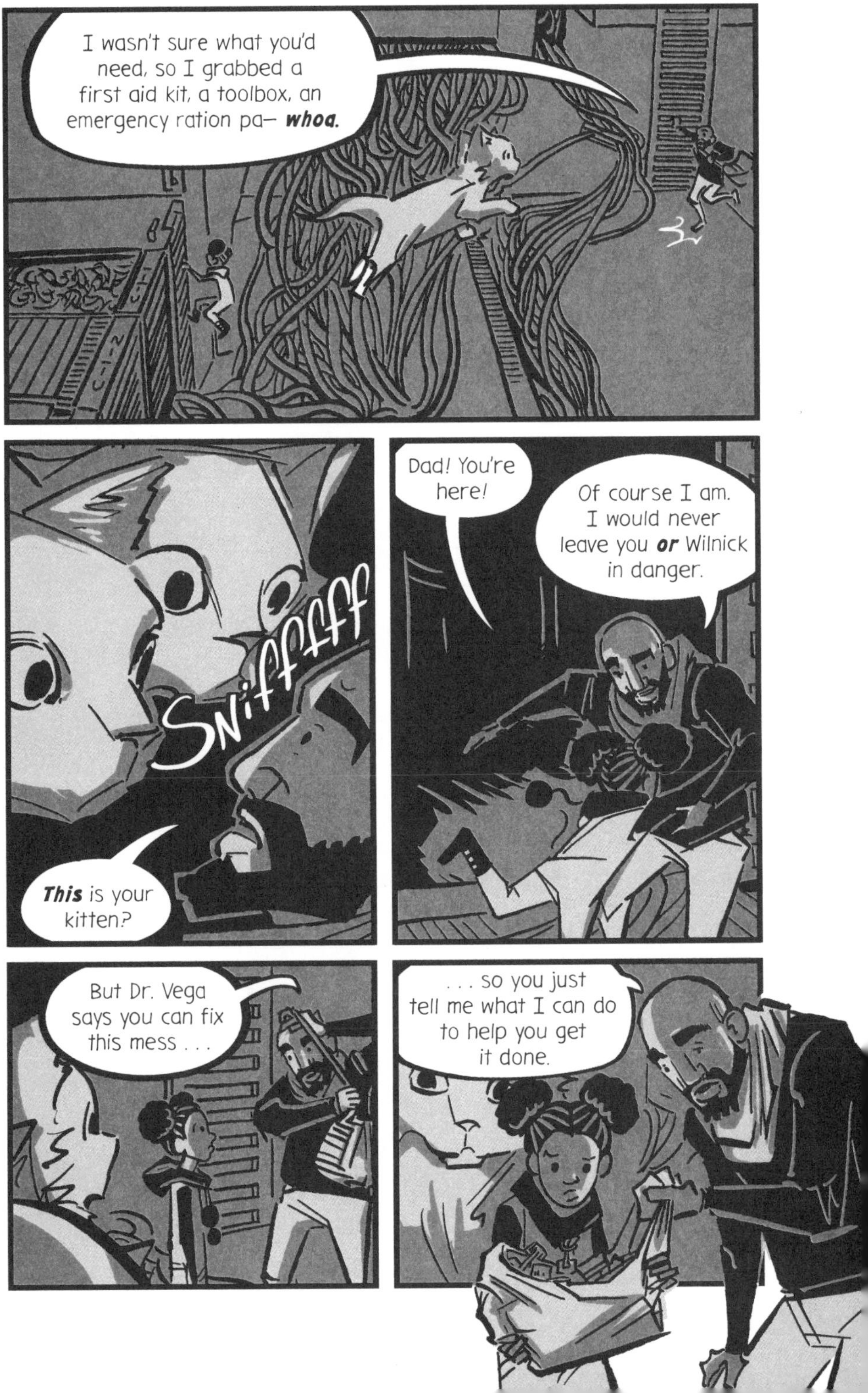
I wasn't sure what you'd need, so I grabbed a first aid kit, a toolbox, an emergency ration pa— **whoa.**
Sniffffff
**This** is your kitten?
Dad! You're here!
Of course I am. I would never leave you **or** Wilnick in danger.
But Dr. Vega says you can fix this mess . . .
. . . so you just tell me what I can do to help you get it done.

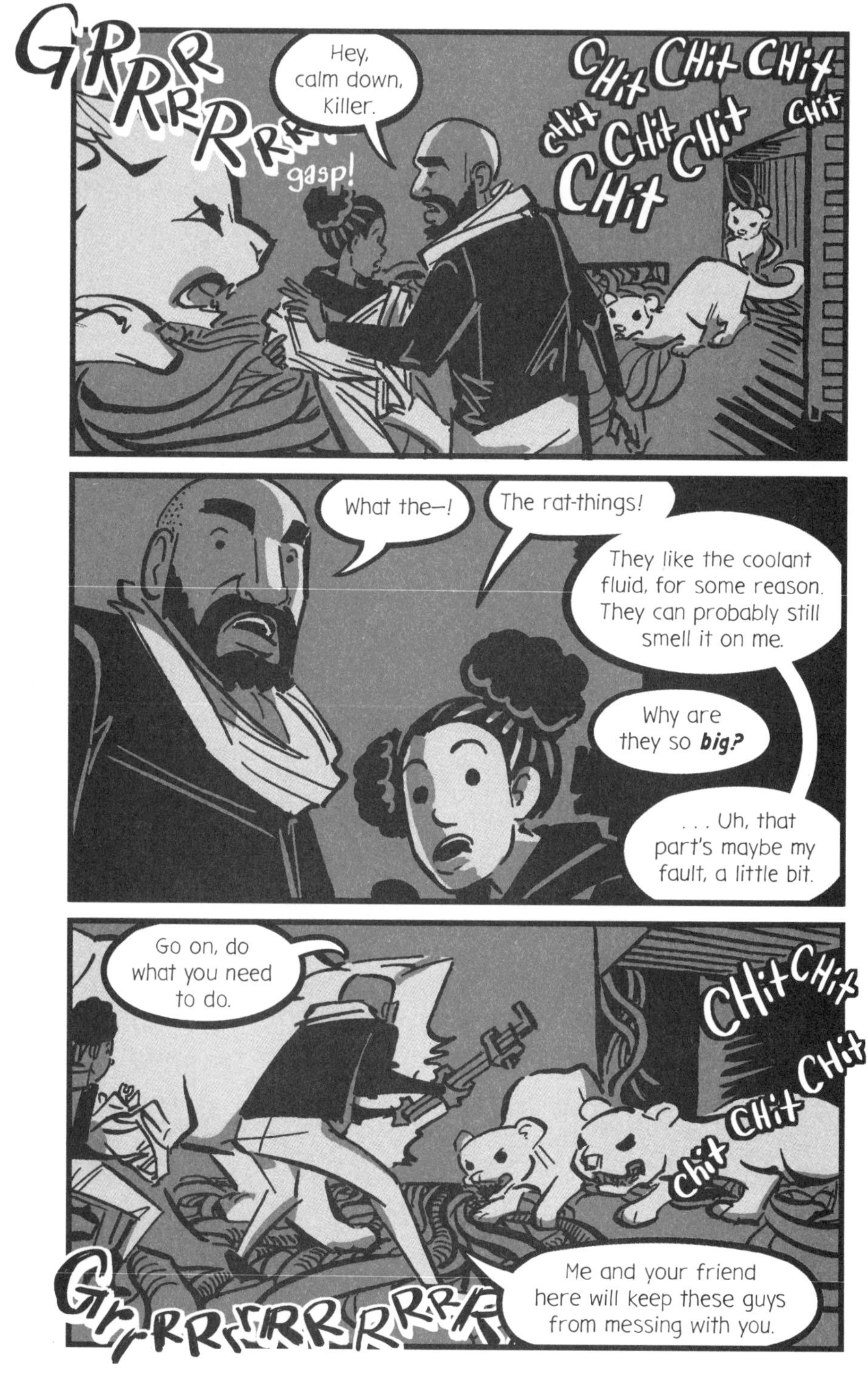
GRRRRRRR
gasp!
Hey, calm down, Killer.
CHit CHit CHit CHit CHit CHit CHit CHit
What the—!
The rat-things!
They like the coolant fluid, for some reason. They can probably still smell it on me.
Why are they so **big?**
. . . Uh, that part's maybe my fault, a little bit.
Go on, do what you need to do.
CHit CHit
Chit CHit CHit
Me and your friend here will keep these guys from messing with you.

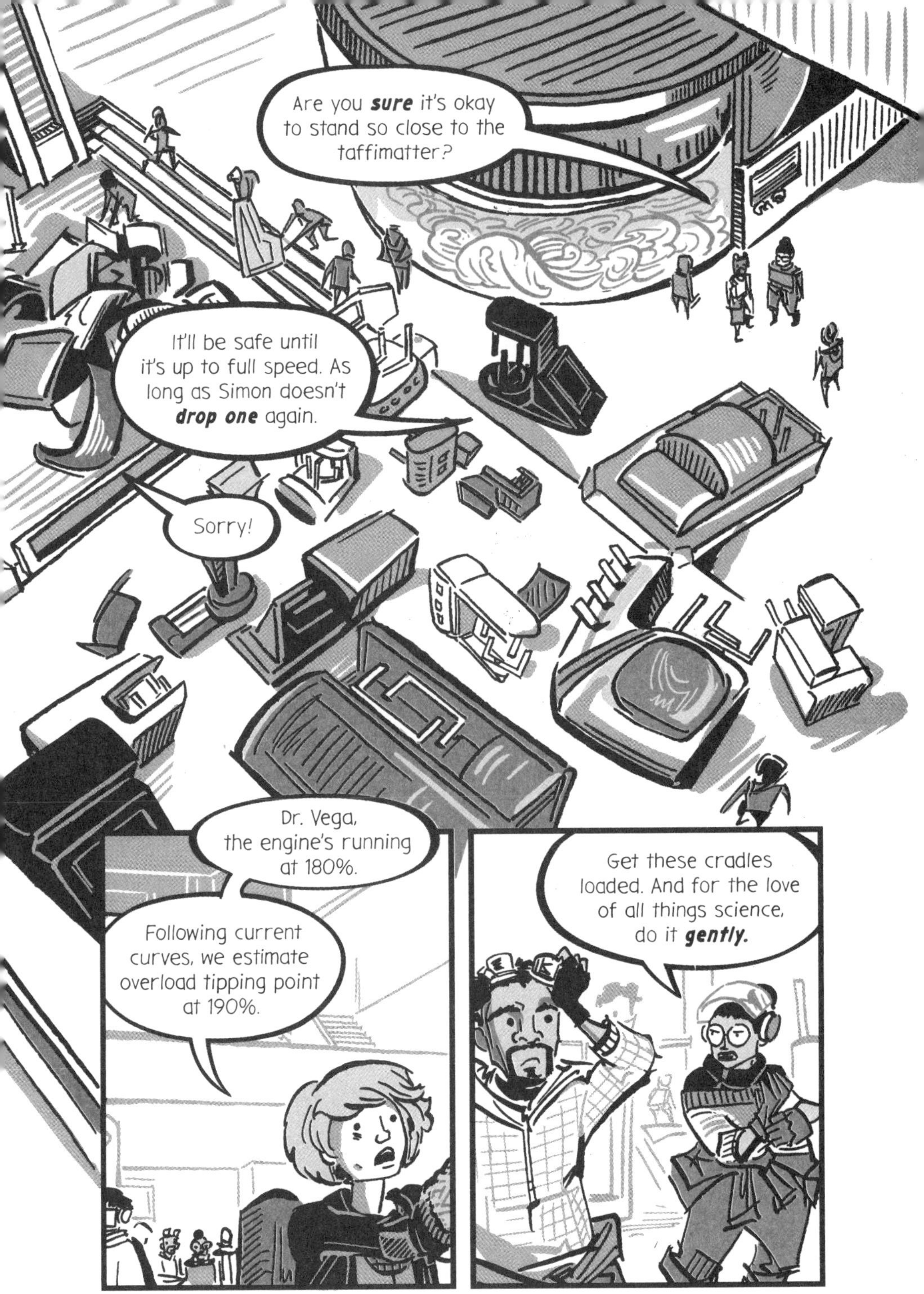
Are you **sure** it's okay to stand so close to the taffimatter?
It'll be safe until it's up to full speed. As long as Simon doesn't **drop one** again.
Sorry!
Dr. Vega, the engine's running at 180%.
Following current curves, we estimate overload tipping point at 190%.
Get these cradles loaded. And for the love of all things science, do it **gently.**

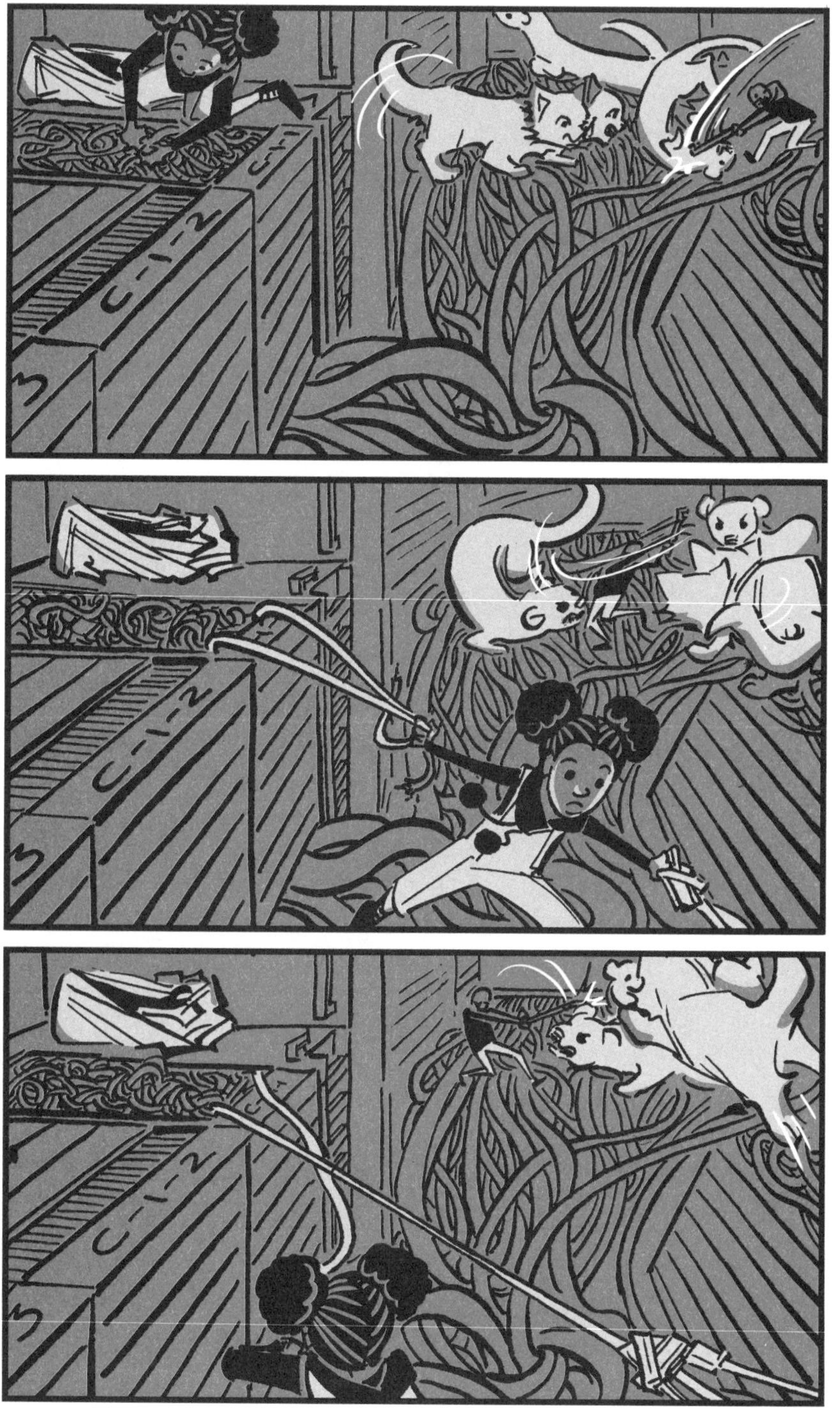
C-1-2
3

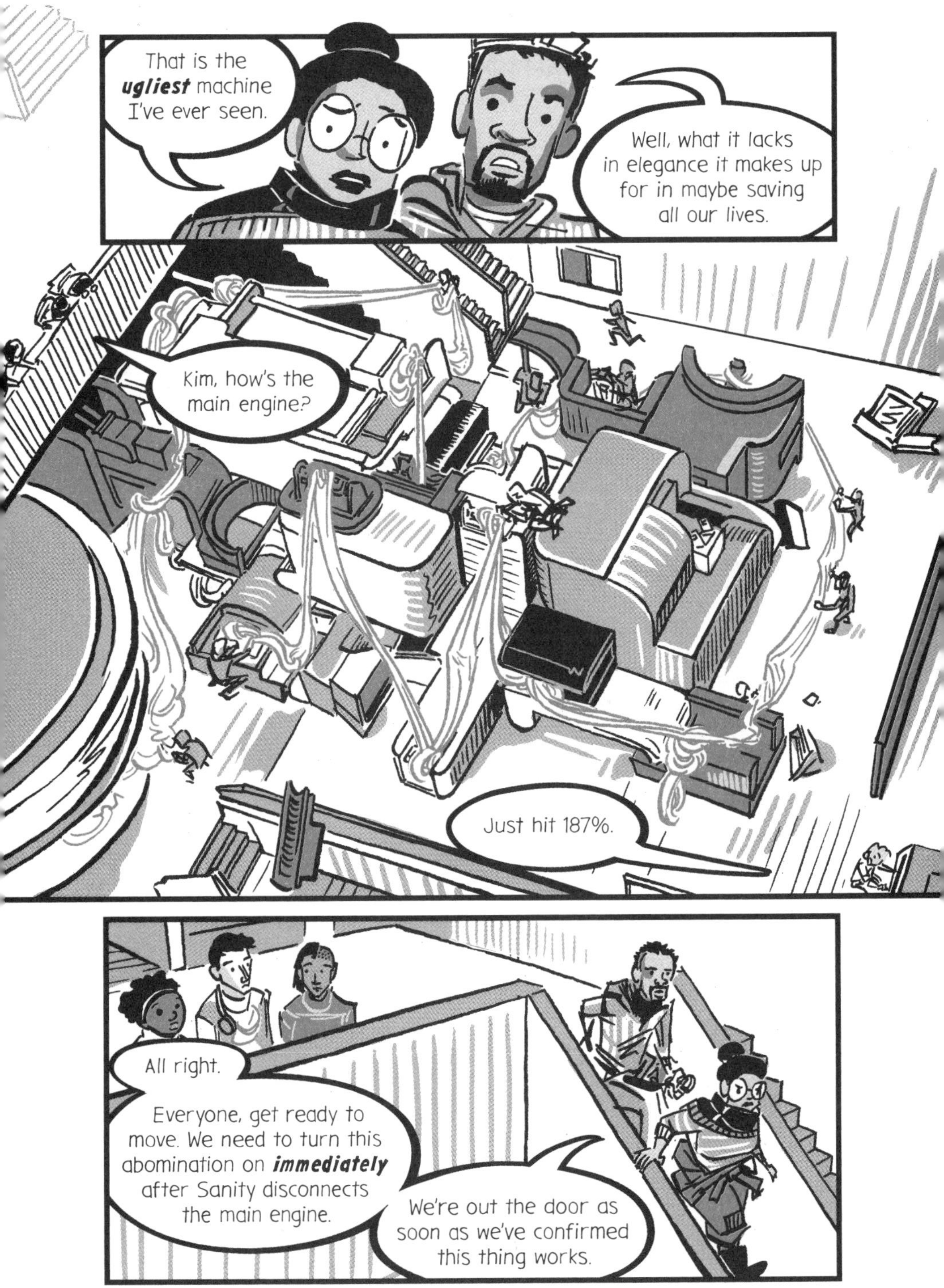
That is the **ugliest** machine I've ever seen.
Well, what it lacks in elegance it makes up for in maybe saving all our lives.
Kim, how's the main engine?
Just hit 187%.
All right.
Everyone, get ready to move. We need to turn this abomination on ***immediately*** after Sanity disconnects the main engine.
We're out the door as soon as we've confirmed this thing works.

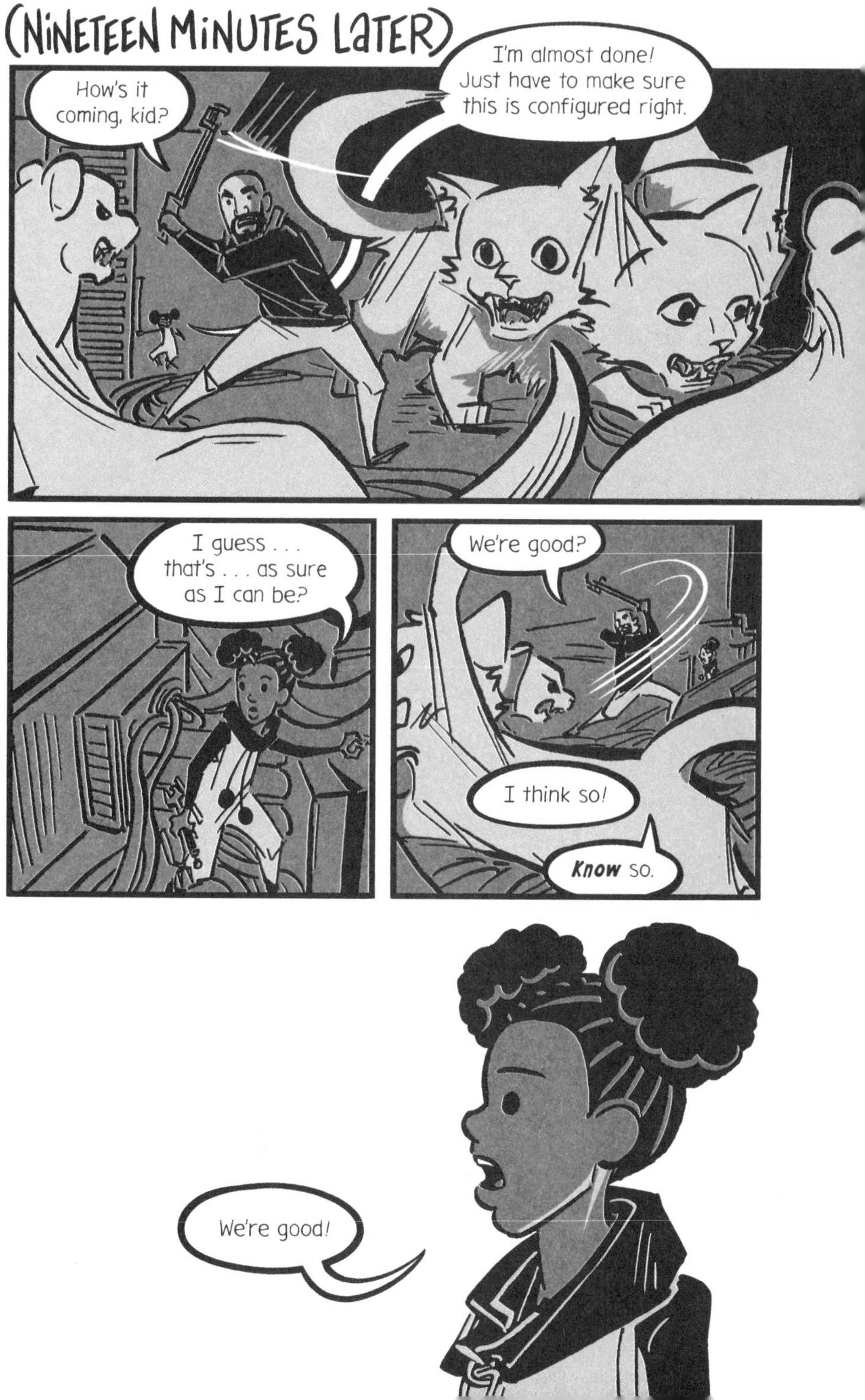
(NINETEEN MINUTES LATER)
How's it coming, kid?
I'm almost done! Just have to make sure this is configured right.
I guess . . . that's . . . as sure as I can be?
We're good?
I think so!
**Know** so.
We're good!

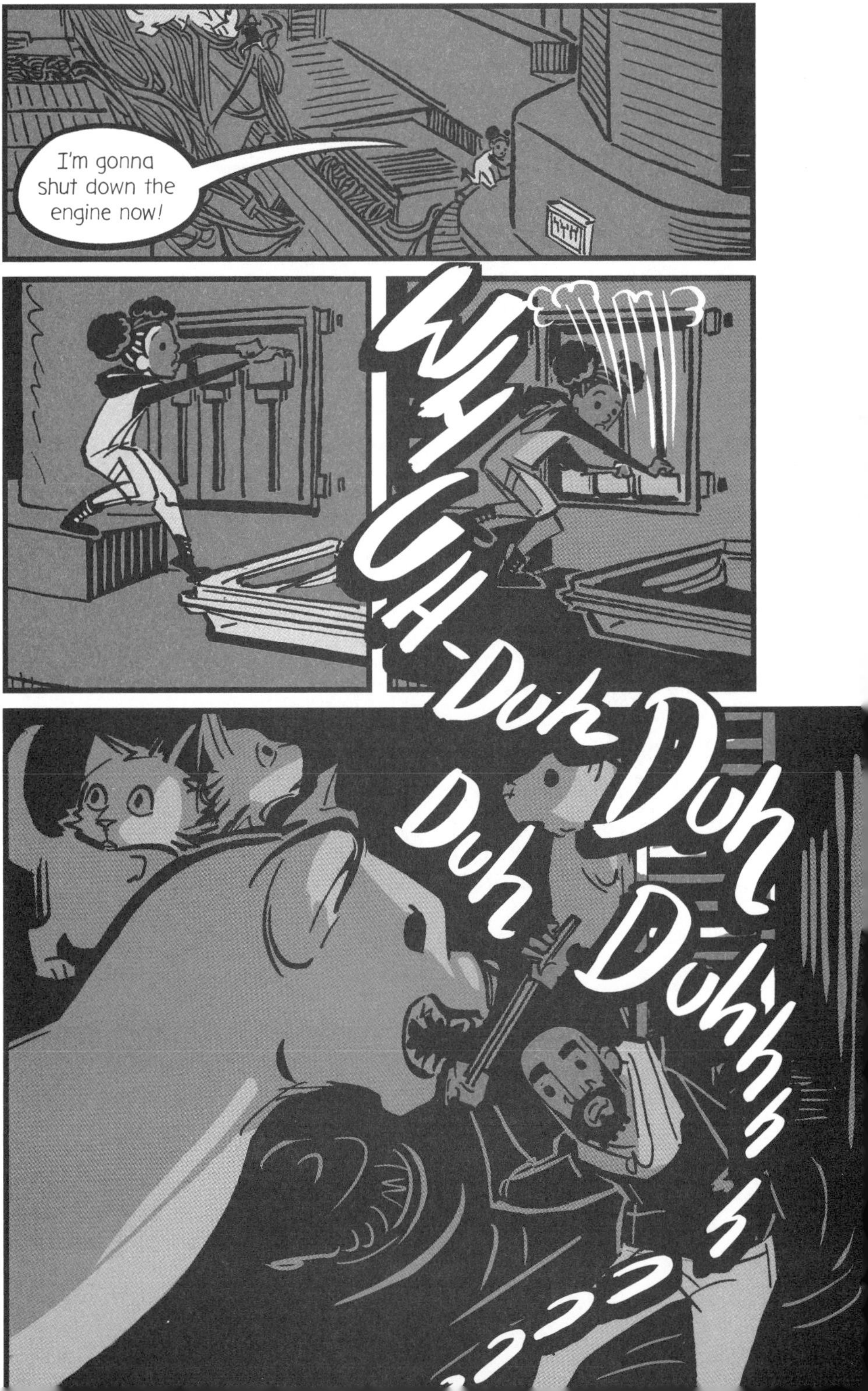
I'm gonna shut down the engine now!
WHUH-Duh
Duh
Duh
Duhhhh

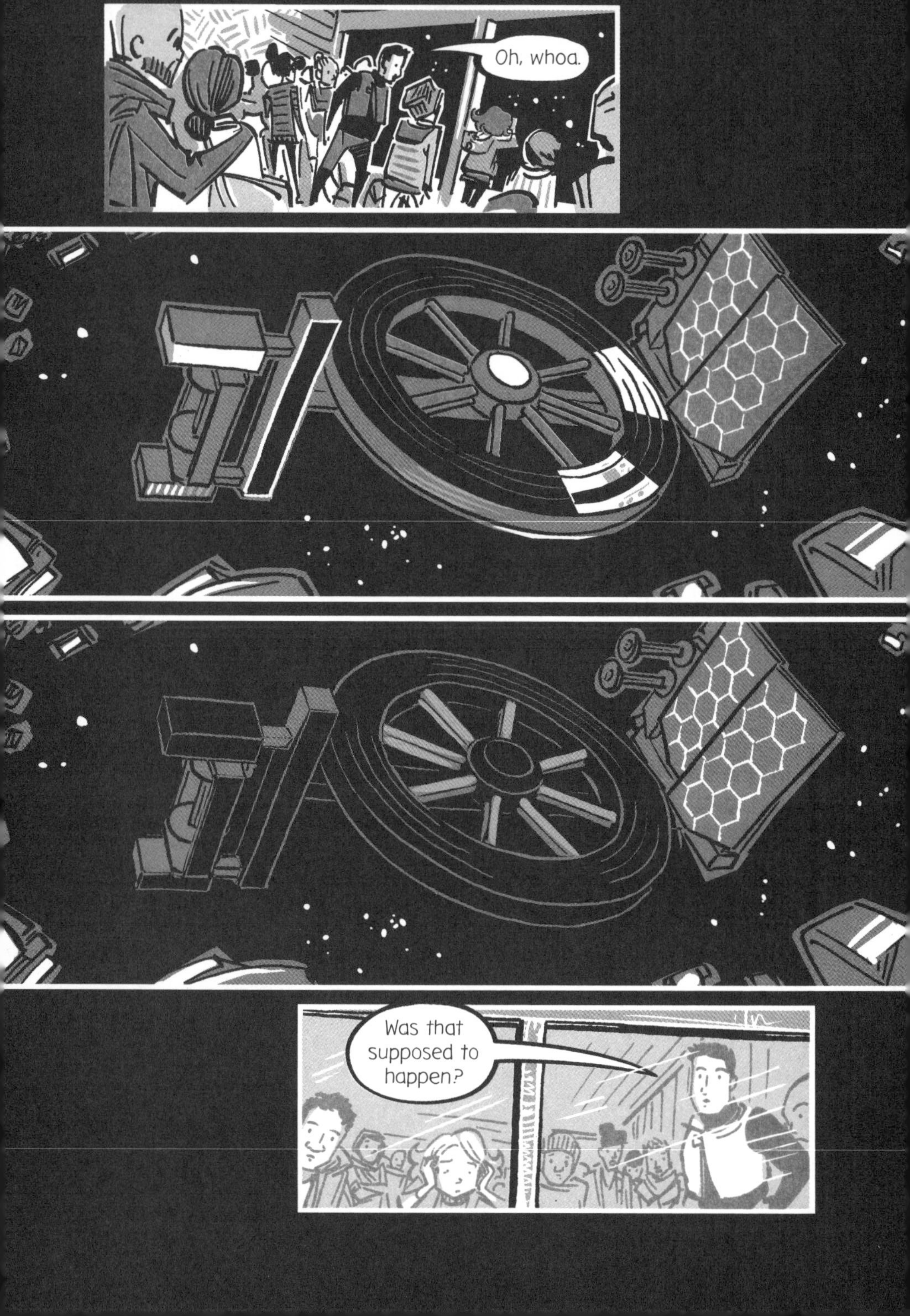

Oh, whoa.
Was that supposed to happen?

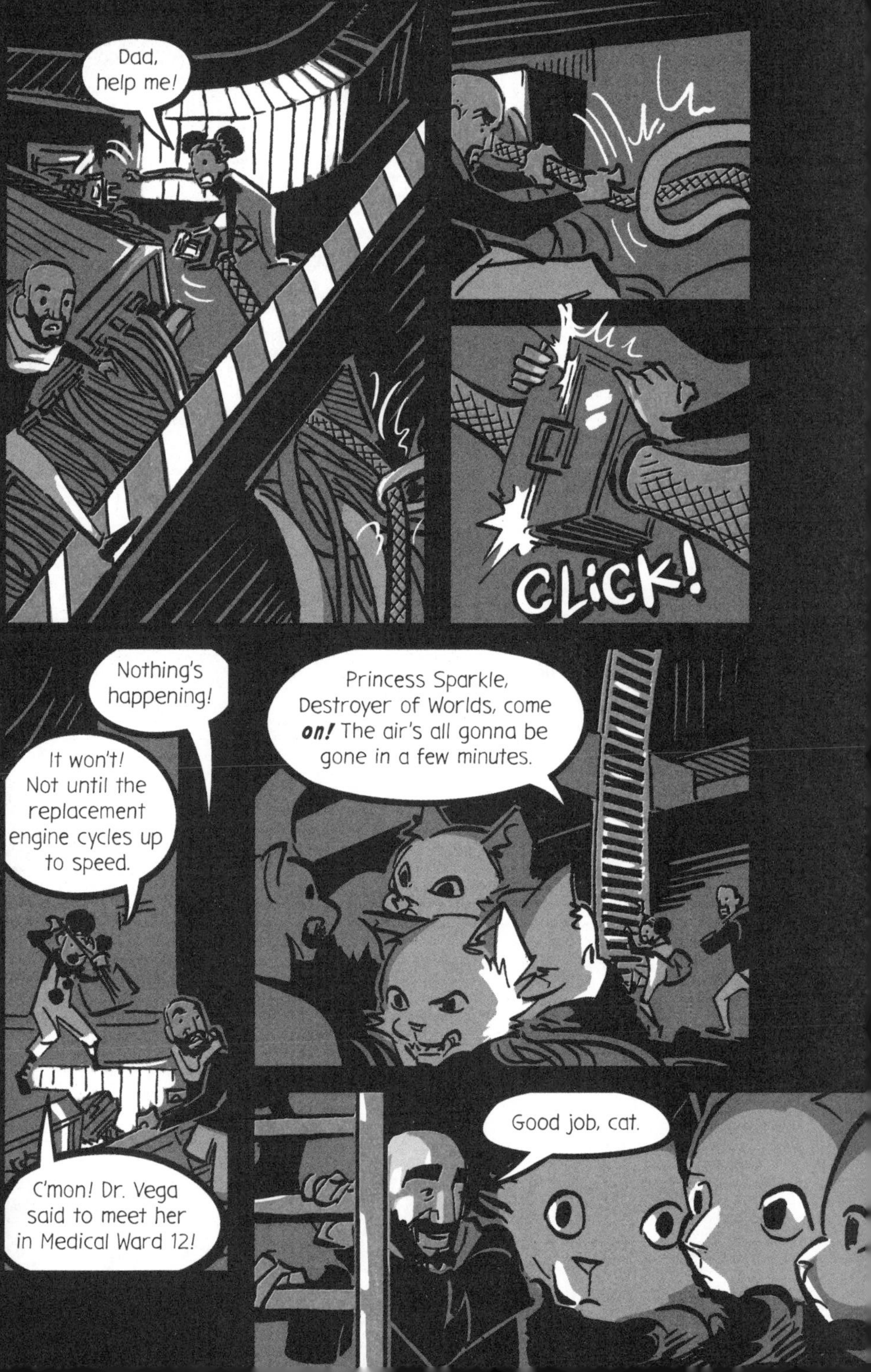
Dad, help me!
CLICK!
Nothing's happening!
It won't! Not until the replacement engine cycles up to speed.
C'mon! Dr. Vega said to meet her in Medical Ward 12!
Princess Sparkle, Destroyer of Worlds, come on! The air's all gonna be gone in a few minutes.
Good job, cat.

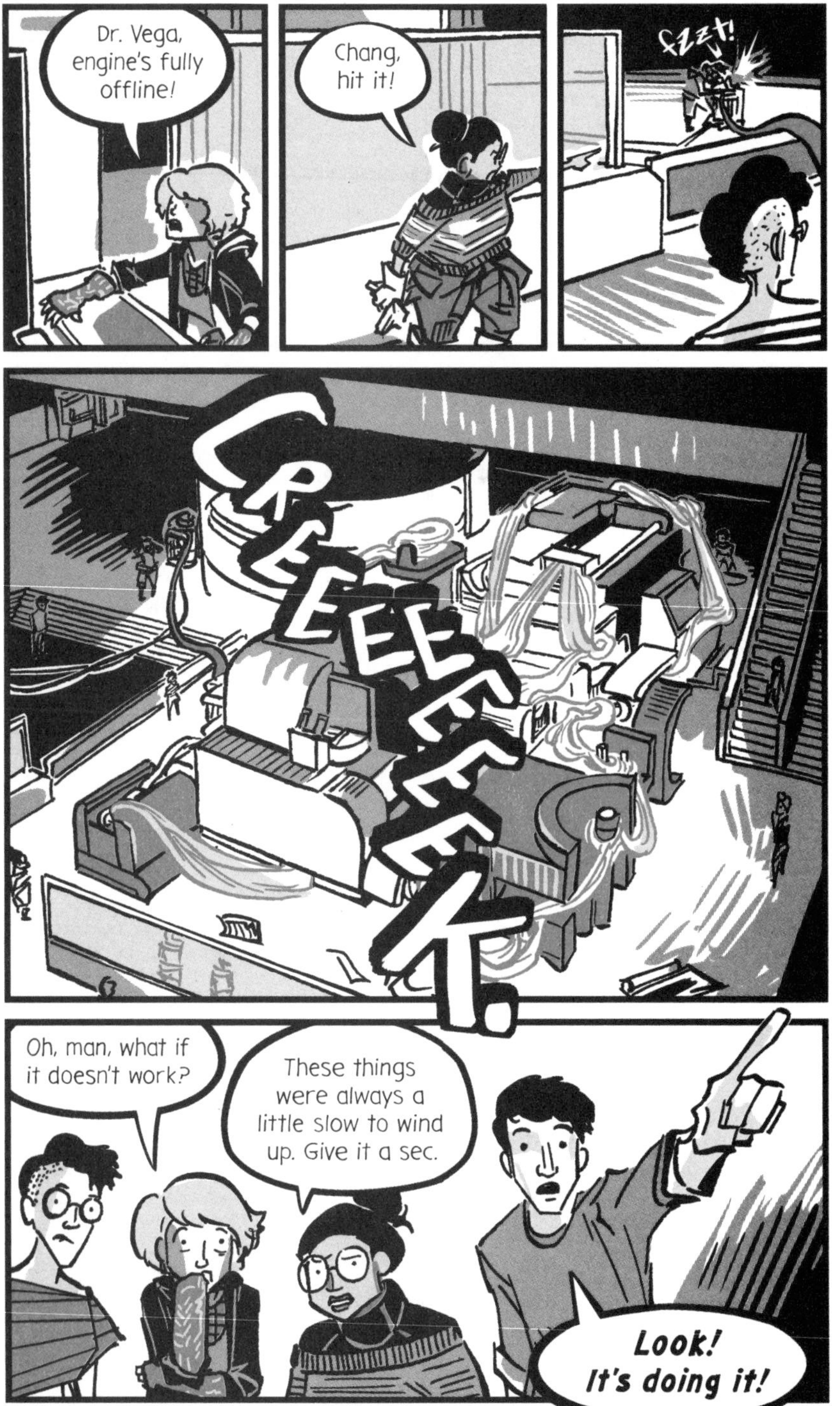
Dr. Vega, engine's fully offline!
Chang, hit it!
FZZT!
CREEEEEEK.
Oh, man, what if it doesn't work?
These things were always a little slow to wind up. Give it a sec.
Look! It's doing it!

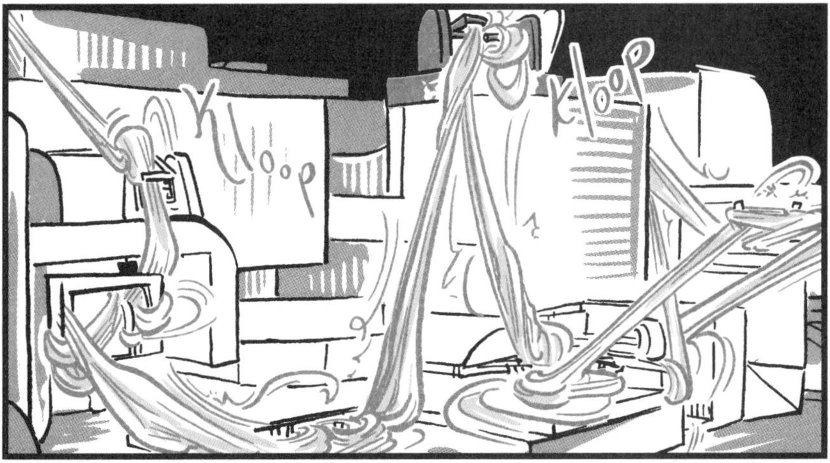
Kloop
Kloop

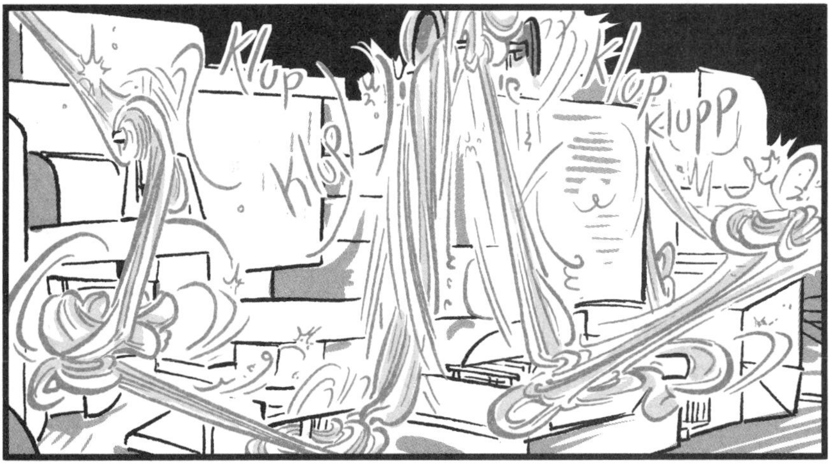
Klup
Klop
Klop
klupp

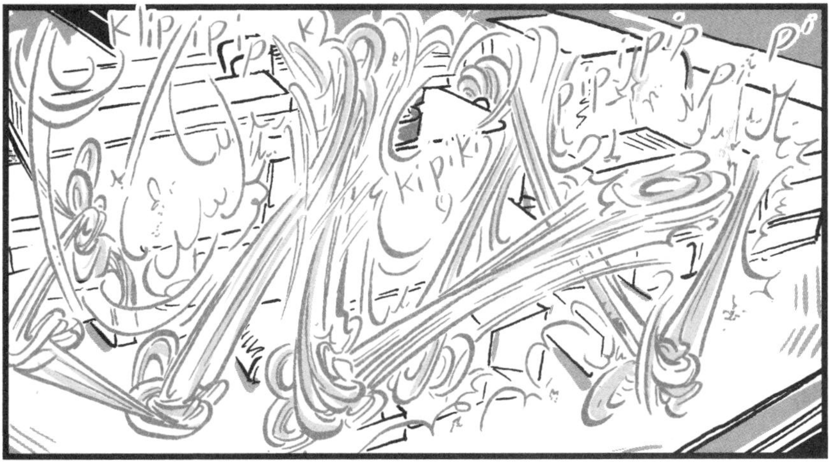
Klipipi
kipiki

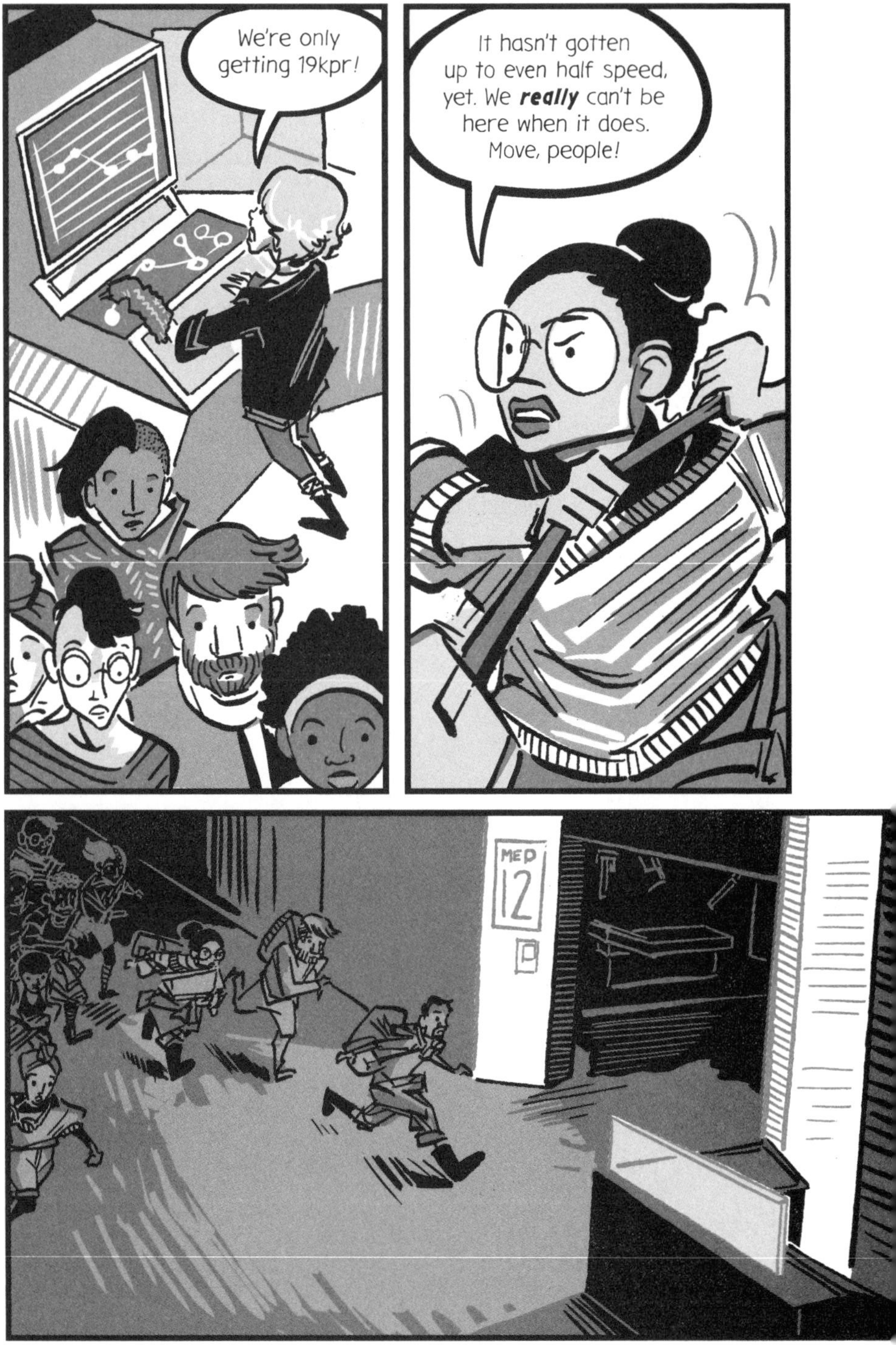
We're only getting 19kpr!
It hasn't gotten up to even half speed, yet. We **really** can't be here when it does. Move, people!
MED 12

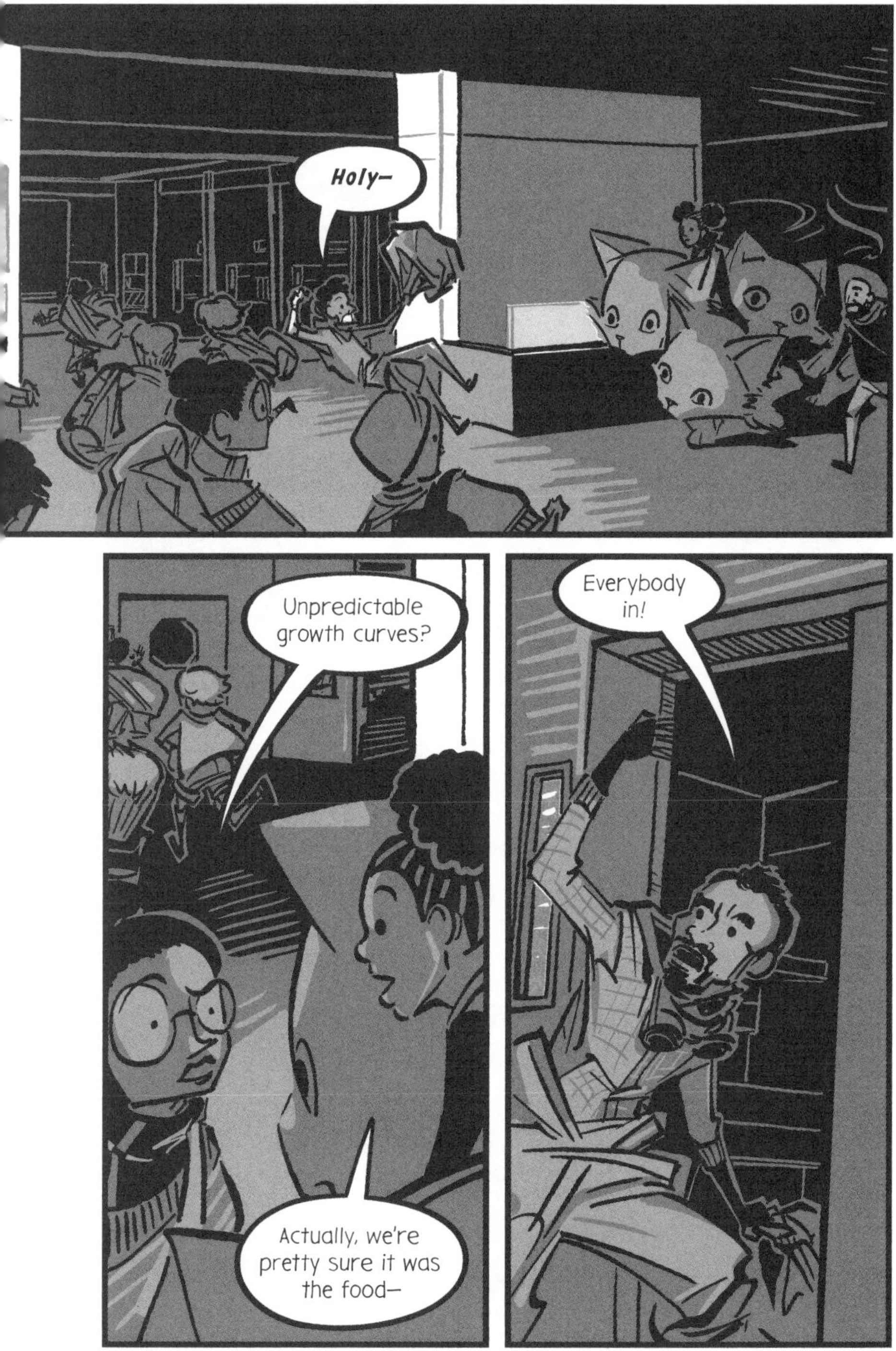
Holy—
Unpredictable growth curves?
Actually, we're pretty sure it was the food—
Everybody in!

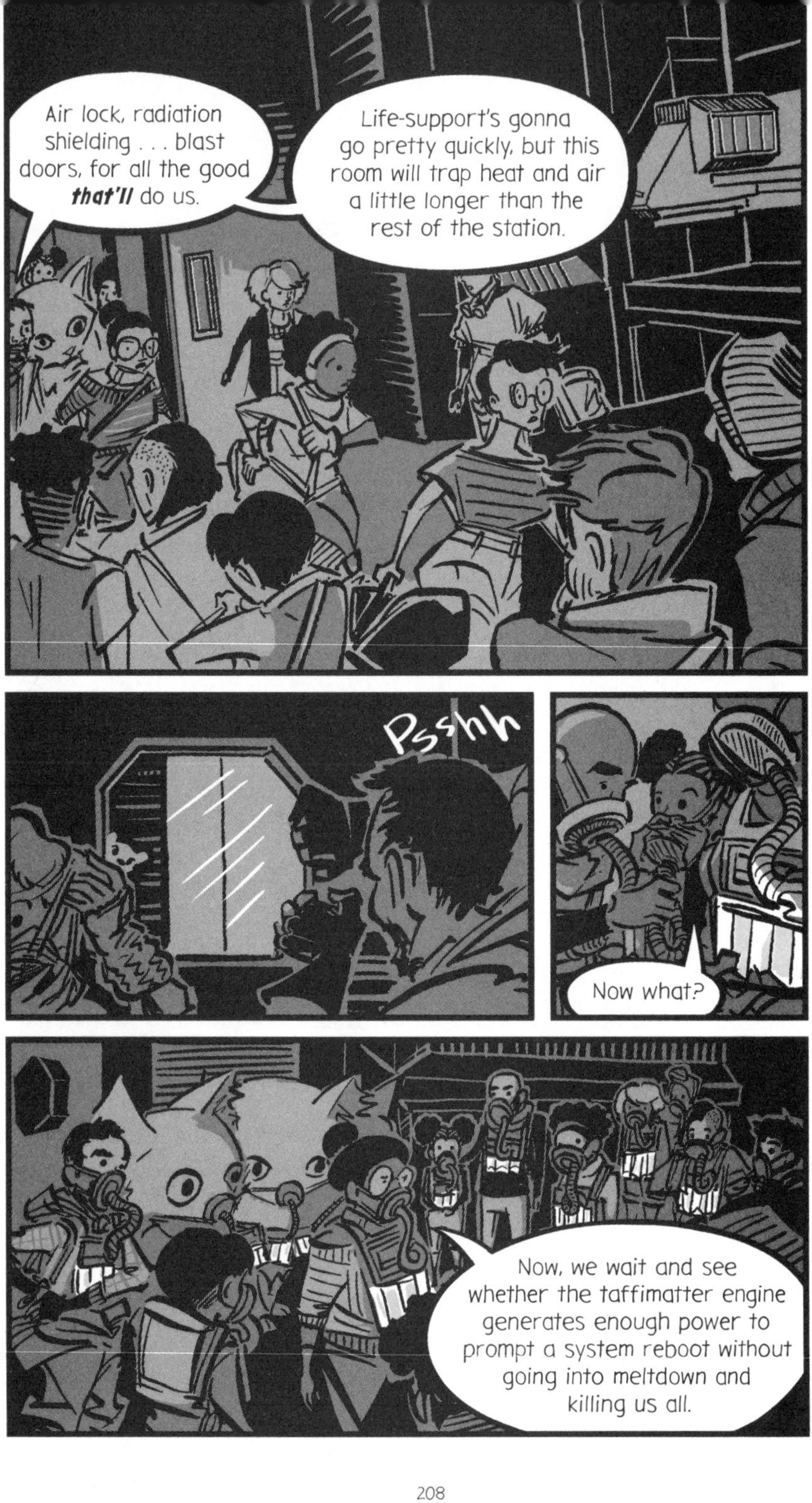
Air lock, radiation shielding . . . blast doors, for all the good ***that'll*** do us.
Life-support's gonna go pretty quickly, but this room will trap heat and air a little longer than the rest of the station.
Psshh
Now what?
Now, we wait and see whether the taffimatter engine generates enough power to prompt a system reboot without going into meltdown and killing us all.

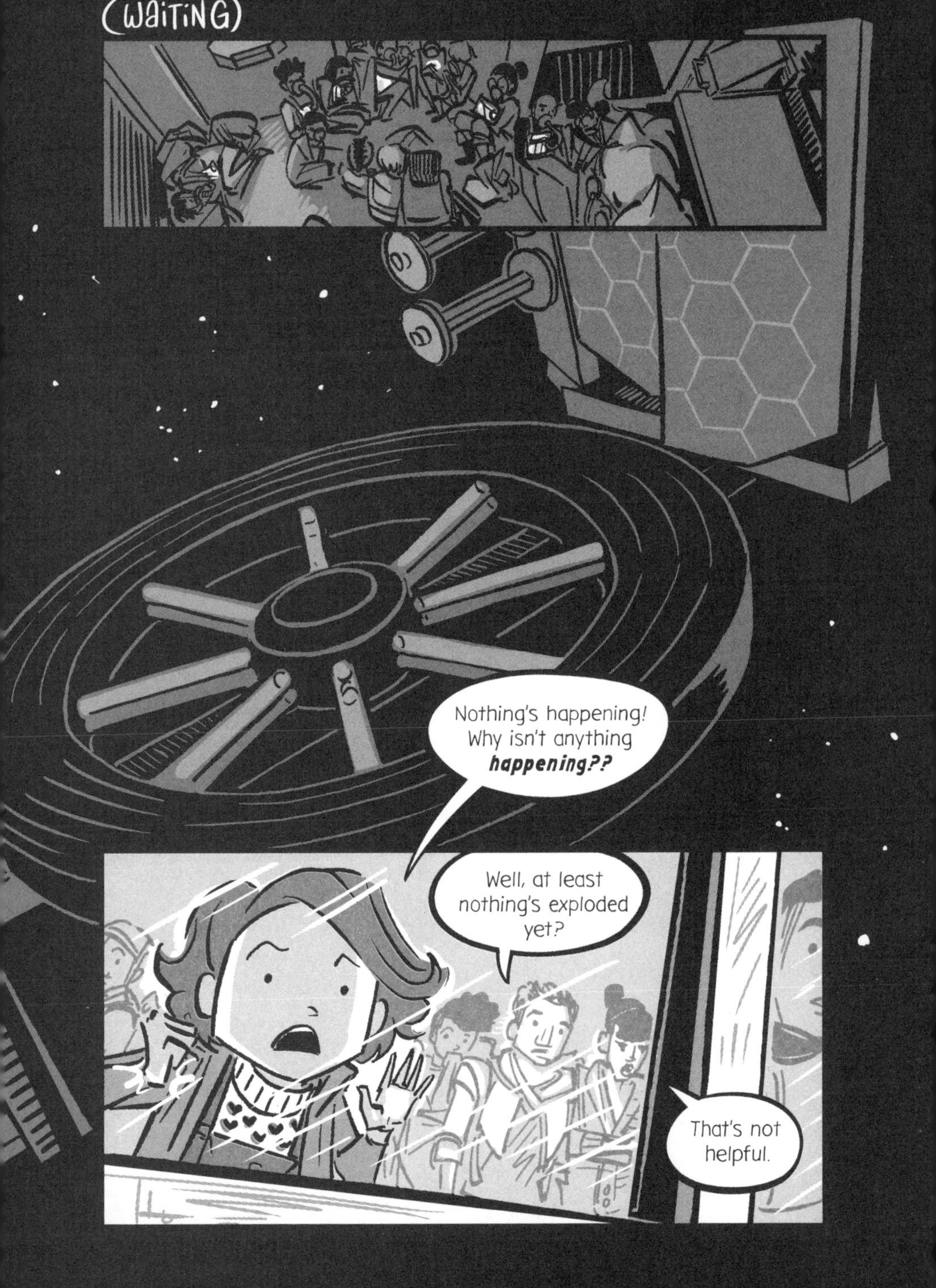
(WAITING)
Nothing's happening! Why isn't anything **happening??**
Well, at least nothing's exploded yet?
That's not helpful.

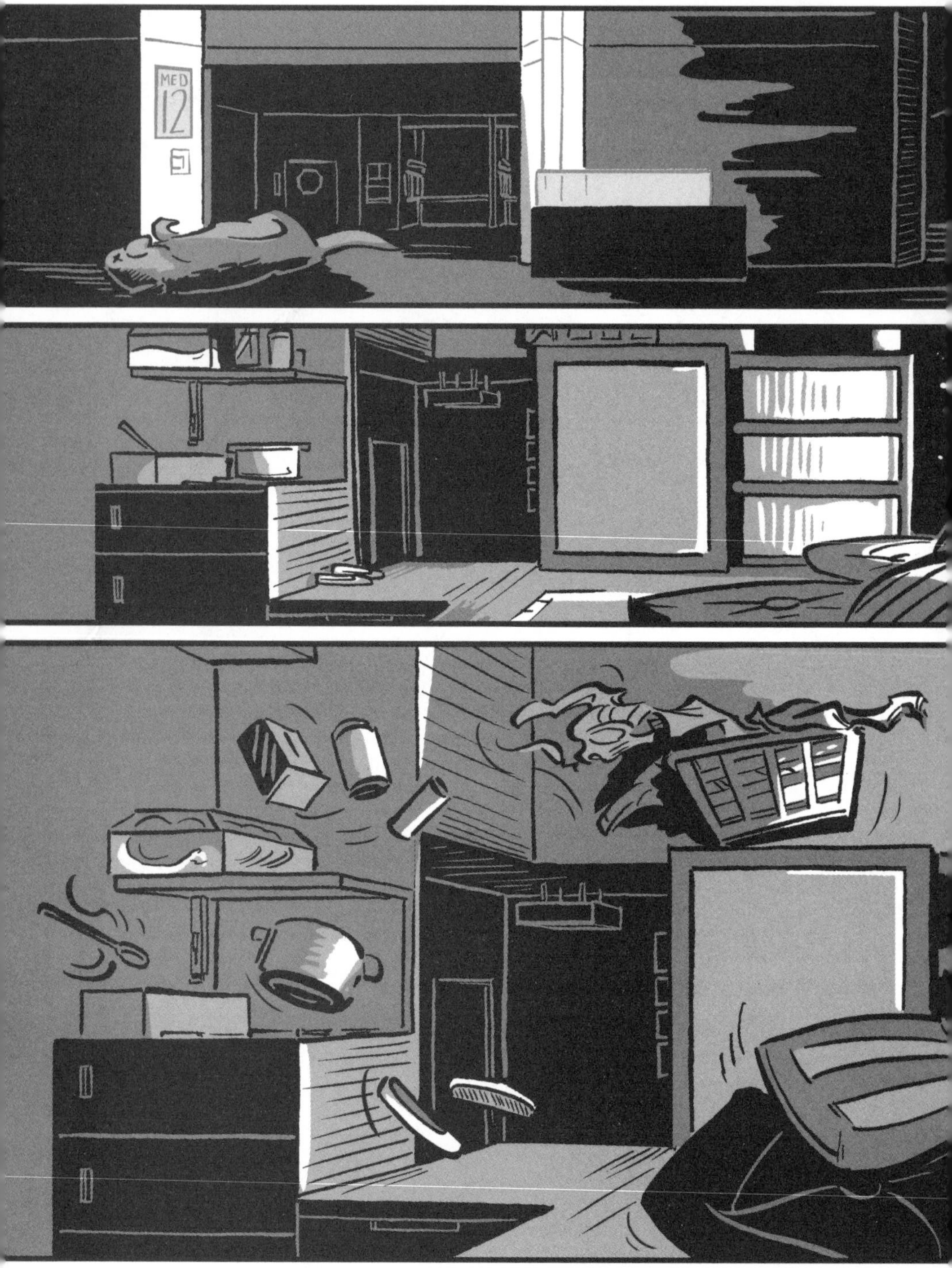
MED
12

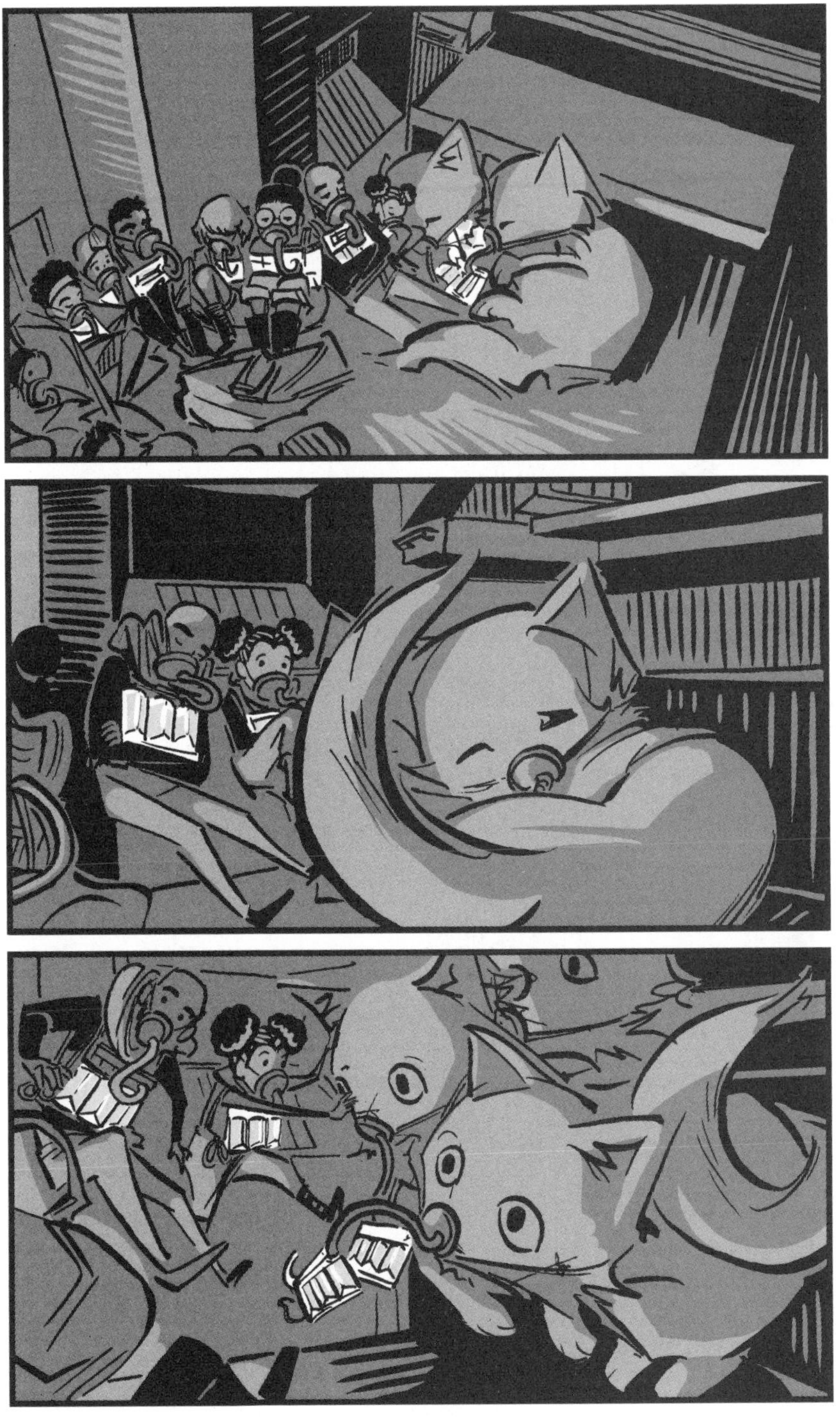

(EVENTUALLY)

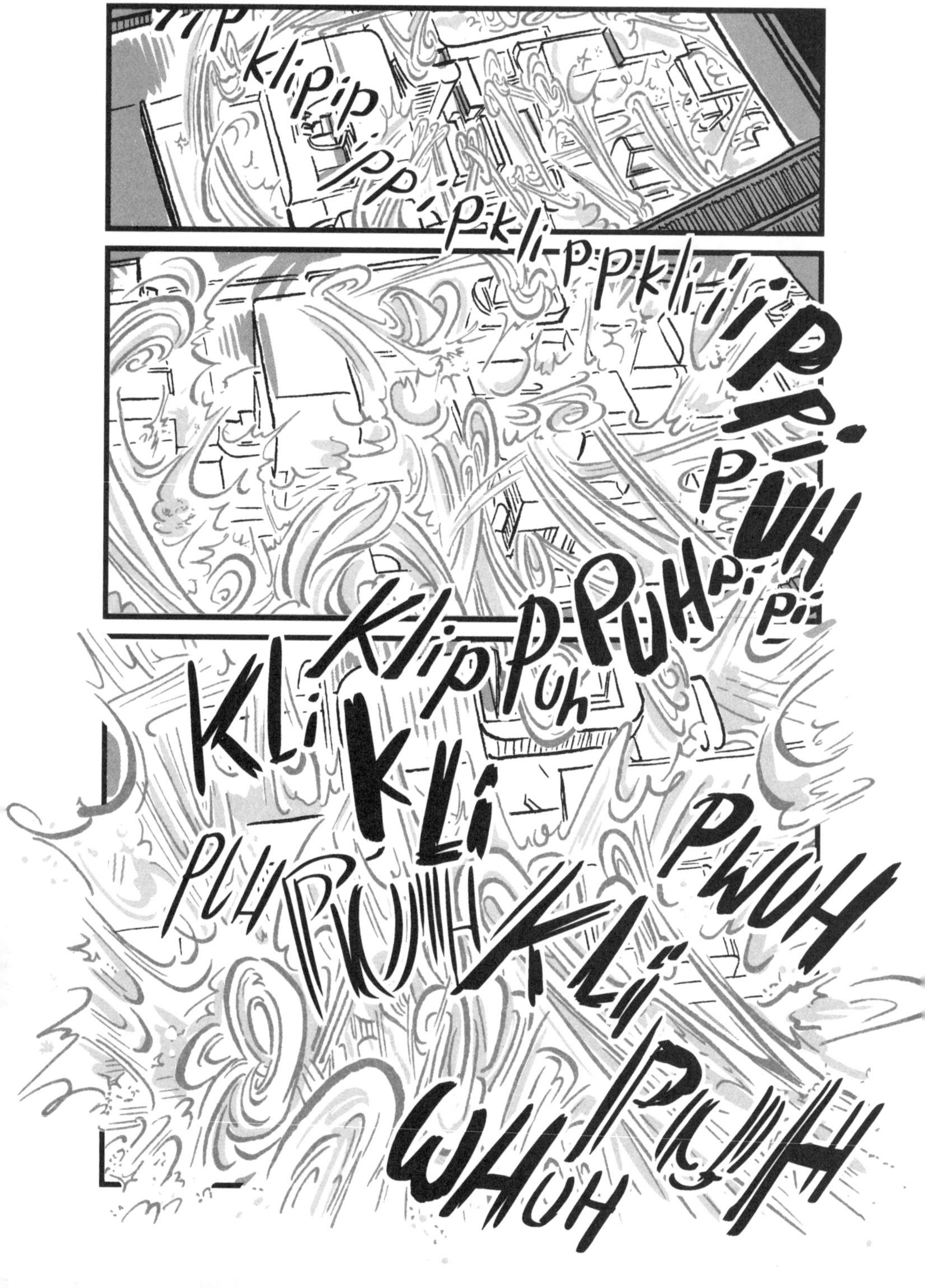
klipip
pp
pklip
pklip
PUH
PUH
KLi
Klip
Puh
PUH
Kli
PUH
PUH
PWUH
KLi
PUH
WHUH

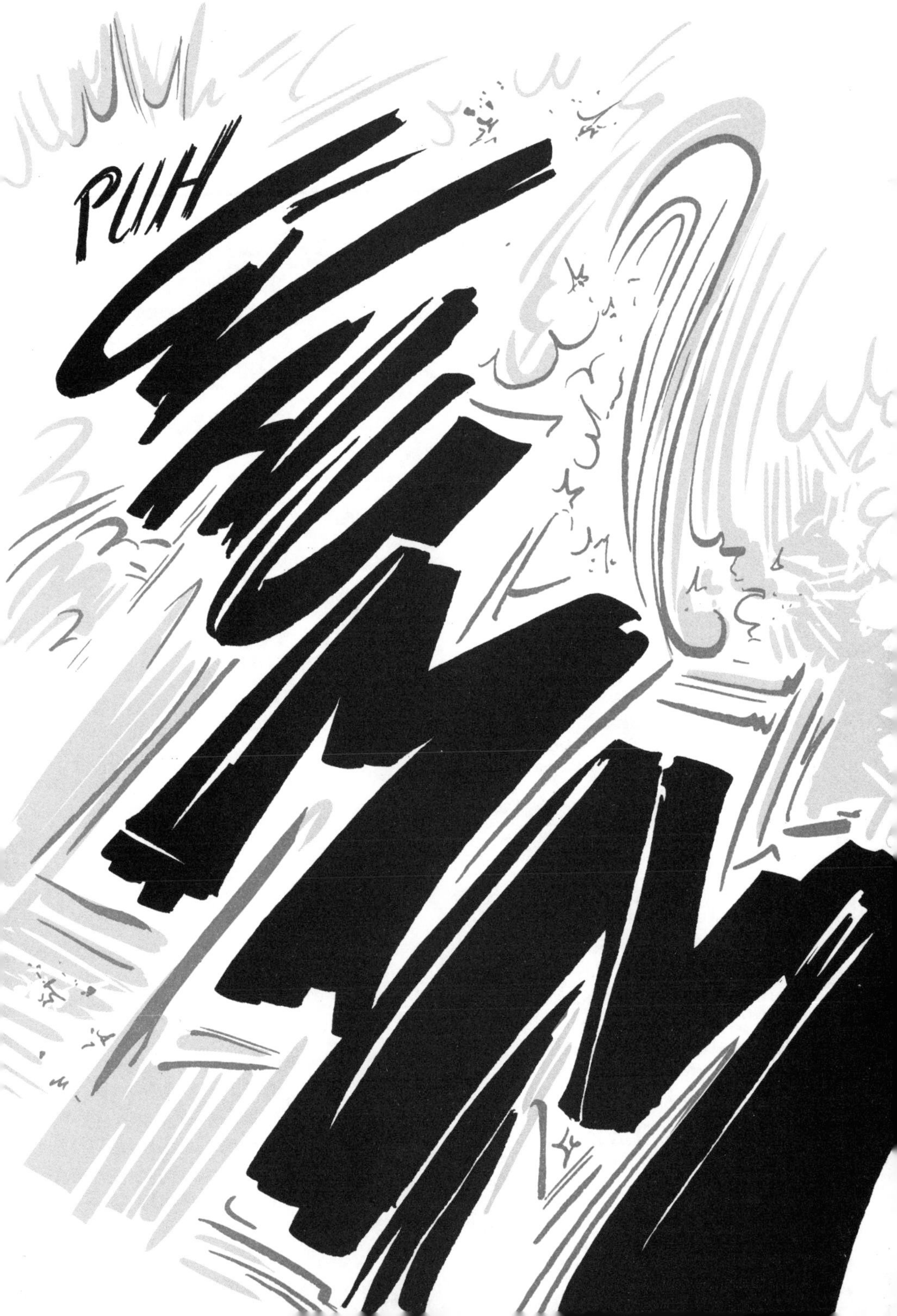
PUH

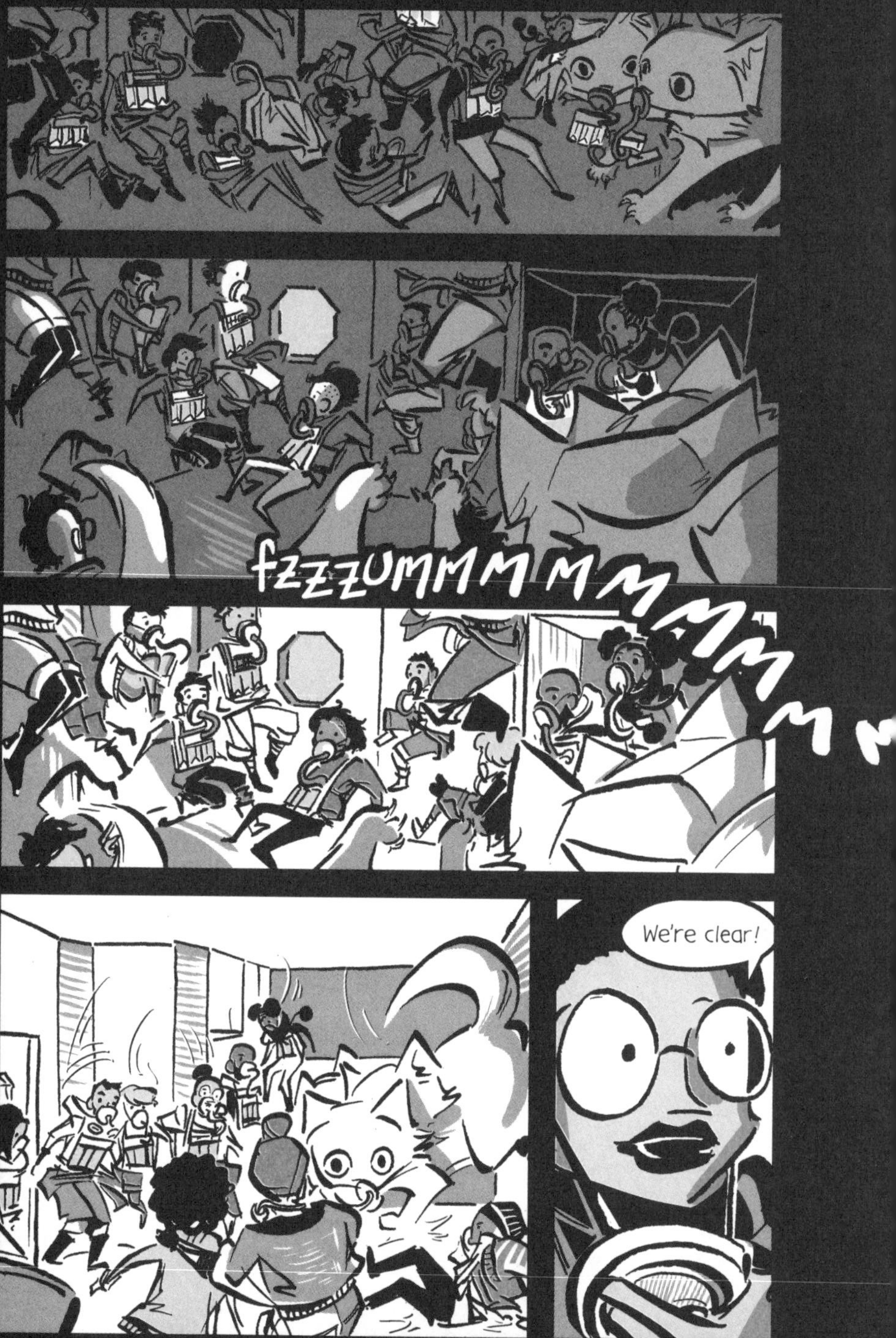
fzzzummmmmmmmmm
We're clear!

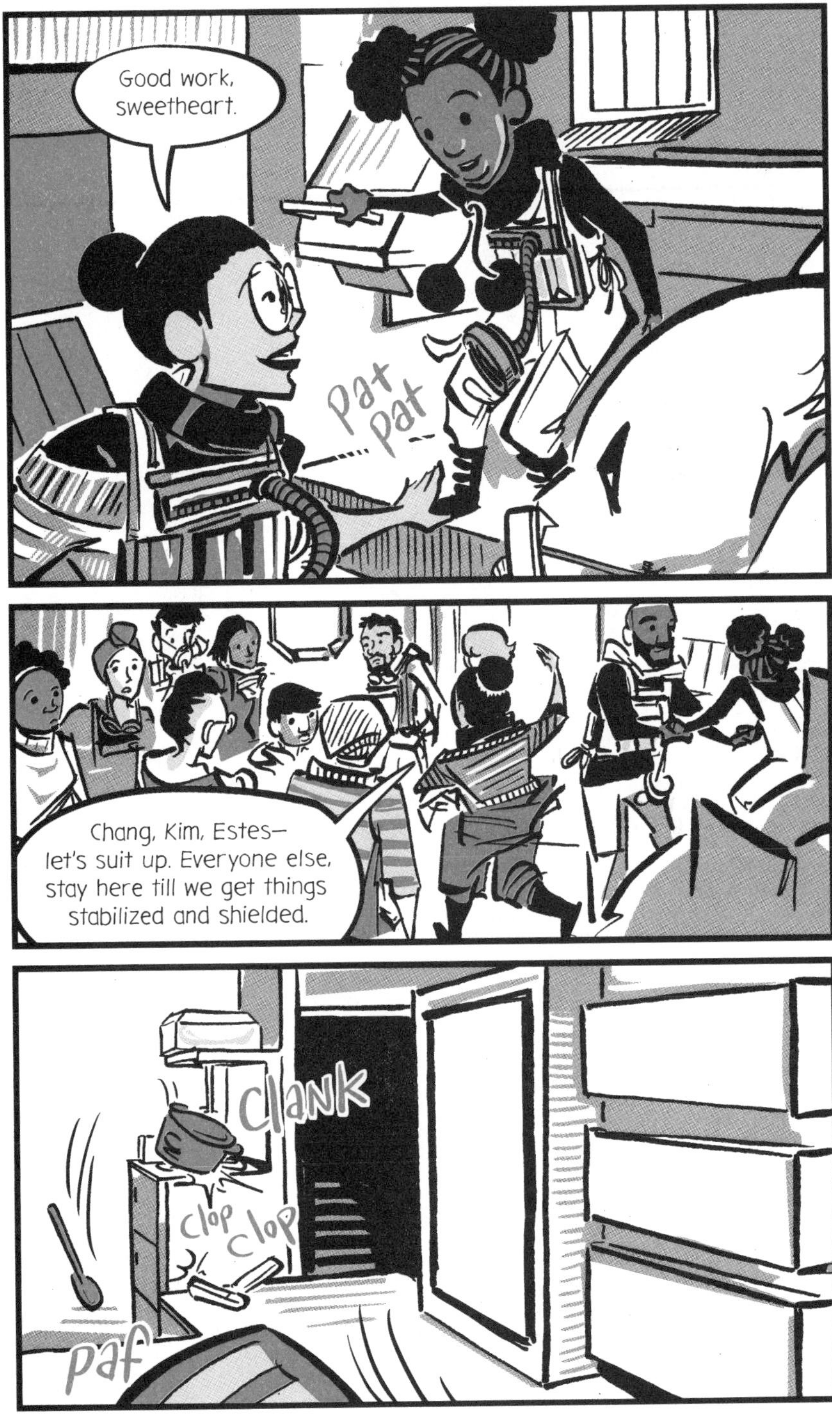
Good work, sweetheart.
pat pat
Chang, Kim, Estes— let's suit up. Everyone else, stay here till we get things stabilized and shielded.
CLANK
clop clop
paf

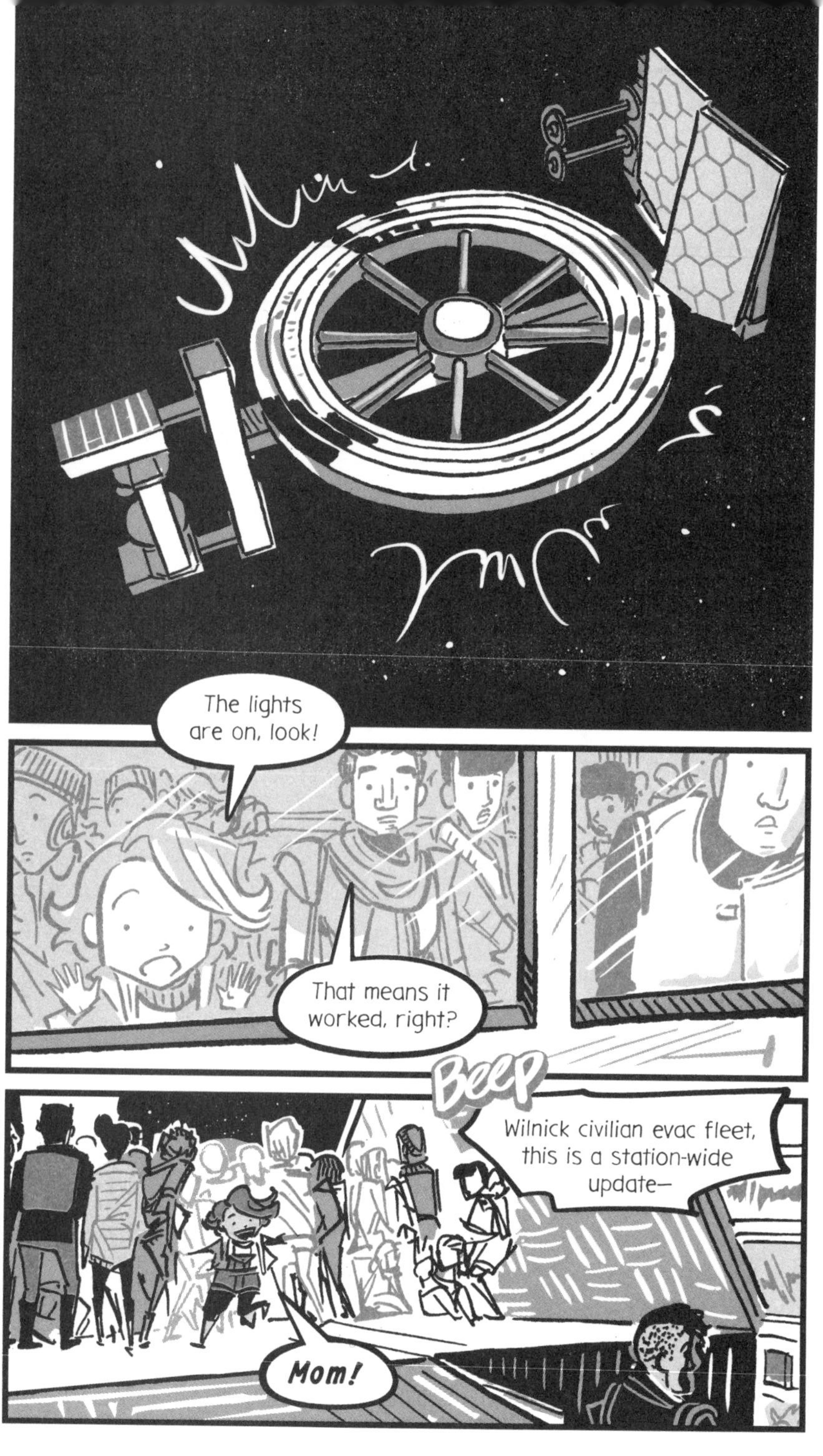
The lights are on, look!
That means it worked, right?
Beep
Wilnick civilian evac fleet, this is a station-wide update—
Mom!

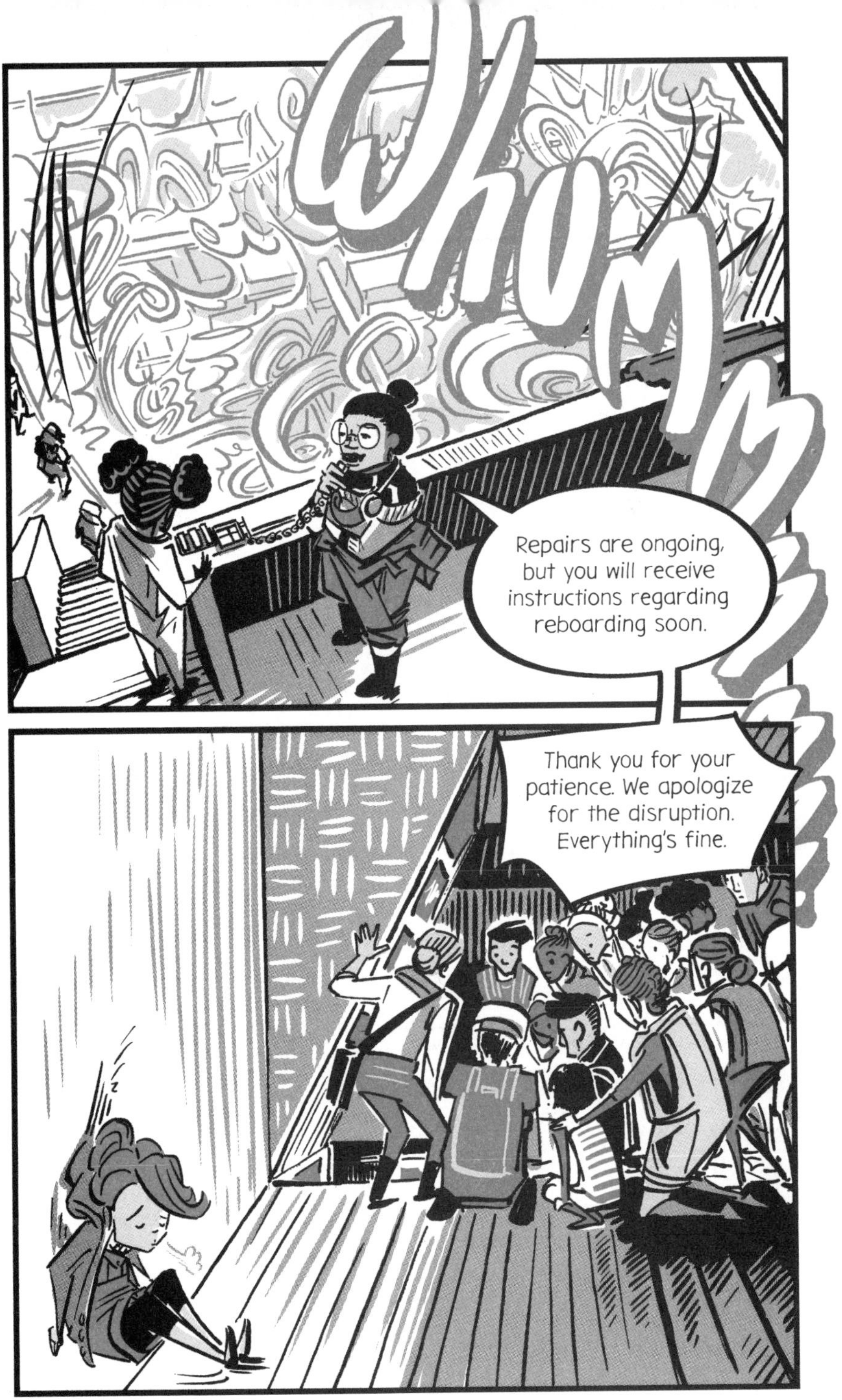
WHOMMMMMM
Repairs are ongoing, but you will receive instructions regarding reboarding soon.
Thank you for your patience. We apologize for the disruption. Everything's fine.

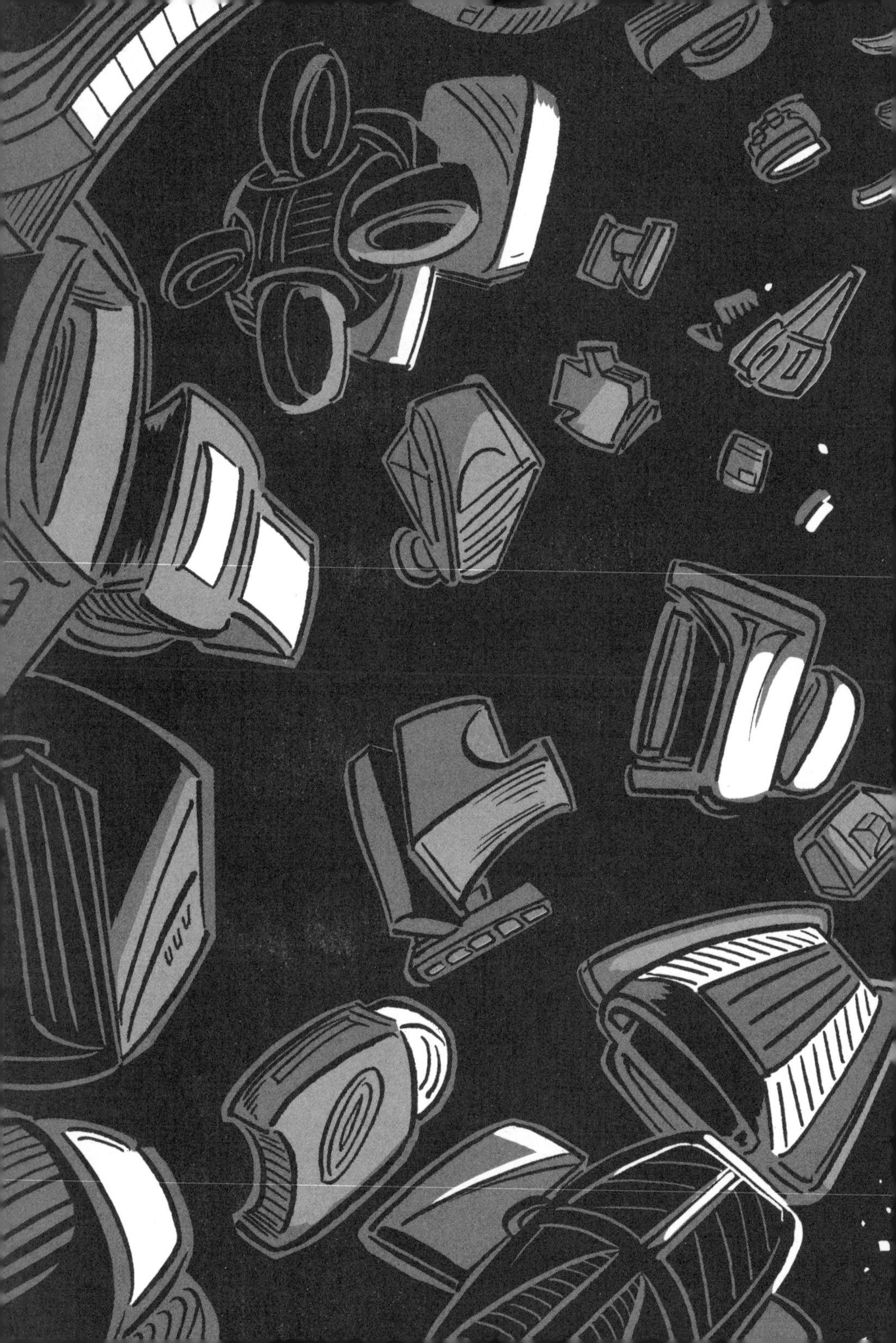

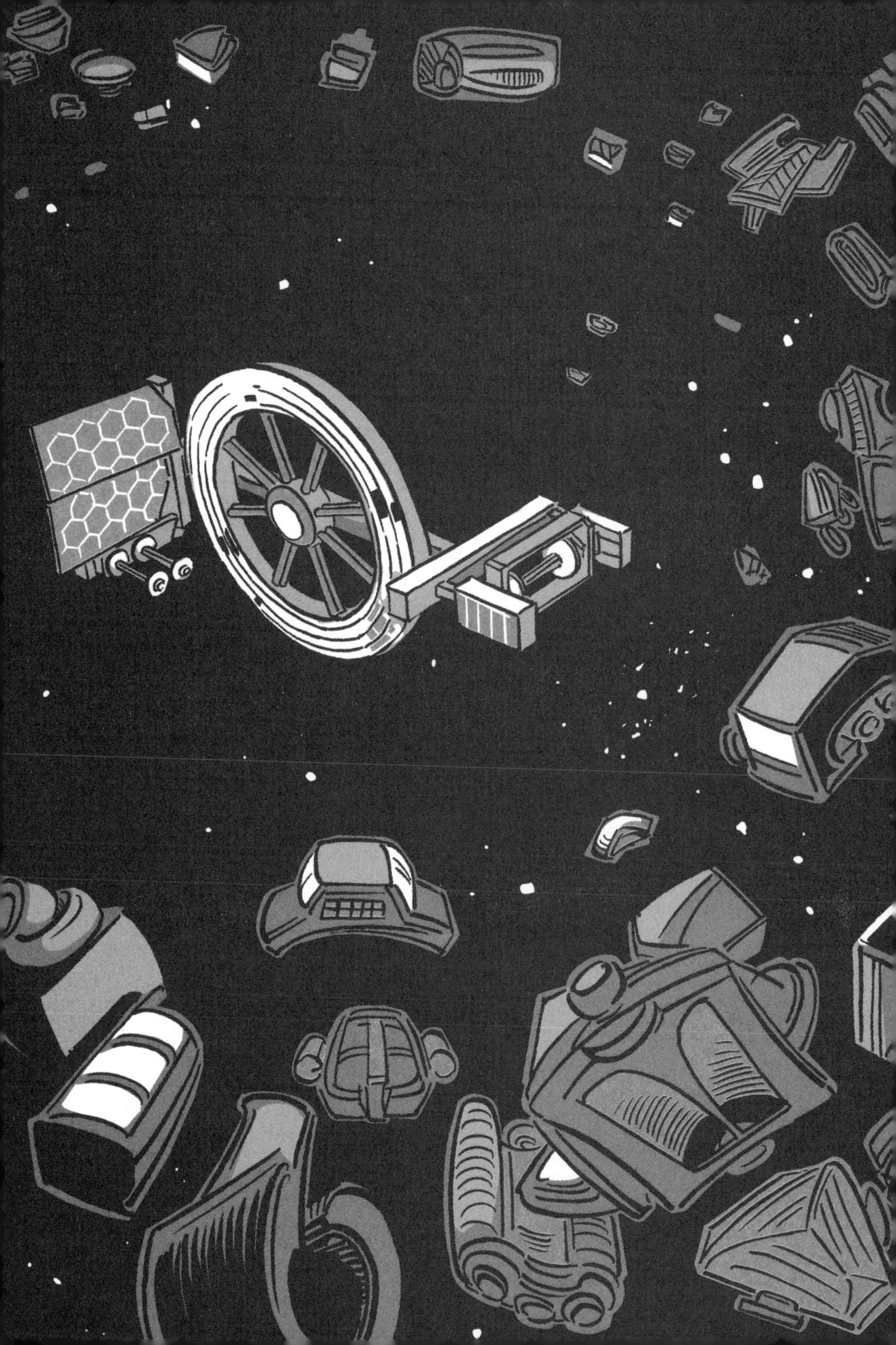

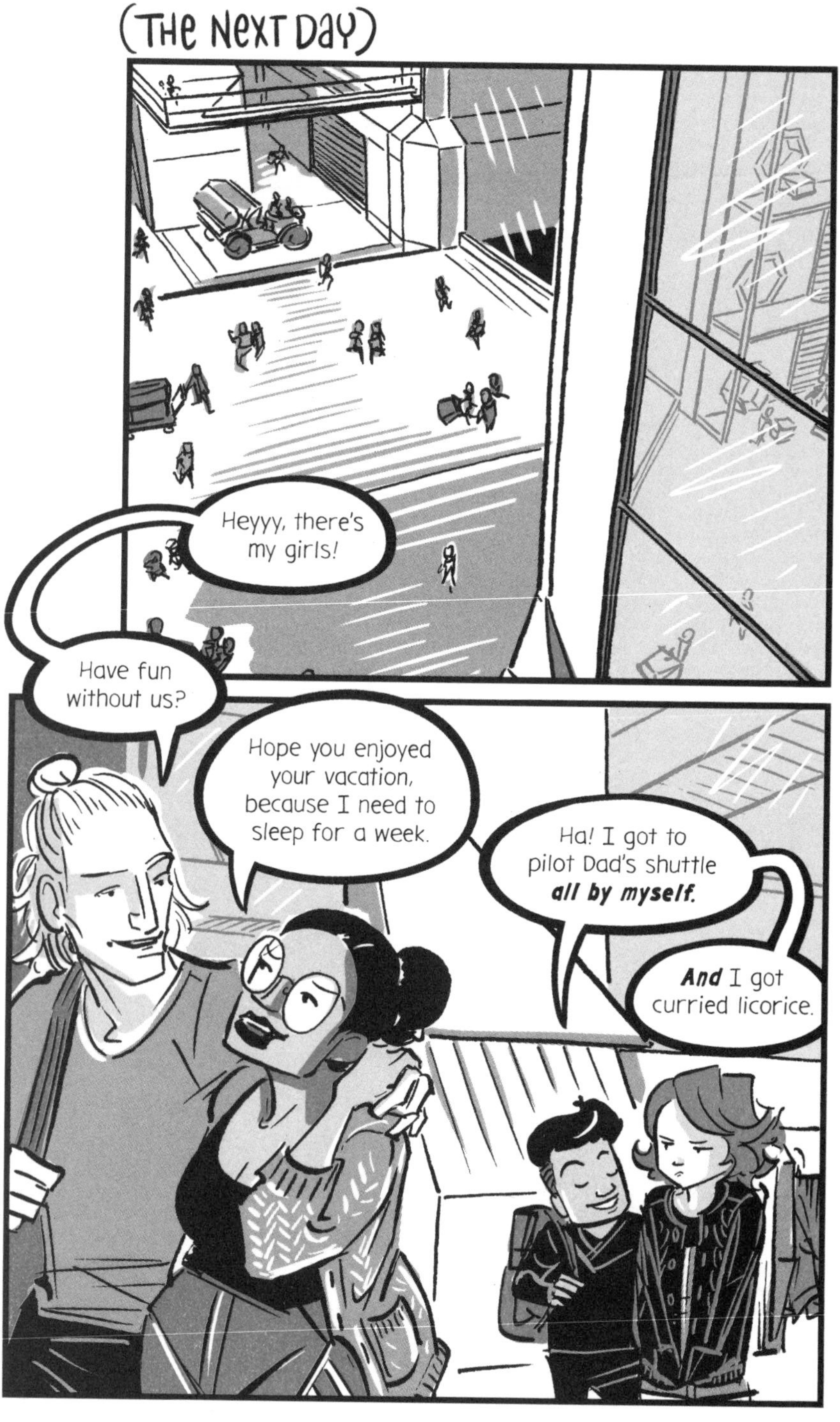
(THE NEXT DAY)
Heyyy, there's my girls!
Have fun without us?
Hope you enjoyed your vacation, because I need to sleep for a week.
Ha! I got to pilot Dad's shuttle ***all by myself.***
***And*** I got curried licorice.

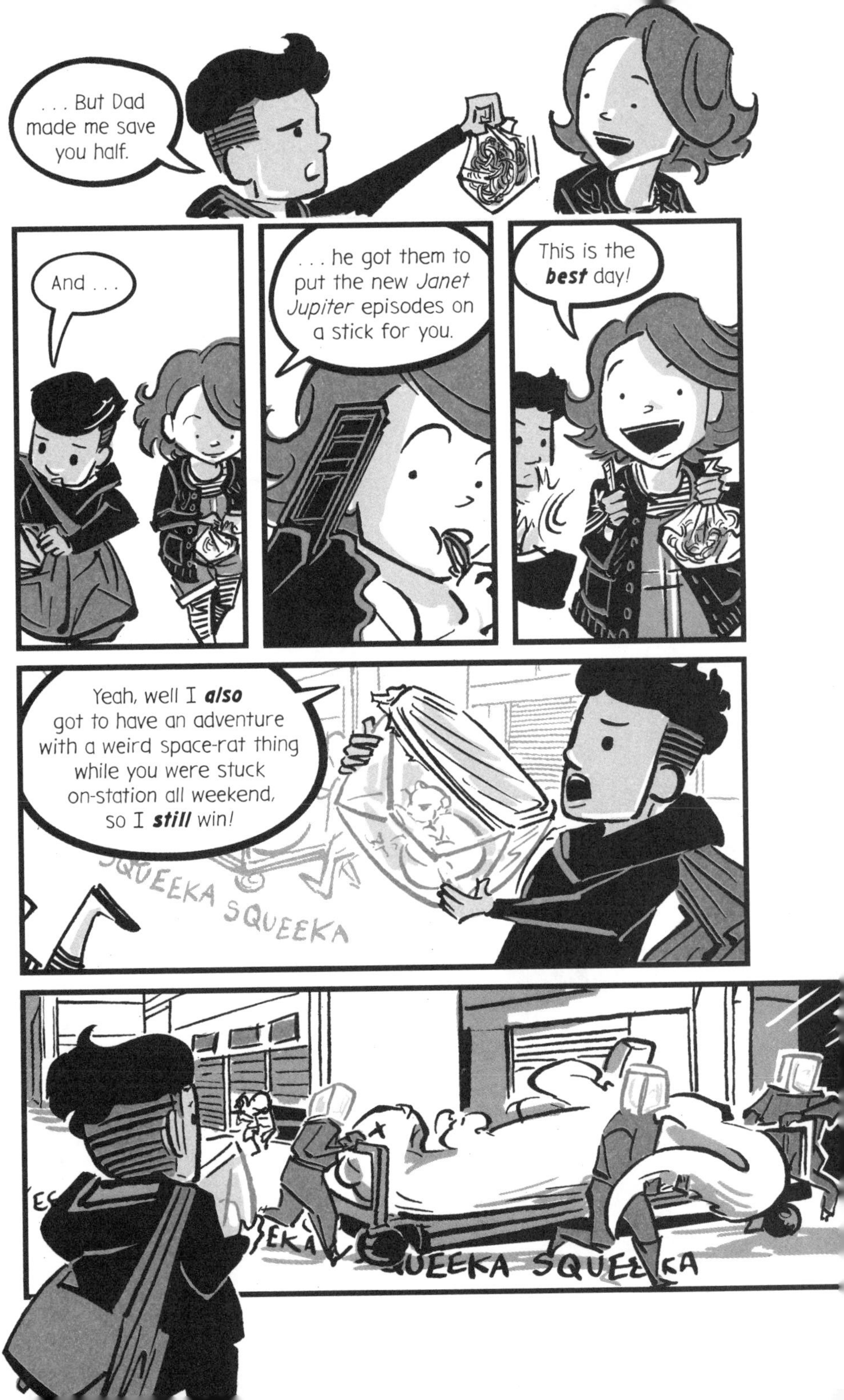
. . . But Dad made me save you half.
And . . .
. . . he got them to put the new *Janet Jupiter* episodes on a stick for you.
This is the **best** day!
Yeah, well I ***also*** got to have an adventure with a weird space-rat thing while you were stuck on-station all weekend, so I ***still*** win!
SQUEEKA SQUEEKA
SQUEEKA SQUEEKA

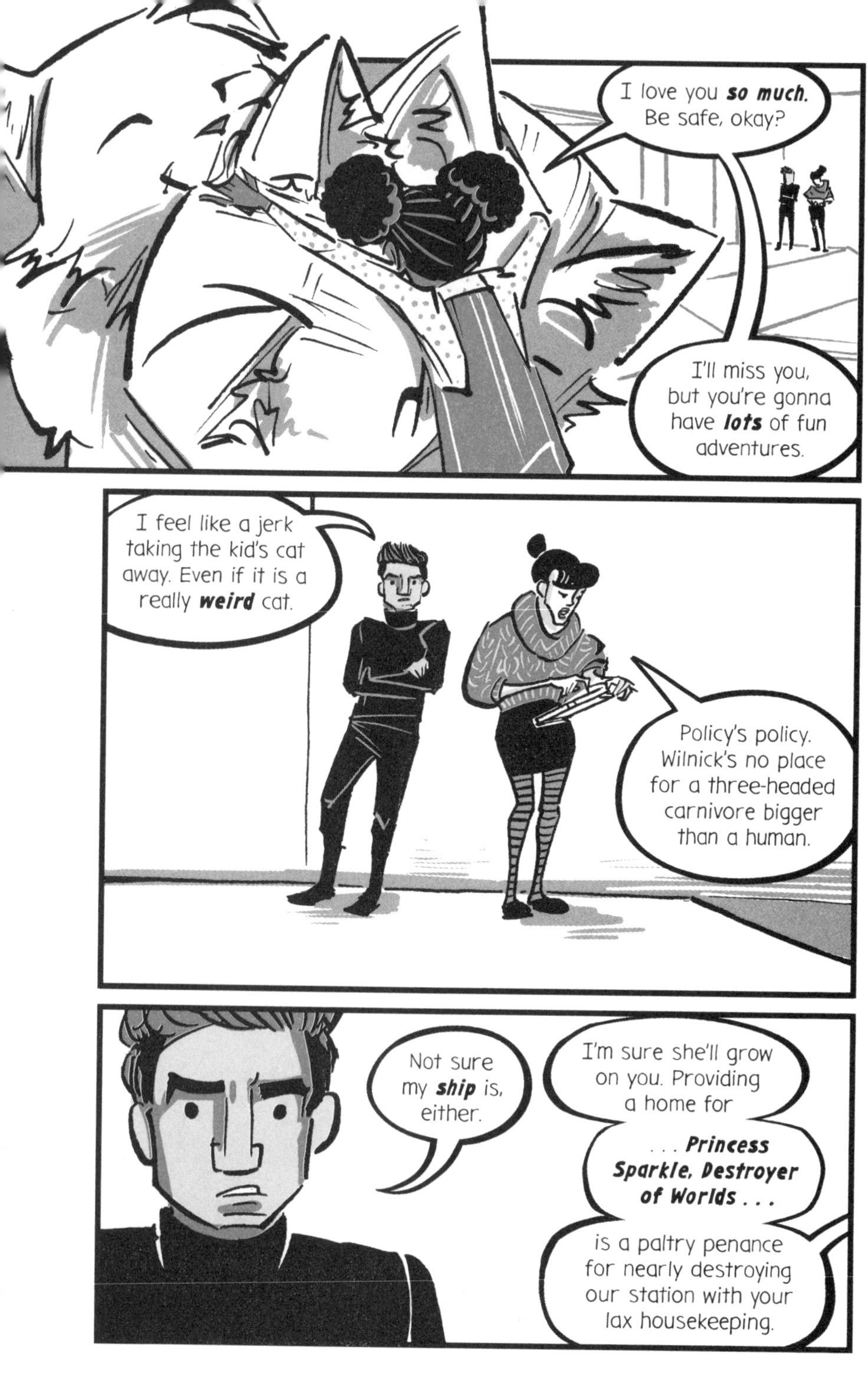
I love you **so much.** Be safe, okay?
I'll miss you, but you're gonna have **lots** of fun adventures.
I feel like a jerk taking the kid's cat away. Even if it is a really **weird** cat.
Policy's policy. Wilnick's no place for a three-headed carnivore bigger than a human.
Not sure my **ship** is, either.
I'm sure she'll grow on you. Providing a home for
. . . **Princess Sparkle, Destroyer of Worlds . . .**
is a paltry penance for nearly destroying our station with your lax housekeeping.

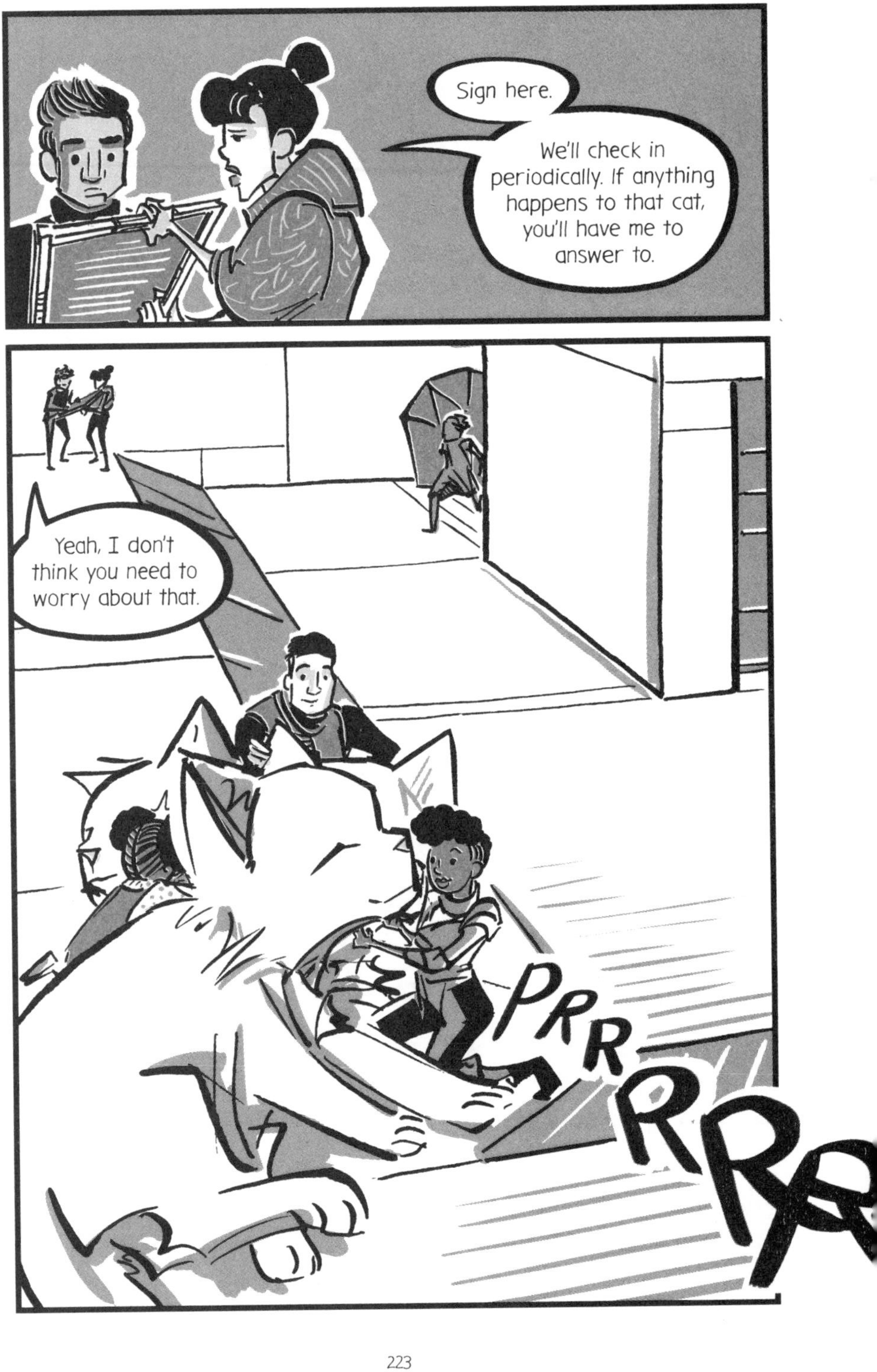
Sign here.
We'll check in periodically. If anything happens to that cat, you'll have me to answer to.
Yeah, I don't think you need to worry about that.
PRRRRR

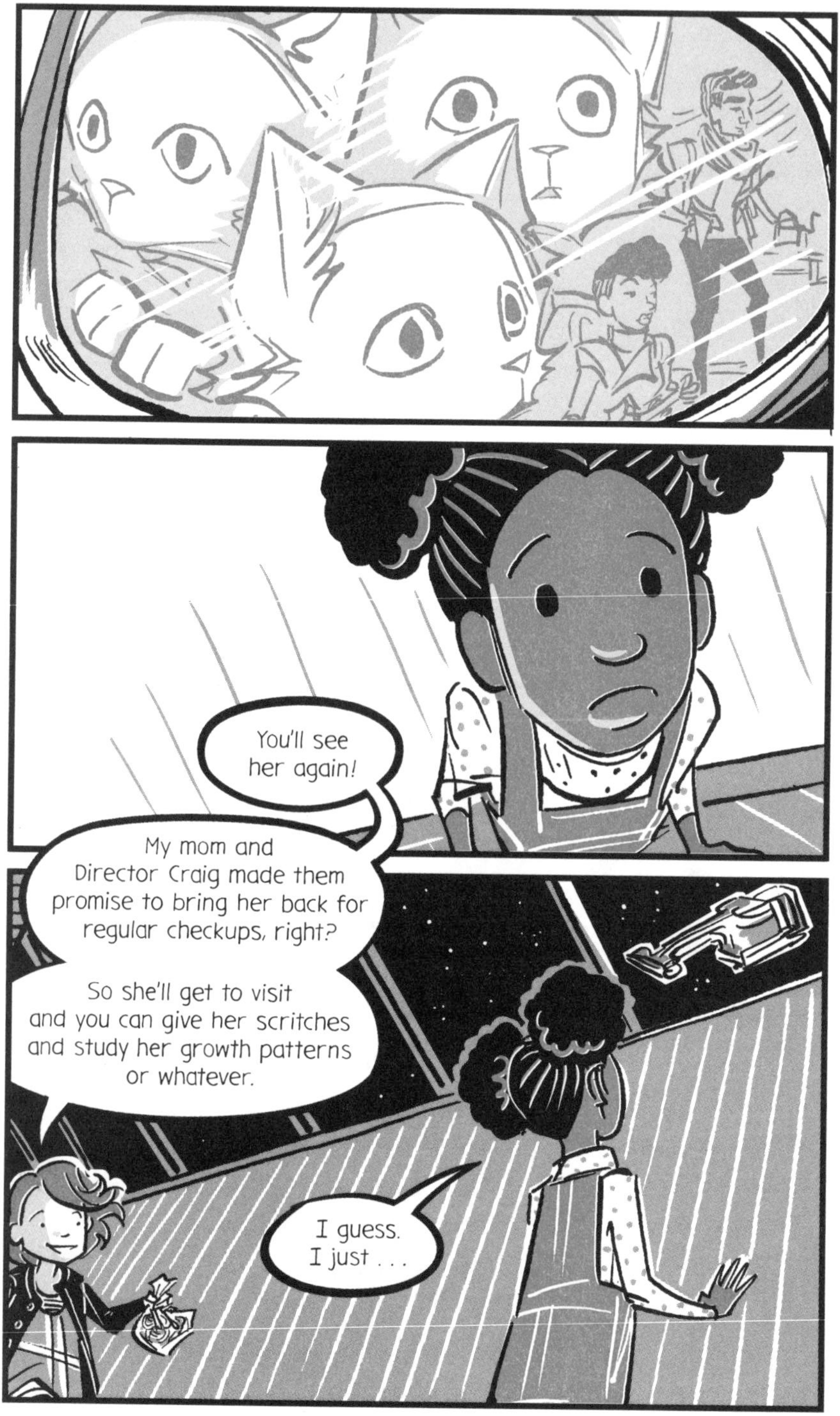
You'll see her again!
My mom and Director Craig made them promise to bring her back for regular checkups, right?
So she'll get to visit and you can give her scritches and study her growth patterns or whatever.
I guess. I just . . .

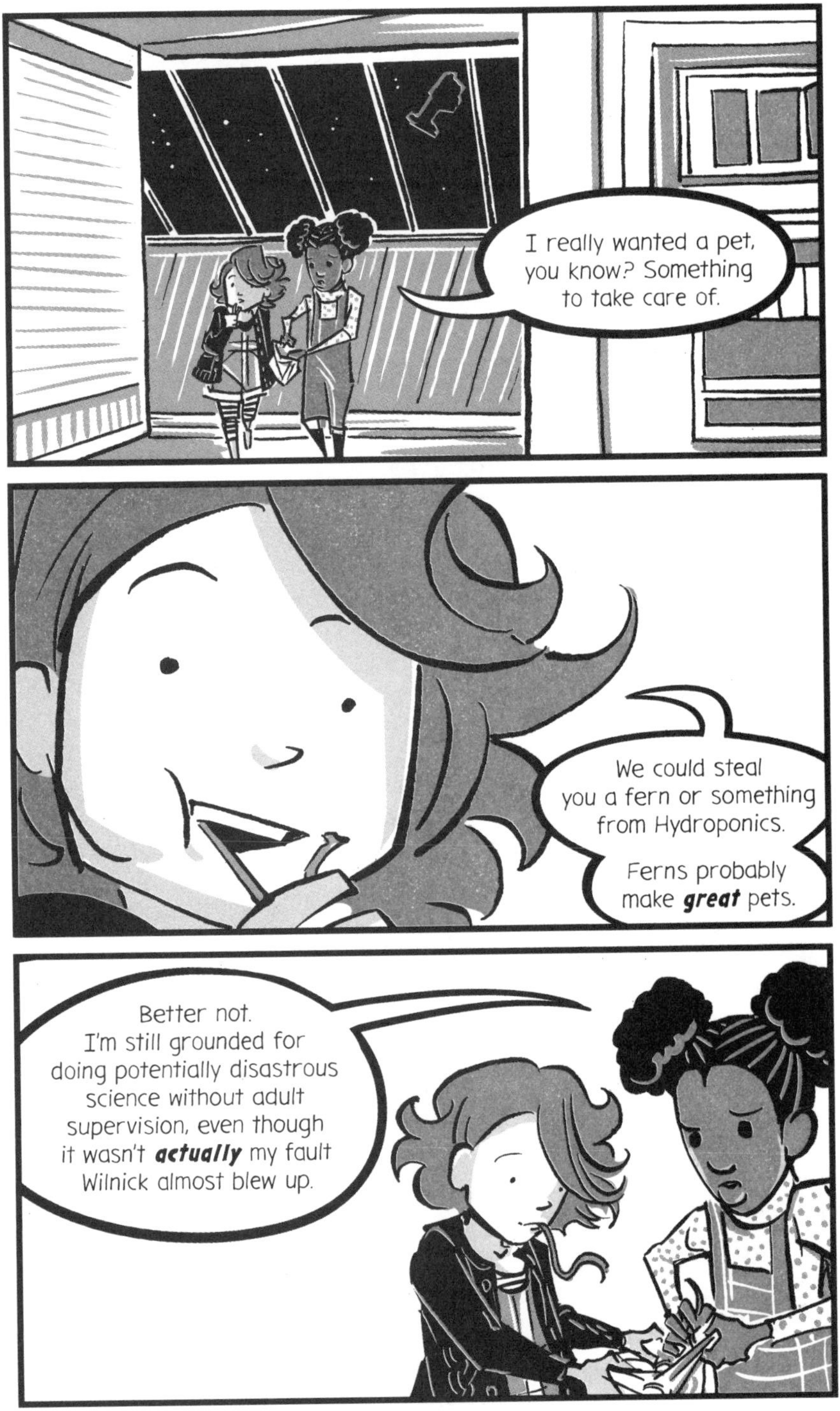

I really wanted a pet, you know? Something to take care of.
We could steal you a fern or something from Hydroponics.
Ferns probably make **great** pets.
Better not. I'm still grounded for doing potentially disastrous science without adult supervision, even though it wasn't **actually** my fault Wilnick almost blew up.

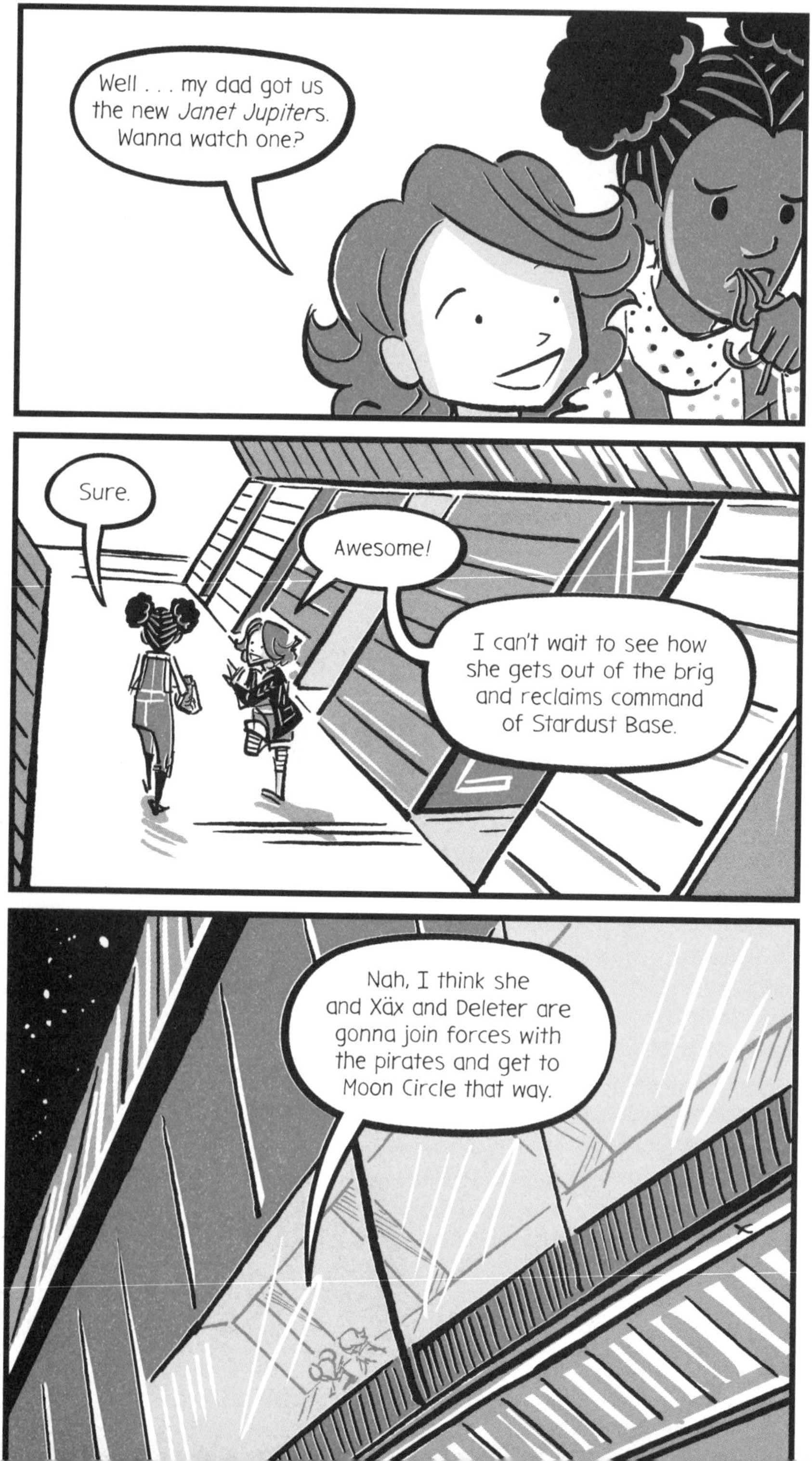
Well . . . my dad got us the new *Janet Jupiters*. Wanna watch one?
Sure.
Awesome!
I can't wait to see how she gets out of the brig and reclaims command of Stardust Base.
Nah, I think she and Xäx and Deleter are gonna join forces with the pirates and get to Moon Circle that way.

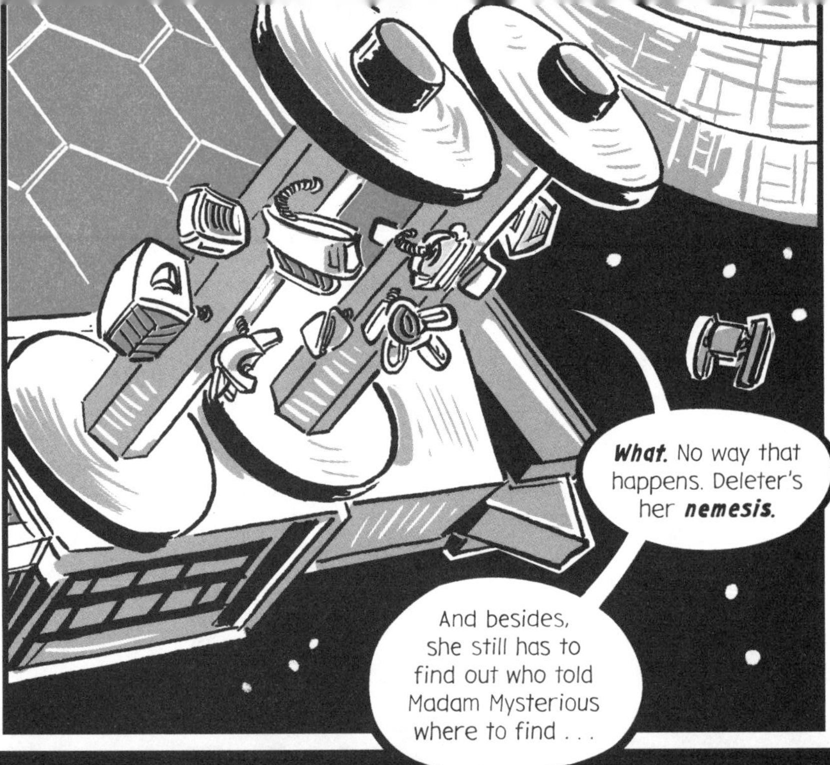
***What.*** No way that happens. Deleter's her ***nemesis.***
And besides, she still has to find out who told Madam Mysterious where to find . . .

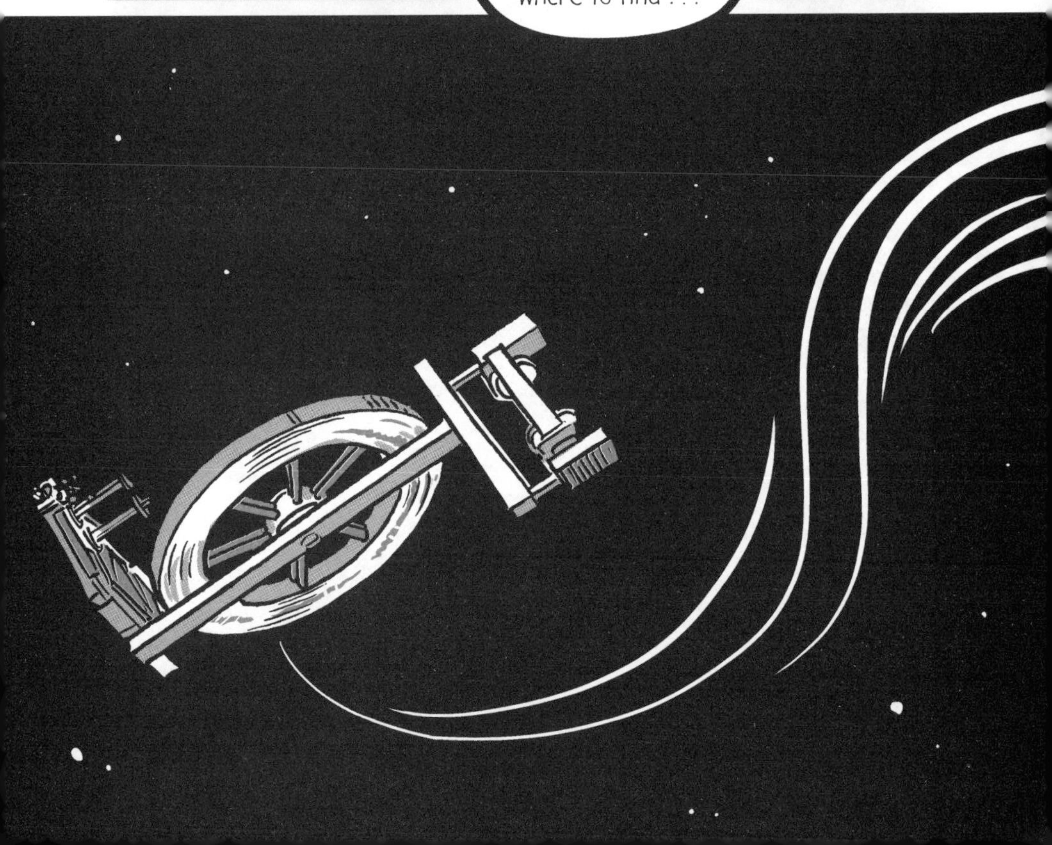

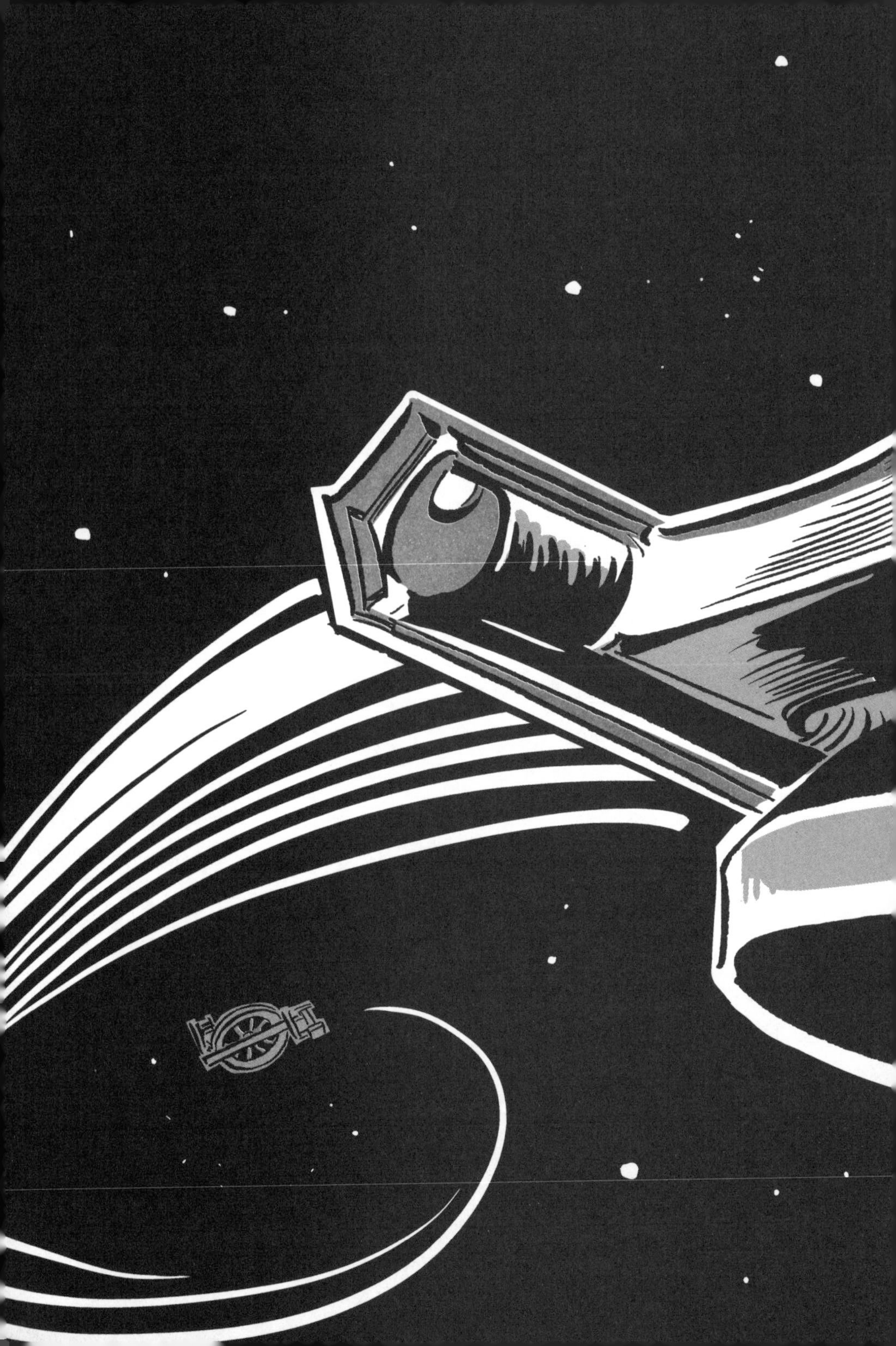

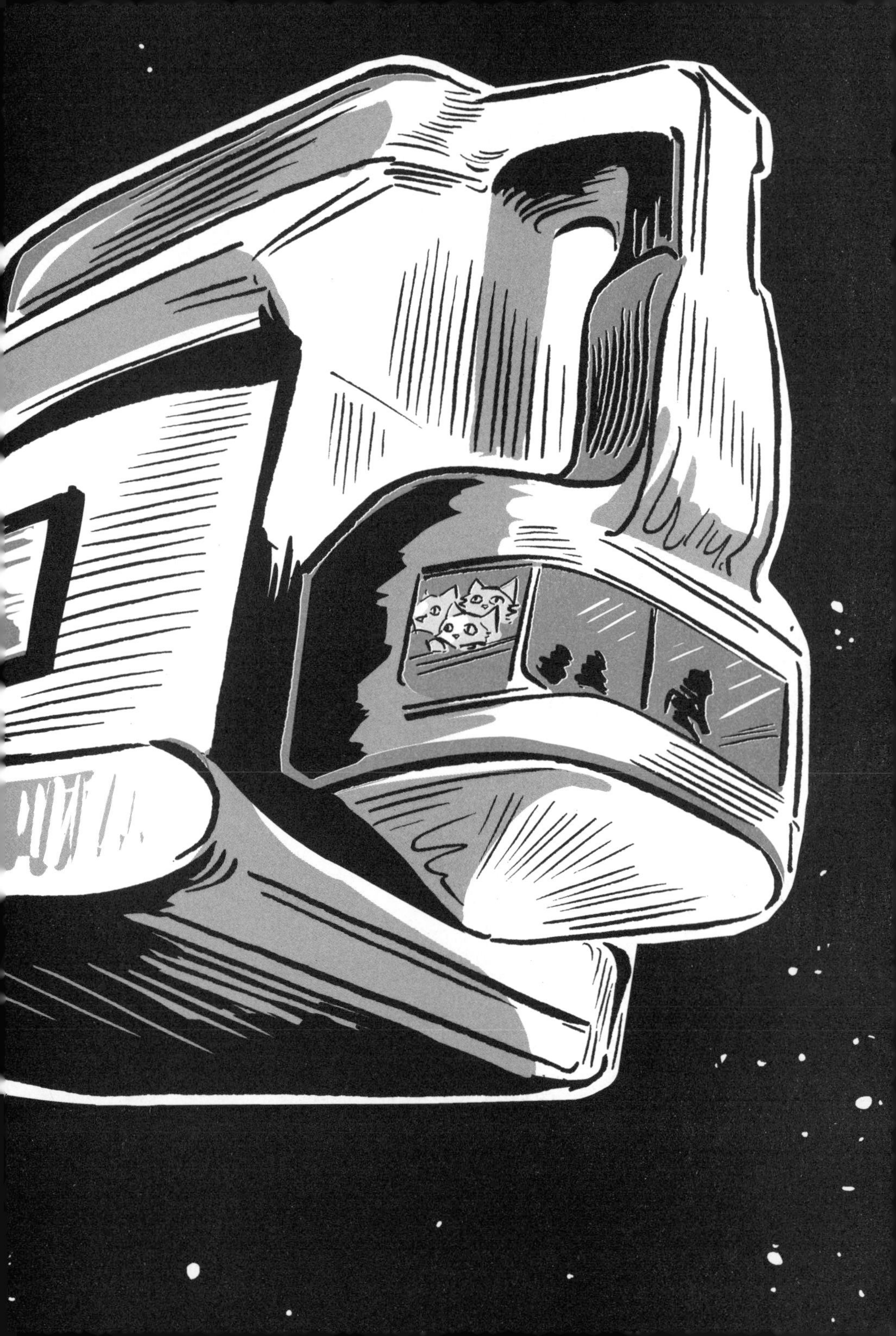

**MOLLY BROOKS** is the illustrator of *Flying Machines: How the Wright Brothers Soared* by Alison Wilgus, and the creator of many comics, which you can see on her website (mollybrooks.com). Her illustrations have appeared in the *Village Voice*, the *Guardian*, the *Boston Globe*, *Time Out New York*, the *Nashville Scene*, the *Riverfront Times*, the *Toast*, *BUST Magazine*, ESPN social, *Sports Illustrated* online, and others. She spends her spare time watching vintage buddy-cop shows and making comics about knitting, hockey, and/or feelings. Molly lives and works in Brooklyn.

Stay tuned for more adventures with

SANITY &

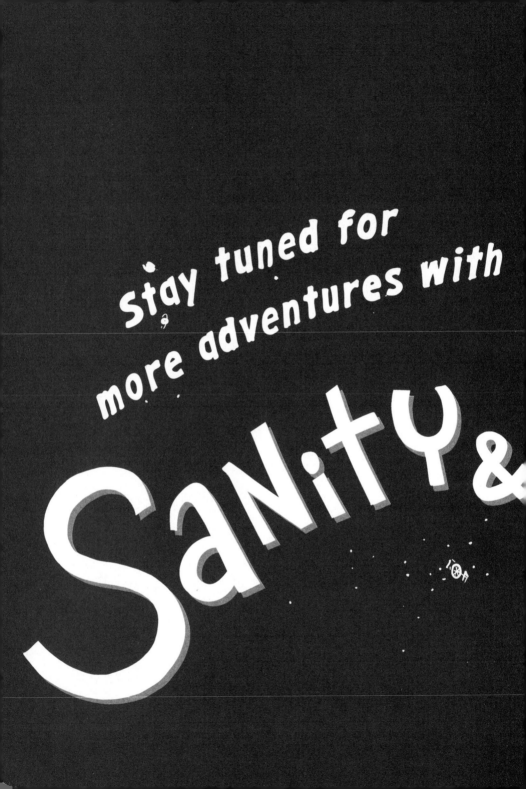

# TALLULAH

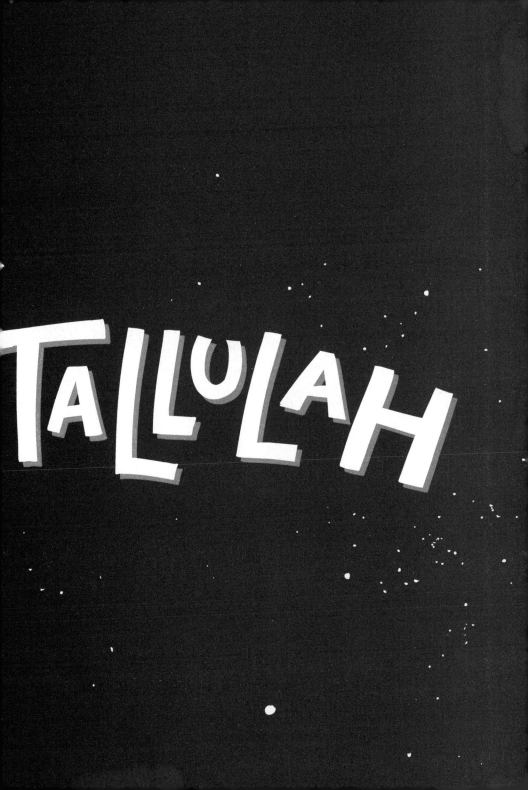